Make Us Yours

Sticks and Stilettos
Book Three

Chloe Rouxel

Author's Note

Make Us Yours was written with the intention to make dreamers fall in love. It contains lots of moments that will have you swooning, laughing with the Griffin gang, and shedding a few tears through memorable and dark times.

Although this is a romance book meant to make you feel good, this story does contain subjects that may be triggering to some, such as: Explicit sexual scenes, vulgar language, multiple deaths, coma patient, abusive parents, abusive/criminal ex, past sexual assault (mentioned), nightmares/night terrors, assault, traumatic pasts, stalking, blackmail, threats, alcohol abuse, PTSD episodes, light BDSM, double penetration, and double vaginal penetration.

If you desire more clarification on these subjects, please feel free to reach out before diving in. Your mental health matters to me above all.

And for those unbothered by these warnings, happy reading!

Please be aware that Make Us Yours may contain a few spoilers to Eternally Yours and Unexpectedly Yours, but it is a standalone and not necessary to have read the previous books.

Mental Health Awareness

If you or a loved one is struggling with mental health, please know that you are not alone and that it's okay to ask for help. Resources are always available to support you, including the 988 Suicide & Crisis Lifeline. You can call and text 988 anytime in the US and Canada, or please reach out to your local crisis hotline for help.

CONTENTS

For those who still feel the invisible shackles of your past weighing you down, who still feel trapped despite how hard you've tried to free yourself from that cage.

I know it's scary and sometimes feels like you'll never break free, like you're walking down an endless dark tunnel with no spec of light in sight.

But you're stronger than you think, BRAVER than you know.
And now, it's time to fight back.

Those shackles? They're made of plastic.
BREAK THEM.
That dark tunnel? It's only a curtain.
RIP IT DOWN.
And that cage? Babe, it's just paper.
Pick up that match and BURN the bitch to the ground.

Chapter One

VERONICA

Never should have looked through those cracks...

~ First Week of June ~

"Yes! Right there, don't stop." My hand fists his hair between my legs as his tongue continues to work its magic against my clit. The sun is now up and shining through my semi-closed curtains, falling along his dark blond hair and giving it golden highlights.

Hmm, I wonder if I should dye my hair blonde next. Could be nice. I'll have to ask Maze. Although she'll probably tell me blonde is too boring, then dye it some awful seafoam green herself. What am I saying? She hasn't steered me wrong yet; why would she now?

"You like that, babe?" He looks up at me with a smirk.

Oh shit. I totally zoned out.

I nod and push his head back down, the need to come rushing back to me. "Yeah, I love it. Now make me come. I have to get up soon," I tell him, grinding up against his face as he chuckles.

"Always so bossy. You're lucky I love giving you what you want." He kisses my pussy and smiles, looking back up at me.

Ugh! What is with all this eye contact today? I force him back down again. "Then stop talking and give me what I want."

He shakes his head slightly with a laugh but dives back in. *All right. Focus, Ronnie. This is good, you like this.* I shift my hips to the side an inch, the flicks of his tongue landing exactly where I need them. *There, that's better.*

I'm not being fair. Nathan is actually really good with his mouth—and his dick. It's why he's the only fuck buddy I keep around. He knows how I am and what I want. He doesn't pressure me into giving him more of myself and doesn't complain when I kick him out after sex or the next morning.

He knows I'm not looking for a relationship and don't want feelings to get involved, which he agrees with. In the last four months of us sleeping together, he's never once made it seem like he wanted more.

He comes over, we fuck, we fall asleep, and then he leaves when we wake up. I know he sleeps with other women, just like I sleep with other men. We just have a good thing going, and sometimes it's nice to have a regular instead of a new hookup every time the itch strikes.

I feel the pressure in my lower belly dissipate. Groaning, I drop my head back to the pillow and throw my arm over my eyes. "Ugh! I don't think this is going to work. Just forget it."

I let go of his head and begin to scoot up the bed, but he quickly grabs onto my thighs, forcing me back into place. My body immediately tenses beneath his touch, and I inhale sharply as my heart rate picks up.

His eyes snap to mine, and he quickly loosens his hold. "I'm sorry."

He knows how I feel about being touched without permission. He doesn't know the reasons behind it, but he accepts it and respects it. That's another reason why our arrangement works so well; he doesn't try to dominate me in the bedroom, instead, he lets me take the lead.

"It's okay," I say quietly.

"Just give me a second. I've got you."

I nod and lie back into place. His hand comes between my legs, and he slowly pushes two fingers into me. Curling them upwards, he moves back and forth, hitting that place that makes me see stars. His mouth drops back to my bud, and he sucks it into his mouth, tongue twirling around it. He's right; it takes him only seconds, and I'm coming all over his fingers and mouth.

"Fuck, yesss!"

He pulls out slowly after cleaning me up with his tongue, bringing his fingers to his mouth and sucking them clean as he stands from the bed and walks to the bathroom. Once I can breathe somewhat normally again, I get out of bed and search my closet for something to wear.

I decide on a high-waisted khaki plaid skirt with thigh-high black stockings and a tight white sleeveless button-down shirt. Tucking the shirt into my skirt, I finish off my outfit with a pair of black stilettos, then exit my closet and sit down at my cosmetics table, where I get ready every morning.

My hair for the moment is half baby blue and half baby pink. Almost two weeks ago I had dyed it pastel pink for the gala, but I wasn't totally in love with it, so I had

Maze make some changes yesterday for my first day at my new job.

I split my hair down the center, dividing both colors, and twist them into two buns above my head, letting a few strands fall loosely around my face. I quickly do my makeup—vibrant pink eyeshadow, dark blue winged eyeliner, mascara, and a dark nude lipstick. *There, all done.*

When I set down my lipstick tube, the bathroom door opens and Nathan steps out wearing only a towel. His muscular body glistens with water droplets, hair damp and tousled.

His hair is short at the sides but longer on the top, it's pretty sexy when he styles it. Actually, he's pretty sexy in general. When he catches me checking him out, he winks, then proceeds to pick up his clothes scattered around my bedroom floor and pulls them on.

Nathan and I met when I was working at a club in New York City. He was a bouncer there, and I was a waitress until I got fired for punching a guy in the face who thought it was appropriate to put his hand down my shirt. And well, Nathan got fired for helping me escape after I threw the perverted asshole's free drink in his face.

Because yes, I lost my job, and he got free booze. Absolute bullshit if you ask me.

"Talk to me, babe. What's got you all distracted this morning? You seem nervous," he asks as he pulls his shirt over his head.

"I'm starting a new job this morning as a housekeeper for some hockey players." I lick my lips and stare at myself in the mirror, going over all my features.

"Don't you know those guys? Why are you nervous? Afraid you won't do the job well?" I give him a frown through the mirror, and he laughs. "You're right, what am I saying? You're practically a clean freak. I'm surprised you don't make me pick up my clothes after sex."

That makes me smile because I think about it every time. "I would, but I'm too exhausted by the time we're done to give you any more orders."

"Nice to know I'm doing my job well." He grins.

"I wouldn't keep you around if you weren't." This time I'm the one to wink at him.

He laughs and sits on the edge of my bed, head turned my way. "All right, all right. Tell me what's going on then?"

I sigh and look down at my makeup brushes placed neatly in their little cubicle, the tip of my finger brushing over each. "I don't know. I mean, yes, you're right, I do know most of them. I've met the whole team a few times, but I don't personally know all of them. And I wasn't informed who exactly I will be working for."

I quickly glance up through the mirror, then look back down. "What if it's someone I don't get along with, and this job doesn't work out?" I let out another breath. "I'm just tired of looking for a new job every other week. I feel like nothing is really made for me."

Nathan gets up from the bed and comes to stand behind me. Slowly, he brings his hands up to rest on my shoulders and waits for my approving nod to squeeze them slightly. "Who is this woman talking to me? Because she's not the Ronnie I know." I smile and roll my eyes.

"You'll do great, Rons. You're a kickass girl and anyone would be lucky to have you work for them. And if they turn out to be assholes, just give me their name and address, and I'll pay them a visit." He winks, then walks back to the bed to put on his shoes.

"Oh, my hero." I swivel in my chair and stand, faking awe as I clasp my hands and press them to my chest.

He looks me over, then smirks. "Fuck, you're sexy. You look like one of those sexy Asian schoolgirls."

"I have no idea if I should take offense to that or not. I'm Italian, not Asian."

"I know, but maybe you could learn a few sexy words in Japanese, then we could get into some roleplaying next time I come over." He looks me up and down, licking his lips.

I swat his arm and head for the door. "You're an idiot. Come on, I have to get going."

He stands and follows me out as we walk to the kitchen, where my roommate Aubrey Ford is busy making breakfast. She turns to us with a blushed face and speaks in a delicate, tiny voice. "Morning."

"Morning, babe," I say, walking to the fridge and taking out the orange juice.

"Well, I'm out of here. Nice seeing you, Brey. Sorry for any noisy inconvenience. Rons, thank you for breakfast." He winks with a smirk and heads for the door as I laugh, while Aubrey flushes a darker shade of red.

"Bye, Nathan," Aubrey and I say in unison as I pour myself a glass and sit down at the island, waiting on Brey's delicious concoction.

"I'm going to have to invest in some very good earplugs. The ones I have are not doing the job as expected," she finally says, and I can't help but laugh.

Aubrey is what you'd consider a prude. Any talk about sex or the opposite gender makes her turn red and uncomfortable, yet she surrounds herself with people who talk about it incessantly. Although I think that's just the innocent virgin in her that makes her react that way. How she even made it to twenty-three, almost twenty-four, without even so much as being kissed is beyond me.

She's a stunning beauty. All natural with long ash-blonde wavy hair and the palest brown eyes I've ever seen. When she looks at you, it's like she can see through your soul. Then there's the splatter of light freckles over her tiny, upturned nose, with beautiful pillowy lips shaped to perfection.

And her body, God. You know those sexy models you see in magazines with flawless curves and tiny waists? Well, that's Aubrey. Even her breasts are perfect, not too big and not too small. Just perfect. Jesus, she never even wears makeup. At the charity gala we attended, she went completely bare with a simple green spaghetti strap dress and still looked absolutely stunning.

I'd kill to look like her, but instead I'm skin and bones with my tiny breasts that I hate. I'm not saying I'm ugly. On the contrary, I make heads turn wherever I go. But I don't have many curves; I'm five-foot-ten with long legs and shoulder-length colorful hair that changes practically every month.

I do have nice symmetrical features, though, tanned golden skin, and dark sapphire-blue eyes. Then there's my full tatted sleeve and piercings, a few along my ears and a septum.

Such a contrast to the girl I used to be...

I offer her a sheepish smile. "Sorry. We'll try to keep it down next time."

"It's fine. I should be used to hearing those sounds by now. My brother was an expert at creating them." She scrunches her nose in disgust and places two plated omelets down on the island, then comes to sit at my side as we dig in. "Today's your first day, right? Do you know whose place you'll be taking care of?"

I wipe my mouth on the napkin she set out beside me. "Yes, and no. Cecilia texted me the address and told me to just say my name and someone would escort me up. But the guys are coming back this afternoon, so I'm supposed to meet whoever it is then. I'm going to head over early to get it all cleaned up and make a good first impression, hoping that will seal the deal."

"That's a good idea. But you'll definitely get the job; your cleaning and organizing skills are impeccable. They'd be stupid not to want you. I'm just surprised Cece didn't tell you who it was." She frowns.

I shrug in response. "She said something about not wanting to give out their information or whatever without their permission. I can understand that." Aubrey nods in agreement.

Cecilia is one of our friends, well, originally Brey's friend since I only met her back in November. She's also married to Silas Hayes, the New York Griffin's team captain, which is how she got me the job.

Aubrey met her three years ago through her brother, Greyson Ford, who's also on the team and one of Silas's good friends. From there, she met Morgan, who's married to Clay Burkley, another player and good friend. There's also Emma, who's dating Greyson. They have a thirteen-month-old daughter named Gracie, while Cecilia and Silas have a seventeen-month-old son named Dante.

That only leaves two others in our little group, Noah Adler and Gabriel Ellis. Also known as the twins. And no, it's not because they're related. They're just two dirty man whores who do everything together. And I mean *everything*.

Noah is a defenseman on the team and Gabriel is a goaltender. Those two are very hands-on and have absolutely no filter when it comes to women. They clearly believe they can get whatever they want thanks to their so-called fame. And apparently, I've become their main target over the last seven months. Something I have no intention of indulging in.

As much as they can get on my nerves, I love them. Every single one of them. When I met Aubrey at NYU, she and I bonded instantly. She was the shy girl, and I was the loud, outspoken one. We had most of our classes together, but outside of school, we didn't see each other much.

That was until she mentioned wanting to move out of her brother's place and was looking for a roommate. At that point, I was living in some shitty little studio that was infested with bugs. So I jumped on the opportunity, and since then, we've spent every waking moment together. Add in the rest of the gang, and we're like a newfound family.

One I desperately needed.

"Well, let me know how it goes. I'm off today, so I'll see you later at Greyson and Emma's for dinner."

"Will do. I'll leave you my car since the address she gave me is close by, then take an Uber or whatever over to Em's." I finish off my plate and orange juice, then rinse them off in the sink before placing them in the dishwasher. "All right, I'm out of here. Wish me luck."

"Good luck!" she exclaims as I head out the door.

Taking the subway, I make the five stops over to my destination. The address isn't super far from where we live, but on foot that's like a forty-five-minute walk. Not that I mind walking; I would have done it if I hadn't been wearing my stilettos.

Once I exit the subway, I do the five-minute walk to the high-rise I will now be calling my place of work. *Wow. This place looks way too luxurious for someone like me.*

The condo Aubrey and I share is really nice and probably way out of our budget, but Greyson didn't like any of the options we showed him that were within our price range. So, he bought us our place, and we pay him rent every month, even if he constantly tells us we don't need to. But we're grown adults, the reasonable thing for us to do is pay rent.

But this place, this place looks like only the rich can afford it, with its around-the-clock doorman, front desk service, and shiny façade. Of course, a fancy hockey player would live here, most likely in the penthouse. From what I hear, most make millions a year.

I walk up to the grand front doors, where an elderly gentleman opens them for me with a tip of his hat. "Good morning, Miss."

"Good morning." I smile at him as I walk past and head for the desk where a man waits behind a hidden computer screen.

"Good morning, how may I help you?" he asks when I stand before him. There's a name tag on his uniform that reads Antoine.

"Um, hi, Antoine. I'm starting a new job here and was told to give my name, and that someone would help me up. Veronica Masters."

"Yes, Miss Masters. We were awaiting your arrival." He smiles. "Graham here will escort you up to the penthouse right away. Here is your key for the future. There's a private elevator to the side that will send you straight up. If there's anything else we can do for you at any given time, please let us know. We'll be happy to help as best as we can."

I take the shiny black keycard from him and place it inside my purse immediately, not wanting to lose it on my first day. "Thank you." I turn in time to see a man, Graham I presume, arrive at my side.

"This way, Miss." He brings me to the side, where I was told the private elevator resides, and places his own black card in front of a sensor seconds before the doors open.

We step in, and he presses one of the three buttons on the panel. P, for penthouse; G, for garage; and L, for lobby. We shoot up and within seconds the doors to the elevator cab open once more. I walk out into the foyer, and my mouth drops open as I stare into the open space of the room, completely stunned to silence.

I hear Graham say something behind me, but my mind is in shock at the view before me, making me only catch the end of his speech. "—should be returning shortly. We'll advise them of your arrival. Have a great day, Miss."

All I do is smile as he steps back into the cab and leaves me to my own in this ginormous place. I put my bag above the small table by the entrance, then wander farther into the penthouse.

Huge wall-to-ceiling windows greet me, giving a beautiful view of Manhattan, with light and dark gray furniture that adds contrast to the white walls. The floors are a form of black wood that would normally have a glossy feature, but they look like they haven't been washed in days, maybe weeks. Off to the left, I can see a beautiful white kitchen with shiny black countertops, and beside it is the dining room that sits on a higher platform but is still open to the rest of the room.

At a quick glance, the place looks pretty well kept. Until you notice the multiple cups spread across the counter, the dining room table littered with random things, dishes in the sink, and very suspicious-looking marks on the glass windows.

Okay, this place is actually pretty filthy.

I give myself a quick tour of the penthouse, trying to determine where to start off. The main floor consists of a home gym, office, library, laundry room, as well as the kitchen and living room. A beautiful dark staircase that looks like it's suspended in the air leads to the second level that contains the master and two guest bedrooms, although they all appear to be similar in size.

By the end of my tour, I've concluded that whoever lives here are massive slobs. Two of the rooms look lived in, while the other looks like a spare room filled with things they don't know what to do with.

And don't even get me started on the bathrooms in this place. *Jesus, I really have my work cut out for me.* With a deep sigh, I go in search of cleaning products and get to work, deciding to start off with the upper level.

As I'm heading back to the main floor, after finishing four hours of work upstairs, my phone buzzes with an incoming notification. I take the final steps to the landing and put the cleaning supplies down in the kitchen, then pull out my phone from the hidden pocket of my skirt.

A shiver runs through me, and small bumps pebble my skin at the sight of a text message from an unknown number. I don't open it, and instead simply stare as the panic starts to set in. *Just breathe, Ronnie. You're fine. He doesn't know where you are; don't let him get inside your head.*

I take a deep breath, shaking off the unease I'm feeling and turn off my phone completely. *There, he can't get to me now.* I have this stupid belief that if you ignore something, it will go away. Emphasize the word stupid, because it's been three years, and he's still not gone. I put my phone back in its place and get back to work, distracting myself with the sweat-smelling gym.

Once I'm done with the rooms down here, as well as the kitchen and dining room, I attack the living room. I pick up any junk that's lying around and throw out at least fifteen granola bar wrappers under the couch. *Jesus Christ, is it really so hard to get up and put it in the garbage?*

Figuring there's most likely more within the couch cushions, I begin taking it apart when my hand catches onto something beneath. I pull it out before fully removing the bottom half of the couch and immediately wish I hadn't.

"OH MY GOD!" I shriek once I notice what I'm holding is an old, knotted condom with dried semen inside the tip.

Without thinking, I fling it in the air where it lands on the floor a few feet away. It's not that I can't handle a condom; I did find several in the bedrooms, but most were in the trash or at least near it. In the couch, though? That's just disgusting.

I shake out my hands and continue investigating the couch with precaution. Turns out, there wasn't just one condom between the cushions, but five. *FIVE!* I have absolutely no words to describe the pigs that live here.

After getting rid of the unexpected findings, I finish off my tasks, cleaning the floors and windows and rearranging everything back into place. By the time I'm done, the place looks immaculate. Everything shines and smells amazing. There's not one hair, or in this case wrapper lying around, not one shoe out of place, and no dirty dishes in view.

The only place I haven't touched yet is the outdoor space because the door is locked, and I can't figure out how to open it. I'll have to wait until Mr. Pig and Mr. Donkey get here to show me how it works.

Just as I'm fluffing up the last throw pillows along the couch, I hear the telltale ding of the elevator, indicating its arrival. *Finally, I'll get to put a face to these slovens.* Slightly bent at the waist, I finish placing the last pillow when I hear an audible gasp.

"NO FUCKING WAY!"

My back instantly straightens at the all-too-familiar voice. *No. Oh God, no. Please tell me this is a joke.*

"Looks like we won the lottery, man!" He laughs loudly before I hear his sneakers jogging up to me. "Hey, Vixen," he says seductively into my ear.

Ugh! Freaking Gabriel Ellis.

I spin to face him with a glare. "This has got to be a joke," I say before squeezing my eyes shut and fisting my hands at my side. "This is just a bad dream. Cecilia wouldn't do this to me. I'll open my eyes, and they'll be gone," I murmur to myself.

"Nope, not a dream. Welcome to our palace, Kitten," Noah adds as he drops onto the couch next to where I stand. "Love what you did with the place. Damn, if we knew how good you were at it, we'd have hired you sooner." He looks around, nodding his head in approval.

"You mean the filthy dump that *I* turned into a palace?" I place my fists against my hips, narrowing my eyes at him.

He smirks. "The one and the same. You'll be generously compensated for your efforts."

Ugh! What an asshole!

"At least now we know why Mama Hayes wouldn't tell us who she hired." Gabe laughs again as if this is the joke of the century. *It might be. The worst joke of the century. I'm going to kill her.*

"So, about your schedule. I was thinking we might need you more often than planned. Say, six days a week? Around the clock. We'll give you Sundays off, because, you know, we're generous men after all." He then winks with that boyish grin of his.

I study Gabe for a moment, then turn and do the same to Noah. "Nope." I shake my head and walk past Gabe. "Not happening. No way am I working for you two. I have enough of seeing you guys with our friends, there's no way I'm spending alone time with both of you."

"Aww, come on, Vixen. It'll be fun! We'll get to know each other better," Gabe calls after me.

"Forget about it! Find someone else to do your dirty work!" I grab my purse and press the call button for the elevator. The doors slide open instantly, and I step in, arms folded over my chest as I spin on my heels.

They both stand by the elevator, apparently having followed me as I stormed off. Noah leans against the wall with his arms crossed along his wide chest, while Gabe grabs the back of his collar and pulls his shirt off with one hand, giving me a full view of his annoyingly delicious abs.

"See you later, Vixen," he says as the doors shut.

"Not a chance in hell," I mutter.

Shit, he means at Emma and Greyson's. God damn it! I'll never escape them.

Chapter Two

NOAH

Ever wondered what thirty thousand tastes like?

"Well, this is an interesting turn of events," I say out loud as I watch the devastatingly beautiful Veronica disappear from view. *Damn, that woman is a goddess.*

I knew it the first moment I saw her all those months ago, but I'm not only talking physically. There's something about her that draws me in. And from how obsessed Gabe has been with her since November, I'd say he feels that same pull.

"You can say that again. Oh, this is going to be fun!" He grins wickedly at me before turning around and heading for the kitchen, most likely to make himself some nasty green smoothie he claims is super healthy.

I stay leaning against the wall a little longer, eyes fixed on the closed elevator doors like she might change her mind and come right back. *She won't. I know she won't.* Veronica is one feisty woman who does whatever she sets her mind to. If she said she was leaving, then she's gone.

"Yeah, that's if we can manage to keep her," I tell him, pushing off the wall and inspecting the open space. Nothing but clean surfaces as far as the eye can see. The floors are shinier than I've seen them in a while, and the place smells clean, like freshly squeezed lemons.

"Don't worry, we will. We just need to convince her to stay." *Yeah, it's going to take some major convincing.* "This is our shot with her, Noh. You realize that, right?" He sets out ingredients on the counter beside the blender.

"Let's not get ahead of ourselves. She's fought us off for the past seven months."

"Yeah, but now we'll be around her three times a week. That's excluding when we're with the rest of the gang. She'll be in our space. All we have to do is kick up the charm factor. She'll give in, trust me."

He's right, she probably will. I've seen her defenses drop from time to time around us recently. What I'm more worried about is what happens after we've had our fun with her. I don't know about Gabriel, but I have a feeling Veronica won't be like all the others—where just a few fucks will be enough to get her out of my system for good.

I think I might want to keep her around after. I'll just need to figure out what his intentions are with her, outside of fucking her brains out.

I watch him blend his shit together then pour half of it into a glass and take his first sip, sighing with pleasure once he's done. "Want one?" He tips his glass my way.

My face contorts in disgust. "Nah, I'm good."

I pull out my phone from my back pocket, checking for missed calls or messages but come up empty, then turn and head for the stairs without saying a word. Gabe is used to my mood swings by now. I may be fun and playful in public, but at home, this is my sanctuary, where I can fully let go and be myself. He gets that and leaves me be.

Gabe and I have been friends for the past five years. We were both traded in at the same time, him from Colorado and me from Los Angeles. We bonded instantly over being the new guys on the team.

Silas, Clay, and Greyson took us under their wing right away, and we all quickly became family. But they were also older than me and Gabriel. We were barely twenty-three at the time, while Greyson was twenty-six and Silas and Clay were twenty-eight. Plus, Clay had just gotten married, so they weren't really the '*going out to clubs*' type.

That's how Gabe and I started getting our reputation of '*always doing everything together.*' At that point, it wasn't entirely true, we just always partied together until one night when this girl wanted us both, and we said why the hell not.

One thing led to another, and we realized how much we enjoyed taking a chick at the same time. From that point, we moved in together as roommates so it would be easier to bring girls home, and the rest is history.

I make my way up to the master bedroom, shutting the door behind me, and lean against it as I take in my new surroundings. My bed is made, and all the clothes that littered the floor were picked up and put away.

I push off the door and walk into the ensuite. Everything sparkles from how clean it is; I can even see through the shower glass walls. They're pristine to the point of seeming almost invisible.

I wander back to the room and into the walk-in closet. *Shit, okay. This girl is beyond good.* All my clothes are neatly hung up and organized by color and season. It looks amazing, but I'll never be able to keep it like this.

I'm not ashamed to admit that I can be a slob. I don't do it on purpose; I just get so lost in my head sometimes that I forget. Then I tell myself I'll pick it up later but forget that, too.

I exit the closet and sit on the side of my bed. She was here, in my room. I can still smell her cinnamon and apple scent through the air. It's subtle, but it's there. *I wonder if she climbed onto my bed to tuck in the sheets. Did she lie down over my pillows, colorful hair splayed out around her like a rainbow?*

My cock thickens against my jeans as I think of Veronica lying on my bed, her skinny body beneath my large one as I fuck her into the mattress. I grab my phone, checking to see if I have time to jerk off before needing to head out. *Fuck, I'm already cutting it close.*

I pass my fingers through my shortly cropped, brown hair and stand, making my way back out of the room and to the elevator. If I don't leave now, I'll be late for dinner tonight, and everyone's going to question where I was, and then I'll be a dick and tell them to mind their own business.

I try to avoid that as much as possible. I know they mean well and just care about me, but this has nothing to do with them, and I like to keep my personal life to myself.

I skip down the stairs, passing Gabe, who's sitting on the couch. "I'm out. I'll see you at Ford's later," I tell him as I step into the elevator and salute a goodbye.

VERONICA

I'm fuming, I feel like I'm going to explode.

I can't believe that sneaky little ant-sized woman!

I'm mad and I'm irritated. *Ugh!* As nervous as I was this morning, I was still excited to have this job. It was a good gig with an amazing paycheck; one I didn't have to kill my back every day of the week to get.

Plus, it's something I'm actually good at and enjoy doing. There's something so satisfying about cleaning and organizing things. It can be a lot of work, but when you're done, the finished product fills you with satisfaction.

But now all that's been flushed down the drain. There's no way I could ever work for Gabe and Noah. I know they won't make it easy for me. They'll corner me at every turn until I give in. I can deal with them when our friends are around, but with no one else to intercept, I don't know how long I'd last.

I hate the way I feel around them, like I want to give them my time, which is something I swore I'd never do again. They make my stomach turn to knots and my heart do somersaults with every little smile and touch.

I can't let that happen.

A little over half an hour later, the cab stops in front of Emma's house, and I pay the driver before storming out and making my way up to the front door. I don't bother knocking or ringing the doorbell, I just grab the knob and push it open.

I find Emma right on the other side with a shocked expression on her face, her purse hanging over her shoulder, and with the look of fear she carries in her eyes, I'd say I probably almost smacked her in the face with the door. *Good. She'd deserve it.* There's no way she wasn't in on this. She and Cecilia have been best friends for a long time; she definitely knew what the little scheming brunette was up to.

I find Cecilia a few steps behind her. *Good. Just the woman I wanted to have a word with.* I fist my hands at my sides, fire blazing in my eyes. "You are all dead to me. *DEAD!* I HATE YOU!" I spit at them.

Their eyes go wide as I storm past them, toward the kitchen. "I need a drink!" I mumble to myself. "I'm taking your most expensive bottle of wine and drinking it all by myself! Try to stop me, Em. *Try,*" I shout over my shoulder and head for the wine cellar.

They both explode with laughter at my outburst, enraging me even more. "THIS ISN'T FUNNY!" I yell back before shutting myself inside the cellar. *I need a moment to collect myself.*

I take a few deep breaths to calm my nerves before scanning the selection in front of me. There's a lot, and if I'm honest, I don't recognize any. *Are they even sorted in a certain way? Price? Taste? Age? Color? Jesus, I'm no expert at this.* I guess that's what happens when you're indebted with student loans and live off a minimal salary. You don't have money for any luxuries.

The door to the cellar opens, and Sam—Dante and Gracie's nanny—walks in. He's a very attractive young man, and sadly for me, not into women. He walks over to a different shelf from the one I'm observing and reaches up high for a bottle.

"Here, this one is exactly what you're looking for," he says with a subtle Italian accent and a smirk.

"How can you tell?"

"My parents are big wine enthusiasts." He chuckles. "That, what you're holding in your hands, is a thirty-thousand-dollar French wine. Also, I'm Italian. We know wine."

My mouth drops at the price but then quickly shuts at his last comment. *"I'm Italian and know nothing about wine,"* I tell him, narrowing my eyes.

"Then I guess that's the difference between a real Italian and an American one." He shrugs, leaning against one of the shelves.

My frown deepens. "You were born in Washington," I deadpan.

"We'll blame it on your youth," he tries again.

"I'm twenty-four!" I gape incredulously at him.

"Exactly!" He snaps his fingers before pointing it at me. "A whole year's worth of extra knowledge up here." He taps his temple, then laughs when I glare at him. "Come on, Bella. Let's go drink some expensive wine."

He throws his arm around my shoulders and pulls me toward the door. Surprisingly, my body doesn't tense at his touch, something I've come to realize only happens, or I should say doesn't happen, with one other man. Noah.

It stunned me the first time he put his hand on me, and I didn't get that itching, panic-filled feeling to push him off. Instead, I felt a sense of calm surrounding him. Even when he drinks, I still feel safe.

But with Gabriel, it hits me every time. It's strong and consuming, yet for some reason, I never push him off right away. Instead, I let him do it more and more, slowly getting used to the feeling of him, something I should be putting a stop to but can't seem to find the strength.

Once back in the kitchen, Sam takes the bottle from my hand and proceeds to open it before taking three wine glasses out and filling them. Cecilia stands on the opposite side of the island watching us but doesn't say a word.

I lean into Sam. "Aren't you on the clock?" I whisper to him.

He chuckles. "No, not necessarily. And anyway, my bosses are pretty cool." He looks up at Cecilia and winks, making her blush slightly in response. She's a bit like Aubrey and blushes easily, although Brey is a whole other level.

"Just don't tell my husband I let you drink. He'll just use it as another excuse for why you aren't good for the job," Cecilia giggles.

She's not wrong; Silas tends to be a little possessive when it comes to her and has been looking for reasons to fire Sam, even though Sam is honestly a perfect fit for the kids and our little group.

He's not like all those other super professional and strict nannies you hear about. He's fun and playful and the kids love him. But the main reason Silas wants him out is because he's a smoking-hot Italian who spends a lot of time alone with his wife. He also happens to be the only one in our group that doesn't know Sam is into men.

Finally, having my extremely deserved glass of wine in my hands, I take a hefty gulp and sigh with satisfaction. "God, thirty thousand tastes good."

"So... I take it you're mad at me..." Cece says as she slides in closer.

I give her a tight smile and chuckle sarcastically, then bring up my hands and begin to undo the two buns over my head, letting my hair fall. I then shake it out and pass my fingers through it before gifting her a reply.

"Oh, mad is not even the right word for how I feel. I can't believe you would do that to me! You know how I feel about the twins. They're relentless! What do you think will happen if I'm constantly around them and in their space?"

I take another sip before continuing. "They'll probably end up kidnapping me and tying me to their bed until I give them what they want! And anyway, how did you even manage to get me up there if they didn't know it was me?"

She gives me an apologetic smile. "Silas still owns the penthouse. They rent it from him, so it was easy to get your name on the approval list of people allowed up."

Her smile falls after as she speaks sincerely. "Look, I'm sorry. I know I should have told you. But you needed a job, and they needed someone to take care of their place. It felt like the perfect solution. Plus, it's with people you know, so they'll give you some slack. And you'd be making way more than you would at any other job you could find."

"I get that, but a heads-up would have been nice."

"If I had told you from the start, you would have refused." She gives me a *'don't bullshit me'* look when I go to protest.

We hear the front door open seconds before the two blondes, Morgan and Aubrey, come into view. "Oh! You're already here. How did it go?" Morg asks, her eyes flicking to Cecilia, before coming back to me with the fakest smile I've ever seen on her face.

"Oh my God! You were in on it too!? Really, Morgan? I thought you were better than this." I fold my arms under my chest, showing clear disappointment.

"I'm sorry! I was going to tell you, but then Emma told me to be quiet. Please don't hate me," she pleads with big blue puppy eyes.

"Wait, what's going on?" Aubrey questions with such innocence. She would never have held information like that if she knew.

"You know my new job I was excited about?" She nods. "Well, it's for Gabe and Noah." I don't need to explain myself further for her to understand.

"Oh..." Her big brown eyes widen.

"Yeah, *Oh*. So now I have to look for another job. Again." I sigh as my shoulders drop.

"What?! No!" Cecilia grabs my hand like that will stop me from not going back to that penthouse.

"Please, just give it a shot. Test it out for one week at least, then you can decide if you want to find something else. You're the best person for the job, Ronnie. No one can put up with those boys like you do. There's a reason they can't keep a cleaner longer than a day, because no one can deal with their shit long enough to see through it."

Everyone nods in agreement. That's true; even if they never truly give up on their pursuit, I do have a knack for being able to put them in their place.

She smiles like she thinks she just convinced me. "But you can. You're tough and levelheaded. It's exactly what they need. Just set them straight, I'm sure it will all be fine from there."

I groan, my eyes closing as I inhale heavily through my nose. I really don't want to work for them. I love those guys as friends, but I don't necessarily want to spend more time with them. I also don't feel like looking for a new job, one I know I'll hate but will force myself to do anyway because I need the money.

"Ugh! Fine. One week. That's all I'm giving them. But I'll need to have a serious talk with them, because what I walked into—no way in hell am I dealing with that every other day!"

"Was it really that bad?" Morgan asks with a worried look.

"HA!" I drain the rest of my glass, then point at it while looking at Sam, who stands quietly leaning against the counter behind us, telling him to top me up. He chuckles as he takes it from my hand and does as instructed.

"Where to start? The place was a total pigsty." I scrunch my nose up.

"Really? I never pictured Gabe and Noah to be that messy." Cecilia furrows her brow, thinking about it. She's not alone. It's not the image they necessarily give off.

"Oh yeah, it was. There was garbage all over the place, shoes and clothes were scattered everywhere. Piles of dishes in the sink and along the counters. The windows were so dirty you could barely see through them anymore. Don't even ask me about the bathrooms."

They all carry a horrid expression. "But that's not the worst part..." I stop to make it a little more dramatic, even if it does deserve the dramatic pause.

"What can be worse than that?" Aubrey questions as she watches me take a sip of my refilled glass.

"Oh, sometimes I forget how sweet and innocent you are." I giggle. "See, there were wrappers all around the couch, so I thought I'd take it apart to make sure there were none beneath the cushions. *Big mistake.*" I widen my eyes as I emphasize the words.

"Oh God, please tell me there wasn't rotten food there?" Morgan looks nauseous as she says it.

"Worse. Condoms. And not just one... Five!"

"Oh! That's not too bad. We all know how sexually active those two are." Cecilia shrugs like it's no big deal. I don't think she's caught on completely.

"No, Cece. Used condoms... as in tied with a knot and dried cum at the end!"

"EWW!" they all say at once, pushing back from the kitchen island like the condoms are lying there.

"Okay, that's nasty. Even for me," Sam says with a revolted look.

"You aren't the one who had to touch them! I don't think I've ever washed my hands so many times in my life." I shudder as my mind is brought back to the incident. *Add buying THICK rubber gloves at the top of the list.*

The baby monitor on the counter next to Sam starts producing babbling sounds, indicating that little Gracie is awake from her nap. Sam turns it off before pushing off the counter. "I'll get the princess. You can finish this conversation without me. I think I've heard enough." He laughs and heads up the stairs.

Dante rushes over to his mom, holding up his favorite miniature hockey stick. That boy carries that thing with him everywhere he goes. "Cie key?" he says to Cecilia. *I have no idea what that's supposed to mean.*

"No, baby. Gracie's still too young to play hockey with you. But maybe Uncle Greyson will play when he arrives. We'll ask him, okay?" she tells him in that sweet, motherly voice.

He drops his arm, then turns and walks back to the living room, where the rest of the toys lie.

"How do you understand what he says?" I ask her, impressed.

"You just pick up on the words and sounds they associate with things they hear. Cie means Gracie and key means hockey. He only recently started trying to say Gracie. It took me a full week to figure it out," she informs us. *Still pretty impressive.*

The girls transition the conversation to hockey and how the guys are doing in the Stanley Cup Finals. I've never been much of a hockey fan, or a sports fan in general, so I sit back and watch them as they talk spiritedly.

You know how they say, *'Pretty people stick together'*? That's definitely the case for this group. Every one of them is gorgeous in their own way. Morgan looks like those blonde barbies you see in sorority houses with her golden hair, crystal blue eyes, and permanently pink-tinted lips. Although, she's nothing like those sorority witches.

Cecilia has bright hazel eyes, rich chocolate-brown hair that holds perfect natural waves, and a killer rack that's hard not to notice. She's also the shortest in our group, standing at five-foot-two, while her husband is a six-foot-four giant. When they stand next to each other, the height difference is pretty comical.

Then there's Emma, who looks like she belongs on every fashion magazine cover. A natural redhead, with a perfect physique and piercing green eyes. Her hair always holds a glossy, vibrant look, most likely from all the expensive products she puts in it. She's the fashion icon of our group, with her expensive designer clothes and a limitless bank account. But we've come to find that she actually has a soft spot for vintage clothes, and is one of the most humble and giving people we know.

Even the boys are in a different league, all tall with delicious muscles you want to lick like an ice cream cone. Hell, even their babies are adorable.

That only leaves me. The tall skinny girl, who changes her hair to a ridiculous color every month, with multiple piercings and tattoos. The badass, as I've been called. Because apparently putting dirty, perverted men who think the world belongs to them in their place makes me a bad bitch. I guess they have a point, since most women would just let it slide or ignore it. But I can't. I've let too much go ignored in my life to keep letting it happen.

I'll never be that girl again.

The front door opens, letting us know of a new arrival, and Greyson stops in his tracks when he finds us all standing in the kitchen, drinking from his wine collection. Apparently during my moment of observation, two more glasses were taken out for Morgan and Brey.

"You okay, Ford?" Cecilia watches him skeptically.

"Yup, it just hit me how strange it is to come home and find a group of women in my kitchen, where none of them are my girlfriend or daughter." We all giggle at his comment.

He's right; it must be weird coming home to find a bunch of people inside when no one was actually home to have them over. But that's just how we are—we're family and all their homes are our homes too.

"Oh, come on, Grey. With all the stories I've heard from Aubrey, you should be used to finding random women in your home." I wink at him teasingly.

From what I've been told, Greyson used to be a pretty big womanizer, with different women in his bed every night. Although that all changed when he found out he had a six-month-old daughter with one of his conquests.

Due to situations out of his control, he gained custody of the beautiful Gracie and hired Emma to watch over her whenever he had other obligations, even though they claimed not to like each other very much. Which is exactly when Aubrey and I moved in together and I came into the picture. From there things escalated between them, and now Emma is, in every sense of the word, Gracie's mother.

"Yes, well, that's in the past," he answers while glaring at his sister just as Sam reappears at the bottom of the stairs holding a miniature version of Aubrey. *Literally, a copy and paste.* "Ah! Much better." He takes Gracie in his arms and kisses her chubby cheeks. "Hey, Buttercup. Daddy missed you so much."

He comes deeper into the kitchen, heading for the fridge, but stops when he spies the bottle on the counter. Frowning, he picks it up, then sets it back down and looks at me with wide, angry eyes. If I didn't know Greyson, I'd probably be intimidated by that look.

"Veronica..." he growls through gritted teeth. "Do you realize how expensive what you're drinking is?" His voice is low and predatory.

I pick up my glass, taking a sip while maintaining eye contact over the rim. "Yup, thirty thousand dollars' worth of good wine. If you have a problem with that, you can talk to your girlfriend. She'll explain to you why I have every right to be drinking it right now." I smile brightly.

I can see the irritation flicking off him as his nostrils flare. I'm pretty sure I even saw his eye twitch. A small giggle escapes Cecilia's lips, and she quickly covers her mouth when he turns his angered gaze at her.

"I'm sorry," she whispers in a tiny guilty voice. She clears her throat, and her face suddenly changes to compassion. "How's Maddison...?"

His whole demeanor changes at the question, a gloomy cloud settling above his head. "Not good. They aren't sure she'll make it through the month..." He bites the inside of his cheeks as he sniffs and looks down at his daughter, his Adam's apple bobbing as he tries to hold his emotions in.

Maddison is a little girl they met during Charity Day that the team hosted, who suffers from some kind of terminal cancer. Emma and Greyson immediately fell in love with the little angel and have been doing everything possible to help her father during these hard times. It's crazy how quickly someone can become important in your life.

"Oh God... poor thing..." Cecilia's eyes water as she places her fingertips to her lips. "If there's anything we can do, anything at all, let us know."

"Yes, please do. Any of us. We're all here for you and her family," Morgan adds tenderly.

Sam rejoins our group with Dante, who tries to pass a small plastic puck between his legs. "I already offered Emma to work more hours if it can help. So don't feel bad if you two want to spend more time at the hospital, I'll be happy to take care of the little princess longer."

"There isn't really much more we can do but be there for her and her father. But I appreciate all the help. Thank you," Greyson says before taking a deep breath and continuing his path to the fridge.

"So, what's the big reason behind you raiding my wine collection?" he asks as he takes a water bottle out and uncaps it while still holding his daughter against his hip.

"Oh, you know, just the fact that Cecilia got me a new job. Except she failed to mention that it was for Noah and Gabe."

He snorts, almost spitting out his sip of water. "Oh, you're so fu...dged," he finishes while looking at his daughter, holding back what he really wanted to say.

Yup, he's right again.

I'm so fucked.

Chapter Three

NOAH

Trial period.

I push the door open to Ford's house, noticing all the cars already in the driveway. Clearly, I'm the last one here. *Great, more questions on my whereabouts.* I don't get why they can't just leave it alone and understand that I don't need to share everything about my life with them.

I make my way inside and find the girls in the kitchen, while the guys sit in the living room with the kids, playing an NHL game on the Xbox. "Ladies." I turn on the charm as I approach them, kissing all their cheeks. First Aubrey, who blushes intensely, then Cecilia, Morgan, and Emma.

I don't miss the glare thrown my way when Grey spots me kissing his girlfriend's cheek. He's a pretty jealous guy. And I'm guessing the fact that Gabe and I have already had our fun with her still pisses him off, even if they were friendly encounters and it happened years ago.

I stop in front of the girl I've been fantasizing about for so many months now. "Veronica." Her name tastes like the sweetest honey on my tongue. "How is it that you keep getting more and more beautiful every time I lay eyes on you?"

She leans back against the counter, hands holding on to either side. A sliver of lust twinkles in her eyes only for a split second before disappearing as a smirk forms on her bow-shaped lips, the lower one being a little heavier than the top.

"Always the charmer, Casanova." *Ah, the famous nickname she gave me the very first day we met.* Not exactly the name I'd want to carry, but since it comes from her, I'll take it.

I slide my hand along her hip, gently resting it there. I give her a second to recognize my touch before leaning in and grazing her cheek with my lips. I never know how Ronnie will react when I get too close, because even though she acts tough, I see the way her body tenses when people come close. The way her shoulders straighten, how the pulse in her neck picks up speed, even the slight tremble in her hands and that faraway look she gets from time to time.

Then there was that time I kissed her at Gracie's birthday party while Gabe and I were having a little fun teasing her with her slim body stuck between ours. When she turned her head my way, I took my shot, which resulted in me getting slapped and being told to never do that again.

I was stunned after the blow, but what really shocked me was the look she held in her eyes. Not anger, but fear. I'm not sure what her story is, but I know there's one. I don't buy the front she puts up for everyone.

I take in a big whiff of her scent before pulling away slightly, my hand staying glued to her hip. When our eyes meet, I find hers searching mine.

"Are you okay?" she asks quietly with concern, as if we're having a private conversation.

Her question startles me for a moment, like it does every time. She never asks where I was, what I was doing, or why I'm late. Instead, she asks if I'm okay. As if she can sense something's off and worries about me.

And even when I lie and say, "Yeah, Kitten. I'm okay." She doesn't call me out on it; she sticks by my side until I finally believe the words myself.

I reluctantly remove my hand from her body and settle beside her against the counter. She takes the smallest step closer to me and bumps her shoulder into mine. Veronica is taller than the average woman, and with her four-inch stilettos, she stands almost as tall as I do at six-foot-two and a half.

That's another thing I love about this woman. I've never really cared for short girls. I like being able to throw my arm around her shoulders properly and kiss her without having to lower myself like Silas does with Cecilia.

"You're late again, Adler." Clay appears in the kitchen, heading to the fridge to grab a beer.

"Yup," I answer directly, not bothering to look at him. I can hear the judgment in his voice.

"Where were you?" He folds his arms over his chest, beer bottle still in hand.

My head snaps his way as I work my jaw. "Does it matter? I'm here now," I bite out.

He frowns as his pale gray eyes assess me. Clay's always been good at reading people. And I'm guessing whatever he reads off me tells him I'm not in the mood and that it's none of his business where I was.

Finally, he nods, but before leaving and returning to his spot on the couch, his eyes flick to Veronica, then back to me. There's a question in his gaze, but he doesn't speak it as he exits the kitchen.

I'm guessing by now everyone knows about me and Gabe's current situation involving Veronica. One I'm thankful no one has brought up yet, but I know we'll have to discuss it by the end of the night. I need to convince her to stay. Not just in our home, but with me.

GABRIEL

"So, what's the deal with you guys?" Greyson asks, pulling my attention away from watching my feisty Vixen.

She stands next to my best friend, their shoulders brushing up against each other. It irritates me that she doesn't pull away, that she doesn't push him off like she does with me. Although I think she may slowly be warming up to me as well. *At least, I hope.*

I don't think I've ever craved someone quite like Ronnie. I can't explain this desire I feel for her; it's as if I was hit in the chest by a lightning bolt the moment she came into my life. Even all my conquests since then have greatly dulled. Of course, there's still a lot of hooking up with bunnies, but I never feel satisfied by the end. Like something is missing, or someone. I don't know what I'll do if she never gives me a chance.

"Who?" I flick my gaze to his before turning it to the TV.

"You, Adler, and Ronnie?" He lifts a brow.

"Yeah, will she really be working for you two? Sorry, but I don't see her wanting to spend more time with you guys." Silas chuckles.

"She will," I say undoubtedly.

"You sure about that?" Clay asks.

I deliver my best grin that charms people instantly. *Well, except for my Vixen, apparently.* "Don't worry about it. We'll convince her to stay on." And finish with a wink.

Greyson scoffs. "If you plan on convincing her the same way you convince women to sleep with you, you'd better start looking for a replacement right away."

I smile and lean back in the armchair. "Nah, you'll see. With those chicks it never takes much convincing. We'll bring out the big guns for Ronnie." He doesn't look convinced, none of them do, but I know we'll win her over.

"If you say so," Clay answers, ending the conversation.

My gaze returns to my dream girl as I try to think of a way to keep her with us. All my attempts up to now have been futile. She's a hard one to crack. I can't figure her out, no matter how hard I try, but I find myself wanting to know everything about her.

If she has any birthmarks along her body or maybe scars? What her feet look like bare. Does she match the nail polish on her toes to the color of her hair? What makes her nose wrinkle up in distaste? What does a real laugh falling from her lips sound like? Because the ones she gives us aren't real, they're all fake. I would know; I deliver them daily.

Sometimes when I watch her, which happens a lot, I notice the small little ticks she has. Whether it's to certain words, loud noises, or people getting too close, her shoulders will tighten and instinctively rise. Her smile will falter for a split second, but she immediately replaces it with a strained one.

Then she'll deliver that fake laugh that has a hint of nervousness lingering in it while her hands ball into fists before stretching out. Over and over again she repeats the movement as if she's trying to convince herself of something, like the feeling of her nails digging into her palm somehow grounds her.

I recognize all of them, all the signs. Turns out, my vixen and I may be a lot more alike than we dare to admit. The difference is, I'm better at hiding them than she is.

NOAH

During dinner, Veronica received two texts, and since she was seated beside me, I caught her peering down at her screen. There was no preview of the messages, and both came from different unsaved numbers. She didn't open them either; she simply shut her screen and slipped her phone back into her skirt pocket.

Her throat worked, then she rubbed her palms down the length of her thighs before plastering a smile on her face and laughing along with everyone else. She was trying to act as if she had been paying attention to the conversation, but clearly something had rattled her.

Everyone is hanging around chatting and drinking. Tomorrow, we only have a late morning training session, so we're taking advantage of not having to wake up too early. The kids are off playing with their toys in the living room, not being a bother at all. I have to admit, Greyson and Silas are pretty lucky to have such calm children, who are easily occupied, and no change of environment seems to bother them.

I wander into the kitchen and pour myself a heavy glass of scotch, my drink of choice after my weekly visits. I try not to touch the heavy stuff too much, but on days like this, it's much needed.

"Hey, you." Cecilia sidles up to my side with a nervous smile.

"What can I do for you, little mama?" I wink.

Her cheeks take on a soft pink tint. "Are you mad at me for the whole Ronnie thing? I know I should have said something beforehand, but I couldn't tell her, or else she would have refused. And if I told you guys, you would have never been able to keep your mouths shut. Well, I know Gabe wouldn't have."

"You're right about that." I chuckle from the rim of my glass before taking a sip. "And no, I'm not mad at you. I actually owe you a big thank you. So, whatever you want—new car, expensive purse, diamond earrings—just let me know, it's yours."

"What do you think I married the big guy for?" she jokes.

"I heard that, Minnie!" Silas calls out from a few feet away, where he talks with Clay.

"You know that's not the only reason I married you... what he carries in his pants is." She lowers her voice slightly at the end, but not enough. I think she may have had a little too much to drink.

"Minnie..." he says again with a warning tone.

She looks over at him, smiling above the rim of her wineglass. "You can punish me later, Big Guy." She blows him a kiss, then giggles. *Yup, definitely one glass too many.* Her attention turns back to me, while mine stays glued to the blue and pink-haired goddess sitting alone on the couch.

From this angle, it appears as if she's watching the kids play. But if you pay close attention, you can see the slight blue reflection on the piercings along her ear, meaning she's looking at her phone discreetly. Whatever those texts are, she clearly doesn't want people finding out about them, which only makes my need to know who they're from stronger.

"So... here's the thing. I convinced Ronnie to give it a try for a week. But you two are going to have to convince her on your own to stay on board. And maybe try and not trash the whole place every day," Cecilia whispers.

"I've heard some things that I would prefer not to repeat. But if every time she comes over, the place looks like a dump, she'll quit. So, maybe make a little effort." She bumps her shoulder into mine—well, tries. That woman is so short that she hits closer to my elbow than my shoulder.

I work my brain to try to figure out what exactly she could be referring to. *Yes, the place was filthy, but I didn't think it was that bad.* I finally just nod my head. "We will."

"Good! I hope it works out. And not just because you guys will finally have a stable housekeeper, but it might also give Ronnie a chance to see that you both aren't the big perves you pretend to be. That you're actually pretty freaking great humans." She winks and walks off to her husband.

I take another sip of my drink, contemplating my next move as I look around at our friends, finding that none seem to have noticed Veronica's absence. I push off from the wall I was occupying and walk over to the couch.

I stop at her feet and wait. She's so engrossed with whatever is on her phone that she doesn't notice my presence. She chews on her lip, hand squeezing her phone so tightly that it looks like it might fold in two.

"Can we talk?" I ask softly.

I think this is a good time to discuss this new situation between us. It's not like I can call her or anything, since I don't have her phone number, unlike Gabe, who had to snoop through Emma's phone to get it.

I know I could ask one of the girls, or even the guys, to give it to me. But I'd rather wait until she hands it over herself, giving her as much control as possible. I have a feeling it's something that's important to her. Control.

She jolts in her seat, a quick flash of fear in her eyes before it disappears, and she rights herself. She presses her phone to her chest swiftly to hide the screen from my sight. "I guess we should." She smiles tightly.

I take a seat next to her, and she doesn't move away. "Let me guess—you're here to convince me to keep working for you guys." Veronica smirks as she puts her phone away.

"That is the plan. I noticed everything you did in our home, and I'm impressed. You're really talented," I tell her truthfully.

"I know," she says with pride.

I chuckle and shake my head. I knew she would say that. "Look, I know we aren't the cleanest people around, but we'll try to keep it decent and not overwhelm you. But we really need you; no one else wants to work for us, and we've practically been blacklisted from every cleaning company."

"I can't imagine why." She gives me a knowing look.

"So, will you consider staying on longer than the week trial you agreed to with Cecilia? We'll pay you double."

"I don't know. That depends on you two." She raises a brow.

"How so?" I frown.

"Well, can you guys manage to behave while I'm around? No sexual comments or jokes. No cornering me or getting handsy while I'm working. And for the love of God, if you bring home women, put your condoms in the trash. I should not be finding those lying around all over." She makes a disgusted face.

I laugh. "So, that's what Cece was referring to."

"Yes. I had to share my traumatic experience with someone."

I nod. "Okay, I think we can work with your requests."

"You sure about that? Will you put a leash on Gabe? He's the one who I'm most worried about," she says with a pointed finger.

"I'll get a handle on him. Don't worry," I promise as I finish my drink.

She watches me finish the contents of my glass with a frown. "You shouldn't drink that shit." There's a bite to her tone as if she has a personal vendetta against the Scotch.

"I know."

Her curious eyes find mine. "Then why do you drink it?"

I shrug and sigh. "Because it helps take the edge off."

I can tell she wants to question some more on the subject but decides to drop it. Although she doesn't lose that worried expression on her face.

I place my arm over her shoulders, slowly bringing her into my side. "You don't need to worry about me, Kitten," I whisper close to her hair. I want to kiss the top of her head, show her a sign of affection. But I'm not sure she'd appreciate that, so I refrain.

Gabe suddenly shows up, plopping himself on Veronica's opposite side. His hand immediately comes down to grab her thigh, half over her thigh-high stocking and exposed skin. Her skirts are always pretty short, but sitting down, her legs are practically fully exposed.

"Hey, Vixen. Thought you could sneak off without us noticing?" He grins at her.

I feel her body grow rigid when his hand connects with her leg. It's momentary but still noticeable. *He must have felt it too.*

"I told you to stop calling me that," she snaps at him but doesn't attempt to take his hand off.

"Not a chance. It fits you so perfectly… just like we would." He winks.

She rolls her eyes. "Ugh! See, this is exactly what I mean." She pushes his hand off and shrugs my arm off her shoulders before standing.

She turns to face us and points a finger at me. "Control him. I'm leaving, but I'll be back tomorrow. Your place was such a dump, I didn't manage to finish everything before you got there," she bites out.

I stand from the couch, bringing my body closer to where she's standing. Just how I like it. "Do you need a ride?" I offer.

"No, my car's outside. And even if I did, I wouldn't be getting in a car alone with either of you." She spins on her heels, kisses the children's heads, then marches over to wish goodnight to the rest of the group.

"Fuck, I love when she gets all feisty like that," Gabe says, watching her walk away.

"Yeah, well, you'll have to tone that shit down if you want her to stay," I rebuke him.

"What did I do?" he asks, acting all innocent.

"Maybe stop being so handsy and flirting with her all the time. She's already made it clear many times that she's not into that. Try being nice and helpful instead, it might win you some points."

He leans back against the couch, stretching both arms wide along the back. "Ahh, I see. So, you're allowed to touch her and flirt with her, but I'm not? What's the matter, Noh? You scared I might actually have a better shot at her than you do?" He smiles devilishly. I know he's just trying to get a rise out of me, but it won't work.

"No. I want you to try and be fucking respectful from time to time. No one wants to work for us, and now we finally have someone willing to give us a chance. I'm telling you not to fuck it up," I scold him.

"Don't you worry. I'll be on my best behavior." He grins brightly with a hint of mischief. "She'll be falling in love with us by the end of the week."

"Did you suddenly become a magician or something?" I scoff. It will take a miracle for that to happen, and certainly within a week.

"No, I just have a lot of hidden talents she hasn't seen yet."

God, I don't even want to know what they are.

Chapter Four

GABRIEL

Wild night or night terrors?

~ The Next Day ~

"Where the hell are you, you stupid fucking boy?!" I hear his footsteps walking down the hall, doors being thrown open as he ravages through every room.

I duck deeper into the pile of clothes in my closet. He already came into my room but didn't think about checking the closet. I just hope he'll give up and turn back to whatever he's been taking that makes him and Mom all sleepy. It's the only time they leave me alone; the only time I don't do anything wrong and need to watch my back.

The only time I'm safe.

"That little piece of shit. He's going to pay when I find him!" he yells from farther away.

For a moment, I can't hear him anymore, and I think, maybe, just maybe, he gave up. But then his steps grow louder as he gets closer until my room door flies open and smashes into the wall.

"I know you're in here, boy. Get out now, and I won't be so harsh on you," he taunts.

But I'm not stupid. I've fallen for that trap too many times. And it's always the same; whether I hide or don't, nothing changes. No more playing his games.

I'm twelve now. Ms. Winslow said I could get emancipated at sixteen. She's tried getting child protective services involved many times, but they never do anything. They never believe me because I'm a reckless child who gets into fights all the time. That's how I end up with so many bruises every week. A black eye, split lip, a few broken bones. Yeah, totally makes sense.

But Ms. Winslow, she believes me. She helps treat my wounds and brings me to the hospital when I need stitches or a cast. She's the only good thing in my life. My math teacher of all people. I hate math. She recently got me to join the hockey team at my school, so that I'll have a reason to be out of the house more often, away from my parents until I can leave for good.

Just four more years.

My closet door is ripped off its hinges, making me yelp in fear. The next thing I know, a hand grabs at my hair and pulls me out of my hiding spot. "There you are, you little fucker!" He continues to pull me out of the closet, then throws me on the floor in the middle of my room.

"You just cost me hundreds of dollars!" He kicks me in the leg as I huddle into a fetus position, trying to cover myself as much as possible. There's no point in fighting back, it just makes it worse. I'm still not strong enough. But one day, I will be.

"What? You thought Mr. Baker wouldn't notice the scratches you left on his car!? You thought you could get away with it? Like you thought you could get away with stealing my money?!" He kicks my arms, then stomps on my shoulder.

I squeeze my eyes shut and bite my lip hard until the copper taste fills my mouth. I will myself to stay quiet, to not cry. The less I respond to his assault, the sooner he leaves me alone.

It wasn't even my fault that our neighbor, Mr. Baker's car, got scratched. Lucas, his son, had gotten a new bike and asked me if I wanted to try it out. I've never had a bike of my own, and his looked cool, so I said yes. But then his older brother, Marcus, arrived. He's three years older than us and a real bully.

He walked up to me and pushed me and the bike into the side of his dad's car. Lucas quickly told him to leave me alone and told me not to worry, that he'd tell his dad he did it. But then Mr. Baker came out of the house, and Marcus told him I ran the bike into his car on purpose. To which Mr. Baker said he would have a word with my parents.

I immediately rushed home and went to hide in my closet, knowing what was coming next. It happens every time, whether it was my fault or not. It even happens if I miss a spot while cleaning the dishes. Really, they just use any excuse to hurt me.

I wish I could say my mother wasn't the same. She may not be as harsh, but she still smacks me every chance she gets or burns things I love. And when she isn't hurting me in some way, she's too high to remember I exist. I think that's probably the point.

I don't even understand why they had me in the first place, since they claim to hate me so much. I don't know why they don't just let CPS take me away and send me off to a foster home. Wouldn't it be better for them if I were gone? They wouldn't have to deal with me or spend more money on food to feed me. They always say they wish they could get rid of me, so why won't they?

And the only reason I took the money, which happened one time, was for hockey gear. Ms. Winslow had found someone who was selling their used equipment for fifty dollars. She wanted to pay, but she had already done so much for me. She still does. So, I told her I could get it. I knew what the consequences would be. But I wanted to prove I was capable, that I could take care of myself.

"You're going to pay for this! Every fucking cent I have to spend to fix that asshole's car! You're always such a little shit! Always costing me money!" He kicks harder, over and over again. Everything hurts, but I keep it all in. Every sound. Until he kicks harder along my side and something snaps. I howl in pain, no longer able to contain my cries.

"There. Now you've gotten what you deserve. Go see your bitch so she can fix you up." He kicks my head one last time for good measure, then storms out of my room as I lie there, balled up on the floor, crying until the pain turns numb enough to get up and leave.

I jolt upright in my bed, gasping for air and panting. My shirt and boxers are soaked through, as well as my covers and sheets. My skin is slick and my hair drips as if I've just stepped out of the shower.

When I look down at my hands, I find them twisted in the wet sheets, tear marks from where my fingers clawed at them. *Great, more sheets to buy. I really need to get these nightmares under control.*

I untangle my hands and pass them through my wet, wavy, dirty-blond hair that reaches my shoulders, pushing them off my sticky face. The movement makes my side ache, and I wince, pressing my hand against the rib that was once broken years ago.

This always happens after my dreams. Depending on which traumatic moment from my past resurfaces, I'll feel the pain where the injury happened as if it were still fresh. Usually all it takes is a cold shower and a few hours in the gym to set me back on my feet.

I glance at the clock on my nightstand. *Five in the morning. Not too bad.* Throwing the cover over the side of the bed, I stand and rip off the shirt that's glued to my body because of the sweat. This is why I usually sleep naked. *I must have knocked out before I could finish undressing.*

I pull at the sheets, removing them fully from the bed and ball them up, then throw them by the door to take down to the trash. Beside my bed, I make a second pile with my comforter, shirt, boxers, pillows, and pillowcases.

I also remove the protective waterproof fitted sheet and add it to the growing pile. I quickly learned about this beautiful invention after having changed my mattress five times in the matter of a year because I couldn't get the sweat smell out of it.

Once my bed is completely bare, I jump into a freezing cold shower, closing my eyes as the ice water hits my back, and try to think of a way to get rid of these horrible nightmares. The truth is, I've tried everything. Therapy, meditation, fucking rock crystals. Nothing works.

With a heavy sigh, I wash myself and then step out. After putting on a pair of joggers and a plain shirt, I head down to the gym for a little workout. I won't overdo it since we're training with the team later.

Two hours later, I've just stepped out of my second shower, and likely not my last of the day. I grab the ripped sheets and carry them down to the kitchen, dropping them off on the counter, then head back up to grab the second pile. As I make my way back down, I find Ronnie standing by the kitchen counter, with my shredded sheets in her hands as she inspects them.

Fuck...

Her head turns my way when she hears me take the final step to the landing. "Wild night?" she asks with a raised brow.

I lean against the ramp with a cocky smile. *I can work with this assumption.* "I can show you just how wild it was if you'd like."

Her features transform into a scowl. "Not even twenty-four hours," she murmurs through her teeth.

Noah appears behind me, smacking me at the back of the head on his way down. "Ellis, quit it," he says harshly, then strides over to Ronnie. "Good morning, Veronica. Would you like a coffee?"

"No, thank you. I had one on my way over. I'll just get to work," she tells him, then puts the sheets back down and walks my way, her hands reaching out for the huge pile in mine. "I'll take those. Wash I presume, or do these all have holes as well?"

"Nope, just needs washing. But I can do it." I hold the items closer to my chest. I know they're still damp, and if she sees them, she'll either assume things or have questions. Hell, I'm surprised she even dared to touch the ripped sheets.

She frowns. "You're paying me to take care of your place. Now give me that and let me do my job." She practically rips them from my hands.

The pile is so big, it almost blocks her entire view, where she needs to tilt her head to the side to see past it. She doesn't say anything or make a face when her hand touches the still wet spots. All she does is turn and head for the laundry room without a word.

I head for the kitchen and open the fridge, taking items out to make breakfast. One of the three things I love in my life. My career, my friends, and cooking. It's fucking sad when I think about it. *I'm twenty-eight years old and can only name three things I love. Pathetic.*

I can feel Noah's assessing gaze on my back as I get to chopping the veggies, but I ignore it. "They're getting worse, aren't they?" He finally speaks up but keeps his voice low so that Ronnie won't hear even if she's down the hall.

Noah is the only one outside of the numerous therapists I've had that knows about my bedtime terrors. Well, there's also that one chick that we paid off to keep her mouth shut. She happened to witness one of my episodes when I had knocked out in bed with them after hours of crazy sex. It's been years now, and I've never heard anything about it, so I'm glad to know she kept it to herself.

"Yup." I chop down harder on the broccoli.

"Maybe you could try seeing someone new to help," he says after a beat.

"You think I haven't already tried? I've seen the best of the best, and none work." I drop the knife on the counter, already irritated with this conversation. "Look, I'm sorry that it interrupts your night. I'll get a handle on it." He never really comments on it, but I'm not an idiot. I know he must hear me through the walls during the night.

"Gabe. It's not about me. I don't give a fuck about the noise you make. It's for your fucking sanity. You can't keep going through this every other night. It's not healthy mentally or emotionally. I'm just looking out for you, bro."

I look down at the cutting board in front of me, both hands now fisting the edge of the counter on either side. "I know. I'll look into a new therapist later today."

He nods his head slowly, then raps his knuckles on the counter. "Good, you deserve a fucking night of peace after all the shit you've been through." He steps away and turns his back to me, heading for the elevator. "I'm going for a run. Save me a plate."

"You know I always do, honey!" I shout jokingly, even if it's true.

VERONICA

Originally, I really did think he had some crazy chick in his bed last night; the claw marks in his ripped sheets were no joke. But now that I'm seeing the rest of the mess created, I'm not sure what to think. I've had some crazy wild sex, but never have I gotten the bed this wet. It's as if he took a bucket of water and dumped it over the mattress, then slept in it.

Maybe he's into some weird, kinky shit... I'll have to ask Emma. Wait, no. What the hell am I saying? I don't want to know or care what Gabe is like in bed. I have zero intentions of going there. Nope. Na-uh. Never.

Once I've started the first load of wash, I walk around the penthouse, taking note of everything I still need to do and things I may have missed yesterday. I attack the home gym first since it's clearly been used in the last twenty-four hours. Weights, empty water bottles, and towels lie around the matted floor.

Jesus, is it so fucking hard to put something back where it belongs or in the trash? These boys seriously need a reality check, and I'm not afraid to give it to them.

Since the office and library don't seem to be rooms they use very often, and I had already passed through them yesterday, I move on to the spare bathroom on the lower level. An hour later, I'm back in the laundry room, starting a second wash and rearranging the cleaning supplies that are hidden behind a wall of cabinets.

I'm on all fours, placing products at the back of the cubicle, when the hairs on the back of my neck rise to attention, a sudden sense of being watched washes over me. I look over my shoulder slowly and find Gabe leaning against the door frame, ankles and arms crossed with a sexy, annoying grin along his lips.

"Damn, Vixen. You have no idea how long I've been dreaming of seeing you bent over like that. Plus, at this angle I can practically see that beautiful..." My eyes turn to slits the more he talks, my irritation showing more and more. He clears his throat. "Right. Sorry."

"Can I help you with something? Or are you just going to stand there all day, staring at my ass like some horny teenager?" I lean back onto my calves, blocking the view of my ass he must have been getting, given the length of my skirt. *I should probably start wearing pants if I'm going to be working around these two.*

"Actually, yes. I was coming to get you. I have something for you." He walks up to me and stretches out a hand for me to take.

I growl. "I swear to God, Gabe. If this is your attempt to bring me to your room and whip out your penis. I will stab you."

He laughs. "I promise it's nothing like that. Noah already warned me to be on my best behavior."

"Sure, that's why you're still making sexual jokes every two seconds," I deadpan.

"I can't help it when I see you." He beams like he just gave me a compliment. *I guess he kind of did.*

I sigh and plop my hand in his, letting him help me up. I expect him to let go once I'm back on two feet, but instead, he pulls me out of the room, dragging me down the hall. Normally, I would protest or snatch my hand from his, but I'm slowly getting used to Gabe's antics.

My phone vibrates just below my ribcage inside my waistband. This high-waisted skirt didn't have any pockets, so I had to get creative. I pull it out, and a little too distracted by Gabriel's pull, I click into the new message.

My heeled feet come to a halt, a lump forming in my throat as the sudden feeling of suffocation takes over. I can hear my pulse beating frantically in my ears as I try to swallow the vomit quickly rising.

One text. One single text can send me spiraling. His others weren't harmful, just simple threats with no real harm, but this one is different.

Unknown

> You can't hide from me forever, Veronica.

He attached it with an apple and skyscraper emojis. *Oh, God. He knows where I am...* I begin to hyperventilate, the tightness in my chest getting stronger and stronger.

"Ronnie? What's wrong?" Gabe's voice filters through my panic attack, but not enough to fully pull me out.

It isn't until he lets go of my hand, that was now clawing into his, and steps in front of me. He places both his hands on my cheeks and forces me to look into his gray eyes that hold a tiny speck of blue in each iris. "Vixen, you're okay. Just breathe," he reassures me with a soft voice.

Finally, something in me snaps, and I jolt out of my shocked state. I take a step away from Gabe, his hands dropping from my face. I blink a few times and take a deep, shaky breath, then plaster a smile on my face.

"I'm fine. Sorry, just got a little winded. All good. Probably from lack of nutrition mixed with chemical fumes." I fake a giggle as I tuck my phone away.

I know he doesn't buy a single word I said; his face says it all, but I can't have him asking questions.

Eventually, he gives me that same fake smile. Although his looks way brighter and more realistic. "Then I guess it's a good thing I came to get you when I did." He reaches out and takes my hand once more, resuming his pace down the hall.

He brings me into the kitchen and pulls out a bar stool by the island. "Sit," he instructs.

I don't fight him on it like I normally would. I lack the energy for it and I'm still feeling a bit dazed. He puts a plate down in front of me and smiles from behind the counter.

"What is this?" I point down at it.

"Broccoli and cheese frittata. And an egg, sausage, avocado, and cheese breakfast burrito." He beams with pride.

I'm kind of impressed; this all looks and smells amazing. "You cooked this for me?"

He chuckles and cups the back of his neck. "I mean, yeah. Well, I always cook around here. Earlier you mentioned you had coffee, but nothing about breakfast. And since you were here early, I thought you might get hungry. So, I made you a plate."

He seems nervous. Gabe is never nervous. This is weird. But I'd be lying if I said I wasn't a bit touched by the gesture.

"I didn't know you could cook." He frowns at my comment. "Sorry, I just always assumed you were the *'eat out or takeout'* kind of guy. Maybe even a chef making all your meals."

"Gabe's dishes are practically his babies. Plus, he's kind of a health nut. Gets mad at me every time I eat something remotely unhealthy." Noah arrives behind us, all sweaty as he lifts the hem of his shirt to wipe his face, showcasing perfectly chiseled, slightly tanned abs. *Ugh, this would be so much easier if these boys weren't so gorgeous.*

I look away and turn back to Gabe, who seems to disagree with Noah's statement. "That is not true. I'm not a total health nut. I do occasionally indulge in a burger and fries, or even pizza."

"You mean the indulgence you have every last Friday of the month?" Noah snickers, then looks at me. "And it's only for one meal, not the whole day."

My mouth opens wide in shock, while Gabe glares at Noah. *Who the hell only eats something unhealthy for one meal throughout the whole month?*

"Will you just shut up and eat?" Gabe says with annoyance toward Noah.

He takes a seat beside me and shrugs. "What? I'm only calling it like it is."

"Well, it's not true. I have sorbet at least once a week," Gabriel responds with satisfaction, like he just proved a point. *He really didn't.* I scoff into my hand, making him narrow his eyes at me. "What?"

"You really think eating sorbet once a week is unhealthy?" I question with raised brows.

"Homemade sorbet," Noah whispers over.

"It isn't. It's full of sugar and low on nutrients," he says defensively.

"Yeah, if you eat a bucket's worth of it! But you make it yourself, which I'm betting you either downsize on the sugar or replace it with honey. And most likely use low-sugar fruits."

"Honey," Noah informs me, and I can't help but giggle.

"That still doesn't make it healthy!" Gabe's voice rises slightly, irritation in his eyes.

"Gabe, sorbet is basically frozen water and fruit. It's like the healthiest freaking dessert you can have!"

"THANK YOU!" Noah exclaims. "I've been telling him this for years, but he won't believe me."

"Wait, hold up." Gabe lifts his hand, stopping mine and Noah's laughter. "Did you just call it frozen water? Like, instead of ice?"

I groan and close my eyes. *I should have known they'd pick up on that.*

Noah laughs loudly and slaps his hand on the island. "She did. I heard it too but wasn't sure if my hearing was playing tricks on me."

"Shut up, okay. It's just a silly thing I picked up as a kid. I thought it would be cooler to call it frozen water instead of ice. But then it grew on me, and now I can't help it!" They both laugh harder, and I feel a smile growing on my face as well. "Can we just eat now, before it gets cold?"

"Yes, please. Dig in," Gabe says once his laughter starts to subside. "Vixen, I wasn't sure if you had any allergies, so maybe name them before taking a bite. Just in case."

"I don't. But thank you for worrying about my health, Pretty Boy." I wink at him, which makes his smile stretch to his ears.

"Good, what would you like to drink with that? We have grapefruit, orange, cranberry, pomegranate, and apple. Of course, there's also coffee, or you could try my green smoothie. I'm about to make one."

"What's in it?" I ask skeptically.

"You don't want to know," Noah tells me as he begins to dig into his plate.

"Okay... well, is it at least good?"

Noah goes to answer, but Gabe cuts him off. "He wouldn't know; he's never tried it. But I promise, it tastes a lot better than it looks."

"I hope it does, because that thing looks like vomit or sewer water," Noah says under his breath.

"Eww, Noah. That's just nasty, we're eating." I turn back to Gabe, who looks excited at having someone try his concoction. "You know what? Yeah, hit me with it. Aubrey always makes me try her weird recipes and food combinations, so I'm pretty sure I've had worse."

"Yes! See, Noh, I always knew she had bigger balls than you do."

I laugh as I finally take a bite of my food and... *Oh my God! This is amazing!* A moan slips out as I take another bite of my burrito with closed eyes. When I open them, I find both men staring at me like hungry vultures. I would normally comment on that, but I'm too busy having an explosive orgasm in my mouth.

"Holy shit, Gabe! Does Morgan know you can cook like this?"

He chuckles. "I don't think so."

"Okay, good. We're never telling her." I shake my head and take another bite. Another moan. I'm pretty sure even my eyes roll back.

"Veronica. I'll have to ask you to stop doing that. We promised to be on our best behavior, but you aren't making it exactly easy right now." Noah frowns.

"He's right. You're not playing fair," Gabe agrees. "But why can't we tell Morg exactly?"

He gets to work on putting his ingredients into the blender as I wipe my mouth with a napkin. "Remember that time Sam made dinner for all of us when we first met him, and Morgan said she was fine with someone else cooking?"

They both nod. "Well, she was lying. The next day, she replicated his dishes and made us girls vote on who did it best. It was easy because both were amazing. But if she went up against you, I'm not sure I could lie to her face..."

He smiles. "I'll take that as a compliment."

I nod my head. "It is. I expect this kind of treatment every day that I'm over. Thank you."

"Your wish is my command, milady." He winks and starts blending his green mixture that truly does look like sewer water and is starting to make me worry. *Oh, good God... what have I agreed to?*

The boys go on to bicker over something else, constantly throwing back and forth friendly insults. It's amusing to watch them go at it, I almost want to ask for some popcorn. I've never seen this side of them, and it's one I quite enjoy. I find myself smiling at their interactions.

I think this is what Cecilia was talking about when she said to give them a chance. That they aren't who I pegged them out to be. The only problem is, this version of them is much more dangerous. Because this version, I can see myself liking, can see myself falling for.

And I can't let that happen.

Chapter Five

NOAH

Ugly yet delicious.

This is nice, sitting here with Veronica, enjoying a meal where we all talk, laugh, and joke around. There are no sexual comments or innuendos, just actual, genuine conversations. We've never had this with all three of us together. I think this might help us gain some points with her. She seems happy rather than annoyed to be around us.

"Here you go," Gabe says as he passes the smoothie over to Veronica.

She picks it up and inspects it with a strange look on her face. She brings it up to her nose for a sniff test and instantly wrinkles it up, then lets out a breath and takes a sip. Gabe and I watch her intently, waiting for a sign of whether or not she likes it.

She swallows and licks her lips. "Okay, wow. This is actually really good. How can something so ugly be so delicious?"

I groan and throw my head back, fully knowing I'll never hear the end of this.

"See! I fucking told you it was good!" Gabe points a finger in my face, then fist bumps Veronica. She smiles with a giggle and bumps her fist against his.

These smiles and laughs are different than the ones she usually presents us with when we're the whole gang together. I'm not saying those are all fake, but these ones seem to come from deep down, like even if she tried to hide them, she couldn't.

She clears her throat after another sip of her drink. "Actually, since I have both of you here. There's something I'd like for us to discuss."

I turn on the barstool to face her, and Gabe leans over the counter. "We're listening." *What could she possibly need to talk to us about?*

"So, I know you need me for cleaning, which is perfectly fine. I was just wondering if you were expecting other things from me as well." She looks at us both, expecting an answer.

Where the hell is this conversation going? I know we've always tried to get with Veronica. But she can't really be offering it that easily... can she?

Gabe peers at me, clearly thinking the same thing as I am, then looks back at her before asking, "Like?"

"Well, I don't know, like groceries or dry cleaning? Maybe some errands you guys don't have time to do with your packed schedule?" *Ah, that makes more sense.*

I clear my throat. "I think those are things we would appreciate if you're offering. We usually order our things online and get them delivered. But sometimes we forget and have to run out and grab stuff or crash someone's house for food."

"Usually Burkley's," Gabe adds in. "Same goes for our dry cleaning. We end up forgetting and have to rush the day before to find somewhere that will do our suits quickly."

"Or we beg Morgan behind her husband's back, and she adds them in with his," I tell her.

Her brows are raised and eyes wide. "Wow, you two really are boys," she murmurs. "Okay, no more depending on Morgan. We're going to turn you into men. If I have to make charts to keep everything up to date, I will." She nods before going on. "I'm going to need a detailed list of your schedules. For food, I want a list of things you like and don't like."

"That might be a little complicated, Gabe can be very picky with the ingredients and all that," I inform her.

It's why I stopped doing the groceries and let him take over. Getting yelled at because I bought the wrong brand of noodles is not something I ever planned to experience. *From my wife, yes. But my best friend? No.*

"That's okay, I was up all night looking into that, and there's actually this app that exists that can be put on your phone, where you add whatever you want to it, with precision. I'll sync all of our devices together; then I'll be able to see your requests and have everything delivered. Here, pass me your phones. I'll set it up right now."

We hand over our devices, and she quickly taps away at Gabe's first, passing it back, then doing the same to mine, although it takes her a few extra seconds. "There, all set. I also added my number into your phone and texted myself," she tells me.

"I think it would be good to have each other's numbers if we have any last-minute information that needs to be passed around. Gabe, I already know you have my number, thanks to the shirtless picture you sent me last month." She narrows her eyes at him.

He passes his hand through his hair and gives her an abashed chuckle. "Yeah... sorry about that." Definitely not one of Gabe's finest moments. He thought it was appropriate and funny to send all the women in our group a picture of himself basically naked at four in the morning.

"Mhmm." She gives him a disappointed look. "Anyway, for the dry cleaning, I'll think of a system for us that works best to have everything ready on time. I was also going to offer working every other day. So, one week, four days, the next, three. Since you two seem to be quite... disorganized. At least until you have a better handle on keeping things in an appropriate state."

That's her polite way of saying we're slobs. Veronica doesn't usually sugarcoat things, so I appreciate the effort. Although I do like her unfiltered mouth.

"That seems like a good plan. We wanted to sound reasonable with three days a week. But if we could have you here every day, we would." I smile, no hidden meaning behind it. I just love having her in our presence, but we don't want to overwork her either.

"Okay then! I'm going to head out and buy some things that I need for here. I'll be here when you two get back from your training." She stands from her seat with one hand placed on the island. "Gabe, thank you for breakfast. It was delicious. Noah, take a shower. You stink."

Gabe and I bellow with laughter. *There's our feisty girl.* She goes to leave, but I jump up from my stool and grab her elbow. She inhales sharply, staring down at my hand. I drop it quickly and take a step back.

"Sorry," I say as she nods in response. "Here, for anything you have to buy. Don't worry about the price." I fish out my wallet and hand her one of my credit cards.

She takes it and turns it over in her hands. "Thank you." She smiles and spins on her heels, walking to the elevator.

I return to my plate, finishing off the last few pieces of my frittata. I stand once more and turn to leave but think better of it. I grab my plate and mug, gulping down the rest of my coffee as I walk over to the sink and deposit the dishes inside. *See? Already an improvement. I didn't leave it on the counter.*

"I'm going to take a shower, then we should head out for practice."

"Wait!" Gabe calls as I turn to leave. "There's something I want to talk to you about."

I face him, taking a few steps closer, and lean against the counter with my arms crossed at my chest. "What is it?"

He looks past my shoulder, toward the direction Veronica left, then back into my eyes, and with the look he gives me, I know whatever he's about to say is serious. "Something's going on with Ronnie," he says in a hushed voice just in case she still may be here.

"What do you mean?" I frown.

"She received a text or something earlier, and it freaked her out. Enough to give her a small panic attack."

My interest peaks instantly. "Did you see it? The text. What did she say?"

"No, I was more focused on trying to calm her down. I didn't think of looking. And she didn't say anything. Once she snapped out of it, she claimed she just got dizzy. Like I would buy that shit." He scoffs with an angry look.

I nod and mull over his words. "It's not the first time she has gotten one. Yesterday at Ford's, she received two messages over dinner. They were strange numbers, like those you'd expect from a burner phone. She didn't open them, but she looked spooked and paled just seeing them pop up."

"What do you think it could be?" Gabe asks, a sense of worry lacing his tone.

I shrug. "A stalker maybe? I really have no clue. It could be a lot of things."

"Well, whatever it is, she should tell us about it if it's affecting her that badly. I'm sure we could help in some way."

"Does Veronica look like the kind of girl who talks about her life openly? And do you really think she would come to us if she had a problem, out of everyone?" I give him a *'you should know better'* look.

"Okay, so we ask the guys. Maybe they've heard something through their wives. And if not, then we get Ronnie to trust us enough until she tells us," he delivers his plan.

I mean, it's a pretty good plan. Although getting her to trust us enough to divulge her secrets might take a while. "Yeah, okay. Let's ask the guys first, then we can move on to plan B and what exactly that would require." I push off the counter and walk out of the kitchen. "Jumping in the shower now. Get ready."

"Ooh, you want me to join you?" he teases childishly, but it still pulls a smile out of me.

"Fuck off."

I finish my last set on the bench press and sit up, wiping my forehead with my towel. I then stand from the bench, wipe it down, and head over to where Burkley and Hayes sit while taking a small break from their workout. A minute later, Ellis and Ford join us.

"Ellis, not your best work today. What's up?" Silas leans in to get a better look at Gabe.

He's a good team captain; I get why he got the position. And there's no doubt when he retires, Clay will be taking his spot if he's still playing. Those two are always attentive to every player and helping out.

"Just a rough night and an extra workout earlier." Gabe shrugs.

"Jesus, I'm too old to be working out twice a day," Clay murmurs as he stretches out his shoulders.

"What's the matter? Age catching up to you, old man?" Greyson chuckles.

"Shut up, doofus. You're only two years younger than I am." Clay furrows his brow in his direction.

Silas laughs at their exchange for a moment but then grows serious and turns his attention back to Gabe. "Rough night or wild night?"

"I wish." Gabe smirks. "Nah, just couldn't sleep. It happens from time to time. Nothing to worry about."

Silas nods, but Clay watches him carefully. He can tell there's more to the story, but like always, he doesn't say anything unless he absolutely has to.

"You know if there's something going on, you can talk to us," Silas offers Gabe, and by the way Gabe's jaw ticks subtly, I can tell he's getting annoyed at having their attention on him. I decide now is the best time to change the subject from him.

"Actually, there is something we wanted to bring up." They all lean in, waiting for me to elaborate. "Have you guys noticed anything strange going on with Veronica?"

Their brows all furrow in confusion.

"Uh, no. Not really," Silas says with a head shake.

"Honestly, I don't pay Ronnie enough attention to notice if something was off," Grey adds with an apologetic shrug.

"That's because you're too focused on Emma to even notice anything else happening around you." Clay smirks.

"Oh, shut up. Like you guys are any better." He rolls his eyes as we all laugh. He's right, though, these guys are all obsessed with their women. I guess Gabe and I can kind of relate.

"But seriously, not even a weird face when she's on her phone? Nothing? What about your girls? They haven't mentioned anything?" Gabe questions.

They all shake their heads at the same time.

"If something were going on, Aubrey would probably be your best shot at finding out. They live together after all," Greyson says next.

He's right. But I have a feeling that if Veronica didn't mention it to the girls, then it's because she doesn't want people to know. We can relate to that.

"Why, what's going on?" Silas looks at us with worry.

"Nothing. She just felt off last night and today again. We were just wondering if there was something we should know." *There, that should get them to drop it.*

Clay snorts. "That's probably because she's now working for you two jackasses."

"Actually, that's been going pretty well. We have been nothing short of polite and respectful with her," Gabe tells them with a proud, glowing smile.

"Ah, you've both been bitten by the lovebug." Silas leans back against the wall, fingers interlocking behind his head as his eyes close. "I swear, that thing is contagious. We went from full-on bachelors to all getting married."

"What? No, we haven't. He's not married," I say, pointing at Ford. "And we're not even in a relationship," I finish, throwing a finger back and forth between me and Gabe.

"Yet. I'm not married yet. But I will be by the end of the year." Greyson's eyes light up at the mention of marrying his girlfriend.

"Does she know that?" Burkley laughs.

"She will soon." He winks back. "And don't rule out so quickly that you aren't going down the same path we are. You two have been obsessed with Ronnie since November. And don't try to pass it off as just wanting to sleep with her, because we all know that's bullshit."

"He's right. I've never seen you guys so hung up over someone before. And now that she's basically surrounded by you two daily, there's no way nothing's going to happen," Silas adds.

"What are you guys gonna do if shit gets serious?" Clay asks curiously.

"What do you mean?" Gabe looks at me with a confused look then back to Burkley.

"Well... there are two of you and one of her."

Shit, I hadn't thought about that...

We exit the elevator in our penthouse, and I immediately feel like something's different; I just can't place what exactly. Gabe stops beside me and looks around with that same expression, as if he's waiting for something to pop out that we haven't noticed.

"Oh! Good. You're back." Veronica comes into view with a smile. "Sit." She points to the couch.

I look at Gabe, and he shrugs, then trots over to the couch and plops down. I walk over and sit next to him, while Veronica comes to stand before us with her hands on her hips.

"So, I've changed a few things around here. As you can see, I've added side tables to the couch." *Ah, so that's what's different.* She frowns. "Let me guess, you didn't even notice?"

"In all fairness, we noticed *something* was different," Gabe justifies.

"So, what you're saying is I could have changed the couch color, and you wouldn't have noticed? Just felt something was off."

I lift a shoulder. "Pretty much."

"Good to know." She nods with a mischievous smirk, but then it drops. "But you see, that's the problem. That's why you're so messy. You guys don't pay attention to things, so it becomes easy to leave stuff lying around without realizing it. Which is why I have added some things around the house to help you in the right direction, without pushing too much."

She claps her hands together. "First off, I've added garbage baskets to every single room, except for those that already had them. Like, for example, there's one right beneath the side table right there." She points to said basket. "You know, so you can put your trash in it, since the kitchen is too far of a walk." She narrows her eyes at us with disappointment.

"Next, I've added a recycling bin and a clothing basket in the gym. One for your water bottles, and the other for your dirty towels. There are also new baskets in your personal bathrooms for your dirty clothes, so no more leaving them in a heaping pile. Just throw it in the basket. That's all I'm asking." We both nod. *We can do that... probably.*

"Okay. I've also installed three hooks behind each of your bedroom doors. Those will be used for anything you might want dry-cleaned. Just hook it up and I'll take care of the rest. Hmm, what else..."

She taps a slender finger to her pretty lips. "Oh! Noah, thank you for putting your dishes in the sink." She smiles at me, and fuck if my heart doesn't do a somersault in my chest.

"Gabe... we need to work on putting things away. You left everything on the counter, so I've added a little bin that hooks to the lower cabinet door. I placed it right below where you use the blender, so when you're done with your ingredients, just slide them right into the bin. As easy as that."

"Wait, you did all that while we were gone? You even built the side coffee tables?"

I ask, now realizing how much she's done.

"I did. It was pretty simple, actually. I had planned on cleaning up the outdoor area, but I forgot to ask you how to open that damn door."

"I'll show you later. But you don't need to clean out there. We never really use it," I inform her.

"That's a shame. It looks beautiful, and the view must be magnificent. With the right outdoor furniture and decorations, it could be spectacular." She sounds almost dreamy as she says it.

"Well then, you have the go-ahead to do whatever you want with it," Gabe offers.

"Oh, I had already planned to," she says matter-of-factly, which makes us both chuckle. "That reminds me." She holds up a finger and walks away, coming back seconds later with a bag in hand.

She opens it up and retrieves what looks like bed sheets. "Here, I got these for you." She hands them over to Gabe for him to look over.

"Umm... there were extra sheets in the linen closet. You didn't need to buy new ones." He looks uncertain of how to react and slightly uncomfortable.

"I know. But these are cooling sheets. They'll help keep your body cool and not sweat as much. And apparently, they're very durable too, less likely to rip." The tiniest hint of a blush forms over her cheeks. This is the first time I've seen Veronica blush, hell, I'm not even sure you can consider it that, but it's a beautiful sight I didn't know I needed.

"Oh... well, thank you," Gabe says with a nervous smile.

"You're welcome. Anyway, I think that was all for now. I hope you'll both make an effort with what I've asked of you. And well, if you don't, there will be consequences." She smiles, but it looks diabolical.

"Wait, wait. What do you mean by consequences?" Gabe sits up and scoots to the edge of the couch.

"Well, Gabe, if you don't at least try, I'll make you eat an unhealthy meal every time you leave stuff around. That should motivate you."

His mouth gapes. "WHAT!? No way."

"Then start picking up after yourself, Pretty Boy." She folds her arms under her chest.

He grumbles something we don't catch, then sighs. "Fine! What about him?" He nods my way.

She looks me up and down, thinking. "Noah, can you cook?"

I go to answer, but Gabe scoffs beside me. "No, he can't cook for shit. Why do you think I'm in charge of every meal around here?"

She smiles wickedly now. "Good. Then every time you leave something lying around, Gabe will not cook for you, and you'll be in charge of making your own meals for the day. No takeout, no leftovers. Seems fair?"

Now it's my turn for my jaw to drop. "How is that fair?!"

"Well, you boys know what to do if you don't want to deal with the consequences. Now show me how to open the patio door so that I can continue working. Gabe, just leave the sheets on your bed, I'll set them up before leaving." She turns and heads toward the outdoor space we have.

"How did we go from hiring a housekeeper to having a mother?" Gabe asks while staring at her back.

"I was wondering the same thing."

"You should have expected it!" Veronica calls out.

We really should have.

Chapter Six

VERONICA

How hard can it really be to make mac and cheese?

I stop at the small deli shop near our condo and order two sandwiches for me and Aubrey before heading to the cute little bakery she works at. Gabe had invited me to stay for dinner, bribing me with more delicious creations, but I had promised to bring Brey dinner since she left hers at home.

I pay for the sandwiches and head out of the shop, walking the two blocks to the bakery as my mind wanders over the day I've had. I must admit, I had a good time with the twins today. It's strange to think that in just two days, I'm starting to see them differently, and I'm not sure how to feel about that.

When we were having breakfast together, it felt good. I didn't feel like I had to force my smiles or my laughs; they just came naturally. I could see it always being like that. Gabe even surprised me by going a full day without flirting, which has never happened since I've known him. He was actually really kind, and it was nice to see under the whole playboy persona he puts on.

Even when I had my little freak out in the hall, he didn't push me for information or make a joke about it like I would have expected him to. Instead, he took my mind off it and acted like it never happened.

And then there's Noah. I can never get a good read on him; I never know what he's thinking. He's always polite with me, a real charmer like always, but it's subtle. Sometimes he looks at me and acts in certain ways that make me question what exactly he might know about me.

I know he's picked up on my dislike of being touched because he refrains from doing so for the most part. And when he does, it's gentle and slow. Like he's waiting to see how I'll respond, waiting for my body and mind to accept him. And somehow, it always does. I always feel safe with his hands on my body. And then I find myself getting lost in his deep brown eyes, that small, secretive smirk he gives me when we look at each other.

Fuck. When the hell did he slip under my defenses? I don't do secret smiles or eye gazing. I don't do feelings, and I most certainly don't do boyfriends. Get yourself together, Ronnie!

I shake my head as I make it to the bakery and pull the door open to the charming little building. I walk up to the counter and order two drinks to accompany our food from the teenage girl behind the counter just as Aubrey walks out of the back door to her office.

I pull out my card to pay for our drinks, but as I go to swipe it, I notice it's black, whereas mine is silver. At first glance, I'm confused, but then I realize it's Noah's card. "Shit." *I never gave it back, and I used it at the deli earlier.* I quickly exchange it for the right card and pay.

"What's wrong?" Aubrey asks in her usual soft voice.

"Nothing, I just realized I used Noah's card to pay for our food. It's fine, though. I'll just text him to let him know so that he doesn't think I'm taking advantage of him." I wave a hand like it's no big deal.

We collect our drinks and take our seats at the corner table, like we always do when I stop by to see my girl at work. I hand over her sandwich and unwrap mine as she places papers on the table beside her.

"What are you doing?"

She looks up from the sheets in front of her and smiles sheepishly. "I'm going over our menu items and seeing what sells and what doesn't. While also thinking about what we could add or change."

"It must be nice to practically be the boss around here." I wouldn't know what that's like, but it seems cool to make all the choices.

"Well, it isn't always easy, and it also means more hours. Having to cover when someone doesn't come in and take blame for anything and everything that goes wrong." She widens her eyes but then smiles with pure joy.

"But I love it. I get to bring in my own little touches here, you know. Having Clara let me take the reins and add my own items to the menu makes me so grateful. And then having clients rave about my creations..." She sighs whimsically. "It's like a dream come true."

"I can tell." In the three years I've known Aubrey, I've never seen her this happy.

"You know, I was afraid I had made a mistake at first, dropping out and taking over here, that maybe my passion was just a hobby and nothing more. But I see it now—this is the best decision I've ever made for myself. This is where I belong. Maybe not this specific bakery, but in this industry."

"Have you ever thought of opening up your own place?"

She blushes at my question. "It would be the goal. But it requires a lot of money, and I don't want to ask my brother for help. He's already done so much for me. It's why I've practically been putting ninety percent of my earnings in a savings account. I'm hoping within the next five to ten years it will be possible to have my own little place."

I place my hand over hers on the table, giving it a little squeeze. "You'll get it for sure. I have no doubt. You're so talented, Aubrey, there's no way your talent stops here."

"Thank you. And thank you for giving me the kick in the butt to go against my brother's wishes and take this route. If it weren't for you, I'd probably still be in school studying courses I don't even like." She giggles.

"Well, you can thank me when you're rich and famous by buying me a nice villa in Italy." I wink as she laughs.

My phone buzzes on the table, and I lift it to see who it could be. At first my nerves kick up, fearing it could be another message from someone I wish had forgotten about me, but when I see Noah's name pop up, a smile forms on my lips. I unlock my phone and tap into the message.

Noah

> I see you're using me for my money. <Wink emoji>

Me

> You should know this by now. All I ever wanted was your money. <Wink emoji>

Noah

> Damn, I should have known you were too good to be true.

Me

> Sorry to ruin your fantasies about me.

Noah

> Nah, you could never ruin those, Kitten.

I bite my lip as I read his text. It's like I can hear him saying it. Hear him calling me Kitten in that deep, smooth, masculine voice. Even when he says my name, it always sounds different coming from him. Over the last few years, I've hated people calling me Veronica. But with him, it makes a knot form in my stomach. And not an unpleasant one.

Another message comes in that makes me giggle.

Noah

BTW, I'm a little disappointed that you'd prefer to have something at a deli rather than eat with us.

Me

I didn't have a choice. I promised Aubrey I'd bring her dinner at work. Or else I could have maybe been persuaded into staying.

Noah

Noted… for next time. <Smile emoji>

Me

Seriously, though, I didn't mean to use your card. I noticed after using it and was going to tell you. I'll pay you back.

Noah

No need, I like knowing you're using me. If it's not for my body, at least let it be my money. <Wink emoji>

Me

You're ridiculous. <Face palm emoji>

"Oh God, not you too…"

I look up from my phone to find Aubrey staring at me with wide eyes. "What?"

"They got to you, didn't they?" she questions.

"No, why would you say that?" I furrow my brows in confusion.

"Because you were just wearing that same goofy smile that the other girls wear every time their men message them."

My mouth opens and closes like a fish. *Was I really doing that?* "I was not," I stagger.

"You were. Trust me, I see that look all the time on Emma's face, as well as Cecilia's and Morgan's." I honestly don't even know what to say about that, so I just stay mute. "I take it today went well?"

I clear my throat, pushing what she said to the far back of my brain. "Yeah, actually, it did. I can't believe I'm saying this, but they're really not how I've always seen them. We actually had a good time and talked like normal people for once. It was refreshing."

She nods. "So, what now? What does that mean for you guys?"

"Absolutely nothing. You know I don't do the boyfriend thing. We're just going to be spending more time together, probably become better friends. But that's all," I say, trying to convince myself more than her.

~ *One Week Later* ~

The boys are coming home from their away game today. This was their third win in the Stanley Cup finals, which means they now have a three-to-two lead. One more win and they take the cup home. It will be their first time winning it in a very long time, so I know how excited they all are. Although I might be dimming that excitement a bit when they get home.

I started redoing the outdoor space two days ago, and I'm glad to say it's pretty much done. It now looks like a beautiful oasis with a magical view of the city. I've set up two outdoor couches, a coffee table, a small outdoor dining table with chairs, some tall leafy plants, string lights all over, and a cute little bird feeder in the corner. It's simple, yet breathtaking.

It gives off this sense of calm and peace. I picture myself coming home after a long day at work, kicking off my shoes as I pour myself a glass of wine. Then I'd come out here to watch the sun set over the city as the birds stop by for their final snack of the day before flying freely back to their nests.

Ugh, I could live here forever.

Except the reality is, this is my place of work, not my home. And I won't get to do those things I dream of. Hell, I'll probably never even get to use it, let alone watch the sunset out here. *How unfair life can be sometimes...*

I finish installing the last throw pillows over the couches outside and place the soft throw blankets into the outdoor waterproof storage bin I got. Then I plug in the little string lights to light up the place. It's still daytime, so it doesn't show off as well as I'd like it to, but I want the boys to see what I've done with the place. And I'm hoping with it looking this nice, they'll use it more often.

I would hate for all this money to go to waste. Noah is going to flip when he sees all the money I've spent since they left. Although now that I think about it, he probably already knows. He most likely gets a notification every time I use his card, since he knew about the sandwiches before I even told him.

Well, that could be fun... I wonder how he'd feel if I started buying some very inappropriate things with it. We'll have to test that out.

I walk over to the adorable bird feeder that looks like a mini toy mansion with seeds flowing from every balcony just as a house sparrow lands on one of them and begins pecking at the grains.

"Hey, little thing," I say quietly, trying not to make any sudden movements to scare it off.

The small brown bird looks at me with the tilt of its head before going back to eating, not seeming bothered by my presence at all. I watch it for a few minutes as it jumps from one balcony to the other, testing out different seeds I've placed in each section until it returns to the first, clearly its favorite.

"You know, this place could be all yours if you decide to come back. I promise to fill it every day, so you never run out." I slowly bring my finger closer to where it's perched and wait patiently.

I've always found birds fascinating—how they get to live their entire lives however they choose, going wherever their pretty wings take them. Nothing holds them back, no invisible chains or bars, no fears. They're just... free.

After a few seconds, it begins to bounce around again, turning in every direction as it seems to inspect my finger before finally landing on it. I smile, feeling its tiny nails biting into my skin as it leans forward to eat some more. As I watch it, I'm taken back to when I had just moved to New York, back to a time when I felt so alone and lost in the world and was looking for guidance, a sign of where to go next, what to do next. A way to survive.

And as I was sitting in my shitty rundown apartment that was only big enough for a single bed, two-seater couch, and stove, a cute little bird just like this one decided to land outside my open window. It stayed there for a good half hour, slightly stepping inside a few times, before finally flying away.

Only it didn't stop there. The next day, I found my new friend perched on the windowsill the moment I entered my apartment. I took that as the sign I was looking for. I didn't lure it back, didn't leave seeds behind in hopes it would return. It chose to come back, just like it did every day for an entire week.

I was exactly where I was meant to be.

I bring my other finger up slowly, petting the back of the little sparrow delicately before it hops off my finger, then turn for the patio doors, knowing the boys will be here any minute. Just as I'm stepping back inside, the elevator dings, indicating its arrival. I quickly shut the patio door behind me as the boys stroll out of the cab.

"Welcome home," I say with a smile.

I'm surprised at how empty the place felt without them here. I've gotten used to seeing them at some point during the day... I hate to admit it, but I missed having them around.

Gabe beams as he strides over to me. "There's my beautiful Vixen!"

I know what's coming next, so I prepare myself for the itchy feeling to set in as he wraps his hands around my waist and lifts me off the ground. "God, I've missed seeing this sexy body."

My legs wrap around his hips and arms around his neck before I even realize what I'm doing. *We'll say it's just instinct, no real meaning behind it.* "You're ridiculous. It was two days." Despite my rigid body in his hold, I feel that icky feeling begin to diminish.

"Still too long, I'd have you with me at all times if I could." He gazes at me with lust-filled eyes. It's like I can see all the naughty thoughts filtering through them.

I unfold my arms from around his head and place my hands on his shoulders, giving a little tap. "All right, that's enough. Put me down, Pretty Boy." He laughs but does as I've asked. Once my feet hit the ground, I walk over to Noah, who waits patiently a few steps away.

"Hey, Kitten," he says with his arms open but doesn't move to take me in, waiting for me to come into the embrace.

I did just let Gabe pick me up, so might as well give him some attention too. I lift my arms and step into him, my body pressing up against his as my arms circle his neck. He stands still for a few seconds before his own come to hug my body tightly to his.

We've never done this before, hugging like this. Side embraces with his arm around my shoulder, yes. But never full-body contact, where my nose presses against his skin and his woodsy scent envelops me. And like always, that itchy feeling never comes.

I don't know what it is about Noah, why his touch is different from any others. Even my ex didn't make me feel this safe in his arms. I find myself craving this feeling more and more with each passing day. A feeling I shouldn't want. But I can't help it, I'm human after all. *Just one more second.*

I let out a breath and untangle my arms from him just as he lets go of me. He smiles, even though there's a hint of disappointment that the hug is over. "I see you're still spending my money." He smirks.

"Oh, yeah. I've been going crazy. I mean, it's not every day you get to use a card with no limit." I wink at him. "But I promise it was all worth it. Come see."

I walk backwards to the patio door, making sure they're following me. I should know better by now; these two always follow me around, never far behind.

"Prepare to be amazed, gentlemen." I slide the door open and step aside, letting them go first.

"Holy shit! You did all of this yourself?" Gabe gasps as he skips over to the couches and throws himself down on one of them.

"I did, I came in yesterday to set most things up and finished it just before you guys got here. I hope it's okay that I came in on my day off?"

"Of course, baby. You're free to use our place whenever you'd like. Even if it's just to crash, there's a spare bedroom. Although there are two other rooms that wouldn't mind having you in them." He winks, then grins when I roll my eyes.

"It's beautiful, Veronica. Thank you for doing all of this. And feel free to use it whenever you'd like. You're always welcome here." Noah smiles at me, then glares at Gabe. "That's what Ellis meant to say."

"Totally what I meant."

I turn to Gabe with a smile. "Sure, it was."

"So, what else have you been up to while we were away? Have any... fun time in our rooms that didn't involve changing the sheets?" He wiggles his brow in that suggestive way.

"Actually, no... I did it on the kitchen island."

Gabe chokes on air as he sits up on the couch, eyes wide like saucers. "You're serious?"

I bite my lip, adding to the convincing play. "Mhmm. I was wearing a similar skirt to this one. I laid back and spread my legs, then took these two fingers." I bring up my middle finger and ring finger as he stares at them with hungry eyes. "And pushed them deep inside me as I thought of you," I finish in a sultry voice.

I swear Gabe looks like he's about to rip his hair out of his head with how hard he's pulling on it. "Holy fuck, that's hot. Did you really?"

I place my hands on my hips and frown at him. "Of course not, you idiot. Do I look like some crazy chick who masturbates on people's counters?"

"I mean... You kind of do look like the type that—"

"Don't you dare finish that sentence, Pretty Boy!" I glare at him.

He lifts his hands up in surrender. "Sorry," he says sheepishly.

"Anyway! I wanted to congratulate you boys on your win last night. Very impressive." I smile at them both.

"Thank you," they both say at once.

"But I have some bad news."

Their faces drop, worried expressions quickly morphing in. "What is it? Are you okay? What's going on?" Noah steps up closer and takes my hand.

I'm momentarily stunned by how genuine his concern seems that I have to blink a few times to remember what I was about to say. "Umm, yes, I'm okay. Nothing's wrong." I smile reassuringly. "But do you two remember when I talked about those consequences for when you leave stuff around?"

Gabe's face turns into a terrified look. "Oh no... no, no, no."

"I'm afraid so. You guys were doing so well. You were both so on top of everything in the beginning. But... Gabe, you left all your fruit peels on the counter. And Noah, you left your dirty clothes littering the bathroom floor." I look from one to the other.

"Also, I found a granola wrapper beside the couch... in front of the garbage basket. I don't know who is to blame for that one, but both of you are in trouble." I pull my hand from Noah's and fold my arms over my chest as I give them a sympathetic look.

"It was an accident. We were in a rush to leave," Noah gives as an excuse.

"Right, yes. Can't we get a free pass for this time?" Gabe pleads.

"I'm sorry, boys, but rules are rules. And if I let this one slide, then I'll let the next one too. If we want you guys to grow into proper men, we need to stick to the rules. And maybe next time before leaving messes behind, you'll think back to this moment and remember why it's essential to do at least the bare minimum."

"Oh God. No, please. Don't make me eat something nasty..." Gabe's eyes are wide with horror.

"Actually, I thought we could make it fun, since it is your first time messing up. Gabe, you're off cooking duty tonight. Noah, you'll be making us dinner." I smile at Noah, who looks just as scared.

"Oh my God, that's even worse!" Gabe exclaims, hands thrown in the air.

Noah swallows. "What did you have in mind?"

"Hmm..." I tap my index finger to my lip as he watches every movement. "How about mac and cheese? That's not too hard to make."

"Will you be staying for dinner?" he asks.

"Of course, who else will make sure you both follow the rules?" I smirk.

He watches me for a moment, then nods. "Okay, I should be able to manage that."

"Kill. Me. Now," Gabe whines as his head drops into his hands, making Noah and I laugh.

"Okay, I think it's ready," Noah calls from the kitchen where he's been cooking for the past hour. I'm not sure why it took so long, but I gave him his space to concentrate.

"What do you mean, you think!? Is it ready or not?" Gabe's eyes widen.

"Shut up." I smack his arm from our spot on the couch. "Leave him alone."

I saunter over to the kitchen, which smells pretty good. *That's a good sign, right?* Then look down inside the pot of mac and cheese he made. "That looks... pretty good for a first attempt." I smile at him, although he doesn't seem to agree with the frown he carries. *Okay, so there are still big lumps of cheese that don't seem quite melted, but the rest looks fine.*

I take out three bowls and forks, setting them down on the kitchen island, while Noah dumps his creation into each, and Gabe fetches out three beers. Then we each take our seats, Gabe to my right and Noah to my left.

"Well, let's hope no one dies tonight," Noah toasts, raising his beer.

I giggle and raise mine as well. "To not dying tonight."

Gabe joins in as we clink our bottles together, then all take a swig before setting them down and looking at our bowls. Gabe sighs and picks up his fork. "All on three?"

I look at Noah, who shrugs, and then turns back to Gabe. "Okay. Let's do it." Noah and I pick up our forks. "One... two... three." We pick at our food and shove it in our mouths.

Immediately, I'm hit with this strange taste in my mouth. Not only that, but it's also very... crunchy. I finish chewing, working hard to swallow, then clear my throat. "Umm... Noah? How long did you leave the noodles on the stovetop?"

"I put them in the water and waited for it to boil, then took them off," he says, staring down at his food with a scowl.

"You put them in the water *before* it boiled!? Oh God! And what is that weird thing I'm tasting?" Gabe tosses his food around with his fork like he's looking for something at the bottom of his bowl.

"I used the smoky barbeque spice you keep beside the stove."

Gabe gapes at Noah like he's lost his mind. "That's a dry rub! It's made for meat, not uncooked noodles with hard cheese! Jesus, I'll probably have food poisoning now!" He takes his napkin, wipes his mouth, and pushes his bowl away.

"No more. I'm done. I'm sorry, I can't do this." He turns to me with begging eyes. "Please, Vixen? Let me whip us up something. Please? I promise I won't leave anything lying around ever again. Just don't make me eat that."

I try my hardest not to laugh. The truth is, I don't think I could eat another bite either. "Okay, fine. But next time, I'm forcing it down your throat!"

"Oh, thank God!" He jumps off the stool and collects our bowls, practically sprinting around the counter to find something else to make.

Noah is quiet beside me, and I kind of feel bad for putting him on the spot like that. I place my hand over his that rests above the countertop. "Hey, if it makes you feel any better, I'm really not a great cook either."

He turns his head to me after gazing at our hands. "Was it really that bad?"

"No... I mean, the noodles could have been more cooked. And next time maybe not use those spices and wait until the cheese is more melted... okay, yes. It was pretty awful." A laugh bursts out of me, and he quickly joins in, shaking his head. "I'm sorry."

"Don't be. Gabe did warn you I couldn't cook." He smiles.

"Still, I'm really proud of you for trying. So, thank you for that," I tell him softly.

His eyes gaze into mine as he says, "Anything for you, Kitten."

And I believe him. Somehow, I know Noah would do anything for me.

Chapter Seven

NOAH

Sleeping beauty.

~ The Next Day ~

"You're heading out too?" I ask Gabe as I watch him pulling on his sneakers.

"Yeah, I have a photo shoot for some ad my agent thinks I should do. I shouldn't be gone too long." I nod at his response. "Where are you going?"

"I have something to do. I'm gonna pick up Veronica on the way and drop her off."

She's not supposed to be working today. But since tomorrow is game day, she offered to come in today so that tomorrow she wouldn't be in the way, and we could fully focus and rest. I told her it wasn't necessary, but she insisted. I'm starting to think she just likes being here or with us. *I'm hoping it's the latter.*

"I don't understand why she takes the subway over. Doesn't she have a car?" Gabe frowns like the thought of being on one of those disturbs him. *Or maybe it's the safety aspect, I'm not sure.*

"She does, but she said she lets Aubrey use it during the day. That's why I offered to give her a lift this morning."

"That's another thing I don't get. Why hasn't Ford gotten a car for Baby Ford? You'd think he'd want his sister to be safe behind a wheel, instead of walking around everywhere." *Ah, so it is about safety.*

I chuckle. "Yeah, that's none of our business. Knowing Aubrey, she probably doesn't want Greyson spending money on her."

"You're probably right. Anyway, I'm out. See you later." He heads for the elevator with a wave.

In the kitchen, I fill two travel mugs with coffee, one for me and one for Veronica. Then I make my way into the elevator and down to the parking garage, where I jump into my silver Aston Martin.

Barely fifteen minutes later, I'm pulling up in front of Veronica and Aubrey's condo. I never realized until now just how close they live even though we helped them move. I make my way to the entrance of the building, noticing there's no doorman or security like at ours. But the door is still locked, so at least it's somewhat safe. I ring the buzzer to their condo and wait.

"Hello?" Aubrey's soft voice filters through the speaker.

"Hey, it's Noah. I told Veronica I'd be picking her up."

"Oh, okay. I'll buzz you in, come on up," she says.

Seconds later the buzzer to the door sounds and I pull it open, then take the elevator to the fourth floor. Once at their door I knock and suddenly start to feel nervous, like when you're going on a first date and picking her up at her door, which hasn't happened in a long time.

I know this isn't the case, but it still feels the same. I could have simply stayed in the car and texted her to come down, but I wanted to see where my Kitten lived, what she was really like behind closed doors.

The door swings open with Aubrey standing on the other side in a camisole and shorts, her long ash-blonde hair up in a messy bun. "Hi, Noah."

"Hey, beautiful." I step in, kiss her cheek, and on cue, she blushes. That girl is always blushing. She really is a beautiful woman, but I'm not into shy girls. Plus, Greyson would rip my head off if I ever went there.

"Ronnie should be out in a sec." She smiles and turns back to their kitchen.

Their place is nice and spacious, all white walls with turquoise-blue accents everywhere and a big kitchen filled with a whole bunch of appliances. I'm guessing Aubrey spends most of her time here, since she's the talented baker in our group.

Voices sound from down the hall seconds before Veronica appears with a big blond guy at her side, his hand resting on her lower back. They stop at the mouth of the hallway, where he places his other hand on her hip and turns her to face him, but she doesn't lift her head.

She keeps looking down, arms wrapped around her stomach and seeming lost in thought. I can't hear what he's saying to her, but she shakes her head, smiles faintly, and places her palm on his bicep while saying something back.

A streak of jealousy rushes through me like lightning. My jaw clenches as I widen my stance and fold my arms over my chest, shoulders wide and head held high. Finally, Veronica steps out of his hold and turns my way.

When her eyes meet mine, she stops, eyes wide and mouth open in surprise. "Noah, I didn't know you were here."

The guy behind her looks me up and down but doesn't say anything. He doesn't look upset that another man is in her space either. He just looks... unfazed, like my presence doesn't threaten him in the least.

"Sorry, I forgot you had company..." Aubrey says in a quiet, apologetic voice.

My teeth grind together. I don't normally get jealous, but I hate knowing Veronica spent the night with another man, especially after she left our place last night. I thought we were getting somewhere with her.

I guess I was wrong.

"It's okay, Nathan was just leaving." *Jesus, if Aubrey knows his name, it's because he's a regular. Not just some random hook up.* Veronica looks back at me with a small smile, not like the one she gave that asshole. "Just give me a few minutes to get my things."

"It's fine. I'll wait for you downstairs," I say a little more harshly than necessary. I know I probably look angry right now, but I don't care. I turn and rip the door open, striding out and back down the elevator.

I get outside to my car and pace a few times, unsure what to make of her and that guy. *Is he her boyfriend? I thought she didn't do boyfriends. Hell, didn't she go home with that Jessie guy the night of the gala? Morgan's billionaire neighbor. Maybe they aren't exclusive? Ugh!*

I pass my hands through my hair, then reach into my car for the two travel mugs. Leaning back against my car, I take a sip from mine and wait, keeping my eyes on the entrance door of their building.

Five minutes later, the door opens, and Veronica walks out with that Nathan guy beside her. They stop, and he opens his arms for her. She seems reluctant at first but finally steps into his embrace. Although she doesn't hug him back, keeping her hands tight around her body.

I can't help the smirk that forms on my lips. She may be intimate with him, but he doesn't give her the same sense of security I give her.

He lets go of her and walks to his car that's parked two vehicles ahead, while Veronica walks slowly over to mine. "Hi," she says softly. "Sorry I made you wait. I didn't know what time you'd be here."

"It's fine." I hand her the travel mug. "It's for you. I wasn't sure how you took your coffee, but you look like a sweets kind of girl. So, I put a bit of cream and two sugars."

She smiles down at the mug as she takes it. "Your assessment is right, but it's three sugars."

I grin back at her before pulling the passenger door open. "I'll remember that.

Come on, let's go."

"Nice car. I've seen it before; I just wasn't sure if it was yours or Gabe's," she says as she sits in carefully.

"Mine, and she's my baby." With a wink, I close the door and head to the driver's side.

"Ah, so I'm guessing no one gets to drive her but you?" She smirks with a knowing look.

"That's right." I nod and start the car, pulling out onto the street.

Veronica makes a weird sound, then lets out a shaky breath. I look at her as we stop at a red light and notice she looks different today. She's not wearing her usual high skirt, stockings, and heels. Instead, she's wearing black and pink leggings with a pink sports bra and sneakers. Her complexion seems pale, her face is makeup free, her hair is down and looks finger-combed, and a lost look fills her gaze.

"Hey, are you okay?"

Her head rests against the seat as she looks out the window. She turns to me, offering a small smile that doesn't reach her eyes as she says, "Yeah, I'm fine."

"You don't look fine," I tell her.

"Thanks, Casanova." She gives me an annoyed look before turning back to the window.

"Kitten." I place my hand gently on her thigh and give it a small squeeze. She looks down at it, then up to me. "That's not what I meant. I just meant that you look tired, maybe even sick. If you want to take the day off, you can."

Her hand comes down above mine. "It's okay. I'm fine. You don't have to worry about me." *Yeah, that's not possible.*

"Okay," I finally say. Clearly, she won't admit what's wrong, so I'll just let it go for now. "Have you had breakfast?"

She shakes her head. "No. Not yet."

"Okay, we'll stop to pick you up some food. Ellis isn't home right now, so he won't be able to make you something. And the groceries aren't set to arrive until later this afternoon, so there's not much in the fridge."

Thanks to the app she's put on our phones, we can see when the deliveries will be made. And yes, I called it home, because even if she doesn't know it yet, that's where she belongs.

"Okay, thank you," she says quietly.

More proof that she isn't doing well. Veronica never speaks in a small voice. Yes, she can be tender and delicate, but she's never sounded like a wounded animal.

VERONICA

A few minutes later, Noah pulls up to a breakfast place and stops the car before turning to me. "Do you want to eat here or at home?"

"At the penthouse, if that's okay?" I'm really not feeling up to sitting in a restaurant around all those people.

As if on cue, my lower abdomen contracts and a blinding pain shoots through me. I fight the urge not to bend in half or cry out by taking deep breaths through my nose. My menstrual cramps have always been tremendously severe.

I've ended up in the hospital more times than I can count over the years, and the doctors never find any reason behind it. I've tried every form of birth control, hoping it would help. None have worked except for the implant, which is what I have now.

Thankfully, I don't get my period every cycle anymore, but every three months or so, it comes, and the pain is horrible once again. Although I'll take that over having it every twenty-eight days. I also have prescribed medication that helps, but I ran out, and with no insurance, I can't afford more right away, so now I'm stuck suffering.

Noah looks at me with worry again, but he doesn't say anything. Instead, he pushes strands of blue hair out of my face and behind my ear with a nod. "What would you like to eat?"

I give him a tight smile. "Surprise me. I'm not picky." My brain is too focused on the pain to think about food, but I know he won't let me go without, so I just agree with whatever he says.

"Okay, I'll be back soon." He steps out of the car, and I watch him go into the restaurant.

I take a sip of my coffee, which was a sweet gesture from him, then rest my head against the seat and sigh. I need something to concentrate on, to take my mind off the anguish coursing through my body.

I gaze around the inside of his car, which is alarmingly clean, almost as if it just came from the dealer. Being my nosy self, I look around, opening the armrest compartment and the glove box, but find nothing. *Jesus, how can he be a clean freak in his car but not his house?*

I rest back against the seat and turn my head toward the driver's side. It's then that my eye catches something white in his door. Given the black and red interior of his car, the white really stands out. I unbuckle my seatbelt and reach for it, despite the pain in my abdomen and lower back. *Like I said, I'm nosy.*

Finally getting it between my fingers, I pull it free and right myself in my seat. I look through the windshield, making sure Noah isn't on his way back, and quickly unfold the sheet of paper.

At first, I don't understand what I'm reading; it all seems like gibberish with big medical terms. It isn't until I see the patient's name that things start to make sense. *Trinity Mary Adler.* And given the date of birth, she's only three years younger than Noah. *This must be his sister. Why didn't I know he had one?*

I don't recognize any of the terms on the paper, but it seems like a request for some form of treatment. Noah's signature is on the bottom, and it's dated a week ago. *Why would he be the one signing off on her medical records? That must be where he goes every time he disappears.*

Movement through the windshield catches my attention, and I look up to see Noah walking toward the entrance door with two bags in his hands. I quickly fold the paper and stuff it back inside his car door before he notices, then buckle myself back up as he pulls the door open and passes me the food.

"I got you a few different things, so you'll have some choice," he says as he backs out of the parking space.

"Thank you. Are you going out today?"

"Yeah, I have a few errands, but it shouldn't take too long. Then I'll be back."

"Okay." *I wonder if he's going to see his sister.*

"I don't want you forcing yourself too much today, just take it easy. Hell, you can even spend the day lying around, I don't care."

I turn and look at his profile—his square jaw covered by a well-trimmed Balbo beard, high cheekbones, long dark lashes, and insanely dark irises. His strong, thick neck, with a pronounced Adam's apple, short, cropped hair, and thick eyebrows, but not bushy. He always seems to wear a stern expression, but when he smiles or smirks, God, do I understand why so many women drop their panties for him.

Noah is sexy, so fucking sexy it's annoying. And that slightly tanned skin he always has that amplifies all his features? Ugh, delicious. *Even his ears are sexy, God damn it.* Sometimes I find myself staring at him and wondering what his neck would taste like. If I used my tongue to lick from the base, over his Adam's apple, all the way up to his jaw. Or how his beard and mustache would feel between my legs and against the inside of my thighs.

"I'm not sure what you're thinking about there, but it did bring some color into your cheeks. And you're staring at me like you want to eat me. So, I'm going to guess you were having naughty thoughts for a sec. Mind sharing?" He smiles.

My eyes widen as I realize I've been staring at him for longer than necessary. I turn my head, look out the windshield, and fold my arms over my chest with a scoff. "I was not!"

He chuckles. "Sure, sure. If you say so. But you know, it's okay if you were. I won't tell anyone." He finishes with a wink, and I roll my eyes. *Yeah, I have no doubt Noah's good at keeping secrets.*

A few minutes later, he parks in front of his building and gets out of the car. He rushes around to the passenger door and opens it before the doorman can get to it, then reaches for the bags of food and offers me his hand. I take it and groan at the next wave of cramps that hits as I stand from the car.

His brows furrow as he examines me. "Remember what I said. Don't overwork yourself. Just relax."

Ugh, what is it with men and always wanting to take care of me? I give him a fake bright smile and flutter my eyelashes dramatically. "Okay, Daddy!" I say cheerfully and a little louder than necessary.

His head pulls back, and his eyes go wide. "Jesus, Kitten. Don't call me that, I do not have a daddy kink." He smiles again. "Though I will accept God, Noah, or even Casanova."

Once more, I roll my eyes at him. "You wish I'd call you God."

"One day." He winks. "Now go. Get inside." He lets go of my hand, hands me the bags of food, and steps out of the way. "I'll see you in a bit."

I nod and walk up the three steps to the entrance. "Good morning, Stanley," I say to the elderly doorman as he pulls open the door.

"Good morning, Miss Masters." He smiles warmly.

Once inside the penthouse, I immediately drop my purse by the entrance and step out of my shoes, needing to feel as comfortable as possible. I walk over to the kitchen and remove everything from inside the bags of food, deciding to eat a bit before attacking today's mess. I definitely need the energy with how low I'm feeling right now.

Turns out, Noah really did get me a bit of everything. And apparently, I was way hungrier than I thought, since I've devoured more than three quarters of the food. Once done, I put the leftovers in the fridge, finish my coffee, then attack the downstairs area first.

After one hour, my cramps have gotten worse, I'm sweating, and I find myself folding in half every few steps. I make my way to the upper level and start with the spare bedroom, which only requires a bit of dusting and a sweep, then move on to Gabe's bedroom. His room is such a contrast to Noah's with his dark gray furniture, black sheets, and dark curtains covering the windows, while Noah's is filled with light grays and whites.

I make his bed, tidy up the bathroom, and fix his clothes in the walk-in that are falling off the hangers. I grab the small amount of dirty clothes in the laundry basket and take them to the laundry room.

The pain becomes unbearable as I head back up the steps to Noah's room, forcing me to my kneel as I try to pass it. My hands shake as I press them into my stomach while taking deep breaths. *In through the nose, out through the mouth.*

My phone vibrates when I finally make it to his door, and I pull it out from the side pocket of my leggings. *Thank the heavens for leggings with pockets.* It's a message from Aubrey, telling me she's having dinner with her parents at Greyson's house and asking if it's okay to use my car.

I send a quick reply saying it's fine and to have a good time. As I'm about to shut my screen, another message comes in, but it's not from Aubrey. It's *him*. Once again using another different number. I block him every time, but it never stops him.

Opening the message, I gasp, my hand covering my mouth as I stare at the image before me. *Oh God no... this is not happening...* It's a picture of me walking out of the deli shop the other day, and it looks like it was taken from across the street.

Oh my God! He was right there... right there, and I didn't even see him. God, I'm such an idiot for thinking he wouldn't come for me after what I did... What am I supposed to do now?

I squeeze my phone in my hands, rage boiling inside of me. "WHY WON'T YOU LEAVE ME ALONE?! JUST LEAVE ME ALONE!" I shout then throw my phone at the wall with all the force I can muster. It falls to the floor on its back, the screen completely shattered and black.

"Shit!" I go to pick it up but am hit with another blinding wave of agony. This one is much stronger than the last, knocking the wind out of me as I drop to my knees and scream. "AHHH!" My arms wrap around my stomach tightly as tears fall from my eyes.

I wait a few seconds for it to pass and try to stand, but a wave of nausea and dizziness hits me, forcing me to lean against the wall as I struggle to breathe. *I need to lie down.* I manage to make it into Noah's room slowly and collapse on his bed, pulling myself into a ball as I cry through the pain.

NOAH

~ After Dropping Off Veronica ~

I watch her walk into the building, then drive off toward the care facility. Guilt fills me for leaving her alone when I know something's wrong, but I don't have a choice. I had planned to visit after coming home from the airport yesterday, but when I walked in and saw Veronica, I found myself not wanting to leave her side.

She seemed so happy and excited to see us and show us everything she had done with the outdoor space. And then she hugged me, and fuck, I could have died in her arms. Having her so close, smelling her perfume directly from her skin, feeling her breath leave her perfect lips and glide against my flesh. I never wanted to let go. But I know Veronica needs time to understand she's mine.

That she's ours.

Once at the facility, I make my way inside. By now, I know my way around this place by heart; I even know most of the staff. It fucking sucks being on such a personal level with them. Knowing that Nurse Jackie's daughter just had a baby boy that weighed eleven pounds, and that Doctor Daltonsen is going through a divorce after finding out his wife has been cheating on him for the past three years with their son's best friend.

But after five years of coming here every week, they've become a form of family to me, and if it weren't for their support, I'm not sure I'd make it out of here on two feet most days. It's not like I can talk about it with my friends, since none of them even know she exists.

It's not that I wanted to keep it from them, but at that time, my career was finally picking up, which meant the media was shining its bright light on me, and I didn't want them around her. I didn't want the focus to be on her, so I kept it to myself and told no one. Not even Gabe.

"Hi, Noah!" Jannice waves from behind the nurse's station.

She started working here when Trinity was transferred and has been by her side ever since. She's a few years older than me, but that hasn't stopped her from trying to take her shot from time to time, although I've shut it down every time. I have no intention of messing around with the staff here.

"Hey, Jannice. How is she today?" I stop by the counter and rap my knuckles against the surface.

"She's good, always an angel." She smiles up at me practically with hearts in her eyes.

"Good to hear. Well, I'll head in. See you later, Jannice." I wave to her as I walk to Trinity's room.

Stepping inside, I close the door quietly and look around the room for anything out of place, anything different. But it's always the same. No one touches anything in this room except for me.

I walk up to the side of the bed and reach up with my hand, pushing dark strands of hair out of her face. "Hey, little sis." Lowering, I kiss her forehead while closing my eyes, breathing her in for a second.

She doesn't smell the same anymore, not like I remember. Instead of the outdoorsy scent she carried from spending so much time in the woods or hiking, she now just smells... clean. Sterile. Like someone who's been washed over and over but never does anything to pick up other scents.

Pulling back, I let my hand glide down her arm to her hand, where I give it a tiny squeeze. I wait for her to squeeze back, for a sign that she's still in there... but she never does.

I let go and sit down in the chair beside her bed, watching her. I never know what to say when I come here; it feels odd talking to someone who will never answer me. But some part of me still hopes that hearing my voice will maybe help her wake up.

I stopped begging, though. I used to. I used to beg and plead for her to wake up, to give me a sign that she would come back to me. But after the first year passed, where all she did was lie there, motionless, I understood that day would never come. So, I've just been holding on, for the both of us.

"Remember that girl I told you about? The one with the funky colored hair that changes all the time and the fiery attitude. Last week, I told you she started working for me and Gabe. But I wasn't sure how that would go since she kind of hated us." I chuckle.

"Well, it's going pretty great. She's been spending a lot of time with us, and it's been really nice. We laugh and have fun. I think I'm finally getting somewhere with her." I stop and look down at my hands, unsure what to do with them. They ball into fists as I think about what I witnessed this morning.

"Well, I thought I was. But now I think she might have a boyfriend or something..." I lean farther back in the chair, my head dropping back as I close my eyes. "I saw her this morning with some guy. Clearly, he had spent the night with her."

I work my jaw as I remember the way he had his hand on her back, the way he hugged her and held her waist. "I've never felt so jealous in my life. I hated seeing them together." I let out a breath. "I don't know what to do, Trinny. I could really use your advice right now."

I open my eyes and bring my head back up, looking down at her tiny form. She's twenty-five now, yet she still looks nineteen. It's as if she stopped aging the moment her accident happened. Or maybe it's just me who can't see the difference.

I stand from the chair and walk around the room to the dresser. Above are photos of my family, me and her, her and Dad, and some with all three of us. I pick up the one with my father hugging us both. It's the last picture we have of him before he died. Just a year before Trinity had her accident.

"She hugged me yesterday, which is new. She's not much of a hugger, and she even held my hand a few times, so I think those are good steps in the right direction. Don't you think?" I look back at the sleeping beauty in bed.

With a sigh, I put the framed picture back down. "She's beautiful, Trinity. I wish you could see her. I think you two would get along. She's only a year younger than you, after all. Plus, she seems adventurous and wild, like you are... like you were."

I walk back to the chair and take a seat once more. "Veronica's always so fierce and stands tall, like she could walk through fire if need be. She looks like a badass, with her full sleeve tattoos, all her piercings, and colorful hair. Can't forget the colorful hair. And before you say it, yes, I know, she's not my usual type." I laugh to myself.

"But I think it's all fake. I think she's just putting on a show to hide who she really is inside. Kind of like what I do to protect you. I'm just not sure what she's trying to protect, and from whom." I sigh.

"I won't be able to stay much longer today, sis. Veronica isn't feeling well, and I don't want to leave her alone for too long. She's a bit stubborn like you and still came in to work, despite it being her day off," I say, chuckling before gazing down at my sister.

She looks so much like our mother; sometimes it hurts to look at her. She doesn't deserve to look like such a horrible person. But nonetheless, my mother was a stunning woman, at least from what I remember before she abandoned us, and my sister took all her beauty.

"I wish you were here, baby sis. I wish you could see how my life turned out, all the amazing friends I've made. They've really become my family. You'd fit right in with all the girls in our little group." My head drops as I rest my elbows on my knees.

"I wish you could have seen me play, Trinny. Just one game. That's all I would have wanted... I miss you, Trinity. I miss hearing your voice. I miss hearing you laugh when I'd try to cook us dinner on those late nights when Dad was stuck working." A broken laugh falls from me.

"I cooked for Veronica yesterday. Let's just say it was horrible and likely won't happen again. But she didn't care, just said she was proud of me. Like you used to say every time." I feel my throat clogging with emotions and decide I've had enough for today.

I stand from my chair and lean over her body, kissing her forehead. "I gotta go now, sis. I'll be back soon. I love you, Trinity."

I leave her side reluctantly and walk out of the room with a heavy heart. Like I do every time.

Chapter Eight

NOAH

Cramps and secrets.

Driving into the underground garage, I park in my usual spot as Gabe's red Porsche pulls up next to me. I kill the engine and step out, waiting by his driver side door as he pushes it open. "Already done with your shoot?"

He joins my side with a beaming smile. "What can I say? Apparently, my face is so perfect that it only took one take to get the perfect shot." He winks arrogantly.

I chuckle and shake my head as we make our way to our private elevator and up to the penthouse. When we enter the foyer, it's eerily quiet, and a sense of worry creeps its way through my veins.

"Veronica?" I call out, walking farther into the living room and looking toward the kitchen.

"Do you think she already left?" Gabe asks, looking around suspiciously.

I shake my head. "No, the groceries are getting delivered later on, and her things are still by the door."

He heads down the hall, looking into the rooms on the main floor, and comes back empty. We both look up the stairs and head up, looking for our girl.

"Vixen? Where are you, baby?" Gabe says once we hit the landing.

I take a step forward, ready to search the rooms up here, but my foot catches onto something. Veronica's phone. I kneel down to pick it up and notice the screen is entirely shattered. Just as I'm about to call out for her again, I hear a faint cry coming from my room. Gabe's head whips my way seconds before we both bolt toward it.

I can't explain the tightness that forms in my chest as I look at the slender body balled up over my cover. She looks so small right now, and I hate it. I hate that I left her like this when I knew she wasn't okay.

Gabe and I rush to her side and drop to the ground beside her. "Kitten, tell me what's wrong? What happened?"

Her complexion is paler than it was this morning, and she has a line of sweat along her forehead. Her eyes are screwed shut like she's in pain, and tears track down her face. From the large wet stain beneath her head, I'd say she's been crying for a little while now. *Shit.*

"It hurts…" she finally cries out.

"Baby, what hurts?" Gabe places his hand on her calf.

She sniffs. "My stomach and my back."

I push hair out of her face gently, placing it behind her ear. "What did you do for it to hurt?"

She shakes her head. "It's… it's my period. It happens every time." She scrunches up her face and brings her legs up closer to her body as she whimpers.

"You go through this every month?!" Gabe asks with wide eyes. I've seen the other girls in a bit of pain during their time of the month, or being cranky and moody, but I've never seen them like this. *That can't be normal.*

"Do you want us to take you to the hospital?" I ask her softly, continuing to play through her hair.

"No. They don't do anything. It's normal." She shakes her head again.

"There's nothing normal about going through this pain every month, Veronica. I may not be a woman or know exactly what you're going through, but I know this isn't normal, and you need to see a doctor."

She cries out again, turning her face into the bed. The sounds falling from her lips rip my heart open. I want to help her, I'm just not sure what to do. I think of what our team physician tells us to do to help with pain. It always involves putting a bit of pressure on the muscles and massaging. *Maybe that could work?* She said it was her back and stomach.

Without wasting another second, I rise to my knees and place one hand on her lower back, wiggling my other against her lower abdomen. Slowly, I apply pressure and gently massage as best as I can with my fingers. At first, she's a little stiff and seems to recoil, but then her body relaxes and I hear her release slow, deep breaths.

"How does that feel?"

"Good." She sniffles again, turning her face back to us. "I've already seen a doctor, and it doesn't happen every month. I got the implant to help, and it does. But every three or so months it pops up, and it's horrible. She's run every test possible, and they can't find any reason for why it's so bad."

"How do you usually manage the pain?" Gabe asks, his hand rubbing up and down her calf.

"I have a prescription I take that makes them milder. But I ran out and couldn't cover the cost since I don't have any medical insurance."

"Jesus fucking Christ, Veronica. You should have said something. We would have covered them for you. Why didn't you tell me this morning you were in this much pain?" I'm angry, but not at her. I'm angry with myself that I didn't notice how bad it was.

"It had calmed down this morning. I thought I was going to be okay." She whimpers as I press a more sensitive spot in her abdomen.

I sigh. "Gabe, can you run her a bath? Then I want you to go get her prescription and anything you think that could help with the pain."

"On it." He stands quickly and rushes into my bathroom to start the water. He then comes back and exits the room, returning a minute later with a handful of products.

"What's all that?" I ask.

"Epsom salt, bubble bath, oils, candles. It's all to help relax her body," he says, pointing out everything.

"Good call." I nod.

"You guys don't need to..." Her arms tighten around her stomach, squeezing me in. "Ahhh!" she cries, folding herself in. "Do that..." she finishes in a tiny, broken voice as tears continue to pour out of her.

"Yes, we do. There's no way we're leaving you like this, Vixen," Gabe says from the doorway of the ensuite, arms folded over his chest as he watches her. "You're our girl," he finishes with a soft smile.

She offers him a small one despite her tormented state, then whimpers again, and I suddenly fear I might be making it worse. "Do you want me to stop?" I begin to remove my hands, but she grabs onto the one that was against her stomach, forcing it to stay in place.

"No, please don't stop. It's helping," she begs.

"Okay." I place it back correctly and resume my movements. It would be easier if she were fully stretched out, but this seems to be the easiest position for her right now.

"Bath is ready. I'm gonna go get that medication, and hopefully you'll be better soon," Gabe says as he walks over and squeezes her pink-socked foot. "Do you need my help getting her in?"

"No, I think I can manage. Just hurry back," I tell him.

"Will do. Hang in there, baby. We've got you," he says before exiting the room.

"You ready to get in the bath?" I ask her.

She nods but seems reluctant. "It hurts to move."

"Do you want me to help you out of your clothes?"

Another nod.

"Okay, Kitten. Can you lie on your back for me? It's going to be easier like that, and I won't have to move you too much."

Slowly, she unfolds herself and turns on her back, whimpering with every movement until she's fully laid out. She closes her eyes and cries silently. I take a deep breath, preparing to see Veronica naked for the very first time.

I start with her sports bra, unzipping it down the valley of her breasts until it falls open. Then I quickly work it down her arms while also trying not to move her too much. As much as I'd love to take my time and explore her body with my gaze, I know this isn't the right moment, so I try my hardest not to peek at her small, perky breasts on display.

I then bring my hands to the waistband of her leggings and ever so slowly inch them down her hips and legs, along with her tiny black thong. I work her socks off quickly, then stand, not daring to look between her legs despite my growing erection.

I've waited so long to see Veronica like this, to have her naked in my bed, but it all feels wrong to look at her right now while she's suffering. Leaning over, I place one hand behind her knees and the other along her back, then lift her off the bed and into my arms. She cradles her head against my neck, arms crossed over her as she covers her chest.

I carry her to the bath and carefully lower her in until she touches the bottom. Gabe filled the tub nearly to the top, which means that by the time she's settled in, the front of my shirt is completely wet. She takes her time lying back against the bath and lets her head drop against the edge, turning it to face me.

I remove my wet shirt and throw it behind me, then sit down on the floor beside the bath in the opposite direction as her so that we're facing each other. I just want to keep an eye on her in case she falls asleep in the tub.

When my gaze meets Veronica's, she's glaring at something behind me. And when I look over my shoulder and spot the shirt I just threw, I chuckle and turn back to her. "I'll pick it up after, I promise."

"Mhmm, you better." She smiles softly.

"How are you feeling now, Kitten?" I bring my hand up and glide it through her hair, her deep sapphire eyes watching my every movement.

"Better. It still hurts, but the heat is helping," she says quietly. "Although it feels weird to have a whole bunch of tiny rocks under my ass."

I laugh. "There's my girl."

We smile at each other for a moment, and I notice this is the second time we've made a comment like that, and she doesn't contradict us like she normally would.

Maybe it's just because of her state, or maybe she's starting to see what we've always seen. I can't help but feel a bit of hope spread through me.

"You didn't even look." Her whispered words pull me away from my thoughts, and I furrow my brows in confusion. "When you undressed me. You didn't look," she clarifies.

"Your eyes were closed. How can you be so sure I didn't?" I smirk.

"I could feel them on me. If you did, it was barely for a second."

"You're right, I didn't," I confirm.

"Why not?" She frowns.

"Because as much as I've been dying to see you naked, today wasn't the time for that. It would feel like I was taking advantage of you, and I never want it to be that way." I bring my hand down to the side of her neck, caressing her cheek with my thumb. "When I finally do get you properly naked, I want it to be because it's what you want, too. Not because you're too weak to fight me or say no."

Something flashes in her eyes for a split second, but it disappears just as quickly. She doesn't answer immediately as her eyes bore into mine, but then she gives the most subtle nod and says, "Okay." *Again, not disagreeing.*

I remove my hand and bring it to rest over my bent knee, feeling she might withdraw after hearing the question I'm about to ask her. She's already let me touch her more than she ever has in the last seven months combined; I won't push my luck.

"Why did you smash your phone, Veronica?"

She turns her head away from me and looks up at the ceiling with a sigh. My Kitten looks ravishing, with her head leaning back, slender neck fully exposed, and her golden shoulders on display with just the beginning of her breasts peeking out through the soapy water. If it weren't for all the bubbles Gabe added, I probably could see them perfectly.

The semi I was still sporting suddenly turns into a full-blown erection. I shift slightly on the ground, dropping my head down and groaning. I haven't had sex in the last week, not that the opportunity hasn't presented itself, but having Veronica around so much has been fucking with my head. I can't seem to think of anyone else but her.

"What's the matter, Casanova? Can't deal with being next to a naked woman?"

When I look up, I find her looking at me with a smirk, and a bit more color has returned to her face. "Glad to see you're feeling a bit better, Kitten. At least enough to give me some of that sass."

She smiles. "I am, this is really helping. I'm not sure what Gabe put in here, but whatever it is, I need to add it to my shopping list."

"We'll buy you a case full. Now, for my question." I raise a brow, knowing she's trying to deflect.

"Ugh." She sinks lower in the water until it hits her jaw. "I was hoping you forgot about that."

"Not likely."

"It's just... my ex. He apparently has a hard time letting go." She peers at me.

"The guy at your place this morning?" I wonder.

"Who?" She seems confused. "Oh, Nathan? No. He's just a friend."

I nod. *Didn't look like just a friend.* "How long has it been? Your ex."

"A little over three years," she says quietly.

My face turns into a frown. "Three years?! Veronica, that's called an obsession, not *'having a hard time letting go'*."

"It's fine. You have nothing to worry about." She looks down at the bubbly water and pops some with her nail. "It just started up again, a little before May. He's just... he thinks I owe him something. We ended really badly, and he's blaming me for it."

I know there's more to the story; I can see it in the way she searches for her words and won't meet my eyes. But I decide to leave it at that for now; she's already admitted more than I expected.

"You're the first person I've told, aside from my therapist." Now she looks at me, and I know she's telling the truth. For her to need a therapist after a breakup means it was a lot worse than she's letting on.

"I feel like a bad friend sometimes. The girls always share all their secrets with me, and yet I don't want them knowing about my past."

I bring my hand over to the top of her knee popping out of the water. "That doesn't make you a bad friend, Kitten. You're allowed to have secrets you don't want to share." She nods with a tight smile.

A need to share one of my own takes over. It's only fair since she's shared hers. "I have a sister."

She lifts slightly from the water, returning to her original position, as her gaze stays locked on mine. She doesn't respond immediately and simply looks over my features until finally she says, "I know."

My brows furrow. "How?" I've never told anyone. No one from my current life knows about her existence, and I've made sure my old life and my new one never crossed paths.

"I may have snooped in your car while you were getting food." She tries to hide her smile when mine grows. I should have expected her to do something like that.

"Her name is Trinity, she's twenty-five," I start, not sure how to just speak about it.

"What happened to her?" she asks softly, taking my hand on her knee and intertwining our fingers.

"She had a hiking accident six years ago that put her in a coma. She hasn't woken up since and most likely never will."

She swallows. "What about your family?"

I shake my head. "My mom disappeared when I was five and Trinny was only two. Haven't heard or seen her since. My dad died seven years ago from lung cancer. And then my sister had her accident on the day of his one-year anniversary." I clear my throat, fighting the surge of emotions taking root.

"They used to go hiking and discover new trails together all the time. I was never really the outdoorsy type, but Trinity and my dad bonded over that. After he died, Trinny started doing more of them; she said it was her way of keeping his spirit alive, that it's in those moments she felt closest to him." I smile sadly.

"Then for his anniversary she went out to do a difficult hike they had always planned to do together. She thought fulfilling their bucket list would bring her closure. Instead, it took her away from me."

"Noah..." She leans in closer, her face scrunching up with the sudden movement, like her pain might be coming back now that the water is cooling down. She takes a deep breath, letting it out, then places her free hand along my cheek. "I'm sorry you've had to go through this alone. It couldn't have been easy."

"It hasn't been. But it was also my choice to keep it to myself." I give her a small smile.

"I guess we all have secrets we don't want to share." I nod in response. "Could I meet her?"

Her question startles me; I wasn't expecting her to ask that. But with the way my heart warms, I realize it's something I want. "You'd want to?" I ask, not wanting to put any pressure on her.

"I would." She smiles.

"Okay, yeah. I'd like that." I grin back.

We're quiet for a moment as we stare at each other until I raise my free hand and grab onto hers that's still resting against my cheek. I turn my head to the side and delicately press my lips to the inside of her wrist. She watches me closely, not saying a word, not pulling away.

"Nathan and I, we're really just friends," she starts, and I'm not sure why she's telling me this, but I appreciate her trying to clear it up.

"We do hook up every week or so, but it's nothing more than that. I had forgotten we made plans last night, and when he showed up, Aubrey let him in. When he found me balled up in bed, he refused to leave and stayed with me until morning. But that's all that happened."

"Okay." I'm not sure what else to say, but I'm glad to know he's not her boyfriend.

"Your savior is finally back!" Gabe calls just as he enters the bathroom. "And I've brought the cure." He lifts the bottle in his hand with a smile.

I let go of Veronica's wrist and untangle our hands as he steps forward and kneels down beside her. He opens the bottle and hands her a pill along with a water bottle. "Here, Vixen. Take this and drink a lot of water. It will help. How are you doing now?" He strokes her hair once she's taken the pill and bottle from him, and I notice she doesn't tense at his touch.

"I'm feeling better already, thank you. The bath really helped." She gives him a warm smile.

"Glad to hear it. I also bought a few things to make lunch. All anti-inflammatory foods, as well as decaf coffee and tea. So finish up here while I make us something to eat, then we're gonna sit down and watch a movie while you apply a heating pad on your stomach."

"Why decaf?" she asks.

"Because caffeine and any fatty foods make your cramps worse. They cause bloating and inflammation," he informs her.

"Shit. I gave her a coffee this morning, and the breakfast I got her probably wasn't the healthiest either." I drag my hand down my face.

"You what?" He glares at me.

"Hey, it's not his fault, I didn't even know that, but it explains a lot. They always did seem to get worse after eating or drinking." She places her hand on his arm that continues to play through her hair.

"Well, not to worry anymore. We'll take care of you from now on." He leans over and kisses her forehead. "Take all the time you need. And when you're ready, come downstairs." He stands and leaves.

"Do you want to stay in here a little longer?" I ask her once we're alone.

"No, I think I'm okay to get out. Plus, the water is getting a bit cold."

"Okay, do you need help getting out?"

I stand and go to reach for her, but instead, she takes my hand and pulls herself up with a slight groan. She seems a lot better, but I can tell she's still not at her best. She stands straight before me and slowly steps out of the bath, her naked body now completely exposed to me once more.

"Fuck, Veronica." I let go of her hand and turn around, quickly grabbing a towel and passing it to her. She's clearly very comfortable with herself.

"You undressed me, Casanova. But this is too much?" She raises a brow when I look back at her.

She doesn't even have the towel wrapped around her and instead wipes herself down with it. I find myself gazing at her as she rubs it down her arms, then over her small breast and down her slim stomach. I usually prefer a girl with a big ass and tits, but Veronica is special. Despite not having many curves, she's still extraordinarily beautiful.

"Shit."

I snap out of my gazing state and find her looking at the towel after having wiped down her long legs. "What's wrong? Are you in pain again?" I go to reach for her, but she straightens and takes a step back, clutching the towel.

"I..." She sighs. "I'm bleeding..."

"What?" I look around, expecting a cut or something. It isn't until I reach her legs that I spot a small trickle of blood sliding down her thigh. *Oh.*

She tightens her legs together. "I got some on the towel," she says quietly.

"That's okay, Kitten. It's just a little blood. Nothing I haven't seen before." I take the few steps separating us and caress her cheek with my knuckles. "Why don't you finish cleaning yourself up, and I'll go grab your bag downstairs? You have what you need in it, right?"

She nods. "Thank you."

I head down the stairs, collect her bag, and rush back up. When I enter my bathroom, I find her sitting on the toilet bowl, naked, which stuns me for a second. I'm not used to seeing a naked woman sitting on the toilet like that. It feels like something you do in a relationship, and my last one was in high school, so we weren't exactly at the stage of doing our business with the door open.

I quickly recover and hand over her bag before she reaches inside and pulls out a tampon. I've seen those before, so I know how they work. She takes the wrapper off and holds the applicator between her fingers. I'm about to turn around and give her some privacy, but then Veronica lifts her butt slightly from the seat, staying in a squatting position, and brings the applicator between her legs, inserting her tampon.

All I can do is stare with wide eyes and my mouth slightly open.

She pulls the applicator back out, puts it inside the wrapping, and throws it in the trash beside the toilet. She then takes some toilet paper and wipes between her legs before flushing, then stands and walks over to the vanity. Still fully naked.

I haven't moved or blinked. I'm not even sure I'm breathing right now. I know how women use those. I've just never seen one do it in front of me, and I have no idea how to feel about this new experience.

She looks at me through the mirror and giggles while washing her hands. "Are you okay there, Casanova?"

I clear my throat. "Yup. Just... might be traumatized for the rest of my life, but that's okay."

She turns to face me as she dries her wet hands with the hand towel, then sets it to the side and presses a hand to her stomach as she closes her eyes. My gaze travels down to her hand, then lower to her sex that's completely bare of any hair. I feel like Veronica is the type to get waxed regularly. I bring my eyes back up when I realize I'm staring at her pussy like a freaking pervert.

"The cramps are starting up again?" I ask with worry.

She nods with a sad smile. "I don't want to put my pants back on, they're too tight around my stomach."

"Okay, we can fix that." I walk back into the room, and she follows closely.

Heading into the walk-in, I grab a baggy shirt at the back, then go through the drawers for a pair of boxers. When I bring them up in front of her, I realize there's no way those will hold up. "Maybe just the shirt and your underwear?"

"Yeah, that will be better than putting on my tight clothes." She takes the shirt from my hands and turns just as Gabe appears at the mouth of the closet.

"HOLY SHIT!" He stares at her nakedness with big googly eyes, jaw basically touching the ground. "Wow... Vixen. Fuck..." He passes a hand through his hair, then rubs his face while keeping his fingers spread to see through them.

"Not the time, Ellis!" I snap.

His eyes finally look away from her and find mine. "Right, yeah. Sorry." He chuckles. "I was just coming to say food is ready. I'll leave you... to finish getting dressed." He turns his back to us and looks down. "Seems we have some fresh material for us tonight, little man."

"Are you really talking to your dick right now?" Veronica asks him.

He looks over his shoulder, clearly wanting one last peek at her exposed body. "Hey, he's standing at attention because of you. I don't have a choice but to talk to him, let him know I'll give him a little attention later."

"Jesus, Gabe. She doesn't want to know that you'll be jerking off to her later." I sigh, exasperated with him.

"Oh, I already figured that was something he did," she says, shaking her head at him when he beams at her.

Chapter Nine

GABRIEL

May the best man win.

I walk out of Noah's room and take a deep breath, needing a second to compose myself. I really wasn't expecting to find my Vixen standing there naked. And fuck, she's even more delicious than I thought she would be.

She's so skinny I'm pretty sure my large hands could wrap around her waist and touch on both sides. But it's not in that skinny, bony way, where she basically looks like a skeleton. I think she's just made really thin.

I've never really cared about a woman's size; I take them as they come. They're all beautiful in their own way. But Vixen, she holds a special place. It's like everywhere she goes, a spotlight shines above her. One that attracts me, pulls me in, and all I want to do is stand in it with her, hold her, and kiss her.

But I know we aren't there yet. She and I don't have the same connection that she has with Noah. I see it. It pisses me off, but I see it. She's closer to him; she doesn't care when he touches her or when he flirts with her.

She doesn't get feisty with him like she does with me, at least, not to the same degree. But I think we're slowly getting somewhere. I'll just have to work harder to make her see there's more to me than what I let on. That she can trust me and love me.

Because that's what I want with Ronnie. I hadn't realized it at first, but now I do. Seeing her with Noah, the way she looks at him, the way she smiles at him. I want that. I want her to see me like that.

I want the same thing Hayes has with Cecilia, Burkley with Morgan. I want what Ford has with Emma. Hell, I'll even take a kid with it too. I love kids. I just need to get my Vixen on board, and I need to have a talk with Noah.

I take the steps down to the main level and over to the kitchen, preparing three bowls of kale and avocado salad with blueberries and edamame. A nice light lunch for my pretty Vixen. Noah and I will most likely eat something else after, but all I care about is making her feel better.

A few minutes later, Ronnie and Noah appear in the kitchen. Noah now has a shirt on, and Ronnie is wearing one of his that ends halfway down her thighs and seems to have nothing underneath. *Fuck, she's so sexy with her long-ass legs and tanned skin.*

She comes to stand beside me, looking down into the bowl I'm holding. "Mmm, that looks delicious."

"I made it just for you." I smile at her.

"You really are my savior, aren't you?"

"That's right, baby. It's about time you figured it out." I wink, and she rolls her eyes at me, causing me to laugh.

"Is your medication working?" I ask as she grabs a fork and takes a big bite from the bowl I'm holding, which was originally mine. *Oh well.*

"Yeah, I still have cramps, but they're tolerable for now," she says around her mouthful. "OH MY GOD! Gabe! How do you make food taste so good!?"

I chuckle. "I don't know, I guess years of cooking for myself."

"Well, whatever it is, I want you to teach me." She takes another bite, while Noah and I watch her with amusement. *I guess she was hungry.*

"Or you could just move in, and I'll cook for you every day." I grin.

Her eyes shoot up to mine as she finishes chewing slowly. "Don't tell Aubrey I hesitated," she finally says. *Which isn't a no.*

Taking yet another bite, she moans loudly and closes her eyes. "AW GAWD! So good. Who knew blueberries would fit so well in a salad?"

Noah and I laugh as she dives in again but then stops and looks at me once more. "This was your bowl, wasn't it?"

"It was, but I'm feeling more in the mood for a sandwich." It's a lie, but she doesn't need to know that. "How about you take my bowl and yours and go sit down on the couch?"

"Fuck me, yes." She pats my cheek. "You know me so well." Then turns and grabs both bowls, bringing them over to the living room.

"Any day, baby. Just say the word," I call after her while laughing.

"I'll think about it," she shouts back, dropping down on the couch.

My eyes widen as I turn to Noah. I'm not sure if she meant the moving in or the fucking her, but I'll take either. I walk over to the fridge with a new sense of triumph. *A sandwich suddenly sounds pretty fucking good.*

An hour later, we're all sitting on the couch with full stomachs. The groceries even came just as we were starting to eat, so Noah and I took care of putting everything away, while Ronnie ate her lunch in peace.

We decided to watch some action movie, since Vixen stated a comedy would make her laugh too much and make her cramps worse. They've already started acting up again, despite her medication.

I'm thinking of looking into finding a doctor who will actually find a way to help her. No matter how many times Ronnie can say this is normal, there's no way it is. Being in pain to the point of being unable to move is never normal. I know a thing or two about that.

She's currently seated between us, carrying an uncomfortable look on her face, and keeps shifting around like she can't find a position that helps. I stand from the couch and get one of the heating pads I had bought. It's one of those that she places on her stomach and straps around her back, keeping it secure in place.

Kneeling in front of her, I catch her gaze. "Scoot closer so that I can pass it behind your back. This should help a bit." She does as I ask before I switch it on, and within seconds it's already warm to the touch. "How does that feel, baby?"

"Good," she says in a small voice, which tells me she's once again in pain.

Noah lifts her by the waist and places her over his lap sideways, then starts applying pressure against her lower back like he did earlier. She leans into his body and rests her head on his shoulder. I take the spot she was previously occupying beside Noah and grab her legs, stretching them out over my lap.

I begin massaging her calves, then her feet, occasionally going up to her thighs but always coming back down. I know that's not where her pain is, but if it can distract her a little and make her feel good, then I'm happy to do it. besides, I just really want to be touching her, too. A smile spreads along my lips when I notice her toenails do match her hair. One foot pink and the other blue. I was expecting to find them nude like her fingernails.

Halfway through the movie, she places her right hand above Noah's, which rests along the heating pad. I watch their hands together for a second, then look away, hating the jolt of jealousy spreading through me.

Noah and I always share women; it's nothing new to see him holding a woman I want. But with Ronnie, it's not the same. I'm not mad that he's touching her; I just wish she would want that from me, too.

As if hearing my thoughts, her left hand reaches out for mine. When I look up into her eyes, she smiles softly at me. I love these kinds of smiles. I love the little laughs she gives us. It all feels so intimate. I always knew they would be beautiful. And if I thought she owned a piece of my heart before I finally witnessed some real ones, she definitely owns it completely now.

I glide my right hand up from her calves and lace our fingers together, then bring it to my lips and kiss the back of her palm. "Why don't you spend the night here?" Her eyes narrow at my suggestion, but I quickly finish what I was saying before she gets the wrong idea.

"You could stay in the spare room. I'd just feel better knowing and seeing that you're okay. Like that, we could check on you throughout the night, and if there's anything you need, we'll be here to take care of you."

Her features soften again, and that soft smile returns. "I'll think about it. It's still early, so we'll see how I feel later."

"Just let us know," Noah says as he kisses her forehead.

Ronnie lifts her head away from Noah, her eyes gazing into his until they fall to his lips. She brings the hand that was holding his up to his jaw, her delicate fingers cupping the side of his face. She then closes her eyes and leans in, pressing her lips to his.

It's not a passionate kiss with an open mouth, tongue, and the whole sexual excitement that comes with it. It's tender, one with a hidden meaning.

After a few seconds, she pulls away, and her hand drops from his jaw. For a moment, she just stares at him, but then her head turns my way, and her gaze falls on me. And instantly, my heart rate skyrockets. Her free hand lifts once again and comes to my cheek this time, where she pulls me closer until our lips are barely an inch away.

I can feel her warm breath fanning against my lips, her featherlike touch against my cheek sending a rush of shivers down my body. All my senses awaken in this one little moment. Finally, she closes the distance between us, and I'm hit with paradise.

It's a simple kiss, yet it's more than I could have ever imagined. Even if it ended as soon as it began, it felt like it lasted a lifetime. I can still feel her against my tingling lips as she pulls away and looks at me.

"This doesn't mean I'm going to sleep with either of you," she says after a beat while eyeing us both. "It was just a kiss. A way to say thank you for all you've done today. It really means a lot to me."

"We weren't expecting anything more," Noah tells her.

She snorts. "Yeah, well, your dicks are telling me something else. One's poking my ass and the other my leg."

"Hey! We can't help it. We're men, and we're attracted to you. This isn't new." I laugh.

"You're right. I should have expected it." She giggles, then returns to her position against Noah.

By the end of the movie, Ronnie has fallen into a deep sleep, with little purrs falling from her slightly parted lips. Lips that were on mine not long ago. I can't stop watching her; she seems so peaceful and content at this moment. *I wonder if she's dreaming. And if so, would she dream of us?*

"Help me bring her up to the spare bedroom?" Noah asks as he stands from the couch with Ronnie in his arms.

I nod, and he turns toward the stairs, taking them one at a time slowly as I watch to make sure he doesn't trip. We get to the spare room, and I open the door for him, then go to the bed and pull back the covers as he gently lays her down.

I replace the blanket over her and brush a few strands of hair out of her face. She doesn't budge at my touch, but a small corner smile appears before her features go back to relaxed. My heart wants to burst at the little gesture she unconsciously made. I lower and kiss her cheek, then pull back. Noah does the same, then turns for the door as I follow him.

Once outside the room, I shut the door silently behind me and find Noah standing there with his arms crossed over his chest, watching me.

"I like her, Noh," is what I find myself saying, needing to make it clear where I stand.

"I know."

"No, I more than like her. I can't explain it, but she's not like the rest of them. She's not a phase I'll grow out of or get bored with. I want her, and not just in the fuck and leave way."

He studies me for a while, not saying anything. Not moving. Finally, he nods, understanding how genuine my words are. "I do, too."

I should have realized this could happen. We do seem to be interested in the same women most of the time. It's why we've always shared them. That was originally the plan with Vixen as well, until I realized she meant more to me than just a quick lay.

"So, what do we do?"

"We always agreed to both have her, I'm still fine with that. I don't want to share her with anyone else. But with you, I can accept that," he says quietly.

I nod. "And what if she only wants one of us?" I swallow around the tightness in my throat, at the thought that she could pick just one of us. That it could be Noah and not me.

His jaw ticks. "Then we man up and wish the other luck." He clearly doesn't like that thought just as much as I don't.

I honestly don't know if I'd be able to deal with watching Ronnie and Noah happy together while I'm removed from the equation. But he's also my best friend, and all I want is for him to be happy. I wouldn't want to lose him over a girl, even if it's my Vixen.

I reach my hand out for him to shake on our agreement. "May the best man win," I say once he grabs mine.

"Let's hope it doesn't come to that," he whispers before leaving for the stairs.

Yeah, let's hope.

~ The Next Morning ~

Ronnie did end up staying the night. Morgan had called during the afternoon while she was still napping, asking if we wanted to come over for dinner. But we told her Ronnie wasn't feeling well, and that we were going to stay home and watch over her.

She made some mushy comments about feeling the love in the air. Which made me laugh, while Noah just shook his head with a smirk.

Once Vixen woke up, we watched another movie while I made dinner, then we went outside to enjoy the sunset on our new patio, talking about everything and anything. Just joking around and enjoying each other's company with a beer or two, except for Ronnie. It's something I could get used to doing.

When we asked Ronnie if she wanted one of us to drive her home, she shook her head and said she would rather stay here for the night. That Aubrey would most likely spend the night at Greyson's, which meant no one would be home, and she didn't feel like being alone. Shortly after that, she wished us goodnight and went up to the spare room.

Having her close by, only a door away, felt right. I wanted to go to her, but I knew it wouldn't be the right move in our new relationship, not yet. Instead, I laid in bed, awake most of the night. I could say that she consumed my thoughts, that knowing she was so close was the reason I couldn't sleep. But the truth is I feared my nightmares would come to haunt me if I did. She's already suspicious about my bedsheets, I don't need her hearing just how bad it really gets.

After managing four hours of peaceful sleep, considering that my sheets aren't clawed off the bed and there's not a sweat stain in sight, I get started with my day by jumping into the shower. Once clean, I head into my closet and get dressed, checking the time on my phone as I head out of my room. 6:30 a.m.

I quietly step out of my room and into the hallway. I know Noah's still sleeping, but he'll be up in about thirty minutes. And from the silence I hear through Ronnie's door, she seems to still be asleep as well, which I expected. Not everyone wakes up early like I do, and Vixen doesn't seem like an early bird.

I slowly crack her door open and look inside to find her balled up in bed, the cover up to her neck, while the rest of the bed is now bare of any comforter. *Ah, so she's a cover hog. Good to know.* Although the chances of us ever sleeping in the same bed are slim to none.

Retreating quietly, I close the door and head down to the kitchen. I place my phone on the counter and start pulling out ingredients from the fridge for a healthy breakfast that everyone will like, including those for my green smoothie.

My phone suddenly rings with an incoming call. *Who the hell calls this early in the morning?* I pick it up, checking the caller ID, and my mood instantly drops. *Marshall.* I growl and silence the call, flipping it face down.

I get back to my task, but now I'm distracted. *What the hell does he want? And why is he calling me so soon?* I try to shake off the sickly feeling that crawls under my skin, but it's no use. He's gotten inside my head with just a simple call.

Fuck it, I guess we're having Greek yogurt with oatmeal and berries. There's no point in making a gourmet breakfast now; it will just taste like shit. *Exactly how I feel.*

Seconds later, my phone starts to ring again. *GOD DAMN IT!* I breathe through my nose, eyes closed as I clutch the edge of the counter. *Just ignore it, Ellis. Just ignore it. He'll give up.* But I know that's bullshit. He never does. He'll just keep calling and calling until he gets what he wants.

I can't deal with this today. Today is game day, our sixth game in the Stanley Cup Finals. If we win this one, the Cup is ours. It will finally be ours. I need to focus on that. I need my head to be in the game, not dealing with my shitbag father.

As expected, my phone starts ringing again the moment it stops. "UGH!" I snatch it off the counter and accept the call. "What the hell do you want?!"

It's silent for a second until his disgusting drunken voice comes through. "I need more."

"You need more!? I just gave you a shitload two weeks ago! We agreed to once a month! You can't just start demanding it whenever you'd like!"

"Listen to me, you little piece of shit! I'll demand it whenever I want it, and you'll give it to me. Unless you want that video of you and your bitch out there. I'm sure some gossip magazine would pay me a nice sum for that kind of information," he spits out.

"Don't you fucking dare!" I bark at him.

He laughs like this is some kind of joke to him. "Then you'd better send me what I want." He hangs up.

"FUCK!" I send my phone sailing across the room and fist my hair. From the sound produced as it makes contact with the wall, it's most likely broken, but I'm too enraged to look. I grab onto the counter like it's a lifeline and bow my head as I try to steady my breath.

"Gabriel?"

My head snaps up at the sound of Ronnie's worried voice. She's never called me by my actual name, which tells me she's more than just concerned.

"Are you okay?" She takes tentative steps toward me, as if she's not sure if it's safe to come near me. I hate that. I don't want her to fear me.

"Yeah, I'll be fine. You don't need to worry about me, Vixen. I'm sorry if I scared you." I straighten and stretch my arms wide. "But I could really use a hug right now."

She smiles and nods, then closes the distance between us and enters my arms. I expected her to resist more, to tell me to find someone else to hug. But I guess she can sense how *not* okay I really am at the moment.

I close my arms around her and take a deep breath as my nose digs into her hair. "Seems we're both in need of a new phone. I'll pick two up on my way back from practice."

She laughs. "You don't need to do that."

"I want to," I whisper. "I'm sorry I won't be making you a fancy breakfast this morning," I say after a beat.

She softens in my arms, hers tightening against my back. "It's okay. You can make it up to me tomorrow." *So, she's planning on coming back tomorrow.* That will make it four days in a row that she's here, and I'm not complaining.

I smile against her head. "It's a deal."

Chapter Ten

VERONICA

Kissing = Thank you.

I'm not sure who Gabe was arguing with on the phone when I came down to the kitchen. I only caught the end of his conversation, where he mentioned an agreement of once a month, and that whoever was on the line couldn't start demanding *it* whenever they wanted.

What is 'it'? And who was he talking to?

Whoever it was, Gabe hates their guts. It showed in his posture, his features, and his tone. His entire body language screamed with pent-up fury. I've never seen Gabe that mad in his life. I didn't even know that was an emotion he had with how happy and goofy he always is. He's like a jokester, the class clown. You'd never expect that person to have a bad temper.

In that moment, he scared me. Without wanting to, my body and mind feared that anger he contained. It reminded me too much of my past, too much of someone I desperately want to forget. But then he asked me for a hug, and despite that smile he carried on his face, there was so much unspoken sadness behind it. Although I could tell from the haunted look in his eyes, it wasn't sadness toward what the person had said. It was something else. Like the person on the phone had evoked a buried past that he didn't want to relive.

And at *that* moment, all I wanted was to run into his arms. To tell him that everything would be okay, the same way I desperately needed someone to tell me that three years ago. But just like three years ago, those words were never spoken. But through my hug, I know he felt them.

I wait around the penthouse for Noah and Gabe to get home before heading out, since Gabe told me I couldn't leave until he arrived with my new phone, even though I reminded him it wasn't necessary. I'm pretty sure I have an old one lying around somewhere in my room that I could use. But he said it was out of the question and that since he was picking one up for himself, it just made more sense to get me one, too.

I walk over to the fridge and pull out a water bottle, then grab my medication bottle from the counter beside it and pop one pill. I could probably go without the medication today, but I'm being cautious. The cramps aren't as bad today, thank God, because I would never be able to sit through a whole hockey game tonight if they were.

I lean my ass against the counter as I wait, bottle in hand, thinking about what little tricks Gabe might pull on me with this phone. Who knows, he might ask for something in exchange. I wouldn't put it past him.

I wouldn't be surprised if, when he hands it over, I find some very inappropriate photos of himself on it. Or maybe he'll text himself from my phone, saying how much I want him and declaring my undying love for him. Then he'll show it to our friends, claiming it was really me who wrote it. The thought makes me laugh from where I stand, the water bottle inches from my lips.

"What's got you laughing over there?"

I look up to find the man in question smirking at me from the couch, his butt leaning against the back of it, feet crossed at the ankles, and arms folded over his large chest. His tight gray shirt clings to his muscular torso and arms that bulge in their position. His damp wavy-blond hair that falls to his shoulders is held back by a backwards baseball cap, and a devilish smirk lies on his clean-shaven face, white pearly teeth glimpsing out from the side.

Gabriel has that boyish charm. The one that makes you want to do wild, crazy things with him. He could ask you to go graffiti the Statue of Liberty, and all it would take is that smile to convince you. He's ridiculously handsome.

"You," I answer truthfully.

His smile broadens as he pushes off the couch and walks toward me. "Glad to know you're thinking about me."

I roll my eyes but still smile.

He comes to stand in front of me and hands me a brand-new iPhone. The newest version, while mine was three generations old. As predicted, the phone is already activated, and everything has been synced from my old one. When I look up to thank him, the mischievous look in his eyes confirms my earlier thoughts. He definitely did something.

"What did you do?" I narrow my eyes to slits.

He holds his hands up. "Nothing. I swear, I'm a good boy."

"The fact that you didn't stop at *'nothing'*, then claimed you were a *'good boy'* tells me you weren't. What did you do to my phone, Ellis?" I raise a brow.

"You'll just have to find out." He winks, then lowers quickly and pecks my cheek.

Noah and Gabe are practically the same height, although I suspect Gabe is maybe half an inch taller, maybe even a third.

When his lips hit my cheek, I expect something to happen, a feeling of unease to wash over me. But again, it never comes. Yesterday every time he touched me, I felt calm. I suspected it was because of my state of mind, but now I'm questioning if maybe something in me has shifted. Maybe my mind and body finally understand that I have nothing to fear from Gabe, that he's harmless.

That he'll never hurt me like Victor did.

"Noh should be arriving soon. He had an interview with a reporter to do before leaving the arena. I'm off to nap. See you at the game later, Vixen." He walks backwards and heads for the stairs as he finishes talking.

"Okay, I'm gonna head out now. Thank you for the phone, and good luck tonight!" I call out as he takes the steps two at a time, up to his room.

I head to the elevator just as it opens with Noah inside. "You leaving?" he asks as we switch positions, him in the foyer and me in the elevator.

"Yeah, but I'll see you at the game tonight." I grab his shirt quickly and kiss his cheek. "For good luck." I wink.

He smiles broadly. "Bye, Veronica."

"Bye, Noah," I say as the doors to the elevator close.

I make my way down while texting Aubrey to find out where she is. She tells me she's still at her brother's house with all the girls and to join her there since she has my car. Once in the lobby, I get myself an Uber and head over to Emma's. Forty-five minutes later, I'm finally at my destination.

"Hello, my beloved puck ladies," I say with a smile as I march into the kitchen where all the girls are gathered around.

"Ugh, we never did end up changing that name. It makes us sound so old," Emma whines while wrinkling her nose.

"Well, last I checked, there were still little humans around with tiny ears. So we can't use the B word anymore," I point out to her.

"I still think it sounds classy," Morgan provides.

"I agree," Aubrey says, nodding her head.

"Of course, you do, Miss Prim and Proper. You just don't like being called a B-I-T-C-H." I narrow my eyes at her, and she smiles.

"How are you feeling today, Ronnie?" Morgan questions softly. "Gabe said you weren't doing so well yesterday."

"He told you that?" I furrow my brows.

"Yeah, I called to invite them over for dinner, but they said you were napping and wanted to stay home to check on you. It's really sweet if you ask me," she finishes with a swoony sigh.

"That's if it's really what was going on." Cecilia smirks.

"It was." I point a finger at her. "Don't start thinking things. Nothing's going on there." I turn back to Morgan. "And I'm feeling much better now."

"Oh, good! I would hate for you to miss their game tonight." She smiles at me. Morgan is a huge supporter of her husband. She practically goes to every single one of his games.

Emma reaches behind her for a wineglass, holding it in my direction. "Want one?"

It's then I notice all the girls already have glasses. I'm tempted to say yes, but then Gabe's warning voice pops into my head, and I groan. "I can't. Gabe forbade me from having anything that could make my cramps worse. He literally made me a list of what I can and can't have. Did you guys know he was such a health nut?"

They all frown as they rack their brains. "Actually, now that you mention it. I don't think I've ever seen Ellis eat anything that wasn't healthy. Even when we've ordered pizza in the past, he always claimed he wasn't hungry because he had just raided Silas's nutrient bars," Cecilia speaks up.

"It's true. Except for drinking beer, I've never seen him eat junk food. He wouldn't even have a piece of cake on my birthday, or at Gracie's," Em says.

"He didn't want any dessert at your baby shower either," Aubrey adds, addressing Cecilia.

"How are we just figuring this out? We spend so much time with those guys." Morgan looks perplexed. "Jesus, I've fed him so many times, and I've never noticed."

Now that actually makes me curious. Gabe and Noah often eat over at Morgan and Clay's, yet Gabe is a phenomenal cook himself. Why eat somewhere else when you can make it yourself? Plus, he really seems to enjoy cooking. It seems both the boys are really good at hiding secrets.

I look around, noticing Dante and Gracie aren't with their toys in the living room. "Are the kids napping?"

Emma holds up a water bottle this time, and I nod as she passes it over. "No, they're out with their grandparents, though they should be coming back soon. We're putting them down a little later, since they'll be up past their bedtime and we don't want them getting cranky at the game."

"Makes sense." My phone vibrates in my pocket, and I pull it out.

"You got a new phone?" Aubrey questions with curiosity as she looks it over in my hand.

"Yeah, my old one broke, so Gabe got me a new one." When I look up, I find all of them staring at me. "What?"

"I don't think I've ever heard you say his name so often in one day." Cecilia stares at me with wide eyes.

"So?"

They all look at each other, then back at me. "He bought you a phone. Did he ask for something in exchange?" Emma asks.

"Umm, no." I furrow my brows.

They give each other that look again. "Wow, could it be?" Morgan questions finally.

"Could what be?" *I'm so confused.*

"That Gabriel Ellis is finally ready to settle down." Cecilia beams with joy.

My eyes widen as my mouth opens wide. "HA! No. Nope. That's not the case. He was getting himself a new one, so he picked one up for me too. That's all. There's no hidden meaning behind it." *At least, I don't think so.*

"Sweetheart, I slept with the guy multiple times. He never even offered me breakfast once. Trust me, this means something to him." Em pats my shoulder.

"You guys are being ridiculous. It's nothing, he's just being nice. And anyway, there's Noah too." *Oh God, why did I just say that?*

"What do you mean, *'there's Noah too'*?" Morgan asks quizzically.

"Wait, you like Noah?" Cecilia jumps in.

"No, that's not what I said. I just meant that... you know, it's always the two of them." They all watch me, waiting for me to go on. But honestly, I'm not even sure what I'm trying to say myself. "Just, never mind. It's not important. No one likes no one. No hidden meaning. No settling down."

My phone vibrates again, reminding me of the notification. I open it up and find a message from *Husband #1.'* I narrow my eyes, confused at what I'm seeing. I don't have anyone in my contact list with that name. I pull up the message thread.

Husband #1

Found it yet? <Wink emoji>

I can't help but laugh as I read the message. *That sneaky little man. If he wrote number one beside his, then that would mean...* I pull out of it and go to my contacts, looking for Noah. And as expected, his name has now been changed to *'Husband #2.'* Going back to Gabe's message, I send him a quick one back.

"He put himself as husband in your phone, but it means nothing, right?" Em says beside me with a smirk as she reads my messages with Gabe.

"She's even wearing that goofy look you get when you talk to Greyson," Cecilia notes.

"Hey! You get it too with Silas, and you with Clay! It's not just me. And I won't even mention Aubrey..." Em peers around me at Brey with a smile.

"I do not get that look!" She turns red as she speaks.

"For a certain head coach of a certain hockey team? Yeah, you do," I say, giggling. She narrows her eyes at me. "You're supposed to be my friend."

"Oh, we all are, Sweetie." Morgan pats her hand from across the kitchen island.

"Speaking of Greyson, where is he?" I ask, just realizing his truck wasn't in the driveway when I arrived.

"He's napping at Cecilia's place with Silas. I told him to go there since we were all going to be here. And I didn't want to risk waking him during his much-needed nap before his game," Emma informs me. "But don't try to change the subject. What's going on with you and the twins?"

I groan, then take a sip of my water bottle, trying to avoid having to answer that question. The truth is I have no idea. I'm confused with everything. After kissing them, I made sure to clarify it meant nothing but a thank you. But then I ended up having a dream about them when I fell asleep. And let's just say, the dream was quite... hot.

Now I'm realizing how much I enjoy being with them, and dare I say... miss them when they aren't around. I don't know what to make of that. I swore off men. I swore I would never let my emotions take over ever again. But missing them? That's an emotion I shouldn't be feeling.

I put my bottle back down, knowing there's no point prolonging the inevitable. With a sigh I mumble, "I kissed them."

They all gasp as their mouths drop open.

"Them... as in, both of them?" Aubrey asks, looking horrified.

"Ugh! Yes, I kissed both of them. It was—"

"Don't you dare say '*nothing*' again," Em cuts in, earning a glare from me.

"Fine! It wasn't nothing. But it was just as a thank you for them taking care of me all day. They were really sweet. They ran me a bath, made me food, and gave me massages while watching a movie. I just felt like I owed them somehow."

"So, you thought a kiss to each would be the right thing to do?" Morgan asks.

"Exactly! Thank you, you get it." I throw a hand her way.

"Do you all say thank you with a kiss?" Aubrey wonders.

"To our partners, yes. Anyone else? No," Cece says, giggling as she looks at me.

"What are you trying to say?" I frown.

"I'm just saying that there might be more to your relationship with Noah and Gabe than you realize. And that's okay."

But it's not. It's not okay. I feel the panic slowly rising within me. *Did I really start something by kissing them without realizing it? Is that why I don't get that itchy sense with Gabe anymore?*

"We're back!" Nancy, Aubrey and Greyson's mother, calls as she comes over to us with Gracie in her arms. She's closely followed by Andrew, their father, as well as

Mira and John Hayes, Silas's parents, who walk behind Dante.

"Oh, there's my little Tulip!" Emma exclaims as she takes her daughter in her arms. "Did you have fun at the park with Grandma and Grandpa?"

"Mama!" Gracie exclaims and tightens her arms around Emma's neck.

I turn to Nancy and Andrew, ready to greet them. "Sir Ford, Lady Ford. Always a pleasure seeing you both." I kiss both their cheeks.

Andrew laughs. "I love this girl. She makes me feel special."

Nancy rolls her eyes. "You say that like I never pay you any attention."

"She calls me sir. You called me an old clown last Christmas."

She huffs out, shaking her head, then turns to me. "How are you, sweetheart? I heard you started working for those two flirts. I hope they're treating you well?"

"I'm good. And they are, surprisingly." I laugh.

"Of course, they are. Have you seen the way they look at her? Those boys are infatuated with that young lady." Mira comes over to me with a warm smile. "Hi, dear."

"Hi." I hug her.

"So, what were you ladies all chatting about before we walked in? I can sense there was a serious topic of conversation happening." Mira loves joining in on our gossip.

"Oh, we were just discussing Ronnie's love life with the twins," Emma informs them, to which everyone chuckles.

"No! There's no love life happening between us." I point a finger at all of them, hoping to make my point clear.

"Really? Both of them?" Nancy asks with raised brow.

"Yes," Cecilia answers for me, just as I was about to say no.

"Does no one listen to me?" I raise my arms at my sides.

"It's okay, Darling. No shame in being with two men at once. Nancy and I once had a threesome with a friend of mine." Andrew pats my shoulder.

"OH MY GOD! DAD!" Aubrey yells in horror, then places her hand to her mouth. "Oh God, I think I'm going to be sick."

"Andrew!" Nancy glares at him at the same time.

"Was it Hugo?" Emma asks, not bothered at all by the conversation.

Andrew snaps his fingers and points at her. "It was!" he exclaims with a smile.

Nancy sighs, looking up at the ceiling. "Can someone please remind me why I married this man?" Her comment is rewarded by a laugh from all of us.

"Hugo? Really, Mom? Wait, Em, how do you know Hugo?" Aubrey looks confused.

"Oh, I don't. But I've heard your parents talking about him often, so I put two and two together." She shrugs.

"This conversation is getting so out of hand." I shake my head.

Mira giggles. "How about you, young lady? Has anything evolved with your man?" She looks at Aubrey.

By now, everyone except for her brother knows exactly who we're talking about. Shane Jefferson, Head Coach for the New York Griffins. Her brother and the boys' coach.

He's not exactly her man, since they don't actually have a relationship. But they're both completely and utterly smitten with each other. They both get tongue-tied in one another's presence and turn red like tomatoes. They also can't seem to keep their eyes off each other when they're in the same room. It's adorable to watch.

"He's not my man," Brey tells Mira while turning a deep pink as she says the words.

"Isn't it funny how she knows exactly who we're talking about, yet claims he's not hers?" Emma giggles.

"She's still trying to deny it," Cecilia informs her mother-in-law.

"Ah, I see." Mira nods, then leans in toward Nancy. "We'll have to come up with something to get those two moving."

Nancy nods in agreement.

"Mom!" Aubrey gapes like a fish. The tips of her ears and nose have turned completely red, like it's the middle of winter and she's been standing outside for hours.

"What? You two would make such a cute couple. Oh! And imagine the babies!?" Nancy gushes.

"Oh, I totally agree. Those babies would be adorable!" Mira coos as well.

This conversation really did get out of hand. At least they aren't talking about my love life anymore. I mean, my non-existing love life with two certain men we won't mention.

After a few more ebullient comments, the conversation is finally changed to safer territories. Cecilia and Emma put Dante and Gracie down for their nap shortly after, during which Aubrey and I head home to get changed for the game tonight.

Emma instructed us to dress fancier than usual, since tonight could be a big night for everyone. We agreed because, as she quoted, *"We don't want to look like garbage in front of the camera."* Then we returned to Emma's to have dinner and finish getting ready before we all headed out the door for the boys' game.

Mira and John get into their car with Dante, while Nancy and Andrew take Gracie into their rental, since they live in Toronto and only came down for the game.

If things go as we're all hoping tonight, the grandparents will be going home with the kids, while we celebrate with the men. And if not, then we'll all be going home and following them to Dallas in three days for the final game.

"Let's go win us a cup!" Emma cheers as the girls and I all pile into her SUV.

I pull out my phone and create a group chat with Noah and Gabe, shooting them one last quick text.

Me

> Good luck again! I'll be cheering for you both.

Husband #1

> That's our girl. Thanks, baby. Do I get a kiss if we win?

Me

> Who knows…

Husband #1

> Oh, we are so winning this game. See you after the game, Vixen <Kiss emoji><Heart emoji>

Husband #2

> What about me? <Wink emoji>

Me

> You boys are so demanding. I swear, worse than puppies.

Husband #1

> But much better looking, right?

Me

> Of course, Pretty Boy. Of course.

Me

> Win the game, and we'll see how things play out after.

NOAH

I glance at the clock. Nine minutes and fifty-seven seconds left. *We've fucking got this.* Turning my focus back to the game, I catch the Ranchers' right winger racing down the ice with the puck, heading for me. I already know what he's going to do and prepare for it.

At this point, they all feel their loss coming and aren't playing strategically anymore. They'll take whatever shot they can and hope luck is on their side. It's fucking stupid if you ask me and a big mistake that won't win them any points.

Time slows as I watch him lift his stick before bringing it back down to the ice, aiming for Ellis's five-hole. *Second mistake.* If this idiot was thinking clearly, he'd know Gabe is amazing at blocking his five-hole, certainly when he's not moving. He shoots the puck as I quickly move into its trajectory, pushing the end of my stick forward at the perfect second to deflect the puck toward Olchkov, my defense partner, who slaps it back down the ice and out of our zone.

Olchkov laughs, his deep Russian accent coming through as the wingers and centers skate after the puck where Clay catches it once it hits the offensive zone. "Feels like we're playing against rookies tonight."

I chuckle along with him. "Couldn't agree more." He's right, I'm not sure what's up with the Ranchers tonight, but they aren't playing as well as they have these past few games. Although they're definitely bringing out the physical game.

As if hearing my thoughts, I spot Greyson being thrown down by the asshole, Eric Gale, who lands right on top of him. But if you ask me, it looks like it was purposely done and most likely is knowing him. Everything from there happens quickly, Ford finally gets back to his skates and chases after him, sending Gale flying into the boards.

"Ah fuck..." I groan, knowing Grey will get in shit for that, and skate forward slowly, wondering if we should interfere. I don't normally get involved with fights and stick by Ellis unless I'm personally aimed, but with this team things often get out of hand to the point where everyone jumps in.

I watch the two battle it out on the ground, blood splattering over the ice until finally they're pulled apart, and I see Ford being pulled over to the penalty bench with a wide grin on his face. "About fucking time!" I shout at him with a laugh as the crowd cheers and Gale gets taken off the ice, blood pissing from his nose.

The play starts up again and the Ranchers are instantly aggressive with every hit as they try once more to score a goal, while Olchkov and I attempt to send the puck back the other way. We're all in each other's faces, bumping into one another while trying to get a hold of the puck when finally, Ellis covers it with his glove in the crease.

I expect the whistle to be blown by the ref immediately, but it doesn't come and our opponents keep jabbing at Gabe's glove with their sticks, trying to free the puck. "Digging!" I call out, hoping to wake up the ref from whatever the fuck he's doing and stop the play.

Finally, the whistle blows and we all move back, but of course, the Ranchers aren't having it and one of the fuckers purposely bumps into Gabe. Within a split second, I'm up right behind him and shoving him to the ground. "DON'T FUCKING TOUCH THE GOALIE!" I yell aggressively and the whistle goes off once more.

"He's lucky you got to him before I did." Olchkov chuckles as we bump fists on my way to the penalty box along with the shit head who started it.

I plop down next to Ford who's almost done with his two-minute. "Good job on Gale. It was time someone put the asshole in his place," I tell him.

He laughs. "Surprised I only got a minor for that one."

"Nah, everyone knows he started that shit and fucking deserved it."

"Well, thanks." He stands and pats my shoulder, ready to get back out there now that his time is up. "And great job on defending our guard dog." He salutes me before skating off.

The next few minutes pass by in a blink with only thirty seconds remaining on the clock. We still have a nine-to-four lead, which if you ask me is unbelievable certainly in the playoffs, but as I said, they've been playing like rookies all night. The girls are already all standing in their seats, clapping hands and cheering for what's about to happen the instant it hits zero.

Gabe laughs his head off while the play is in the offensive zone. "We fucking did it! Holy shit, we fucking won!" he shouts, the widest grin plastered over his face as I look over my shoulder and find him moving around and wiggling his ass. "Come on, Adler! This deserves a victory dance!"

I shake my head at him despite the grin I carry and join in, moving my hips as Olchkov does the same a second later. I'm sure we look like idiots, but Gabe's right, this deserves a victory dance.

Finally, the buzzer goes off and the crowd goes wild. Gabe quickly leaves his post and tackles me into a bear hug, Olchkov doing the same as the rest of our team jumps over the boards in front of the players bench and skate our way with Ford, Burkley, and Hayes. Soon, we're a huge pile of hockey players on the ground, all laughing and shouting, unable to believe what just happened.

That we finally took the Stanley Cup home.

From there it's all a blur of congratulations and cheers as the cup is brought out and we all get a chance to hold it. The families and friends then join the ice, and hugs are passed all around while others take picture with the cup. I spot Veronica congratulating the guys through the crowd and begin skating over to her, but Gabe beats me to it and whisks her off her feet from behind, doing a little circle around the rink as she laughs away.

He finally sets her down when I reach them and beams at her as she fixes her short dress back into place. It's a nice sparkling gold number that ends mid-thigh with long sleeves, accompanied by a pair of thigh-high black stiletto boots. Her makeup is the usual blue winged eyeliner with subtle gold eyeshadow, giving her that feisty look I adore, while her blue and pink hair is curled with one side tucked behind her ear.

"God, you boys smell terrible, and now I'm all sticky." Veronica wrinkles up her nose while wiping her hands along her dress as Gabe and I laugh. "I understand why Em said it was mandatory for us to bring spare clothes for the celebrations later on."

"Ah, come on, Vixen. It's not that bad," Ellis says as he places his hand on her hip and tries to pull her in once more, but she pushes against his chest.

"It is. Don't touch me."

He gives her big puppy eyes and pouts. "But what about my kiss? You said if we win, I get a kiss." A smirk grows on his lips as her eyes narrow to slits.

"Actually, I never said that. You did. I said we would see."

"She's kind of right." I shrug when Gabe frowns at me.

"Bro, I'm trying to win us a kiss here and you're not helping."

Veronica rolls her eyes at us. "Ugh, you boys are truly way too demanding," she grumbles then fists the front of Gabe's jersey and pulls him down, smacking her lips to his before letting go. She turns to face me next, grabs my jersey forcefully and does the exact same, delivering a bruising yet powerful kiss. "There, happy?"

Gabe's grin grows even wider than before, now full open mouth, making him look goofy as hell, and all I can do is chuckle at how ecstatic he looks.

"Oh God! Stop that, you look ridiculous!" Veronica looks away with wide eyes, seeming extremely embarrassed, but then shrieks when Ellis wraps his arms around her once more and lifts her off the ground. "Pretty Boy, no! I said stop it. Put me down! What don't you understand with *you smell like shit*!?"

He laughs and lets her go. "I just wanted a hug. We did just win a pretty big game, you know."

"Fine," she mumbles, delivering that eye roll again, but I don't miss the smirk playing along her lips right before she glances my way. "Let me guess, you want one too?"

I smile and open my arms, letting her come to me. "I wouldn't say no."

"Might as well since I already smell like crap." She steps into them immediately and I slowly wrap mine around her. "Congratulations, Casanova," she whispers into my ear.

"Thank you, Kitten."

Chapter Eleven

VERONICA

Clayton and his flowery blanket.

~ The Next Day ~

"Ughhh..."

"Why is it so... bright?"

"Can someone shut off that damn music?!"

I scrunch my face before blinking my eyes open. Everything is blurry, and nothing comes into focus right away. *Where the hell am I?* I can hear voices talking around me, everything sounding like grunts or whines, but it's all fuzzy.

Suddenly my vision begins to come back, blinding light piercing my eyes as I try to bash it away. *Oh God, that hurts.* Almost as much as the splitting headache that I'm feeling. My throat feels dry as I try to swallow around the lump of clay stuck in it. *I need to drink something.*

"Shut off the music!" someone groans louder.

What music?

But then I finally hear it, although I don't recognize what it is. *Country? Who the hell is playing country music this early in the morning? Wait, what time is it?* I try to sit up, opening my eyes at the same time, but knock right back down as the heaviness in my head and body weighs me down.

"Fuck..."

I rub my fists into my eyes, blinking again as the ceiling comes into view. I look at my hands, then down my body. *I'm still wearing last night's clothes, that's good.* Looking to one side, I discover that I'm lying on one end of a couch. I stretch out my body, and my hands connect with a body part at the same time as my feet touch another, grunts coming from both ends as I hit them with my limbs accidentally.

I peer down first, noticing Gabe at my feet, my toes touching his silky hair, while his legs hang off the arm and back of the couch. I then gaze up behind me and find Clay in a ball on the armchair next to the couch. I nearly giggle at the sight.

Clay always looks like a grumpy, mean giant, even if he's really not. Seeing him right now in that chair with a flower-printed blanket covering him is epic. "Someone take a picture," I mumble hoarsely.

"A picture of what?" Aubrey asks, clearing her throat a few times. *Wait, she's here? Where?*

I look around the room quickly and find her on another armchair across the room. "What?"

"You said someone take a picture. Of what?" she mutters again.

Oh, I hadn't realized I said that out loud.

"Never mind," I say with a sigh as I close my eyes and drop my arm over them, trying to lessen the brutal assault happening inside my head, which makes me realize the music is still playing. "Can someone stop that fucking music?! Where is it even coming from?"

A few seconds later, I hear faint footsteps walking around, and finally the music goes mute. A chorus of sighs happens around the room.

"Fucking finally!" someone says from beside me. *But I'm on the couch; that makes no sense.*

I force myself to roll over and look down at the floor, only to find Noah lying on the ground with a pillow beneath his head. He squints one eye open and peeks at me. "Hey, Kitten."

"Hi," I whisper back. "What are you doing down there?"

He looks around him like he hadn't noticed he was sleeping on the hard wooden floors. "I have no idea."

I giggle and turn back onto the couch, starting to feel dizzy and nauseous from moving too much. "Where are we?" I ask no one in particular.

Gabe lifts his head slightly, turns it from side to side, then drops it back to my feet. "Hayes's house," he rasps out in a scratchy voice.

"Was that music playing all night?" Aubrey asks suddenly. She's so quiet I keep forgetting she's there. "And where's everyone else?"

"Yes, it was. Although you've all only been sleeping for two hours." Morgan suddenly appears behind the couch near my head, nearly giving me a heart attack. "Em and Grey are in one of the spare rooms, and Cece and Sy are in their room."

"Well, that explains why I feel like shit. How are you up and walking?" I eye her suspiciously. *I don't even think I can stand.*

"I guess I just tolerate alcohol better than all of you." She shrugs and smiles.

"Or you stopped drinking before all of us," Noah mutters from below.

Last night took us all by surprise. Well, not really. We knew the boys would win. They had played so well all season and were killing it in the playoffs. But it still was a shock to realize it was really happening as we watched those last seconds tick down, knowing what was coming. It was magical. The screams surrounded us as we all jumped in place with joy for our partners and friends. It was amazing.

Then, of course, there was a lot of celebration happening. And I mean, A LOT. The last thing I remember was taking shots at the club. I'm not sure how we made it back here, but I'm glad to see everyone is in one piece. Or somewhat.

"Wait," Aubrey starts. "I'm still confused about the music. Why was it even on in the first place? No one here listens to country music." The poor girl never gets drunk. She's probably so lost right now that her only hope of sanity is to focus on that specific subject.

"Well, you guys decided you weren't done celebrating. And you also wanted to camouflage the sound of Emma and Greyson going at it like rabbits. For the country part, I have no idea."

Oh, that's right, I remember hearing them. They were a little wild, although we can't really blame them after what finally happened last night at the game. So naturally, Greyson was really excited to celebrate a different kind of win with her. And it showed.

"It was this crazy witch's idea." Clay's hand comes down to my head as he ruffles my hair.

"Me!?" I gasp.

"Mhmm. Claimed you could two-step and wanted to show us."

"OH GOD! I've never two-stepped in my life!" I bury my face behind my hands.

"It was pretty cute to watch." Noah chuckles.

"Shut up, Casanova. If I find out someone filmed me, they're about to die." I look around, waiting for someone to admit to it.

"Aubrey did," Gabe mumbles.

I gasp even louder. "You traitor."

"I'll delete it, I swear... once I find my phone," she says from her spot. No one in the living room has moved yet. We're now all talking, but everyone is still lying down, clearly trying to gain their bearings before daring to stand.

My stomach suddenly claws at my skin, grumbling to life. I press a hand down on it, but that doesn't help. *I need food.* I wiggle my toes, and they catch in Gabe's hair once more. His hand comes back and latches onto one of them, bringing it down the side of his face as he kisses the top of my foot, then lets it go.

I manage to turn around on the couch, placing myself on my stomach with my head where my feet used to be, and bring myself up close and personal with Gabe. "Pretty Boy, wake up." I look down at him.

He smiles but doesn't open his eyes. I brush a wavy blond strand away from his face. "Come on. Wakey, wakey."

"What can I do for you, milady?" he says, still not opening them.

"Can you make me that green smoothie of yours? I feel like it would make me feel so much better right now." I beg with pretty eyes and a smile.

He peeks at me through one slit, then beams and closes his eye again. "It would, but I can think of other things that would help, too."

I smack his naked chest. "Stop being naughty. Make me my drink."

He laughs and finally opens his eyes, grays rendering me speechless. Those tiny specks of blue shining brighter as they gaze into my deep sapphires. Gabriel Ellis has beautiful eyes. Those that seem to hold you captive when they fall on you.

My head is held up completely above his as I rest on my elbows, arms on either side of his head as I stare down at his upside-down face. My hair falls down around my face, and with how close we are, it practically serves as a curtain of privacy.

He reaches up and tucks one side behind my ear. "Can I get a kiss?" I narrow my eyes at his request. "You know, for getting up while I'm still drunk and making you our special drink?"

I pucker my lips, thinking it over. Finally, with a grunt, I lower the few inches separating us and press my lips to his quickly. I'm not even sure it lasted a second. But he also didn't specify the length of time required. "There. Now can I have my drink?"

He pushes himself up as I pull back into a kneeling position on the couch. "Right away, baby." He stands and stretches himself out. Arms folded above his head as he flexes his back muscles, making them all ripple in effect.

Fuck, that's sexy as hell.

A warm tingle spreads in my lower abdomen as I grow hot and fuzzy inside while watching him. *Holy shit, I'm turned on. Gabriel Ellis just turned me on...* My eyes go wide at the realization. *This has to be because of that stupid dream.*

The dream where I was lying in bed, sprawled out between the both of them. Their hands all over my body, touching every inch of my skin and setting it on fire. Feeling them spread my legs and taking me in turn, while the other devoured my mouth and played with my body.

Jesus, I'm getting wet just thinking about it.

I force myself to look away, my gaze falling on Noah, who watches me intriguingly with a smirk. He brings a hand up to the side of his lip and taps it. "You have a little drool there."

I gasp as he laughs, taking the pillow behind me and throwing it at his head. "Shut up! I do not!" I wipe my mouth for good measure, just in case.

When I look around the rest of the room, I find Clay still in his position, clearly not having moved an inch and not planning to. But then I fall on Aubrey, who stares at me with wide eyes, and Morgan, who smiles like a mother watching her child fall in love. But she's not my mom, and I'm not falling in love.

Definitely not. Never happening.

"Baby, we have a problem. Our smoothie won't be exactly the same since Hayes doesn't have all the ingredients I need. But I promise it'll still be delicious," Gabe calls from the fridge.

I turn to smile at him. "That's okay, but I also want food. You promised me one of your gourmet breakfasts."

He pops his head out from the fridge, grinning back at me. "Anything for you, Vixen."

"Wait, why are you asking Gabe to cook for you? I can make you something," Morgan asks with a frown.

Shit... I forgot she was there.

"Umm..." I look around, wanting to cover my face with the pillow I had, but remember I just threw it at Noah. "Because Gabe is a good cook," I mumble quickly, hoping she won't hear me.

"What?" She leans in like it might help her hear me better.

I sigh and close my eyes, dropping my head back. "Because Gabe is a phenomenal cook, and his food is to die for!"

When I open my eyes, I find her gaping at me, looking completely flabbergasted. Suddenly her face contorts into an angry scowl as she turns her attention to the man in question.

"I have been feeding you for years! And this whole time you could cook!?" she shouts, her voice going to a concerning high pitch. "I took pity on you, thinking you didn't know how to make your own food!"

He chuckles and rubs at his neck with a slightly embarrassed blush on his cheeks. "Yeah... sorry about that."

"Why are you guys yelling?" Emma appears with Greyson in the kitchen, followed by Cecilia, Silas, and Milo, their dog.

"Gabe can cook." Morg flaps her hands at her sides. "And apparently, as my supposed friend Ronnie pointed out, he's phenomenal at it!"

"Oh, you should have kept your mouth shut about that, Sweetie," Cecilia says with a giggle, but then scrunches her face and rubs at her temple.

"I'll get you some Advil." Silas kisses the top of her head, then looks up at us. "Anyone else need?" There's a series of grunts and raised hands. He chuckles and turns for the hall. "I'll just bring the bottle."

"How is he in good shape, too? What is this magic cure you two seem to possess?" I ask astounded, as I watch him walking away like he's in top shape, then turn to Morgan.

"I have a better question. How did we get here? I can't remember anything," Aubrey admits in a small voice. She looks so uncomfortable.

"I stopped drinking pretty early on, so I drove one car home. And Silas only had one drink, so he took the other." *Oh, that's right.* I forgot Silas only ever has one drink. The poor thing is still traumatized from what happened with his wife the last time he got drunk.

"Now that I think of it, I thought you weren't supposed to be drinking either?" Em calls as she wanders over and plops down beside me on the couch.

"Shit, that's right." Noah sits up and rests his hand on my knee. "Are you feeling okay?"

I place mine over his and give a reassuring squeeze. "I'm fine, I promise. The cramps usually only last about twenty-four hours, and then they're pretty normal if not gone altogether."

"Okay, but if you feel anything, let us know." He smiles tenderly.

"I love how much these two worry about you. It's like one of those *why choose* romance books you read, Cece," Emma says as she looks up at Cecilia, then back down to me. "It's okay to love them both." She pats my other leg with a wicked smile.

"I did," Aubrey finishes.

"Where have I heard that before?" I rack my brain for that specific quote.

"Vampire Diaries," the girls all answer at once. *Oh yeah, now I remember.* Morgan had started watching it a few months back and roped us all into it.

"Hey, if you three get serious. How would that work with kids and marriage? I mean, would the child call both of you *Dad*? And you can only marry one person, so that kind of leaves the other one left out," Clay asks out of nowhere, still huddled under his flowery blanket.

"Clay," Morgan warns, clearly telling him to shut up.

"What? I'm curious how a relationship like that would work. Like, do you all share one bed? Date nights happen all together? And sex, are you allowed to sleep with just one at a time or like always together?" he continues. "Imagine the introduction to the parents. *'Hey, Mom and Dad. These are my boyfriends.'*... Awkward..." Clay chuckles, and I'm starting to suspect he's still not sober. He's usually pretty quiet, always serious, and never really makes jokes.

"CLAYTON JOSEPH BURKLEY! Stop talking this instant. Their relationship is none of your business. Let them figure out their story on their own," Morg barks at him with her hands on her hips.

"It's not my fault my brain is going crazy with questions. It's your fault I drank so much," he grumbles.

"Hold up!" Gabe shouts from the kitchen. "Your name is Clayton?!"

Clay groans.

"How is that possible? I've seen your driver's license. It only says Clay Burkley," Emma adds in.

"I had it changed when I was eighteen," he grumbles again.

"Clay!" Cecilia gasps. "How could you have hidden this from me? You're supposed to be my brother." They aren't actually siblings, but they have a really close friendship.

"Sorry, C. No one but my wife, Silas, and my parents know that horrendous name exists."

She turns to her husband with a gaping mouth. "You knew about this and didn't tell me!? I'm shocked. Absolutely shocked."

"Sorry, babe. I'll make it up to you later, promise. But Clay's got a point, though, how would that all work out?" Silas asks with a raised brow.

I grunt. "Can we stop with this ridiculous conversation? There's no relationship. I'm not getting married. I'm not having any babies, and I'm not dating either of them. So, drop it!" I shout, causing silence to fall on the room. I get a mumbled apology from Silas and Clay as everyone else carries on with their own things.

When I gaze down at Noah, I find him looking down and frowning, then I turn to Gabe in the kitchen and notice him carrying a sad expression as well. I instantly feel bad for my comment, but I shouldn't. This is my life. I decide who I want to be in a relationship with. I decide who I want to marry and have children with.

So why do I feel like shit knowing my words may have disappointed them?

Chapter Twelve

NOAH

Heated passenger doors and gym mirrors.

~ One Week Later ~

I'm anxious as I make my way up to Veronica's condo. Today is a big day for me, something I never thought I'd ever be doing. I'm taking her to see my sister.

When she asked to meet her, I didn't think she'd want to go so soon. Another part of me thought she might have offered only to be nice but didn't actually want to. But then yesterday, she asked when I was planning on going and if she could come along. So I told her I was going today, and here we are.

I knock on the door and wait. Aubrey opens it a few seconds later since she rang me in and knew I was coming up. "Morning, sweetheart." I kiss her cheek like I always do.

"Good morning, Noah," she says as she turns bright red.

I chuckle. "What are you going to do when you have a boyfriend, Aubrey?"

She smiles with a soft giggle. "Hope he finds my incessant blushing endearing. At least long enough to fall in love with me."

"If he's smart, he'll fall in love the moment he lays eyes on you," I tell her, genuinely meaning it. I've known Aubrey for a few years now, and aside from her shyness, I've yet to find any flaws.

Her blush deepens. "That's really sweet of you to say, Noah."

I smile and go to reply but spot Veronica coming into view from the hall, and my mouth goes dry. Veronica always looks good, but right now, she takes my breath away.

She's not in her usual clothing I've grown used to. Instead, she wears a short, dusty blue dress that seems to be backless from what I can see. Thin spaghetti straps rest on her shoulders, a slightly flared skirt falling from her hips, with her usual thigh-high stockings and black stilettos on her feet. She's also curled her hair beautifully with one side tucked behind her ear, and her makeup is stunningly done with dark blue eyeliner that wings at the tip and nude lipstick.

She smiles once she catches me staring and walks over. "Hey, Casanova."

I swallow. "Hey, Kitten. Ready to go?" She nods in response.

"Where are you guys going?" Aubrey asks from beside us as she watches our interaction.

My mind suddenly goes blank as I open my mouth while searching for a good reason. Veronica came over yesterday, so technically, it's her day off, and Aubrey knows that.

"There are a few things I want to buy for their place to help with the organizing system I've put in place. I asked Noah to come with me to have his input as well, since he and Gabe will be the ones using it mostly," Veronica provides quickly as an excuse, then smiles up at me.

God, I could kiss her right now.

"Oh, okay. Well, have fun," Aubrey says sweetly.

"We will," I call back as we head for the door. Once back outside and in the safety of my car, I turn to Veronica. "Thank you for that, what you said to Aubrey."

She leans her head against the seat and looks at me. "I wasn't going to tell her where we're really going. I know you don't want others knowing, and I respect that."

"Well, again, thank you." I take her hand, locking our fingers together, and kiss the back of her palm.

In the three weeks she's been working for us, the progress in our relationship is striking. Holding hands has become something we do regularly. Even the eye rolls or feisty comebacks have lessened, although Ellis still gets those occasionally.

"You look beautiful, by the way," I tell her, before starting the car and pulling out onto the road.

"Thank you," she says with a soft smile when I peek at her. "Do you think she'll like it?" She plays with the hem of her dress.

I frown in confusion. "Who?"

She's quiet for a second before answering my question. "Trinity."

My heart squeezes at the single word spoken from her lips. The single name. She's talking as if my sister will be sitting up, waiting in her bed for us. Not an immobilized vessel just waiting to die.

I swallow around the lump of emotions fighting in my throat and clear it. "Yeah, Kitten. She'll love it. Blue is actually her favorite color."

She smiles again. "I can't wait to meet her." She squeezes my hand, then turns to look out the window.

The rest of the drive is done in silence as my nerves grow with every mile we gain until we reach the facility, and I find my hands clammy. I let go of Veronica's and wipe them down my jeans, taking a deep breath. I can sense her watching me from the side, but I don't dare look.

I don't understand why I'm freaking out right now.

"If this is too much, Noah, it's okay. I can just wait in the car while you go see her." She places her slim hand on my forearm.

I look over at her, taking the time to breathe, then shake my head. "No, I want you to come with me. It's just all new. I'm used to being alone."

"Well, you don't have to be alone anymore, Noah. You have me," she whispers.

I don't think she realizes how desperately I want those words to be true. How deeply I want to have her as mine in every sense of the word.

I nod and open my car door, stepping out, then walk over and open hers as I help her to her feet. She takes my hand in hers with a smile as we make our way inside. Once on the right floor, I spot Jannice and Everly, another nurse, chatting behind the counter. I walk up to them, unsure how to do things from here.

"Hey, Jannice. Everly."

"Oh! Hi, Noah!" Jannice beams up at me.

"Congrats on your big win! We were all rooting for you guys," Everly says.

"Thanks." I smile, then look over at my Kitten. "This is Veronica." I hesitate for a split second before deciding on what to say. "My girlfriend." I'm not sure how she'll react to that, but I thought it was the best way to get her in. I'm not even sure if I'm allowed to bring people with me or not.

Veronica's expression doesn't change. She keeps that pretty smile on her face, but I didn't miss the slight squeeze in my hand when the words fell out of me. "It's a pleasure to meet you both."

Everly and Jannice smile at her and introduce themselves in return. I notice Jannice peeking at me with a sliver of disappointment in her eyes, but I ignore it. There was never going to be anything between us, and after five years, she should have realized that.

"So, do I have to sign her in or something?" I finally ask.

"Oh, no. You can just go on. But if you want to give her access to come alone, then yes, you'll have to sign an authorization form. But we can take care of that after the visit is done, since it takes a little time to fill out," Everly informs me.

"Okay. Well then, we'll head in."

I turn away from the counter and guide Veronica toward Trinity's room. When my hand reaches for the knob, I notice a small tremble in it. I'm never nervous. Not like this. But something about this moment tugs at every cell in my body.

I guess the fear of not knowing how Veronica will act once she's faced with my practically lifeless sister's body is starting to grow stronger. But I shove those worries down and push the door open.

Taking a few steps in, she lets go of my hand and walks farther into the room, looking around as I close the door silently behind me. I don't move from my spot, simply examine her as she gazes at the pictures on the dresser with a smile, then turns to look at my sister and back at me.

"May I?" She tilts her head toward the chair beside Trinny's bed.

I nod, unable to speak at this moment.

She wanders over slowly, then sits down beside my sister. "Hi, Trinity. It's lovely to finally meet you. I wish I could say I've heard a lot about you, but your brother tends to like keeping you to himself." She chuckles.

"I'm not sure if you know who I am, but my name's Veronica, and I'm a good friend of Noah's." She shakes her head. "Actually, what am I saying? Of course, you've heard about me. This guy is practically obsessed with me. I bet he spends all his time talking about me when he's here." This time she really laughs. "We'll just pretend I don't know about it." When she peeks back at me, she winks, then returns her focus to my sister.

Veronica gazes down at my sister with a tender smile. "You're very beautiful, Trinity. I bet you made your brother's life hell growing up, with all the boys that must have been running after you."

I snort because she has no idea how true that is. I feel like all my youth was dedicated to batting away all male species from my sister. They were drawn to her like moths to a flame.

She leans in closer to her and says in a whispered voice, "So, tell me. Do you have any embarrassing stories about Noah when he was younger? Maybe some bad acne when he hit puberty? Trying to do the dirty with a pie and burning himself? Making out with his cousin before finding out she's related to him?"

I laugh, unable to hold it in. "Where are you getting these ridiculous ideas?"

"Shush, this discussion does not concern you. It's between me and Trinity." She bats me away with her hand.

I step closer to them and sit on the edge of the bed. "Actually, I'm pretty sure it does. Since I'm the main topic."

She rolls her eyes. "Ugh, men." *So, I guess we aren't exactly done with the eye rolls for me either.* She grabs my sister's hand and gives it a small shake. "Come on, girl. Don't leave me hanging. You need to give me something I can tell all our friends about. Just one story. I refuse to believe he's this perfect."

"You think I'm perfect?" I ask, shocked.

She opens her mouth to say something but then shakes her head and lifts her free hand at her side. "I plead the fifth."

I chuckle as she looks at me with a smile.

"I think you and I are going to get along great," she whispers to my sister and touches her hair delicately. "I'll be able to tell you all about your brother and the things he probably doesn't mention to you. Like how he's a pretty messy guy. Well, actually, I think it's just laziness, but we're working on it. Which makes absolutely no sense because he keeps his car squeaky clean."

I zone out from there as she keeps chatting to my sister. I love the way she talks to her as if she's really here. Like she might answer or make a comment, laugh along with her. It's beautiful to watch.

I was nervous about bringing Veronica here this morning, but now I realize it was the best decision I've ever made. Watching them together makes my love for Veronica grow a thousand times stronger.

After an hour of the two girls talking—well, Veronica talking and pretending my sister was answering—she stands from the chair and comes in front of me, her hand falling on my shoulder. "Do you want some time alone with her? I can wait outside in the hall."

"No. That's okay, Kitten. Are you ready to go?"

"I think so." She bites her lip and looks back at my sister. "Would it be okay if I came back to see her some time?"

I watch her for a second. "You mean alone?"

She nods. "Only if you're comfortable with that."

"Yeah, I think that would be okay." She smiles in response. "We'll go fill out the paperwork on our way out."

I place my hands on her hips and slowly bring her body between my spread legs as she places her other hand on my shoulder as well and looks down at me. "I'm sorry for calling you my girlfriend."

"It's okay," she whispers.

"I wasn't sure if I was allowed to bring someone, and I thought it would pass better if they thought you were with me," I tell her truthfully. I hadn't planned on saying it; I know how Veronica feels about dating. But I can't hide how amazing it felt to call her mine.

"It's okay, Casanova. I understand." Her hands move along my shoulders, slowly going down my arms, then back up. She traces her movements with her eyes, no longer meeting mine.

"It's just a word... it means nothing... right?" Finally, she looks back up as she swallows, and I see an inkling of fear in her eyes.

I nod slowly, even though every cell in my body is telling me to deny her claim, to tell her *this* means something to us. That she means something to me. But I know she needs me to agree with her, to reassure her. "Yeah, Kitten. It's just a word."

She nods and takes a step back as I stand. I walk over to my sister and lower, kissing her forehead. "Bye, sis. I love you."

Veronica stands behind me, smiling at my sister. "Bye, Trinity. I'll be coming to see you again soon."

I take her hand as we make our way over to the nurses' station to fill out the forms. A little while later, we head out to my car together, still hand in hand. When we get to the passenger door, I go to pull it open, but Veronica leans against it, eyes searching mine.

I can tell something's running through her mind; I'm just not sure what exactly. Until she presses her hand to my chest. I take a step closer and place one hand on her hip, the other coming up to cradle the side of her face as her eyes widen, lips parting slightly and pupils dilating.

My gaze falls to her lips momentarily, then back up to hers as I take another step, pressing our bodies together. Her hand that lies on my chest slides up to my nape in the process. I give her a second to come to terms with what I'm about to do, what is about to happen between us.

I catch her gaze falling to my lips as her chest rises and falls against mine, and when she looks back up, she gives me a subtle nod. I'm not sure if she even realized she did it, but I take that as the green light I've been waiting for and slowly descend my lips to hers.

Veronica instantly melts in my arms, a soft moan falling from her lips, and I capture it. I deepen the kiss when she opens up for me, my tongue sliding between her lips and into her mouth as hers twirls around mine. Her hand moves into my hair, pulling me even closer as she becomes desperate for my touch.

I feel my shaft turning to stone inside my boxers as I thrust softly against her, causing her to whimper. I bite her lower lip and do it again, needing to hear her perfect little noises once more. This time she moans my name, her head slightly dropping back as she tries to fist my short hair. "Noah..."

I kiss her again, never getting enough. Wanting more. This isn't like the first time she kissed me, where it was just lip against lip and lasted barely five seconds, or even the one during our big win. This one is deep, feverish, and holds passion. It holds everything I've ever wanted from her.

We're lost in the moment as we claim each other with our mouths, electricity shooting through the air around us. That is until a car horn blares from nearby and snaps us back to reality.

I pull away slightly as we look at each other, both breathing heavily, pupils fully blown on both ends. For a moment, she seems frozen in place, like the realization of what just happened between us is finally hitting her. But then she smiles, and it nearly knocks me to my knees. I bring my lips down to hers one last time, kissing them delicately, then step away.

She moves aside and lets me open the car door for her, where she slides in quietly before I walk around and settle into the driver's seat. When I look at her, she seems lost in thought. "Do you want me to drop you off at your place?"

She eventually turns to me, looking over all my features. "Is it okay if I come back to the penthouse with you?" she whispers. "Aubrey will be working later, and I don't feel like sitting around alone doing nothing."

"Of course, Kitten. It's *our* home, you're always welcome there."

GABRIEL

I grab a water bottle from the fridge and take a much-needed gulp as the elevator dings. I'm expecting to find only Noah making his way over but spot Ronnie at his side as well.

"Vixen." I grin. "I didn't know you were coming today."

"I wasn't planning to." She looks up at Noah for a second before turning back to me. "But I was getting bored at home and texted Noah to see what you guys were up to. He offered to bring me over here on his way home."

I nod, a little irritated that she texted him and not me, but I swallow it down. "So, what's the plan for the day?" I ask, hoping they didn't already make plans without me.

Plans that don't include me.

"Not sure, we haven't discussed anything yet," Noah informs me. *Thank God.*

"What would you like to do, baby? It's your call. Anything you want." I beam her way.

She looks at both of us, then bites her pillowy bottom lip. "I've always wanted to go to Coney Island."

"You've never been?" Noah asks as he brushes her hair back behind her ear, to which she shakes her head while gazing at him.

I clap my hands, pulling them out of whatever little moment they're having. "Then I guess it's settled. We're going to Coney Island." The excitement that lights up Ronnie's face at my statement makes this impromptu trip totally worth it.

"I'm gonna grab a shower first. Then we can go," Noah tells us.

"That's okay, I was in the middle of my workout anyway. Just came to get some water since the mini fridge is out. I'll finish up quickly, then jump in the shower as well, and we'll leave after."

"Okay, I'll fill up the fridge in the gym. I forgot to do it yesterday, sorry," Ronnie says as she moves into the pantry and grabs a case of bottled water.

I take it from her hands as she reaches for a box of protein bars as well. "That's okay, baby. No need to apologize, it's not the end of the world." We walk together toward the gym while Noah heads upstairs.

Once inside the weight room, I get back to my workout. From the corner of my eye, I catch Ronnie watching me from time to time as she fixes up the fridge. A few moments later, she finishes up her task, and I expect her to leave the room and wander off to do something else. But instead, she gets closer, standing against one of the mirrors along the wall and watches me.

She doesn't say anything, and neither do I. But I feel her heated gaze traveling down my body with every move I make. And it's fucking euphoric. Finishing up all my sets, I drop to the ground to finish off with my regular stretches. As a goalie, it's important to stay flexible and have your joints loose. The season might be over, but I like to stay at the top of my shape even during the off-season.

As I twist from side to side, stretching my hips and legs out, I find Ronnie with hooded eyes, lips slightly parted as she leans her back into the mirror. One dainty hand falling over her chest delicately as it rises and falls. *My little Vixen is turned on.* I give her a wink and a tiny blush forms over her cheekbones.

She clears her throat, lifting her head and pushing her shoulders back, acting like she's not affected by me in the slightest. "I never realized how flexible you were. I always thought it was just all the pads that made you look that way."

"Nope. All me, baby." I grin as I stand.

"It must come in handy, being flexible," she says softly.

I take a few steps toward her. "You have no idea."

"It makes sense now, why all the girls are so crazy about you. I mean, you must be able to do some pretty crazy things." She wets her lips as I get closer.

Only a few inches separate us now. Her chest moves more rapidly now, eyes dilating further as she watches my every move. "Would you like to find out, Vixen?"

She visibly swallows, lips parting more as she goes to answer. "I... I..."

But I don't let her finish. I don't give her time to think or doubt. I don't give her fears time to take over. I take the final step, grip her face between my palms, and crash my mouth to hers. She stiffens in my hold, her body going rigid as she tries to push me away with her hands against my chest.

But I don't let her; I stay rooted in place and continue to kiss her. Whatever her fears are, they're the ones pushing at me. Because her lips, they're kissing me back, and that's all her. She just needs to move past them, push through whatever is scaring her.

So, I continue my assault on her mouth until I feel the snap happen. The energy shifts in the room, and suddenly her hands pull me closer instead of pushing me away. Our kiss turns frantic as our tongues dance together, teeth scraping one another. Her hands move up to my hair, arms folding around my neck.

I grab onto her thighs and wrap them around my waist, pressing her body into the mirror as we consume each other. She whimpers when I push my hard length against her warm center. I can feel her wetness slowly piercing through my workout shorts and it drives me fucking wild. I move my lips to her jaw, her ear, her neck, biting down as she moans repeatedly.

"Gabe..." she cries out when I thrust harder into her. Over and over until she's grinding herself down on me as well, chasing her own release. "Oh God, Gabe."

"Fuck, Vixen." *I fucking need this woman.*

I feel precum leaking out of my cock as I continue to rock against her. I slide my hands higher up her smooth thighs until I reach her ass, giving it a firm squeeze before digging a little further until I feel her drenched panties.

I go to push them aside, an urgent need to be inside of her taking over. But one of her arms leaves my neck, and she quickly grabs onto the one about to touch her perfect pussy. "Gabriel, wait!"

I pull away from her neck and look at her. Her pupils are fully dilated, and the tiny portion of her irises left has turned to a deep, blazing blue. We're both panting as we watch each other.

Finally, she shakes her head. "No."

And suddenly everything clicks. What we're doing. What I'm doing to her. I've pushed her too far. *Fuck!* She was finally opening up to me, finally accepting me. And now I've taken it too far. I got greedy and ruined everything.

I let go of her, putting her back on the ground, and take a step back, passing my hands through my hair as I pace back and forth. "Fuck, Ronnie. I'm so sorry. I shouldn't have done that. I didn't mean to force you into anything."

"It's okay," she says quietly, but my mind is spiraling.

"No, it's not okay. You didn't want it. You were pushing against me, but I wouldn't let go. I should have stopped."

"I said it's okay, Gabe." She tries to reach for me, but I step aside, still frustrated with myself.

"But it's not! Don't you see that? You've always had boundaries with me, and I forced you to ignore them. That's not right." I stop pacing and stand before her, freaking out internally. *She's going to retreat into herself. She won't want me anymore.* "Please don't hate me. I'd never hurt you. You know that, right?" My own fears begin to creep in.

What if I'm just like him? What if I am capable of hurting someone? I basically forced myself on her; isn't that the same thing? I gasp for air as panic sets in. *I feel like I'm suffocating.*

She steps into me, her hands framing my face as she presses her lips to mine. Her body leans into me as she moans softly when I kiss her back. This kiss is different; it's tender compared to the heated one from a minute ago. And instantly, my panic subsides, turning to a simmer until all I feel is her.

She pulls away slightly, her forehead resting against mine. "I know you'd never hurt me, Gabriel. I don't hate you, and you didn't force me to do anything I didn't want." One of her hands falls to my chest as she lifts her head to look into my eyes. "Do you hear me? I wanted it. I wanted you to kiss me. I wanted you."

I nod.

She leans back in for a second, pecking my lips again. "But I'm still confused with everything that's going on between us. Not just me and you, but Noah too. And I'm just not ready to take things further yet."

"Okay, I can respect that." I wrap my arms around her waist and sigh. "I should go shower if we want to make it to Coney Island."

She puts her arms around my neck and kisses me again. "Okay." I'm not sure if she's just trying to prove that she wants me or if she really can't get enough of kissing me. But whichever it is, I'm good with it.

I smile against her lips, kissing her back once more, then pull away. As I turn to head out of the gym, I spot Noah leaning against the door, watching us. Joy spreads inside me once I realize that he witnessed our moment.

But when Ronnie finally sees him, she freezes slightly and looks uncertain about how to proceed. The look of guilt on her face tells me all I need to know. She didn't kiss me first. She kissed him.

Now I can't help but wonder if she only kissed me out of pity.

Chapter Thirteen

VERONICA

Flirty transactions.

~ Three Days Later ~

"You're not going to Noah and Gabe's today?" Aubrey asks as she steps into her shoes and grabs her purse from the small rectangular table by the entrance.

"What's the matter? Were you getting used to having the place to yourself?" I laugh from my spot on the couch before pausing the show I was watching. "And for your information, no. I thought a day off was much overdue."

She giggles. "You have been spending a lot of time there, much more than what you originally agreed to." There's a hint of suspicion in her smirk, but she doesn't voice it.

"Exactly why I'm staying home today, giving myself a bit of me time."

The truth is, after what happened with the twins three days ago, I really needed a moment alone to think about everything. I also feel like something shifted in Gabriel's mind after our kiss. He's still being his usual flirty and charming self, but every once in a while he goes quiet whenever I'm giving Noah attention.

I'm not sure if it's a jealousy thing, which would be weird since they've always shared girls and I shouldn't be any different, but that's what it feels like, and I hate it. I don't want either of them to be jealous of each other; I certainly don't want to cause a rift in their friendship when I still don't know exactly what's happening between us.

I also think Gabe knows I kissed Noah before him, which would explain the hint of jealousy he's experiencing. I'm not sure if it's Noah who told him or if he just figured it out, but I wish he wouldn't feel this way. I don't see it as who I kissed first or who I want more; it was just a spur-of-the-moment reaction with both.

When Gabe and I were in the home gym, I wanted him just as much as I wanted

Noah in that parking lot. And if I wasn't still so confused with my thoughts and feelings involving them, I would have let Gabriel have me entirely against that mirror.

"You're heading to work already?" I frown. It's only ten in the morning, and she isn't supposed to start until three.

Aubrey sighs with her hand on the door handle. "Yup, one of the girls working the day shift claimed having a stomachache and left before even giving me time to find a replacement, so I need to go in."

"Ugh, that sucks. Well, I hope it turns out to be a slow day and that you get to just sit back and relax. You deserve some time off, too."

She laughs and pulls the door open. "Isn't that why we're going on vacation next week?"

"It is, but why not add an extra day to it?" I wink and blow her a kiss.

She smiles and shakes her head. "Well, you have fun on your day off. I'll see you later. Love you."

"Love you, too!" I call back right before she steps out and closes the door behind her.

I press play on the TV remote and sit back against the couch, trying to pay attention to the show playing, but my eyes keep drifting to my phone. I pick it up and tap into my messages with Gabe. Even though we have a group chat going with all three of us, I like sending each special little messages individually once in a while.

Me

What are you doing?

Husband #1

Just lying in bed in the spare room where the sheets still smell like you. It's amazing, almost as if you were right here with me. <heart eyes emoji>

Me

Oh my God! No, you're not, and no, they don't! <Laughing emoji> I washed those a few days ago.

Husband #1

Damn, you caught me. <Wink emoji>

Husband #1

> The better question is, what are you doing texting me out of the blue? I thought you wanted the day off?

Husband #1

> Would you happen to be missing me, my little Vixen? <Smirking emoji>

I laugh with an eye roll and text back my reply.

Me

> Shut up.

Husband #1

> I'll take that as a yes. <Grinning emoji>

Husband #1

> So… What are you up to?

Me

> Just watching a show, might ask one of the girls if they want to go shopping or something… and MAYBE I was thinking about you a bit.

Husband #1

> I like when you think of me. <Smirking emoji> <Heart emoji>

I can practically feel his wide and happy grin through the phone right now.

Me

> I'm sure you do.

Husband #1

> You know what else I like?

I'm pretty sure I have a good idea, but I'm going to stop you right there, Pretty Boy. Stop being naughty.

Okay! Fine. <Whining emoji>

But you should definitely go shopping. Go treat yourself to some sexy outfits, and you know, don't hesitate to send me pictures if you aren't sure. I was told I give very good advice. <Wink emoji>

<Laughing emoji> We'll see. <Blowing kiss emoji>

I exit our messages and go through my contacts, deciding to call Emma. She's been dealing with a lot lately, and I think a little shopping session would do her some good. I press the call button and set her on speakerphone as I get up and wander into my room to get dressed.

"Hey, babe," her quiet voice comes through the phone along with a tiny sniffle, which is very telling of her current mood. Emma is never quiet.

"Hey, you okay?" If she's crying right now, there's only one reason for that, and it breaks my heart to think about.

"Yeah… I just left the hospital. It was a rough day, but I don't really want to talk about that because then I'll start crying again and spiral, and we all know how that goes…" She clears her throat, sniffles again, then takes a deep breath. "So yeah, what's up?"

"I get it. No talking about that." I force a small smile even though she doesn't see me. "I was just calling to see if you were busy and maybe wanted to go shopping with me."

"You know what, shopping sounds really amazing right now and would definitely cheer me up. Grey went to the water park with Little Tulip, so I've got some free time on my hands. Want me to pick you up?"

"Sounds like a plan."

"Good. See you in a bit, babe." She hangs up and I quickly move to my closet, picking out my outfit of the day before attacking my hair and makeup next.

Twenty minutes later, I step out of my building and climb into Emma's SUV. "Surprised you aren't with the twins today," Emma says with a smirk the moment I shut the car door.

"You do know I have my own life, right? One that doesn't revolve around them." I narrow my eyes to slits while buckling myself in.

"Could have fooled me," she mumbles as I smack her arm and she laughs.

"No, but seriously, babe, talk to me. How are things really going with them? You three seemed pretty cozy after the big win, but well, I know they can be... a lot to handle, certainly when it involves you." Emma shifts in her seat slightly to look at me.

We're still parked outside my place rather than driving away like I thought we were going to do. I mean, the whole point of going shopping was to try and take my mind off the whole Noah and Gabe thing. But I know this is Emma's caring nature taking over, and she won't move from here until I reassure her that everything is fine.

I sigh and lean back against my seat. "It's... going. We may have had a little moment the other day, but—"

"I'm going to cut you off right there. You are not permitted to say *'it means nothing'* at any point today. I get that it's scary sometimes feeling things we didn't expect, but saying it doesn't mean anything diminishes the value it may have and will only hurt you in the end."

I roll my eyes at her and giggle. "What I was going to say before you interrupted me is that now I feel even more confused than I did before. As much as I hate to admit it, you girls were right. Gabe and Noah are truly great guys, they're amazing..."

"But?" She tilts her head to the side, eyes roaming over all my features.

"But I'm terrified of letting myself venture down that road," I admit while looking out the windshield.

"You're afraid of getting hurt again," she whispers with a knowing look.

"Yeah... something like that." It's more than just about getting hurt. It's about learning to trust again, something I swore I'd never do. I turn my head to the side, finding her eyes still solely focused on me. "When you broke up with Tommy and started seeing Greyson, how did you just move on from all the shit he did to you?"

She chuckles and leans back against her seat. "I didn't, at least, not entirely. I was over Tommy, that was for sure, but that fear of being hurt again still lingered even if I pretended it didn't. Eventually, Wolf showed me that I could trust him with my heart, not necessarily through words but through actions, and slowly it made it easier to just... let it happen."

I sigh. "I wish it could be that simple." Doing that would mean letting my relationship with Noah and Gabe evolve and dropping all my walls. But how am I supposed to do that when I don't think I'm even capable of letting them down long enough to try?

"You know, it's not really about moving on from what this person did to you, it's about letting go of the pain it caused you."

"Isn't that the same thing?" I raise a brow.

"No." Em giggles quietly. "One is a physical event that took place, while the other is an emotional one. You've already moved on from the situation. What you haven't moved on from is the emotions that came from it. Once you're able to let go of that emotion still holding you captive, facing your fears will be a lot easier." She reaches out and places her hand over mine. "Although if I'm being honest with you, Ronnie, I think you're already letting go without even realizing it."

"Look at you being all wise and shit. It's like you just channeled your inner Morgan and Aubrey in one sitting." I snort when she throws her head back and laughs.

"I know, right? Grey would be proud of me for being so serious for longer than five minutes." A dazzling grin spreads over her lips as she takes my hand in hers, her smile turning tender. "But seriously, you know you can always talk to us about anything, right? We're here for you, Ronnie, and we'd never judge you, no matter what it is."

"I know, and thank you for the advice and all the words of wisdom." I squeeze her hand.

"Anytime. Now, let me guess. This impromptu shopping trip is you trying to distract yourself from the twins a bit and clear your mind?"

"Yup, pretty much. Although that kind of backfired when I told Gabe I was thinking about going, and now he expects me to send him naughty pictures in sexy outfits." I laugh and shake my head.

Emma suddenly gets that devilish grin that tells me she has some mischievous plan forming in her mind.

"What?"

"Did those boys leave you one of their credit cards?"

"They did... Why?"

"Well, if their card works anything like Grey's, they'll get a notification every time you buy something with it." She's grinning so wide right now that I'm surprised her cheeks don't hurt. Hell, it even looks scary now.

"And what did you have in mind?" My own smirk comes into play.

"Let's make them sweat a little with a different kind of shopping." She sits herself properly in her seat and starts up the car before pulling out onto the street.

"Oh, you are bad!" I laugh.

"I know, but it'll be fun." She joins in on the giggles. "Plus, Wolf will be more than happy to see me come home with some fun things for us to play with later tonight."

NOAH

"Fuck, that was incredible." Gabe grins from beside me as we sit on the couch watching a replay of the Stanley Cup Finals.

"Tell me about it. I feel like I'm still high off that win." I chuckle and pick up my beer from the side table.

Victory night was something we had all dreamed about for so long. All year we played extremely well and knew we would make it far in the playoffs; it was like a gut feeling. But that night, we played better than we ever had, and it showed. It feels fucking amazing, and I hope we get to experience that feeling again.

Today Veronica messaged in our group chat early that she wouldn't be coming over, which sucked if I'm being honest. We've gotten so used to having her here that when she's not, we have no idea what to do with ourselves. *Talk about being dependent and obsessed...*

My phone suddenly vibrates in my short's pocket, pulling my attention away from the screen. I drag it out and smile when a text notification with Veronica's name fills my screen, or should I say Kitten since I changed it to that last week.

I know she was texting with Gabe earlier, thanks to him practically rubbing it in my face that she somewhat admitted missing him. Was I a bit jealous? Sure, but seeing the goofy grin on his face made that unwanted feeling go away just as quickly. Although I was still hoping she'd reach out to me too at some point.

Kitten

I hope you boys are behaving and keeping the place clean.

I scoff at her message and smile while typing out my reply.

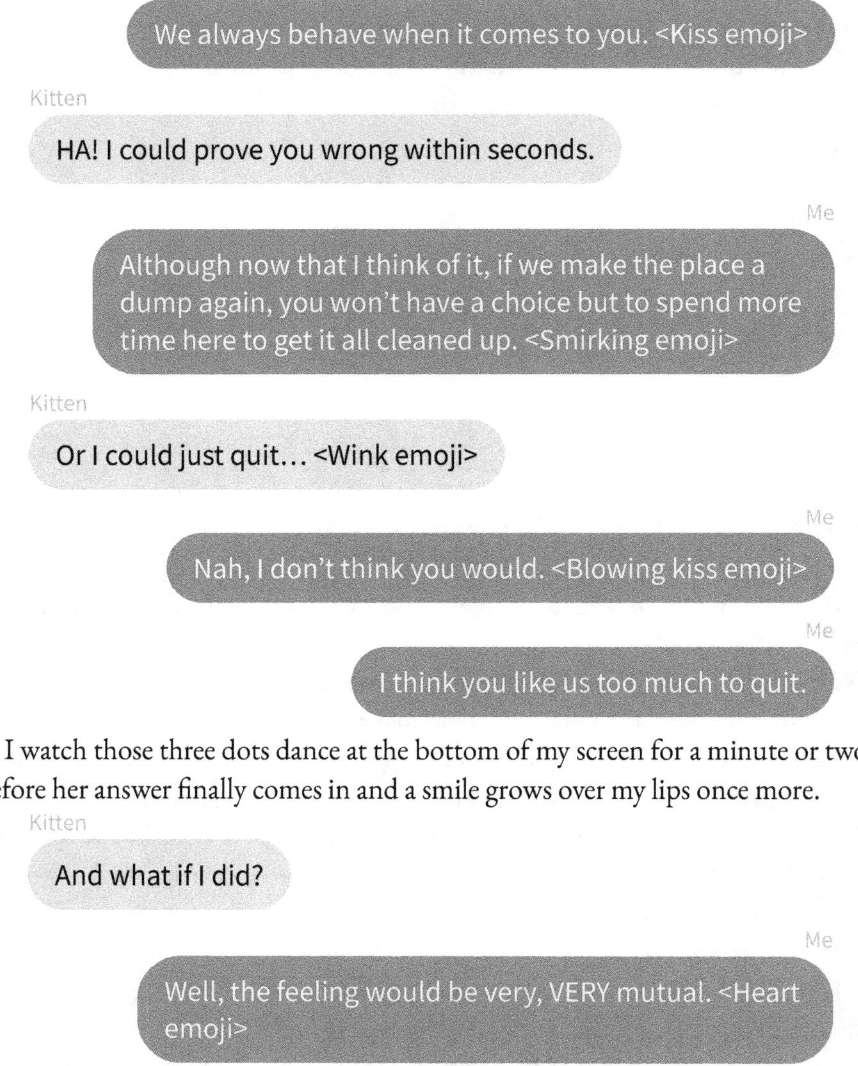

I watch those three dots dance at the bottom of my screen for a minute or two before her answer finally comes in and a smile grows over my lips once more.

I set my phone down on the side table as Gabe gets up to get us two more beers.

When he gets back, I take a few gulps and refocus on the TV. Five minutes later, a notification comes through, and I tilt my screen to read it with my beer bottle to my lips. I instantly choke on my sip when I notice it's a purchase alert on my credit card... at a lingerie store.

What the hell? Last I checked, Veronica still has my card. Maybe she lost it?

"You good?" Gabe eyes me curiously.

I clear my throat and hit my chest a few times while sitting up and setting down my beer. "Yeah."

I quickly return to my text exchange with Veronica and shoot one off.

Me

> Do you still have my credit card?

Her response comes in immediately.

Kitten

> Um, I should. Let me check.

Kitten

> Yup, still got it.

She follows that message with a picture of it in her wallet.

Hm, so my naughty little Kitten was out buying lingerie and probably used my card without realizing it. I wonder why she felt she needed lingerie and who she intends to wear it for.

Kitten

> Why?

Me

> No reason. Just curious.

Kitten

> Oh, okay. Well, it's still safe with me. <Smiling emoji>

I try to forget about what I just witnessed as Gabe starts talking to me about the hat-trick Ford made during the game, but my mind keeps drifting back to Veronica as I picture her wearing whatever sexy outfit she just bought.

Suddenly, another notification comes through. I quickly grab my phone, eyes bulging wide as I see this new purchase was made at a sex shop. *What the hell is she doing?!* I try to control my breathing and stop my heart from racing as I tell myself it's nothing, that she's allowed to treat herself. But when another one comes in for over five hundred dollars at a different sex shop, I find myself choking on my beer all over again.

"Jesus, what the hell is going on with you?" Gabe slaps my back a few times.

I take deep breaths, clearing my throat a few times until it's safe to speak, and turn my phone over to him. "It seems our girl is going on a little shopping spree."

His eyes narrow for a second as he reads each transaction, then widen just as quickly as he throws himself back against the couch and belly laughs. "Oh God! That is epic! When she said she wanted to go shopping, I didn't think it was *that* kind of shopping!" He gasps for air, wiping his tears away. "Fuck, now I wish I had offered to go with her. I wonder what she bought at that price."

"Yeah, me too. But the better question is, why is she using my card? We paid her this week, right?"

"We did, but let her have fun. I told her to treat herself, and clearly that's what she's doing." He chuckles again. "And if you want my opinion, she's doing it on purpose. One slip up? Sure. But three in a row? Highly doubt it. Vixen is anal with that shit. You see how much she pays attention to everything. There's no way she hasn't noticed by now that she's using the wrong card."

A smirk spreads on my lips when I realize he's right. She is very attentive to those things usually, which means she's trying to get a reaction out of me. I pull up our conversation once more and type out a text.

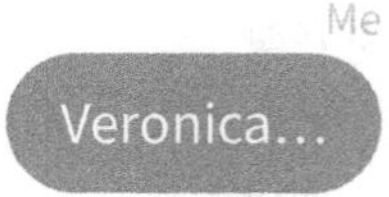

The bubbles appear instantly after hitting send. *She was expecting me to message and waiting in our chat.*

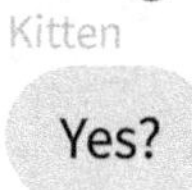

Kitten

What do you mean? I'm not doing anything. <Smiling emoji>

Me

Mhm, sure.

Me

So, I see you're doing a bit of shopping.

Kitten

How do you know? Oh, Gabe must have told you.

Me

Yup, that's EXACTLY how I know. But I'm curious, what did you buy?

Kitten

Oh, you know, just some very useful things I was in deep need of.

Me

Mind sharing? <Smirking emoji>

Kitten

Mmm, sorry, Casanova. That's only for me to know. <Wink emoji>

Me

And me to find out?

Kitten

Who knows… <Wink emoji>

"Oh, she is *definitely* playing with you!" Gabe bursts with laughter once more. "This girl is going to be the death of us."

"One hundred percent."

Chapter Fourteen

VERONICA

365 reasons.

~ Four Days Later ~

Aubrey and I are currently at the mall for some last-minute shopping before we leave for our vacation in three days. I'm beyond excited. I haven't been on a vacation to a tropical island in years. Plus, the whole gang is going to be there, so it will be a blast. Two weeks of fun in the Fiji Islands, with the people I love most in the world.

The boys rented out a whole island for us, which means aside from the staff for the resort, it will be just the thirteen of us. Clay and Morgan, Silas and Cecilia with little Dante. Greyson and Emma with Gracie. Noah and Gabe, Aubrey and me, as well as Sam, the kids' nanny.

It seems extreme to rent a whole island just for thirteen people, but I understand that the boys like their privacy. And like that, we're free to do whatever we want, including nude tanning, which I will one hundred percent be doing.

We start off with swimwear because I'm in desperate need of a new one. And a small part of me really wants to make Noah and Gabe just a little crazy looking at me in a sexy bikini. I already know their minds are going crazy wondering what I bought at the sex shop a few days ago; might as well torture them a little more.

Emma's plan was diabolical, but I loved every minute of it. Noah never did outright tell me he knew I was using his card, but his messages had Emma and I in a giggle fit throughout our shopping session. And when I showed up at their place the next morning, it was evident they knew about where I had been the previous day. Again, they didn't say a word, but their hungry eyes were all telling.

I'm still not sure exactly what is going on between us, but ever since those wicked make-out sessions a week ago, things have changed. Gabe sends me a message every day at sunrise saying, '*Good morning, beautiful.*' And Noah wishes me good night every single time I get into bed.

I haven't kissed either of them since then, but there's been a lot of flirting and intimate little touches when we're around each other. And the more time I spend around them, the more I find myself craving them. But it's not just sex, and that's what has me most confused. I crave their attention, their eyes on me, their laughs, and their smiles.

I swore I didn't want a relationship, that I had no intention of getting into another one. I swore I would never let myself get close to those two men, who have started to haunt my dreams. But now I find myself smiling at every new message, having a skip in my step when I know I'll be seeing them soon. I feel myself turning back into the old me, the one before everything happened.

And that terrifies me.

I don't want to turn into that girl again. That stupid, naïve girl who falls head over heels and ignores every red flag, every instinct in her gut telling her to get out. I swore I would never let my heart lead me again, yet I feel it slowly taking over once more. And I don't know how to stop it.

I grab a few different models of bikinis and a couple sexy one pieces, while Aubrey takes pretty boring options into the dressing room. *I'm going to have to sneak in a couple of riskier ones into her suitcase.* I plan on taking plenty of nice pictures of our girl on vacation and sending them to Shane. Maybe that will give him the push he needs to finally ask her out. I don't have his number, but I'm pretty sure I can convince one of the boys to give it to me.

Or I could secretly upload them to her Instagram, since I know he follows her on there. That could work too. There's no way he won't notice them like that, but Brey is a pretty reserved kind of girl, so she'll definitely freak out if I do that.

I try on a half-white, half-black tiny bikini that leaves little to the imagination. Liking what I see in the mirror, I snap a quick picture and send it to the boys in our group chat.

Me

What do you boys think?

Within seconds, I'm receiving replies from both.

Husband #1

FUCK ME! YESSS! <Drooling emoji><Heart eyes emoji>

Husband #2

Use my card and buy everything you'd like, Kitten. Then come back here and model them for us. <Wink emoji>

Husband #1

Fuck that, I want to see you trying them on right now. Where are you, baby?

Husband #2

Even better.

I giggle and send them the address of where we are. This could be fun, seeing their reaction firsthand. Two minutes later, they tell me they're out the door and on their way.

Brey and I finish up with the swimwear shortly after, where I ended up buying six different pieces and Aubrey bought two. Although I snuck one into my pile for her, as planned. We walk down the halls to the mall, slipping in and out of shops along the way.

"By the way, Gabe and Noah are joining us. They should be here soon."

She gives me a surprised look, then smiles. "So... things are going well with you guys?"

I bite my lip and shrug. "I guess. It's a little confusing, though."

Her eyes stay focused on me as she watches my every expression. "Do you have feelings for them?"

I told her about what happened last week in detail instead of vaguely like I did with Emma, so she's aware that things have somewhat escalated between us three. And I'm guessing the fact that they pick me up every work morning gives it away, too, since they refuse to let me take the subway over.

I know I could always just use my car, but I like leaving it for Aubrey. She's the one who usually does our groceries and goes out more often. I honestly don't even know why I have one. But since all our coupled friends live just on the other side of the Hudson River, it's much easier to get there by car. So I guess it does come in handy at the end of the day. Aubrey and I, as well as Gabe and Noah, are the only ones still living in New York City.

"I don't know, maybe? I do feel things around them, like these knots forming in my stomach, and I guess that's what makes it confusing. Because I feel it for both, and that's never happened." I shrug.

"I've been with two men before, like in bed. But I've never had feelings for two guys at the same time." I know I keep denying with the rest of our friends that anything is going on between me, Noah, and Gabe. But I can't hide it from Aubrey.

"Yeah, I can understand that. Just having those feelings for one man is confusing to me. I can't imagine two." Her cheeks turn pink as she looks down at the ground. It's in those subtle comments that she admits her attraction to Shane without even noticing.

"Can I ask you something?"

"Always." She smiles at me.

"Why are you still a virgin?" She furrows her brows, but I grab her arm. "I don't mean it as an insult, Brey. I'm just curious as to why you never gave it up. Because I know you've had opportunities. I just wonder what made you decide not to ever, you know, go for it?"

"Honestly, I'm not sure. And it has nothing to do with waiting until marriage. It's silly, and I probably sound crazy, but sometimes I get this little voice in my head telling me to wait. I'm not sure for what, but I think I'm supposed to." She's blushing as she talks, this conversation clearly making her uncomfortable.

Aubrey has never been in a rush to lose her virginity. But she's already admitted to me once that she felt like something was wrong with her for not just doing it like the rest of us.

"You're waiting for your *one.*' There's nothing wrong with that, Brey. If that's what your gut is telling you to do, then listen to it." I smile reassuringly.

"But doesn't that make me sound stupid? Some people don't find their *'one'* until they're forty. Others never even find it. What if that happens to me? What if I never find my one and end up wasting all this time for something so stupid?"

I turn in front of her, stopping Aubrey in her tracks and grabbing both her arms. "There's nothing stupid about that, Aubrey. This is your virginity, your body. Who you decide to give it to is important. Hell, even I wish I would have waited sometimes. And for what it's worth, I think you've already met your one. Your story just hasn't started yet."

She turns a deep shade of red at my words because she knows exactly who I'm referring to. "Maybe..." She bites her lip and smiles.

"Come on, let's find a lingerie store for when Noah and Gabe get here. I want to see them lose their mind in person." She laughs as I pass my arm through hers and turn us toward the store I have in mind.

But the minute I'm facing the right way, my eyes catch on to someone. Someone I haven't seen in years. Someone I wished never to see again. *Victor.*

I freeze in place, color draining from my face, my heart battling inside my chest, blood pounding in my ears as this sickening feeling takes over. I take a step back, nails digging into Aubrey's arm as I pull her along with me. He's staring straight at me, his venomous eyes on me, a satanic smirk on his lips as he watches the fear consume me.

"No... no, no, no. This can't be happening..." I shake my head, gasping for air. My vision blurs. *Oh God, I'm going to faint. I'm going to be sick.*

"Ronnie? What's going on? You're scaring me," Aubrey says in a worried voice, but she sounds distant, her voice muffled by the panic settling in.

"We... we need to go. We need to go. Now!" I take another step back, pulling her with me. I'm scared to turn around, scared to lose sight of him and not know where he goes.

Will he come for me? Will he keep following me until I'm alone? But I can't stay here. I need to leave. I need to get away from him.

I turn around quickly, ready to run, but smack right into a big muscular chest. Their arms grab hold of me as I try to fight him off. "Vixen! Hey, it's me! It's me."

My vision finally regains focus and falls onto Gabe's gray orbs. My body loses the fight as the realization that I'm safe now grows. Tears begin to pour from my eyes as I cry out, my body falling against Gabriel's.

"What's going on, baby?! Talk to us," he says with worry while petting my hair.

"He's here! He's here," I sob in a panic.

Gabe pushes me off him, holding me at arm's length, a raging look in his eyes. "Where!?"

I turn to look over my shoulder, ready to point out the man who I've been running from. But when my gaze falls to the place that I last saw him, he's nowhere to be seen. I turn in Gabe's arms, looking around frantically. "He was right there... I know I saw him. I'm not crazy."

Noah comes to my side, cupping my wet cheek. "No one thinks you're crazy, Kitten." He looks around the place with a stern expression, then back to me. "I think that's enough shopping for today. We'll take you girls home."

"Take her back with you. I don't know what's going on, but I don't think she should be alone right now. I have to work soon, so I won't be home to stay with her," Aubrey tells them, and they both nod.

We walk Aubrey to my car and wait for her to leave, making sure no one's following her, because I wouldn't put it past him to do something like that. Then the boys take me to Gabe's car, and we make our way to the penthouse.

I don't talk the whole drive home, I'm too lost in my head, and they don't pressure me to say anything, not until we get inside. "Veronica, I think it's time you tell us what's really going on," Noah says.

I sit down on the couch with a sigh, looking down at my hands. *They're right... I can't keep hiding this.* "I don't even know where to start..." I whisper.

Gabe comes to sit beside me, taking my hand in his. "Start from the beginning," he says while Noah takes a seat on the coffee table in front of me, placing his hands on my knees as he leans in.

I swallow and take a deep breath. "Victor and I met when I was sixteen. He was the older bad guy that girls fall for. Driving a motorcycle, tattoos all over, long hair that he kept tied up in a bun. That sense of danger that followed him everywhere he went, yet you couldn't help yourself but be drawn to it. He swept me off my fucking feet the moment I laid eyes on him."

"How old was he?" Noah asks, his jaw muscles tensing.

"Twenty-six."

"What the fuck?! Vixen, he was a full-grown adult preying on a child!" Gabe growls.

"I know, okay? Now I see it. But at the time, I didn't. I was a rebellious teenager growing up in a religious home with a pastor as a father. I went to church every freaking Sunday without missing a beat." I pass my hand through my hair.

"I never swore, never drank, never went out with my friends. I had a fucking curfew and never once passed it by a minute. Can you understand why I was so drawn to him? He was everything I craved. He was my ticket out, the freedom I was dying for."

"Your father's a pastor?" Gabe gapes at me. "I really never could have seen that coming." I giggle in response because no one ever does.

"So, what happened?" Noah asks, encouraging me to continue my story.

"He used to drive by my house every day. When I'd walk to school, he'd always pass me. Every time he'd slow down and smirk, giving me time to look at him as he looked me over. That went on for over two months, until one day I found him waiting against his bike by the sidewalk, exactly where we'd always cross paths."

I look up at them, and they're both staring at me, listening carefully to every word falling from my lips. "He asked me if I wanted a ride, which was stupid because my school was literally down the road. But I think it was more his way of seeing if I'd actually do it. Testing to see how much of a good girl I really was. It's what he used to call me. His good girl."

I swallow again, wishing I had a drink in hand or something. Liquid courage always helps. Noah must sense my need because he stands quickly and wanders over to the kitchen, grabbing us each a beer, then coming back to his spot.

"I feel like we'll all need this by the time you're done." *He's not wrong...*

I take a big gulp, then focus on the bottle as I continue. "I wasn't going to, I knew it was wrong, but a part of me wanted to feel alive just for two minutes. So I got on the back of his bike, and that was the start of it." I close my eyes momentarily, wishing for the millionth time I could go back in time and never get on that damn bike.

"From there, we spent all our time together. I started skipping school, drinking, smoking. I'd show up late for my curfew, or not show up at all. I gave him my virginity. I became wild and did everything to please him." I laugh humorlessly, unable to believe how stupid I was.

"Soon my parents figured out what was going on and kicked me out, disowned me, and told me I was never allowed back into their home until I regained my faith. Victor took me in right away, and life was perfect for a little while. I was in love. I had the guy of my dreams. Well, that's what I thought at the time."

I take another sip. "He was nice to me. I had never feared him even though I knew he was dangerous. Not until I turned eighteen... that's when things started going south. I always knew he was involved in some questionable things. He was always secretive about what he did." *I should have paid attention to the signs. They were all there, right in front of me. And I ignored every single one of them...*

"He'd have late-night meetings with the rest of his crew. Sometimes he'd come home all bloody and would ask me not to question it. He didn't want me to know what he was doing, which was probably the only good thing he did."

I take a deep breath, knowing we are getting to the darker parts of the story. The parts that have me needing a therapist because of all the trauma it caused me.

"Once I turned eighteen, he let me see his true colors. He gradually became violent. At first it was verbal, but then it turned physical... he would hit me every time I did something wrong. Beat me when I'd ask too many questions or disobeyed him..."

My throat clogs as horrific memories resurface. Memories I've tried to bury for so long. I feel a tear roll down my cheek and onto my forearm while Gabe's hand in mine shakes with rage.

"He... he started f-forcing himself on m-me whenever he felt like it. No matter how m-much I screamed or begged him n-not to... no matter how many ti-times I said n-no and cried... And then he... h-he'd pass me around to his f-friends..." I sob out the broken words.

"Fuck..." Noah comes to the couch and takes me in his arms as I cradle into his chest, crying against him.

"I t-tried to leave… I did, but he thre-threatened to k-kill me. He went after my parents t-too. Sending me p-pictures taken f-from in their room while they s-slept… I didn't know what to d-do."

"Shh… It's okay, Kitten. You're safe now. We won't let him hurt you again," he says, stroking my back.

"But I'm not," I cry harder. "He's back… He's f-found my number somehow, and he's been t-texting me pictures of myself. Th-threatening me. Telling me that I ca-can't hide. He's been following me." I shake my head against his chest and weep.

"How did you finally get out of it?" Gabe asks quietly after giving me a few minutes to calm down. And when I turn my gaze to him, I don't understand the look in his eyes. He seems… lost.

I wipe my face with the back of my hand and try to steady my voice with a few calming breaths. "I was out doing the groceries, one of the rare times he ever let me out. An FBI agent approached me and gave me his card, told me to call him when I could talk alone. I refused to talk to him at first. I was so scared of what Victor would do to me if he found out. But after a week of going through more of his cruel touches, I couldn't do it anymore. I had to get out, and I was willing to risk it even if it killed me."

I push back from Noah, needing a moment to collect myself. Gabe gets up to get some tissues and passes them to me. I wipe myself again and focus on my breathing. Aside from my therapist, I've never told anyone about what happened. About Victor.

"On my next trip out. I used a public phone to call the agent. He told me to meet him at a café just around the corner in five minutes. That's when he explained that they had been trying to infiltrate the gang Victor was a part of. That they had been trying for years to take them down. Apparently, they were involved in drug shipments, and Victor was even suspected of murder. They wanted my help. Anything I could tell them."

I remove myself from Noah, sitting back down on the couch between them, and pick up my beer bottle that now sits on the table. I hadn't even realized it was taken away from me. Draining the last of it, I finish my story.

"It took us three months of meeting once a week, giving them as many details as I could. Since Victor wouldn't share much with me, it took more time than I had hoped. But finally, a plan was in motion, and all I had to do was act naturally. But somehow, Victor found out about the takedown at the last minute, and he escaped. Everyone else was arrested but him."

"Shit... and he figured out it was you?" Noah asks.

I nod. "While the takedown was happening, I packed my bags and bought a bus ticket out of there, as far as I could get from him, just in case. I guess my gut told me something was gonna go wrong. And I was right." I shrug a shoulder and force a small smile.

"It's how I ended up in New York City. I thought a big city crowded with people would make it harder for him to find me. I only found out the next day that he hadn't been caught, and I knew once he got home and noticed me gone, he would put two and two together."

"That's why you change your look every month," Gabe says, putting the pieces together.

I nod. "I didn't have a choice. It was the only way for me to stay hidden without having to move nonstop. So, every month, I dye my hair a different color. I got tattoos and piercings. Everything to look different. I never even dressed like this until I ran away."

"The other day, you told me it's been over three years since you last saw him. How do you think he found you after so much time?" Noah questions with a furrowed brow.

"I'm not sure... the only thing that's changed in the last months is you guys. Maybe he saw me on TV at one of your games or fell on a picture of me with the girls online. I don't know."

Gabe nods. "That must be it. Even if you aren't directly in the spotlight. There are tons of pictures of you with the team or the wives of players. Cecilia was often in the headlines, and she has pictures of you on her Instagram, so does Emma. If he somehow fell on those, it would be easy to narrow down where you are."

My head drops into my hands as I push the heels of my palms against my eyes. "Fuck. I got careless; that's what happened, and now he's found me..."

"We won't let him get to you, Vixen. I promise." Gabe takes my hand once more.

"Maybe you should think about staying here from now on, with us. Just until we figure out what to do. I don't like knowing he's out there following you around," Noah offers.

"I don't know. I don't want to feel caged in again, like I can't leave the house without being afraid. I've been going through years of therapy because of that. I feel like it would be taking a step back if I started hiding out here." I shake my head.

"But I also don't want to put the others in danger or make them a target. I don't know what he's capable of exactly. But if what that agent had told me was true, then it could get really bad..." I chew on my lip, hating how weak I feel in this moment.

Hating that one sight of him made me turn back into the small little girl that I fought so hard to break free from.

"Kitten, you wouldn't be caged in. We'd still let you do whatever you wanted. But at least here, you'd have two people watching over you, two people who would have your back if anything happened. Plus, this place is super secure; there's no way he would get in here," Noah says as he puts his hand on my thigh.

"Just think about it. But until then, we'll continue to pick you up and drop you off when you work. And if you need to go shopping or whatever, I'd feel better if one of us stayed with you during those times. Just to make sure you're safe." He smiles tenderly.

"Okay," I say softly.

As much as I hate feeling like I'm regressing, I'm happy to know I won't be alone in this. Not like the first time. I know I can count on Gabe and Noah. I know I'll be safe with them.

I sit back against the couch, closing my eyes for a moment with a deep sigh. Reliving those memories was painful, but it feels good to finally talk about it. I feel like a weight has been lifted off my chest.

"But wait, weren't you studying at NYU not long ago? Wasn't that risky, since you had to give all your documents and shit?" Gabe questions with furrowed brows. "Weren't you afraid he'd find you like that?"

I shake my head and look at him. "I had fake documents made when I arrived here with my grandmother's last name. Even my driver's license says Veronica Sillienna. Aside from Aubrey and my therapist, you guys were the first ones I introduced myself to as Masters."

"So Aubrey knows?" Noah frowns, not understanding since I told him no one knew about my past.

"No, but she saw my birth certificate in my car when we started hanging out. I told her it was my real last name but that I used my grandmother's when signing up for school. I guess I just knew I could trust her and that she wouldn't tell anyone, so I wasn't really worried about her knowing that little detail. Although, I might have to fill her in now on everything after what she witnessed today." I sigh, closing my eyes once more.

"So... where are you really from?" Gabe questions.

I smile, keeping my eyes closed, despite the damper mood in the room. "Arizona."

"Holy shit! You really didn't mess around." He stares at me with wide, impressed eyes when I finally peek at him.

"And your parents, have you talked or seen them since?" Noah squeezes my thigh lightly as I turn to look at him.

I shake my head. "I haven't had any contact with my parents since they kicked me out. I can't imagine what they'd think if they saw me now." I laugh.

"You really look that different?" Gabe cocks a brow.

I hold my hand out. "Give me your phone." He unlocks it and hands it over.

My eyes widen when I realize his wallpaper is a picture of me. I'm not sure when exactly he took this picture, but I'm sitting outside on one of the couches with a coffee mug in my hands, looking out at the birds eating from the bird feeder. It seems to be early in the morning.

When I turn to look at him, he squeezes the back of his neck and a pink hue forms over his cheeks. "Yeah, I forgot about that." He chuckles.

I let it be for now, unsure how to react to this new information. I tap into his Facebook and search myself up. I might not have any social media accounts now, but I have an old account on there that's still activated. I find it within seconds and pull up the images, passing it back to Gabe.

"You tell me if I still look the same."

His mouth opens and closes. He blinks a few times, looks from me to the screen, over and over, then leans in closer to the phone. "How is it possible? You don't even look like the same person." He hands the phone over to Noah, whose eyebrows shoot up to his hairline.

It's a picture of me on my sixteenth birthday, before my life took a turn. I was wearing this hideous flower-printed turtleneck dress that ended mid-calf with ruffled sleeves. My straight mocha brown hair falling to the center of my back, pearl earrings and necklace on display. Not a touch of makeup, not a piercing in sight. No ink crawling up my skin. Just pure, innocent virgin me, who had no idea how much her life was about to change.

Noah turns to another picture; it's one with me and my parents. I looked so happy there. I hate how much I ruined everything. I loved my parents; they were like my best friends, but I hated the religion aspect of our lives. I had never really cared about it, never truly believed in it, but I did it to please them. And then I went and fucked it all up because I wanted a taste of freedom.

I look away, blinking the tears out of my eyes, my throat growing tighter with each swallow. *I miss them so much.* "Fuck. I'm gonna have to book another session with my therapist."

I already know what happened today will mess me up some more, so talking to her about it will help. Besides, she'll be happy to know I finally opened up about my past to someone else. *Two someones.*

"Do you see her often?" Noah passes the phone back to Gabe.

I nod. "Once a month for the past three years, although it was every week in the beginning."

"And does it work...?" Gabe asks quietly, a sliver of hope in his voice.

"It does. I saw a few different ones at first, but it all felt like it was a waste of time. Until I found her. She didn't ask me the same stupid questions they all do; instead, she asked if I wanted to play a game of cards with her on my first appointment. We didn't even talk about my problems, nothing. We just played cards until my time was up." I laugh remembering how confused I was that day.

"When I got up from my chair to leave, I felt like I had once again wasted my time. She stopped me and said, *'I don't know what he did to you, but he's a piece of shit, and you're worth so much more than that'.*" I shake my head, smiling to myself.

"I was so shocked at her crude words because all the therapists I had seen before were so polite. I didn't even make it out of the building before having another session already booked with her, and I haven't stopped going back."

I lean my head against Gabe's shoulder, sensing him overthinking. I don't know what his story is yet, but I can tell there's one. Every now and then, he gets this faraway look in his eyes, like his mind is taking him someplace else, somewhere dark and lonely. I hate seeing him like that.

"I could give you her number... if you want," I whisper to him.

His shoulder stiffens slightly, and I feel his heart thumping rapidly. I place my hand over his heart for a few seconds, then glide it higher up his neck, over his jaw, and to his cheek. I then turn his face down to me while lifting my head and bring my lips to his, kissing him softly until I feel his body relaxing.

I pull away and look into his eyes. "It's okay to need therapy, Gabriel. There's nothing wrong with that. It doesn't make you inadequate or stupid for not being able to face your demons on your own. Asking for help doesn't make you weak, it makes you brave."

His throat bobs as he nods slowly. "Okay," he murmurs back.

I smile at him, pressing my lips delicately to his one last time before sitting back down properly in my seat. I lift my right arm, stretching it out to show them my sleeved ink. "She's the reason I have this. After a month of sessions with her, I was still in a really dark place. I had no desire to live. I felt dirty and used no matter how many times I washed myself." I swallow, remembering how many times I came close to just ending it all.

"She gave me a journal and told me to write down one word a day for an entire year about something that made me happy during that day. Even if it was as silly as a little bird sitting on the windowsill." I glide my finger over my tattoo of a bird sitting outside a window and smile.

"After a year of doing it, I took my journal to Maze; she's my tattoo artist and hairdresser. I told her I wanted her to take every word in that book and turn it into a tattoo all over my arm, and this is what she came up with."

My eyes travel over every little image like I'm seeing them again for the first time. "Now I have three hundred and sixty-five reasons to be happy forever with me," I finish quietly.

Although at this moment, I feel like I have three hundred and sixty-seven.

Chapter Fifteen

GABRIEL

Jealousy looks cute on you.

~ Three Days Later / July ~

I'm still seething. It's been three days, seventy-two hours since Ronnie told us what that piece of trash did to her, and I'm still enraged. I just want to find him and rip his throat out for hurting her.

But fuck, she's so strong. My beautiful Vixen. She's the bravest person I've ever met. How she can still stand so tall, after everything she's been through, makes me fall for her even more.

I know she's still living through her trauma, still working on getting better. But she's doing it; she's fucking trying. She sought out help on her own and has been doing everything in her power to heal. She isn't hiding from her trauma. She's facing it straight on.

Unlike me.

I knew our wounds were similar in some way; our stories may not be the same, but in the end, we were both brutally hurt by people we thought loved us. Aside from Noah and the people who helped me get out, no one knows my story.

I've never wanted to share it with the world. I just wanted to ignore it, pretend it didn't exist, and hope it would go away. I'm the funny guy, the flirt, the guy who always smiles and laughs.

What would they think of me if they knew just how broken I really was inside?

But Ronnie knows. She might not know the story, but she sees my pain. She sees right through me. It's why she offered her therapist. It's why she told me I shouldn't be afraid to ask for help, because she knows how desperately I still need it even if I pretend to be fine.

I don't think I'm ready to try therapy again, despite me telling Noah I would go.

I've tried so many times, and it just makes me feel worse in the end. But now that Vixen has shared her past with us, it makes me want to share mine with her. I just don't know how to bring it up. How to just... say it.

Like, *'Hey! Remember that time you found holes in my sheets, and I claimed it was because of wild sex? Yeah, well, that was bullshit. The truth is I have night terrors about my past because my parents used to beat the shit out of me daily, to the point of almost killing me a few times. So yeah, want to toast to our shared trauma?'* God, that just makes me sound even crazier.

I'm jolted out of my thoughts when Vixen's hand taps against my thigh. We're currently seated by our boarding gate, waiting for the rest of the gang to get here. We picked up Ronnie and Aubrey at their condo this afternoon before heading to the airport.

Vixen has her head leaning against Noah's shoulder as they watch something on his phone together. She's not looking at me, but her hand still reaches out for me, hitting against my thigh, then higher up until she lands on my forearm.

From there, dark purple fingernails drag down my forearm, into my palm until they slip between my fingers and curl. I bring her hand that now holds mine up to my lips and kiss it. She still doesn't look my way, but her lips spread into a heart-melting smile.

God, she's mesmerizing.

The day after her encounter with her ex, I brought Ronnie to see her friend Maze, who dyed her hair a nice orchid purple. She's a pretty cool chick with a flashy pink pixie cut and tattoos from her toes to her neck, from what I could tell. A little heavy on the makeup, but she has this whole punk rock look going on that seems to fit her perfectly.

What freaked me out a little was that she called me by my name the minute I walked into her little hidden workspace, located in the middle of nowhere. She didn't say it out of recognition from being a fan or seeing me on TV. She said it like we were old-time buddies and knew exactly who I was.

After seeing my stunned face, she laughed and revealed that Ronnie often talks about me and Noah to her. Well, complains would be the correct word, which I'm not surprised about. Vixen has never been shy to speak her mind, and I know we were very determined when it came to having her, which meant we pissed her off most of the time. But I'm hoping that will change, or maybe it already has.

Because ever since that day in our home gym, things have been escalating between us at rapid speed. Every day feels like we're getting closer to her. And since the episode with her ex, our relationship has developed even more.

She kisses us at least once a day. Once a day, I get to feel those perfect pink lips against mine. It's not like that scorching hot session, where I was ready to make her scream my name. But it's still her and me, and I happily die a little more inside every time she melts into my arms and moans into my mouth.

When I look in front of me where Aubrey sits facing us, she smiles with a pink tint covering her cheeks, which makes me chuckle and shake my head. This girl and her uncontrollable blush.

"We're finally here!" Morgan calls as she rushes over and kisses all our cheeks in greeting.

"Vacation time, baby!" Emma shouts as she plops down beside Aubrey. "Are you excited too, little Tulip? We're going to have so much fun!" she says to her daughter, who claps with joy in her arms.

Cecilia comes over next, doing the same as Morgan did while holding her son's hand. I lean forward to get as close to eye level as I can with him and stretch out my free hand to him, palm facing him. "Hey, little man. You excited to spend some time on the beach with your favorite uncle?"

He tries to high-five my hand with a stuffed pillow shaped like a hockey stick. "Ockey!"

I lean back in my seat and laugh. This kid cracks me up. His obsession with hockey is borderline unhealthy.

"Ugh!" Cecilia groans. "I can't wait for this idiotic phase to be over. It's getting ridiculous. You should have seen the tantrum he gave us because we weren't bringing his hockey stick with us." She shakes her head. "Sy had to run out and go from store to store until he found this pillow-shaped stick. It was the only way to get him on board with leaving his favorite stick behind."

Silas comes up to her side with a wide grin and kisses her head. "What can I say? He's my son after all," he says, to which she rolls her eyes.

Noah chuckles. "What did you even do to get him so obsessed with it?"

"Probably decorating his room with nothing else but hockey gear wasn't the best idea," Silas replies with a snort.

"And may I remind you that all the gifts I received from you guys at the shower had something to do with hockey? I literally have twenty miniature hockey sticks, so you're all to blame for his obsession." Cecilia gives us all the stink eye.

"I'm just happy Gracie isn't obsessed with anything yet." Grey sits down beside his girlfriend and daughter. "As much as I love hockey, I could not stand hearing that word every minute of every day." He laughs.

"Dada! Miam, miam," Gracie says and reaches out for her father.

"You hungry, Buttercup?" He takes her into his arms.

"I'll go buy her something," Em says as she stands and kisses her daughter's cheek.

"I'll come with you." Aubrey quickly gets up and joins her.

"Me too. Sam, can you watch Dante while I'm gone?" Cecilia asks the kids' nanny.

He walks over and takes Dante's hand from her. "No problem."

"I'm right here, you know." Silas frowns. "His *actual* father."

She giggles and pats his cheek. "I know, honey." She's totally doing it on purpose to ruffle his feathers at this point.

"So, Sam. You excited for a nice tropical vacation?" I ask him, bringing my hand that still holds Vixen's onto her lap, needing to feel her smooth skin some more. She's still leaning against Noah but is now paying attention to all of us.

Sam looks down at our hands, then to Ronnie and Noah, and smirks. "Yeah, a free paid vacation filled with fun. How could I not be?"

"You're here to watch the kids. Not have fun," Silas scolds him.

"Oh, don't be so grouchy, Sy. He can have fun as well. We're eleven adults with only two children. We can all watch them. Sam's mostly here to give you guys a break when you want some time alone with your wives. But that doesn't mean he can't still enjoy his vacation," Morgan tells him.

Silas groans and drops down in a seat. "I guess," he grumbles, not looking pleased.

Suddenly a group of four teenage boys wanders over, all with excited grins on their faces. "Hi!" one says. "We're really huge fans. We were at your game when you guys won the Stanley Cup."

"It was epic!" another shouts.

"Seriously amazeballs! Mr. Ford, you killed it with that hat trick!" a third one adds. "Could we get your autographs and some pictures?"

The last one rips out his phone. "Oh, yeah! My brother will totally be jealous. He's been a fan for so long. He would die if I came home with your autographs all over my shirt and selfies."

"Thank you," Greyson says to the third one. "And sure, why not." He smiles, then turns to Morgan. "Mind holding her for a sec?"

"Not at all." She beams and takes Gracie from him.

The boys come in closer, all going to each of us as we fish out our permanent markers from our carry-ons. It's become a habit to always wander around with a few markers in our pockets. Fans stop us often, wanting autographs, and don't always have things to write with.

I release Ronnie's hand to write properly on all their shirts or papers and take pictures. Soon, we're gathering a crowd of more people wanting some and congratulating us on our win. By the time it dies down and we're doing the last pictures and signings, the girls have already returned with food and drinks for everyone.

I'm just taking the last picture with a woman who claims it's for her son when two chicks walk up to me. When I look up at them, I notice they're identical twins and seem oddly familiar.

"Hi, Gabe!" One waves. "Remember us?"

They're both fluttering their fake lashes and sticking out their chests in my direction. *Shit, I hate these moments.* I feel like an ass for not remembering names, but when it's only about sex, I don't find it necessary to remember it.

"Umm…" I look them up and down, searching for something that might jog my memory. I catch sight of a tattoo along one of their wrists that reads *'Sh-elly'*. And it clicks. "Shelly and Elly," I say, hoping I'm right.

The other jumps on the spot, squishing her breasts between her arms as she offers me a huge pearly white smile. "YES! I told you he remembered us," she tells her sister.

She comes closer and presses herself to my side, her hand running up and down my chest. "We've missed you."

The other comes to do the same on my other side. "You should give us a call soon. We had so much fun last time, remember?" She leans in closer and licks my ear. "There are so many more tricks I want to show you."

"All right, that's enough," I hear Ronnie say from behind me, seconds before I'm pulled back and out of their grasps. "He's not interested." She gives them the fakest, bitchiest smile I've ever seen her wear as she takes my hand and places it around her waist.

The twins watch us with wide eyes. "Oh," one says. "We're sorry, we didn't know you had a girlfriend now."

"Must be pretty recent." The other offers Vixen a similar smile, then turns her gaze to Noah. "How about you, Noah? We haven't forgotten about you either." She winks.

Ronnie reaches out for Noah, who stands not far away, and grabs his hand, locking their fingers together. "Yeah, he's not interested either, so why don't you back off and go shove your fake tits in someone else's face?"

The whole gang snickers behind us as the twins gasp, then turn on their heels with fuming expressions. "What a bitch!" one calls as they storm off.

Noah chuckles as I smile and turn to Ronnie. "I didn't know you were so jealous,

Vixen." I kiss her cheek.

"Shut up and sit down," she says with an angry look as she lets go of us and drops down in her seat. I take my seat beside her, and Noah takes her other side.

She folds her arms over her chest and scowls. "I can't believe you remember their names," she grumbles.

I laugh at how cute she looks all jealous and angry. "I didn't. But there was a tattoo on her arm with their names written together. It was an easy guess."

"Whatever," she says but doesn't look any less mad.

"Baby, you have no reason to be jealous. I had no intention of taking them up on their offer." I lean in closer, whispering into her ear. "The only girl I plan on having from now on is you."

She turns to look at me, her lips practically grazing mine. Her eyes pierce into mine for a moment, then drop down to my lips. "Good," she whispers, then turns back to our friends, acting like she didn't just have a mini jealousy fit in front of everyone.

"So, are the kids going to be okay on the plane?" she asks, looking from Cecilia to Emma.

"I think so. Gracie's pretty used to flying now," Emma tells her.

"Dante, too. He's usually pretty calm on the plane. But we brought toys and snacks just in case. We also have some things to help them sleep if they get too fussy. It's a pretty long flight, so I would expect them to get annoyed at some point," Cecilia says, leaning against her husband.

She's right about that. Originally, we had planned on renting a yacht and traveling to a nearby destination. But then the girls got a little carried away, and we ended up with a whole island reserved just for us.

Which now means we have an ungodly number of hours sitting on a cramped plane. Starting off with a six-hour flight to LA, then a three-hour layover there, before boarding our next flight for a total of eleven hours to Nadi International Airport. Where we'll then get on a much smaller plane for thirty minutes to Pacific Harbour and finish that with a thirty-five-minute speedboat ride to our private island.

Like I said, long ass travel plans. But it will totally be worth it if it means spending every single moment with my Vixen for the next two weeks.

NOAH

Veronica being jealous of those two girls took me by surprise. I never would have expected her to react that way, since she's still claiming nothing is going on between us to our friends. Even though she's being extremely touchy and kissy with us around them. But her little moment of jealousy pretty much clarified where we all stand. She's ours, and we're hers, even if she's still living in denial.

Our first flight to Los Angeles went over smoothly, as well as the layover there. Now we're on our overnight flight to Nadi, and everyone on board seems to be asleep, except for Veronica and me.

We're watching a movie together on my tablet with her head rested on my shoulder. Gabe knocked out an hour ago with his AirPods in his ears after taking some medication to help him sleep.

At first, Sam was supposed to be seated with us on the overnight flight and Veronica with Aubrey two seats down. But he quickly offered to change his spot with her so she would be seated between us for the night. Which we gladly accepted, and Kitten didn't seem too upset by the change either.

Veronica lifts her head from my shoulder and looks at me. "Are you doing okay?" She looks beside her at Gabe, making sure he's really asleep before whispering, "With... you know. Being away for two weeks?" She's talking about Trinity.

The truth is I'm pretty nervous about being so far away from her for so long. I hate not seeing her for more than a week. But I made sure the staff was aware that I would be away and checked with my service provider to make sure my phone would be working in Fiji. I also gave them the number to the reception desk at the resort, just in case they couldn't reach me.

And I know I'm not the only one who's nervous about this two-week trip. From what Greyson told us, Maddison, the little cancer girl, isn't doing so great, to the point that Emma was ready to back out of the trip. But with a little convincing from everyone, Maddison included, she conceded. Emma has been putting on a bright face for all of us, but the dark circles under her usually glowing face tell a whole different story, one that Greyson confirmed. She's not doing well.

"Yeah, I'm okay." I smile and kiss her forehead.

"Did you give them the number to the resort? Just in case. I know they also have my number, but sometimes cell reception can be shitty." *She's so adorable, being all worried for me.*

"Yeah, Kitten. I did. Everything will be fine. You don't have to worry." I kiss her lips this time.

She sighs happily against mine before whispering, "Okay."

She pulls away and returns to my shoulder as I play through her hair. "And you, have you gotten… anything since?" I ask, referring to the only person on this planet I'm debating on killing.

She shakes her head. "No. Nothing, not even a text. I don't know what he's playing at, and that worries me. He would send me a message at least once a day before, but now it's been three days of radio silence."

"Think about what we offered you, Veronica. It would only help make you feel a little safer. I promise we won't coddle you."

She nods. "I'll think about it. Just give me these two weeks to make my decision."

"Okay." I kiss her crown. I can't get enough of kissing her. I have this vibrating need to always touch her in some way, and I love that she now comes willingly.

"Hey, are you guys up?" Emma appears in the narrow walkway with Gracie in her arms.

"Yeah, what's wrong?" I ask her.

"Gracie's having a hard time falling asleep, and I really need to use the washroom. Everyone else is sleeping. Would you mind watching her while I go take care of business?"

Veronica straightens and reaches out with her hands. "Of course, take all the time you need." She takes Gracie from Em's outstretched arms. "Come here, princess. You're gonna spend some time with Aunty Ronnie while Mommy goes to tinkle." She places her down on her lap, facing her.

"Thank you so much! Those bathrooms are so tiny, going in there with a toddler is horrible." Emma widens her eyes, then rushes off to said bathroom.

"What's going on, princess? Why aren't you sleeping like the rest of these muggles?" she asks Gracie in a hushed tone.

I chuckle. "Did you just call us muggles?"

"Don't judge me. I've been binge-watching Harry Potter in my spare time."

"Are you going to start casting spells on us? Make a glass of scotch appear with…frozen water inside?" I cover my laugh with my fist.

She glares at me, which only makes it harder to stop laughing. "I can't just make things appear for you. That's not how magic works."

"Okay, okay, Hermione Granger."

"Shush it." She bumps her shoulder into mine.

"Do you want kids?" I have no idea where this question's coming from, and by the wide eyes Veronica gives me, she doesn't either.

"Umm... I don't know. Honestly, I never saw myself having kids. I love Gracie and Dante, but I don't know if motherhood is for me." She won't meet my eyes now, like the question is making her uncomfortable.

I hum in response. Her answer kind of bums me, and I'm not sure why. Like her, I've never really seen kids in my future. I'm not opposed to it, but it's never been on my list of needs. It's not something I've given much thought to, not like Ellis. Despite his shitty past, he really wants kids.

I still remember the way his face lit up when we found out Cecilia was pregnant. He was so happy that there would finally be a baby around us. It was like he was the husband finding out his wife was pregnant.

"You?" she whispers eventually.

"I'm a little indifferent to the idea. If I have some, great, but I'm also fine not having any," I tell her truthfully.

She nods, seeming lost in her head, then turns to look at Gabe, who's still sound asleep. "But Gabe wants kids, doesn't he?"

I'm not sure where we're going with this conversation. We're nowhere close to being ready to talk about the future and babies. I'm guessing Clay's comment two weeks ago got inside our head without us realizing it.

I nod. "He does."

She chews on her lip with a frown while cradling Gracie to her chest, and I place my hand on her knee to get her attention. "Hey, it doesn't matter what we want or what you want right now. We're just getting to know each other better. How about we just focus on our relationship first and see where that goes before even thinking about potential kids? There's no need to stress about anything like that."

I smile at her. "If whatever is going on between us three does develop into something more down the line, then we can reevaluate and have a more serious conversation about it. But that won't be any time soon. It was just a simple question, Kitten. Nothing more."

"Okay." She sends me a small smile in return.

"Thank you so much!" Emma shows up again. "I thought I was going to burst in my seat. Come on, little Tulip. It's time to go night-night." She reaches out as Veronica passes Gracie back.

"You're welcome. If she doesn't end up sleeping and you want a little break, don't hesitate to pass her over again," Veronica tells her.

"I should be fine, but I'll keep that in mind. You two should try and get some sleep, too. We have a big day ahead of us." She grins and walks away with Gracie.

I look at Veronica as she turns to face me. "Are you tired?"

"Not really, I slept through the whole first flight," she says, shaking her head. "And I'm a little excited to arrive on the island."

"You know what I'm excited for?" I grab her chin and pull her closer to my lips.

"What?" she breathes against them.

"Seeing you in all those pretty bikinis you bought, or maybe even without them." I bite her bottom lip delicately.

She smiles with a soft giggle. "Of course you are, Casanova."

She brings her hand up to my nape and fuses our lips together, shutting me up for the rest of our flight.

Chapter Sixteen

VERONICA

Perfect angels.

We made it. We finally made it to the island.

I stretch my arms out into the air as I take in the fresh, peaceful breeze around me, while Gabe and Noah carry our suitcases off the speedboat. It took us several trips to all get here from Nadi Airport since we couldn't all fit in the little plane and speedboat. Which means Noah, Gabe, and I are the last ones to arrive at the resort.

An arm comes behind my knees as I'm swept off my feet and into someone's arms. I yelp as Gabe presses me to his chest and spins us around in a circle. "Look at this place, baby! We're gonna have so much fun!" he says with a huge grin while laughing.

His laugh is so contagious that I can't help joining in as I throw my arms up and shout, "Woo-hoo!"

He carries me down the dock, where we are greeted by the manager of the island, who proceeds to bring us over to our own little villas. Aubrey and I had already decided to share one together. And from what I've gathered, Noah and Gabe are in the one next to us, only a two-minute walking distance away.

I enter our split-level villa and am immediately gasping for air. When I picture a dream luxury vacation, this is what I see. It's paradise. That's the only way to describe it.

Dark wooden beams, light-beige walls, sliding glass doors that open up the whole wall, giving you direct access to the large deck that wraps around the front of the villa. A perfect view of the lagoon in front of us with water for as far as the eye can see.

Taking a few steps in, I drop my luggage by the door and walk past the living room and kitchen area, all the way to the back deck, needing a closer look at the scenic view before me. *Oh my God! There's a pool. We have our own plunge pool! I am definitely going skinny-dipping in that tonight!*

"Finally! You're here!" Aubrey appears to my right on a higher-level section of the deck. She walks down a few steps and reaches me.

I take her into my arms. "I didn't know you were still here. I thought you might have met up with the rest of the gang already."

She pulls back and smiles. "No, we're all meeting up for lunch. But I wanted to wait for you to get here so we could go together."

"Okay, let me just put my luggage away, get changed, and we'll head out." I turn back toward the villa, looking inside.

From out here we can clearly see the layout of the place. In the center is the main living space with a seating area and kitchen, then on each side there's a raised floor with two identical bedrooms.

Each bedroom has its own bathroom and king-size bed. And like the main floor, a full wall of sliding glass doors opens the bedrooms to the deck. *Holy shit, this place must have cost a fortune.*

"You know we'll be paying Emma back for the rest of our lives." Thanks to our amazing and beyond loaded friend, Aubrey and I were able to join the gang on this luxury vacation. Because without her, there was no way we could afford coming here.

"Oh, I know." Aubrey giggles and pulls me in toward my luggage.

Thirty minutes later, I've taken a quick shower and changed into a simple white, spaghetti strap, mini summer dress. Beneath it, I'm wearing my sexy black and white bikini with white wedge sandals on my feet, showing off my newly done dark purple toenails.

"You ready to go?" I call out to Aubrey as I stand by the door.

She comes down the few steps to her room and strolls over. "Ready." She's wearing a similar dress to mine, except hers is a little longer, ending right above her knees, and it's turquoise blue rather than white.

A smile forms on my lips. "Nice dress. You know what it reminds me of?" I smirk.

She looks down at it, her hands gliding down the flowy material. "What?"

"Shane's eyes." I press my lips together not to laugh.

She's so obvious, it's blinding. Over the years of being friends, her favorite color has suddenly changed from soft purple to blue. And not any kind of blue, turquoise blue. The exact color of Shane's eyes. She even decorated our place with a shitload of things in that specific color. But she still believes no one has noticed. I mean, maybe she hasn't even realized it herself.

Her eyes grow wide, cheeks, nose, and ears burning up with how hard she's blushing. "Really?" Her voice comes out a whole octave higher. She clears it and tries again. "Really? I hadn't noticed."

"Mhm, sure you hadn't." I raise a brow. "What color's your bathing suit?"

She folds her arms over her chest. "That has nothing to do with it. You know it's my favorite color." From the small straps I can see, I'd say it's the exact same color, as well as her sandals. *She's obsessed.*

"I wonder why," I murmur under my breath with a snicker.

"Come on, let's go. Everyone's waiting for us." She loops her arm through mine and pulls me out of the villa.

On our way down the trail to the main reception hall where we all agreed to meet, we bump into Gabe and Noah. They stop walking ahead of us the minute they spot us. Gabe comes skipping back toward me and lifts me in his arms, twirling us around. "God, you're so fucking sexy, Vixen." He kisses my neck then sets me back down.

"Thank you, Pretty Boy."

He turns his back to me and squats down. "Piggyback ride?"

"Is that just an excuse to have me riding up against you?" I raise a brow.

He looks over his shoulder with a smirk. "Hell yeah, it is." *This guy.*

I shake my head but still hop onto his back. He stands and begins to carry me down the pathway with Aubrey beside us. Noah falls into step beside her, chuckling as he watches Gabe trotting ahead with me on his back.

"There you are! We were about to sit down without you guys," Silas calls when he sees us approaching.

"Sorry!" I shout. "We're here now." Gabe lowers and sets me on the floor.

"Let's eat! I'm starving," Gabe declares, patting his belly.

We follow an employee to a long table set up outside by the water. Stacks of food are already set up in the center in a buffet style, just waiting for us to dig in. We all take our seats, and of course, I end up sitting between Noah and Gabe.

A waiter comes around, offering us different wines, to which we all agree. When he reaches Morgan and goes to fill her glass, she places her hand above and says, "No, thank you."

I snort in surprise. "Since when does Mrs. Burkley say no to wine?" I say jokingly, but then my eyes widen.

The table goes silent. All you can hear is the soft breeze blowing through the nearby leaves and the two toddlers babbling away as we all stare at Morgan. Waiting.

She looks at every one of us, then turns to her husband, who smiles proudly down at his wife. A breathtaking grin splits her lips before she says the words we've all been dying to hear leaves her mouth. "We're pregnant."

"Oh my God! Really!? Are you really?!" Emma brings her hands up to her mouth, waiting for confirmation that we all heard right.

She turns back to us, tears filling her eyes as she nods. "We are," she cries happily. "It's still early, so we aren't telling people yet. But we knew we couldn't keep it from you guys for much longer."

"Oh, dear God!" Cecilia exclaims as we all jump out of our chairs and rush over to congratulate the soon-to-be parents.

Everyone is emotional as we each take Morgan and Clay in our arms, joy radiating for as far as the eye can see. All the girls are in tears, even Clay has glassy eyes as his friends all slap him on the back. Hell, even I'm getting emotional for them. They've been trying to have a baby for over two years without success. But their time is finally here, and we couldn't be happier for them. They deserve it.

After several more minutes, we finally sit back down to eat. "How far along are you?" Aubrey asks in her usual soft voice.

"Eight weeks."

"Eight weeks!? So when we went wedding dress shopping, you were already pregnant?" Emma asks while wiping away her tears.

Morgan nods with a soft smile. "I was, but my doctor says we must have miscalculated when I ovulated, and it was still too early to tell, which is why the blood tests came back negative."

"Wow, and did you just find out?" Cecilia questions next.

Morg shakes her head. "No, we found out the morning of the Stanley Cup win."

I gasp, slapping my hand on the table. "That's why you were in such good shape the next morning! You didn't even drink!"

She giggles. "I was passing all my shots and drinks to Clay."

"That makes so much sense now. I had never seen you that drunk before, man. I was starting to wonder if it was the old age hitting you hard." Gabe laughs beside me.

"F-off!" Clay chuckles.

"But wait." Em lifts her butter knife in the air that she was using to butter a little bun. "You had a glass of wine during the day with us at my place."

"Actually, I didn't." Morgan smiles sheepishly. "You poured me one, and then I waited until no one was looking to occasionally pour some into the sink and act like I was drinking it."

"Oh, you sneaky girl." Em laughs.

"You threw my wine down the drain?" Greyson glares at Morgan, but there's not much anger in the look.

Emma pats his chest. "It's okay, Wolf. I'll buy you a new one." He nods in response.

I still don't understand what Greyson's deal with wine is. He mostly only drinks beer when we're all together, yet he has a huge selection in his wine cellar with bottles worth thousands of dollars. The whole collection together must be worth more than three million dollars. When we asked Emma about it, she told us he really likes wine but only drinks it on his downtime, that they often have a bottle at night together before heading to bed.

"Is it weird for you to know that your girlfriend has more money than you do?" Gabe asks Greyson as his hand comes to rest on my thigh.

"Ellis, why do you always have to ask questions that make people uncomfortable?" Silas sighs with his head thrown back.

"I can't help it. I just say whatever's on my mind." Gabe shrugs.

"It's fine." Greyson waves his hand then answers Gabe. "No, not really. I don't care about her money, and Bunny doesn't care about mine." He takes Emma's hand and kisses it.

"Do you even know how much money she has?" Noah questions next, his hand now settling on my other thigh. Their knuckles rub up against each other, but neither one moves.

"I'm actually curious about this, too. How much money you got, Em?" Clay sits up, joining in on the conversation.

She laughs. "Let's just say, I'm not a billionaire. But I'm really, *really* close to being one."

A few gasps sound around the table. Even I'm shocked. I knew she had money, but not that much.

"Wait a second! So you're saying you could have paid for this whole trip without a problem? That we could have taken a private jet over here instead of that long ass flight? What the heck, Mackenzie!?" Silas stares at her with his jaw practically scraping his plate.

"I offered! But you men and your egos wouldn't let me pay!" she states. "Now you boys can all sit there feeling stupid for refusing my offer." She goes back to eating her chicken salad with a satisfied smile on her face. "Now for the private jet, I have no idea why none of you thought of that to begin with."

It's silent for a few seconds until Gabe loses it and slaps his free hand on the table, bellowing with laughter. "Ford! You found yourself a sugar mommy!" He laughs some more, holding his stomach. "Now how does it feel knowing just how loaded she really is?"

"I have money too, you know?" Greyson glares at Gabe, who can't help himself.

Noah snickers. "Yeah. But compared to her, you're basically broke."

Greyson's glare turns to Noah, then to me. "Ronnie, you can do better," he declares.

I gape at him. "Me? What did I do? Why am I being brought into this ludicrous conversation?"

"I'm just saying. You can do better than these two dummies." He furrows his brows. "Are we allowed to say idiot in front of the kids?" He turns to Emma.

She looks up from her plate with a frown. "I mean, it's not a nice thing to say, but it's not a bad word. So, I guess, yes?" She shrugs with uncertainty.

"Wow... he even has to ask for permission to talk... she really is his sugar mommy," Gabe whispers loud enough for everyone to hear, earning him a few chuckles around the table.

"Shut up, Ellis!" Greyson shouts at him.

"Now *that*, you can't say," Emma scolds him.

"Wait. So, he can say *idiot*, but he can't say *shut up*?" Clay frowns. "I'm confused. That makes no sense."

"Well, I don't want my daughter saying shut up to a stranger," Emma informs him.

"But calling someone an idiot is okay?" Silas asks with amusement.

"Oh..." Em's eyes widen. "You have a point." She nods. "Okay, no more saying idiot or shut up from now on!" she states to the table.

"Shu up."

We all gasp and turn to Dante, who's looking at us with a pleased smile, right before repeating in his tiny toddler voice, "Shu up."

"OH MY GOD! EMMA!!" Cecilia yells.

"Hey! I'm not the only one who said it!"

"Yeah, but you did kind of repeat it often." I giggle.

"You, be quiet." Em points a finger at me.

"Shu up, shu up, shu up!" Dante giggles as he repeats the words over and over.

"No, no, baby. We don't say that. It's a bad, bad word." Cecilia tries to quiet her son, but that seems to only make him find it even funnier.

"Shu up!"

"Oh God! Honey! Do something!" She turns to Silas with a panicked expression. "Why does he have to be a fast learner! Next thing we know, he's going to be obsessed with that word and hockey!"

"Ockey!" Dante exclaims with his tiny fists in the air. He looks just like his father, it's actually really cute.

"Oh, thank the lord. We're back on track." Cece places a hand over her heart and sighs in relief. She then points an angry finger at every single one of us. "No more saying any word we wouldn't want our kids repeating to someone. Understood?!"

We all nod and chuckle. *God, I love these people.*

"So, what's the plan for today?" Sam asks once everyone has settled down. *Jesus, he's so quiet in his seat I forgot he was there for a moment.*

Morgan shrugs. "We thought we could just enjoy the beach today. I think we're all pretty exhausted after all that traveling. I'm honestly a little confused at what time it actually is."

"Ugh, I hate jetlag," Emma whines.

"I think the beach is a good idea," Gabe says, then leans in and whispers into my ear, "We'll finally get to see you in that sexy bikini."

I turn my head to face him, our noses brushing up against each other. "And here I thought you would prefer seeing me without it." I stick out my tongue and flick his lower lip.

His eyes darken, a soft growl producing from his throat. "Oh, I'd much prefer that." He leans his head to the side, coming in to nip at my neck with his teeth. "My naughty little Vixen."

I can't stop the small moan from slipping past my lips as my eyes close and my head leans to the side, offering him more skin to caress with his tongue.

"Guys! Seriously? We're eating," Greyson whines. "None of that at the table."

I rub my lips together, trying to hold in my giggle. "Sorry."

Two hours later, we're finally all on the sandy beach. Despite the heat, there's a cool wind making it just perfect to stay out in the sun, and the water is to die for with its beautiful crystal blue color. The pictures we saw online didn't do it justice. I could stay here forever.

We lay our towels down on the sand, then rip off our clothes and head for the water to cool off. After a few minutes of splashing in the water, I return to my towel and lie down on my stomach, getting ready to work on my tan. A few seconds later, a big shadow appears behind me, moments before a dripping wet body presses itself against my back as it crawls over me.

"It looks even sexier in person," Noah whispers against my nape as he kisses me there, then down my shoulder blade.

I lift my ass slightly, rubbing it against his crotch where I get a faint feel of his growing erection in his swim shorts. "Glad to see just how much you like it." I smile, tilting my head to the side.

"If you need help taking it off later, I'd gladly lend a hand." His lips come back up my body until his face is inches from mine.

I lift my head, turning even more until my lips capture his. "I'll let you know." Then push against him. "Now go away. I'm trying to tan."

He chuckles and kisses my cheek before removing himself from my body. I decide tanning from the front first might be a better idea, like that I'll see the boys coming beforehand. Switching onto my back, I'm about to settle back down when I catch Aubrey slowly coming out of the water.

The one-piece she chose is actually really hot. It practically looks like a two-piece, with the sides cut out, showcasing her waist. Only a small strip of fabric down her stomach holds the top and bottom together. The top portion dips low, displaying her cleavage beautifully, and ties behind her neck. And you guessed it, it's turquoise as I had predicted.

I quickly grab my phone from my bag and snap a picture of her as she brings her hands up and slides them over her head and down her hair. I look down at the picture and whistle quietly. Not going to lie, it's fucking sexy. It's like she's posing for a photoshoot.

Her body is fully stretched out, chest pushed out with her peaked nipples pressing against the fabric, eyes closed and face serene-looking, with her lips slightly parted. *Oh my God, Shane is going to die seeing this!*

I rush over to Emma, who's also lying on her towel. I look around to make sure no one is in earshot, then kneel down beside her. "Hey," I whisper. "Do you have Shane's number?"

She pushes her sunglasses over her head and looks at me quizzically. "I do. Why?"

I get even closer to her. "Quick. Send him this, then delete it." I send her the picture as she grabs her own phone.

"Holy shit! He's going to love this, but Baby Brey will kill you if she ever finds out." She giggles.

"That's why I'm telling you to do it fast and delete the evidence." I motion with my hand, telling her to hurry.

She quickly types out a message to Shane with just one simple word, 'Enjoy,' and the picture. Within seconds, the message is read, and the little bubble icon appears, indicating he's typing back. But then it leaves... and comes back... and leaves again.

"Oh, the poor guy. He doesn't know how to respond to this," Emma coos.

Finally, after a full two minutes a message, comes through with a simple, *'Thank you.'* I instantly giggle. *He's so polite.* "How much you want to bet he's jerking off right now to that picture?"

"Oh, definitely. And it won't be a one-time thing. I bet he'll save it in a hidden folder or something like Greyson does." Emma smiles and shakes her head.

"Okay, delete it now. No evidence of what just happened can be found. We did nothing. Perfect angels."

She deletes the text as well as the picture as I do the same. "There, perfect angels." She pulls her sunglasses down and smiles mischievously.

Greyson suddenly appears and plops down beside his girlfriend. "What are you two whispering about?" He kisses Emma's cheek, then looks from her to me.

"Oh, nothing. We were just commenting on how much Aubrey has grown over the last few years," Emma provides. *Okay, not too far from the truth.*

"Ugh. Don't remind me. Thank God, she's still not dating. I don't know how I'll deal with that," Grey grunts out.

"You do know it will happen one day, and you won't really have a say in it. Who she chooses to be with is her decision, not yours," I tell him.

"As her brother, I do get a say. If he's not good for her, then I don't want him near my sister." He frowns at me.

Emma subtly shakes her head, telling me to drop it. They've probably already had this conversation, and it never goes anywhere. Poor guy when he finds out who she's actually into.

Hell will definitely break loose.

Chapter Seventeen

VERONICA

My queen.

~ The Next Day ~

We're only on day two of our vacation, and I already have a gorgeous tan on top of my natural golden skin. I can't wait to see what I'll look like by the end of our stay. It will definitely make for some nice pictures with the girls.

I bet my boys will look quite nice as well.

Today everyone is off exploring the island and doing their own thing. Morgan, Clay, Emma, and Greyson are gone snorkeling, while Cecilia and Silas are doing some Hobie Cat sailing. Aubrey, on the other hand, decided to stay back with Sam and the kids to spend the day in the pool.

Which leaves me and the two men who never leave my side. We weren't sure what to do at first but finally decided to explore the island on our own. The island manager offered us a tour guide, but we thought it would be more fun to venture alone. We started off by following the shore then went into the more forested section of the island.

It's so quiet and peaceful here; all you can hear is the distant sound of waves crashing along the cliffs and tropical birds chirping within the trees. I hadn't realized how much I miss the quiet after spending the last three years in the city. No horns blaring, no people shouting, no bumping into pedestrians along the sidewalk, or zipping through endless traffic. It's just us and this big, beautiful island, surrounded by nature. A part of me wishes we could live here forever.

After a few hours of walking and exploring, we find a secretive little beach on the other side of the island. There's no pathway or trail to it, so I'm guessing no one ever really comes here. I kick off my sandals and walk into the water, dipping my hands in and bringing them back up to glide over my skin, cooling it down from the heat.

We left the resort in only our swimsuits and shoes, planning on getting in the water whenever we could, so it made sense to bring no extra clothing or bags with us. The staff assured us there was no way for us to get lost, that no matter which way we walked, eventually we would return to the resort.

Noah comes into the water behind me, one hand coming up to my neck as he brushes my hair to the side and kisses the spot between my neck and shoulder. His other hand moves around my waist, pressing me into his hard, sculpted body.

"I love this bikini so much more than yesterday's." He kisses up my neck.

"Oh, yeah?" I tilt my head back, giving him better access.

"Mhmm, you wanna know why?" He flicks my earlobe with his tongue.

"Tell me," I say breathlessly, eyes closing as I let his seductive voice travel along my skin, through my body, down to my core.

"This beautiful white top when wet…" His hand that brushed my hair away earlier slides down my front. Tiny bumps scatter my skin as his finger delicately trails lower, over my breast. "Becomes practically see-through."

The tip of his finger glides over my pebbled nipple as he swirls it around a few times before cupping my breast in his palm. His huge hand looks enormous as he squeezes my breast in his grasp.

I moan as the wild sensation brings my body to life. I've always been very sensitive; whether it's my breast or between my legs, every touch feels like a bolt of electricity passing through me.

"Which gives me the perfect view of these perky little tits." Noah bites my ear delicately over my piercings before the hand around my waist dips lower until it's resting at the side of my bikini bottom. "And these silly little strings…" He pulls on it slightly, then growls. "One little tug and everything comes loose."

I moan again, tempted to tell him to do it. Wanting him to do it. These last few days have been torture with their hands constantly touching me, their lips always on me. It's all I can think about. Wanting. Needing. The throbbing between my legs has been persistent lately, begging for attention. Their attention.

I'm about to grab his hand at my hip and bring it down to my center, needing his touch there when Gabe yells out at us, stopping me. "Hey, guys! Come see what I found!"

Noah removes his hands from me with one last lingering kiss to my neck before giving me that devilish smirk. He laces our fingers together and walks us over to Gabe, following him along the shore until the sand stops and is replaced by big boulders, where we're forced to walk in the water.

"It's right after the rocks," Gabe says with an excited smile.

Once we've passed the huge rocks, the terrain turns flat and shows an opening to a hidden cave. "Oh my God, there's a cave? Did you go in?" I ask him, to which he smiles and nods. I smack his arm instantly. "Gabe! That's super dangerous. You shouldn't have gone in alone."

"You worried something might happen to me, baby?" He winks and pulls me by the waist, pressing my front against his chest.

"Yes," I answer honestly.

"Aw, Vixen. My heart." He presses his hand to his chest between us.

"Shut up." I smack him again.

He laughs. "Come on, you don't need to worry. It's just a small hole, practically an alcove. But there's a small body of water inside."

"The water must get in during high tide, so we need to make sure to be out before that happens," Noah says.

"We'll just go in for a bit. Then we'll head back to meet the rest for dinner." Gabe beams as he lets go of me and steps up onto the flat surface, then begins to walk into the cave's opening.

He's right; it really isn't big. Well, the cave is pretty large, but it doesn't go deep at all. And as he mentioned, right in the center, the stone floor dips in, and whatever water comes in with the tide remains trapped.

"Wow, this is beautiful." I gaze up and around.

"This could be our secret little hiding place for the next two weeks." Gabe wraps his arms around me from behind.

"Hmm, and what would we do in our hiding place?"

"Anything you want, Vixen," he whispers in my ear.

A shiver runs down my spine as my imagination runs wild. "That could be a dangerous offer," I say, stepping out of his hold with a devilish smirk thrown over my shoulder.

I walk over to the small pool of water and dip my toe in. The water is warm and clear; you can see the stone flooring at the bottom. It's not too deep either, maybe waist height. "Can we get in?"

Noah inspects it for a beat, then slowly steps in, walking around a bit before coming to stand in front of me, although now he's eye level with my pussy. He slowly looks up, a wicked smirk landing on his lips as he gazes between my legs, before his eyes travel the length of my body, up to my face.

He finally reaches his hands out for me to take. "Come here, Kitten."

I take a step closer, placing my arms on his shoulders instead as he grabs my waist and brings me into the water, while Gabe jumps in seconds later beside us.

"Be careful, some of the rocks are a little slippery. We wouldn't want you to hurt yourself," Noah says, still holding on to my waist and only lets go once I'm on steady ground.

I walk around a little, then dip below the surface of the water, coming back up and swiping my wet shoulder-length hair back. When I open my eyes, I find both men watching me with hungry eyes.

Getting back to the side, I pull myself out of the water and sit on the edge, feet dangling in the water. They both walk over, settling on either side of me but staying in the water, their gazes permanently fixed on me. I feel them lingering over my body. Everywhere.

"Have you two ever done stuff together?" I ask, my curiosity piqued. I know they share women often, but I don't know just how much they share.

"What do you mean?" Noah asks.

"Like, when you share. Is it just with the girl, or do you two... you know." I look from one to the other.

"Have we ever done shit together?" Gabe laughs. "No. Never."

"Not even a kiss?"

"Nope," Gabe says with a smile.

Noah just shakes his head. "We aren't into each other if that's what you're asking."

"Why? You thought there was something between us?" Gabe questions.

"No. But you two are really close, and you always have sex together. So, it could have been a possibility." I shrug.

"Well, there have been the occasional touches; for example, let's say one of our hands are occupied, and we need help with positioning. So, yes, I've grabbed his dick and he's grabbed mine," Gabe starts.

"Same goes for double penetration. If we're working the same entrance, then we're sliding up against each other. But there's no emotional connection or whatever between us. We're just in the moment, so we don't care. But he doesn't get me hard, and I sure hope as shit I don't get him hard." He finishes with a chuckle, while all I can do is stare at him with wide eyes.

"I promise you, you don't," Noah tells him.

When they both turn to me and notice my shocked expression, they chuckle. "Have you never been with two men before, Veronica?" Noah asks quietly.

"I have."

"Then why do you look so stunned?" Gabe smirks.

"Just the same entrance comment startled me a little." I feel heat rising to my cheeks. *Jesus, why am I blushing?* "I didn't know that was really a thing."

Gabe lifts himself out of the water to my left, settling beside me as his chest presses against my arm. "Oh, it's definitely a thing. And it feels fucking amazing."

I scoff. "I'll be the judge of that."

Noah climbs out as well, seating himself to my right and mimicking Gabe's position. "Are you saying you'd let us have you like that, Kitten?"

Gabe kisses my shoulder. "Not right now, of course. That takes practice and patience." His wet lips trail up my neck. "Something I don't have right now."

Noah comes in too, pushing my hair back to nip at my jaw, then my ear. "We'd take really good care of you. You wouldn't regret it."

I tilt my head back, mind swimming in a sensual sea of touches. I sigh with content as my body erupts in goosebumps.

"What do you say, Vixen? Will you gift us this enchanting body of yours?" Gabe's hand comes to my hair, fisting it as I close my eyes on a gasp. He tilts my head his way as Noah's mouth travels to my collarbone.

"Let us be yours, Vixen," Gabriel whispers against my parted lips.

"Say yes, Kitten. All we want is to be yours. Make us yours," Noah murmurs against my skin as his hand glides against my stomach to right below my breast.

"Yes," I breathe against Gabe's mouth.

In an instant his lips fall to mine, devouring me as Noah cups my breast, kneading it. Gabe continues to ravage my mouth while his hand releases my hair and goes to the tie behind my neck, tugging on it until it falls loose. And Noah wastes no time in bringing it down my front, exposing my breasts to him as he captures one nipple between his lips.

I moan into Gabe's mouth at the sensation blooming inside me. Suddenly, a hand trails down my body to the waistband of my bikini bottom; it tickles my skin, back and forth, before finally dipping in.

For a moment, I'm unable to identify whose hand is slowly creeping through my legs. But then I feel Noah grab hold of both my breasts as he sucks one nipple into his mouth before moving on to the other. It immediately becomes clear whose long, thick fingers are slipping between my slick folds. I gasp when the tip of his finger collides with my clit, sending a shock wave into my lower belly. My body arches upwards, my chest pressing further against Noah's mouth.

"You're so fucking wet, Vixen. I could easily slip inside of you," Gabe says as he removes himself from my lips and kisses my neck. "Just like this."

He shoves one wide digit into my tight channel, making me cry out from the sudden intrusion. Noah lets go of one breast and begins to tug at the strings on one side of my bottom until they fall apart, giving Gabe better access with his hand. Noah then returns his attention to my chest as Gabe finger fucks my pussy.

I'm panting, moaning, and whimpering at the explosion of sensations taking over my body. I'm not sure if it's the combination of them touching me everywhere at the same time or if it's just *them*. But nothing has ever felt this good in my life.

I'm already so close.

Noah suddenly bites hard onto my nipple, and I lose it. My body jumps over the cliff's edge as I squeeze down on Gabe's finger. He continues to push into me, rougher, eager to feed my orgasm as I cry out, over and over, moaning as they keep working me through this eruption that makes my body quiver against them.

When my orgasm begins to dwindle down, I open my eyes wide, feeling almost in shock at how quickly they were able to make me come. "Holy shit..."

Gabe chuckles. "That felt so fucking good around my fingers." He brings his lips to mine once, then pulls back. "Look at that, Noh. Look how beautifully her pupils are blown. Fucking sexy, Vixen," he says, looking me over.

I peer down just as Noah removes his mouth from my breast. He licks his lips before a seductive smirk takes over. "Magnificent," he replies in his deep, smooth voice.

I feel a blush creep over my cheeks as he watches me. I shouldn't be blushing over a compliment like that; these two constantly tell me how beautiful I am. But every time Noah looks at me the way he is now, I feel like he's seeing into my soul. Like he sees me. And it makes that knot in my stomach tighten harder, makes those butterflies flutter faster.

Makes my heart beat stronger.

His eyes darken as he reads me, as if he knows exactly what I'm thinking, as if he sees the effect he has on me. He comes back up to my face, his hand cupping my cheek. "My turn," he tells Gabe as he crashes his lips to mine.

I remove one hand from the stony surface and bring it up to his nape, pulling him closer as I melt against him. Gabe slowly removes his finger from inside me, and I whimper at the loss of his touch and open my eyes once more, while Noah kisses along my jaw. I watch as Gabe brings his slick fingers up to his mouth and licks them clean.

I hadn't even realized they were still in me, and there were three. That's how quickly my body got used to his presence, as if having three of his thick fingers deep inside my pussy was an everyday thing.

I stare, completely entranced, as he finishes swiping his tongue around his fingers. "Good," he finally says to Noah. "Because I was planning on devouring something else next." He smirks, then jumps back into the body of water and grabs hold of my thighs, spreading my legs wide open for him in one quick move.

My body stiffens on instinct. This is the part I hate, the one where men try to take charge, where they place you how they want you and press down if you try to move. But that's not how I work, not anymore. I take over in the bedroom. I decide what I want to do or not. It's the only way for me to feel in control. Something I desperately need.

My therapist says it's a form of PTSD from all the unspeakable things Victor and his friends did to me. That certain touches, movements, noises, or even smells will trigger me and take me back to those days. Make my brain react as if I was still there, still trapped under his evil hand.

It's what I feared most about being with Gabriel.

He's unpredictable. He acts on instinct. If he wants to hug you, he'll hug you. If he wants to kiss you, he'll kiss you. No warning, No notice. He just takes what he wants. Whereas Noah always gives me time to adjust, always signals me first before making a move. And even when he does, it's always tentative. Cautious.

I feel the panic setting in as I watch Gabe's hands holding my legs in place. My heart beats overtime as I try to regain some semblance of control.

I'm here.

I'm now.

I'm with Noah and Gabe.

They don't want to hurt me.

They won't hurt me.

I'm here.

I'm now.

Noah pulls away from me; I can feel his eyes reading me once more. But I can't look away; I can't take my eyes off his fingers that dig into my thighs. But they're not Gabriel's anymore... they're Victor's.

"Ellis," Noah says calmly, but I hear the warning in his voice. He knows I'm seconds away from freaking out.

I'm about to push away, kick him off. I'm about to tell them to stop, to get up and leave. But then Gabe looks up at me with that beautiful, dazzling smile. The smile I once found annoying, but now find endearing.

And something happens. The panic that was on the verge of bursting suddenly fades until I can no longer feel it sizzling inside of me, vanishing completely. Now all I feel is warmth at the smile he's offering me.

His hands lose their grip on my legs as he begins to glide them up and down in a soothing way. "You still with me, Vixen?" he asks softly.

"I'm still with you," I whisper back as I let out a breath and blink away the fog in my mind.

"That's my girl." His smile glows brighter.

Noah's hand comes to my hair, fingers gliding through the strands. When I turn my gaze to him, I find his eyes roaming over my features. "Are you okay?" I nod with certainty as I continue to do my breathing exercise. "Good, can you lean back on your elbows for me? And scoot closer to the edge for him."

I bring myself closer to the edge as instructed, keeping my legs spread, then lean back on my elbows. Noah comes back down to my mouth, our tongues colliding with each other as they reacquaint like long-lost lovers.

A trail of wet kisses climbs up my leg, starting at my ankle, up to my knee, then right along my inner thigh until I feel Gabe's warm breath over my center. But then it disappears, and the kisses resume on my other leg. Finally, I feel him again where I desperately want him.

I pull away from Noah to watch Gabe as the tip of his nose presses against my clit, and he breathes me in. "Mmm, you smell delicious, Vixen." He brings his tongue out, barely grazing my bud with it. But still, I feel it everywhere. "How many orgasms should we give her, Noh?"

Noah kisses my shoulder, his hand kneading my breast once more. "Hmm, eight."

My eyes widen as I turn to him. "Eight?! Why eight?"

"For how many months you've made us wait." Gabe smirks before grazing my clit with his teeth.

"Ahh!" My head drops back. "I can't come eight times. That's too much."

They both chuckle as I look back down at Gabe between my spread legs. "We'll see about that." He winks, then dives in. His mouth wraps over my pussy, tongue lapping up my folds, then circles my little bud filled with nerves.

"Oh, fuck me! Yes!" I moan out as Noah comes back to kissing every inch of my skin.

His hand works around me to undo my bikini completely. First the top, throwing it to the side, then the bottom that was still attached at one end, letting it fall fully open beneath me.

I can see the outline of his thick cock through his rapidly tightening swim trunks. I reach my hand out that's closest to him and glide my fingernails over it before gripping it through his shorts. He growls in response to my touch, and his shaft twitches in my hold.

He comes back to play with my nipples as I continue to rub him through the fabric. *I'm starting to think he's a tit guy. Sucks for him, I don't have much to show.* My body hums with pleasure as Gabe continues to work my pussy with his mouth. I feel my core tingling as another orgasm begins to build slowly within me.

I reach higher to his waistband and begin to slip my hand in, but Noah places his over my wrist, stopping me. "You don't have to do that, Kitten. We only want to please you."

"I want to, Noah. I want you in my mouth," I breathe.

He growls again but lets my wrist go. I slide it in, wrapping my fingers around his girth as he sits up on his knees and lowers his shorts, letting me pull it out and into view. My eyes hood with lust as I watch my hand stroke up and down.

He has a beautiful dick, matching the rest of him. I never thought I'd say a penis was beautiful, but Noah's is exactly that. Its thickness is just perfect, where I can wrap my hand around it with just a little gap left between my fingers. Which tells me I'll feel him deliciously without it stretching me out painfully.

But the length. *Wow.* That's a long dick, I'm not sure he'll be able to fit it all inside me. The best part, though, the one that has me squirming and my stomach tightening even more, is the slight curve near the head of his cock. A curve that will definitely make him hit my G-spot with every thrust.

I lean in as best as I can while still supporting my upper body weight and flatten my tongue against his shaft, starting at the bottom, all the way up to his mushroom head. I lick up the white bead of precum that's slipping out as his eyes blaze with fire while watching me.

Gabe suddenly sucks hard on my clit while pushing a finger inside me at that exact moment, making me open my mouth wide and cry out with the tip of Noah's length brushing against my lips.

He caresses my cheek with the back of his knuckles as I lick my lips once, then part them again and bring them down his long cock. I take him as far as I can, but even once he hits the back of my throat, I can still wrap my hand around him with some wiggle room left.

I moan around his shaft, eyes rolling back in my head as my legs begin to tremble. I pull back, swirling my tongue around the tip, then take him into my mouth again. When he touches my throat this time, I take a deep breath through my nose and relax my jaw and throat, letting him slide even deeper in. *Thank the gods for not having a gag reflex.*

"Fuck, Kitten. Your mouth feels fucking amazing. All wet and warm." His head tips back as he closes his eyes for a moment, but then his gaze comes back to me.

"Can you take it all?" he asks.

There are still a few inches of him left, yet he's already in my throat. I'm panting and squirming against Gabe's hand and mouth, whimpering and moaning as he brings me to the edge, over and over again. But right as I'm about to tip over, he slows his pace, changing position.

He's torturing me.

I nod in response as I continue to bob my head up and down his length, taking him farther every time. A desperate need to feel all of him inside me takes over, whether it's my mouth or my pussy.

"You're such a good girl for us, Kitten," he praises me. I expect those two words to hit me and send me spiraling again, but they don't. Not when they come from them. *I want to be their good girl...*

His hand moves to my nape, slightly tugging on my hair as he pulls me off his dick. "Take a deep breath for me, sweetheart." I do as he says, despite my need to cry and moan at Gabe's touches.

Noah nudges my lips with the head of his cock, and I open for him. He pushes all the way back as I breathe out but hits a bit of resistance on the way. "Relax, Kitten. Another deep breath through the side of your mouth. Then breathe out through your nose."

Once again, I obey as he pushes the rest of the way in with one thrust. *Holy fuck.* I've never had a dick that far down before. And it feels amazing to hear the grunts coming from his mouth.

He moves his hips slightly, not enough to pull out completely, but just enough to feel him going up and down. I take small calming breaths along the way every time he pulls back and exhale when he pushes back in. His free hand comes up to cup my cheek, while the other stays behind my head.

"So perfect," he whispers as tears begin to leak from the corner of my eyes, then he turns his face toward Gabe and smirks. "Make her come."

Either they're in sync, or Gabe was just waiting for the word, because the second Noah tells him to make me come. It happens. With one powerful suck on my clit and the curl of his fingers inside me, I'm crying out around Noah's cock, coming out all muffled as I fight for air. My hips buck up against Gabe as he rides out my orgasm with me.

I feel Noah's hand against my head, holding me in place. But he's not really; there's no actual pressure against it. If I wanted to pull back, I could. But I don't want to. There's something euphoric about this feeling, having Gabe eating me out while Noah's deep inside my mouth. I want more of it; I want both of them inside me.

Once I finally come down from an orgasm that felt like it lasted a lifetime, when in reality it was only seconds, I pull away from Noah, gasping for air just as Gabe finishes cleaning me up with his mouth.

"Two," Gabe says with a smirk as he kisses my inner thigh. "You need to have a taste, Noh. Come taste how delicious she is."

"That's exactly what I planned on doing," Noah answers as he dips down to press his lips to mine.

He then disappears into the water, while Gabe hops out and takes Noah's place at my side. Noah's hands take hold of my legs as he lifts them slowly over his shoulder; his eyes stay on mine the whole time as he brings his hands to my hips next.

"Is this okay?" he asks quietly, pulling me slightly closer to him.

"Yes."

They barely give me any time to adjust to the changed positions before Noah's mouth is devouring my pussy. His facial hair tickles my sensitive skin, making me shiver all over, while Gabe pushes down his swim shorts.

He fists his cock, stroking it a few times as I whimper and shake against Noah's tongue. I'm so sensitive right now that every little flick makes me see stars. *I'll never make it to eight without passing out.*

Gabe's cock is just as beautiful, yet completely different from Noah's. His isn't as long and doesn't have a curve at the tip, but it's much thicker. Much, much thicker. *Ooh... That stretch is definitely going to hurt a little. But it's a sexy dick, so totally worth it.*

Jesus, what have they done to me? Is every penis suddenly beautiful? Or am I simply so far gone that everything about them appeals to me?

Gabe fists my hair with one hand as he guides my open moaning mouth to his cock. He swipes the tip along my lips first, spreading his precum all over them as I slip my tongue out to lick them clean, humming with satisfaction.

"You like how I taste, Vixen?" He grins.

"Yes. I want more," I beg breathlessly.

"Then open wide." And I do just that as he pushes my head down his shaft. "Fuuuuck! Your mouth might be my new favorite home." His words encourage me as I bob up and down greedily.

"That's it, baby. Suck my cock like the fucking queen you are."

My eyes snap open at his choice of words as I look up and find him smirking at me. Memories of our first encounter flash before my eyes, his words sounding just like those I once spoke to him.

~ *Eight Months Ago* ~

I stand in the middle of Aubrey's brother's kitchen, surrounded by a whole bunch of strangers and feeling entirely out of place, when a devilishly sexy blond man with a boyish smile walks up to me.

"Hey, I'm Gabriel. Famous goaltender for the New York Griffins." He takes my hand in his and kisses it. "How about you and I spend some alone time after we're done here?" he says with a smile.

The throat of a man equally as handsome with short dark hair clears next to him. "Unless you don't mind my friend here joining us," the blond tells me with a signature grin I'm sure makes all the women he tries to conquer melt.

Wow. This guy really has no shame.

A giggle leaves my lips as I close my eyes and tilt my head down timidly, pretending to be falling for his charm. If he knew anything about me, he'd know that I'm far from timid and that I despise men like him who think they can have whatever they want.

Gabriel's smile widens as I open my eyes, clearly thinking he's won another foolish woman over with his charming smile. Fluttering my lashes seductively, I take a step into him and rest my palms against his chest, playing along with the game.

"You know what I love?" I begin with a sultry voice. "A man who treats his woman with respect and dignity, who treats her like the queen she is. One who would do anything for her, who would give her anything her heart demands. A man who worships the ground she walks on, who attends to all her needs. All her deepest desires."

I slide my hand up to the back of Gabriel's head, fisting his shaggy blond hair through my fingers, and bring my lips an inch away from his as I peer down at them. "And you, Pretty Boy, are anything but." I let go and push him away. "So, if you ever plan on getting into my pants like you seem to desperately want, prepare to beg on your knees." I turn my back to him, my electric blue hair whipping him in the face as I walk away.

~ *Present Day* ~

He grazes my cheek with his knuckles as I keep watching him, seeing him under a new light. "My queen," he whispers. "You've always had me on my knees, Vixen.

Right from the very start."

And with his final words, I fall apart once more. I come all over Noah's mouth as his hands tighten around my hips slightly to keep me in place, my body jerking violently against him. Within seconds, my arms give out, no longer able to support me as I continue to tremble. My mouth pops off Gabe's length as I crash to the hard surface beneath me, panting crazily.

"Oh my God..."

Chapter Eighteen

NOAH

What's the magical number?

I watch Veronica's body collapse to the ground, her limbs still twitching from her latest orgasm. We'll never be able to give her eight in one session. She's already super sensitive as it is, but now I can visibly see her pulse throbbing in her clit. One little touch there now feels like a torch to her.

Gabe lowers himself above Veronica and kisses her parted lips. "Three." He smiles down at her.

I jump out of the water and settle on my knees at her other side, brushing the wet hair away from her sticky face. "You good, Kitten?"

She giggles a bit deliriously. "So good."

"You want more?"

"Yes," she whispers. "I want all of you." Then reaches up with one hand, pulling me down and pressing her lips to mine. "Both of you," she finishes, turning away from me to do the same to Gabe.

"We're all yours, Vixen. But we have a problem," Gabe says, making a face.

"What is it?" Veronica furrows her brows.

"We didn't bring any condoms." He gives her a disappointed smile.

"I told you I have the implant. And I'm always safe." She offers with a small shrug.

We all know it's risky. And normally I would never promote the thought of unprotected sex. But I've craved Veronica for so long, I fear going without her for even just an extra hour might kill me.

"We get checked regularly, and we never go without. It's our general rule. Plus, I haven't had sex since my last testing," I tell her, hoping that might seal the deal. *At least, for me.*

"You haven't?" Gabe frowns. When I shake my head, his frown deepens. "Neither have I..." Now it's my turn to frown.

The realization hits us right in the face at the same time. Gabe and I have always had a hookup at least twice a week. I know that might make us sound like pigs, but it was our thing. We were single, we enjoyed women and having fun, so we didn't care what people thought and simply lived our best life. But now that Veronica has finally come into the picture, it's like we completely forgot about our previous lives and only focus on our new center. Her.

"Why do you both look disappointed with that revelation?" Veronica asks with a soft laugh. She's still lying on the floor, looking up at us both.

Gabe shakes his head. "Not disappointed. More like we didn't notice how long it had been."

"Why? When was your last test?"

"Beginning of June," I say as I push my fingers through her hair at the side of her head.

She snorts. "Does this not happen often?"

Gabe and I both shake our heads. "Never," he says.

Her eyes widen when the date registers. She looks at Gabe, then at me. "I never asked you guys to do that…"

"We know. But why go sleep elsewhere when the woman we really want is standing right in front of us? Finally, giving us a chance," Gabe says with a warm smile.

"Tell me something, Veronica. Have you been with Nathan recently?" I'm not judging. Even if she says yes, it won't change a thing. But I have a feeling I already know the answer to my question.

She goes to respond but then closes her mouth and frowns, similar to what we did minutes ago. "Actually, no. The last time was the day I started working for you two." *Exactly what I thought.*

"And why is that?"

She looks at me, eyes searching mine for a few seconds. "Because it didn't feel right," she whispers quietly, like a secret she'd normally never dare speak.

"Now you understand why we haven't either," I say, lowering to claim her lips again.

Gabe kisses her neck, then down over her collarbone and to her breast, sucking a nipple into his mouth. "So is that a go, Vixen? Because I really want to be inside you right now."

She moans. "I want you inside of me, too."

"Fuck yes!" He moves to her legs but stops. "Can you move up for me, baby?"

She scoots backwards, giving Gabe room to settle between her legs as he picks her bikini bottom out from beneath her and tosses it to the side. He then takes his shorts off completely and kneels between her spread thighs. He fists his cock and leans in over Veronica's body, his free hand supporting him beside her waist.

"You still wet for me, Vixen?" He presses the head of his dick against her entrance, rubbing it up and down as I watch them with hungry eyes.

I've always been into watching people have sex; it's as much of a turn-on as doing the act itself. The way their bodies move, the way they respond, the noises they make. How if you watch really carefully, you know exactly when the woman is about to come. It's enthralling. I guess that makes me a voyeur.

"Of course, you still are," Gabe continues. "You're such a good girl for us." He begins to push in slowly.

Veronica's back arches slightly as he intrudes her body, a gasp falling from her lips. "Oh fuck!"

Her hand comes down to my thigh as I kneel beside her, nails digging into my skin. She brings her other hand up to her lips and bites down on her knuckles, muffling her sounds of pleasure as he stretches her out.

I lift my hand to her mouth, softly taking her small wrist between my fingers and pulling it away. "Don't hide those beautiful noises from us, Kitten. We want to hear every single one of them."

"Oh God, holy shit!" she cries out as he seats himself fully inside her.

"Fuck, you're so tight around my cock, baby. You feel so fucking good," he groans. "I don't think I'll last very long," he admits with a chuckle, then begins to rock his hips slowly.

Veronica cries out as he picks up speed, thrusting more brutally into her within seconds. I fist my cock and begin to stroke myself leisurely, and my Kitten's eyes fall on my hand as she licks her lips, her chest rising and falling heavily.

"Do you want me in your mouth again, Kitten?"

"Yes, please." I have a feeling our girl loves giving head. And she's damn good at it.

Not a lot of women are able to take me all the way. I know I'm longer than average, and even those who can deep throat don't usually take me to the hilt. But Veronica, she did it like a pro and was even able to keep me down her throat, without panicking, for longer than I thought. Which doesn't seem to be an easy task since most can't manage it.

She lifts to her elbows like she was earlier as I move closer to her, then eagerly takes me into her mouth, humming as her eyelids flutter with satisfaction. Like she can't get enough of my taste on her tongue. With how powerful Gabe rocks into her, causing her body to jerk back and forth, it makes it hard for her to bob properly. So with one hand cupping the back of her head, I help guide her down my shaft.

"That's it, Kitten. Take me as deep as you can." She takes me all the way once more, and my eyes roll to the back of my head. *Fuck, this feels so good. I could come right now, but I won't. The only place I want to come in this moment is deep in her pussy.*

She pulls back quickly, her hand jerking me off instead as she whimpers and moans. "Oh fuck! Yes, yes. YESSS! Don't stop! Holy fuck, I'm gonna come!" Her head falls back as she cries out his name. "Gabriel!"

Veronica falls back down, body arching fully off the ground as she quivers intensely. Her hand still holds tightly onto my dick, squeezing it to the point of pain as droplets leak out of my tip.

"That's it, baby. Milk my fucking cock." Gabe thrusts into her one last time and holds still. "FUCK, VIXEN!" he growls with a moan as he shoots his load deep inside her, then drops down on top of her as they both pant, coming down from their explosive moment.

Eventually he lifts his head and kisses her belly as he murmurs, "Four."

"I can't do eight. I can't. There's no way," she says, still gasping for air.

"Then one more will have to do for now." I remove her hand from my dick and lean in to kiss her. "You'll give us the remaining three tonight." I smile against her lips and pull away, moving to her parted legs that lie limp on the ground as Gabe moves out of the way.

He settles behind her head and lifts her up by the armpits until her back rests on his chest, with his own leaning against the wall behind him. He reaches forward and grabs hold of her thighs, lifting them up and open for me, securing her in place and preventing her from moving.

Instantly, I see this position won't work. She wakes up from her dazed state in a flash, and a look of panic sets in her eyes. She begins to shake her head from side to side, fighting against his hold. "No... no, no, no. Please. Please, don't hold me down..." she urges out in a hurry.

"Ellis, let her go," I bark out quickly.

He drops her legs immediately, letting them fall back down to the ground, and keeps his hands up. Gabe understands how PTSD works; he lives with it daily. There's a reason why Gabe never gets into fights and does everything to avoid them. It's one of his biggest triggers.

Sometimes I wonder if that's why he chose to be a goalie, since it's the position that rarely gets in any fights. Ellis is a fantastic hockey player and could easily play any position and be great at it. From what he told me, he played defense up until college, where he then changed it up to goalie.

I focus back on Veronica, who's taking deep breaths as she tries to shake herself back to the present. Carefully, I press my hand to her thigh and rub up and down. "Kitten, you know we would never hurt you, right?"

Her eyes flick up to mine as she swallows, then nods slowly. "I know. I'm sorry."

Gabe's hands come down to her arms, imitating my movements. "You have nothing to be sorry about, baby. We understand you have limits, and we'll work with them." He kisses the side of her head. "We'll figure it all out together, Vixen."

"Okay," she says quietly.

Having the green light, I pass my arms beneath her legs until the backs of her knees rest on the inside crook of my elbows. My hands grab her hips as I lift her pelvis slightly off the floor. The position brings her lower on Gabe, her head now resting on his abs instead of his chest.

"Is this okay?" I ask once I'm properly positioned. My dick is still hard, and if I'm being honest, I don't think it ever softens around Veronica.

She nods as Gabe's hands begin to fondle her breasts, bringing her mind back into the moment. She whimpers when he pinches her nipples, twisting them around and pulling slightly. I look between her legs and see some of Gabe's cum leaking out of her, but it doesn't bother me.

I'm used to it by now, and it only serves as extra lube for me. Which means there's no need to go in slowly. Gabe has already stretched her out. Mine might not be as wide, but it's much longer. So, I'll be hitting spots deep inside her he didn't, and that's a turn-on in itself. I'll cause her a different kind of pain, one she'll love and lose her mind over.

While she's focused on Gabe's hands playing with her body, I grab hold of my cock and position it at her entrance. Once I'm well aligned, I replace her leg properly and thrust into her in one swift movement.

"AHHH! FUCK! OH FUCK, fuck, fuck!" Her muscles stiffen, her thighs trying to close but my arms and body prevent them from doing so. Her pussy clenches around my girth, squeezing it painfully. She's already close. "Oh God! I'm going to come again!"

I tighten my grip on her hips and slam repeatedly into her as she tries to squirm out of my hold. *Fuck, she feels deliciously good. Now I see why Ellis said he wouldn't last. I don't think I will either.* I grunt and groan as I continue my assault on her beautiful, tight pussy. Despite her tan, a sexy blush spreads over her entire body as she comes undone for the fifth time.

"OH, NOAH! Yes! Oh my God, Noah, Noah, Noah!" she chants as her walls pulse around me, and her legs shake against my arms.

I don't let up. Even when her orgasm subsides, I continue to plow into her forcefully with everything I have. Sweat drips down my forehead and back, the sound of skin slapping against skin reverberating within the walls of the cave.

Releasing one hip, I adjust her legs higher until they both rest on my shoulders. With one arm, I hold her legs in place, and with my free hand, I bring my thumb down to her clit, pressing down on it.

"Ow! Oh God, no. I can't! No more. No more." Veronica shakes her head from side to side briskly.

"You can, Kitten. Just one more," I tell her, not slowing down my thrusts.

"Give us just one more, baby, and we'll let you rest after. I promise," Gabe whispers to her as he glides his fingers through her purple hair.

I rub my thumb in circles over her clit softly. I know she's beyond sensitive right now, and I don't want to hurt her. It only takes a few swipes of my thumb and a few deep thrusts into her pussy to have her coming all over again, screaming at the top of her lungs. She crushes my cock in a vice grip, making me explode inside her, my seed filling her tight channel to the brim.

My vision goes fuzzy, spots dancing in my eyes as my knees weaken, and I lose my grip on her legs. Her body falls back to the ground as I tumble above her, catching myself at the last second before I crush her.

"Holy shit," I gasp. I've never come so hard in my life. I swear I was seconds away from passing out.

Veronica lies against Gabe, mumbling incomprehensible words with her eyes closed, her body still twitching every few seconds. Gabe looks down at her and chuckles. "Bro, I think we broke her." He smiles and caresses her cheek. "You did so well, baby."

She hums and smiles, turning onto her side and cuddling into him as I remove my body from above hers.

I sit back on my heels and watch the mixture of our arousals drip from her swollen cunt. It's a beautiful sight. One I want engraved in my mind forever. A soft snore pulls my gaze up to her enchanting face.

"And she's out." I laugh quietly, looking at Veronica's sleeping form.

"I'm guessing six is the magic number to knock her out then." Gabe laughs along with me, then sighs. "Fuck, it's going to be a bitch carrying her back."

I frown. "Why? She's lighter than a hockey bag."

"I don't mean her. I mean the paths we took to get here are going to be tough while holding her."

"Shit, I didn't think about that." I rub the back of my neck.

"Yeah, well, we put her into a coma, so we gotta suck it up and find a way. Because I'm getting hungry, and we have a few hours of walking ahead of us."

His choice of words makes my mood dim slightly as my mind wanders to my sister. *I'll have to call the facility when we get back to the villa, just to make sure all is okay.*

I stand and walk over to my discarded swim trunks, pulling them on, then pick up Veronica's. "Help me get her dressed and we'll head back."

I pass her top over to Gabe and get to work on her bottom. Turning her slowly onto her back, I lift her hips slightly, just enough to get one side of the material beneath her. I pass the top portion between her legs, covering up her still-filled pussy and securing each side in a bow tie.

Gabe remains seated behind her as he works on tying a knot behind her neck, then placing each triangle over her breasts. I get up close and grab each end of the strings at her sides as he lifts her off him. Passing my hands behind her back, I tie another knot there. Then with one arm behind her knees and the other along her back, I lift her off the ground and into my arms. She cuddles up against my chest with a soft sigh and a smile lingering along her lips, head resting in the crook of my neck.

Gabe stands and pulls on his shorts, then exits the cave with me in tow. He steps down from the flat surface and into the water outside the small cave, stretching out his arms my way for me to pass over our sleepy girl. I do just that, and we make our way back to the resort after collecting our footwear at the little hidden beach, exchanging Veronica every thirty minutes or so as to not get exhausted. She barely stirs the whole way back, mumbling occasionally, but never waking.

We really did fuck her to sleep.

Once back at the resort, we debate whether to bring her back to our place or hers but end up deciding hers might be best. She may have agreed to what happened in the cave, but that doesn't mean she'll agree to spend the night with us.

We walk up to her villa and knock on the door, hoping Aubrey is there so we don't have to go hunt her down and explain to everyone why we're carrying Veronica around while she's out cold.

The door swings open seconds later. "Oh, thank God you guys are back. We were starting to get worried." She presses a hand to her chest but then looks down at our girl. "Oh my God! What happened?! Is she okay?"

Gabe smiles brightly. "Oh, baby Ford, she's more than okay. Don't you worry, we took good care of her."

Aubrey blushes intensely in an instant. "Oh lord..."

"Can you show us to her room? So that she can sleep it off a bit. I don't think she's ready to wake up just yet," I ask her.

She nods and moves to the side. "Yes, of course. Just this way." She begins to walk to the right and heads up the few steps to a room.

The layout of their place is identical to ours, so we know our way around immediately. Once I've set her down in bed, Gabe goes into the bathroom and comes back with a warm, wet washcloth. I remove her bikini bottom to let him clean her up as I hunt through her things for something else to put her in.

I find a large gray shirt in one of the drawers that, without a doubt, must belong to a man. I push the irritation of knowing she carries a man's shirt around with her down and bring it over to the bed.

When Gabe's done cleaning her up, he helps me pass her arms and head through the shirt before we put her back down and cover her body with a thin blanket. Then we both kiss her forehead before walking out of the room.

"Fuck, I'm starving," Gabe declares as his stomach growls angrily.

"Do we just leave her here? The gang's already waiting on us to have dinner..." Aubrey seems reluctant to leave Veronica on her own.

"I'll stay back until she wakes up. You guys go eat," I offer.

"You sure?" Gabe asks.

"Yeah, I'm fine. I'd rather she not wake up alone. She might be disoriented a little." *Plus, it will give me time to make my call in private.*

"Okay, we'll let the others know. There's a bit of food in the fridge if you're hungry," Aubrey says as she comes to kiss my cheek, blushing once more.

I don't think Aubrey is attracted to me at all. She just can't hide her emotions even if she tries. And the act of affection, even a friendly one, makes her react. "Thank you for watching over her."

"We'll bring you guys back some food if you aren't there when we leave," Gabe calls as they walk out of the villa.

I go back to Veronica's room and lie down in bed beside her. Instinctively, she turns toward me and places her hand on my chest. "Noah," she whispers in her sleep as she cuddles up to my side. I bring my arm up around her and under her head, placing her how I always wanted her.

Hearing my name fall from her lips as she sleeps tugs at my heart. I can't help watching her, wanting to kiss her and hold her forever. I knew this would happen. I knew she was different.

I knew once I had her, everything would change, that I'd never want to let her go. That she'd become my sole purpose. The center of my universe.

And as of right now, I can say it without a doubt.
I've fallen madly in love with Veronica Masters.

Chapter Nineteen

GABRIEL

Really, Sy? Your mom?

"So… is this like, just for fun? With Ronnie I mean." Aubrey blushes at my side as we walk down the path to reach our friends. "I know Ronnie always says she doesn't want to date, but I think that's a lie. I think she's just afraid to let anyone in. And I know I shouldn't be saying this, but right now, she's confused about her feelings for you both. I just don't want you to hurt her if it is just fun for you guys," she finishes softly.

I look down at my feet. *Do we really come out as such assholes who only think about fucking chicks?* I guess that makes sense since we've never had a relationship with a woman of any type to show them the contrary. But I don't think it's because we didn't want one. We just hadn't found someone we wanted to take that next step with, someone we couldn't stop thinking about. Not until Ronnie.

When I take too long to answer, she continues. "Look, I've known you guys for a while now, and I love you both, but Ronnie's my best friend. I would hate for something to go wrong and then have things be weird between all of us, or her not wanting to hang out with the gang anymore."

I place a hand on her shoulder, stopping her from taking her next step and turning her to face me. "Let me stop you right there." I smile. "I care deeply about Ronnie, and so does Noah. Whatever happened between us three today wasn't just about sex, it was more, and I'm just hoping she saw it that way as well. So maybe if you could put in a good word for us, that would be cool." I chuckle, then sling my arm over her shoulders as we begin walking again.

"I understand your worries, baby Ford. Noah and I haven't shown you the best example of boyfriend material, or any, for that matter. But I promise you, we only have Ronnie's best intentions in mind. I swear." I kiss the side of her head. "Plus, have you ever known us to pursue the same woman for eight months straight without giving up and moving on?"

She giggles. "I guess you have a point there. You two were really pissing her off with all the flirting non-stop."

"Yeah, but she secretly loved it." I look down at her and wink.

"I'm starting to think that may have been the case." She smiles with a soft blush over her cheeks.

We finally make it to our friends, who sit at a long table inside an open-air restaurant. There's a roof, but no walls, giving you direct access to the beach.

"Finally! We were about to start eating without you," Emma calls. "Where's Ronnie and Noah?" She looks behind us, searching for the two missing bodies.

"Ronnie's sleeping, and Noah wanted to stay by her side until she wakes up," I inform her as I take a seat next to Clay, who sits at the head of the table. While Aubrey goes to sit beside Emma on the other side of the table.

"You guys screwed her into a coma, didn't you?" Greyson asks from his seat between his daughter and girlfriend.

I throw my arms up, clasping my hands behind my head with a satisfied grin. "That we did."

"Poor girl." Clay chuckles.

Cecilia giggles. "It's about time."

"I'm honestly surprised it took that long. How long have you two been trying to get her attention? It feels like it's been years," Morgan asks as she stuffs her face with bread in front of me.

"Eight months. Eight orgasms for eight months."

Silas, who's sitting at the other end of the two empty chairs beside me, chokes on his beer, then slaps his hand on the table before bellowing out with laughter. "You guys gave her eight orgasms!? No wonder she's out cold!" He continues to laugh. "The last time I did something like that to Minnie in a short amount of time, she was delirious for a few hours. I honestly started getting worried and wanted to take her to the hospital."

"Actually, she only made it to six, then started babbling stuff that didn't make sense and passed out." I shrug, still smiling smugly. I know I'll probably get yelled at by Vixen once she finds out I've informed all our friends about our little cave experience.

"Still pretty impressive." Sam laughs from his spot between Aubrey and Morgan.

Cecilia narrows her eyes at her husband from her seat at his side, Dante also munching away on bread to her left. "Thank you for telling everyone at the table about our sex life."

"I'm just letting *everyone* at this table know how well I satisfy you," he answers back, enunciating the word *'everyone'* as he looks directly at Sam. *Jesus, he's still going on about this?*

I guess we should put the poor guy out of his misery. He becomes all macho man for no reason every time Sam is around, which is practically every other day since he takes care of the kids. "Hayes, Sam's not going to steal your wife. He's gay," I blurt out.

The table falls silent as Silas frowns and turns to me. "How do you know he's gay?"

"Because he's checked all of us out more times than I can count. Just yesterday at the beach he was eye-fu–" I look at the kids before finishing the word. *Shit, how am I supposed to censor that word?* "Eye-humping you when you were getting out of the water. The man is into you, not your wife!"

His jaw drops open, then he looks around the table as everyone nods, and Sam just shrugs with a smirk. "You all knew?" he asks, appalled.

"Yup. Caught him checking me out the very first day." Greyson chuckles.

"Same here," I add.

Silas turns to Clay next. "Yeah, I've seen him looking a few times, too." He lifts a shoulder. "Plus, Morg told me."

Silas's brows lift to his hairline as he shakes his head a little. "Wow... Minnie, I don't really like our friends right now. Can we temporarily add them to your hit list for the time being?" He looks down at his wife, who's trying desperately not to laugh and gasps. "You knew, too?!"

"I'm sorry." She breaks out in a fit of laughter.

"You let me go on for months about him!" He peeks at Sam. "Sorry about that, man. Didn't mean to be such an A-hole to you. But you get it, right?"

Sam waves him off. "Yeah, I get it. All's good."

"By the way, I'm not into dudes. But I'm flattered."

I laugh. "I'm pretty sure he knew you didn't roll that way, Hayes."

He glares at me. "Just pointing it out." He looks back at Cecilia, keeping the glare on his face, but there's no real anger to it. "You really are an evil woman."

"HA!" She gapes at him. "Me? Evil? You just told everyone at this table that I went coo-coo after you gave me too many orgasms."

"So did he!" He points at me.

"Yeah well, I'm sure Ronnie won't be too happy about that either." She looks at all of us with a wicked smile. "By the way, what he forgot to mention about that story is that he called Mira after."

"Really, Sy? Your mom?" Emma scrunches up her nose.

"I didn't know what to do, she was mumbling non-stop and rolling around in the sheets like someone possessed! I freaked out!" Silas exclaims as a chorus of laughter breaks out.

"You could have called one of us, literally any of us," I tell him, laughing along with the group.

"Seriously," Greyson adds. "That's really weird. I feel so bad for Mira now."

"Imagine me when she asked how I was doing after my orgasm high over family dinner!" Cecilia covers her shame-filled face with her hands.

"Spence must have had a field day with that." Emma giggles.

Spencer, Silas's younger brother, loves to tease people, certainly his older brother. We don't see much of him, but every time we do, he finds something to say to get on Silas's nerves.

"Oh, he did. Still does every time we see him and almost causes a fight between them every single time," Cecilia tells her.

"Okay, how about we eat and stop talking about orgasms? I'm starving! And I feel like Aubrey's about to pop a blood vessel or something with how red she is." Morgan giggles.

We all look at the poor, shy girl, and sure enough, she's redder than I've ever seen her. It's almost alarming. "Sorry, baby Ford. Didn't mean to make you uncomfortable," I offer.

She clears her throat. "It's okay. I'm fine." She smiles timidly now that all the attention is on her.

The girls go on to chat about the foundation that Cecilia and Emma have created, which will be debuting at the end of the month, as food begins to arrive. It's like one of those eight-course meals, where they bring you a bit of everything that's on the menu, one plate at a time.

I watch Morgan continue to pick into the breadbasket every few minutes, her eyes going wide with hunger. She's practically salivating as she spreads a bit of butter over the piece of dough. It's adorable to watch.

"You look absolutely beautiful, Morgan. Pregnancy really suits you," I tell her tenderly.

She looks up as she brings the bread up to her lips but stops short, her eyes glossing over as she smiles. "Thank you, Gabe. That really means a lot." She looks down at the bread, then back up at me as a pink tint appears on her cheeks. "Sorry, I'm just always hungry now. It's horrible."

"You're growing a little human in there, no reason to apologize." I smile.

She smiles back and proceeds to eat. When I look to my side, I find Clay watching her with love in his eyes. This man is obsessed with his wife; they all are. And I get it now, because it's how I feel about my Vixen.

"How does it feel to know you're going to be a dad in just a few more months?" I ask him quietly, not needing everyone to join into our conversation.

He doesn't take his eyes off her as he answers me. "Like freaking bliss." He then swallows and turns to me. "You know, for a moment I started wondering if I was the problem. I had an appointment booked for after the playoffs to check if everything was okay."

Morgan places her hand above his that rests on the table. "I never doubted you. It just took us a little more time than others, but it will have been a thousand percent worth it."

He lowers in to kiss her, and instantly, I wish Ronnie was here. *I miss her already.*

A few hours later, Aubrey and I are walking back toward our villas. Ronnie and Noah never showed up for dinner, so I'm guessing they're still back at her place. I won't hide the fact that I'm a bit jealous that he got to spend all this alone time with her, but I know I need to deal with that. She's our girl, both of us, which means we have to share in every way.

We arrive at the big mahogany doors to Aubrey and Ronnie's villa. Brey grabs onto the handle, ready to push the door open, but stops herself and spins to look at me, her cheeks growing pinker by the second. "What if they're... you know?" she whispers with wide eyes.

I chuckle and shake my head at her innocence. "They're not." *At least, I hope they aren't.* That would piss me off a bit. We haven't discussed whether one-on-ones are permitted or not.

"Are you sure?"

"I promise." I smile, hoping like hell I'm right.

She lets out a breath. "Okay."

"Shouldn't you be used to hearing people fuck by now? I mean, you did live with Grey for some time. And from what I've heard, Ronnie did bring men around too." I laugh.

"Yes, but that doesn't mean I enjoy hearing it, least of all seeing it. I've seen and heard enough. If I can avoid it, I do." She finally takes the handle again and swings the door open.

We step in, and in the distance, I spot Noah and Ronnie on one of the lounge chairs on the deck outside. Cuddling. *Oh, thank God.* We walk over to them, and once Ronnie sees me, she smiles with affection.

"Gabriel." *Fuck, I love hearing my name on her lips.*

I lower in front of her, just as she reaches up to cup my cheek, sweeping my lips over hers. "Hi, baby. How are you feeling?"

I pull back and glide my fingers through her humid strands. *She must have taken a shower recently.* A quick glance at Adler tells me he wasn't in there with her since he doesn't have that freshly showered look.

"I'm good, although I don't remember getting back to my room." She giggles softly.

"Yeah, we figured you might be a little disoriented when you woke up. Have you been awake for long?"

She shakes her head as Noah answers. "She woke up half an hour ago and hasn't eaten yet." *Fuck, I forgot to bring them back food like I said I would.*

I smile down at her. "Are you hungry, Vixen?"

Her eyes glitter with excitement. "Starving."

"Want me to make you something?"

She grabs onto my hand as if I might take back my offer. *Never.* I love cooking for my woman and watching the joy light up her face as she takes the first bite.

"Oh, please! I was a little bummed I wouldn't be getting any of your special cooking for two weeks. I mean, other food is great, but it's not yours," she finishes softly, stroking my ego just right.

God, she's perfection.

I cradle her face with my hands, grazing her lips with mine. "I'd cook every day of my life for you, Vixen. Any place, any time. If it puts a smile on your face, I'll do it all for you." I seal our lips together as she sighs with content.

I stand back up and walk over to their kitchen, looking at what I have to work with before getting to work on feeding my girl.

An hour later, we're all seated outside on the deck. Ronnie and Noah have both eaten the entire platter of fresh fruits and sandwiches I made them. There weren't many choices in their fridge and pantry, so I went simple.

"God, Gabe. How is it possible that even a basic sandwich tastes amazing coming from you? I make some like this all the time, and they don't taste half as good. What's your magic trick?" Ronnie asks as she shoves the last bite into her mouth.

"I make them with love?" I offer with a shrug.

Everyone laughs. "That sounds like something my mom would say," Ronnie says, still laughing, but then it ends in a sad sigh.

"Do you miss them?" I ask quietly.

She looks at me and smiles sadly. "Yeah... despite everything that went down, I love my parents. It's been hard staying away. This is the only thing I have left of them. It was my dad's," she says, touching her baggy shirt.

The mood instantly dims around us. I don't know how Ronnie feels; I never had a loving relationship with my parents. But as I picture my friends, my newfound family that I love, if I ever had to leave them behind, it would devastate me.

"Why do you have to stay away?" Aubrey asks softly. Sometimes she's so quiet and still that we forget she's there. Like in this moment, where I talked about something Ronnie didn't want people to know.

I look at Ronnie and mouth, "I'm sorry," with an apologetic tight smile.

"It's okay," she whispers back from her seat beside me.

Aubrey looks at all of us, waiting for an answer. "Does it have something to do with whoever you saw at the mall?" She's quick to put things together.

Ronnie takes a deep breath, then lets it out. "Yeah, it does."

Brey nods her head in comprehension, then reaches across the table and squeezes Ronnie's hand. "You don't need to tell me anything if you don't want to."

Ronnie shakes her head. "No, I should. You're my best friend, Brey. You always have my back, even when you don't know what's going on. You did that day at the mall, so you deserve to know."

She takes another big inhale and begins to tell Aubrey about her past, her parents, and Victor. Although she doesn't go into detail about what exactly he did to her, like she did with us, which is for the better. Aubrey is innocent; she shouldn't be subjected to the cruel parts of this world even if she knows they exist.

Aubrey has tears in her eyes as she listens carefully to Ronnie's story. "And you went through all this alone? You've been living with this fear for years on your own?"

"I didn't really have a choice. What was I supposed to do? Tell everyone and have them all worry about me? I don't want to be seen as the poor, scared girl anymore. I worked too hard on myself not to be that way and let others treat me as such."

That's my girl, always so brave and strong.

"You're right. I'm still sorry you went through that, but you have us now, and we'll always be here for you. And you don't need to worry; I won't tell the others." Aubrey smiles, still holding her hand.

"Thank you."

Feeling like it's time to change the mood and subject, I spring out of my chair.

"How about a midnight swim before bed?" I point at the pool behind us.

Ronnie smiles brightly. "I'm in! Brey?"

"If you guys want to be alone, it's fine. You don't need to include me." She shrugs.

"Don't be ridiculous, baby Ford. Jump in the water with us." I grin, then slip into the pool. I still haven't changed since we left the resort this morning, so all I've got on are my swim shorts.

"Okay, let me just get changed first," Brey says.

"Yeah, me too. We'll be right back," Ronnie says as they scoot out of their chairs and wander indoors together. While Noah gets into the pool and sits on the same bench as me, leaving just enough space between us for Vixen.

"Is she really okay?" I ask him now that we're alone. A small part of me worries that Ronnie might regret what happened today.

He smirks. "Yeah, just a little sore. We'll have to go easy on her tonight."

I grin. *Good, we were on the same page. She does still owe us two orgasms after all.*

"GABRIEL, I DON'T KNOW WHAT YOUR MIDDLE NAME IS, ELLIS! You told everyone about what happened at the cave?!" Vixen comes marching back with an angry scowl a few minutes later.

I give a disappointed look at Aubrey, who stands behind her. "You told her?"

"Don't be angry with her, I'm happy she told me because I don't think you would have. I can't believe you did that, Gabe! Do you know how mortifying that is for me?!"

"Oh, come on, it's not that bad," I whine.

"It really was," Aubrey says.

I point at her. "No. It wasn't. Your virgin ears might have been horrified, but everyone else just found it funny. Then Silas and Cecilia had one of their fake fights that ends in punishing sex, and that was the end of that. No one said another word about it." I shrug. "Oh! But Silas now knows Sam is gay, so that was pretty funny to watch."

"Shit, I can't believe I missed that." Ronnie comes over to stand behind me and Noah. "His reaction must have been priceless."

"It was. I don't think I've ever seen him so shocked in his life." I chuckle.

She comes into the water and settles between me and Noah, while Aubrey sits on the opposite bench. I place my hand on her thigh under the warm water and glide my thumb along her skin.

"I'm sorry I told everyone what we did. But they practically guessed it on their own."

She sighs and drops her head to my shoulder. "I forgive you. But maybe next time, don't share *all* the details."

"Okay, promise." I kiss the top of her head, then sigh with content now that my girl is at my side. After a few minutes of peaceful silence, I speak up once more. "I can't believe Morgan and Clay are finally having a baby."

"Oh, I know. I'm so excited for them. They deserve it so much," Aubrey says with so much love lacing her voice.

"Isn't it crazy how much our group has changed in the last years?" Noah chuckles. "Just a few years ago, we were all bachelors. Well, except for Clay. Now we're all settling down and having kids."

"Right?" I say, agreeing with him. "But I'm happy about all the changes. I love our little family." I squeeze Ronnie's thigh a little in my hand. "Although, you know what that means?" I smile, turning my gaze to Aubrey.

Her eyes widen. "What?"

"There's only one of us left to settle down," Noah tells her, and I hear Ronnie giggling softly against my shoulder.

Aubrey's brows furrow. "Who?" she asks ignorantly.

"You." I beam.

Her eyes almost bug out of her head, heat rising along her face. "Oh, no. No, no. I'm good alone."

"Ah, come on, baby Ford. There must be a man out there that you're interested in."

The tips of her ears turn red, along with her neck and nose. "Nope." Her voice comes out squeaky. She clears her throat before speaking again. "There's no one." She then gives us the fakest imitation of a yawn and stands from the pool. "It's getting late, I'm going to head in. Goodnight, guys." She quickly scurries into the house.

"Aw, Aubrey. I didn't mean to make you uncomfortable. I'm sorry," I call after her, but she's already vanished. *Shit, now I feel bad.*

"It's okay, just leave her. It's a touchy subject," Vixen whispers to us. "There's someone, but it's complicated."

Noah and I share a look. We aren't stupid; we've seen the lingering looks between Aubrey and Coach. But I get what she means; that is a complicated situation. If I had a baby sister who had a thing with my much older boss, I would probably lose my shit. But Aubrey is so pure and kind; she'd never put that kind of pressure on her brother. Which explains why the conversation makes her uncomfortable.

Having enough of talking about other people. I pass my hand through Ronnie's hair and pull her head back. "We're finally alone," I breathe against her parted lips.

"On a scale of one to ten, how sore are you right now?"

She moans softly as my hand trails up her thigh to the junction of her legs. "I can't remember," she whispers.

I smile. "That's our girl." Then I claim her lips as Noah detaches her bathing suit and kisses her neck.

We end the night taking turns in making our girl come repeatedly until she's a gabbling sweaty mess and can no longer stand on her own. *I'm guessing eleven orgasms in less than twenty-four hours will do that to you.* We then bring her to bed and cuddle with her until she falls into a deep sleep.

Once she's gone for the night, I climb out of bed, waving goodnight to Noah, and head over to our villa. Where I jump in the shower and get changed, then settle into my bed, wishing I was still with my Vixen.

But I can't risk it, as much as it kills me to be away from her.

Chapter Twenty

VERONICA

Mommy card and heartbreak.

~ Two Weeks Later ~

We're finally on our way home from our amazing getaway. As much as I loved our vacation, I'm happy to be home. I've missed the city and all its noise. I've missed the people and having everything a step away. There's always something new to try in New York City.

But most of all, I've missed coffee. There was some on the island, but it just didn't taste the same. *Okay, that's a lie. The thing I've missed the most is Gabe's cooking. And he promised me a five-star dinner when we get back. So... YAY!*

Most of our days on the island were spent exploring, swimming, tanning, experiencing a new culture and their dishes. We also went to the mainland a few times to visit the city, then came back to the island and played games and danced the night away.

And then there were days when Gabe, Noah, and I stayed in and spent the day in bed, or returned to our little hideout and reenacted our first time out there. Then we'd head out to the deck once the sun had set and spent hours watching the night sky with its millions of stars shining down on us. It's one thing I hate about living in the city; we never get those kinds of views.

The plane begins to descend as we approach landing at JFK airport. I can see Emma a few rows up front, getting jittery the closer we get to disembarking. We all are. Our overnight flight went smoothly, and we were all excited to get home. Then we had a small layover of three hours at LAX, which is when things took a turn.

A few minutes before boarding, Emma received a call from Bryan, Maddison's father. He was clearly having a meltdown. We could all hear him crying through the phone as he told her they didn't think Maddison would make it through the night.

That Maddie was crying and begging for Emma.

Emma promised they would be on their way to the hospital the minute the plane landed, then she broke down and collapsed in Greyson's arms. I had never seen Em in such a devastating state. It was heartbreaking to watch.

We immediately made a plan of action for when we would arrive. We switched up our seats so that Em and Grey would be seated closer to the front of the plane. Then when they got off, they would head over to the hospital right away, while we'd collect their luggage and Gracie, who is currently seated on Sam.

Originally, the plan was for all of us to go home and rest since it's nearly one in the morning. But now we'll all be heading back to Greyson's place and waiting around until they get back.

Sam had offered to watch Gracie for the night so that we could all go home. But we're a family and all want to be there for Emma and Greyson in any way we can, even if it's just as moral support or making sure they have food.

The instant the seatbelt signal turns off, Emma bolts out of her seat along with Greyson. He grabs their carry-ons and waits for the flight attendant to open the door. A minute later they're walking out with Greyson mouthing a *'thank you'* to us as they leave from view.

Once we're all off the plane, having collected our luggage and made our way to the parking lot, we pile into our cars and head over to Greyson and Emma's place. A little over thirty minutes later, we arrive at our destination and walk inside.

Sam and Cecilia go up to Gracie's room to set down the kids for the night while we all stand around in the kitchen, unsure what to do next. There's a somber mood settling in the room. We all know what's about to happen next, and we all know the next few days won't be easy for this household.

I look around at Morgan, who's cuddled up against Clay; she looks exhausted. I walk over to them and place my hand on her shoulder. "Hey, why don't you guys go take one of the spare rooms? Get a few hours of rest. We'll wake you when they come home."

"Are you sure?" She seems reluctant to sleep when something terrible is happening to our friends.

"Yes, Morg. There's nothing we can do right now but wait. It's the middle of the night. Go rest, you need it too. I want my future niece or nephew to be healthy."

That puts a small smile on her face. "Okay. But wake us up the minute they arrive."

"We will. Promise," I reassure her as they head up the stairs.

"You and Cecilia can take my old room as well," Aubrey offers Silas.

"You're not going to sleep?" he asks.

"I'll just crash on the couch. It's a king-size bed. It would be stupid for me to take it alone and have you two on the couch instead." She lifts a shoulder with a soft smile.

"Okay. Thanks, Aubrey. I appreciate it." He hugs her, then turns to me. "Same rule goes for us. When they arrive, let us know."

"Will do, Cap." I smile.

He chuckles with a head shake, then heads up as well, just as Cecilia stands at the landing. She smiles sadly and waves goodnight. A second later, Sam strolls down the steps, his hair ruffled and clothes crinkled. He stretches his arms above his head as he yawns.

"Sam, why don't you head home? You're probably excited to have a day off and away from us," I tell him, feeling bad for the poor guy.

"Nah, it's okay. Surprisingly, I actually like you guys. And I love the kids, so it's a win-win." He winks at me.

I laugh quietly. "We like you too, Sam. But you deserve a day off. We aren't going anywhere for the next twenty-four hours. So, you might as well take advantage of it. Go sleep, then see your family or friends. Go on a date, or even just spend the day lounging around at home. You can come back after tomorrow."

"Are you sure? I feel guilty leaving." He scratches the back of his head.

"We're sure," Aubrey steps in. "Emma doesn't like getting emotional in front of people, even us. She definitely won't want you to see her crying. We'll be here to take care of Gracie. But you might be needed for the whole week once you come back. So, take the day off we're giving you."

"Okay, yeah. I'll head out. But tell them I'll be back Wednesday morning." He hugs us both, then waves to the two dead men on the couch as he walks to the door.

I turn to face Aubrey as she's checking her phone. "Anything?" I know it hasn't been long, but we never know.

She shakes her head. "Nothing yet."

"You should take the couch in Em's office. It'll be much comfier than the armchair. I'll take the baby monitor. I slept the whole flight over, so I don't plan on sleeping."

"Okay, I'll keep my sound on just in case Grey texts." She hugs me and wanders off down the hall.

I pick up the monitor from the kitchen counter and go over to the living room, where Noah is already asleep on a recliner and Gabe is lying down on the couch. I thought he was asleep, but now I see the blue-tinted light reflecting on his face as he scrolls through his phone.

I place the baby monitor on the coffee table and crawl over Gabe, lying over his body as he closes his phone and places his arm around me. I look up at him and kiss his jaw, watching the smile spread on his lips before he gazes down at me and caresses my lips with his.

We've all gotten really close over the last two weeks. Spending every moment of the day with them has been wonderful, and I'm realizing more and more how wrong I was about them. They're so caring and attentive to me. They dote on me around the clock, and I'm gobbling it all up.

And to think a little over a month ago I was dead set on not getting in a relationship or getting near these two. Now I can't seem to walk away from them. *Who was I kidding?*

We haven't established where our relationship stands yet, but the boys have made it pretty clear with their subtle comments that we're a thing. I know we'll have to discuss soon how all of this is going to work, because I've never been in a relationship with two men before.

I don't know what they expect of me and what I should expect from them. *Are we exclusive? Do I call them my boyfriends? Whose bed do I sleep in?* The more I think about everything, the more I understand where Clay's curiosity came from. *This is confusing.*

But right now, I'm worried about Gabe. Something isn't right, but he won't talk to me about it. For the past three days, he's been checking his phone as if he's waiting for something. I caught him a few times going through gossip magazines and the news. I just can't figure out what he's looking for.

And when I ask, he puts his phone away and tells me it's nothing, but I don't miss the worried look in his eyes. He's also very antsy, with his knee constantly bouncing when he sits down or his foot twitching back and forth like right now.

I glide my hand up his chest as we break apart. "Is everything okay?"

He brings his own up and passes his fingers through my locks. "Yeah, baby. Everything's fine." He kisses my forehead.

"You know you can talk to me about anything, right?" I try again.

He sighs and wraps his other hand around me. Now one along my back and the other in my hair, holding me close. "I know, Vixen. But it's nothing you need to worry about," he whispers into my hair.

So, he is admitting there's something. He just won't tell me what. I'll give him today, but when we get home, I'll push some more. *Home... is it bad that I already love how that sounds?*

We're quiet for a moment until he speaks up again in a low voice. "Is he the reason why you don't let your hair grow out? Or do you just prefer having it short like this?"

I shrug. "I cut it when I got to New York since I needed to look different, and I've just gotten used to having it like this. But sometimes I miss my long hair."

He pulls slightly on my hair, lifting my gaze to his. "If you miss your hair, then let it grow out. If you miss your natural color, then let it come back. If you want to start dressing like a goody-two-shoe, praise-the-lord-gal again, then do it." I giggle softly at his last comment. "Stop living your life in fear of him, Vixen. Don't let him control you like that. We're here now, we'll keep you safe."

He's not the first to tell me that. My therapist has been trying for years. Maze, even though she doesn't know the story, reminds me every time I see her. And despite how many times they were repeated to me, I couldn't let go. *I didn't know how.*

But somehow, someway, Gabe's words rattle through my bones.

I'm tired. I'm so tired. I don't want to do this anymore. I don't want to hide anymore. To pretend I'm someone I'm not. To pretend I'm okay. That I'm not terrified every time I turn a corner late at night.

I'm done. No more hiding. I'm fighting.

A lone tear slips down my cheek, his thumb coming to wipe it away. "Okay."

He cups my face and kisses my lips. "My brave, brave girl."

Two hours later, Aubrey comes walking into the living room holding her phone. "Hey." She kneels down next to me. "Grey just texted. They're five minutes out. I'm going to go let the others know."

I climb off Gabe and stand from the couch, while Gabe sits up and scrubs his face, then passes his hands through his hair. We both haven't slept, simply cuddling, talking, and kissing since everyone went to bed.

"Okay, I'll get coffee running. We'll definitely need it," I say, stretching out my body.

"I'll help you and see what I can make to eat. Someone's probably gonna be hungry." He stands behind me and kisses my shoulder before walking away to the kitchen. I watch him go with a smile on my lips.

When I turn back to Aubrey, a warm expression crosses her face. She takes my hand and squeezes it. "I'm happy for you," she whispers, then smiles and heads to the second level.

I start brewing coffee as Gabe goes over to a cabinet along the far wall that holds several rows of mugs. He pulls one glass door open and reaches in to pick one up. "No! Not those ones," I whisper-shout just as his fingers wrap around it.

He turns to me slowly with the mug in his hand, a frown lining his face. "Why not?"

I sigh. "I don't know. Em said they were special mugs only she and Grey could use. She forbade all of us from using them."

He chuckles and places the mug back. "They have some weird kind of obsession with mugs, don't they?"

"It's their thing." I shrug and point to the kitchen cabinet that contains the ones we can use.

He takes out several mugs and sets them down on the counter beside the brewer, then stands behind me, arms circling my waist. "Will we have an *our thing*?"

I turn in his arms and place mine around his neck. "What if you two are my thing?"

He brings his mouth down to mine. "Even better."

We kiss for a minute until I hear footsteps above and pull away smiling. "I'll go wake up Noah."

Stepping out of his hold, I wander over to the other man who occupies my thoughts. He's still fast asleep in the recliner with his feet kicked up. I sit on the armrest delicately and lift my hand to his face, stroking his cheekbone with my thumb, then I lean in slowly and brush my lips against his.

"Wake up, Casanova," I breathe against him.

He groans, his hand coming around my waist and pulling me closer as I fall on top of him in the seat. I squeal at the sudden movement, a heartfelt laugh falling from my lips while his free hand comes to cradle my head, right before he kisses me back.

"I could wake up like this every day for the rest of my life," he says once his lips move down to my neck.

"Stop." I giggle. "Come on, babe. They're gonna be here any minute. Come have a coffee."

I maneuver myself away from him and regain my footing on the ground. He pushes the legs of the recliner down but doesn't make an attempt to stand. He's just sitting there with a goofy grin on his face.

"What?" I raise a brow.

"You called me *babe*."

I roll my eyes despite the slight blush and smirk that threaten to break loose. "Are you gonna get all sentimental on me now? Do you need me to get you a tissue or something?" I pop a hip and fold my arms over my chest.

A wicked smirk appears on his face, mischief twinkling in his deep brown eyes.

"I love when you get all sassy with me." He finally gets up and leans in to bite my earlobe. "It makes me want to fuck it right out of you."

My core clenches despite me still being sore from our last session. I swat him away playfully and head back over to Gabe, who holds out a mug filled with coffee for me. A minute later, everyone joins us in the kitchen, all taking a cup of coffee greedily. Except for Morgan, who accepts a mug of hot chocolate when Gabe offers it, since there's no decaf.

Shortly after, headlights shine through the window from the driveway, and everyone goes quiet as we wait to see what is about to walk through the door. With how emotional Emma was getting off the plane, I have a feeling it won't be pretty.

A loud wail sounds from outside, having us all gasping. Silas quickly walks over to the door, whipping it open just as Greyson strides through the door with a sobbing Emma in his arms. "Can someone get our things in my truck?"

"I'll get them," Noah says as he marches out of the house.

Grey swallows and nods. "I'm going to take her to bed," he says over her sobs as she buries her face into his chest.

We watch as he climbs the steps to their bedroom, her cries getting louder by the second until she screams.

"We should get the kids and bring them down here," Cecilia says while rubbing her chest. I can see the tears shining in her eyes as she listens to her friend's heart being ripped to shreds.

"I'll get Gracie," Aubrey tells her softly, looking just as emotional.

They hurry upstairs, coming back down a few minutes later with the kids, and Silas and Clay quickly put up the playpens to lay them back down. Despite the screams taking place on the upper floor, they fall right back to sleep.

They all come to stand around the kitchen, the atmosphere dark and gloomy as everyone holds on to each other, listening to Emma's piercing cries and wails that reverberate through the walls. Morgan weeps softly against Clay, Cecilia sits in Silas's lap on a bar stool as tears track down her cheeks, even Aubrey wipes at her eyes every few seconds.

Gabe removes the pan of eggs he was cooking from the burner and sets them aside. He turns and takes Aubrey in his arms, holding her close to his chest as his hand sweeps through her hair. He smiles tenderly my way, and I'm grateful to him for taking care of my friend in this heart-wrenching moment.

Noah's arms circle my waist from behind as I lean into him. I haven't known Emma as long as the rest of them, but she's become a true friend to me. A sister. And hearing her fall apart nearly brings me to my knees.

We didn't know Maddie personally, but we understand the pain Emma and Greyson feel at this moment. Some people just come into your life out of the blue and instantly gain a place within your heart. Just like everyone in this room became a part of mine, Maddison became a part of Greyson and Emma's family.

Half an hour later, the house falls silent once more as we all sit down in the dining room situated beside the wine cellar, some of us munching quietly on the early breakfast Gabe made us. It's only four in the morning, so the kids are still asleep for now.

Greyson shows up in the opening of the room looking exhausted. "She finally fell asleep." He gives us a mournful smile. "Sorry about all the noise, I hope we didn't wake the kids?"

"Don't apologize for what you two are going through." Cecilia gets up and rounds the table, wrapping her arms around his waist. His own come up slowly to hug her back as his head leans over hers, his shoulders rising and falling as he takes a deep, shaky breath.

When they pull apart, he sniffs and looks at us with red-rimmed eyes. "Thank you all for being here. For taking care of Gracie." He swallows.

"We're family, Grey. We'll always be here," Morgan says sincerely.

He nods as his eyes water.

"Why don't you go rest? We got this. I'll go pick up the dogs later from the sitter, and we'll take care of Gracie for the day," Silas offers.

"You guys don't have to do that. I'll just lie down for an hour or two until she wakes up," he begins to protest.

"No. What you're going to do is go back up there, hold your girl until you fall asleep, and spend the day with her. She needs you right now. We'll take care of everything," Clay says sternly, leaving no room for negotiations.

"Okay, yeah. Thank you again. These next few days won't be easy, so I appreciate the help." He waves with a sad smile and heads back to his girlfriend.

~ *The Next Day* ~

We got back to the penthouse last night, after another rough day of hearing Emma crying. It was brutal having to sit around and not be able to physically help her in any way.

Greyson popped in occasionally to collect food for them and to see his daughter, but Emma didn't leave the room once. We all went home after Aubrey offered to spend the night with them and watch over Gracie until Sam arrived in the morning.

Noah, Gabe, and I were so exhausted from these last forty-eight hours that no playtime took place. The second we walked through the door, we showered together, then dropped into Noah's bed and cuddled until exhaustion took over. Which was about three minutes, give or take.

I wake up to the sound of shouting coming from downstairs. I blink my eyes a few times, unsure if I'm imagining the sound, but then it happens again. I can't make out who it is, but something's clearly going on. Looking from side to side, I realize I'm now alone in Noah's bed. I'm also not sure what time it is.

"FUCK YOU!"

The roar is so loud, I shoot up in bed, quickly scrambling out of the covers and to the door. I don't know what's waiting for me down the steps, so I creak the door open slowly and slip out of the room.

I go down the stairs as quietly as possible, and once I reach the final step, the voice becomes clearer, and I realize it's Gabe's. He seems to be on the phone because I can't hear anyone talking back. I look around and don't see Noah anywhere. *He must be out for a jog.* I know he's not with Trinity, because he told me we'd go together later.

When I look toward the kitchen, I find Gabe with his back to me. His hand is pulling at his hair brutally, and the other holds the phone to his ear. He's pacing back and forth, head tilted downwards.

The penthouse is practically all open-spaced, and the railing to the stairs is glass. If he turns around, he'll spot me right away. But I have a feeling this conversation might be the key to what has been going on with Gabe.

So instead of making my presence known, I quickly take the few steps toward the foyer and hide behind the wall. From here, he won't be able to see me, but I'll be able to hear him. And if Noah gets back before I hear the end of the phone call, the elevator will signal me.

"I fucking told you I would be out of town for two weeks and that I couldn't be reached! What the fuck don't you understand?!" Gabe growls into the phone as I peek around the corner.

"It's not your fucking money! You aren't the reason I made it big; I don't owe you shit!" He stops pacing, turning around now. He seems distressed, or like he's seconds away from going on a rampage.

"Thanking you? I SHOULD BE THANKING YOU?! You didn't keep me alive; you nearly killed me more than a dozen times! You wanted nothing to do with me. You wanted me gone!"

He picks up a glass from the counter that still contains some of his green smoothie and whips it into the sink, the green liquid splashing all over with shards of glass. The crash makes me jump in place, and I quickly cover my mouth with both hands to hold in my gasp.

"Well, I fucking left! I got out of your shitty fucking life and made my own! You were finally fucking free of me, so why couldn't you just forget I exist like you wanted for so long?!" He paces again, listening to the other person on the line.

"No! I want it. No more of this bullshit. How much is it gonna take for you to give it to me and lose my number?" His eyes widen. "Are you fucking kidding me?! I don't have that kind of money! And even if I did, I can't just withdraw that kind of sum!" He walks around the kitchen island and takes a few steps in my direction but stops as I quickly glue myself to the wall, hoping he won't come closer.

It's quiet for a full minute, and I start to wonder if maybe he ended the call. I'm afraid to look in case he's much closer than I think, but then his yell shakes my core. "DON'T FUCKING CALL ME SON!" His voice cracks. "You don't get to play the mom card with me. You're no longer my mother..."

Oh, Gabriel...

My heart breaks for him. He's losing this battle; I can hear it in his voice. Despite what he just said, it's hard for any child to fully let go of their mother, no matter how horrible they may be. A mother is supposed to be a part of your life, supposed to love you and cherish you. Not do whatever this is. *I can't let her break him.* He keeps saying he'll protect me, well it's my turn to protect him.

I push off the wall and step around the corner. When he sees me come into view, his eyes widen in shock, and he freezes. I quickly march over to him, rip the phone out of his hand, and end the call.

He snaps out of it and tries to grab it out of my hands. "No, Vixen! Don't—"

"That's enough, Gabriel!" I bark out as I step back and hold the phone away. "I don't know what the hell that call was, but I heard enough to know that it's wrong. Whatever they asked for, you're not doing it. End of story."

"You don't understand, I don't have a choice!" he cries out.

"Then help me understand!" I throw the phone onto the couch a few feet away and take a step into him, my hands holding his cheeks.

"Please, Gabriel. Talk to me. I hate seeing you like this and not being able to help because you shut me out. Please don't shut me out." I kiss his lips softly before whispering against them. "Please..."

His arms wrap around me. "It's not a pretty story..."

I pull my head back, looking into his eyes. "Neither was mine, but you still listened to it. Now I want to listen to yours."

He breathes out, some of the tension leaving his body. "Are you sure?"

"Isn't that what couples are supposed to do? Support and be there for each other?"

A smile appears on his lips. "So, we're a couple? Does that mean I get to call you my girlfriend? Because I'd really like that."

"Of course, you would." I smirk. "But wouldn't it be called a throuple? Is there an actual term for a three-person relationship?"

"I think they call it a polyamorous relationship." He chuckles. His mood already greatly shifting from mere seconds ago. "So, do I?"

"Only if you tell me what's going on," I answer.

I'll let him call me his girlfriend even if he doesn't, but I'd really like to know. I don't like seeing him this way; he's supposed to be my happy, goofy boyfriend. Not the sad, seconds-away-from-breaking-down one.

He pulls me back in, placing his hand at the back of my head for me to lean onto his shoulder. For a moment, I'm afraid he won't do it. That he'll say he's fine and act like I didn't just hear everything he said. But then his soothing voice filters through the quiet surrounding us.

"Okay."

I look up at him and smile. It's one of those rare moments when I'm actually shorter than him rather than standing almost as tall, since I'm barefoot and not in heels. "Really?"

He gives me a hesitant smile in return. "Yeah. But can we go up to my room?"

My features shift to unimpressed. "Is that your way of trying to get me alone in bed?"

He chuckles. "No, but that's not a bad idea." I smack his chest, and he sighs. "I just... I don't want you to look at me with pity in your eyes. I couldn't stand having you look at me like that. It's dark in my room, it will make it easier for me..."

I place my hand on his chest, watching the vulnerability swim through his eyes. "I get it." I kiss him one last time and take his hand in mine, leading him up the stairs and into his room.

Chapter Twenty-One

VERONICA

Unwelcome delivery.

I push the door to his room open, and as he mentioned, it really is dark in here. With the blinds closed and the dark color of his walls, it almost looks like it's the middle of the night. We climb onto his bed, and he settles in with his back against the headboard. While I place myself at his side, my head resting on his chest and my arm holding his waist.

"What time is it?" I realize now I still have no clue if it's early in the morning or the middle of the afternoon.

"Just past nine. Noah's out running." The rumble of his voice vibrates through his chest and into my ear that lies against him.

I nod. "Does he know what's going on?" I ask softly.

He sighs. "No. He knows about my past, but he doesn't know about my present situation."

"Okay." I don't push for more and instead wait until he's ready.

It feels like a lifetime before he finally speaks up, his fingers gliding through my strands. "My parents never liked me. From the moment I was born, they hated me, and I still don't know why. I don't know what I did wrong or what I said wrong for them to wish my inexistence. I can't remember a time when my mother hugged me, kissed me, or told me she loved me. And my father, he just ignored me. Until he didn't."

He kisses the top of my head, inhaling my scent like it might help steady him. "I was five the first time my father hit me. A nasty backhand to the face. I had a black eye the next day, and my mother told the school I had a fit because they wouldn't let me do some shit, and I tried to run away and smacked into the door. When the reason he hit me was because I didn't get up fast enough to give him a beer from the fridge." He scoffs.

"It didn't happen every day at that point, it was more verbal than physical from both of them. But soon, everything I did or didn't do was never good enough. His punishments went from yells to punches every day. If there was a dish in the sink, whether it was his or my mother's, and I didn't clean it right away, I'd be punished." He breathes out, his voice staying low and calm as he continues to work his fingers into my hair.

"If he ran out of beer, if the car didn't start, if my mother forgot to get groceries because she was too high off her ass, it was all my fault, and I would pay the price for it. But every time, they had a reasonable excuse for why I was all black and blue, and I quickly gained a reputation of being a troubled kid who got into fights. Even though I had never fought anyone in my life. By the time I was twelve, I had already broken both my arms twice, one leg, and a few other fractures, along with two of my ribs."

Tears well in my eyes as I try my hardest not to let them out. I want to be strong for him at this moment, but all I picture is a little innocent blond boy fighting for his life. And it breaks my heart.

I turn my head, kissing his chest through the fabric of his shirt, and pull my arm tighter around his waist. "CPS didn't try to get involved? No one found it weird that you were always beaten up?"

"They did, but it never came to anything. My parents put on bright faces and pretended we were a big happy family. And since they had been spreading their lies for as long as I can remember, when they questioned my teachers or anyone else involved in my life, everyone gave the same story."

I shake my head, disgusted with how little effort the system might have put into his case, disgusted with how easily people believed the lies. No matter how troubled a child might be, no matter how many fights they might get in, there's always a reason behind it, and it usually has to do with their home environment. They should have fought harder to uncover the evil truth that lurked behind his door.

"Did you ever try telling them? No one believed you?"

"There was one. When I was in seventh grade, I had a math teacher, Ms. Winslow. After the first couple of bruises or casts, she started watching me closely. It didn't take her long to realize I wasn't a troubled kid." I can hear the appreciation in his voice that he has for this teacher with how he says her name.

"One day after class, she held me back and sat me down, refused to let me leave until I told her the truth. She called CPS right away. She really did try to help, but when she noticed nothing was coming from it, she took matters into her own hands."

I look up and kiss the underside of his jaw. "I'm happy you had someone there for you. Someone who believed you," I whisper.

He tilts his head down, a sad smile lining his lips. His hand comes up to cup my cheek, his eyes roaming over my features before he kisses me tenderly. He pulls away, leaning his head back, and continues his story as I listen to every word that falls from his beautiful lips.

"Since I was only twelve and couldn't get emancipated until I was sixteen, she got me into hockey. With all the practices and games, I was out of the house most of the time. She also found me a little job cleaning tables and washing dishes where I was paid under the table. Anything to make sure I spent as little time in my home as possible. If I wasn't at hockey, I was at the diner." His hand glides down my arm as he strokes up and down with the tip of his fingers.

"You had a job cleaning tables and washing dishes for years... yet you're incapable of doing it now," I deadpan.

He chuckles and kisses my head. "I never said I was any good at it."

I roll my eyes and shake my head against him before letting him continue with his past.

"Evelyn, that was her name, let me store all the money I made at her place. She only lived a few blocks away, a ten-minute walk. She even got me a cheap phone so that I could call her or the authorities if I ever needed. And whenever I was too weak to walk after another one of his brutal punishments, she would come pick me up."

"Your mother... did she hurt you too?" I swallow the bile rising in my throat at the thought of a mother doing that to her child.

"My mother, in some ways, was more evil than my father. She didn't use her fists often; instead, she played with my emotions. Anything I loved or grew attached to, she would rip it away from me and force me to watch as she burned it or broke it." He lets out a breath.

"Whether it was a new pair of shoes or a picture of me winning my first hockey game. She didn't care. If it were something I cared about, she'd destroy it. I quickly learned to stop bringing anything I cared about home."

I can hear the sadness seeping through his words. All he wanted was a mother who loved him, and instead he got two parents who wished he was dead. Life isn't fair.

"Anyway, when I turned sixteen, Evelyn helped me get emancipated. It worked. I was finally free of them. Even though she wasn't my teacher anymore, she still helped me and took me in, and my job started paying me properly. Things were finally going well for me."

He swallows, and I have a feeling I know where this story is going and why his parents still have a hold on him. "She never tried to seduce me in any way, never showed any interest. But I was a sixteen-year-old boy filled with testosterone. I had grown into my shape. I was tall and fit with all the workouts and hockey. And I mean, look at me. Hard to resist, right?" He chuckles when I smack him.

But he's right, the man is gorgeous and apparently impossible to resist.

"One night after a win, she offered me a congratulatory beer. One thing led to another, and we had sex. I was so nervous. It was my first time, and she was beautiful and much older than me. It was intimidating." He laughs, remembering the moment.

"She freaked out in the morning, but I reassured her I wouldn't tell anyone. It didn't happen again for a few weeks, but then it became a regular thing. We were always careful, never showing any signs of affection in public. And like I promised her, I never told a soul."

"How long did it go on?"

"About two years, until I went off to college. No one knows about my relationship with her, not even Noah. You're the first person I've told. It's why he doesn't understand why I'm..." He trails off.

I lift myself from his chest and look at him. "Why you're having nightmares," I finish for him.

I had already put it together, the state of his sheets every couple of days. How he never wants to spend the whole night in bed with me, and I find him sleeping somewhere else in the morning.

He sighs. "Yeah... he knew I had some occasionally. But ever since my parents came back into the picture, they've gotten worse. I don't know how they found out about me and Evelyn, but somehow, they did, and they claim to have evidence."

"They're blackmailing you for money?" I ask.

He nods. "We had agreed to a once-a-month payout, but now they are demanding more money and more often. If I don't pay up, they'll make it public. I can't let that happen. I don't care about my reputation, but even if it was years ago, she'll still go to jail for it. After everything she's done for me, I can't let that happen to her."

"Have you ever seen it? The evidence. You said you two were really careful; how would they have gotten any?"

He shakes his head this time. "No. And I have no idea, but they swear they have it, and I can't risk it."

I climb on top of him, straddling his thighs as I take his face between my palms. "Listen to me, you won't pay them a cent again. Ignore their calls, block them. They don't have any evidence, I promise you."

"How can you be so sure?" He frowns.

"When was the last time they demanded money?"

"Six days ago."

"And have you paid it yet?" He shakes his head from side to side again. "That's what I thought. If they had evidence, they would have already sent it out or threatened you with proof."

"But what if they really do? What if it's not a bluff?" he asks with worry.

"They don't, trust me. If there's one thing Victor taught me, it was how to call a bluff. He would always say, *'Someone who threatens twice is a liar.'* He showed me exactly what he meant by that a few times. He told me that you only ever threaten someone once, and that if you have to do it again, you give them an example of your threat. The next time they don't listen, you perform the threat."

I drop my hands from his face and close my eyes momentarily as unwanted memories of him flood my mind and a shiver runs through my spine. Gabe must sense it because his hands suddenly settle along my arms as he rubs up and down, bringing me back to the moment.

I open my eyes again and smile at him. "It's how he knew if someone was lying to him. If they kept threatening but never actually did anything about it, it's because whatever they claimed they had or would do was bullshit." I place my hands on his chest. "They might know about it, but they don't have any proof, Gabriel. Trust me. No more money, no more taking their calls."

"But what if we turn out to be wrong?"

"We aren't. I can feel it in my gut. Someone told me not long ago to stop living in fear of someone else. To stop letting them control my life." I cup his cheek once more.

"He sounds like a really smart guy."

"I think he may be." I smile, leaning in and kissing his lips. "I just hope he takes my advice."

He kisses me back, brushing my hair behind my ears. "Okay, no more money." His shoulders drop as his body loses tension, like a weight has finally been lifted off his shoulders.

"Thank you for telling me," I whisper against him.

"Thank you for being patient with me." He pulls me back in for another kiss. "Although I may be a ball of nerves for the next few days." He chuckles.

"That's okay." I'm expecting it. At least until he realizes I'm right and nothing comes from their threats. "I know a few ways to calm you down." I feel him harden beneath me as I begin to kiss down his neck and rock my hips slowly. These two men have turned me into a starved woman.

"Mmm, I like where your mind is going." He holds my hips, helping me grind against him.

"Am I interrupting something?"

We stop moving and look back to the door, finding Noah leaning against the door frame with his arms folded over his chest and a smirk on his lips. His sweat-soaked shirt sticks to his deliciously thick muscles.

"Nah, our girl was just hungry and needs to be fed." Gabe smiles and scoots us over to the side of the bed with me still over him. He lifts us with ease and chuckles. "You really are lighter than a hockey bag." Then he begins to walk toward the door and out into the hall.

"Wait, where are we going?" I'm confused why we can't just have sex in his room since we're already all here.

"I just said I was going to feed you." He laughs and carries us down the stairs while Noah heads for his room, likely to take a shower.

"That's not the kind of feeding I wanted!" I whine, which only makes him laugh harder. I can even hear Noah from inside his room laughing as well.

NOAH

~ One Week Later ~

"Do you guys mind if we stop at my place before heading over to Morgan's? I want to grab a change of clothes since I'm spending the night here," Veronica calls as she comes down the stairs with her shoes on and purse hanging off her shoulder.

The whole gang is heading over to Burkley's place for dinner. Greyson is supposed to propose to Emma today. And if all goes well, she'll say yes, and we'll be celebrating their engagement at Clay's house.

Emma is still in a funk since Maddison's passing, still hardly leaving the bed and functioning. She's spiraling into a depression, and Greyson is starting to freak out.

Originally, he had planned to propose at their launch party this weekend. But with her state of mind, he thought proposing earlier might get her out of depression in time for her and Cecilia's grand opening.

Cecilia has been picking up the slack with the rest of the girls' help to get everything ready and moving for the launch party and their first day of work. But she can't do it all on her own; she needs her business partner.

"Yeah, of course. You can even pack up all your things while you're at it and just move in." Gabe shines a blinding smile at her.

She stops in front of him, patting his chest. "One thing at a time, Pretty Boy. One thing at a time." She steps away and heads for the elevator.

Gabe leans in, hands in his jean's pockets. "She didn't say no."

I chuckle and shake my head at him, then follow after Veronica.

We take Gabe's Porsche over to Veronica's condo, since my car only fits two. We're just turning onto her block when she pushes her head between us from the back, arms bent and supporting her body on either side of our seats.

"You know..." she starts, then smiles devilishly at me. "If we ever have a baby, you'll have to get a new car since yours is only a two-seater."

My eyes grow wide as Gabe hits the brakes hard, sending us all flying against our seatbelts, except for Veronica, who doesn't seem to be buckled in. I quickly put my arm in the way, stopping her from flying out the windshield.

"HOLY FUCK! I'm sorry. Shit, fuck, sorry. I just... I think I just came in my pants." Gabe shuts off the engine and turns in his seat, beaming at Veronica. "Is it time? Are we really having this conversation now? Because I'm ready. I'm so, so ready."

He practically bounces in his seat with excitement. "We can do it right here, right now. Or in your condo, since we're already here. I'm going to put so many babies in you, Vixen. Fuck, I'm hard just thinking about it. I can't wait to see you all swollen and emotional."

"Jesus, that turned scary real quick," I mutter, still shocked from what Veronica spurted out of the blue.

Gabe glares my way. "There is absolutely nothing scary about a pregnancy. It's one of the most beautiful moments in a woman's life. Don't say shit like that, she might take it back!"

Veronica suddenly bursts into a high-pitched hyena laugh, holding on to her belly as she falls back into her seat. I swear if there was more room back there, she'd be rolling all over and kicking her feet in the air. "Oh my God! That was hilarious! I should have filmed it."

I give her a reproachful look. "This is funny to you?"

She takes a few deep breaths as she steadies herself and sits back up properly. "Oh, come on, it's a little funny. I just wanted to see his reaction. I mean, look at him." She nods toward Gabe. "He's like a big golden retriever puppy all excited to chew on his new toy." Gabe narrows his eyes at her, and she quickly places a hand over her mouth to suppress her giggle. "Look, now he's pouting because we took away his toy."

I can't help but laugh as I watch Veronica giggling her heart away at Gabe's expense.

"I hate you both," he declares as he faces forward in his seat and crosses his arms, sulking like a child.

Veronica goes to the back of his seat, her arms coming around to hold him. "Aww, no, you don't. I think you still like me very much."

"You're right, I think I do. But only because you're fucking hot and I really want to fuck your brains out tonight." He turns, grabbing her head and kissing her.

"Way to make that sound romantic, Pretty Boy." She laughs against his lips just as her phone begins to ring.

She pulls back and takes it out from her purse, frowning as she sees who's calling. She quickly answers it and puts the phone to her ear. "Hey, Nate." *Nate? Who the fuck is Nate? Nathan? And if so, why the fuck is he calling her?*

"Yeah, actually I just got to the condo." She listens for a moment. "Oh okay, sure. We haven't gone in yet, so I'll just wait before heading up, so you don't have to ring... Okay, see you in a bit."

She hangs up and looks at us. Apparently, I'm not the only one not enjoying that phone call. One look at Gabe and he looks ready to rip someone's head off.

"So... Nathan's coming to pick up some of his stuff he left at my place a while back. He was supposed to collect them before we left on vaca, but he had an emergency, so he canceled. He said he was right around the corner and asked if he could stop by," she clarifies for us as she looks out the window. "Oh, he's already here."

Veronica quickly steps out of the car as Gabe and I follow suit. She walks over to him as he opens his arms, only hesitating a second before reaching up and accepting his hug. I hear a growl erupt from Gabe's throat at my side as he watches them.

Veronica must hear it too, because she swiftly steps out of his embrace and glares at Gabe. She then smiles awkwardly at all of us before snapping out of it. "Um, Nathan, this is Noah and Gabriel. Noah, Gabe, this is Nathan."

We nod at each other in acknowledgment. "So, you're the friend?" Gabe says in a not-so-friendly voice.

Nathan smiles broadly with another nod, then looks at me. "And you're the boyfriend."

Now it's my turn to smile and quickly turn it into a smirk. "One of them."

His eyebrows rise as he turns to Veronica. "Damn, Rons. You went from not wanting to date to having two boyfriends?" He throws his head back and laughs. "Good for you." He finishes with a smile aimed at her.

She punches his arm. "Shut up." Then rolls her eyes. "All right, well, let's go inside. Unless you guys want to start a pissing contest or something."

Gabe takes a step toward her and throws his arm around her shoulders. "Come on, baby. I can't wait to see your room so we can get started on that baby making." He turns her toward the entrance to her building.

"Oh my God, Gabe! I was joking!"

He kisses her temple and laughs. "Whatever you say, Vixen."

I chuckle at the same time as Nathan does. *Okay, maybe he's not too bad of a guy.*

We enter the building and step into the waiting elevator, making our way to the fourth floor. No one says a word, all standing awkwardly around Veronica, until Gabe breaks the silence. "Now I understand how Silas must have felt when he was around Ford after finding out he slept with his girl." He whistles. "Fucking unpleasant."

"Jesus, Ellis. Shut up," I grunt out.

Nathan shakes his head with a smirk. "For what it's worth, Rons and I were only ever friends with the occasional hookup."

"Not helping at all," Gabe grumbles.

"Boys, behave," Veronica chides us.

"By the way, congrats on your win," he says with a genuine smile.

"Thanks, man." I smile back. I have no idea if he has any intentions of staying in my Kitten's life, but might as well get used to it now.

We finally reach her floor and enter her condo to find Aubrey standing in the kitchen. "Oh, hey! I thought you were already at Morg's," Veronica says as she walks over to her.

"Not yet, I had a few things to do at the bakery before heading over, and I spilled coffee on my shirt, so I came in to get changed." She smiles, then her eyes turn round when she notices us all standing by the door.

"Oh, wow... hi everyone..." She waves hesitantly, then turns back to Veronica. "This is weird, right?"

"Very weird." Kitten giggles. "Nathan just stopped by to collect some things of his. And I wanted to grab some spare clothes, since I'm spending the night with these two giants."

"I'm just gonna head back and grab my things, if that's okay?" Nathan steps up to the girls, pointing toward Veronica's room.

"Yeah, just go ahead."

"Thanks. Hey, Brey." He smiles at her before heading down the hall.

"Hi, Nathan." She blushes for a moment, then shakes it off. "Oh! This came in for you as I was stepping into the building."

Veronica's brows furrow as she inspects the rectangular package. "That's weird, I didn't order anything." She picks it up and shakes the box as something rattles inside. She goes to open it just as Nathan reappears.

"Got everything. I'm gonna head out, my shift starts soon. See you around, Rons. Don't be a stranger. Bye everyone." He hugs her again, then waves and leaves with two or three items of clothing and a watch in hand.

Veronica gets back to opening her package, ripping through the tape with one hand while holding the box with her other. She pushes the flaps open and looks inside. A loud gasp leaves her lips, making all the little hairs on my body stand to attention. The color drains from her face as the box falls from her hands.

"Baby, what's wrong?" Gabe rushes to her side, taking her in his arms as she begins to shake.

I go to reach for the package just as Aubrey looks inside the box. "Oh my God..." She covers her mouth with her hands while looking down in horror.

I pick it up and look inside.

"Oh fuck..."

This guy isn't messing around anymore.

Chapter Twenty-Two

GABRIEL

Pizza, beer, and surprises.

I'm not sure what's in that box, but with the look on the girls' faces and the way Noah whips his head my way, I'm not sure I want to know.

"We have a problem," he says with a hard yet worried expression.

I gulp. "What kind of problem?"

He takes a step toward me, angling the box for me to peer in. My insides instantly tighten, bile rising to my throat as I look at the images of the girls in the box. Each one of them individually taken at random moments during the day. There's even one with Cecilia and Dante standing outside their home.

Fuck. This guy isn't a joke.

I'm not sure what we're dealing with, but if the contents in this box and what Ronnie said to me a week ago are anything to go by, it's nothing good. Victor is much more dangerous than we initially thought. And now he's coming after our women.

"I did this. This is all my fault." Ronnie begins to cry in my arms. "I should have stayed away. I should have kept moving around like I planned on doing," she sobs. "He's going to go after them. He's going to hurt them."

"No, we won't let that happen," Noah tries to reassure her, but there's no use. She's stuck in her head right now.

She pushes against me and rushes to her room. We quickly follow her and find her pulling out a huge bag, throwing clothes into it haphazardly, which is very unlike Ronnie. She always keeps everything tidy. Even at the resort, she took all our clothes out of our suitcases and folded them into the dressers.

"Kitten, what are you doing?" Noah asks, stepping cautiously toward her.

"If... if I leave, he'll follow me. He won't come after you all. He'll leave you alone. You'll be safe if I'm gone." Her voice cracks as she whimpers.

"No, baby, this isn't the way." *Fuck being cautious. She needs to know we're here and that we aren't going anywhere.* I stride over to her and grab hold of her hands, stopping her from filling the bag. "You leaving isn't going to solve anything. You'll just have to keep running forever. That's not a life, Vixen."

She looks into my eyes, tears tracking down her face. "I don't know what else to do, Gabriel. I can't let him hurt them."

I release her hands and cup her cheeks, using my thumbs to wipe away her tears. "He won't. I promise you, Ronnie. We won't let him. What did we talk about last week? Don't live in fear of him, don't let him control you. We'll figure it out."

"How?"

"We'll have to tell the others, at least the guys. It might be best if the girls don't know, so as to not cause more panic. We'll hire security for the time being until we can catch this guy," Noah tells her, coming in to stroke her hair.

"And how are we supposed to catch him? He's everywhere, and yet we don't ever see him! And what security would accept watching people without them knowing?"

"We might have to go to the cops with this. Do you still have that detective's number or name? He might be able to help." She nods in response. I don't always agree that getting the authorities involved is a good thing, but I really don't know what else to do.

"We could ask Julian," Aubrey says quietly, still standing by the door.

Noah and I furrow our brows as we turn to her. *Who the hell is Julian?*

"Who?" Noah asks.

"Julian Storm," she clarifies. "His brother lives in front of Morgan's. They own one of the best security services in the world. I'm sure he would know what to do in a case like this one." She blushes slightly.

"Oh shit, I forgot about those guys," I say, dropping my hands from Ronnie when it finally clicks who Aubrey's talking about. The three billionaire brothers. I'm not exactly sure what they do security wise, but Morgan and Clay swear by their company.

"That's actually a really good idea. We'll talk to him before going to the cops with anything. See what he suggests. We'll just have to find a time to get to him as well as tell the guys, without Morgan, Cecilia, and Emma noticing." Noah nods as a plan forms in his head.

Veronica lets out a sigh as she sits on the corner of her bed. She looks exhausted with this whole situation. "We could try to distract them, maybe give you boys a reason to leave the house all together."

I nod this time. "That could work. We'll inform the guys, then sneak over to the neighbor's house and explain the situation. Hoping he's there."

"Or we could just ask Shane." Brey instantly turns red. "I mean Coach Jefferson.

He's good friends with Julian. He could probably get you in touch."

"You really are the smartest one in our group." Noah smirks at her, causing her to go a deeper shade. "All right, I'll give Coach a call, but I want you two to pack your things. You'll both be staying with us for the time being."

Aubrey's eyes go wide. "Oh... I don't know if that's necessary."

"Of course, it is, Brey. I'm hardly ever here lately, and there's no way you're staying here alone. If you prefer, you can stay at your brother's place. We can tell them a pipe broke and we're having repairs done. You'll keep my car so that you can get to work from there easily," Ronnie says.

"Okay, yeah. I already have a room at his place anyway," Aubrey agrees.

"Good, everything is set now. Let's go, ladies. Go pack some things so that we can get out of here. We're already late for Burkley's," I announce with a clap of my hands as Noah walks out of the room with his phone to his ear.

Aubrey rushes over to her room as Ronnie stands from the bed slowly, chewing on her lip. "Are you sure this is going to work?"

"We'll make it work, baby. I promise we'll keep you safe. All of you." I cradle the back of her head with one hand and pull her in as she circles my waist with her arms.

"It's done. They'll all be in front of Clay's place. He said it's something that will take time to discuss. And since we don't want to raise any suspicions with the girls, he thinks it's best if they come over to *'celebrate'* with us," Noah says as he comes back into the room.

"We'll say we bumped into them on our way back and offered them to come over for dinner. But you'll have to try and keep the wives away from the men while we discuss. Think you can do that, Kitten?" he asks Ronnie.

She nods. "Yeah, I think I can manage that."

"Good. Are you done getting your stuff?" She looks at the bag that hasn't been touched since I pulled her away from it.

"Umm, no. Just let me grab a few more things." She rushes off to her closet and brings out a stack of heels. *Jesus, women and their shoes.*

I chuckle and head toward the door. "I'll go check on Aubrey, see if she needs any help."

"I'M GETTING MARRIED!" Emma bursts through the door at Burkley's house literally seconds after we stepped in with her arms thrown in the air as she squeals with excitement.

The sound of barstools scratching against the floor rings out seconds before Morgan and Cecilia come running over to her and demand to see the ring. Aubrey and Ronnie quickly take Emma into their arms, their high-pitched screams nearly bursting all our eardrums. Ford wears the proudest smile I've ever seen on his face as he listens to the girls fawning over the engagement ring, then shakes his head with a chuckle.

"About time!" I clap him on the back.

"Congrats, man." Noah does the same.

He beams. "Thanks, guys."

We leave the girls behind and join Silas and Clay in the kitchen as Clay comes to Greyson, taking him in for a man hug. "I'm happy for you, bro. And glad to see she seems a little better." He steps back and nods toward Em as the girls slowly make their way over.

"Thank you. And yeah, for now. I just don't know how long this happy state will last with the funeral coming up in two weeks." Greyson shrugs and looks at his future wife with a sad smile.

Silas pushes Clay aside and takes Greyson into a big hug, slapping his back a few times until Grey winces. "Welcome to married life, brother. Where your balls are no longer your own."

We all laugh as the girls finally join us once more, then congratulate Emma as well. She radiates with joy and excitement, bouncing up and down as she throws herself into her fiancé's arms. "I love you so much, Wolf. I can't wait to marry you."

"Soon." He grins at her before sealing their mouths together for a passionate kiss.

After a few seconds of smooching, Em pulls away quickly. Her eyes widen as she stares up at Greyson. "Uh-oh…" She suddenly pushes off him and rushes to the sink, bending her head in and emptying her guts down the drain.

We all stare with wide eyes at what is unraveling before us. She turns on the tap once she's done, wiping her hands and mouth quickly before rinsing out the sink, then turns to face us with horror-filled eyes.

"This is normal, right? Being too excited can make you sick, right?… Right?!" Her gaze bounces over all of us.

"Well, yes, technically it can. But I've seen you excited many times, and that's never happened." Aubrey smiles sympathetically at Emma.

Emma's eyes suddenly fill with rage as her head whips toward Greyson.

"WOLF!!!" she shrieks. "You knocked me up, didn't you?!"

He sucks in his lips, trying his hardest not to laugh. "I'm... sorry?" Unable to contain himself, he folds in half and cracks up, wiping the tears from his eyes.

"This isn't funny!" Em stomps her foot on the ground like an angry child. "We agreed to wait, Wolf. Gracie just turned one barely three months ago! This isn't waiting!!" she whines. "This is all your fault!"

"My fault? I'm not the one who forgot her pills when we left for vacation." He raises a brow.

"YOU DISTRACTED ME WITH SEX!" she shouts. "That's why I forgot them!"

Greyson walks up to her, his hands falling to her waist. "You're right, I'm sorry. We did agree to wait, but a baby isn't the end of the world, Bunny."

"But I'll look fat in my wedding dress." Emma pouts, looking up at him with tears in her eyes.

"No, you won't. We're getting married in just over four months. You'll only have a small bump by then. And even if it were huge, you'd still be the most beautiful woman in the room." He beams at her and kisses her pouty lips.

"Wait, you guys already have a date set?" I frown in confusion.

"Mhmm." Em smiles now. *Jesus, this girl is already a rollercoaster of emotions, it's going to be something once she's further along.* "December twenty-third. Greyson joked about it with our parents, but apparently, it wasn't a joke, and he already booked the place for us."

"Wow, so we'll all be spending Christmas together then?" Silas asks.

"That's the plan. Of course, your families are invited as well. But you're also free to fly back home on the twenty-fourth if you'd prefer," Grey informs us.

"We also have some news we'd like to share." Morgan places her arm around Clay's waist as his drapes over her shoulders. "We had our first ultrasound yesterday..." They look at each other with a smile that would even make the Grinch's heart melt. "We're expecting twins."

"Oh my God!" Emma jumps away from Greyson and practically tackles Morgan. "I told you there was a reason it took so long; now you're going to have two babies! And we're going to be pregnant together, I'm so excited! We can do all our shopping together."

She squeezes Morgan in her arms, then looks back at Greyson. "Although if you put two babies in me, you can say bye-bye to your balls, Wolf!"

"Don't you want to make sure you're actually pregnant first, Em?" Ronnie giggles as she goes over to hug Morgan as well, Cecilia and Aubrey following behind.

"You're right, I should probably do that." Emma nods.

"I still have some tests in the bathroom, if you want," Morgan offers.

"We should probably take some of those, too. Since Vixen said she's ready for baby-making season." I grin at everyone who seems shocked by my declaration.

"I did not say that!" Ronnie points a finger at me with a glare. "I was making a joke. No baby making! Get that thought out of your head, Pretty Boy."

"We'll convince her soon," I whisper, which only makes her angrier, while everyone laughs. "Hey, where are the kids, anyway?" I look around searching for the two little toddlers but come up empty.

"Gracie is with my father and his girlfriend," Em says.

"And Dante is with his grandparents," Cecilia adds.

"Shit, I forgot it was your day with the Cup," Grey says as he peers into the living room at the huge trophy sitting up on the coffee table.

Noah and I turn around, looking in the same direction and then to the keeper sitting quietly on the couch nearby. "Holy shit, he's so quiet and still; if you hadn't pointed out the cup, I probably wouldn't have noticed he was even there for another twenty minutes." I laugh.

The keeper smirks. "Only here to watch over this beauty, not disrupt your moment with it."

Ford walks up to the Stanley Cup, eyes roaming over every inch of it. "Seeing it never gets old." He smiles down at it like it's the most beautiful thing he's ever seen. Come to think of it, it's a lot like how he looks at Emma, which is hilarious if you ask me.

"Tell me about it." Burkley chuckles as we all join him and take in our latest victory. "I haven't stopped staring at it since this morning."

"We should eat ice cream out of it. I'm so down for ice cream," Morgan calls as the girls join us.

"Ooh! I could totally go for ice cream!" Em bounces excitedly.

"By the way, I haven't made anything for dinner. The smell of cooking has been making me nauseous lately." Morg makes a face. "I thought you could cook instead, Gabe."

"Or we could order something?" Ronnie looks at me with wide eyes, clearly trying to pass a message. "Tomorrow's supposed to be your cheat day, right, Gabe? Why don't we move it up and have some pizza and fries tonight? Beers, the whole thing. Make a real celebration out of it."

She comes up to my side, wrapping her arms around my neck as I place mine on her hips. "You boys could go out and get everything we need, and we ladies will start talking wedding and babies."

"That's a good fucking plan, I haven't had pizza in forever," Noah steps in. "We could even open the fire pit later, do some smores." *Ah, now I get it.* It'll help sell our plan for dividing the group so that we can talk to the guys and have a reason to invite the brothers over.

"That's a fantastic idea," Cecilia chimes in. "We don't often get a night together without the kids, let's make it wild."

"I mean, we do have two reasons to celebrate, or three actually." Emma grins at Greyson, but within seconds her smile drops. "Ugh! But I can't drink," she whines.

"Hey, neither can I. So, you won't be alone," Morgan says.

"We'll get you some non-alcoholic bubbly stuff if you want," I offer them.

"Ooh yes! I want to pretend to be drunk so that Wolf can unleash his beast on me tonight." Emma waggles her brows at Greyson, which only makes us all laugh.

"How about we make you take that test first to see if you really can't drink? You boys go before these pregnant ladies get hangry," Ronnie says, taking Emma by the arm as they all head toward the bathroom, already picking out baby names.

"She's gonna be worse than Minnie pregnant, you know that, right?" Silas laughs and slaps Grey on the back.

"Remember when Cece had her meltdown during her baby shower?" I tell them while chuckling.

"Oh God! Please don't remind me..." Ford's eyes widen.

"That really was scary to watch." Clay looks equally terrified.

"Well, you both are about to live it. Better stock up on tissues while we're out. You'll need it. And if she tells you she wants freaking Chinese food at four in the morning, get her the damn Chinese food." Silas goes on to give them advice as we all walk out of the house, Clay and Greyson getting more worried with every word that leaves his mouth.

This is going to be epic.

We all climb into Emma's seven-seater SUV and buckle up. Ford and Burkley up front, Noah and I in the middle row, and Hayes behind us in the last seat. We're pretty big guys, so even in a five-seater car, we don't fit very well.

The minute the car pulls out of the driveway, Noah wastes no time to broach the subject we desperately need to acknowledge. "Guys, we have a situation we need to discuss. Gabe and I already took the next step, but we think it's best if the women aren't aware of what's going on. Of course, Veronica and Aubrey are in the know, since they were there when the problem showed up. But they won't say a word to the others."

"Is this why we were all forced out of the house when only two of us could have gone to get the food and drinks?" Clay smirks smugly. *Ever the Mr. Know-it-all.*

"Yes, it is. It's a delicate subject, and the girls might get freaked out if they know about it," I tell him.

"Okay... so what's going on?" Greyson looks up in the rearview mirror quickly with a worried expression, then focuses back on the road.

Noah and I glance at each other, not really sure how to say it without freaking them out either. Finally, he sighs and speaks. "Veronica has a really bad ex who won't leave her alone. And when I say bad, I don't mean an asshole who doesn't understand they're over, like Emma's. I mean a dangerous criminal."

"He's been threatening her, and now he's taking pictures of the girls," I finish for him.

"WHAT?!" Silas shouts in my ear with rage.

Greyson quickly pulls the car over to the curb, shutting off the engine, and turns in his seat to face us at the same time as Clay. "Explain. Because I'm seconds away from losing my shit," he says sternly.

"Look, I won't go into details about Veronica's story because that's her business. But the guy was abusive, and when she found out he was involved in criminal things, she helped the cops take him down. Things went south, and he didn't get caught, and Veronica has been hiding out since," Noah begins to tell them.

"But now he's back and has been stalking her. He's clearly not happy about what went down and wants her to pay. Today she received a box with photos of all the girls that were clearly taken within the last week. Some of them coming out of our homes."

"I don't fucking like this one bit," Clay mutters.

"You're telling me someone's stalking our girls, and we just left them at the house, *ALONE?!*" Greyson barks.

"Are you two fucking kidding me? Ford, get us back to the house *now*," Silas instructs him.

"No, wait! It's fine." I place my hand on Greyson's shoulder, stopping him from starting the car. "The girls already have security watching them."

"What do you mean, *they already have security watching them*?" Clay frowns.

"I got in touch with Julian Storm. He has someone watching them right now from the outside, and he and his brothers will be over later to discuss everything. Veronica and Aubrey already know to keep the girls distracted while we talk," Noah says.

"It's why we're having a big *'celebration'*—to make it look more believable that we'd invite them over. Coach will also be with them," I add in.

They all mull over what we've just said for a moment until finally Grey nods, then Clay. I turn to look at Silas, expecting him to be on board as well, but he still doesn't seem convinced.

"Are we sure they'll keep them safe?" He looks us all over. "If something happens to Minnie or my son... you guys know I can't go through that again..." He swallows as emotions flash in his eyes.

"Hayes, normally, I wouldn't trust anyone to keep my wife safe but myself and you guys. But Julian really is the best of the best. If he says he'll keep them safe, he will. Let's hear him out, see what he has to say and thinks we should do, then we'll make a decision and go from there," Clay tells him calmly.

Silas passes his fingers through his hair. Finally, he nods in agreement and blows out a breath. "Okay, yeah. If you trust him, then I do too."

"Okay, good. Now that everyone is informed and on board, let's go get everything the girls are expecting us to come back with, then get some clarity to this shit show," I declare as Grey starts up the car and pulls away from the curb.

"Do we even know what this guy looks like?" Ford asks as we make our way to the pizzeria.

"Veronica gave me his name, and I searched him up. Apparently, he's still wanted by the feds. She also gave me the detective's number that she was in touch with back then. I don't know if he's still on the case, but we'll probably have to inform them of what's going on." Noah takes his phone out and swipes through it until he lands on a picture of the massive biker.

He turns it around, showing it to everyone. One after the other, their faces drain of color. We might be big and tough, but that guy is on a whole other level. I'm not afraid to admit that Victor could crush us all in an instant.

What the hell was Ronnie doing with a guy like that?

Chapter Twenty-Three

NOAH

Nice hair, Shane.

We make it back to the house and step out of the huge SUV, with Hayes carrying six boxes of extra-large pizzas, while Burkley and Ford hold cases of beer and drinks. Ellis has two bags full of different ice cream flavors, and I have an equal number of bags filled with snacks.

"Are you sure he has someone watching the girls right now? Because I don't see anyone looking suspicious." Silas looks down both sides of the street.

"Yeah, the only cars parked on the street are like ten houses away. If that's really how he's watching the girls, I'm not sure I trust the guy." Greyson frowns.

"Gentlemen."

We look across the street and find Julian crossing the road in what seems to be his everyday wear, a suit and tie, as he adjusts his cufflinks with a glare. Cropped black hair, stubble along his tight jaw that never seems to relax, and electric green eyes. *I swear, the guy always looks pissed off.*

Behind him is his younger brother, Jason, who looks like a menacing military sergeant ready to put you to work. With his huge build, tattoos littering his body, hair tied back in a bun, and thick beard. And just like his brother, a stern expression rests on his face and in his equally piercing green eyes.

Then there's Jessie behind him, the youngest of the three, who's dressed casually and looks way too excited at the thought of being in a house with our women. He seems to be all warm and sunshine, with a constant smile on his clean-shaved face. Same identical eyes as his brothers and short cropped black hair like his oldest. One look at them, and there's no doubt they are related.

His arm is awkwardly looped around our coach's neck, pulling him along. Shane Jefferson is just a bit taller than Silas, hitting the six-foot-five mark, while Jessie is around my height. A clean face as usual, and dark hair that seems longer than what we're used to seeing. He's dressed pretty casually as well, with gray golf shorts, a white button-down shirt, and white sneakers.

The closer he gets, the more nervous he seems, which is so unlike him unless he's in the presence of a certain someone.

Shane is a really good guy and an outstanding coach. He's so different compared to all the others I've had in the past or heard about. Where they tend to be more aggressive with their players to get the message through, he's always so calm and collected and treats us like equals. I don't think I've ever heard him raise his voice at anyone.

Most might think that's not a good coaching technique and that he should be sterner with his players. But it works for us and helps us thrive to our fullest potential. And in the end, we respect him even more for it.

"Julian." I reach out with my hand once he stands before me and shake his. "Jason, Jessie, Coach." I nod to the others. "Thank you for coming on such short notice, but this was a matter that couldn't wait."

"Completely understandable." Julian dips his head.

"So, where's your guy? Adler said you had someone watching the girls, but we didn't see anyone," Silas asks from beside me.

The side of Julian's mouth twitches. "If you could see him, then he wouldn't be doing his job properly, would he?"

"How do we know you're not full of shit?" Greyson narrows his eyes at him from Silas's other side.

Julian sighs heavily and closes his eyes momentarily, clearly annoyed with us already. He pulls out his phone and types out a message quickly. A few seconds later, blinking headlights down the street catch our attention. When I look the other way, the same thing happens. Two different cars at opposite ends.

"What the fuck! They're watching from all the way down there?!" Gabe steps up, anger and disappointment in his eyes. "They can't even see the house!"

"This is why I hate dealing with amateurs," Julian mutters under his breath.

"Julian," Coach warns him.

He sighs again, then tells us what we want to know. "There are microscopic cameras hidden around your house, and we have taken the liberty of installing some at your homes as well. Except for the penthouse, but we have hacked into their security system and will be keeping a close watch on everyone who enters and exits the building." He looks all of us over.

"There is no way someone could get within ten feet of your property without us being notified. And if by some miraculous way someone did make it inside without our knowledge, I have infiltrated your security system and have been listening every few minutes. If someone unwanted entered the house, I would have known." *Okay, this guy really is good.*

"What the fuck? You've been listening in on them? Through my security system that's supposed to be hack-proof. Isn't that against contract policies?" Clay glares at him.

Julian's lip twitches with amusement again. "It is hack-proof to anyone else but him." He nods toward Jessie.

"I created the impenetrable algorithm, which means I'm the only one who knows how to get in. They don't call us the best for nothing." Jessie winks with a beaming smile.

"Still, that feels like an invasion of privacy." Silas frowns.

"Do you want me to keep them safe or not?" Julian asks sternly.

"We don't actually have to listen in. The program picks up on every voice in the house, matching them with the person. Every time a new voice is heard, it notifies us, and we'll be able to pair it with its owner. It also sends out a different notification if a scream or loud noise is heard," Jessie informs us, settling our nerves slightly.

"Which I must inform you has happened quite frequently while you were all away. I understand congratulations are in order to the both of you." Julian looks from Clay to Greyson.

"Thank you." They both smile at the mention of the new changes in their lives.

"May we go inside now, or will we be standing out here all day?" Julian asks, once again looking annoyed as he swipes through his phone like he has better things to do than talk with us.

"Yeah, I'm starving. And I happen to know there's a party going on in there that I'd really like to see." Jessie grins with his hands in his pockets as he rocks back and forth on the heels of his shoes.

"You do know all those women in there are taken, right?" I ask him with furrowed brows.

"Oh, I know." He looks over to Shane with a smile, then back at us. "But it doesn't hurt to look." He shrugs. This guy is constantly flirting with any woman he sees. I honestly think he might be worse than Gabe and I were before Veronica.

"All right, let's go." Clay turns around and walks up to his front door, all of us following behind.

We enter the house and immediately understand Jessie's reference to a party as loud music blasts from the entertainment room. We wander over with curious eyes and find the girls all dancing and singing together in the middle of the room.

'Made You Look' by Meghan Trainor plays loudly on the speakers, and the Stanley Cup that was in the living room a few hours ago now sits on a table in the center of their dance party.

The girls haven't noticed our arrival and continue to sway their hips to the beat, hands in the air as they turn and rub their bodies up against each other. It's a fucking sight to see. We all wait by the open double doors, eyes glued to their movements. Although my focus is stuck on only one of them.

Veronica swings her ass around in that cruel short high-waisted skirt, thigh-high stockings rubbing together, knees slightly bent with stilettos on her feet. A tiny white crop top covers her breasts but exposes a portion of her tanned stomach and ribcage.

Her hands are up as she dances against Aubrey, who wears a spaghetti strap flowy blue dress. They're back-to-back, eyes closed as their asses rub up against each other. *God, I can't wait to get home and rip those schoolgirl clothes off her slender body and devour it.*

When I look over at the guys, I find them all watching with hungry eyes, except for Julian, who looks bored, and Jason seems to find this amusing. Gabe bounces with excitement at my side, while Jessie looks extremely pleased with the sight in front of him.

When I glance at Coach, his eyes are wide and unblinking. A light blotch of pink settles over his cheekbones as his gaze tracks every single movement a young blonde in a blue dress makes, his chest rapidly rising and falling. I bet if I got close enough, I could hear his heart racing a thousand beats a minute. *Jesus, both of them are completely gone for each other.*

Veronica turns around, spinning Aubrey with her so that they now face each other. She places her hands on Brey's hips, making her dress slide up her thighs a fraction. She says something to her that we can't hear over the music, and Aubrey throws her head back and laughs. When her face comes back down, her eyes open and finally fall on us.

She gasps loudly and takes a step back, straightening herself. "Shane!" That catches the attention of the other girls, and now all five sets of eyes lie on us as Aubrey blushes violently.

"Hi." Her voice comes out squeaky, making her clear her throat. "Your hair. You haven't cut it. It's... really nice." She quickly glances at her brother, then back at Coach, turning a deeper shade of red. "It suits you, I mean."

The girls all watch the awkward encounter unfold, unsure how to save her from this one. But then Greyson laughs, clearly not picking up on their attraction. "Jesus, Brey. That was embarrassing even for me. Come on, you've been around Coach for some time now, shouldn't you be past all this shy stammering stage?"

She giggles nervously as everyone chuckles.

Emma picks something off the table and comes running up to Greyson, throwing herself in his arms as he catches her. "It's positive! We're having a baby!" she squeals.

He looks over the pregnancy test and smiles tenderly at her before kissing her lips. "I love you. Are you happy about it now?"

"So happy! Gracie's gonna be a big sister. I can't wait to tell our parents."

"Your dad's going to be ecstatic," he tells her.

"Oh God... he's going to go crazy. Maybe we should wait a little before telling them finally." She stares at him with wide eyes as he chuckles. Emma then climbs out of his arms and looks at the newcomers. "What is this? Are you all friends now?"

"We bumped into them outside and invited them over to celebrate," Clay clarifies.

"Oh, playing the friendly neighbor now, are we, Clay?" Cecilia wanders over with a smirk.

"Shut up, C." Clay smirks back.

"Hey! Don't tell my wife to shut up," Silas interjects, making Julian groan.

"I'm already regretting coming in here," he grumbles.

"Oh, shush. We aren't that bad." Veronica comes up with Morgan and Aubrey.

Jessie offers Veronica a flirty smile. "Oh no, you definitely aren't."

"Back off, man," Gabe growls as he reaches a hand around Veronica's waist and pulls her in. She melts against him with a sigh as I kiss her temple.

Jessie only chuckles with a small head shake, then smiles broadly at the girls. "Hello, ladies."

"Hi, Jessie," they all say at once.

Julian steps up to Aubrey and takes her hand. "Hello, Aubrey. It is lovely seeing you again." He kisses the top of her hand.

She instantly blushes all over and glances at Shane quickly. "Hello, Julian. It's a surprise to see you here."

A smile graces his lips as he watches her, but it's not an affectionate one. It's the kind that says, '*I know how uncomfortable I'm making you, and I'm enjoying it. Plus, I really like to piss off my friend who has a crush on you.*' "I told you we would be meeting again."

"Yes, you did." She turns a deeper shade of red.

Greyson watches them interact with a very displeasing frown.

"All right. How about we get this stuff to the kitchen and grab some food? I have ice cream that's melting and an empty stomach," Gabe says as he backs out of the room, still holding on to Veronica with one hand and the other holding the two bags of ice cream.

Once we get to the kitchen, the girls begin putting things away while we guys take out plates and set things up to eat outside by the pool.

"Question, who brought the cup into the entertainment room?" Silas asks as he grabs a couple of beers between his fingers.

"We did." Cecilia smiles up at him and plants a kiss on his lips when he lowers for her.

"You're joking, right!?" Gabe stares at her with wide eyes.

"They better be joking! You know you're not allowed to carry anything heavy, babe!" Clay whips his head toward his wife.

"You shouldn't be either, Bunny." Greyson points at Emma.

She rolls her eyes at him. "We didn't. Those three did all the heavy lifting." She points toward Cecilia, Veronica, and Aubrey.

"Oh God... We're doomed..." Gabe whines and drops his head.

"We're kidding." Cecilia giggles and squeezes his arm. "We know all about your superstitions. Nigel carried it over." She nods to the keeper, who is once again sitting so quietly in the living room we forgot he was there.

"Oh, thank the lord." Ellis sighs and places his hand over his heart.

He's a bit intense with the unwritten rules when it comes to the Stanley Cup. For example, no touching the cup until you've won it, no touching at all of any other trophy leading up to the cup, and the winning team must drink from the cup. But the one Gabe was just freaking out over was the rule about only the winning team members or the keepers are permitted to carry the cup. Others can touch it, but they can't lift it.

"Did you seriously think they actually carried it?" I snort. "From Emma and Morgan? Yeah, I could picture it. That woman is scary strong, and I've seen her lift heavy things before." I point from Em to Morg, then move on to Aubrey and Cece. "But Brey is way too delicate to do anything like that, and let's be real, the cup is almost as tall as Cecilia. No way she could pick that up."

"Wow, I see how much faith you have in me." Cecilia frowns at me as a few of the guys chuckle.

"Just calling it like it is, Mama." I wink at her.

"And what about me?" Veronica smirks when my eyes widen slightly and I swallow, realizing I may have fucked up here.

She has one brow raised high as she walks over leisurely, that devilish look in her eyes. "What's the matter, Casanova?" She rests her hand on my chest as she leans into me, my arms coming around her waist. "Don't think I'm strong enough to lift it?" She flicks my lower lip with her tongue before biting it softly and pulling it back slightly.

Pleasure shoots through my body, my blood running south toward my growing erection that presses against her tight little body. *Good, she's being playful. I can work with that.* "Oh, I know just how strong you are, Kitten."

Gabe comes up behind her, pinning her between us. Her free hand lifts and comes to wrap around his nape. "After all, you do take our brutal pounding quite well," he says, kissing the crook of her neck.

"Dear lord, that is not information I needed to hear." Julian runs a hand down his face.

Veronica squeezes out from between us and strolls over to him. "Oh, come on, Mr. Storm. Lighten up, relax." She undoes the button of his suit jacket and begins to shrug it off his shoulders as he glares at her, like touching his suit is a forbidden act. "Take a load off."

"HA!" Jason exclaims, a deep, rough laugh expelling from his lungs. "You're telling M*ister Uptight and In Control* to relax? Good luck with that, sweets."

"He's right, I've known that guy since we were kids, and I've rarely seen him loosen up," Coach says with a soft chuckle.

"He's the definition of a control freak." Jessie laughs.

Julian turns his glare on them, then takes Veronica's wrists in his grasp swiftly. Her body goes rigid instantly in his hold as she gasps. His head whips back to her, picking up on her sudden change in demeanor, and quickly releases her wrists. "Apologies, but please do not touch the suit."

She steps back, giving him a stiff nod and a tight smile. "If you don't want me to touch it, then take it off. We aren't going to a business meeting; we're just friends celebrating together."

"Yes, Julian. Take it off! We wanna see what's under that armor," Emma encourages.

"Bunny," Greyson growls with a warning.

"What?" She looks at him. "We did it to Shane, now it's his turn." She looks back at Julian, pumping her fist in the air. "Take it off! Take it off! Take it off!"

Immediately, Morgan, Cecilia, and Veronica join in, while Aubrey blushes madly. And us men? We just frown in disapproval. *What else can we do?*

"Man, just take it off. They won't stop until you do," Silas tells him with a sigh.

"They might even tackle you to the ground and take it off themselves. I wouldn't put it past this one." Greyson points a thumb at his fiancée.

Julian looks at all the girls with irritation, then turns on his axis and marches out of the kitchen and toward the front door.

The girls quiet down their chants as they all look from one to the other. "Did he really just leave?" Morgan asks.

But then Julian returns in only a black dress shirt, rolling up the sleeves on his way over. The jacket now gone from sight. "Happy?" He stretches his arms out.

"Well, I'll be damned. Who knew all it took was a bunch of women yelling at him to convince him into something?" Jason guffaws loudly. His laugh is infectious enough to make us all join in, despite the daggers Julian shoots at us with his eyes.

Two hours later, we've all eaten, and the girls are now inside cleaning up and preparing the snacks for the fire pit. I overheard Veronica mention babies and wedding plans, so we know that should keep them occupied for a little while.

"I have already been in touch with the agent you sent me. He and I have worked together in the past, and he happened to still be working on Victor's case, although it had run cold until now," Julian says quietly with an evil smirk. "He will be in touch with Miss Masters in the next few days to collect the evidence and talk with her about his latest methods of contact."

"Good." I nod to him.

"And are we still agreeing to not tell the girls?" Greyson asks, looking uncertain.

"Yeah, what if they put themselves in a dangerous situation without even realizing it?" Silas adds, holding that same look on his face.

"It is best not to involve them in this current predicament. Women tend to act on impulse, certainly mothers. It is instinctive for them. And the three women who are not aware at this moment are either mothers or soon-to-be ones," Julian informs them.

"He's right," Jason starts. "I've done a lot of security detail involved with threats. And most times when things went south, it was because the woman made an impulsive decision that only further put her in danger. I'm not saying all women are the same, and I understand their need to protect someone they love. But sometimes, to keep them safe, it's best to keep them in the unknown."

"Cecilia would never do anything reckless like that," Silas argues.

"She would." Everyone turns to me. "Cecilia would risk her life without a second thought if it meant saving her child or family. So would Morgan, Emma, and Aubrey. Hell, the minute Veronica saw what was in that package, she was ready to pack up her things and disappear just because she thought it would keep everyone safe." I smile sadly at my friends. "They're right. We can't tell the girls. It's the only way we can truly protect them."

"You have nothing to worry about. Their every movement will be followed, as well as yours. He may have threatened the women only, but I would not put it past him to come after you as well," Julian says.

Clay huffs out, dropping back against the chair as he passes his fingers through his short hair. "Okay, so what do we do?"

"Nothing. The best thing to do is to act naturally. If he gets a whiff that you are being protected, he might back away, and that is not what we want. We want him to come out so that we can catch him," Julian tells him.

"My guess is that he was only trying to scare Veronica by sending her those pictures. He wants her to act out, do something crazy that might put her in a vulnerable position. I think he'll keep his target on her; that's why we'll be putting extra protection on her and around the penthouse," Jason reassures Gabe and me. It's what I thought as well.

"Do you have cameras installed within the penthouse?" Jessie questions.

I look at Gabe, who shrugs, then to Silas. It's technically still his, so if anyone knows, it would be him.

He shakes his head. "No. There were some when I first bought it, but I had them removed."

Jessie pulls out his phone, tapping away at it quickly. "We'll get some installed tomorrow morning." I'm about to protest when he lifts his hand to stop me. "And no, we won't be listening in or looking at the feed. It's simply a precaution."

"Wait, what about Aubrey? I know Ronnie spends most of her time with you two, and I don't feel safe letting her stay in that condo alone. Certainly, since that's where the package was delivered." Greyson shakes his head.

"We already discussed this with her. She has a suitcase packed in Ronnie's car. We'll tell the girls that a pipe broke in the condo and that there are renovations to do. Which gives her a reason to stay with you and Emma, while Veronica will stay with us," I inform him and watch the worry melt off his features.

"I will be in touch if our men get a sighting of him, you will be in the loop the whole time. And if there is any news that comes to light, please notify me right away," Julian finishes as he looks over to where the girls are now in view and coming our way.

"Of course," Gabe tells him quietly. "Thank you again for this."

Julian nods just as Veronica plops down in my lap and kisses my neck affectionately. "I tried to stall them as long as I could," she whispers against my skin.

"We're all good, Kitten. You don't have to worry anymore," I murmur back, turning my head to the side and capturing her lips.

Delivering a silent promise to do everything in my power to keep her safe.

VERONICA

It's a little past ten as we sit around the fire pit, everyone nursing beers, except for Silas, and sprawled out along the chairs and couches. Couples cocooning together as they make pretty eyes at each other with tender kisses.

The Storm brothers and Shane are still here, laughing along with Noah and Gabe. Well, all are laughing except for Julian, who only smirks occasionally. *That man is as serious as a funeral home.*

It's surprising to see them get along so well. The few times they've interacted in the past, it felt like we were seconds away from a brawl. I expected them to leave the second dinner was over, Julian mostly; he seemed so uncomfortable around us. But to my surprise, he hasn't made any attempt or excuse to leave. *Yet.*

Aubrey and I are seated on the opposite side of everyone else, simply people watching through the licks of orange and red. A soft, warm blanket rests over my shoulders and back, bundling me up in my seat. Despite it being late July, a cool breeze settles in late at night.

Shane stands from his chair, excusing himself as he walks toward the patio doors, glancing up at Aubrey on his way in. Their gaze locks on each other, passion and longing swimming in their eyes.

Brey's cheeks warm with a pink hue before she shivers slightly, and a quiet gasp falls from her parted lips. She quickly looks away, and disappointment flashes in his vibrant blues before he refocuses his gaze on the doors and heads inside.

"Ugh! What is wrong with me?" she mumbles as she buries her face in her hands.

"Hey, it's normal to be nervous around someone you like," I say quietly as I place my hand on her thigh.

She looks up from her hands with a sad expression. "I can't even look at him for a long time without losing my cool. How will I ever have a proper conversation with him?" Her head drops back down. "He probably thinks I'm an immature freak."

"Are you kidding me, Brey?" She looks up once more, resting her back against the couch we're sitting on. "That guy is crazy about you, and he knows you're shy.

You have nothing to worry about. When the time comes for whatever is happening between you two to evolve, you'll both find a way. I know it." I smile genuinely at her.

"That's the problem, Ronnie. It can't evolve. But I don't know how to stop it, and I don't know if I want to anymore..." she whispers in a small, uncertain voice.

I squeeze her thigh. "Then stop fighting it, your brother will come around. He'd be an idiot not to see how great you two could be together." She tries to smile at my comment, but it's weak. "Plus, I mean, have you seen the guy? I almost fanned myself when he walked in. If I had a sister, I'd want her to be with a hunk like that."

This time she giggles. "He really does look nice. I like what he did with his hair." She looks down at her hands with a smile as a beautiful blush forms.

"Ah, yes. The hair—you've mentioned that earlier." I giggle and bump my shoulder against hers.

"Oh God, don't remind me. That was mortifying, I swear I thought I was going to catch on fire."

We're both giggling when a form passes in front of us. When we look up, Shane stands before Aubrey with a blanket similar to mine in his hands. He opens it up and places it over her shoulders.

"You seemed a little cold. I wouldn't want you getting sick."

As he finishes wrapping it around her, his face inches from hers, she looks up into his rich blue eyes. "Thank you, Shane."

His eyes drop to her plump rosy lips; he swallows, then his gaze returns to her pale browns. "You're welcome... Aubrey," he breathes out, her name rolling off his tongue like a sweet caress.

Jesus, even I'm getting hot watching them.

He straightens and passes his fingers through his rogue wavy strands, pushing them off his face. But the second he removes his hand, they fall back down and frame the side of his face beautifully.

Aubrey whimpers as she watches him. Her eyes go wide when she realizes what she just did, a blush spreading like wildfire over the tip of her ears and neck. Shane chuckles softly and gives her a dazzling smile, deep dimples making an appearance.

He takes a step over to the empty spot on the couch, pulls his shorts up slightly as he sits down beside her, thick thighs fighting against the fabric. He leans in, placing his elbows on his knees, fingers laced together between his spread legs. Massive biceps strain the material of his shirt, and his back ripples with strong muscles. He might not play hockey anymore, but he definitely still has the shape of one.

Aubrey leans back against the couch, watching him. She turns to me quickly with those big eyes again, then back to him. He stares down at his hands for a while, then tilts his head to the side, his eyes roaming over her features.

"Are you okay?" She frowns a bit, confused by his question. "With everything going on?" he clarifies, looking around to make sure no one is paying attention to us. "And you as well, Veronica?"

"Oh! Yes, I'm fine. I'm okay. Peachy," Aubrey rambles quickly, then squeezes her eyes shut and shakes her head slightly.

Shane smiles at her as I giggle. "Yes, we're fine. A little shaken, but we trust your friends. Thank you for asking," I tell him.

"Good." He nods, then looks back down at his hands once more, grazing his bottom lip with his teeth before giving Aubrey his attention once more.

He glances at Greyson quickly, who's busy doting on his fiancée, then back to his desired target. "You know, if you need a place to stay, I have a room... I mean, spare rooms. You could stay with me if... if you'd like." He swallows again and clears his throat.

Aubrey's eyes practically bug out of her head as she stares at him without blinking, mouth opening and closing repeatedly like a fish. *This is pretty comical to watch.* I fold my arms and lean back against the couch, waiting to see what she says.

She bites her lip and glances at me for guidance, but all I do is shrug. In the end, it's her choice. She looks down at her feet and sighs, and by the look on her face, I already know what she's about to say.

"I can't... Greyson already knows I'm staying with him. I don't think he'd take it very well if I told him I'd rather stay with you." She finally gazes back up at him with a sad smile. "I'm sorry, Shane."

He nods, looking a bit defeated. "No need to apologize, I completely understand. It was simply an offer, one that stays if you ever change your mind. You'll always be welcome in my home, Aubrey."

She blushes and smiles at him. Actually, they're both just smiling at each other now. I almost feel like I'm interrupting something magical just by sitting here.

"By the way, you looked beautiful on your vacation trip." Something close to desire flicks through his eyes. "The tropical sun really suits you, I... I really liked your bathing suit."

Oh God! Shane, no! Why would you say that?!

Aubrey practically melts at the compliment, leaning slightly toward him. "Oh, thank you, Shane." But then she straightens, catching on to the last part. Her brows furrow. "Wait, how did you see my swimsuit? I haven't posted any pictures of it."

Shane's eyes shoot up to me, then over to Emma, before returning to Aubrey. She tracks their movements, quickly putting the puzzle pieces together. She shifts in her seat toward me with a nervous look.

"What did you do?" she hisses through gritted teeth.

I catch Shane's apologetic smile over Aubrey's shoulder. "It's nothing, we just sent him a few pictures of you while in Fiji." I shrug like it's no big deal. But the look of horror on her face tells me it is.

"Who's we?" she questions.

"Just me and Em..." I give her a strained smile.

"Oh my God!" She hides her face behind her hands, then sticks one out toward me. "Show me them. Show me the pictures." *Shit! I was hoping she wouldn't ask that.*

"Umm... we sort of deleted the pictures after sending them so you wouldn't find out..." I giggle nervously. "Sorry. But I'm sure Shane still has them. Don't you?" I look over and find him staring like a deer caught in headlights.

"I... uhhh... maybe... yes, yes... just... give me a minute." He pulls his phone out quickly, fumbling a little as he opens it.

He tilts the phone slightly so that we can't make out what's on the screen, then passes it over to Aubrey. His eyes bounce between her and the phone, an anxious look in them as if she might fall on something she's not supposed to see.

After a few seconds and fifteen pictures later, Aubrey gasps, shutting the phone and pushing it back into Shane's hand. "Oh, God! I'm so mortified!" she whispers behind her hands that cover her face once again. She's now practically red from head to toe with embarrassment.

"Don't be." Shane grabs her wrist gently, tugging it down to her lap. He then peeks over at Grey, making sure we still don't have his attention. "You looked absolutely gorgeous in every single one of them." He smiles and releases her wrist.

She brings her second hand down and breathes out, as if she'd been holding her breath the whole time his hand was on her. "Still, I'm sorry my friends bothered you with that."

"I'm glad they did, I really enjoyed them." A tiny speck of pink appears on his cheekbones.

I snort, then mumble, "I'm sure you did."

"Ronnie!" Aubrey hisses at me.

"Well, gentlemen." Julian rises from his seat, gathering all our attention. "And ladies." He graces us with a small, tight smile. "It has been a delightful evening, but I am afraid we must get going. Some of us do not have the luxury of only working half the year."

"Yes, thank you for the invite. We should do this again. Ladies, I wish you all a good night." Jessie beams as he stands as well, following behind his older brother.

"Goodnight, Jessie," us girls all call at once, gaining a choir of groans.

Jason walks behind, wishing us goodnight with a nod. He doesn't seem like much of a talker. Shane stands with a sigh, a regretful smile on his face as he looks down at the woman he longs for.

"Goodnight, Aubrey," he says softly as his fingertips skim over her knees.

Her breath catches, lips parting, pupils slightly dilating at the small intimate touch of affection. "Goodnight, Shane," she whispers breathlessly.

They smile at each other for a moment until Jessie's voice snaps him out of his daze.

"You coming, Shay?"

He looks up, nodding. "Yeah, I'll be right there." Then he turns to wave goodbye to everyone. "Goodnight, guys." He gives one last lingering look at the pretty blonde before walking away, through the house and out the front door with the Storm brothers.

"You two are so hot together. Jesus, I think my panties might be wet just from watching you both." I giggle. "By the way, that was a good start to a conversation with him."

Aubrey quickly grabs hold of my arm, forcing me to look into her huge eyes. "He saved them. The pictures. They're saved into his phone, in a file named 'My Angel'!"

Wow, he really has it as bad as she does.

I take both her hands in mine as we sit sideways to face each other. "I told you he liked you."

A breathtaking smile splits over her face, lighting it up like a thousand fireflies floating through the air on a warm summer night.

Chapter Twenty-Four

VERONICA

One unfulfilled skittle.

~ One Week Later / August ~

Noah and I exit his car parked along the street before he walks around the hood and takes my hand on the sidewalk. He kisses the back of it with tenderness as I guide him toward my main girl's shop in Brooklyn, pushing the door open as the bell chimes, indicating a new client's arrival.

"Hey, Bear!" I wave to the big burly man sitting on his rolling stool as he prepares his equipment for his first client that waits patiently in the tattoo chair next to him.

"There's my favorite Skittle girl! It's about time you graced us with your presence. These big boys keeping you locked up in their big fancy tower or what?" he calls back, laughing.

"Aw, did you miss me, Pooky Bear?" I pout my lips, sarcastically fluttering my eyelashes at him, to which he barks out a laugh and shakes his head.

I turn to Noah and lean into his side, my hand falling to his chest. "Casanova, this is Bernard, but we all call him Bear." I turn back to the big mountain man. "Bear, this is my boyfriend, Noah."

"You mean one of them." Bear laughs as Noah chuckles.

"Shut up. Maze in yet?" I smile.

"Yeah, she's in her section waiting for you. Head on back." He points with his thumb behind him.

"Thanks!" I call as I pull Noah along with me to the divider at the far end that separates Maze's section from the rest of the tattoo parlor. "Hey, babe." I smile once I see her lounging in a laid-back chair, scrolling through her phone.

She puts her phone away instantly, throws her legs over the side of the chair, and hops off before striding toward us with a devilish smile. "Ah, I get to meet boyfriend number two today. Hey there, Noah. I was wondering when she'd drag you along."

He smiles. "Hey, Maze. I've heard a lot about you. Nice to finally meet the person behind my Kitten's colorful appearance." He reaches a hand forward and shakes hers.

"All good things, obviously. I'm a saint." She winks at him, then claps her hands. "So, what are we doing today, girly? You giving me free rein?"

I smile up at Noah. "Actually, I was thinking you could pick."

"Me?" he questions.

I wind my arms around his neck as he circles my waist. "Yeah, whatever color you want." I press my lips to his, smiling against them.

I haven't been this happy in a long time, and it feels amazing. Noah and Gabe are bringing the old me back, day by day. The one who smiled at everything and saw only the good in the world, the one who didn't fear anything. And I can't thank them enough for it.

"Okay." He smiles back. "Maze, let's turn her into a real-life skittle," he says without taking his eyes off me.

"Yes! I knew I'd like this guy." She pumps a fist. "Come, my darling. Let's make you the prettiest fucking rainbow we've ever seen." She brushes her fingers through the end of my hair. "Same length too?"

"Actually, no more cuts. Just the ends and the dye."

Maze's eyes bounce up to mine, a wide grin spreading on her lips before she looks over to Noah. "Whatever you're doing, keep doing it. It's about time she let go." She then grabs my arm, spins around, and drags me toward the chair.

Four hours later, we're walking out of Maze's shop with my new skittle hair. Flashy orange, red, yellow, blue, purple, and green all over. It's a little crazy, but I love it. She also took the time to style my hair into beautiful curls, and now looking at my reflection in Noah's car window, I feel like a thousand bucks.

He comes up behind me, holding onto my hips, and presses a kiss to my shoulder. "You look absolutely stunning, Kitten."

"Thank you. You picked well." I turn in his arms and seal my lips to his, melting against him with a soft moan. "Can we go see Trinity now?"

He pulls away with a warm smile. "Yeah, let's go."

We buckle up inside the car and make our way over to Noah's sister. My phone starts pinging with new messages from my group chat with the girls. Cecilia is sending us pictures of the setup for the birthday party they're organizing today for a little ten-year-old boy who suffers from Paraplegia. He's really big into Mario and Luigi, so the whole room is now decorated like the Mushroom Kingdom.

Their launch party last weekend was beyond successful. It was amazing to watch them talk about their cause and goals for the future with so much devotion. *The Mackenzie Rose Funhouse Foundation* might seem like a silly organization to some, but I personally think it's wonderful what they're doing.

Their main goal is to host pro bono events for children who come from low-income families. Whether it's birthday parties or graduation parties, holiday parties or charity events for orphanages and churches. They simply want to help the community by giving them their very own special day.

They already had a handful of sponsors and donations before the actual launch even happened, thanks to the boys constantly bringing it up with the media and reporters. But from what I've heard from Em and Cece, the launch brought in so many more, and they are now booked solid through the next year.

They're already planning on hiring more employees and eventually expanding to a bigger location to host more events at once. It's beautiful to see them at work. You can tell just how much they love what they're doing, that they've finally found their calling. I'm beyond thrilled for them, but a part of me can't help but feel envious of what they have.

All my friends have a purpose in life, a goal, a dream. Morgan has her own interior design company. Cecilia and Emma now have their rapidly growing foundation. Even Aubrey has been saving up for the past few years to open her own bakery. She has the whole five-to-ten-year plan written out and already has a book filled with her own recipes for when she finally opens it.

And then there's me. Me, who has no idea what she's doing with her life. Me, who's never had a goal or a dream, a path she wanted to follow. And I hate that. I want to be excited about something. I want to have a purpose like they all do. I want a job that brings me joy and makes me smile knowing I'll get to do something I love every single day.

"Hey... what's that sad look in your eyes for?" Noah watches me as we stop at a red light, his hand coming to my thigh and squeezing lightly. "What's going through your mind, Kitten? Are you worried about Victor?"

Hearing his name used to make my skin crawl, but now that I have Noah and Gabe, it doesn't have that same effect anymore. I feel safe with them, and I guess knowing we're constantly being followed by Julian's men helps a bit, too.

I shake my head. "No, it's not that."

"Then what is it, Kitten? I can tell something's bothering you."

I sigh as he turns his attention back to the road but glances at me every few seconds, letting me know that I still have his attention. "It's just that seeing Cecilia and Emma so happy with what they're doing kind of makes me feel…" I trail off.

"Unfulfilled?" he finishes for me.

I rest my head against the seat. "Yeah… They all have these great plans and accomplishments. And I just have… nothing. I don't even know what I'd want to do if I had the opportunity."

"Hmm," he hums, not saying more for a minute. "What is it you like doing, Veronica? Even if it's simple, what brings you joy when you do it?"

"I don't know. Being with you and Gabe makes me happy." I smile when he does.

"You make us happy too, Kitten. But that's not really something you can do as a career. Although I would pay you to stay with me forever." He chuckles. "Tell me, do you like what you're doing right now? Working for us, I mean."

"I guess, yeah. I mean, I've always liked cleaning and keeping things neat, but I prefer the organizing part. I really like doing those things for you guys and making it simple and easier to use. There are so many different ways it can be done, and the finished product always makes me smile. It's crazy how even the messiest place can look beautiful once it's well organized."

When I gaze over at him, he stares at me with wonder. "You see what just happened there? You lit up talking about that. If it's something you enjoy doing, why not make a career out of it? You could start your own business. Doesn't have to be big or take up all your time. It can just be a small thing that you do for fun and get paid at the same time."

That piques my interest but also makes me a bit nervous. "I wouldn't even know how to start a business, and I don't know many people like you guys do. How would I even get customers?"

He smiles but keeps his eyes on the road. "That's simple; we can help you with getting it started. You could even ask the girls for help since they're all involved in the business world," he suggests.

"And when it comes to customers, ear-to-mouth is always the best way to start, but having a website always helps too. You could take pictures of the things you've done in the penthouse and use them to show off your work. Then we'll all help spread the word and get you some customers," he finishes as his thumb caresses my thigh.

"Is there even a clientele for that kind of business? Do people really hire others to organize their stuff for them?" I have a hard time believing there's such a thing.

Noah snorts. "You'd be surprised at the number of rich people who hire people specifically for that simply because they're too lazy to do it themselves or want to make it look like they have their shit together. Trust me, Veronica, you'd have many requests."

"Okay, and how much would I charge for my services? I don't even know what people in that line of work charge." I nibble my lip, a thousand questions and thoughts popping into my head.

"One thing at a time, Kitten. We'll do research on it and everything. I'm not telling you to start right now, but if it's something you think you'd like to do, then it's worth exploring. Just take your time and think it over." He takes my hand and brings it to his lips, kissing the back of it.

"Okay, yeah. I'll think about it." I smile when he looks over at me, feeling like I'm finally moving in the right direction.

"But you do know that you don't need to work, right? Gabe and I can easily take care of you if you'd prefer. We don't have a problem with that. You could even stop taking care of the penthouse if you wanted, and we'll find someone else to do it. We just want you to be happy."

I squeeze his hand with my fingers. "I know, babe. But I've lived most of my life depending on someone else, first my parents, then Victor. But these last few years, it's been just me, and I've gotten used to taking care of myself. I don't want that to change. I don't want to become dependent again."

"I get that, and I admire you for it. Just know that we're here for you." He releases my hand and brings his to the back of my head, pulling me in to kiss my forehead. "Whatever you want, Kitten."

"Thank you." I smile, then rest back in my seat with a giddy feeling inside of me. "Damn, who knew I'd end up so lucky? Not one, but two sugar daddies. That's a pretty big win if you ask me."

A melodic laugh bursts from Noah's lips, everything about him softening as the happiness takes over. This time, I'm the one to lean in and grab his chin, tilting his head to the side to kiss his smiling lips.

God, I'm crazy about these men.

We arrive at the care facility thirty minutes later, ready to chat Trinity's ears off. But the moment we make it to the nurses' station and see Jannice and Everly carrying a sad smile, we know things aren't going to go as planned.

"Hey, Noah... I was just about to call you..." Jannice stands from behind the desk.

His body tenses beside mine, hand tightening against my own. "What's wrong?"

"I think it's best if you speak with Dr. Daltonsen. I'll page him to let him know you've arrived, and he'll come see you right away." Everly speaks up for Jannice, whose eyes begin to water.

Noah swallows, jaw straining. "Just tell me what's going on," he barks out, but it's not aimed at them. He feels exactly what I'm sensing, that we're about to receive bad news.

Everly sighs. "Trinity isn't doing too well... we had to place a ventilator because her oxygen levels are dropping and she's struggling to breathe on her own... she—"

Noah doesn't give her time to finish. He tightens his hold on my hand and marches over to Trinity's room. He swings the door open quickly and walks to the end of her bed, standing in place like a frozen statue as he stares down at his sister.

One look at her, and I know this is bad. She doesn't look like the Trinny I saw just four days ago. Tubes and wires spill out from everywhere, with new machines placed beside her bed. Her skin has turned a pale ashy color, making her look like she aged ten years in the blink of an eye. Jesus, she even looks like she lost weight.

I take a step closer, blinking back the emotions that threaten to surface. I delicately place my hand on Noah's arm, looking up at him. He still hasn't moved, hasn't said a word. "Noh..."

He clears his throat and shakes his head, taking a step away from me. My hand drops from his arm, landing at my side. I try to ignore the sting of rejection as he turns his back to me. I know it isn't about me; he's hurting and fighting his emotions. Having me here is probably making it harder.

I take a step back toward the door. "I'll wait outsi—"

"No," he says harshly, making me jump, but then falls silent for a few seconds. "Please don't leave..." he finally whispers, and my heart breaks at the pain in his voice.

I quickly walk up to his back that still faces me, wrapping my arms around him and resting my cheek against his stiff muscles. "Okay, I'm not going anywhere." I kiss his back and sense him take a deep breath.

Letting go, I walk over to Trinity's side and settle into the chair, reaching out to hold her cold hand. "Hey, beautiful." I smile sadly, tears welling in my eyes as I rub my thumb back and forth over her hand.

"I know we saw each other a few days ago, but I really wanted to show you my new hair. Your brother picked it out for me. Do you like it? Don't tell him I said this, but I'm starting to think he has really good taste. First me, now my hair. What's next?"

I turn to the sound of Noah's soft chuckle; he breathes out and offers me a gratified smile, then mouths, "Thank you."

I smile and nod just as the door to Trinity's room opens, and in comes Dr. Daltonsen. Noah swivels and reaches him near the door, shaking his outstretched hand. "Noah, I'm happy you could make it in today. And I'm sorry this isn't under better circumstances." He looks past Noah and directly at me. "Hello again, Veronica."

"Hi." I give him a small wave, then redirect my focus to the angel resting in bed.

They cut to the chase, and Dr. Daltonsen divulges the situation at hand, going into technical terms and explaining what they are doing. I try to listen in, but he tends to talk like everyone around him is a doctor and understands medical terms and codes. After so many years, I know Noah does, but I'm still new at this. So besides small recognizable words, I still don't have a clue what's happening to her.

I stand and kiss Trinity's forehead, my hand slowly leaving hers as I walk over to Noah, coming into his side as his arm holds onto my waist. He turns his head to me and kisses my temple. "What's going on?" I ask quietly.

Noah gulps thickly before talking. "She has an infection."

"Oh, okay. Can we treat it?" I ask, feeling hopeful.

The doctor gives me a despairing look as Noah faces me and cradles the back of my head with one hand, the other still around my waist. He brings my head down to his shoulder, kissing my forehead with a sigh. "There's no point..."

"Why not? Why would you say that?" My voice cracks, emotions clogging up my throat. I don't move; I need his comfort just as much as he needs mine in this instant.

"Her organs are failing..." Those words are like a direct stab to my heart. I turn my head into him as the tears that have been on the verge of falling since we walked in finally let loose.

"I'm sorry," Dr. Daltonsen says softly.

Noah nods against me. "I knew it was a matter of time." I lift my head and look into his sad, heartbroken eyes.

Dr. Daltonsen steps closer, placing his hand on Noah's back. "We'll continue to treat her, give you both time to come to terms. But you should know that it won't be long despite our best efforts."

He squeezes my arm then retreats. "I'll leave you both. If you have any questions, please don't hesitate to call. Again, my sincerest apologies." He turns and exits the room.

We stand there for a moment, not wanting to pull away, not knowing how to accept this. Eventually, Noah takes my hand and brings us over to Trinity. He sits down in the chair and pulls me into his lap. And for the next two hours, all we do is sit there in complete silence, staring at the young girl who lost her life too early.

The car ride home is silent, so are the next few hours in the penthouse. Noah busied himself with drinking the minute we stepped out of the elevator, then went up to his room after a few heavy glasses. I'm not taking it personally; I understand he needs his space right now, so I busy myself with cleaning, since it is still my job here.

It's four in the afternoon when Gabe finally gets home. He had some photoshoots and a commercial to do with some sponsors, so he's been out of the house most of the day. And I think it was for the best. Noah still doesn't seem to want to tell people about his sister, and I'm not sure how we could have hidden his current mood if Gabe had been home.

"Damn, Vixen!" He comes up behind me, wrapping me in his arms and kissing my neck. "My girl is sexy as fuck!"

I giggle and turn to face him, throwing my arms around his neck and legs around his waist as he lifts me. "I missed you today."

A heart-stopping grin reaches his ears. "Yeah, baby?" I nod. "I missed you, too. I always miss you the second I step out." He brings his lips to mine, showing me just how much he missed me with his mouth. I moan and wiggle in his hold as heat begins to bloom in my core.

When we finally come up for air, my gaze falls on Noah who stands on the opposite side of the kitchen island, watching us. Gabe sets me down on the ground, and I pad over to Noah barefoot.

My hands slide up his chest, one going into his hair as he rests his on my hip. His hair is still damp from the shower he must have taken recently. I pull him down to me, claiming his mouth like Gabe did to me seconds ago.

Since I temporarily moved in last week, I've been sleeping in Noah's bed, and every night, we fall beneath the sheets all together. A mess of tangled limbs, sweaty bodies pressed up against each other until we give in to exhaustion. And in the morning, when the sun rises, it's only Noah and I in bed.

I hate waking up without Gabe, but I also love my little intimate moments with Noah, where he cuddles me and kisses every inch of my body. Where we talk like normal lovers about everything and anything. It makes every kiss shared between us feel different, deeper, as if we share something that's just between me and him.

I love it. But I wish I had this with Gabe as well.

When I pull away and look into his deep chocolate eyes, all I see is love shining back at me. My heart dances in the most beautiful way every time he looks at me like that. Who knew this would be waiting for me on the other side once I finally gave into them?

Is this what the girls feel when they look at their partners? This warmth that keeps on growing, this need to have them at your side? To have all their little smiles, little touches, little whispers?

Because if it is, then I was wrong about Victor. I never loved him the way I thought I did. What I had with him never felt all consuming. Never felt like he was my reason for breathing, my reason for existing. I never felt a fraction of what I feel for these two men who worship the ground I walk on.

Which only leaves me with one realization.

I've fallen madly, head over heels, irrevocably in love with Noah Adler and Gabriel Ellis.

Chapter Twenty-Five

GABRIEL

Fried brain and tequila shots.

"We should do something tonight, something different," Ronnie says as she lies down over mine and Noah's legs. Her butt is between us, thighs over me and head resting on Noah as he passes his fingers through her locks.

Something's up with him; I don't know what it is, but I can feel it. He's been quieter than usual, seeming lost in his head. He's also been drinking much more than I'm used to seeing him do. Every few minutes, I notice Ronnie looking up at him with a question in her eyes. One he clearly hears and offers her what I can only describe as a reassuring smile back. But it's small.

Something happened today, and Vixen knows what it is, but she hasn't said a word. Neither has he, and I can't help but feel a bit unsettled by it. I know they spend more time together than she and I. They clearly share a deeper connection, and it makes me jealous. I hate it, but I don't know how to change it.

I rub my hand up and down her long, smooth legs. "What did you have in mind, baby?" If there's one great thing about living in the city, it's that there's always something to do, no matter the time.

"Let's go wild, get drunk and dance the night away. I haven't been to a club in so long!" She pulls her legs off mine and sits up between us with a huge grin, grabbing on to both our thighs.

"Yes! I'll dress all slutty in a super short dress, show off my new hair. We'll take a car out. You can pretend you don't know me and try to pick me up at the bar. Then we'll dance, and you'll take me back to your lair to do all those filthy things you've dreamed of doing to me." Her fingernails trail up our thighs, closer to where we want them. "Unless you two are too old for that."

Noah snorts as my mouth drops open. "Excuse me?"

"Well, what? I am much younger than you two. It's understandable if staying up past midnight is too hard on your thirty-year-old bodies." She sucks in her lips to suppress her giggles, eyes bouncing with amusement at my astounded expression.

"First of all, we're twenty-eight, not thirty." I grab her hips, lifting her into the air and making her straddle my thighs. "Second, you're only four years younger than us, little lady."

I nip her chin as she throws her head back and laughs, my fingers digging into her ribs as I tickle her. "And third, this body works overtime to be at its absolute best, around the clock. So you can bet that sexy little ass of yours that it can keep up with you."

I capture her open mouth quickly, tongue tangling with her as she moans. My hand comes up to fist her hair, angling her head exactly like I want it. I deepen the kiss until she's squirming in my hold, hips rocking back and forth as she chases more friction.

I release her hair and grab hold of her hips, stopping her movements. She whimpers as I pull away. "Later, baby. I promise we'll take good care of you." I kiss her pouting lips one last time. "What do you say, Noh? You up for a wild night with our girl?"

He picks up his amber drink from the side table, downs the rest, and sets it back down. "Sure. Let's do it."

"Yay! Give me an hour, then we'll go. I'm going to make you boys drool tonight." She stands from the couch, kissing us both, then turns to leave.

"As long as I get to see your ass every time you bend down, I'm good," I call after her as she reaches the stairs. She grabs hold of her short skirt and flips it up, giving us a delicious view of her ass.

I lean back against the couch, laughing away. "God, this girl is going to be the death of me."

"You and I both, brother." Noah chuckles while shaking his head.

An hour later, we've all showered and changed. Noah and I are dressed in dark blue jeans and a nice dress shirt, his white, mine powder blue. A pair of Oxfords on both our feet. Noah's sleeves are down, while mine are rolled up, the first two buttons at our collars undone.

I pass my fingers through my hair, pushing the medium-length strands back and over to one side, the way I know my Vixen loves it. She's always gliding her fingers through them and placing them slightly to the side. I love when she plays with me like that. I just love everything about this woman.

Heels clicking against the wooden floor catch our attention. We look up in time to see the beautiful siren slowly descending the stairs. Like a queen making her entrance at a ball, she captivates everyone's attention, enchanting us all with her sublime beauty.

Golden, open-toe stilettos make their way down, one step at a time. Long bare legs on display, a tiny excuse for a dress barely covering her body. Cobalt blue fabric hugging her curves delicately, tied at the nape, backless down to the dip right before her ass. A low V in the front and slits on either side of her thighs, giving us hungry men an easy access to her hypnotizing palace.

And yes, if she bends down, I can see her ass beautifully.

She's re-curled her rainbow hair and done her makeup in a dark blue shade, with a shiny lip gloss on her heart-shaped lips. While her fingernails and toenails are painted a powder blue that matches my button-down.

Holy shit, she wasn't joking about making us drool. My mouth waters just at the sight of her. I have a feeling I'll be sporting a semi all night.

"Hello, gentlemen," she purrs once she reaches the last step.

Noah walks up to her quickly, his arm wrapping around her waist, and pulls her in swiftly against his body with a growl. "You're not leaving our side at any point in the night, not even an inch. Do I make myself clear?"

She brings her hand up, index and middle fingers walking slowly up his torso and over his pec, stopping at the collar of his shirt. "Are you jealous that other men will see me like this, Casanova?" she asks seductively.

"I don't want anyone else thinking they can have what's mine. What's ours."

"Don't worry, babe. You two are the only ones who get to see me naked at the end of the night." She leans in and flicks his lips with her tongue, then steps out of his hold and turns around, winking at him over her shoulder as she sashays over to me.

Jesus, she's a fucking tease tonight, and I'm living for it.

He growls once more, watching her ass sway, then pulls out his phone from his pocket and mutters he has to make a call while turning down the hall and leaving Ronnie and I alone.

"Hey, Pretty Boy." She wraps her arms around my neck, pecking my lips.

"You look ravishing, Vixen. I can't wait to devour you tonight." I bite her neck.

"It's all I want," she breathes, head tipping back.

I look down the hall to where Noah ventured and hear his faint voice filtering through the air. "Is he okay?" I ask, nodding his way.

Something in her eyes flashes—sadness and worry. "He's going to be. You don't have to worry, okay? I'll take care of him." I'm about to question what's going on, but she shakes her head before I can voice my thoughts.

"Please don't ask me to tell you," she begs. "Just like you, Noah has secrets he doesn't want to share with others. I promised I wouldn't say anything, so I won't. Just know that I'm here for him, and I'll help him in any way I can, just like I'm doing with you.”

I nod. “Okay.”

She searches my gaze for a moment before speaking again. “How are things going with you know? Are they still harassing you?”

“They keep trying, even though I’ve blocked all their numbers. They just find other phones to call or text me from, but I never answer. You were right; I don’t think they have any evidence. It’s been two weeks, and nothing’s come up. If they did, they would have already used it.”

She beams at me. “I told you it would all work out. I’m proud of you, Gabriel.”

“It’s all because of you, and I can’t thank you enough, Vixen. I’ll owe you for the rest of my life.” I glide my fingers through her curls. If it weren’t for her, I’d still be trapped under their hold. I’d still be a slave to them, forced to obey their every command.

“The only thing I want is you, Gabriel. You and Noah.” She caresses her cherry-tasting, glossy lips against mine.

I love this change in her. I’m not sure exactly when it happened, but things between us all keep shifting for the better. She openly talks about her wants and needs now—her feelings for us—and I find myself craving more and more of it. More and more of her. Like the way she talks about the future and forever. Those words light me up like the night sky on the Fourth of July and make me fall in love with her even more.

“Just keep making us yours, and you’ll have us forever,” I tell her as she hums against my lips.

“I like the sound of that.”

“Me too, baby. Me too.”

“Last shot, baby. After that you’re sticking to water.” I chuckle at her little pouty whine as I hand her the tequila shot.

“You’re no fun, Pretty Boy.” She huffs and takes the drink.

I pass one over to Noah, but he shakes his head. He’s been nursing the same glass of scotch for the past hour. His third since we got here two hours ago, and that’s not counting the ones he had at home. I don’t even know how he’s not hammered by now. But he's barely taken a sip of this one, only looking down at it and hardly engaging in any topic of conversation.

"I may be no fun, but I don't want you sick." I kiss her temple as she grumbles.

We tap our shots together and throw them back, the burning sensation making its way down my throat. Tequila isn't my drink of choice, but Ronnie wanted to take shots, and she chose this one… five times. And we all know by now, I'll do anything to make my baby happy.

Her eyes light up when she spots Noah's untouched one. "You're not having it?"

"Nah, Kitten. I'm done drinking for the night. You can have it." He brushes his knuckles over her cheek and smiles at her.

"Yay! More for me." She quickly grabs the shot glass before I can stop her and downs it.

"Vixen," I warn.

"I know, I know. No more now." She rolls her eyes then perks up. "Ooh! I love this song! Let's dance."

She crawls over my lap, pecking my lips before standing outside the VIP booth we have back here in the club. Despite our last-minute decision to come out, I happened to know the owner, and he got us on the list when I called in a favor.

"Come on. Come, come. I want to feel you guys pressed up against me." She reaches for my hand and practically pulls me out of the seat.

I stand at her side with a chuckle as she looks back at Noah, who still hasn't moved despite her energetic demands. "Babe? You coming? I can't dance with only one of you, I want both my boyfriends with me." She pouts out her lip dramatically.

He smirks and shakes his head. "How can I say no to that." He finally stands, leaving his drink behind and taking her free hand as she drags us to the dance floor.

She stops us right in the center, sweaty bodies surrounding us. This is the third time she's pulled us out to dance. Well, actually, the first time she wanted to go alone, but there was no way we were letting that happen. Even now, I spot all the hungry male eyes roaming over her body, and it makes my jealousy spike.

She squeezes her body between us, Noah at her back and me at her front, as she begins to sway to the music with her eyes closed. The music enchanting her body, like a cobra drawn to a sensual melody. My hands are on her hips, while Noah has one on the outside of her thigh and the other along her ribcage.

A hand suddenly trails up my arm from the back, making its way to my shoulder before a warm, booze-induced breath fans my ear, tongue coming out to lick the shell of my ear.

"Hey, Gabe. I've missed you," the feminine voice says in my ear. Her other hand trails around my hip and slithers between mine and Ronnie's body, seconds away from grabbing my crotch.

I move my head to the side, away from the woman's mouth, just as my Vixen's eyes snap open, likely having felt an extra hand that shouldn't be there. Rage flicks through her eyes as she takes in the woman rubbing herself against my back and where her hands are placed.

She grips the woman's hands painfully enough to make her cry out and throws them to the side. "Don't fucking touch him! He's not yours!" Ronnie yells at her.

"Fucking psycho!" the woman screeches, holding her wrist before stomping away.

I wipe my ear, then smile at my girl, who's still following the woman with her angry eyes. "My little psycho."

"I hate them. I hate them, Gabe. I hate that everywhere we go women throw themselves at you both. Call you by your names like they personally know you because they most likely do." There's a sense of sadness and defeat in her voice that instantly dims my mood and makes the smile on my face vanish.

"I'm sorry, baby. I wish there was something I could do to make them back off." I cup her cheek as Noah rubs up and down her thighs.

"Make me yours, Gabriel. Both of you." She looks back at Noah then returns to me. "I'm tired of everyone thinking you're still single. I want the world to know that you're both mine. That I'm yours. Make me yours."

I bring my second hand up, caging her face as I capture her lips with mine, savoring the taste of tequila, cherry, and her. She moans into my mouth when my tongue swipes against her lips, begging them to open for me. Her hands clutch my shirt, pulling me in for more.

A strong, rough hand takes hold of my wrist, pulling my hand away from Ronnie's face. I pull back and open my eyes, taking note that it's just Noah, waiting patiently for his turn. Or not so patiently. He grabs her chin, tilting her face to the side and swallowing her next hums of pleasure.

I press my leg between her thighs as she grinds herself down on it. My hands roam over her body, from her thighs, up her waist, over her pebbled nipples that poke through the fabric of her dress. God, I want to lean in and capture one between my teeth. But that's not very appropriate to do in public, and I don't want anyone else getting a view of my Vixen.

Noah's hand releases her chin, sliding down the slope of her neck until it rests at the base, where he then lightly circles it, gaining a whimper from her beautifully swollen lips. Ronnie rocks herself harder against us, heated pussy against my thigh and greedy ass against Noah's erection, which I'm sure is painfully hard if he's as affected by her as I am.

She places one arm behind my head and the other behind his, turning her face to mine to kiss me again, then back to him. I can feel a humid spot forming on my leg from how wet she is. Hell, even I'm slowly leaking in my boxers from how hot this moment is. I don't know how much longer I can wait before I claim her again.

Thankfully, she takes us out of our misery pretty quickly.

"Take me home. I want both of you inside me tonight, at the same time." Her sultry voice speaks the most erotic words we've been dying to hear.

Noah quickly grabs her hand, leading us out of the nightclub without looking back. Just as we're about to exit, Ronnie digs her heels into the ground, head whipping back. But she's not looking at me; she's looking past me. Her gaze darts swiftly from side to side, searching for something.

"Baby, what is it?" I look behind me, trying to see what's caught her attention.

She shivers slightly, rubbing her arm with her own hand. "I don't know, I just got this feeling like someone was watching me..." Her eyes keep bouncing from one corner to the other.

"It's probably just Julian's men." Noah stands behind her, kissing her shoulder.

"Yeah, you're right." She smiles, that unsettling feeling leaving her body and grabs both our hands, pulling us out of the club.

Once outside, Noah calls our car, and within three minutes the black SUV we arrived in earlier pulls up to the curb. We quickly climb in, Ronnie sitting between us. The privacy divider is already up, giving us the intimacy we desperately need.

She takes advantage of the moment, hands trailing up our thighs to the waistband of our jeans. Where she then makes quick and impressive work of undoing them with one hand and pulling down the zippers. She then frees us from our boxers, and both of our rock-hard cocks spring out of their cages. A soft whimper falls from her lips as she looks from one to the other, grabbing hold of us in each smooth warm palm.

"Fuuuuck." I drop my head back against the seat, eyes closed as I take in the magical feeling of her hand on my dick. I hear Noah's rumbled groan from her other side, clearly enjoying her touch as much as I am.

I grab onto one of her thighs, just as he does the same, spreading her wide open for us. Our hands skim up her soft skin to the junction of her legs, our knuckles bumping into each other, but we don't care. Our sole purpose is to give our beautiful, mesmerizing girl the pleasure she deserves as she strokes our shafts simultaneously.

His fingers brush over her soaked panties, earning us a moan, right before I push the fabric to the side, exposing her to the cool air. Noah swipes through her slick folds, then circles her clit as I push a finger inside her tight wet cunt.

She cries out, whimpering and moaning with her eyes closed and head resting back. But she doesn't stop the torturous movements of her hands, her thumb coming up to swipe the pearly beads leaking out of us over the head and using it to lubricate us.

I remove my single digit and push two back in, just as Noah removes his from her clit and comes to cradle the back of my hand. Two of his fingers sliding in along with my own, stretching her around us deliciously.

"Oh God! Yes!" Ronnie's thighs begin to tremble, her walls contracting against us, her hands now moving to the same rhythm as we pump in and out of her.

With a few more pumps, she combusts around us, squeezing us in a vise grip, hips bucking wildly as she lets her orgasm take over. Her hands stop their stroking movement and simply tighten their hold on us, nearly making me choke. When she finally comes down from her high, we pull our slick fingers from her wet heat and bring them up to our mouths, savoring her sweetness.

"Fuck, that was so hot." She quickly scurries from the seat, dropping onto her knees in front of us. Leaning in, she licks the tip of my cock, then starts again at the base, all the way up. Finally, she spreads her puffy lips over the head and swallows me down.

"Jesus, Vixen. I'll never get enough of your mouth." I fist her hair, helping her up and down my length as she moans at my praise.

After a few more mouthwatering swallows, she pops her lips off my shaft. Leaving a glistening trail of saliva, she does the same to Noah, taking him into her mouth as he moans with satisfaction.

"You feel so good, Kitten." He strokes her cheek with his thumb as she hums a sigh around him.

Ronnie takes him in as deep as she can while jerking me off. Every few pumps, she switches from one to the other. It's the most delicious kind of torture. I could have her on her knees like this all day.

The car suddenly stops, and I'm snapped out of the moment, only now remembering where we are. Noah cups her face, lifting her off his cock as her lips leave an audible *pop*. "Time to go, Kitten."

She retakes her seat between us as we tuck ourselves in quickly. The back door opens seconds later, and Noah climbs out first, followed by Ronnie, then me.

We wish goodnight to the driver, then head up the three steps to the high-rise we call home. An elderly man waits for us by the door, pulling it open once we reach the second step. "Good evening, Mr. Ellis, Mr. Adler, and Miss Masters."

"Good evening," I say, walking by.

"Thank you." Noah nods next.

"Good evening, Stanley. Or should we be saying good morning, given the time?" Ronnie giggles.

"Well, I do suppose you are right." He chuckles along with her. "I hope you had a fine night, Miss Masters."

"With these two, always." She points at us.

"Well, enjoy the rest of it." He beams at our beautiful girl.

"Thank you, Stanley. We will. Goodnight!" She follows us in, waving at him as we make our way to our private elevator.

I give a quick nod to the man at the reception desk, who watches us closely with a strange look on his face. He forces a smile when he notices me looking at him, then nods back before quickly looking down at the computer in front of him. *Weird...* I shake my head and step into the elevator with Noah and our girl.

"You know his name?" I question once the doors close, coming back to the conversation she just had with the doorman.

"Of course, I do. Stanley's practically there around the clock. I swear, whether it's morning, day, or night, he's always there," she says with a frown as if I'm asking a ridiculous question, then her eyes widen. "Please tell me you knew his name?"

Noah and I shake our heads, feeling a bit like uptight assholes for not knowing someone we've seen regularly for the past few years.

"Jesus. And how long have you lived here?" She looks at both of us with disappointment.

"Umm, since a little before Hayes's wedding." Noah shrugs.

"Are you kidding me!? That was like three years ago, no?" Her eyes are big and round once more.

I cup the back of my neck, an embarrassed chuckle falling from my lips. "Yeah, something like that."

She narrows her eyes at us, pointing a finger. "Do. Better. That old man stands there, all day, every day, waiting to serve you. The least you can do is acknowledge him and learn his fucking name," she says sternly. "It's not because you're rich and famous now that it means you get to treat people with less respect than they deserve."

Jesus, I feel like I just got chastised by my mother. But she's right, as little as it seems, we have been treating him unfairly. Hell, it's been over three years, and I don't think

I've ever had a conversation with that man. Let alone anyone else in this building that I see almost on a day-to-day basis.

I grab hold of her hips, pulling her in toward me as her hands settle on my chest. "You're right, I'm sorry. I'll do better, okay? It's a promise."

Noah comes up behind her, petting her hair and kissing her temple. "We both will."

"Are you mad at us?"

She sighs. "No, I just don't like when people are treated like less."

"How can we make it up to you?" I kiss along her jaw, down her neck.

She giggles and bites her lip. "Well, that's a pretty good start."

Noah imitates my movements, nibbling on the other side of her neck, her ear. "What about giving you orgasms all night? Would that do the trick?"

She leans her head back, exposing her neck as Noah presses into her back, pushing her front against me. "Mmm, that does sound kind of nice."

"Only kind of?" I chuckle, running the tip of my nose against her slender shoulder. "What if we took turns pounding into this tight pretty pussy until your legs turned to jelly?"

I bring one hand down between her legs and beneath the skirt of her dress. A desperate moan falls from her lips as I rub small circles over her clit, through her panties.

"Then we'll run you a nice bubble bath, a massage, and finish with a few more orgasms with our mouths." Noah's hands slide between mine and Ronnie's body, cupping her breasts then pinching her nipples. This time she whimpers.

"What about my ass?" She grins when our movements temporarily stop at her question.

My own spreads wide from cheek to cheek. "That's right, I do recall you saying something about wanting us both inside of you."

"Please," she moans.

"Soon, Kitten. We'll give you anything and everything you want the second we step inside."

"What the hell is taking so long? Shouldn't we already be in the penthouse by now?" Ronnie whines with impatience.

She's right; it usually only takes seconds to make it up. I look at the side panel and throw my head back with a laugh when I notice the problem.

"What?" Noah looks up with a frown.

"We never pressed the button... we're still at the lobby." I drop my head against Ronnie's shoulder, chuckling.

"Oh my God!" She reaches out and presses the 'P' for Penthouse with a huff. "You two are frying my brain."

I grab her chin between my thumb and finger, bringing her lips to mine. "Now you know how we feel every time we look at you, Vixen."

Chapter Twenty-Six

VERONICA

Closed for business until tomorrow.

A few seconds later, we finally make it inside our home. And the second we pass through the threshold, all clothes are abandoned as Noah carries me in his arms up to his bedroom.

He sets me down on the edge of the bed then pulls down his boxers, the only piece of clothing that was left while I sat with my legs bent and spread, leaning back on my hands completely nude.

Gabe stands proudly beside Noah, buck naked with his fists on his hips, erection pointing at me and the widest grin on his face. *God, I love my happy Pretty Boy.*

Once they both stand equally proud, they look at each other, a silent conversation passing between them. "I call dibs. You'll get it next time," Gabe says, earning a shrug from Noah.

"Dibs on what?" I frown as Noah comes over, lying down on his back beside me and flips me over him in the process, making me yelp.

He pulls me up his body until my thighs straddle his head. "On this sexy little ass of yours." He smirks. I shudder in response at the first swipe of his tongue against my pussy.

Gabe comes up behind me, standing on his knees, legs on either side of Noah's torso with a bottle of lube in his hand. I have no idea where and when he got that.

He places a hand along my back and pushes me slightly. "Bend over for me, baby. Let me work on that gorgeous ass while he gives you what you're craving."

I do as I'm told, leaning over as Noah continues to deliver delicious flicks over my already pulsing clit. His hands grip the back of my thighs, keeping me spread open.

They've slowly worked up their way to manhandling me more and more. Where I used to freak out from being held down, I now enjoy it with them. I trust them, and I know they'll never hurt me.

Cool droplets fall over my ass, down my crack. I look back at Gabe, who spreads a generous amount of lube over his fingers while moaning and panting in response to Noah's touch.

"Has anyone ever played with this ass before, Vixen?" I nod my head and he smiles. "Ah, so this pretty tight hole is used to being fed a big dick, isn't it?"

"Not as big as yours," I say breathlessly and bite my lip as his thumb circles my puckered hole.

"Don't worry, baby. We'll work you up to it. In no time, I'll be seated deep inside of you, and I can't fucking wait." He beams, then slowly pushes his thumb in. I whimper and drop my head. The slight burn fades pretty quickly, and in comes the pleasure as he pulls it out and pushes it back in repeatedly.

"Oh God, that feels so good," I moan.

He retreats his thumb fully, squirts more lube over me, and pushes two fingers inside my ass. Noah removes his hand from my thigh and passes his arm between my legs by the front. He circles my entrance with the tip of his fingers before slipping two inside my pussy.

"Ahh... mmm... yes!" My body begins to rock against both their hands.

I look back over my shoulder at Gabe, who's staring at my ass while jerking himself off. And from the arm I can see running beneath him, Noah seems to be doing the same. Watching them stroke themselves always does something to me; I love the sight of it.

I feel myself leaking all over Noah and down my thighs, a slight tremor setting in as my core tightens, heat blooming at the base of my belly and spreading rapidly. They both remove their hands at the same time, and I whimper at the loss. But it quickly turns into a gasp as three fingers are pushed into both my holes simultaneously.

"Ahh!" I cry out.

Noah groans against my pussy, then sucks my clit into his mouth. I keep my focus on Gabe, watching his hand grip his cock as he squeezes it roughly. Beating up and down its length, deep moans fall from his lips as he watches his fingers slide inside my ass and stretch me out.

I'm panting and squirming, grinding against them both. Stars dance in my eyes as heat crawls over my pebbled breasts, up my neck, and spreads on my cheeks. I can feel it everywhere in the most delicious way.

"Fuck, Noh. You should see her right now. Pupils fully blown. Skin flushed. She's a sight. Looks like fucking paradise, and I'm more than ready to pass through those golden gates."

Despite the phenomenal sensations coursing through my body at their actions, Gabe's words are what really set me off. Causing the stack of dominoes to tumble until they all crash and spread out within me. Detonating the bomb inside of me, hitting the big red button that sends me into oblivion.

His words always have a way of digging deep within my heart, making it feel like they're more than *just* words. They touch my soul, leaving a mark in its wake every time.

My eyes roll back in my head as I cry out, hips jerking as I ride Noah's face. Their fingers slipping in and out of me with brutal force, riding the wave of bliss with me until my mind and body come crashing back down to earth and I collapse. My legs and arms give out at that exact moment, suffocating Noah beneath me.

I feel and hear him chuckle as they withdraw their fingers, and he grabs my hips, lifting me slightly and slipping his head out from under me. Someone smacks my ass as I stay lying in a daze with my eyes closed.

"Come on, Kitten. Wake up. We're not done with you yet." Noah grabs my ankles and pulls me back down to the edge of the bed.

I groan. "I don't think I can stand." My voice comes out muffled against the covers.

Two large hands hold onto my waist, lifting me straight off the bed like I weigh nothing. "That's okay, baby. We'll do all the heavy lifting. You just let us take care of this beautiful body." Gabe kisses the back of my neck then throws me into Noah's arms.

They're both standing off the bed now. My legs wrap around Noah's hips as my arms circle his neck. I rest my head against his neck and watch Gabe lather up his length with lube. Noah suddenly fists my hair gently and pulls my head back enough to cover my mouth with his. I open up for him instantly, deepening the kiss and feeling it all the way down to my toes.

My hips start to move on their own, searching for a way to settle the ache forming between my legs once more. He releases my hair, and the next thing I feel is the head of his shaft swiping through my folds before he pushes in with one slow thrust, all the way to the hilt.

I cry out, his mouth swallowing every little sound leaving my lips, the deep stretch bordering the line between pleasure and pain. He pumps leisurely in and out of me as Gabe comes to stand behind me. His lubed fingers circle my tight ring once more before a much, much larger object presses against it, demanding entrance.

"You ready, baby?" He kisses my shoulder. I pull away from Noah and look back at him, nodding tentatively.

One of his hands comes to my waist, holding onto me tightly, while Noah holds me up by my thighs. I move one of my arms back, grabbing onto Gabe's nape as my fingers slide through his hair at the base of his neck.

He pushes in slowly, stretching me wide open with the head of his cock as I groan out, inch by torturous inch sliding deeper into me. He then pulls out a bit and presses back in further until he's fully seated inside my tight asshole that stings around his girth.

"OH FUCK! Fuck, fuck, fuuuuck!!! Oh God!" I feel my eyes rolling to the back of my head. I've never been this full; I can feel them everywhere, like they're ripping me in half. My body quivers in their hold, another orgasm on the brink of erupting just from having both of them inside me. I'm panting and gasping for air, yet they aren't even moving. "Holy shit..."

"You okay, Kitten?" Noah kisses my jaw.

"Is this too much, Vixen?" Gabe murmurs against my neck.

"No, it feels amazing," I breathe.

"You feel amazing, baby. We're going to start moving, okay?" He kisses up my neck to my ear.

"Okay." And they do just that.

It starts off with slow thrusts, but they quickly pick up the pace more and more until I'm a delusional, jabbering mess. I scream every profanity my mind can make up as they plow into me with vicious, ruthless thrusts. I don't know how they do it, but their movements are in sync, and it's driving me crazy in the most blissful way.

Two sets of hands are on my thighs, one pair near the curve of my ass, the other just before my knees, spreading me wide open. I'm not sure which is which, and I really don't care. Having both their hands on me always feels euphoric. My hands fist both their hairs as they grunt and groan with every flex of their hips.

"Fuck, Vixen! You're squeezing the life out of me. I want to live in this tight asshole forever." One hand near my ass leaves my leg and comes up to cup my cheek.

Gabe turns my head toward him and devours my mouth as he fucks me harder. His palm leaves my cheek and trails down my neck, over my collarbone, and to my breast. Where he then pinches my nipple between his thumb and forefinger, twisting and pulling.

I whimper, moan, scream, mewl, any noise my lungs can create expels from my throat. Another hand leaves my opposite leg seconds before Noah fists my hair and crashes his lips to my gasping ones.

Suddenly it's too much, my body overheats with stimulation and sensations. Hands everywhere, tongues dancing, moans filling the room, my body being brutalized and turned inside out as I shake violently in their hold, seconds away from flying off to Neverland.

I rip my mouth off Noah, fingernails digging into the back of their scalps. "OH MY GOD! I'M GONNA COME. FUCK YES, YES, YESSS! DON'T STOP, DON'T STOP!" I whip my head back against Gabe, screaming at the top of my lungs as my body convulses in their grasp.

They ram erratically into me, fingers biting into my skin until they roar ferociously, like two fierce lions claiming their territory. Filling me up beyond belief, their warm sperm drips out of me as they slow their thrusts.

My ears are ringing, vision filled with spots, body turned to mush as our harsh pants overlap each other. "Holy fuck! Noh, you got her? Because my knees are about to give out." Gabe gasps as he kisses my temple.

"Yeah, I got her." Noah adjusts his hold on me as Gabe's hands leave my body, and his still half-erected dick slips out of my ass, causing me to whimper at the ache left behind.

I hear him plop down on the bed, seconds before Noah sets me down beside Gabe, who now lies on his back with his arms up over his head. Noah climbs up the bed beside me, lying on his side with one hand draped lazily over my body.

"Best fucking sex of my life." Gabe laughs breathlessly.

"Right with you on that one," Noah says, smiling.

I want to agree with them, but no words leave my mouth. Almost like my mind and body are no longer connected together. My eyes are open, but I feel like I'm sleeping, like I'm dreaming. I hear them, but they sound distant. Even their touch feels numb, but not in a bad way.

Noah frowns when he notices all I've been doing for the last minute is staring at him without moving. "Kitten, you okay?"

"Umphm." *Wow, seems I can't talk either.*

Gabe laughs and rises to his elbows. "What was that, baby?"

"Nnnhg... sex." I squeeze my eyes shut, shaking my head from side to side as I try to pull myself out of this strange yet heavenly subspace.

Noah chuckles. "I think we broke her again."

Gabe leans in, cupping my face. "What is it, Vixen? You want more sex?" He smirks.

My eyes pop open faster than lightning striking the ground. "Noooooo... uh-uh. No. Nope. No more." *Finally, some real words.*

"You sure? Because I could probably go again, just give me a few more minutes." He lowers himself and grazes my nipple with his teeth.

"AHH! No!" His touch feels like a million needles poking through my skin with how sensitive my body is right now.

I push him off, rolling over Noah's body and almost falling off the bed in an attempt to get away from Gabe. Noah catches me by the waist seconds before I slip past the edge.

"Woah there, Kitten. Don't want you getting hurt." He sets me back above him, my back to his chest.

Something pokes at the base of my spine, and my eyes widen. "What the hell? How are you hard again?? I just died!"

He chuckles as Gabe laughs harder. "Someone's being dramatic."

I glare his way.

"All right, up. Let's clean you up, then bed. Unless you want that bath and more orgasms that we talked about?" Noah asks, pushing against my back until I'm sitting up above him.

"Oh, no. I am closed for business until tomorrow." I shake my head.

"Tomorrow as in... when we wake up? Or tomorrow right now? You know, since it's way past midnight." Gabe winks.

I point my finger at him. "Don't get smart with me, Pretty Boy." He only laughs.

"Okay, come on, in the shower. You're leaking all over me." Noah grabs my waist and hoists me in the air just as Gabe gets off the bed and takes me from Noah's outstretched hands.

It's pretty funny how after sex, they like to pass me around like I'm a baby. They'd be great dads, no doubt about it. *Oh... oh no! Where the hell did that come from!? No! No baby thoughts! Out! I banish you. Obliviate!*

I wrap my legs around Gabe's waist and look back over my shoulder at Noah, who stands from the bed, pools of cum leaking down his lower abdomen. "Oopsie." I giggle nervously.

We step into the huge gray tiled shower, and Noah walks over to the control panel, turning on the rain shower above us. Warm water pours over our bodies, steaming up the room within seconds. There's also jets along the walls aiming in every direction, but we rarely use those.

We've quickly gotten into a routine when it comes to shower time. Noah washes my body while I wash Gabe's, then Gabe washes my hair while I wash Noah's body. After that, the boys finish off with washing their own hair as I watch them with hungry eyes.

I like these moments with them, something we share every night that bonds us together. It's intimate and sweet. The attention they give me makes me fall for them a little more every second we spend here. Sometimes we even go as far as having naked bubble fights that end with some steamy sex against the glass wall, or the floor, or the bench. Really just anywhere. I love it all.

Once we're all clean and dry, we get back into the room and climb into bed naked. Well, Noah and I do, but Gabe just stands off to the side looking despondent.

"Gabriel?" I know what's coming, but I wish he wouldn't.

"I'm gonna head to my room, it's late and I'm exhausted. You two get some sleep as well," he says quietly.

"Gabe... you don't have to leave. I don't care about your nightmares." I stretch my hand out and grab his. "Just stay..."

I know he still gets them, despite having gotten rid of his parents' blackmailing threats. It doesn't happen every night, but on the nights it does, I hear him through the walls. I hear him screaming and crying in agony. It rips my heart to pieces, and all I want to do is run to him, to help him. All I want to do is save him from those demons that still haunt his mind.

But Noah stops me every time, telling me that he'll be okay and it'll soon be over. So instead of going to him, I spend the next hour awake, listening to his cries until they finally stop and I know the nightmare is over. Then I fall back asleep, wishing I could help him somehow...

"I can't, Vixen..."

Tears well in my eyes at his words. I don't want this to be our life. I don't want him to have to sleep in a separate bed when we should be together. I want to fall asleep next to him and wake up in his arms, the same way I do with Noah. I want us to talk for hours until exhaustion takes over and kiss the second we open our eyes in the morning.

Gabe crouches down beside the bed, gliding his fingers through my hair. "No, baby. Please don't be sad. I want to stay, believe me. There's nothing I want more than to spend the night with you at my side. But it's better this way. Safer." He kisses my forehead, then my lips. "I'll work on it, okay? Just be patient with me. Can you do that?"

"Okay," I say softly.

"I promise, I'll get a handle on it. I'll figure something out." He kisses me once more and stands, his hand falling from my hair. "Goodnight, my beautiful girl." He nods to Noah, turns, and leaves, closing the door quietly behind him.

Noah doesn't say a word as he turns off the bedside lamps, then pulls my body to his. My front to his side as I rest my head on his chest, his fingers smoothing down my hair. "I hate this, Noh. It doesn't feel fair."

"I know, Kitten. It isn't, but there's not much we can do," he murmurs against my head before kissing my crown.

"Maybe he could see a therapist or something… I'm sure someone knows what to do." I let my finger trail the grooves of his abs as my mind thinks of ways to help Gabe.

"He's already seen a couple and doesn't want to do that anymore. We can't force him."

"But this isn't how it's supposed to be. We're supposed to be all in it together, the three of us. Him not sleeping in the same bed ever feels like we're excluding him, and it makes me feel guilty."

"I know, my love. I know." We fall silent for a moment, both of us lost in our own thoughts until eventually he speaks again in a pained voice. "You do realize that we won't be able to have everything, don't you?"

His question startles me a bit. I lift my head from his chest, peering at the outline of his face until my eyes connect with his. It's dark, but within a few seconds I can make him out. "What do you mean?"

"This kind of relationship comes with complications a normal one wouldn't have. Things we probably should have talked about before getting seriously involved." He brushes his knuckles over my cheekbone.

I frown, a dreadful sense settling in my belly. "Like what?" I whisper.

"Like the fact that we'll never be able to marry you, at least not both of us. Which means one of us will be left out."

"We don't have to get married. I don't need a wedding or anything," I say quickly.

He smiles and kisses my forehead. "But then you'd never carry our name. And what about kids? Whose name do we put on the birth certificate? And date nights? Do we each take our turn or go all together? You know people will talk and judge. The media will have a field day with that when our relationship comes to light."

What the hell is going on? Why is he saying all these things now? Like he's rethinking everything that's happening between us.

I sit up in bed, bringing my knees to my chest as I face him, feeling the emotions slowly making their way back up. "Why are you talking like you regret it? Like you regret being in this relationship?" I blink away the tears, but one manages to slip out.

I'm finally ready to admit my feelings for them, finally ready to let myself love them to the fullest. And now he's pulling away? I don't get it.

He quickly sits up against the headboard and wipes my tear away. "No, Kitten. I don't regret it for a second, I could never. I love what we have, it's all I ever wanted. I just want to make sure you know and understand what you are signing up for." He gathers me in his arms and sets me down sideways over his lap.

"I don't want you to end up miserable five years down the road, because things won't be easy. Because no matter how hard we try, Gabe and I won't always be able to give you what you want," he whispers, fingers gliding through my hair.

"Because sometimes we'll have to compromise and make decisions that will leave someone out. Because even five, ten years down the line, people will still judge our relationship. But not only us, our kids too." He tightens his hold around me, pressing his lips to my temple for a long time.

"I just want you to take the time to think about all of that, if it's really what you want. I don't want to be the reason your dreams don't come true, and I know Ellis wouldn't want that either. Even if it means letting you go."

I move around, straddling his thighs completely naked, and grab his face between my palms. "Stop, just stop. You think I haven't thought about this? Because I have, Noah. I don't care if I never get married. I don't care if I never wear your name or Gabe's. I don't care whose name is on the damn certificate, as long as our children have both your last names attached to theirs and call you both *Dad*."

"Veronica..."

"No, I'm serious," I cut him off. "And fuck whoever judges us. I couldn't give two shits about those people. Let them talk, let the media say what they want to say, it doesn't matter to me. The only thing I care about is that you two are in my life. I meant what I said earlier..." I bring my lips down to his, kissing him softly. "Make me yours, Noah." *Kiss* "And I'll make you mine." *Kiss* "Forever."

My hands drop to his chest as he brushes my hair behind my ears, eyes bouncing over every feature of my face. Then something settles inside him, I see the change in his eyes, but I'm not sure what it is. Worry? Fear? But whatever it is, it's gone now and being replaced with a dashing smile that makes my heart skip a beat.

He traces my lips with his thumb as he cradles the side of my face, the word falling from his lips like a secret promise. "Forever."

Chapter Twenty-Seven

NOAH

Sweet dreams, precious Sleeping Beauty.

~ Three Days Later ~

Three days.
    That's how long it took for her body to fully give out.
    For her lungs to stop breathing.
    For her heart to stop beating.
    Three days of coming to see her every day.
    Watching her body weaken.
    Watching her complexion die.
    Watching her fade from existence.
    Three days...

Veronica stands at my side, holding my hand as we watch the nurses remove all wires and equipment from the room. It might be a beautiful August morning, but nothing about this day *feels* beautiful. No matter how bright the sun may shine through those curtains, the room has never felt darker than it does at this moment.

Everyone works in silence, but I don't miss the small sniffles every few seconds as they try to compose themselves. Despite them not knowing Trinity personally or her knowing them, she became a part of their everyday life. They all talked to her daily, even though she never responded. She became a friend. She became family.

And now it's time to say goodbye.

I knew this moment was coming; I've known it for a while. Even though the staff tried to keep my hopes up, telling me that some patients just need more time to wake up. I knew deep within my soul that my sister was gone.

The truth is, she's been gone since the moment she fell.

I just wasn't ready to let her go.

I look down at my beautiful girl, who stands so tall beside me, unshed tears in her eyes that she desperately tries to hold back. There's a slight tremor in her hand, her throat working constantly to swallow the cry that's begging to break loose. But she won't let it. She's keeping it together for me, being strong for me.

My brave, brave girl.

I bring up our joined hands and kiss the back of hers. Her gaze falls to mine, and a weak smile forms over her lips before vanishing once more when her eyes return to my sister who lies so peacefully in her bed.

I watch as they finish putting everything away, preparing to leave this occupied room for the very last time until someone else comes in to take my sister's place. I've already removed all the picture frames and things that belonged to Trinity from the room, leaving nothing behind but the vessel that no longer holds life.

I clear the thickness in my throat before addressing them all. "I'd like to thank you all for everything you've done for Trinity. I'm deeply and will always be grateful to every one of you." I look from one face to the other, recognizing every single one of them. "Trinity's funeral will take place next week, and you are all welcome to attend. So again, thank you. Thank you for being here when I couldn't. Thank you for treating her like a friend, like a sister, like family."

They all walk out, squeezing my arm and hugging Veronica, offering us their condolences. When I look back at my sister, I find Jannice at her side, holding her cold hand. "Goodbye, sweet angel," she whispers, then steps back as tears roll down her cheeks.

Everly steps up next, doing the same. "Rest in peace, beautiful soul." She releases Trinity's hand and puts her arms around Jannice, guiding her out of the room.

I stop them just as they come to pass us, letting go of Veronica and taking Jannice into my arms. She crumbles against my chest, tears soaking through my shirt as I pet the back of her head. "Thank you, Jannice. Thank you for everything."

Despite her constant obvious flirting, she's the one who's been most involved with my sister. Whenever I had long away stretches during hockey season, she would spend time with Trinity, even coming in on her days off to talk and read to her. She's been a real friend through it all.

She nods against me and steps out of my hold, wiping her wet cheeks as Everly comes in for a hug as well. "I know you have no reason to come back here, and probably don't want to, but know that you'll always be welcome here, Noah." She smiles, taking a step back and looking over at my Kitten. "You too, Ronnie."

Veronica hugs them both next. "Thank you."

"We'll leave you to say goodbye. Take all the time you need," Everly says as they exit the room, closing the door behind them.

Veronica steps into my arms, pressing her cheek against my shoulder. "You ready?" I nod, and she laces our fingers together and walks us over to the bed.

She lets go and takes my sister's hand, then passes her fingers through Trinity's hair as a lone tear finally falls. "Hey, girl, I'm going to miss seeing you, talking to you. But this isn't a goodbye, Trinity. I know we'll see each other again someday, and then you'll finally get to tell me all those stories you've been dying to say about your brother. We'll finally be able to get those mani-pedis like we talked about." She laughs sadly through her cries.

"Sweet dreams, Trinity. Watch over your brother from wherever you are." She kisses her forehead and turns, wiping away her tears as she walks over to the door, giving me space.

I step up closer, my fingers trailing over the features of her face, down her arm, to her hand, then back up the same path. Something inside me breaks as I realize this will be the last time I'll ever get to touch her, to hold her. To look at her beautiful face.

I take a deep breath and lean in, cupping the side of her face as I plant my lips over her forehead, my thumb strokes back and forth along her cheek. "Goodbye, baby sis. I'm sorry it took me so long to let go, but you're free now... Say hi to Dad for me. I miss you both... I love you, Trinny."

I give her one last kiss and straighten, taking one final look at the little girl I've loved since the day she was born. Then join my girl by the door, take her hand in mine, and walk out for the very last time.

We make it to my car and Veronica stops me at the hood. "I know no one drives your car, but let me. You might look put together, but I can see it in your eyes that you aren't. Let me drive us home."

I don't even fight her on it, simply nod and climb into the passenger side. She's right, I'm not okay. I feel... hollow, empty, numb. I haven't cried, and I won't. I never cry. I didn't when my father passed, I won't for my sister either despite the pain and heartache I feel inside.

The last time I did was when my mother walked out on us. And I swore I'd never do it again. People die and leave all the time, why waste my time crying? What good does it really do? Nothing. So instead, I hold it together and move on.

Tomorrow is Maddison's funeral, and we all promised Emma we would be there. Even if we didn't know her, we'll attend to support our friends, our family. The only one I have left. *I don't know how I'll sit through that after everything that happened today.*

Two days ago, I made all the funeral arrangements for Trinity. Veronica told me I should have spaced it out a little longer, given myself time to grieve, but I wanted it over and done with as soon as possible. It's easier that way, and it's not as if we're making a big event out of it.

The only people outside of me and Veronica that will attend are those who knew of her existence at the facility. Even when she was living her life, my sister wasn't very social. She didn't have any friends she kept in touch with or any boyfriends. It was just the three of us. Then my father died, and it was only her and me.

Veronica takes my hand once we're seated in my car, and given her height, she barely has to adjust anything in my car to fit her. She offers me a tender smile, kisses my hand, then pulls out of the parking lot and drives us home.

VERONICA

~ The Next Day ~

Noah hasn't been the same since yesterday. When we got home, he excused himself to his room and hasn't left it since. I brought him food and asked him to come watch a movie with me and Gabe, but he wouldn't. Just shook his head and went back to drinking in one of the chairs and watching the TV in his room. He's barely spoken since either, and it has me worried.

Gabe knows something happened, but he doesn't ask any questions like I asked him not to. He's trusting me in helping Noah, but I don't miss the worry and pain in his eyes for his friend. We've been busying ourselves with a *Harry Potter* marathon and Gabe trying to teach me how to cook. It's been fun, distracting. But it's all hard.

I keep a smile on my face when I'm around Gabriel, but late at night, when I crawled into bed with Noah, I let my tears fall as he held me in his arms. I feel guilty for being the one crying when it should be him. But he tells me it's okay, that I have every right to cry.

Today is Maddie's funeral and I don't know how I'll keep it together, knowing that in just a few days we'll be attending another. One that belongs to a person that quickly became important to me.

I finish straightening my hair and applying my makeup, then slip into my little black dress. Half sleeves wrap around my arms with the top portion of the dress hugging my chest before flowing down from the waist to my knees, and a pair of black pumps on my feet.

I collect my little black purse and make my way down the stairs to my boyfriends, who wait in the living room. One stands in the center of the room, the other sits on the couch with a drink, both dressed all in black with Gabe's hair styled backwards with some gel.

I head over to Gabe first, pecking his lips as he tells me I look beautiful, then over to Noah. The second I'm within a few inches of him, I can smell the booze oozing off him, and his eyes look a bit glossy and distant.

He stays seated on the couch and lifts his hand to drain the rest of the Scotch in his glass, but I take it away before he can. Walking to the kitchen, I dump it in the sink, then get back to his side and pull him up off the couch. He sways a little but rights himself quickly.

Jesus, this is not a good start to the day.

"You've had enough," I tell him quietly.

All he does is scoff and head for the elevator.

My heart breaks as I watch him go, but I need to stay strong. Gabe comes to my side and takes my hand, gifting me a small smile. I let out a breath and return the smile. "Let's get this day over with."

An hour later we arrive at the church in Gabe's car where the funeral service is being held. Then we'll be going to the gravesite for the burial and after the funeral reception that Emma and Greyson are kindly hosting at their home. They didn't want Bryan to have to deal with all of it after losing his child, so they took everything into their own hands and even paid every expense for the funeral.

We step inside and make our way over to the grieving father, offering our condolences, then over to our friends. All of them are already here. Morgan and Cecilia lean against their husbands, while Aubrey and Sam hold Gracie and Dante. Greyson has his arms around Emma as she cries softly against his chest.

"Hey…" I place my hand on her back.

She looks up and turns from her fiancé's hold, wrapping her arms around me as I do the same to her. "Thank you for coming."

"Of course we'd be here, Em. We're family." I let go and hug Greyson next while

Gabe goes to Emma.

Noah comes in after, pulling Emma in. She scrunches up her nose, then smells him and looks at his face. "Are you seriously drunk right now?" she whispers harshly. "This is a funeral, Noah. Couldn't you have at least waited until the reception?"

"You wanted me here, I'm here. If you're not happy with my state, then I'll just leave." He takes a step back, ready to head for the door, but I grab his wrist before he can.

"No, don't go, okay? Just go sit down and I'll join you in a minute." He works his jaw then nods, going down one of the wooden pews as I release my hold on him.

I sigh and turn back to our friends, who all look over at Noah, not understanding what's going on. "Look, Noah's going through some things... He doesn't mean to be disrespectful; it's just a hard time for him..." It's the best I can give them, and I hate it. Because they deserve to know, and Noah deserves to have their support as well.

"Whatever, get him under control," Emma says, then turns and walks over to Bryan. I know she doesn't mean to be rude, but I also understand her anger.

I join Noah in the pew, taking his hand as Gabe sits beside me. I lean my head against his shoulder, my thumb rubbing soothing circles over his skin as the ceremony begins. When Emma takes the stage, delivering her eulogy, Noah's hands begin to shake. His leg bounces up and down as he becomes restless.

Suddenly he rips his hand out of mine and moves over, raking his fingers through his hair. "I'm sorry. I can't do this." His eyes plead with me to understand, and I do. He looks over at Gabe next. "Take her home when you guys are done." He stands and walks out, catching all our friends' attention, including Emma's.

I watch him leave, every cell in my body screaming at me to go after him, to hold him, to plead with him to talk to me. To beg him to let out this pain he's burying deep inside.

But I don't do any of that because no matter how much my heart bleeds for Noah, this moment is about my best friend and her own grief. So instead, I turn to Gabe as he wraps his arms around me. Then I rest my head into the crook of his neck and let myself cry in the comfort of him.

~ *Five Days Later* ~

Today is the day. The one I've been dreading all week.

The weather couldn't be more fitting. Dark gray clouds cover the normally beautiful bright blue skies, weeping with us. Mourning along with us.

Noah keeps getting worse every day. Drinking more, talking less. He barely kisses me, hugs me, or holds me. Most nights he isn't even in bed when I fall asleep. He hasn't been on his morning runs since his sister's death either and hasn't been working out.

All he does is drink...

Drink...

And drink...

I miss him, I miss my boyfriend, my lover.

I miss the man who calls me his Kitten.

I miss my Casanova.

We're currently getting ready in his room, the same black dress I wore a few days ago, back against my itchy skin. The same black suit against his emotionally aching body. We don't talk as we get dressed. We don't look at each other. I'm desperately trying not to take this personally, but it hurts... It hurts so much... I feel like I'm losing him, and I don't know how to get him back.

The funeral isn't for another two hours, but Noah wants us to leave while Gabe is occupied in the gym. Where he won't notice our choice of clothing, where he won't notice us leaving.

I turn my gaze to Noah as he pulls his black dress shirt on, passing the buttons through the small loops. His head is down, a gloomy look on his face. None of this feels right; we shouldn't be doing it like this. We should be with our friends, our family.

They may not have met Trinity, but they would still be here for us. I know they would. I wish Noah would change his mind, I wish he would reconsider. None of this is healthy; this isn't how people are meant to grieve, to heal.

I know I made a promise to him not to say a word, but my soul is screaming at me, begging me to do the right thing. Even if he hates me in the end. I don't want him to go through this day alone and end up regretting it, because I know he will.

With that decision in mind, I grab my phone and head to the door. "I just need to grab something from my other purse in the kitchen. I'll meet you by the elevator."

He doesn't even look up, only nods as I walk out of the room.

I hurry down the stairs, into the gym where I know Gabe is in the middle of his workout session. The second he spots me, taking one look at my outfit, he rises from the ground and walks over to me.

"Vixen? What's going on? Why are you dressed like that?" Worry seeps through his voice as his eyes bounce over my features.

"I don't have much time to explain, but I need you to do something for me. It's urgent. Noah can't know," I rush out quickly, looking over my shoulder to make sure Noah isn't down to the main floor yet.

"Anything, baby. What do you need?"

I quickly fill him in on what I need from him. The more I say, the more the heartache for his friend becomes visible in his eyes. Once I'm done, he grabs my face and crashes his lips against mine.

"Thank you for being here for him. But you're doing the right thing," he breathes against my mouth.

"I hope you're right."

He steps back, quickly going to his phone and shooting off text after text after text. I scurry out and lock myself into the laundry room. I swipe through the contacts on my phone and call up the person I'm looking for. The one who will understand this situation more than anyone else.

It rings three times before the line connects. "Hey, Em… I know you're still upset with Noah for what happened at Maddie's funeral… but I really need you right now… he needs you. All of you." I let out a breath, praying she understands. "But I understand if this is asking too much after what he did… I wouldn't blame you for not wanting to help me. But I promise, Em… once I tell you this, everything will make sense."

She's quiet for a minute, and I wonder if she hung up on me. I pull the phone away, but no, the line is still on. I bring it back in time to hear her deep, long sigh. "What do you need my help with?"

NOAH

We stand in the middle of the cemetery, the heavy rain pouring down on us. Umbrellas open as we wait for the ceremony to start, the dark sky crying along with us. We're only ten people in all, and that's including the funeral conductor, Veronica and I, Everly and Jannice, Dr. Daltonsen, and four other staff members from the care facility.

I understood that not everyone could be present given the short notice and some having to work, but I'm grateful at least a few could make it. Although it's still sad to see the outcome.

Some part of me feels guilty for not telling the people I consider my family about today, about Trinity. For keeping my sister's memory only to myself. Maybe I'm just being selfish... but it's too late now.

"Is everyone present?" the conductor asks, looking from Veronica to me.

I nod and say, "yes," just as Veronica says, "no." My head whips to her with a frown, confused at the word she spoke.

"We're just waiting on a few more. They should be here any moment," she tells the conductor, who nods with a soft smile.

When she looks up at me, I see it in her eyes before she even voices it. The guilt, the apology. "I'm sorry, Noah. I know I promised you I wouldn't tell anyone, but none of this is right. None of this feels right, can't you see it?"

Just then, ten or so black cars pull up along the road, bodies all dressed in black descending from the cabs and making their way toward us. My family. My friends. My team. They're all here. My heart squeezes at the sight, my throat clogging as my eyes fog over.

"Hate me if you want, but please don't hate them. We're a family, Noah. We should all be together at this moment. Trinity would want that," she says softly, tears tumbling from her eyes.

I pull her in, wrapping my arms around her shoulders and swallowing past the lump in my throat. "Thank you," I whisper with a heavy breath, my voice cracking at the end.

And when I squeeze my eyes shut, burying my face into her hair, I feel it. The first tear in thirteen years slips past my lid and falls into her skittle hair.

This beautiful fucking woman. How did I ever get so lucky? She knew exactly what I needed, despite me saying otherwise. She did all of this for me. How could I not be in love with her?

Within a few minutes, they've all joined us, standing behind us and squeezing my shoulder on their way past. Emma comes to stand before me with an expression I can't read as she stares at me. I know I owe her an apology for the way I acted the other day, but I can't get the words out, not right now.

Luckily, she does it for me, circling her arms around my neck and pulling me in. I hug her back instantly as I whisper the words in her ear. "I'm sorry…"

"I forgive you, Noah, but I wish you had told me. I feel guilty for being mad at you when you were going through the same thing I was."

"You couldn't have known. No one but Veronica knew, and that's on me," I admit with a sense of shame.

She pulls back, hands along my arms, and smiles warmly up at me. "No more secrets, okay?"

I know I can't make that promise, given that both Veronica and Gabriel have their own. But I can still answer for myself, at least for this part. "Okay."

She joins the rest of our friends behind us, just as Gabe takes her place in front of me. He looks mad, a deep frown on his face as he watches me for a moment. But then he takes me into a tight hug, squeezing me in.

"Don't ever do that again, you hear me? You're my best friend, Noh. We're supposed to have each other's back. You've had mine through all my bullshit; you should have let me be there for yours." I hear him sniff as he tries to be strong despite the hurt that he feels right now, and all it does is increase my guilt.

"I know… you're right, I'm sorry…"

"Enough of that, let's get through this ceremony. Then we'll go home, and you'll tell me all about her." He releases me and pats my back. "I love you, man."

"I love you too, brother." I smile through my tears that keep coming.

He moves over to Veronica's other side, taking her hand and kissing her temple. I do the same to her, breathing in her cinnamon and apple scent as I close my eyes. "Thank you, Kitten. You are the very best thing in my life, and I don't know what I'd do without you. I hope you know that," I whisper against her hair.

She turns and gazes deep into my eyes. "I know," she breathes, then presses her lips to mine.

Chapter Twenty-Eight

GABRIEL

Better luck next time.

I was shocked.

After Ronnie told me what was going on with Noah, that he had a sister that had just died, I was shocked beyond belief. I was hurt that he would keep this from me, angry that he didn't trust me with his secrets. Jesus, we've lived together for the past five years, we do everything together, yet I didn't know about her existence.

What kind of friend does that make me? A shitty one.

I should have questioned him more every time he left the house and wouldn't tell me where he was going. I should have pushed harder for answers. I should have followed him. I should have put two and two together.

After the funeral, Ronnie managed to convince Noah to go over to Hayes's place. He was reluctant at first but eventually agreed. I know he didn't owe us anything, but we all wanted answers.

So, we sat down together in their living room with a beer in hand, except for Noah, who wanted his heavier drink of choice. *One I've realized he's becoming too friendly with. Something we'll have to watch out for with preseason starting up soon.* Then we waited patiently for him to be ready to share with us, and he did. He told us every possible memory he could think of involving his sister. He filled us in on his life, about his mother leaving, his father passing, then what happened to Trinity.

It fucking crushed me knowing he went through all of this alone. But at least he had Vixen in the end when it truly mattered the most. *I just wish I could have been there for him, too.*

I get why he did it, though. I get that hiding it from us wasn't intentional. When her accident happened, our careers were just taking off. The spotlight was shining on us, and the media and reporters wanted to know everything about us. Where we went, what we did, where we ate. They dug up everything they could about us.

How he managed to hide his whole family from them is actually pretty impressive. Although I get it, because I did the same with mine. I gave them my attention by partying and going crazy with the female fans, like that their focus was on my present and not my past. He did the same.

I just wish he would have come clean at some point, would have told us what he was going through. We would have been there for him. We would have helped him in any way we could. But I get it, it's why I'm putting my feelings aside and focusing on him, because he's my best friend and he's what really matters at this moment.

After a few hours with our friends, Noah started retreating and we understood it was time to go home. He needed his space and time to grieve on his own. The car ride home was made in silence, and so is the elevator ride up to the penthouse.

Ronnie stands at his side, head leaning on his shoulder, body pressed up against his with his arm around her waist. We haven't had sex since the night we went out clubbing, and it had been driving me crazy, but I understand why now. Their minds weren't in it, rightfully so.

We enter the penthouse and I head for the living room. "You guys want to watch a movie?" It's pretty late, but I'm not really tired yet, and another lonely night without my girl is not something I'm looking forward to.

"Sure." Ronnie smiles my way.

"Actually, I'm gonna head up. You two watch it without me." Noah throws his thumb over his shoulder in the direction of the stairs.

Ronnie's face drops. "Oh…"

He turns her in his arms, hugging her. "I'll see you later in bed."

She offers him a sad smile. "Okay," she says quietly as he kisses her for a second then retreats up the stairs.

I walk over to her quickly and take her against me. "We'll get him back. He just needs a little time." I kiss her crown.

"I know… I just miss him… I miss us," she murmurs against my chest.

"VERONICA!"

Ronnie and I pull apart suddenly, looking up the stairs where Noah's worried voice travels down, seconds before she sprints up the steps with me on her tail. I don't have time to see what's going on before her loud gasp fills my ears. Her hands are pressed to her mouth as she stares down at the bed.

Above the perfectly made bed lies a certain blue dress neatly, one I easily recognize. It's the same dress she wore to the nightclub. There's a white piece of paper lying above it. Ronnie steps up tentatively and reaches out with a shaky hand. Noah stands to the side of the bed with a glare while I take a step closer to Ronnie's back, reading over her shoulder what's written on the note.

"You always did look good in blue," I say out loud as realization sinks in. "That bastard was at the club."

"Oh my God! He was here... he was in our room!" She drops the paper like it's just burnt her hand and steps back quickly, bumping into my chest as I grab her arms.

"Oh God. He got into the penthouse." She begins to hyperventilate, her entire body shaking violently as tears start to fall from her eyes. "He got in..."

"Take her back downstairs. Wait in the living room while I check out the rooms to make sure he's gone, and call Julian," Noah instructs.

I nod and lift Ronnie into my arms as she sobs, then carry her downstairs and sit her down on the couch while pulling out my phone to call Julian. He picks up on the first ring.

"Storm."

"We have a problem. He was in the penthouse," I tell him.

"We are on our way. Marcos and Ricky will be up in a few seconds to scope out the place. They are the security details that have been assigned to you." He hangs up without letting me get another word in, and true to his word, two huge men walk out of the elevator seconds later.

They introduce themselves quickly, telling us to stay in place while they look around, just as Noah comes down the stairs. "I just checked upstairs but haven't done the main floor," he tells them, joining us on the couch.

"We'll look again, just to make sure. These kinds of people can get creative with their hideouts," Ricky says as they both head off farther into the penthouse, Marcos on the main floor while Ricky heads upstairs.

I settle down beside Ronnie and lift her into my lap. "It's okay, baby. If he's here, they'll find him."

She sobs louder. "It's not okay, Gabriel. He was here. He touched our things. What if this wasn't the first time? Maybe he's been coming and going. Oh God, what if he came in during the night when we were sleeping, and we didn't even know?" She begins to gasp for air again.

"Shh, everything will be okay, love. Just breathe. I promise you. We won't let anything happen to you." Noah rubs his hand up and down her back, kissing her shoulder.

"We can't stay here. We can't risk it," she cries and buries her face into the crook of my neck.

She's right, I'm not sure staying here is a good idea anymore. If he was able to get past security and up to the penthouse when it should have been impossible. Who's to say what else he can do?

Fifteen minutes later, Julian, Jason, and Jessie stride out of the elevator. Julian taps away on his phone, Jason looks mighty pissed off, and Jessie carries an open laptop as he punches on keys at lightning speed. He's also wearing glasses, which is a new look I haven't seen before.

Marcos and Ricky march back into the living room at the same time. "All clear, boss," Marcos announces to Julian.

"Any bugs?"

"None that we could find," Ricky tells him next.

"My device isn't picking up on anything either, except for ours," Jessie tells him, not looking up from his screen.

Julian nods. "Good." He puts his phone away and angles his attention our way. "We have run through the footage. He is gone, but he left us a message." He turns his head to Jessie. "Show them."

Jessie comes over as I place Ronnie between Noah and me. He sets the laptop down on the coffee table and presses play. It's footage from inside our penthouse. We see Victor strolling out of the elevator, casually walking through the penthouse, looking everything over.

Jessie presses a button and the camera changes to the one at the top of the stairs. We see him head up and walk directly into Noah's room first. A few seconds later he walks out and goes down the hall to mine, then the spare. He comes back into view and returns to Noah's room, where he stays for a few minutes, clearly setting the dress down and writing the note.

He finally exits the room and goes back to the main floor. Once again Jessie changes the camera as we watch Victor head to the kitchen, pull open the fridge, and take out an orange. He then proceeds to bite directly into it like an apple.

I scrunch up my face in disgust. "What the hell? What kind of savage eats an orange like that?" I mutter out loud.

Victor then leaves the kitchen and comes to stand in front of the camera, one hand on his hip as he looks around and continues to eat his orange. Or should I say, my orange. Eventually he chuckles and looks directly into the camera with a smirk. Ronnie gasps, her nails digging into my thigh.

"Tsk, tsk, tsk. Better luck next time, boys." He shakes his head as if he's disappointed that he didn't get caught right then and there. An evil smile suddenly takes over his face, disturbing enough to make my skin crawl. "Sweet dreams, Veronica." He then steps into the elevator and disappears.

"Oh God! I'm going to be sick." Ronnie stands quickly from the couch and runs to the bathroom on the ground level.

"I'll go check on her," Noah says as he hurries to his feet and follows after her.

Barely a minute goes by when the elevator dings and the doors open. A man I don't recognize walks in, but Julian turns and greets him immediately. "Agent Callahan, thank you for coming." Julian shakes his hand.

So this is the agent Ronnie was in touch with. Originally, we were meant to meet him last week to drop off the box Victor left her, but he had other obligations and sent his partner instead.

"No, thank you for informing me right away." He nods and steps toward me. "Hello, my name is Agent Scott Callahan. I work with the Federal Bureau of Investigations and am the one who has been assigned to Victor 'Snake' Cordova's case for the past four years."

I stand and shake his hand. "Gabriel Ellis, Ronnie's partner."

At that moment, Ronnie and Noah re-enter the room. "Agent Callahan?"

He turns and smiles warmly at her. "Hello, Veronica. It is nice to see you in person again, although I'm sorry it must be under such circumstances once more."

"So am I." She sighs, shaking his hand, then sitting back down on the couch.

"Noah Adler, Veronica's partner." Noah takes his hand as well.

Scott chuckles when he catches on to our relationship. "Agent Scott Callahan."

Noah takes his spot as well as we look up at everyone standing in our living room. "What do we do now? How the hell did he even get into the penthouse? You need a keycard to access the elevator. How come your men and cameras didn't pick him up?" Noah asks Julian furiously.

"Because he never came into the building," Julian says calmly.

"What do you mean he never came in?! He was clearly here!" I'm getting aggravated. They are supposed to be the best in the business, yet Victor got by them.

"What I mean is that he never entered nor exited the building, at least not in a way that can be detected. We have access to every camera in this building. Jessie and his team have been going over this past week's footage with facial recognition, and he has not appeared once. Not even someone with a similar look or build."

"How is that even possible..." I mumble to myself.

"As for the lobby footage, the only people who have used your private elevator are yourselves and a man by the name of Graham Stevenson, who escorted a deliveryman with groceries. Which means he came in from the underground garage. Unfortunately, the camera for the garage does not give us a clear view of the elevators, but we will be rectifying that immediately."

"Oh my God... he's still in the building..." Ronnie stares ahead with wide, terrified eyes.

"That's what we believe. I'm working on getting a search warrant for every condo in this building, but it will take some time," Agent Callahan informs us.

"But wait, that dress he picked out was one I wore a week ago. He was clearly at the club or near it to have seen me, which means he had to have left the building that night." Ronnie shakes her head with confusion.

"Like Julian said, he wasn't on any of the cameras. So if he is coming and going, he's doing it in a way that can't be seen," Jessie says.

"Which means?" I ask.

"The only way I can think of is in the back of a car, which tells us he has inside help. And since he clearly has a keycard, I'd put my finger on it being an employee." Jessie sits down beside me and turns the laptop toward him, typing away on it once more.

"Jess, get your team to go through everyone who lives in this building, every employee, every friend of a friend of a friend. Distant family, everything," Julian instructs his brother.

"Already on it."

"We will be changing the codes for the pad to the elevator and giving you new cards," Julian tells us.

"Isn't that all kind of illegal?" I raise a curious brow.

Jessie chuckles. "Let's just say it's in the gray zone." *That's what I thought.*

"And you're letting them do this?" Noah asks Agent Callahan.

He shrugs. "Look, my only goal is to catch this fucker. If I have to turn a blind eye to this in order to catch him, I will."

"Should we move out? Go stay somewhere else until he's caught?" Ronnie asks next.

"No. Staying here is our best option." Callahan shakes his head.

"You're joking, right? You want us to just stay here and sit around until he shows his face again?" I gape at him, completely astounded by his decision.

"I understand you are all worried right now. But my guess is he won't show his face again for a few weeks. If he's smart, which unfortunately he is, he'll lay low for a while in hopes that we give up our thorough search. You running will only make it harder for us to catch him."

"He is right," Julian starts. "We have it narrowed down now to where he can be; it will be easier to search for him this way, rather than starting off somewhere new. He may be smart, but his obsession with Veronica is what will get him caught."

"And you guys acting as if his presence isn't bothering you will only make him act out more, make him come out of hiding. He wants you afraid, he wants you to run. But once he sees that his plans aren't working, he'll make himself known, and that's when we'll be able to catch him." Jason speaks for the first time since he entered the room. That man is so quiet, despite his huge form, it's easy to forget he's even here.

Ronnie chews on her lip, still not certain that staying is the best option for us.

"Look, Ronnie." Jessie reaches over and places his hand on her knee. Noah and I both look at it with a frown. "I get that you don't trust us for now, but I promise you, we're the best at this. We'll catch him, and we'll keep you safe. Do you really want to keep running forever? Or would you rather stick this out a bit longer so that you can finally be free of him for good?"

"I want him gone... I don't want to be scared anymore," she admits in a quiet, broken voice. *Fuck, I hate seeing her like this.*

"Then trust me when I say this will work. We'll get him, and he'll never bother you again." He smiles tenderly as she nods.

But the fucker still hasn't removed his hand, so I pick it up, squeeze his wrist a little harder than necessary, and throw it back his way. All he does is chuckle and shake his head, going back to his computer. *Asshole.*

"We will be adding two more guards to your watch, and Jessie's team will be keeping an eye on camera footage around the clock. So please, limit your late-night activities to the bedroom until this is all over," Julian says, then pulls out his phone, tapping away on it once more, then placing it back inside his suit jacket's inner pocket.

"Jess, can you head down with Agent Callahan and get to work on the new keycards as well as putting up a camera near the elevators in the garage and inside the cab? I want full coverage of the underground space, no blind spots." Julian comes over just as Jessie stands and walks to the elevator with the agent.

He sits down in Jessie's spot and pulls something up on the laptop screen before passing it over to Ronnie. "Veronica, I want you to go through all these pictures. Tell me if someone stands out that you recognize outside of here. Not because they work or live here, but because you have seen them in the past somewhere else."

"Okay." She leans in, going over every single image. There has to be at least two hundred of them, and I don't recognize three-quarters of these people.

After about twenty minutes of her scrutinizing every picture, she sits back and shakes her head. "I don't recognize any of these people outside of here. No one stands out. I'm sorry."

"No need to apologize, it was simply a quick search. We will keep looking into everyone's past and any connections they may have to Mr. Cordova." He closes the laptop and stands, nodding to Marcos, Ricky, and Jason. "We will leave you all for the night, and I will be in touch if anything comes up."

Jessie and Agent Callahan re-enter the penthouse at that moment. Jessie passes us each a new card as well as one to Marcos and Ricky. I'm not sure how he got new ones without our authorization at the security desk, but I'm guessing it's part of the gray zone he was referring to earlier, and I won't question it.

Although Julian assured us that there was no way of Victor getting another keycard and that even if he managed to get one from the front desk again, it wouldn't work. Apparently, Jessie blocked the front desk's access to creating any more active cards for the penthouse elevator.

He also added that Ricky or Marcos would be escorting any deliveries or anyone on the approval list up from now on, since they're the only others to have a keycard aside from us three. Which also means that if we lose ours, we'll need to contact the Storms directly for a new card.

Agent Callahan collects the note Victor had left, and they all climb back into the elevator. Just as Julian is about to step in as well, he turns to us. "Adler," he calls out to Noah. "My condolences on your loss."

Noah swallows and nods. "Thank you."

He nods in return and leaves.

We all just stand in the foyer, unsure what to do now.

"Well, this was one hell of a day..." I mutter.

Ronnie comes into my side, hugging my waist. "I know it's late, but I don't think I can sleep right now... Can we still watch that movie you offered earlier?"

I kiss the top of her head. "Of course, baby. Anything you want." I look over at Noah, who seems to have retreated back into his head. "You joining us?"

He works his jaw then shakes his head. I sigh and look down at Veronica, who seems sad once more that he's pushing us away. He comes in and kisses her cheek, wishing her goodnight, and heads back to his room. She watches him go but doesn't say anything.

Hating the look of rejection on her face, I grab her chin and turn her gaze back to mine. "Want me to make you something to eat? I can whip us up that blueberry salad that you loved."

She smiles now. *There's my beautiful Vixen.* "Please?"

I let her go, bopping her nose. "Anything for you. Now go pick out a movie while I get my queen what she wants." I wink and turn away as she giggles and rushes over to the couch.

When I'm done making our late-night snack, I settle in beside her on the couch and she immediately cuddles in against me with her bowl in hand. I press play on the remote and realize she's put on the last *Harry Potter* movie. I chuckle and kiss her head. *Not that we literally watched it two days ago, but whatever.*

"What? They're amazing, okay!?"

I laugh again. "I didn't say anything. You're right, they are. But here's a question for you, how many times have you watched all eight movies this year?"

"Four…" she grumbles.

"Oh, you're adorable." I kiss her head again. "So does that make you a little wizard nerd?"

"Shut up!" She smacks my chest then laughs along with me. When our laugh subsides, she looks up into my eyes with such tenderness it squeezes my heart. "Thank you, Gabriel."

"What for?" I ask softly, passing my fingers through her hair.

"For being your goofy self when I need it the most. For making me smile and laugh when all I want to do is cry." She takes my bowl and hers, setting them down on the coffee table, then takes my face between her palms. "For showing me that you aren't the man I thought you were. For being an amazing friend and lover. For being patient with me, for protecting me. For always knowing how to comfort me."

She presses her lips softly to mine then pulls away, her eyes once more on mine. "For watching the same movie over and over, simply to please me. For making me food all the time. For trusting me with your problems. For not giving up no matter how mean I was to you in the past. Just thank you for being what I didn't know was missing from my life."

She sniffles and smiles. "I don't know how I'd get through all of this if it weren't for you and Noah. So, thank you for showing me that I could learn to trust again, to love again. That not everyone in this world is evil… Just thank you."

I fist the back of her head and pull her into me, smashing her lips to mine in a fierce, passionate, soul-shattering way. Those three words so close to slipping out as I make love to her mouth.

Because I feel them everywhere. I've felt them for so long. But right now, at this very moment, that feeling is like a tsunami hitting me at full force. And I'm not sure how much longer I'll be able to hold on. I'm not sure I want to hold them in anymore.

I've thought about saying them many times already, but I always doubted that Ronnie felt the same way. But after what she just said, I don't doubt it anymore.

She loves me.

Chapter Twenty-Nine

VERONICA
Shackles and Cages.

~ The Next Day ~

Last night was terrible. All I did was toss and turn all night once I climbed into bed with Noah, waiting for Victor to appear, waiting for the sound of footsteps to approach our bedroom door. I'm not even sure I slept a total of two hours.

Even now, my mind is still all over the place and filled with anxiety. I'm jittery and can't stand still. I hate this, I hate this nervous and scared version of myself. I feel like I'm once again trapped in those god-awful months after contacting Agent Callahan as I waited for the outcome I knew wouldn't work.

I check the time on my phone before grabbing my purse from the counter and slipping into my heels, my gaze constantly flicking toward the elevator as I try to calm my nerves. I jiggle my hand, once again lighting up my screen as I wait for Morgan's text to come in.

Once again, Gabe is out shooting a commercial for one of his newest brand deals. Mind you, it's for a cookie brand, which if you ask me is hilarious since he doesn't even eat any sweets. And Noah... well, I have no idea where Noah is.

When I woke up this morning after the little sleep I managed to get, he was already gone from the room. I thought he may have gotten up earlier and headed down to the kitchen for breakfast, but when I reached the main floor, all I found was Gabe. And the sympathetic smile he gave me when he noticed me standing by the stairs, confirmed my suspicions. Noah was gone.

I've texted and called him several times, left numerous voicemails, but all have gone unanswered, and that only increases my worries. I know I need to give him time to grieve and heal on his own, but with how much he's been drinking these past few days and how quiet he's gotten, I'm afraid of what he might do.

I'm pulled out from my train of thought when my phone vibrates in my hand.

Morg

> About five minutes out.

I sigh with relief as I read over her message, then send one off to my boys in our group chat.

Me

> Heading out, Morgan's here.

Husband #1

> Okay, baby. Stay safe and call if there's anything. I'll be home soon. <Heart emoji> <Kiss emoji>

Me

> I will. Can't wait. I miss you. <Heart emoji>

Husband #1

> I miss you, too, Vixen. I promise when I get home, I'm gonna snuggle the shit out of you. <Wink with kiss emoji>

Me

> I like the sound of that. <Wink emoji>

The chat goes quiet as I stare down at my screen for an extra minute, waiting and hoping for a message from Noah to come through, but it never comes in. I put my phone in my purse and walk to the elevator, my anxiety rising with each step I take as I press the call button and the doors slide open.

I'm excited to spend some time with Morgan, mostly because I won't be by myself for much longer. But I'm also extremely nervous about being down in the lobby and in the open, even if it's just for a minute.

I know I'm not technically alone, since there's always someone at the reception desk and Marcos and Ricky are right outside, or whoever the two new bodyguards are that Julian promised to have added. But despite knowing they are there, it doesn't stop the panic from setting in.

I know how quick Victor is when he has something in mind, I know how easily he can get past anything. Last night was clear proof of that. So if he wants me to disappear in broad daylight, he'll find a way to do it, even with people watching.

That thought unsettles me as I ride down the elevator to the lobby.

Once out of the cab, I glance around and notice there's no one else here but Antoine, the desk clerk, and Stanley standing by the door outside. I let out a breath and start walking toward the glass doors, knowing Morgan will be here any second to pick me up. All my senses heighten instantly—how loud my breath is, how fast my heart is beating, how loud my heels are clicking against the marble floor. And when Antoine calls my name out of the blue, I nearly jump out of my skin.

"Miss Masters! Good afternoon." Antoine beams at me, but there's always that little nervous tick happening at the corner of his mouth.

I squeeze my hands into fists, breathing in then letting it out slowly before turning to him and plastering a bright smile on my face. "Good afternoon, Antoine."

"Would you like me to call a car for you?"

My brows raise slightly at his question, but I quickly cover my expression. "Oh, no thank you." He asks me this every time, so it's not an unusual question. But after last night, I'm now second-guessing everything.

"Are you certain? It is quite hot outside today; you shouldn't have to walk to your destination in this heat. Please, I insist. It's complementary of the building, no hidden charges."

I feel my heart pounding a little harder in my chest the longer I stand here out in the open. "No, really, it's okay. My friend is picking me up; she should be here any second." I smile tightly and continue walking to the doors, not letting him get another word in as Stanley pulls one open.

"Miss Masters, always a delight to see you. Where are we heading to today?" Stanley gifts me his usual charming grin that reminds me of my grandfather's when I was a child before he passed away.

"Afternoon, Stanley. Just spending the day with my friend before my boys get home. Talking about them, have you happened to see Noah leave this morning? It would have been quite early." I stand beside him, looking down both sides of the road for Morgan's car.

"I have. I believe it was just past five when Mr. Adler drove by the front of the building after exiting through the garage." *So he left the moment I fell asleep... Which means he was just pretending to sleep while I was awake all night.* "Honestly, I'm quite surprised either of them agreed to leave your side today."

His question startles me and I slowly turn to look at him. "What?" That uneasy feeling returns instantly despite how hard I try to hide it.

Stanley smiles tenderly. "As you know, I'm here very often. And with how much time I spend outside these doors, I notice things. Lots of things. Like cars parked along the sidewalk every day in the exact same spot, yet no one ever enters or leaves the car except to grab something from the little café right there or use their restroom." He nods toward the cute coffee shop. "And how that same car follows behind every single time you leave this place. Although it's a different one when Mr. Adler or Mr. Ellis leave."

My mind races with a million thoughts as every word he speaks crawls up my skin like an unwelcome touch. *What is he trying to say? Does he know about Victor? Has he seen him? What isn't he saying? Oh God... I need to get out of here... I'm going to be sick again... I need this fucking nightmare to end!*

"I also happened to have been here last night when those three gentlemen arrived. I recognized them from the paper I read daily. And well, the last fella that came in a few minutes later looked exactly like what you'd expect an undercover cop to look like." *He's talking about Agent Callahan.*

Something in my gaze must show how close I am to freaking out, because in the next second, the sweet old doorman places his hand on my arm as the look in his eyes softens yet fills with worry. *Stay calm. Act normal. Stay calm. Act normal. Stay calm. Act normal.* I repeat the words the Storm brothers instructed us to do over and over in my mind.

"I'm sorry, Miss Masters, I did not mean to frighten you. All I meant to say was that I hope everything is all right and that if you ever need anything, I am always here. I may be an old man, but I still have a few tricks up my sleeves." He winks and removes his hand from my arm as I let out a breath.

I'm just paranoid. He's only being kind and watching out for me. Nothing more. I mean, if I were the one to witness the events from last night, I'd offer my help to the victim too, and I'm sure that's why Antoine was so insistent on getting me a car as well. Just like Stanley, Antoine works a lot and is here more often than any of the other receptionists. I could put my hand down that he was here last night when Jessie and Agent Callahan demanded to use his computer.

I'm just being paranoid...

I force another smile and nod just as Morgan pulls up in front of us. *Finally!* My body instantly relaxes as she waves through the passenger window with that bright grin lighting up her face.

"I need to go, my friend's here." I point to Morg's car and walk down the three steps.

"I have the evening off tonight, so I won't be here when you return. But I do hope you have a wonderful day, Miss Masters," he calls after me.

With my hand on the doorhandle, ready to pull it open, I focus on relaxing my nerves and look back at the kind old man who means no harm. "Thank you, Stanley, you too. And while you're at it, you should take the week off. You deserve a little break." My next smile is more genuine.

He laughs and places his hand over his heart. "I'll definitely think about it."

I finally climb into my friend's car and let out a heavy sigh while buckling myself in.

"Sorry it took a little longer to get here. I was stuck behind a delivery truck trying to parallel park in a spot that was *WAY* too small for the size of his cargo. And no matter how loud I shouted at him that he wouldn't fit, he didn't listen." Morgan rolls her eyes and pulls away from the sidewalk.

I chuckle at her frustration. "It's okay, I didn't mind waiting."

She glances at me quickly before refocusing on the road, but I don't miss the hint of worry in her eyes. "You sure? You seemed a little pale and lost back there when I pulled up."

Shit, she saw me on the verge of freaking out. How do I play this off? "No, I'm okay, I promise. Just something Stanley said about Noah leaving this morning that had me worried." *Let's hope she buys that. It's not technically a lie.*

Her gaze fills with compassion. "How is he really doing? I know he tried to put on a brave face for us yesterday, but he didn't fool any of us."

I sigh once more. "Not great. I know it's only been a day, but ever since we found out about her condition getting worse, he's been spiraling. All he does is drink no matter how much I try to get him to stop. Apparently, he snuck out this morning before Gabe and I woke up, and he hasn't responded to either of us since. I know I need to give him time to grieve, but I'm worried if I let him go too much, he'll just get worse. He's already started shutting me out..." I look down at my hands, trying to ignore the sting in my heart.

"I can't imagine any of that is easy," Morgan says as she takes my hand in hers. "I wish I could give you some advice on Noah, but the truth is, we've never seen this side of him before. He's always been, well, a slightly calmer version of Gabe with us." We both giggle at that. "But this new quiet and withdrawn version is one we aren't used to and don't really know how to handle either."

"That's what I'm most worried about. That none of us will know how to really help him." I lean my head back against the seat, staring out the window as we zoom past parked cars.

"Hey." She squeezes my hand. "We'll figure it out, okay? I do think giving him a bit more time is the right thing to do right now. Everyone grieves and responds to rough situations differently, and if we try to push them out of that stage too quickly or before they're ready, it will only make things worse. But we'll all step in to help when the timing is right."

"I know, I'll try not to be too hard on him right away."

"And how about you? How are you holding up?" I frown for a second, my mind instantly going to Victor and what happened last night. *But that doesn't make sense; the girls aren't aware of any of that.* "I know she was Noah's sister, but she still meant something to you as well, even if it wasn't for as long." *Oh, she means about Trinity. Jesus, I really need to get a handle on my nerves.*

"I'm… doing okay, I guess. I'm sad and all I want to do is cry when I think about it. I'll miss going to visit her, but I think she's at peace now, and that's what's really important." I shrug, not really knowing what the right response to this is. Sure, I've been going to see her regularly for the past two months and I grew close to her, but I also feel a bit guilty for being so upset that she's gone when I didn't know her as deeply as Noah did.

"You know you're allowed to be upset about it, right?" Morgan smiles tenderly, clearly reading my mind. "It's not because you only knew her for a short period of time that it means your emotions about the situation are less valid. Just look at Em and how hard Maddison's death is hitting her, yet she only knew her for barely two months. Sometimes people walk into your life out of the blue and become important instantly. The length of time that you've known them shouldn't dictate how you feel."

"You're right. And thank you for asking how I'm doing." I squeeze her hand back before letting go.

"Of course, Ronnie. I know you probably still feel like the newest addition to our little gang, but we care about you just as much as any other. We're family now," she says softly.

"And family sticks together," I whisper the end of their saying. I've heard them say this particular phrase to each other so many times over the past nine months that it's impossible to forget now.

Morgan beams at me as her eyes gloss over. "Oh God, these hormones are really getting the best of me. I swear, I'm tearing up every day." She quickly fans her face and laughs. "You know, I have no idea how we even started saying that, but it's like we heard it one day, and it just stuck with all of us."

"I couldn't tell you, but it's definitely a beautiful saying and fits perfectly with this group." I look at her and grin as she gazes back and does the same once we hit a red light.

"It really does."

We start moving again and I decide to brighten the mood with a topic I know will have Morgan lighting up. "So, are you excited to see those two little munchkins again?"

I swear, her entire body glows instantly. "So excited, but also super nervous. I don't know why I get like that every time I have an appointment, even if it's just a little regular checkup where we only get to listen to their heartbeats." She gets teary-eyed once more. "I guess I'm just terrified that if something goes wrong... Clay and I have spent the past two years getting bad news every month, so now that it's really happening, I feel like I need to expect the other shoe to drop at some point..."

"Hey, none of that negative talk." I take her hand once more. "Nothing's going to happen to those beautiful babies. It's finally your time now, and I'll be damned if something goes wrong. Hell, I'll become your personal bodyguard if you want and walk around you with a baseball bat in hand around the clock. I'll even stand in the corner of your room while you sleep to make sure Clay keeps his hands and feet away from that baby bump. No one messes with my nieces or nephews."

She laughs and wipes her tears. "Thanks, I might take you up on that. It would definitely help with all this stress and worry. Although Clay has been just as protective." She radiates with joy instantly simply from speaking her husband's name. "I swear if it wasn't for him having to go to his meeting today with a possible new sponsor, he would never leave my side."

"Hey, do you mind if we stop somewhere before you drop me off? I promise I won't be long," I ask Morgan as I climb onto the passenger seat after leaving her doctor's appointment.

I'm glad I got to tag along and see those two little shrimps inside her belly. It filled me with a strange feeling that wasn't necessarily unwelcome. Don't get me wrong, I'm nowhere close to wanting or being ready for kids just yet, but I now understand the desire for it a little more. It's a feeling you just can't experience any other way.

"Not at all, Clay won't be home for another hour, so I have some free time on my hands."

She pulls out of the parking lot, and I notice a black sedan backing out of a different parking spot seconds later. The same one that was parked across the street from the little café near the penthouse. *That must be Marcos and Ricky.*

When they go to exit the lot, a grey SUV slows down in front of them, and the driver nods at the black sedan before coming up behind us. *And that must be the guy following Morgan.* They're following much closer than I expected them to, but maybe that's the point, to act natural. I just hope none of the girls picked up on it.

"Where did you want to go?" Morgan asks, pulling me out of my thoughts.

"Um, to the graveyard. I know we were just there yesterday, but I feel like I could really use a little chat with Trinity right now."

During Morgan's appointment, I tried to call Noah three times and texted him a handful of messages, but he never answered any. I even called Gabe to see if he got any news from him, and he told me he hadn't but that he'd try again.

"Of course, sweetie." Morg smiles before driving us to our next destination.

Twenty minutes later, we arrive at the cemetery, and Morgan parks the car as close to Trinity's gravesite as possible. "Take all the time you need." She smiles and squeezes my hand before I open the door and step out.

As I walk over to where Trinity rests, I spot the black sedan once more in the distance, parking right at the entrance of the cemetery. While the grey SUV goes all the way around and parks facing Morgan but farther back to not draw any suspicions. The man even gets out of his car and walks up to a grave, pretending to pay their loved ones a visit.

I focus back on where I'm going and finally reach Trinity's burial spot where the ground is still fresh from yesterday. But what has me frowning slightly is the single blue flower resting at the foot of the headstone. *Could Noah have been here earlier and left it behind?*

I kneel down beside the fresh dirt, not caring that it's most likely getting my thigh-high socks dirty, and pick up the flower. "Hey, Trinny. I know we saw each other just yesterday, but I could really use your advice." I sigh, delicately gliding the tip of my finger over the soft blue petals. "I'm scared of how quickly Noah is derailing. I'm scared that I won't know how to truly help him when he finally lets me back in. All he's been doing for the past ten days is drinking, and now he's disappeared on us all day."

I wipe the single tear that falls and set the flower down, then look behind me as the sense of someone watching me makes my body erupt with shivers. But it's just Julian's men; no one else is here. I bring my attention back to the beautiful girl who left too soon, trying to ignore the anxiety coursing through my body at the thought that Victor could be somewhere out there right now watching me.

"I'm so worried about him, Trinity, and it's even worse now that Victor's popping up again…" I cover my face with my hands when the tears begin to flow freely. "Fuck… I'm so tired of being scared… of having to look over my shoulder everywhere I go… I hate it…" I pass my fingers through my hair, taking a few deep breaths.

"I feel like this fear inside of me is even stronger now than it was before because it's no longer just about me… and I'm terrified of what he'll do to my boys if he ever gets to them…" I cry quietly with my head bowed, hating that I once again feel like the weak little girl I tried so hard to break free from. "I'll never survive it if something happens to either of them…"

I give myself a few more minutes of silence to collect myself before getting to my feet and heading back to Morgan's car. When I climb in, she immediately reaches for me and takes me in her arms. "Everything's going to be all right. Just breathe through it and stay strong," Morg whispers in my ear before pulling back and smiling at me with her hands still on my arms. "You're our bad B-I-T-C-H. You've got this."

We both giggle at the fact that she spelled out the word rather than say it, but Morgan's been intense with the no cursing, even when there aren't any children around. She's going to be a phenomenal mother to these babies with how much she's always thinking ahead of everything.

"Thanks, I think I needed that reminder." I smile at her.

"Anytime, sweetie."

One hour later, I'm sitting outside on the patio, gazing at the cute little birds chirping away as they jump around their birdhouse and peck the seeds, when Gabe arrives home. He leans against the open patio doors, that dazzling grin over his lips as he watches me apply the last coat of nail polish on my toenails.

"You're finally home." I can't help my smile from growing at the sight of him.

"Hi, baby." He walks over as I close the bottle and kiss him. "Missed me?"

"I always miss you when you're gone," I admit while he takes a seat next to me on the couch and places my feet over his thigh.

"Pretty," he whispers, looking down at my rainbow toes that match my hair, then begins blowing softly on them.

"Have you heard anything?" I swallow, already knowing the answer.

Gabe shakes his head. "I'm sure he's fine, he probably just needed a day to himself," he says, but even I can tell he doesn't believe his own words.

"Do you think we should call Julian? Didn't he say he had someone on all of us? Maybe he knows where he is."

He cups my cheek, forcing a smile for me. "I already did, and he assured me someone was watching over Noah, but he refused to tell me where he was out of respect for his privacy." My face falls instantly. "I know it sucks and it's not the answer you wanted, but we need to give him time." *There goes that famous advice again.*

"I know..."

"Come here." He moves my feet off his legs and opens his arms.

I quickly get up and sit down sideways on his lap, my feet on the couch cushion beside us with my arms around his torso and head nuzzled beneath his chin as he kisses my crown. For the next few minutes all we do is watch the birds in silence as Gabe glides his fingers through my hair and I listen to the sound of his heart beating.

"Have you ever thought about getting a bird as a pet? You seem to like them a lot," he suddenly asks.

I shake my head against him. "I could never own one."

"Why not?" I can hear the frown in his tone.

"I've spent the last eight years of my life feeling like a bird trapped in a cage. Even once I was free, I could still feel the weight of its shackles wrapped around my ankles, tying me to that cage. The last thing I would ever want to do is take away that innocent bird's freedom."

His arms tighten around me once more, soothing me with his touch as he kisses the top of my head again.

Chapter Thirty

VERONICA

Baboons and horny hippos.

~ Two Days Later ~

I wish I could say that things are getting better, but they aren't.

Although there hasn't been any sign of Victor since, *thank the heavens,* Noah is still spiraling. He spends most of his time either drinking at home or going out to God knows where to get drunk, then stumbles in smelling like cheap beer and women, and I hate it. I don't think he'd cheat on me, but I can't stop my mind from wondering where he goes and what he does when he leaves the house.

Gabe tells me not to worry, that Noah would never do something like that. That wherever he goes women probably cling to him, but that he remains faithful to me. *I hope he's right...*

Outside of the whole Noah and Victor situations, Gabe and I have been spending a lot of time together. He does everything to keep my mind occupied, whether it's staying home or going out to wander around New York. He always finds us something fun to do, every hour of the day, and I'm so grateful to him for it. He's the best boyfriend I could have asked for.

Gabe had a meeting with his agent this afternoon, something about a new sponsor. I swear he has something new every other day. The public really can't get enough of him, although I am starting to get a little jealous. *I thought hockey players had the summer off?*

And then there's Noah, who has once again been MIA since this morning and hasn't been answering his phone... again. So I've been alone for the past three hours, busying myself with cleaning and trying to get the alcohol smell out of the rug in Noah's room, from where he spilled his drink last night.

After spending forty-five minutes scrubbing the rug clean, I move on to the laundry basket in the bathroom. I carry it back into the room and sort through the clothes over the bed before bringing them down to the washing machine.

I fall on one of Noah's white shirts that he wore out two days ago, and a red spot by the collar catches my attention. I lay it on my lap and glide my fingertips over the smudged lipstick, thoughts racing through my head as my eyes well up. I wipe away the tear that slips out furiously and throw the shirt back into the basket.

"I didn't cheat on you." I look up to find Noah standing by the door, watching me. "I know where your mind is going. I didn't do any of that."

"Then where have you been, Noah? Where do you go every time you leave the house? Why don't you ever answer your phone when you're gone for hours and come home at odd hours of the night?" I'm trying to keep it together, but the pain resonates in my voice.

"I just wander around, find a bar along the way, and have a few drinks. That's all. It's no big deal." He shrugs.

I stand from the bed, angry that he doesn't see how much he's hurting me. "But it is a big deal, Noah! You shouldn't be driving if you're drinking. You shouldn't be going hours without answering your phone and not telling anyone where you are." My eyes well once more. "What if something happened to you? Do you know how worried I am every time you leave? How I can't fucking fall asleep until you get home, because I'm terrified something may have happened to you?!" My voice wobbles with emotions.

I know I could probably beg Julian to tell me where Noah is, or even ask Jessie, but it shouldn't have to come to that. He's my boyfriend, he should be the one communicating with me because that's what we do in relationships.

"Fuck." He scrubs his face with his palms then walks over to me, taking me in his arms. "I'm sorry. I didn't mean to worry you."

A sob breaks out despite how hard I'm trying to keep it in. "I know you're hurting, Noah, I get it. But please, you can't keep going like this. This behavior is destructive... It's not only hurting you, but also me and Gabe as well. Please just try to answer your phone sometimes and no more taking your car if you're going to drink... I can't lose you."

"I can't lose you either, Veronica... I can't... I don't think I'd survive it..." His voice cracks as my heart breaks for this beautiful man who's suffering.

I reach up, my hand coming into his hair as I seal my lips to his, promising to never leave him with my mouth, to love him forever. Within seconds, our kiss turns heated, and we're ripping at each other's clothes, sending them flying around the room until we're naked. I push him down on the bed and climb above him while he lies in the middle of it.

He's already hard beneath me as I rub my aching clit against him, my wetness spreading along the length of his cock. We haven't had sex in two weeks, and I'm dying for it. I lift onto my knees, grabbing hold of his shaft and positioning myself over it, then cry out as I slide all the way down. He grabs my breasts, twisting and pulling my nipples as I ride his dick.

Everything is frantic, rough, desperate. We don't give each other time to settle on a perfect rhythm, we just fuck like animals, panting and groaning as we near our point of ecstasy. I lean in, claiming his lips as he thrusts his hips up, fucking me with all the strength he can muster.

"You'll never lose me, Noah. I'm yours forever," I breathe against his lips.

"Forever." He fists my hair and devours my mouth.

Barely thirty seconds later, I'm crying out against his lips, moaning through my orgasm as my hips buck uncontrollably against him. He pumps in a few more times, then tightens his hold on me as he spills his seed deep inside my pussy with a deep, long grunt.

Noah turns us to our side, pulling the sheet over our bodies. I rest my head on his arm, my forehead against his lips as he passes his fingers through my hair. We don't say anything, simply breathing in each other's presence. I've missed him these last couple of days.

"Hey, I'm..." Gabe appears at the entrance to Noah's room.

The smile he was just wearing vanishes from his face as he takes us in, a sad, rejected look filling its place instead. I see his Adam's apple bob in his throat as he takes a step back.

"I'll just get dinner ready." He turns quickly and bolts down the steps, his retreating footsteps echoing loudly in my ears.

Guilt begins to build in the pit of my stomach as I realize what has dimmed the light in his eyes with our current situation. Last night, Gabe tried to touch me, and I stopped him, telling him it didn't feel right doing anything without Noah. And now here I am, having just had sex with Noah while Gabe was gone.

God, I'm such an idiot!

I sit up in bed and bury my face into my hands, unsure how to fix this.

"Hey." Noah runs his knuckles against my spine. "He'll be fine."

"I feel guilty... We've never had sex just one-on-one, and yesterday I told him we couldn't, but now I'm doing just the opposite. I feel like I'm betraying him..."

"But you're not, Kitten. Yes, we're all in this relationship, but it doesn't mean we have to always do everything together. It's okay for you and me to do things alone, like it's okay for you and him to have moments together too." He sits up and kisses my back. "Why don't you go see him while I grab a shower?"

"Yeah, okay." I scoot out of bed and grab one of Noah's baggy shirts from the walk-in. Passing it over my head, I hurry down the steps in search of Gabe. Noah's sticky cum makes my thighs slippery, but I don't care, seeing Gabe is more important right now.

I find him standing in the kitchen, staring down at the stovetop with a pan resting on one of the burners, but there's nothing inside it. His hands are fisted against the edge of the counter on either side of the stove, head bowed.

"Gabriel?"

He doesn't respond immediately, but the strained muscles in his back tell me he heard me. "You know, I've been trying to wrap my head around why you'd tell me no but say yes to him."

"It wasn't like that, Gabe." I step around the island, getting closer to him.

He turns just as I'm about to reach for him. "Really? Because it sure as shit seems like it. You think I haven't noticed the connection you two have? You think I don't hear you guys talking and laughing every morning together in bed? I get it. You like him more." He swallows, his jaw working back and forth. "But I thought that after these last couple of days, things had changed between us, that maybe you liked me as much as I do you. But I guess I was wrong." There's so much pain in his voice, and it kills me that I'm the reason he feels that way.

I grab onto his forearm, pleading with him. "That's not true, Gabe. Don't say that. I don't like one of you more than the other, because if that were the case, I wouldn't be in this relationship. What I feel inside my heart, I feel it for the both of you."

He rips his arm away from me. "Bullshit, Ronnie. Because if that were true, you wouldn't have rejected me last night, claiming you didn't want to leave Noah out. You wouldn't have slept with him while I was out. Who's to say that was even the first time it happened? For all I know you two have been hooking up behind my back since the start."

"Stop it, Gabe! We haven't, okay? That was the first time, and I'm sorry I pushed you away last night. I didn't intend on having sex with Noah today, I just fucking missed him, and I was angry at him when he got home. One thing led to the other and we had sex."

I take a step closer to him, forcing him to look at me with my hands. "I'm sorry if I made you feel rejected. I never meant to hurt you. I care about you so much, Gabe, don't you see that? I love every moment we share together. I crave them all the time.

Don't ever think what I feel for you is less than what I feel for Noah, because it's not. You have no idea how guilty I feel right now for what I've done."

He stares at me and for an instant, I think I'm finally getting through to him. But then he grabs my wrists, forcing my hands away and turns his back to me. "The only reason you feel guilty is because you got caught," he says then heads for the fridge, pulling out items. "Just go back to him. I'll call when dinner's ready."

What the fuck is happening?

I feel like we've been cursed or something. How did we go from such a happy relationship to this? Because that's all it's been since the beginning of the month. Shit, after shit, after shit. I'm already having a hard time getting through to Noah, I can't be dealing with this nonsense on top of it with Gabe.

"No."

He sighs, dropping his head. "Ronnie, please just go upstairs."

"No, I won't go."

"Well, I fucking want you to!" he shouts, turning to face me.

"No, you don't! You're just mad at me, so take it out on me."

"No." He fists his hands at his sides.

"Yes. I want you to. Use me. Fuck me like you hate me, I don't care. Just take all that anger you have inside right now and give it to me. Show me how hurt you are. Make me pay."

I walk up to him, chest grazing his as we stare down at each other. I know I've been getting used to their touches and manhandling, to the point where I no longer get any icky feelings or slight moments of panic. But one thing I haven't let them do is get extremely rough with me. It's a hard line for me to cross and requires a lot of trust.

"You don't know what you're asking for," he whispers.

I look into those beautiful gray orbs that plead with me to ease this pain he feels inside and smile. "I do, and I want it. No holding back, give me your all." It may be a hard line, but I trust him. I trust both of them.

His jaw ticks, nostrils flaring, pupils dilating, and for a second, I think he's going to refuse me again. But in the blink of an eye, he jumps me, fisting my hair painfully, lips bruising mine in a punishing kiss. Then he yanks his hand back with my hair still in his grip and flips me around, bending me over the counter as I yelp.

I hear his pants hit the floor as he pushes my shirt up, then smacks my ass hard before leaning against me. "Tell me, Vixen, is his cum still inside of you?" he growls into my ear.

"Yes," I say breathlessly.

He chuckles wickedly. "Good." Then rams into me. No foreplay, no checking to see if I'm wet, simply forcing himself into my tight cunt.

"AHHHH!" I scream as my head drops forward, but he quickly tightens his hold on my hair and pulls me up, forcing my head back and arching my body.

My palms lay flat on the surface of the kitchen island, mouth wide open as I cry out repeatedly. The edge of the counter digs into my hips as he plows into me with powerful, relentless thrusts. I know I'll have bruises there tomorrow, but I don't care.

"You like that, baby? Do you like me fucking you like I hate you?"

"YES!" I shout, tears rising in my eyes at how brutally he's fucking me, but I don't stop him. We both need this.

The grunts he releases are feral, unhinged. Like a beast that's been trapped for years, finally breaking free. I've never seen this wild unrestrained side of Gabe before, and I realize now that this is the side of him my subconscious used to fear. But now that I know the real him, now that I've fallen for the real Gabriel, I'm not afraid anymore. I want all of him, his good and his bad, and I love every version of him.

Noah marches down the stairs and comes over to the kitchen, taking a seat at the island in front of me. Gabe doesn't seem bothered by his presence, in fact, it seems to fuel him. He fucks me even harder, one hand pulling my hair and the other leaving bruise marks on my hip.

I'm gasping and panting, moaning and screaming, nails clawing at the flat, smooth surface of the counter. Noah leans in on his elbows, his face inches away from mine. His eyes are focused on mine, moving from one to the other. I feel my face flush at being examined while also being fucked.

"She's close," he tells Gabe with a smirk.

"Oh, I know. I can feel her pussy shaking around me. She's choking my dick to death, and it feels fucking amazing." He laughs. "Isn't that right, baby? You gonna come all over my cock like a good girl?"

"Oh God! Yes!" I cry out.

"Then fucking come!" He yanks on my hair harder, my scalp feeling like it's been set on fire, and releases my hip to smack the side of my ass cheek hard.

I detonate on a scream. "GABRIEL!!!" My arms give out beneath me, just as he untangles his fist from my hair. Noah places his hand beneath my head seconds before it smacks against the counter.

Gabe takes hold of my hips, lifting me off the ground as he continues to brutalize my pussy with savage thrusts. My thighs, ass, and hips burn from the assault, but my body loves it. Wants more of it. Wishes it would never end, and that Gabe would touch me in this consuming way forever.

But within a few more strokes, he releases a barbaric roar and slams into me one last time, filling every inch of me until I feel him running down my legs.

He sets my feet back to the ground and leans over my body, kissing my shoulder lovingly. "I could never hate you, Vixen," he whispers against my heated sticky skin.

~ *Two Days Later* ~

Gabe and I pull up at Morgan's house just as Aubrey steps out of my car beside us. I climb out of Gabe's car quickly and rush over to her, taking her in my arms. *God, it feels like I haven't seen her in forever.* When we lived together, we used to see each other every day, now I'm lucky if I get to see her once a week.

"Ugh! I've missed you so much!" I squeeze her tightly against me.

She giggles softly, pulling me in as well. "I've missed you too, Ronnie. It's so weird not living together."

I pull back as we hold each other at arm's length. "How are things going with living in the Ford Manor?"

She laughs elegantly. I don't know how she does it, but everything Aubrey does is done gracefully. I swear she must have been a princess in another life. "It's hardly a manor, but it's been... fine."

I scrunch my nose and let go of her. "Oh no, don't tell me they're going at it like horny hippos?"

"Horny hippos? Really?"

Gabe joins our side and kisses Aubrey's head then throws his arm around my shoulder as she flushes. "Oh yeah, you should see how they woo their female companion. It's pretty disturbing yet impressive."

"I'm so confused right now..." She stares with wide eyes.

"Don't ask, we watched a very strange documentary about animal reproduction last night." I giggle.

"It's given me a whole bunch of new ideas to get in your pants." He nibbles at my earlobe, flicking my four piercings with his tongue.

I slap his chest with the back of my hand. "Don't even think about throwing your shit around to get to me. I can assure you, that will not work in your favor," I warn him as he laughs.

"Well, for your information, yes, they are. I really have no idea how Gracie sleeps through all of that. I really didn't miss hearing my brother... doing that. I think it makes it even worse that it's with one of my best friends." She blushes once more talking about it.

"Do you think you're going to turn red like a tomato every time you have sex, baby Ford?" Gabe asks, chuckling behind his fist.

I smack him again. "Shut up. Leave her alone."

She looks behind us, peering at the car. "Noah's not coming?"

A tightness forms in my chest at her question. "No..."

She offers me a sympathetic smile and rubs my arm.

A voice across the street catches our attention, and we all turn to watch Shane stepping out of Jessie's house as he waves goodbye. He takes the few steps down, watching his feet, but then looks up and stops in his tracks when he spots us and stares straight at Aubrey.

I turn my head to her, finding her blushing with her lips slightly parted. I elbow her and whisper through my smile, "Say hi."

She jumps into action, throwing her hand up high. "H-hi, Shane!" she shouts a little too loudly. She quickly pulls her arm back down and rests her hand along the base of her neck as her cheeks burn brightly. "Oh God... that was embarrassing."

I turn in Gabe's arms, hiding my face in his chest as I try not to laugh, but it's impossible. I feel Gabe's chest rumbling as he tries to suppress his own laughter. When I peek a glance toward Shane, I find him smiling brightly at her, he slowly raises his hand and waves back.

Aubrey quickly grabs my elbow and pulls me away from Gabe. "Okay, I said hi, now let's go inside before I do something stupid again." She drags us along toward the front door as Gabe and I wave to Shane as well.

We step into the house and find Clay, Morgan, Cecilia, and Silas sitting around in the living room. Cecilia notices us first, climbing off Silas's lap. "Yay! You finally made it." She claps her hands together and comes in to hug us all.

I giggle. "You thought we wouldn't come?"

"No, of course, I knew you would. But I feel like we haven't been all together under good conditions in a while." She smiles tenderly.

"Yeah, you're right. These past two or so weeks have been pretty brutal for all of us, I think." I sigh.

Morgan joins her side, coming in for a hug as well. "They have. How are you holding up?" She leans back and cups my face like a mother would, and it instantly makes me long for my own.

"I'm... still okay, I guess. Gabe has been wonderful for my spirit." I smile at him.

"I knew he would be a good boyfriend someday." Morgan beams with joy.

Once she steps back, Gabe takes a good look at her as his eyes widen. "Oh wow, look at you! Your little bump is starting to show already!"

"I know! The doctor says it's normal since there are two of them, even though I'm only fourteen weeks along." She lights up at the mention of her babies, and we all can't help but smile along with her.

"Hey, where's Adler?" Silas calls as we finally sit down on the couch, Gabe taking the end seat with Aubrey beside him, while I sit sideways on his lap.

That tightness I felt earlier in my chest now moves to my throat. I shake my head. "I don't know."

Clay frowns. "What do you mean, *you don't know*?"

I look down at my hands as I fiddle with the hem of my skirt. Gabe slides his fingers through my hair soothingly and kisses my temple. "He's been... disappearing during the day. Sometimes late into the night as well."

"And you don't know where he is?" Cecilia asks softly.

I shake my head again. "He won't answer his phone, and he won't tell me where he goes. We talked about it the other day, and he said he would tell me from now on. But he still doesn't, and he ignores all our calls and texts." I feel the tears swelling in my eyes as I sniff.

Aubrey takes my hand in hers, rubbing soothing circles over my palm. I take a deep breath and look at everyone who holds commiserated expressions on their faces. "Can we please change the subject? I really don't want to cry right now. But I could really use a glass of wine, though." I giggle humorlessly with a sad smile.

"Of course, sweetie." Morgan smiles with sympathy, understanding exactly the emotions I'm feeling after our talk, and stands from beside Clay. "You too, Brey? Gabe, beer?"

"You rest, little mama. I'll get our drinks." He lifts me by the waist and sets me down in his vacated spot, grabbing my chin and tilting my head up as he kisses me. He pulls back with a beaming smile that makes me melt. "Have I told you how beautiful you look today?"

I giggle. "Only seven times."

"Then let me say it again." He pecks my lips once more. "You look beautiful today, Vixen."

I bite my lip. "Thank you." He straightens, winks, and heads to the kitchen, while all I can do is watch his retreating form with a breathless sigh and turn to mush in my seat.

"Aww, you guys are adorable!" Cecilia coos with hearts in her eyes.

I laugh. "Gabe is a very attentive boyfriend. Honestly, he's amazing. But don't tell him that, it will only boost his ego," I whisper to them.

"And to think you hated his guts not too long ago." Silas laughs.

"There's a very thin line between love and hate." Aubrey smiles. "Just look at Grey and Em."

"I don't think Greyson ever really hated Em. He just couldn't stand her craziness." Cecilia points at her in a knowing way.

"And look at him now, can't get enough of it." Clay chuckles.

Gabe returns with two glasses of white wine and a beer, handing the wine over to Aubrey and me as I stand to let him take his spot. His hand circles my waist and pulls me back to him, then he kisses my shoulder.

"Speaking of Grey and Em, where are they?" I ask, just picking up on the two missing members of our group. Well, aside from Noah.

"They had an ultrasound this afternoon to check on the baby. We picked up Gracie earlier since it's Sam's day off. Her and Dante are down for their nap upstairs," Cece informs us.

"And how are things going with the business?" Gabe asks, taking a swig of his beer.

"Oh, it's doing amazingly! The outcome is so much more than we could have imagined. We've had to hire five more event planners, and we're visiting a new location tomorrow." Cecilia grins broadly. "We hadn't planned on having to expand until next year, but things are moving so quickly, and we have so many new demands coming in daily. Plus, the donations, God, we keep receiving more and more; it's almost overwhelming." She bounces in her husband's lap excitedly.

"Would you be moving the whole foundation if you like this new place?" Aubrey asks with interest.

"Oh, no. It was our goal at first. But the place we are seeing tomorrow is actually a huge industrial building that was remodeled into four separate halls. But the owner abandoned the project halfway, now all that's left is to put up the walls and the finishing touches. Which means we would be able to plan four different events at the same time, on the same day. Plus, the one at our headquarters; it would give us an opportunity to host more people at once."

"Wow, that's incredible!" I gush in amazement.

The front door bursts open, making all of us whip our heads in its direction. "NO, GREYSON! Never again! You are never touching me ever again!" Emma comes stomping in, throwing her bag onto the ground dramatically.

"TWO OF THEM! There are two of them!" She stretches her hands at her sides, emphasizing her point.

"What's two of them?" I frown.

"That..." She flaps her hand around in Greyson's direction, who leans against the wall with clear amusement. "Baboon, put two babies in me! Two! Do you realize what that's going to do to my body!?"

She turns to face Greyson. "You can say goodbye to that tight little pussy you like so much, because it's never coming back! BYE-BYE! Adios! And even if it does, you're never putting your hands on it ever again!"

"Did she just call him a baboon?" Gabe asks with a chuckle.

"Shut up, Gabe! It's all I could think of under pressure. Can't you tell I'm having a major crisis right now?! By next year, I'm going to be fat and give birth to two huge babies! When I didn't even want one right now!" She whines, stomping her foot repeatedly.

"Hey! You said I was lucky to be having two." Morgan narrows her eyes at her.

Emma's eyes go wide as she hurries over to Morgan, kneeling before her and taking her hands in hers. "Oh, but you are! I'm happy that you're gifting us two beautiful babies. Me? Not so much. I'm getting married at the end of the year. How will I even fit in my dress? And I already have a daughter, now I'm going to have two screaming babies and a toddler. Oh God!"

She stands and begins to pace the room. "But it's okay, yeah, everything is fine. It'll be fun, right? We'll dress them in matching outfits, go shopping for double strollers, and two cribs, and two highchairs, and two baby swings, and two car seats." She lets out a hysterical laugh that sounds extremely scary before her face falls and eyes go wide once more.

"Oh God, we'll need to get a second nanny, because there's no way Sam can take care of twins on top of Gracie and Dante. And we'll need to turn one of the spare rooms into a second nursery. And get a bigger play area in the living room and more storage bins." She starts to hyperventilate, flapping her hands in her face.

"Guys... I think she might be having a mini panic attack," I say cautiously.

"Oh, no. I'm fine, totally fine." She laughs hysterically once more and bends in half, placing her hands on her knees as she continues to pant.

Greyson hurries over to her side, resting his hand on her back. "Bunny, you need to calm down. This can't be good for the baby."

She stands quickly, pushing him aside. "Don't you freaking put your hands on me, Greyson!" She reaches for a throw pillow beside Aubrey and begins whacking Greyson with it repeatedly. "THIS IS ALL YOUR FAULT! You did this to me, you asshole who can't control your fucking sperm! And it's BABIES! PLURAL!!!"

She continues to smack him as we all break out in a fit of laughter at the episode unfolding before us. Poor Greyson covers his head and face as he lets her unleash her anger on him.

Silas slaps his leg as he bends forward, almost knocking Cecilia off his lap in the process. "Oh God! This is beyond epic!"

"I warned you, Wolf! I told you what would happen if you put two of them in me! Those balls are mine now! Call up your doctor, schedule an appointment to get them cut off!" She throws the pillow away with a huff and fixes her wild red mane.

Greyson lifts his hands from his face slowly, looking at her with a barely restrained smile. "That's not how it works, Bunny."

"Oh, but it is. You thought I was crazy to start with? Well, you haven't seen anything yet. We're getting you castrated. I want those balls gone! And then I'm gonna bring them home and turn them into stress balls. And every time those kids of yours drive me crazy, I'm going to take them out and squish them between my fingers in front of you," she whispers menacingly as all noise dies in the room.

Greyson visibly pales as he watches the evil look on her face, the smile falling from his lips as he gulps.

"Shit... that's dark as fuck..." Clay mutters behind them. "Even I'm a bit terrified right now."

"Same here, man..." Gabe swallows with wide eyes.

"And I thought you were crazy pregnant. Thank God it wasn't that bad," Sy says to his wife.

Cecilia turns to face him with a frown. "You thought I was crazy? You said I was adorable pregnant!"

Silas's eyes widen as he quickly tries to cover his fuck-up. "Oh, yes. Yes, you were totally adorable... when you weren't crying or losing your shit for no reason," he mumbles the end.

"Oh, you are so sleeping on the couch tonight!" She folds her arms over her chest.

"No, please, Minnie. Not the couch again! I'm sorry, okay? Fine, I admit, you were a little crazy at times. But compared to this," he nods toward Emma and Greyson, "you were a saint. The most beautiful and perfect pregnant woman."

She narrows her eyes at him for a minute. "You're lucky I love you and that you gave me a beautiful son." She rights herself and drops her back against him.

"So... no couch?" he asks tentatively, rubbing his hands up and down her arms.

"No couch... for now."

"Yesss." He pumps his fist.

"See! You men are all the same! You knock us up and then complain that we're losing our mind while carrying your child! You're all assholes!" Emma turns around, heading for the kitchen. "I need a fucking drink." She then spins on her axis and throws her arms out while facing us. "Oh! But guess what? I CAN'T FUCKING HAVE ONE!"

The baby monitors come to life on the coffee table, letting us know that nap time is over. "Great! I woke up the kids!" Emma says frustratedly as she heads for the stairs instead.

"Hey, little Tulip, guess what? You're not just getting one sibling, but two! Better start saying bye-bye to ever having anything of your own, because your brothers or sisters will be taking up *A LOT* of room! You can blame Daddy for that!"

Greyson stands silently in the middle of the living room, watching her leave with a petrified expression on his face. "What have I done..." he mumbles to himself.

We all explode with laughter as Silas stands and slaps Grey's back on his way up to get his son. "Good luck, man. You'll need it."

"This is just the beginning," Clay tells him.

"I'm fucked," Grey says as he turns and drops into an armchair.

Chapter Thirty-One

VERONICA

Stay out...

After dinner, Gabe and I make our way home. I'm a little antsy in my seat as I try to call Noah for the millionth time today. And once again, it goes to voicemail. I don't bother leaving one, since he hasn't responded to all the others I've left.

Gabe takes my hand in his, kissing the back of it. "I'm sure he's fine. But we'll need to get a handle on this soon, with training camp starting up next month. He needs to get back in shape."

"I know... I'm thinking of booking him an appointment with my therapist. That's if he would ever come home." I chew my lip.

With everything that's been going on with Victor, I've started seeing Dr. Hallaway every two weeks, instead of only once a month. I might seem and feel fine, but I'm not dumb. I know this whole situation is affecting me deep down, and the stuff happening with Noah is just adding onto it.

Gabe's phone begins to ring through the cab, the word *'Lobby'* appearing on the display screen of the car. He frowns as he looks down at it but answers the call. "Yes?"

"Hello, Mr. Ellis. This is Antoine, from the front desk. I'm sorry to be bothering you this late into the evening, but we seem to have a situation."

My mind immediately jumps to Noah and every worst-case scenario that could have happened. And with the way Gabe's eyes flick to mine, I know his did too. "I'm listening. What's the situation?"

"There's a woman down here in the lobby asking to see you. We haven't let her up to the penthouse since she isn't on the guest list, but she's becoming agitated and causing a commotion. I'm afraid we will have to call the authorities."

"What's her name?" Gabe asks the man on the phone.

"She claims to be a Mrs. Courtney Ellis."

Gabe's swallow is audible as he leans his head back against the seat. "Tell her that I'll be there in five minutes. If she causes another scene before I arrive, you have my permission to call the police."

"Very well, sir. We'll notify her."

"Thank you." Gabe ends the call and lets out a sigh.

I'm afraid to ask, because I have a feeling I already know the answer, and I don't know if I'm prepared for it. "Who is she?"

He turns to look at me as we pull into the underground parking lot. "My mother."

Gabe pulls up in his spot, and I notice Noah's car still isn't here, despite me pleading with him not to take it when he's drinking. Gabe turns the engine off and simply sits in his seat for a minute, eyes closed, not saying a word.

I bring my hand up and cup his cheek. "Hey, do you want me to go up there and throw her out?" I don't even understand how she's here. Gabe told me his parents still lived in Colorado from what he last heard.

He smiles. "No, it's okay. I knew this would happen eventually. I think it's time I face them and end this for good."

"Do you want me to stay with you?" I ask softly.

"Please?"

I lean in, cupping his other side as well and delicately pressing my lips to his. "Anything for you, Gabriel."

We pull apart as he takes my hand and kisses the inside of my wrist. "I thought that was my saying?" He smiles.

"I think it works both ways." I smile back.

He takes another minute for himself, then we exit the car and head up to the lobby. The second we exit the elevator, a shrill voice pierces through the room. "This is unacceptable! Call him up right now and tell him he can't keep me waiting like this! I did *not* drive all this way for nothing!"

"Ma'am, please, I'm going to ask you to calm down. He—"

"What are you doing here, Courtney?" Gabe asks as we step closer to the deranged-looking woman.

She whips around, greasy long blonde hair almost slapping her in the face as she swivels. "Finally!" She flaps her arms at her sides, then takes quick, hurried steps toward us.

"I asked you a question." Gabe stops a few feet away from her, holding my hand.

She comes up even closer, looking up at him from her short height. Gabe clearly gets his height from someone else. "Is that any way to speak to your mother!?"

His jaw ticks, but he stays calm. "You aren't my mother."

"Bullshit!" she spits with anger in her eyes. "I fucking carried you for nine god-awful months. If it weren't for me, you wouldn't be here!" She points a finger in his face, and on instinct, I slap it away.

"Don't fucking touch him."

Her intoxicated eyes turn to me with clear disgust, a reddish tint over the sclera, and fully dilated pupils. Clearly high. "Who the hell is this tramp?" Her gaze turns back to Gabe. "Is *she* the reason you've been ignoring us? You always did act like a wimp for every woman who spread her legs."

Oh, I am about to lose it on this woman! I take a step closer, but Gabe puts his arm to stop me. "That's enough. Either you tell me why you're here or get the fuck out."

She fists her hands at her sides, nostrils flaring. She sniffs and lifts her hand to wipe her nose, then looks from side to side like a paranoid woman who's being watched. "They took your father. I don't know where he is," she whispers harshly.

Gabe frowns but with little care. *Good, they don't deserve his pity.* "Who?"

"The people we owe money to! Who else do you think, stupid boy!" she hisses.

"Watch your tone because I'm seconds away from slapping you," I growl like a lioness protecting her king.

"Don't fucking talk to me, little girl! You have no place here," she says, trying to sound threatening, but it comes out anything but.

"Okay, but that doesn't explain why you're here," Gabe says, trying to defuse the tension. A clear reminder that he doesn't like altercations, at least not the ones involving him.

"It's your fault they came to get him! If you had just sent us the money you owe us, we wouldn't be in this mess! I couldn't stay there. I had to get out before they came back for me."

"And you thought by showing your face here, I'd give it to you?" He scoffs. "YOU FUCKING OWE US!"

He takes a step closer to her, and she instantly cowers. "I don't owe you shit!" he says through clenched teeth, then takes a step back. "We're done here. Get out and don't come back." He turns his back to her, still holding my hand, and walks us toward the elevators.

"I'm going to make you fucking pay for this! You'll see! I should have fucking killed you the moment I found out about you!"

My patience snaps. I rip my hand out of Gabe's, turn and march over to her so quickly, she doesn't have time to react. Pulling my fist back, I smash it against her face, feeling something crack from the powerful punch. I bring my fist to my chest, cradling it, then shaking it out with a hiss.

Courtney stumbles back with a scream, falling to the floor as she clutches her face with both hands, blood already pissing from her nose. "YOU BITCH! YOU BROKE MY NOSE!"

"Threaten him again, and it won't just be your nose," I snarl above her.

"So you can threaten me, but I can't?!" She wipes the blood away from her face with a glare, spreading it everywhere.

"Oh, hun, that wasn't a threat. It was a promise." I smile wickedly and turn around to find Gabe smiling proudly at me a few steps away. I reach him, taking his hand with my uninjured one, and kiss him passionately.

When we pull apart, he looks over to the front desk, where Antoine stands a little shocked, yet holds a small, satisfied smile. "If she doesn't leave on her own within the next two minutes, call the cops. I'm sure they'll be happy to pick her up."

We head into our elevator and jump each other like wild animals the second the doors close. Once in the penthouse, our clothes leave a trail from the foyer to the couch, where Gabe lays me down and fucks me with fierce passion into oblivion.

Two hours later, when the movie we're watching ends, Gabe yawns and looks at his phone. I lift my head from his shoulder and kiss his cheek. "You can go to bed if you're tired. It's okay."

"Are you sure? I'll admit that after the events in the lobby, I'm a little beat. But I can wait up a little longer with you." He cups my cheek, stroking it with his thumb.

"No, baby, go to bed. I'm gonna head in as well." I stand and grab my phone from the side table, waking the screen to see if I have a message from Noah. It blinks back at me empty, and my heart cracks a little more.

Gabe lifts from the couch and takes me in his arms. "He'll come home."

"I hope you're right..."

We turn off the lights in the penthouse and head upstairs, hand in hand. Once on the landing, he brings me to Noah's door and opens it. His fingers slide through my hair as he pulls me in, tilting my head back and capturing my lips between his. I melt against him, hands fisting his shirt, a soft moan falling from my lips as he swallows it up.

"Thank you, Vixen," he whispers against me.

"You never need to thank me, Gabriel. I'll do anything for you." I kiss him again.

"Anything for you," he repeats.

I lean back, staring into his vibrating grayish-blue eyes. "Anything."

He smiles lovingly, pressing his lips one last time to mine. "Goodnight, my beautiful queen."

"Goodnight, Gabriel."

I step into the room and close the door behind me, heading into the ensuite to brush my teeth and clean my face. Once I'm done, I turn off all the lights and climb into bed with my phone in hand as I lie on my side. Facing where Noah should be sleeping with the cover tucked under my chin, I dial his number one last time and bring the phone up to my ear.

"This is Adler. Leave a message." It doesn't even ring, sending me straight to voicemail.

"Hey, babe. I was just wondering where you were.... I'm worried about you... we all are..." I sniffle as the tears begin to run freely down my cheeks. "I miss you... please come home, Noah... please." I end the call, throwing my phone down on his pillow and curling into a ball as I cry into my pillow.

Two hours later, I'm tossing and turning, still unable to fall asleep as worry eats at me from the inside. I sit up, passing my fingers through my hair. *I don't want to be here. I don't want to be in this bed alone, when he's out there, somewhere, doing God knows what. I don't want to be alone anymore.*

I flip the covers off my body and climb out of bed, walking to the door and out into the hall. I look toward Gabe's room, then down the stairs. I know he doesn't want us to sleep in the same room because of his nightmares, but right now, I don't care.

The only place I want to be is in his arms. Because over the last few days, he's been the only thing keeping me together when all I want to do is fall apart. He's been my saving grace, my comfort, my happy place. And at this moment, I really need my happy place.

I need him.

I turn back to his room and walk over to the door. I press my ear against it, listening in to see if he's awake, but I don't hear anything. I slowly turn the knob and quietly step in, closing it softly behind me. I stretch my hands out in front of me and tiptoe cautiously toward his bed. It's so dark that I can't even see my hands before me, but I've been in this room so many times that I know the layout by heart.

Bending slightly, I move my hands around until I feel the comforter. I slide my hand up slowly, trying to determine where exactly Gabe is in the bed. My fingers collide with his arm, and I stop, waiting to see if the touch might wake him, but he doesn't even stir.

I lift the cover slowly and sidle underneath it, then lie on my side, facing him, and close my eyes as I breathe in his scent. I can never put my finger down on what exactly he smells like, but it's spicy with a hint of citrus, and I love it.

As if he can sense me near, he turns from his back to his side, his arm reaching over my body and pulling me into him. I curl up against his neck with a blissful smile resting on my lips as I fall asleep to the sound of his beating heart.

One that beats for me, the same way mine beats for him.

GABRIEL

I gather the warm dish from the oven, carrying it over to the dining room table with pride. Looking down at the smoked salmon, roasted asparagus, and white rice with slices of lemon, I place it down on the center of the table and take note of the four place settings. Two on each side of the table.

When I look up, I find my mother and father sitting on the other side of the table, a disgusted look on their faces as they take in the dish. I stand straight, confused by their sudden presence in my home. "Mom?... Dad?... What are you doing here?"

Ronnie grabs my arm and forces me down in my seat beside her. Her beautiful rainbow hair perfectly styled with big curls. "Come on, Gabriel. Don't be like that. Let's enjoy a nice meal with your family," she scolds me with warning eyes.

I don't understand... Ronnie hates my parents, why would she want to have dinner with them? Why are they even here?

I swallow the lump in my throat, forcing the bile rising to my mouth back down, and nod. I can do this. I can sit through one meal with them, then send them on their merry way and never see them again.

"Aren't you going to serve us, boy?" my father starts. "Or is that what your bitch is for?"

I clench my jaw, nostrils flaring as I glare at him, squeezing my fist around the butter knife that rests beside my plate. "Don't call her that!" I bark.

He laughs in my face as if this is some kind of joke. "I'll call her whatever the hell I want." He smiles ominously at me, then turns his beady eyes on her. "She is a pretty bitch. I understand why you're so protective of her." He licks his lips with hunger in his eyes. "I wonder what she tastes like, what she feels like."

Anger bursts through my veins as I try to stand from my chair. But I can't move, I'm glued to my seat, gravity placing all its weight on me. "SHUT UP!" I spit at him with rage.

My mother snickers at his side and leans in toward my father. "I hear he likes to share her with his best friend. I wonder if he'd share her with you." She runs her dirty yellowish nails up his arm. "I'd love to watch our son cry while you fuck his girlfriend."

I try to move again, the chair rattling in place, but nothing happens. I bang my fists against the table with frustration. "NO! Don't you fucking dare! She's not yours! She's not yours!"

My father chuckles. Ignoring my threats, he lifts his hand and beckons Ronnie over to him with a finger. "Come here, cunt. Let me see what this boy is so obsessed with."

I turn my head toward my girl and find her smiling back at my father with a flirty gaze. She twirls a strand of hair around her manicured finger, then pushes out of her chair and stands.

No, this isn't Ronnie. She would never do this. She would never.

I try to stop her, try to grab her wrist, but I can't let go of the knife in my hand. I can't move. "No, baby, please. Please don't go. Please don't do this!" I plead with her, but she doesn't listen.

She walks around the table and stands by my father's side. "It's okay, baby. Don't cry. You know how much I love having another dick inside of me. Why do you think I always want Noah with us?" She smiles sweetly at me.

This isn't her. This isn't my girl, my Vixen. She wouldn't do this to me.

I feel the tears running down my face, my body rocking from side to side as I try to jump out of my chair. Try to stop this from happening.

My father's bony hand touches her knee first, then trails up her thigh until it disappears under her skirt. She moans loudly once his fingers make contact, leaning in, hand falling on his shoulder as she uses him for support.

"NO! NO, NO, NO! PLEASE, STOP! PLEASE! I'M BEGGING YOU!" I shout at the top of my lungs, devastation in my voice. "Please don't touch her! I'll do anything! Stop, please!" I feel like my heart is being ripped out of my chest as I watch them, unable to tear my eyes from the horrid sight.

Oh God, I'm going to be sick!

My mother throws her head back, laughing hysterically while pressing her hand to her chest. "Look at him, he was always such a pussy, crying over everything."

My father chuckles along with her, then refocuses his attention on Ronnie, who grinds down on his fingers. "That's it, bitch. Rock that greedy pussy against my hand."

Ronnie suddenly cries out as she orgasms with my father's help. I watch in horror as her juices flow down her beautifully tanned thighs before she smiles down at him. "You do it so much better than him," she whispers, then leans in, pressing her lips against his.

And I snap.

I fly out of my chair as it clatters to the ground behind me. The knife hits my plate with a clanking sound, right before I throw myself above my father. My hands circle his neck as I watch the life drain from his eyes.

Chapter Thirty-Two

NOAH

I'm here... I'm now...

I wake with a start as a car horn honks nearby, my throbbing back and aching legs making themselves known as I shift in my seat. I press my palms into my eyes, scrubbing the blurriness away, then push my fingers against my temples as I try to dull the headache pounding in my skull.

I adjust myself in my seat and start my car, glancing down at the time on the display screen that reads 4:13a.m. "Fuck!" *Veronica is going to kill me!* I buckle myself in quickly and put myself in gear, driving away from the roadside I had parked at last night.

I hadn't planned on spending most of the night in my car. It was only supposed to be a quick snooze. Two or three hours until I got some of the liquor out of my system and was once again capable of driving myself home.

I know I promised Veronica I would keep in touch while I'm out, that I wouldn't take my car if I were planning on drinking. But then I did the stupid thing anyway, left the penthouse early in the morning, and took my car. I drove around for a few hours until I found an empty, grimy roadside bar, where the likelihood of someone recognizing me was slim. Unfortunately, luck wasn't on my side, and after a few glasses, someone did.

I got up, jumped in my car, and found a liquor store instead. Then I drove some more until I ended up in some sort of countryside, where all that waited for me was long green fields. I parked myself halfway on the grass, got out, and sat down against my car.

I then drank everything I had bought until my mind was too hazy to think properly anymore. Until my thoughts could no longer torment me. It's pretty much all I've been doing since Trinity's funeral. I leave the city and wander into another, one where I'm not immediately recognized, and head into a bar or a club. Anything that will serve me something to numb the pain.

And when the place gets too crowded and women begin to circle around me, I leave and find somewhere quiet to try and clear my mind. I know I'm losing it; I know I'm spiraling out of control, but what I don't know is how to stop it.

How do you stop your brain from thinking the worst? From realizing that you're now all alone in this god-awful world. That everyone you grew up loving, idolizing, has now vanished from existence? Gone forever. That the only family I have left is a woman who couldn't care any less if I were dead?

I know technically I've been alone for a while, but it wasn't the same. Even if my sister was unconscious for the past six years, she was still here. She was still with me physically. I could still see her, talk to her, hold her. Now she's gone as well. And all that's left is me...

After the sun had gone down and I had nearly drunk myself to death, I stumbled my way into my car. I started it up, tried to buckle my seatbelt but failed, then turned on my wipers because I thought it was raining outside, but it turned out to be my eyes crying. I decided it wasn't safe for me to drive in this condition, and I know my Kitten would have had a fit if I did.

I grab my phone from the cup holder, switching it back on after having turned it off earlier in the night. I didn't want to ignore Veronica, but I just couldn't face her, couldn't listen to the hurt in her voice. The one I've caused and keep causing over and over.

Unread messages litter my screen, some from Veronica and others from Gabe. I head into my voicemail and play the last two I haven't listened to.

Gabe's frustrated voice filters through the car speakers. "Bro, I get you're going through some shit, but this isn't cool. You're making her worry nonstop. Just answer her fucking calls or come home. Get your shit together. If not for you, then do it for her."

I continue on to the last message. The recording begins to play, and all I hear is the rustling sound of fabric being moved and soft sniffling. But then her beautiful broken voice echoes loudly in my car, even though the volume is set to low.

"Hey, babe. I was just wondering where you were.... I'm worried about you... we all are..." She sniffs again, a quiet cry falling from her lips. "I miss you... please come home, Noah... Please."

"Fuck..." I close my eyes and bang my head against the headrest but quickly reopen them when I remember I'm driving. "I'm so sorry, Kitten... I'm so fucking sorry," I mutter to myself as I press on the gas and hurry home.

An hour later, I'm stepping out of the elevator and into the quiet penthouse, although it doesn't stay that way for long. A high-pitched scream pierces through the air, making my skin pebble and bones rattle.

"VERONICA!!!" I shout as I sprint up the stairs so fast I nearly trip and fall face-first once I hit the landing. I push my bedroom door open in a panic, expecting to find a distressed Veronica in bed, but the room is dark and void of any presence.

I step in, about to look inside the ensuite, when another scream coming from Gabe's room resonates through the walls. This time it seems gargled or muffled, like something is stopping the sound from traveling properly. "Oh God, no. Please, no!"

I skid across the hall, throwing his door open as it bangs against the wall. The image before me nearly brings me to my knees. Gabe is kneeling above Veronica, hands around her throat as she fights him for dear life. Her legs kick repeatedly, nails clawing away at his arms and face as she tries desperately to free herself from his death grip.

I jump into action, running over to the bed and tackling him to the ground. Veronica tumbles along with us as his hands finally let go of her neck. She gasps for air, sobbing as she crawls backwards, far away from us until her back hits the wall. Where she then brings her knees up to her chest, holding herself while crying hysterically.

Gabe continues trying to fight me, his hands now grabbing at me, reaching up to choke me the same way he was doing to her seconds ago. His eyes are wide open and stare straight back at me, but I know he doesn't see me. He's still stuck in whatever sickening nightmare this is.

I quickly knock his arms back, pinning them down to the ground as he tries to shake me off with his body. "Stop it, Gabe! Wake up!" I shout, lifting his wrists and smacking them back against the floor, hoping the hit will shake him out of this confused state.

"It's me, Noah. Your best friend. You're safe." I try to sound calm, despite hearing Veronica's sobs behind me that are tearing my heart to shreds.

Gabe manages to free one of his hands and punches me in the jaw, sending me to my side as he climbs above me. But I regain the upper hand quickly and get him on his back once more, and this time I don't try to reason with him.

I raise my arm and backhand him right in the face. "WAKE THE FUCK UP!!!"

The fight suddenly leaves his body as his arms and legs lose their strength and stop moving. His eyes blink a few times before I see recognition flick through them.

I pant, rolling off him and dropping to my ass. "Finally."

He doesn't say anything, just lies there for a moment, and it's then I realize Veronica's no longer crying. Instead, she's mumbling something over and over again. I look over to the corner she's now crouched in, arms around her knees as she rocks herself back and forth. Her eyes are wide and look a little unhinged.

"I'm here, I'm now, I'm with Noah and Gabe, they don't want to hurt me, they won't hurt me, I'm here, I'm now. I'm here, I'm now, I'm with Noah and Gabe, they don't want to hurt me, they won't hurt me, I'm here, I'm now. I'm here, I'm now, I'm with Noah and Gabe, they don't want to hurt me, they won't hurt me, I'm here, I'm now," she repeats in a hushed voice.

I stand slowly from the ground, taking cautious steps over to her. I place my hands in front of me, showing her that I intend no harm. "Veronica?" She doesn't answer, doesn't acknowledge me as she continues to chant. I kneel down tentatively before her. "Kitten? It's me, Noah. Can you hear me, love?" I place my hand hesitantly on her knee.

She flinches at the contact, blinking once, then twice. She looks down at my hand, then back to my eyes. "You still with me, Kitten?"

Her face scrunches up as the tears begin to pour once more. She sobs as she stretches her hands out toward me, begging me to hold her. "I'm still with you," she cries as I take her in my arms, and she crumbles against me, turning into a small, frail version of herself.

"Oh, no... no, no, no..." Gabe stands, rushing over to us, but stops himself halfway.

His cheek is red and a bit swollen from where I hit him, and his arms and jaw are covered in scratch marks with small little beads of blood breaking through the surface. "Baby... I'm... I'm so sorry... I swear... I swear I didn't mean to."

He takes another step closer, but Veronica turns herself more into me.

He drops to his knees, eyes turning glassy with unshed tears. "You have to believe me... you know I would never hurt you willingly. You know that, don't you? I'm so, so sorry. Please, forgive me. Please, Vixen..."

"Just give her some time, Gabe. She's still in shock right now," I whisper quietly while stroking her hair. "I'll take her into my room and try to calm her down." I manage to stand from the floor with Veronica in my arms, clutching at my clothes like they're her lifeline.

His eyes bounce from me to her and back to me. "I... okay... yeah, okay..." He stands as well and steps back, giving us more room. "I'm so sorry, Ronnie... please don't hate me..."

As I head out the door with our trembling girl, the guilt seeps its way through my veins. If I had come home earlier... if I hadn't drunk so much... if I had just answered her calls... she wouldn't have put herself in a dangerous situation. She wouldn't have gone to Gabe for safety and comfort. She would have stayed in bed with me, and none of this would have happened. I put her in this situation. It's my fault she got hurt.

It's my fault if she never forgives Gabe...

Once in my bedroom, I lay us down in bed and pull the covers over us. She sticks to me like she wishes she could crawl into my skin, and it fucking hurts. It hurts seeing her like this... I continue to glide my fingers through her hair as I hum to her. I'm not even sure what I'm humming, but I remember my dad doing this to my sister when she was little and couldn't understand why our mother left her. And just like Trinity, Veronica's cries slowly subside until her breathing turns to a dull rhythm, and she falls asleep.

I want to stay with her forever, never leave her side again. But I also know my best friend is most likely freaking out right now and needs someone to talk him out of doing something crazy. So I wait until she's heavy in my arms, then untangle myself from her delicately and exit the room, leaving the door slightly ajar for me to hear her if she wakes up.

I go to Gabe's room first but find it empty. Heading down the stairs next, I spot him sitting at the kitchen island with a cup of coffee in hand. When I get closer, I notice the tremble in them as he clutches them around his mug. His eyes are wide and red as he stares straight ahead.

I come up to the counter slowly, reaching up in the cabinet for a mug and pouring myself some coffee as well. When I'm done and turn around, I find his gaze on mine, deep remorse burning in his eyes. "I swear I didn't know what I was doing... I would never do that to her..."

"I know," I tell him genuinely. Gabe is far from a violent guy, and he loves Veronica deeply. I know he would never wish her any harm.

"How... how is she?" He swallows, a shiny layer glossing over his eyes.

"She's sleeping."

He nods and looks down at his mug. "I should probably go while she's still sleeping... She won't want me here when she wakes up."

"Don't be ridiculous. She's in shock right now, but it will pass. She knows you, Ellis. She knows you would never want to harm her, and she'll know how much you regret what happened. Veronica is strong, she'll be okay." I take a sip of my coffee. "She knew you had nightmares, Gabe. She still chose to go into your room. Don't beat yourself up over it."

His head whips up, a glare aimed my way. "So, you're saying it's her fault I nearly killed her?! Because that's what would have happened if you hadn't shown up on time. She would be lying in that bed, lifeless, and I wouldn't even be aware of how it happened!"

"No. I'm saying it's my fault... if I had been here, she wouldn't have gone to your room." I work my jaw, feeling the need for something stronger than coffee quickly rising.

"Maybe, but that doesn't change the fact that I shouldn't be here. What I did was unforgivable. I'm supposed to protect her, and instead I hurt her... It's best if I go." He drops my gaze again.

"Just wait until she wakes up... see how she's doing and let her decide what she wants. We don't know how she'll be when she wakes."

"I don't want her to be scared of me again, Noah..." A tear slips past his lid. "I don't know how I'll live with myself if she is..."

"She won't, our girl is stronger than you think. This won't tear her down." I shake my head, emphasizing my point.

He just watches me for a moment before speaking again in a whisper. "I hope you're right."

VERONICA

I wake up just as Noah enters the room. "Hey," he says quietly, coming over and sitting down on the bed beside me just as I pull myself up against the headboard. "How are you feeling?"

I'm not exactly sure how I'm feeling at this moment. I know in my moment of panic a few hours ago, I clung to him out of fear. But now that the feeling has faded, all I feel is anger. I'm angry at him, I'm hurt that he's been pushing me away. I'm upset that he doesn't realize that I might be hurting, too.

I may not have known Trinity for a long time, but I grew close to her. I miss going to see her every other day, I miss holding her hand as I told her all my deepest secrets knowing she'll never share them with anyone else. I'm sad that she's gone and that I'll never be able to see Noah's face light up again, the way it did every time he looked at her.

"I'm fine." I push the covers off my legs and step out of bed. "I'm going to take a bath," I say, not looking at him as I pad over to the bathroom.

"Do you want me to stay with you?" he asks when I reach the door.

I stop, hand gripping the doorway, and look over my shoulder. "No." I walk in and close the door behind me, locking it. I need to be alone right now, I need time to think and process everything. Having him beside me won't help me think clearly.

I turn the water on in the tub, grabbing a bottle of bubble bath and Epsom salts that Gabe left here for me, and pour a generous amount into the warm water. Then I remove my panties and Noah's shirt I had slipped on last night before stepping into the tub.

After an hour of relaxing and clearing my mind, I emerge from the bath and grab the towel hanging on the rack. I quickly pat my body dry, then towel-dry my wet hair as I walk over to the mirror. My hands stop their motion when I notice the red marks along my neck.

I place the damp towel on the vanity and look at myself in the mirror, my fingers delicately passing over the red fingerprints. Regardless of what happened and how scared I was at the moment, I'm not angry with Gabe. I don't blame him, and I know he didn't do it on purpose.

I understand how sometimes your nightmares can trap you in, make you imagine things that aren't really there. How they seem so lifelike and all you can do is fight back. And even though I was on the receiving end, I'm happy he finally fought back, even if it was only in a dream. But knowing Gabe, he's most likely beating himself up with guilt over this.

I take a step back from the vanity, getting a better view of my body in the mirror. My fingers leave my bruised neck and travel down to my breast, over the little love bites Gabe left there yesterday. Then further down to my hips that still hold his handprints from how hard he took me.

A smile forms along my lips as I remember it all. I don't want him to think I hate him, that I blame him in any way. I need him to know that I'm okay and that I forgive him. That this changes nothing between us.

How could it? Gabe has been nothing but wonderful to me. He's been here, by my side, doing everything in his power to make me happy. He never once made me feel abandoned like Noah has these past few days. I can't have him distancing himself from me because of this. I won't let him.

I pick up the towel and wrap it around my body, then unlock the door and pull it open. When I step out, I find Noah sitting at the end of the bed, elbows on his spread knees, head in his hands.

He looks up the moment he hears me. "I know you said you didn't want me to stay, but it didn't feel right leaving you..."

"Oh, now it doesn't feel right?" I scoff and turn for the walk-in.

"I'm sorry, Veronica. I know I messed up." He drops his head back down.

I pull on a pair of white lacy panties with a tiny white camisole, then step back out of the closet with the towel in hand. "Where the hell were you, Noah? Where the fuck have you been for the last week? I asked you to give me news, to not take your fucking car when you're drinking! You told me you would, yet you're still acting recklessly! I get you're hurting, Noah. I fucking get it! But you're going to kill yourself if you keep going like this."

He doesn't even look up, doesn't explain himself. All he says is a simple, "I know."

His reply infuriates me even more. I stomp into the bathroom, throwing the towel into the laundry basket, and walk back into the room, stopping right in front of him with an outstretched hand. "Give me your keys."

This time he lifts his head, looking at my hand. "What?"

"I said give me your keys. I can still smell the alcohol on you, so give me your fucking keys. I'm cutting you off." I motion with my hand, telling him to hurry. He sighs and digs into his pocket, dropping his car key in my palm.

"You want to fucking go out all day and night and get drunk, find your own way." I turn and storm out of the room. *If I have to play the evil girlfriend to potentially save his life, then so be it.*

I head into Gabe's room and straight into his walk-in, where I pull down a big black hoodie from one of the hangers and slip into it. The thing is so huge it covers me up to mid-thigh. It also covers my neck slightly, which is what I was hoping for. I know if Gabe sees the marks, he'll never forgive himself.

I then walk barefoot down the steps, looking for my poor broken man. He isn't in the living room or the kitchen. I stop quickly in the laundry room, stashing Noah's car keys in the back of the cleaning products cabinet.

He'll never think of looking there, and if he knows what's good for him, he won't even try to look for them. Then I head for the home gym next, which is usually his sanctuary, but come up empty.

Where the hell is he? He'd better not have left!

I turn back down the hall but stop in front of the library. We never come into this room; I know Silas or Cecilia must have used it when they lived here, but I'm pretty sure it's been vacant ever since Noah and Gabe moved in. Except for the weekly sweeping and dusting I do in here, no one ever sets foot inside.

I turn the knob slowly, push the door open, and immediately, my gaze falls on the man I've been searching for. His back is to the door, but with the way his muscles tense up and his demeanor goes rigid, I know he senses me. And I love that about him, I love that the moment I enter a room, he instantly turns, instantly knows I'm here.

I walk up to the back of the couch where he sits, going around it to face him. But his head is down low, fingers entwined at his nape, elbows resting on his knees. "Gabriel, baby? Look at me."

It's so quiet in the room, all I hear is his deep, harsh breath. "I can't..."

"Yes, you can." I lower to my knees at his feet and cup his face with my palms. "Please, baby. I need you to look at me. I need you to see that I'm fine." His hands drop their hold around his neck as I gently push his head up.

"But you're not. I hurt you, Vixen..." His eyes are red, the skin around them slightly swollen, likely due to crying. There are also red scratches all along his jaw that I know came from me when I tried to fight him off. *Oh, my poor Pretty Boy.*

I smile at him, hoping to reassure him that I am, in fact, fine. "It was an accident. I know that, and you know that. I don't blame you for this, baby. Not one bit, and I don't want you blaming yourself either."

"How can I not?" He delicately takes my wrists, removing my hands from his face, and I notice all the marks on his arms as well, causing the ache in my heart to grow. "Why don't you hate me right now? I can't be trusted around you. I hurt you when I swore to protect you. I can't risk harming you again, Ronnie. I could never live with myself if I ever hurt you again."

He releases my wrists and looks away as his eyes fill with tears. "You mean too much to me, Vixen... I would never forgive myself if I were the reason you left us," he says on a shaky breath.

I push against his shoulders, forcing him back against the seat with my hands, then straddle his thighs before he can stop me and place my hands on his chest. "I could never hate you, Gabriel. And I'll never leave you. You're my forever. I trust you with all my heart, and I know we'll figure it out together."

His eyes bore into mine with so much pain in them. No matter what I say, his mind keeps telling him the contrary. "How?... I'm exactly like him... Victor... I'm exactly like them..."

I grab his face once more. "Listen to me, you are *nothing* like them. *Nothing!* I love you, Gabriel Ellis. I fucking love you. And I refuse to let this destroy us, because there's no way I can live without you."

His eyes widen once they register what I've just said, and it makes my heart bloom, doing a tiny somersault in my chest. I bring him closer, his lips a hair's length away from mine. "I love you, Gabriel," I whisper against his lips before closing my eyes and sealing them to his.

He doesn't immediately kiss me back, still in shock with my declaration, but then he catches on. Bringing his hand up into my hair, he deepens the kiss, angling my head to the side and claiming me as his as my body melts against him.

"Please let me show you how much you mean to me," I beg against his mouth.

He untangles his finger from my hair and grabs the hem of his hoodie on my body, lifting it over my head. When his eyes find the marks along my neck, he freezes, his hands losing their grip on the hoodie and letting it fall beside us.

"Oh, fuck... Oh fuck, fuck, fuck. God!" His voice cracks as those tears return, this time a few falling free. "I'm so sorry, baby... God, I'm so sorry..."

I bring my arms up around his neck and pull him in as his forehead falls to my shoulder. "It's okay, baby. I promise you, I'm fine. I promise. But I need you to stop blaming yourself. I need you to forgive yourself because none of this is your fault. It was just an accident. One we'll figure out how to avoid."

"How?" he cries against my shoulder, and it breaks my heart to see Gabe in this state because of this. "I've tried everything... nothing works. They won't go away."

"I could take some Krav Maga classes or something. Like that, next time you jump me, I'll kick you in the nuts. That should wake you up pretty quickly." I smile when he chuckles against my skin.

He lifts his head slowly, peering at me with hopeful eyes. "You'd really do that?" he asks softly.

I brush my lips against his, then pull back and remove one arm from his neck to wipe away his tears. "I'd do anything for you, Gabriel. Anything." I peck his lips, then slant my head back, exposing my neck to him. "I want you to kiss it better for me. Will you do that?"

He swallows and nods. "Anything for you, Vixen. Anything," he says, repeating the promise I just made him as he leans in hesitantly and grazes his soft swollen lips against my skin. He starts on one side, then moves to the other side as he sniffles.

"I'm sorry, baby... I love you so much. I'm so sorry," he whispers, kissing the bruised flesh.

I fist his hair delicately and pull him back, capturing his mouth with mine. "Make love to me, Gabriel. Please make love to me."

He reaches for my camisole, taking it off as I rip his shirt over his head. I lift my hips slightly as he wiggles out of his sweatpants before grabbing each side of my thong. Ready to slide them down my legs, but I place my hands over his. "I want you to rip them off."

Gabe looks into my eyes with uncertainty, so I offer him a reassuring nod. He twists the material around his fists and gives it one quick tug. The cheap, thin fabric rips apart easily, leaving a sharp sting against my hips, but I couldn't care less. He slides my panties out from under me and throws them aside.

He swipes his fingers through my folds to see how wet I am, which is extremely, then grabs the base of his cock and holds it in place as I slowly lower myself down his shaft. He groans as I moan, circling my hips to adjust to his girth. Then our mouths reconnect as we grind against each other.

There's nothing rough or feral about this moment. No slapping skin, no screams, no heavy panting, or powerful thrusting. It's just him and me, connecting in a way we had yet to discover. Lips and tongues exploring each other, hands roaming all over, heart pounding together as we consume each other to an earth-shattering orgasm. Crying out into one another's mouth as we fall apart in each other's arms.

"I love you, Vixen." His soft breath tickles my swollen lips, sweaty foreheads pressed against each other.

The smile that graces my face can be felt down to my toes. "I love you, Pretty Boy."

Chapter Thirty-Three

VERONICA

Silas's bathroom... again.

After redressing, we walk out of the library hand in hand, and all feels right in the world. That is until we emerge into the kitchen, and I spot Noah sitting alone in the living room with a glass in his hands.

"You're still here?" Gabe asks Noah as he heads for the fridge. "Are you hungry, baby?" he questions next, looking over his shoulder.

"Famished." I smile, then look over to Noah. "He's sulking because I took away his car privileges."

"Ouch..." Gabe chuckles, then gets to work on preparing us breakfast. Or I should say lunch since it seems to be noon already.

I watch the blissful smile on his lips as he moves around, and it makes my heart pound even louder in the best possible way. It's crazy how three simple little words can completely change your mood. But I get it, because hearing him say them to me lit me up like a firecracker.

With a sigh, I head over to Noah. I've fixed one situation today; it's time I fixed this one too. Once in front of him, I grab the Scotch glass from between his fingers, walk back over to the kitchen, and dump it in the sink. He doesn't say anything, but I feel his glare on my back the whole time.

I lift onto the tips of my toes and kiss Gabe's cheek. "I'm going to clean up quickly and get dressed, I'll be right back," I tell him, feeling his cum leaking from my core.

I hurry up the stairs and into Noah's bathroom, clean between my legs with a warm washcloth, then dress in my usual thigh-high black socks. But instead of a skirt, I pair it with light-blue denim short shorts, a black sports bra, and a baggy gray crop top that falls off one shoulder.

I slip my feet into black laced-up platform stiletto ankle boots, then head back into the bathroom to do my makeup and hair. I apply some concealer over my neck, trying to hide the marks as best as I can, then go through my usual routine and finish with a double-winged purple eyeliner and a dark pinkish-purple matte lipstick.

From there, I decide to separate my hair in half, leaving the bottom loose and tying the top into two buns over my head. I leave a few strands framing my face and slightly curl the bottom portion of my hair. It's grown a lot since my last cut before our vacation and now passes my shoulder blades. I hadn't realized how much I missed my long hair until now.

Happy with my look, I return downstairs to the delicious aromas of Gabe's fine cooking. But my mood instantly sours when I notice Noah now has a new tumbler in hand as he sits on one of the barstools at the kitchen island with his legs spread, one foot propped up on the footrest.

His back is to me, so he doesn't get the joy of witnessing my reaction, but Gabe does. He offers me a tight smile and returns to plating our food. I march over to Noah and snatch the drink from his hand with force, nearly spilling some over the rim. And once again, head to the sink to dump it down the drain.

"Veronica…" he warns.

I set the glass down on the counter with a loud clank and turn back to him. "Do not *'Veronica'* me. That's enough, Noah. It stops now."

He rubs his palms into his eyes. "It's not that simple," he mutters quietly.

I walk over to him, standing between his thighs and taking hold of his wrists as I force his gaze back on mine. "I know it's not that simple, but you can find another coping mechanism. One that won't ruin your life. Because I won't stop, if I have to keep dumping that toxic shit down the drain for the next fifty years, then that's what I'm going to do. Because I love you, Noah, and I won't let you kill yourself. I won't let you wreck what we have. And continuing down this path you've taken, will."

He looks down at my hands still holding onto his. "I don't know how to stop them… I don't know how to quiet those voices in my head reminding me that I've lost everything," he whispers.

I cradle his face and bring his eyes back up, getting even closer. "Then we'll get you help, Noah. Both of you," I say, turning to look at Gabe, then back at Noah.

"I have a therapy session in two hours, and I'd like you both to attend it with me. And starting tomorrow, we're gonna go on your morning run together. Just you and me. You'll also start working out again, because you have less than a month before training camp, and we need to get you back into shape."

A small smirk appears on his lips. "You're going to run and work out with me?" he says it like it's the most unrealistic thing he's ever heard.

I press my hand to my chest, clutching my invisible pearls, and feign offense. I then climb onto his lap, feet dangling between his legs, and throw my arms around his neck. "I'll let you know that I know very well how to jog and work out."

His smile grows as his hand rests on my lower back and the other on my thigh. "That doesn't mean you're any good at it."

"Oh, you are just looking for trouble, aren't you?" I laugh softly. "I guess that makes me lucky to have two men who will teach me how to do it right." I grin at him, then bring one hand back to caress his cheek. "Thank you for not fighting me on this."

"I'm not saying I won't be tempted, but I'll try. For you, I'll try." He kisses the inside of my wrist.

"And I'll be tempted to keep dumping your drink." I graze his lips delicately with my own.

"By the way..." he starts.

"Yes?" I pull back slightly, looking into the depth of his deep chocolate eyes.

He places a strand of hair behind my ear and smiles, his eyes tracking his movements before coming back to my blues. "I love you, too, Veronica," he says softly, and my heart explodes.

I crush my lips to his, pouring all my soul into it as our tongues collide. I've missed him so much, and I'm overjoyed to see him smile again, to have him holding me, wanting me. I know the next few days won't be easy; that he might withdraw some more until we find the right outlet for him. But I'll stick by his side the whole way. I won't let him run anymore.

We eventually come up for air, and I find Gabe grinning behind us. "What's that smile for?" I laugh.

"Just happy to see us back to this place. Plus, I feel like we're making some good progress to baby-making season." He winks and sets our plates along the kitchen island.

I jump off Noah's lap. "Get your mind out of the gutter, Pretty Boy. This factory is closed for business." I pat my belly.

"Closed permanently? Or temporarily?" He beams as Noah shakes his head. *God, I've missed this carefree behavior between us.*

"We'll say temporarily, but that doesn't mean I'm anywhere close to wanting a baby." I point at Gabe. I'll admit that the thought of having a child with these two is a pretty appealing image.

"Did you hear that, Noh? She said temporarily, which means we'll be dads sometime soon." He sits down two stools over from Noah.

I lift my arms, gaping at him. "I *just* said... You know what, never mind. Clearly, whatever I say goes in through one ear and out the other." I shake my head and settle in between them.

"That's not true, I remember you telling me you loved me." He winks again, gaining an eye roll from me.

A thought comes to mind that I know will quickly diminish his cockiness. "Oh, I forgot to mention something earlier."

"What is it?" Noah gives me his attention.

"I'm afraid I have some bad news." I force a sad pout.

"What news? Did that asshole try to contact you again?" Gabe jumps into the conversation, sounding a bit distressed.

I place my hand above his that rests on the black marble surface. I love the contrast of this kitchen with the pure white cabinets and black countertops. "No, nothing like that. Victor hasn't made any appearance since the one in this penthouse. Which is starting to stress me out a bit, but let's not focus on that right now." I smile reassuringly.

I take my hand back from Gabe's, placing it in my lap as I look from one to the other with a sweet smile that holds just a touch of mischief. "You remember those rules I talked about when I first started working here?"

Gabe's eyes widen in horror as Noah drops his head and groans. "No..." Gabe whispers. "Oh God... no... please not that again!"

I sigh. "I'm afraid so. Noah, you've been leaving everything lying around all week. And Gabe, there's a pile of clothes on the floor in your walk-in." I pat both their thighs. "You know what this means, right?"

"Please don't say it..." Gabe begs, clutching my hand in his big ones.

"Tomorrow night, Gabe, you're off cooking duty. Noah, you're back on." I laugh when they drop their heads back and whine, like they're both in physical agony.

"No whining, you know the rules. Now let's eat up so that we can get to our first therapy session together, and then we're having dinner at Cecilia's place with the gang." I pat their legs once more then begin to devour my plate with a satisfied smile.

"Did I tell you how beautiful you look right now, baby? Flawlessly elegant. Gorgeous. Stunning," Gabe says, leaning in and kissing my cheek.

"The most magnificent woman I've ever seen," Noah finishes, pecking my other side.

"Aww, thank you, baby." I turn my head to Gabe and kiss his lips, then do the same to Noah. "Thank you, babe." I return to my dish smiling, still feeling their eyes on me. "But flattery won't get you anywhere. I won't change my mind." They groan and turn back to their plates.

An hour and a half later, we're entering my therapist's office, hand in hand. Her back is to us as she begins to speak. "Hello, Ronnie. I hope you're having a good day. Mine has been disastrous. Poor Tom was having another one of his meltdowns about his wife. The woman left him twenty years ago, move on already." I giggle to myself as I listen to her.

This is why I've kept her around all these years. She gets straight to the point, doesn't bullshit around, and whines along with me. She complains to me about her other patients, even though legally she's not allowed, but she knows I would never tell a soul.

She swears and laughs when I start crying for stupid reasons. Most people would be offended by her professionalism, but then again, she's not made for everyone. And I love her just the way she is. She's a breath of fresh air.

"Anyway! I'm glad I end my day with your nutty self instead of him." She finishes arranging the papers on her desk and spins with a beaming smile, but it drops the moment she notices I'm not alone. "Oh... I'm sorry, I didn't realize you were bringing company." She looks from one man to the other.

"Dr. Hallaway, these here are my boyfriends, Noah Adler." I point to him. "And Gabriel Ellis." I finish toward Gabe and smile back at my therapist. "Boys, this is Dr. Susan Hallaway, my therapist. We're in need of a group session," I tell her.

"Oh... OH! Your boyfriends! Oh my... this is some twisted shit right here, if I may say so." She laughs. "I was not expecting there to be two of them."

I frown, confused at her statement since I've mentioned them a few times already. Then it hits me. "Oh my God! Did you think I was crazy and that they were in my head?!"

"Oh no, dear. I just thought you were dating one man who may have multiple personalities and goes by different names depending on the day." I gape at her as she smiles and claps her hands. "But all is well now. I'm glad to see you weren't changing up one crazy guy for another. Although this is an interesting turn of events."

"Well, let's not speak too soon. They have their issues as well," I inform her.

Her brows raise high. "Oh, okay. Like what?" We're all still standing in the center of her office.

I point with my thumb to Gabe first. "He chokes me in his sleep because of nightmares," then point to Noah, "he's quickly becoming an alcoholic because his sister passed away," and finally turn my thumb on myself, "and Victor broke into our home and left me a message."

"Wow... okay, let's have a seat." Noah, Gabe, and I all head over to the couch, sitting down with me in the middle as Susan takes her wingback chair.

"So... let's start with the murderous one, Gabriel, is it?" She looks at him with her hands clasped as he nods, then she leans in on her arms. "Have you ever thought about having a therapy pet?"

GABRIEL

"I can't believe she called me a murderer..." I say, stepping out of the car in Hayes's driveway.

"Hey, she compared my ass to a corgi's and said that I needed to pull my head out of it. I can't even tell if that's an insult or not. You think that's any better?" Noah states, following beside us up to the entrance.

"Corgis are cute. So yes, that's a lot better." I glare at him.

"I think she was just pointing out that you had a nice ass. I saw her checking you both out when we were leaving." Ronnie giggles.

"You know your shrink's crazy, right?" Noah raises a brow her way.

She laughs and pushes the door open. "Oh, I know. She sees a therapist once a month."

Noah and I both stop, looking at each other, then back at Ronnie. "And you expect us to trust an expert who needs therapy themself?" I gape, which only makes her laugh harder.

"I wonder what it says about a therapist who needs a therapist..." Noah chuckles.

The second we step through the threshold, we're greeted by two friendly dogs. Milo, a beige and white Alaskan Klee Kai with vibrant blue eyes, who belongs to Silas and Cecilia. And Daisy, a pure white Pomeranian who's Emma and Greyson's pup.

"How about a dog?" Ronnie asks as I crouch down to show them some love.

"Eh, I don't know. I love them, but I feel like with our career, it's not the best lifestyle for them. Besides, if we were to get a dog, I'd rather have an actual backyard for it, rather than just the back patio."

I know technically she's living with us for now, so our puppy would never be alone, but I don't know if she intends to stay once everything with Victor is over...

if it ever is. At this point it seems like the guy is impossible to catch.

"Okay, so how about a cat?" she questions.

I look up at Noah, who shrugs, then Vixen, who smiles down at me. "A cat could work. Although I don't see how a lazy feline will do any good with my nightmares." I stand, dusting my hands from all the fur.

"You'd be surprised what animals can do." She kisses my cheek and heads over to our friends who litter the kitchen.

"Hey guys! Happy you could make it." Cecilia comes over, hugs Ronnie, then me, and stops in front of Noah. "Hey Noah, it's good to have you back. It's not the same without you."

He wraps her in his arms, squeezing tight. "Yeah, sorry about that, Mama. Just needed a little time to myself."

"I get that." She smiles warmly at him.

"Everyone," I raise my voice, gaining everyone's attention. "We have some news." I beam while Ronnie eyes me suspiciously, even Noah's frowning beside me.

"Oh my God! You're pregnant too?!" Emma shrieks with excitement.

"NO!" Ronnie shouts, holding her hands up in front of her. "No, I am *not* pregnant." She glares at me.

"Of course not, your men have good seeds who know how to stay put," Em grumbles.

"Wait, so I have bad seeds because I knocked you up?" Greyson frowns.

She whips her head his way with a glare. "Twice! You knocked me up twice!"

"I see she's still mad about that." I chuckle, whispering over to Ronnie, who giggles.

"What's going on? What are they talking about?" Noah leans in, asking quietly.

"Emma found out yesterday that she's having twins, and she's not very happy about it," Ronnie murmurs.

"It was epic. She was beating him with a pillow, then made a very disturbing visual of what she was going to do to his balls." I chuckle.

"Damn, that must have been something," he says, but I can tell there's a hint of sadness in his voice. Ronnie must pick up on it as well because she wraps her arms around his waist and leans into him.

"Okay, okay. We get it, you're still mad about the twin thing," Clay says with a hand up to silence their bickering. "What's the news, Ellis?"

Oh right, I forgot about that for a second. I puff out my chest, a prideful beam shining at them. "Ronnie said she loved me."

I hear Ronnie groan into Noah's chest as the room silences to the point that crickets could be heard. Then everyone explodes with laughter.

"I thought you were going to announce you guys were moving in together permanently, or buying a house, not this!" Silas laughs harder, slapping his thigh.

"Why not this?" I ask, confused.

"Because, sweetie, we already knew she was in love with the both of you." Morgan smiles.

"Well, I'm still proud to announce that she finally said it." I stand tall.

"And you have every right to be." Aubrey comes over with a sweet smile. "I'm happy for you guys, truly." Her gaze falls to Ronnie's, but within seconds, her smile disappears, and a frown appears on her face.

"Ronnie? What's this?" She reaches up to touch Vixen's neck, where her concealer has started wearing off.

Ronnie's eyes widen, and she quickly covers the marks with her hand. "It's nothing."

Aubrey's gaze bounces all over Vixen face, then mine, and I can see the moment she spots the scratches along my jaw that Ronnie tried to hide with a concealer as well. She looks around, noticing no one is paying attention to us anymore as she comes closer and whispers, "It doesn't look like nothing... did he... do that?"

Ronnie furrows her brows. "What?" Then she catches on. "Oh! No. No, it's not him. We just... we get a little carried away in bed sometimes. That's all." She grabs Aubrey's hand with her free one. "I promise it's nothing you need to worry about."

I know Vixen didn't need to cover up my mistakes, but I'm grateful she did. I don't know if I could have faced the humiliation so soon. Even though we're on good terms, better terms than we've ever been, the guilt still eats away at my skin.

Aubrey chews on her lip with uncertainty. "Okay... if you say so."

The sliding patio doors to the backyard open, and in comes two toddlers with their nanny. Sam seems to be pretending to be a dinosaur that's chasing after them as they screech with laughter. I watch them in awe, wondering if one day I'll get to do the same with my kids.

"Unc Gay!" Dante screams as he runs toward me, throwing himself into my open arms as I crouch down to catch him.

His pronunciation isn't on point yet, but I understand it's his way of calling me, and I love it. He started calling me that on vacation, and I was thrilled to be the first one to gain the uncle title out of our group. I guess repeating it to him constantly when no one was around did help, but I won't tell the others that.

"I've got you, little man! I'll keep you safe!" I spin us around, putting my back to Sam as he comes in and tries to grab hold of Dante, who bubbles with joy.

Gracie hides herself between Ronnie's legs, then throws her hands up, indicating she wants to be taken. "You want me to protect you, baby girl? Good choice, if anyone will keep you safe from the evil dinosaur, it's me!" She picks her up and runs around in circles with Gracie as Sam abandons Dante and chases after the girls.

She comes to my front, hiding behind my massive frame, with both kids stuck between us. They deliver some lung-filled shrieks whenever they feel Sam's hands trying to grab them, and I watch Ronnie radiate with happiness as she laughs away with them.

I can picture it. I can see us, just like this. My wife with our two rowdy kids, playing *save the princess* right before dinner time. I want that. I want it with her.

"All right, kids. Time to settle down. Give poor Sam a break, he has other things to do than watch you two hooligans." Emma comes over and pats Sam's back. "You're too good with them." She then collects Gracie from Ronnie's arms and brushes their noses together. "Come on, little Tulip. Let's get you cleaned up and ready for dinner. You got mud all over your hands."

Dante squirms out of my arms and runs to his mother. "You too, baby. Let's go wash your hands." Cecilia takes him by the tiny hand and brings him upstairs, following behind Emma.

Vixen continues to carry a breathtaking smile along her lips as she watches them go before turning to me. "They're adorable."

"They really are." I grin. "You'd be good at it," I tell her sincerely.

"Being a mom? Maybe." She bites her lip as she studies me. "Do you want a lot of them?" Her question startles me for a moment. Ronnie never wants to talk babies, unless it's as a joke.

"I mean, I don't need a certain amount. I just know that I want some, or at least one. I've always wanted to get married and have kids. Although, in this situation, I'm guessing two would be better than one." I nod toward Noah, who's busy talking with Greyson.

She smiles his way. "Yeah, it wouldn't feel fair only having one in this case." She looks back at me, her smile slipping slightly. "But Gabe, you do realize that marriage wouldn't be in our future, don't you? I can't marry two people, and it wouldn't be right for me to marry only one of you..."

My smile dims as well. I know she's right. I've thought about it before. I just wish there was a way around it. "That's okay, Vixen." I wrap my arms around her waist and pull her into me. "All I care about is that my future is with you." I press my lips to hers.

"It is," she breathes against mine.

"All right!" Sam claps his hands to get everyone's attention. "Everyone out of the kitchen, the chef needs room to work." He smiles wide.

"You're cooking?" I ask him.

"He offered to since I'm still not past this nauseating stage apparently," Morgan informs us.

"Want some help?" I offer to Sam.

"Are you any good?" He quirks a brow.

"Oh, he's phenomenal." Ronnie beams excitedly.

"Then come on up over here. I love a man who can cook." He winks at me, and I laugh.

I kiss Ronnie one last time before letting go, just as Noah comes up behind her and kisses her neck with his arms around her. "God, you're fucking sexy. Wanna sneak away to the bathroom for a little bit?" he whispers to her.

She bites her lip with a giggle and nods. He releases her and takes her hand, dragging her away as she looks over her shoulder at me and mouths, "I love you."

My heart swells as I mouth it back, "I love you, too."

A few minutes later, Silas comes over to the kitchen. "Where's Adler?" he asks while grabbing a water bottle from the fridge.

I refrain myself from smiling as I shrug. "I think he went to the bathroom."

"Hm," he hums as he takes huge gulps of water but then stops and looks around the room as he brings the bottle down from his mouth. "Where's Ronnie?"

This time my smile breaks free, but I don't answer. *He'll figure it out.*

"No... NO! No, not again! Not my bathroom!" He sets down his bottle and runs to the bathroom on the main floor.

He bangs loud enough for us all to hear and most likely scare the shit out of Vixen and Noah. "GET OUT OF MY BATHROOM! You can't do that in there! Stop it right now!"

Noah shouts something back that sounds a lot like, "Fuck off." But it's a bit muffled by the door.

Silas comes running back into the kitchen. "MINNIE!" Then continues to the group in the living room. "Minnie! They're going at it! I can hear them! They're doing it in my bathroom!" he whines to his wife, who's watching their son play hockey with Greyson and Clay in the mini arena they built at the far end of their living room. *I'm definitely getting one of those for my kids, too.*

"Just let them be. You remember what it's like when all you want to do is jump each other at every moment of the day. We were those people, honey." She brushes him off with the wave of her hand.

"But it's my bathroom…" He pouts.

"Then put up a sign next time." I can feel her eyes roll all the way from the kitchen. Sam and I chuckle as we continue preparing the meal.

"Yes! I'm going to make a sign. Right. Now." He storms back toward us, ripping a drawer open and retrieving a white sheet with a permanent marker. "No more funny business in my bathroom!" he grumbles as he begins to write in huge letters, '*NO FUCKING IN MY BATHROOM!*'

I laugh as I watch him dig the marker into the paper with irritation. "Maybe try something a little less angry and a little more polite. You want people to obey you, not tell you to fuck off."

"Right, right. Good point." He grabs another sheet and starts again, this time writing, '*No fornication in these premises.*' He holds it up for us to see. "Better?"

Sam chuckles. "Much better."

He grabs some heavy-duty tape and walks over to the bathroom door, taping away at it. I walk over to the hall, needing to see this for myself. Just as he finishes putting up his sign, the door swings open. He glares at them and smacks his hand below the sign on the now open door.

"READ THE SIGN!" he says, then stomps away.

Ronnie comes over laughing. "I think he's mad."

"He was seconds away from having a meltdown." I laugh along with her and wrap my arms around her neck as she places hers on my waist. "You smell like sex," I tell her, breathing her in.

"Sorry." She smiles sheepishly.

"Don't be sorry, it just makes me excited to have my turn." I kiss her temple. "I can't wait to get you home and fuck you until you lose your mind."

"I can't wait either." She bites her lip and steps out of my arms, her hand grazing my semi-hard dick as she walks away with a smirk.

Chapter Thirty-Four

VERONICA

Day six out of seven.

~ One Week Later ~

Noah growls from behind me as I bend in half and touch my toes, finishing off my stretches. "You know, this is a bigger torture than not drinking. If I had known this is what I'd have to suffer through before each run, I wouldn't have agreed to let you jog with me."

I laugh and straighten, placing my hands on my hips as I turn to him. "Oh, stop it. This," I gesture to my outfit, "is motivation. Gives you something fun to run after, and who knows, maybe you'll get lucky once you catch it." I wink at him before skipping over to Gabe standing in the kitchen, watching me with that adorable grin on his lips.

"You say that like I'm not the one constantly jogging ahead of you." Noah snorts, and it makes the amused smirk on my lips fall instantly.

"Do you want to get lucky when we get home, Casanova? Because these comments are not winning you any points right now, and I have no issues with taking my offer off the table." I raise a brow, giving him a look that tells him just how serious I am.

"Nope, shutting up now." Noah tightens his lips together while waiting for me near the couch.

"That's what I thought." I giggle and wrap my arms around my favorite blond boy. "Be good for me."

"I'm always good for you." Gabe smiles against my lips before sealing them together.

"Mmm, that you are, Pretty Boy." I peck his lips one last time then step back. "I'll see you soon, don't think of me too much while I'm gone."

"Impossible not to think of you when you're wearing that." He winks as I wander back to Noah's side, and we head for the elevator.

The truth is, I've been purposely wearing very eye-catching and revealing clothes for our morning jogs all week. I could tell it was a bit of a struggle for Noah to get back into his usual routine, so I thought I'd make it a little more fun for him in some way.

Today's outfit consists of a crisscross type of black sports bra, both in the front and back that was very complicated to get into, and despite my girls being on the very smaller side, they look pretty nice in this top. For my bottom half, I put on these new tight, high-waisted white workout short-shorts I bought two days ago, with string ties on each side that give me one hell of an ass. And of course, I finished the ensemble off with my signature thigh-high white socks and black running shoes.

Honestly, I look hot as hell, and I get why Noah considers this torture to look at. *Oh well.*

We start off our usual jog with a half hour run through Central Park, where Noah constantly teases me about being slow, then move onto the busy streets not too far from our place. We're usually gone for a good hour and a half to two hours total, although that's most likely due to me constantly having to slow down. I swear, every time I call timeout and bend in half to catch my breath, Noah has a good laugh at how not in shape I am. I want to smack him every time, but honestly, I'm just happy to see the old Noah returning.

After my seventh break, I check the time on my phone. It's only been one hour and twelve minutes, but I'm ready to call it a day. Besides, we're only ten blocks away from the penthouse; might as well end our jogging session now.

"Are we almost done?" I pant, putting my phone away and taking the last few gulps from my water bottle that I've had to refill midway.

Noah throws his head back and laughs. He's all sweaty as well, yet doesn't seem nearly as out of breath as I am. "You know, you're really bad at this."

"Shut up!" I throw my empty water bottle at him and he catches it effortlessly. "Jesus, you'd think after the workout you two put me through daily, I'd be in much better shape... Apparently not."

He chuckles and comes to stand behind me, kissing my sticky neck before pinching my ass. "Come on, Kitten. Just ten more blocks, you can do it."

I yelp and push him away before moving once more. When we reach our building fifteen minutes later, Stanley laughs the moment he sees us coming up the steps. "I take it the workout didn't go as planned?"

"Stanley, jogging is torture. I don't know how people do this daily, but I give up,"

I declare from my comfy spot on Noah's back. It took a total of two blocks for me to stop completely and decide I was taking a taxi the rest of the way, to which Noah claimed I was ridiculous and instead offered me a piggyback ride home.

Stanley shakes his head with a chuckle and pulls the door open for us, letting us through. Noah carries me to our private elevator, only setting me down once we're inside and the doors have shut.

"What am I going to do with you?" he says as he takes a step closer and corners me against the wall behind me next to the button panel.

From the look in his hungry eyes, I can tell exactly where his mind is going, and my body instantly heats in response. "There's a lot of things you could do with me," I whisper back as I drag my fingernails up the front of his soaked shirt.

"Is that right?" He smirks, grazing the side of my neck with his lips as I moan softly and tilt my head back. "Have anything in mind?"

"Mmm, a few things." I claim his lips when they move up to mine. We're still at the lobby, neither one of us ready to break this moment. "We could go up to the penthouse, and you and Gabe could go feral on me for the next few hours," I suggest first as I bring my hand back down to the waistband of his shorts. "Or you could be entirely selfish and take me right here, right now in this elevator." I dip my hand into his shorts, fisting his hard shaft as he moans with pleasure.

If I thought we were fucking a lot all three together, it's nothing compared to how many times these two corner me one-on-one. Any chance they get, I'm being stripped and railed in places I never even thought would happen. Just yesterday Gabe fucked me while I was bent over inside the cleaning cabinet sorting through the products. And an hour later, Noah sat me over the mini fridge in the gym and ate me out until I was squirting all over the place.

"Fuck the penthouse. Too far," he mutters as I giggle before capturing my lips once more and pressing his body into mine.

We make out like starved creatures for barely thirty seconds before Noah spins me around, forcing me to let go of his cock, and pushes my front into the wall. His hands move to my shorts, where he rips them down my hips and leaves them right above my knees. Given how tight my shorts were to begin with, the material wraps snuggly around my legs, making it almost impossible to move or spread them. Which I have a feeling was exactly what Noah wanted.

In the next second, his shorts hit the ground, and I feel his fingers sliding through my wet folds before replacing them with the head of his cock. He pushes in swiftly, making me cry out as my eyes roll back. No matter how many times we have sex, the length of his dick always sends the most delicious shiver through my body when he seats himself completely. The same thing happens with Gabe as well, although for him it's that painful stretch because of how wide he is.

Noah grabs onto my waist and slams into me repeatedly as I fist my hands against the wall, trying desperately to hold onto something. "Holy shit, Kitten. You have no idea how fucking incredible your pussy feels right now with your legs squeezed tight together like that," he grunts, fingers biting into my hips with every thrust.

Sweat drips down my back, quickly reminding me of our messy state. But despite how sweaty and stinky we are right now after our run, my core clenches in response, and I feel that ball of fire igniting within my stomach. *Definitely going to need an intense shower after this.*

Noah suddenly releases one of my hips and grabs my wrist, slowly removing it from the wall and pulling it down behind me until it folds at my back. My mind freezes for a moment, and I swallow. I can take the manhandling, the throwing me around, and the rough sex. I can take them holding me in place with their hands if I'm really in the moment. But having my own arms or legs restrained is a hard limit for me, and I'm not sure if I'm fully ready to surpass it.

His eyes stay locked on mine as he sees the fear slowly rising within me. "Do you trust me, Veronica? Be honest with me." He stops thrusting altogether, giving me time to think over his question as he waits for my reply.

"I-I..." The single word comes shaky as I swallow again, feeling the fabric around my legs getting tighter as I try to wiggle them around and his grip squeezes around my arm. I know none of that is really happening, but my mind is struggling not to think that way, not to imagine the worst.

"Hey," Noah whispers as his eyes soften and he lets go of my wrist to caress my cheek. "It's completely okay if you don't with this. I won't be angry, Kitten. I promise. We're in this together, remember? We're learning as we go."

I'm about to tell him I'm not ready for that, but as I stare into his warm chocolate eyes, I find the panic and fear inside of me fading, and I realize that I do trust him. *They won't hurt me.* I close my eyes for a second, letting go of those invisible chains still gripping me, and place both my arms behind my back, wrists one above the other as my cheek rests against the wall.

His cock twitches inside of me when he realizes what I'm doing, but still, he doesn't grab onto them, doesn't start moving. "Are you sure?"

I open my eyes and smile at him. "I'm sure."

His entire face lights up instantly. "I fucking love you," he whispers, quickly kissing my lips before pulling out only to slam back in.

I moan loudly, instantly brought back into the moment as he gently grabs onto both my wrists with one hand and pulls me away from the wall. Noah places us right in the middle of the elevator facing the doors as he reaches to the side with his free hand and presses the 'P' button. Then he wraps my hair around his fist and begins thrusting violently into me once more.

"How about we go give Gabe a little show?" He chuckles as I feel myself nearing the edge every time his length touches that magic part inside of me.

My legs shake by the time we reach the penthouse, thighs slippery with my own juices, ass cheeks burning from how roughly Noah continuously rams into me, and throat raw from how loud I've been screaming in the short few seconds up. Noah isn't normally this rough with me, that's all Gabe usually, but despite this sudden change and the way he's restraining me, my body hums with pleasure and begs for more.

The doors to the elevator ding open just as an orgasm hits me at full force, and I cry out, body trembling against Noah as he keeps me upright and continues to fuck me. Gabe quickly appears in the entrance hall, a confused look on his face at what he just heard, but it instantly morphs into amusement and hunger when he takes us in.

"Well, not exactly what I was expecting for your return, but I am not complaining." He grins as Noah chuckles behind me. Gabe steps closer, placing his hand along the side to keep the door open, and lets his eyes roam over my entire body as I feel another climax quickly building.

"Hm, this is new," he says softly, fingers stroking the side of my folded back arm and sending a rush of shivers down my spine. "Think you can lower her for me?" he then asks Noah.

I'm confused by his questions, only slightly listening to what they're saying as my body and mind focus on Noah's long shaft still spearing me, making my walls contract around him repeatedly. But when Noah shifts us slightly and I see Gabe quickly pushing down his shorts, everything clicks.

Gabriel caresses my cheek as Noah releases my hair and instead places his hand along my back, forcing me to bend forward while still holding onto my wrists. Gabe's fingers slide into my hair next as he strokes himself leisurely before nudging against my lips with the head of his stiff shaft. I open wide for him instantly, and he smiles, his foot now resting against the side of the elevator to make sure the doors don't close on us.

"That's it, baby. Take my cock in your mouth while he fucks your tight pussy like the good girl you are for us."

I shiver once more at his words as he bobs my head up and down, Noah's rocking motion forcing Gabe down my throat with every thrust as I salivate all over him. I begin to pant, my thighs squeezing as that ball of nerves in the pit of my stomach grows more and more for the second time.

"Fuckkk, she's squeezing the shit out of my cock. I'm seconds from blowing." Noah grunts as his movements become slightly erratic, his need to come taking over as well.

"Good, make her come at the same time. I want to feel her screaming around my cock." Gabe tightens his hold on my hair and thrusts his hips faster. "I'm gonna fill this pretty throat while he fills that insatiable cunt of yours. You ready, baby?"

I nod as best as I can, despite barely being able to move in this position. Noah readjusts his hold on my arms, now gripping them with both hands while Gabriel steps closer to me. A part of me feels caged in for a split second, but the feeling vanishes instantly when they both thrust simultaneous and my eyes roll back.

Five pumps later from both ends, I'm detonating on a scream as I feel both of them swelling inside of me, one in my pussy, the other deep in my throat. Their warmth fills me from both ends, and my scream quickly turns into a choking fit when the sensation of suffocating on Gabe's cock becomes too real. He holds my head down in place, most likely enjoying the feeling of my throat closing up around him as he empties himself, but the panic intensifies the longer he holds me down.

I squeeze my eyes shut, willing myself to calm down, to ignore the fear rising inside of me, but it's no use. My nails dig painfully into my forearms as I begin to thrash from side to side, the pressure at the back of my head getting heavier, the grip around my wrists tighter.

I'm trapped. I can't move. I can't breathe. No. No... I'm hallucinating... I'm okay... I'm...

"Let her go," Noah suddenly says, but it sounds distant as my mind takes me to that faraway place I used to escape to when trapped under Victor's evil claws. "Let her go! ELLIS, LET HER GO!"

Within the next second my body is released, and I collapse to my knees, hands coming in front of me just in time to catch my fall. My body shakes violently as I stare down at my hands gripping the floor of the elevator. I gasp for air while taking in the reddish tint around my nails from having ripped my skin open, my mind slowly coming back to the present as I repeat the words that have grounded me for the past three years.

"I'm here... I'm now... I'm here... I'm now..."

"Fuck... Vixen... I didn't mean to hold you down like that..." Gabe says quietly, their voices sounding more in the moment now.

"I should have known you weren't ready for that. I'm sorry for pushing you too far, Kitten," Noah whispers next from behind me. "It won't happen again."

I stop chanting and shake my head, taking a few more deep breaths. "I'm okay," I murmur. "I just need a minute."

The doors begin to close now that Gabe has taken a step back, but he quickly smacks his hand against it, opening them fully once more. "Take all the time you need."

My phone begins to vibrate against the side of my breast from inside my sports bra, but I ignore it as I continue kneeling there on the ground. I know I must look like an idiot right now with my shorts down and ass out, but I know I'm not entirely ready to move just yet.

After another minute or so of sitting in silence with both my boys watching me, I look up and find Gabe still with his shorts at his feet, limp dick hanging out, then I glance back and notice Noah in the exact same situation. They've been so hyper-focused on my state that they haven't even bothered redressing themselves, and something about that makes my heart melt even more for them.

"I think I'm okay now," I say, holding up my hand for Gabe to help me to my feet as my phone vibrates once more.

He quickly takes both my hands in his as Noah holds onto my waist before pulling my shorts back up. I see the pain and guilt in Gabe's eyes instantly as he takes in the small blood smudges around my nails and the scratch marks on my forearms.

"I'm sorry," he whispers, and I quickly wrap my arms around his neck, then my legs when he lifts me off the ground.

"You don't need to apologize. You did nothing wrong, Pretty Boy." I kiss him, then look back at Noah as we finally step out of the elevator with me still in Gabriel's arms. "You either, Casanova." I try to reassure them. "Sometimes my mind just... tricks me into thinking and feeling things that aren't really there..."

"We'll try harder to pick up on the signs when you get to that point," Noah murmurs against my shoulder before kissing it softly. "Now why don't we all go shower, and then we'll bandage these up, okay?" I nod in response as they carry me up the stairs.

An hour later, Gabe sits me down on the kitchen island while Noah brings over the first aid kit as well as my phone. Gabriel gets to work on adding ointment to one arm before wrapping it up as I check my messages that I still hadn't gotten to.

"What is it?" Noah asks when he notices me frowning.

"Just Julian. He asked if I was okay," I tell them as I go to type out a reply, but my phone starts ringing instead with a call from him. "Hello?" I put the phone on speaker and set it down beside me as I hold my second arm out for Gabe.

"This is Storm. Are you all right?"

"Umm..." I'm confused by his question once again and unsure how to answer it.

"Veronica. It is the simplest of questions. Are you all right? Yes, or no?" Julian says sternly in a way that has my back straightening instantly.

"Yes, I'm okay... Why?" My mind instantly goes to Victor as I wonder if maybe he knows something we don't yet.

"Well, seeing as you are currently being bandaged up in the middle of your kitchen, I believed asking about your condition was the correct thing to do. Now has something happened that you may have not informed me of yet?"

I look up at the camera in our kitchen, only now remembering about all the others in the penthouse. "Oh, no. It was nothing like that. We just got a bit carried away."

"Very well then, since all has been cleared, may I remind you all that every room in your home, excluding your bedrooms, are under twenty-four-hour surveillance. Please refrain from performing any type of intimate activity in public spaces—that includes the elevator. Thank you." He hangs up the moment the last word leaves his lips, and we all fall into a fit of laughter.

"I swear, I keep forgetting about those damn cameras." Gabe shakes his head with a goofy grin on his lips before kissing both my newly wrapped forearms.

"Well, at least someone got quite the show." Noah snorts.

I giggle. "Yeah, I'm not sure how I feel about that."

Both their faces fall instantly. "Shit... I'm sorry. It was just a joke, but we should have thought about it." Noah cups my face, worry shining in his eyes.

"Guys, I'm fine. Everything is fine. You don't need to keep apologizing." I smile, reaching for both their hands. "We're constantly having sex all over this place; I'm sure it wasn't the first time someone got an eyeful and probably won't be the last. Besides, if they work for Julian, I'm pretty sure they have some huge NDA contract signed that won't allow them to speak or do anything with whatever they see."

"Yeah, most likely," Gabe says, returning my smile, but it doesn't reach his eyes. I get it; they're both worried about me and the fact that we still haven't heard anything from Victor. They know it's starting to really mess with my head despite me trying to act like it's not.

"I need to get going." Noah looks at the time on his phone, then puts it away and kisses my forehead.

"Are you nervous?" I search his eyes for how he might truly be feeling.

Today is Noah's first one-on-one appointment with Dr. Hallaway. She knew there were things the boys might not want to share in front of me, or maybe even be embarrassed to speak of, so she thought all of us having private sessions as well as a group session every other week would be good. Tomorrow will be Gabe's first session alone, I'll have mine the following day, and next week we have our second group session.

"Not really nervous, just... trying to put myself in the mindset of having to open up and talk about my feelings." He smirks, knowing it's the thing he struggles with the most.

"You can do it, babe. I know you can, and I promise you'll start feeling a lot better after." I pull him in for a kiss.

"I know," he breathes against my lips before stepping back. "I'll see you later, Kitten."

The moment the sound of the elevator shutting echoes in the quiet space, Gabe wraps his arms around my waist from where I'm still sitting on the kitchen island. "Mmm, finally, I have you all to myself."

"Oh, shush. You act like you never get me alone." I giggle as he starts peppering my neck with kisses.

"Not enough." He nibbles on the skin beneath my ear as I swat him away. "It's almost lunchtime. Have any requests?"

"Hm, how about my favorite salad? I want you to teach me how to make it." I grin up at him, my arms now wrapped loosely around his neck as he chuckles.

"You say that like you're planning on making it yourself one day." He raises a brow as I snort.

"Not a chance. You're my personal chef from now on until we're old and gray." I laugh.

"Good to know, because I plan on cooking for you for the rest of our lives." He claims my lips as I melt against him.

I love these little moments with Gabe so much, where he's all playful and touchy and talking about our future together. I still can't believe there was a time when I couldn't stand this man, when his goofiness and flirting ways would get on my nerves. And now, I can't imagine falling for any other version of him but this one.

"All right, up you go. If my lady wants her special salad, then we best get to it." He bops my nose before lifting me up by the waist and setting me down on the floor.

Gabe moves over to the fridge, where he pulls out all the ingredients we'll need, then places everything in front of me, along with one big bowl, two smaller ones, a knife, and a cutting board. I watch as he sets a pot of lightly salted water to boil on the stovetop while washing my hands, then wait for him to turn back to me with a warm smile.

"Okay, first, we're going to start with chopping up the kale. Think you can do that without cutting yourself?" He smirks as I narrow my eyes at him.

"That was one time! And for the record, that cucumber was super slippery. It's not my fault the knife slipped over to where my fingers were." He laughs the same way he did when it happened last week, still not believing my story. I roll my eyes and pick up the knife he's set aside for me. "Shouldn't we wash it first? You're always going on about having to wash things before eating them."

"No need, I washed them this morning." Gabe comes up behind me, resting his hands on my hips and kisses my shoulder.

"You washed the kale this morning?"

"Mhm."

"Why?"

"Because you ask me for this specific salad once a week, and it has now been…" He thinks for a moment. "…six days since you last requested it. I had a feeling today was the day, and would you look at that, I was right." He laughs at me once more and bites my neck. "Now focus, or else we'll never get this food done and you'll end up with another cut."

I get to work on chopping the kale, and honestly, it looks like shit compared to how I've seen Gabe do it. His is always so perfectly done and a decent size between cuts, while mine has some huge pieces and others extremely small.

"Slowly, Vixen. It's not a race, take your time." He kisses my temple and goes back to the stove now that the water is boiling and adds in the basket of fresh edamame pods.

When I'm done chopping everything up as best as I can, Gabe picks it all off the cutting board and puts it into the big mixing bowl. "Now you're going to massage it."

"Excuse me?" I pull my head back and turn it to the side to look at him.

"God, you're adorable." He laughs and takes my hands, placing them inside the bowl. "Play with the leaves a bit. We want them nice and soft."

"That sounds so wrong." I giggle but do as he says while his hands stay in the bowl with me and help me feel the difference.

Leaning back against him, I tilt my head to the side and close my eyes momentarily, enjoying this simple yet intimate moment. "I love you, Gabriel," I find myself whispering as my eyes flutter open and find his.

I've never really been the type of person to say those words unnecessarily. Even in the early days with Victor, those weren't words I'd say very often. But with Gabe, I find myself wanting to say them repeatedly simply to see his face light up the way it's doing right now.

The brightest grin takes over his face, like he truly can't believe I would choose to love him, before he lowers his face closer to mine and claims my lips. "If this is a dream, I never want to wake up from it," he breathes against my lips after a few seconds.

"If this is a dream, I hope we get to stay in it together forever. You, Noah, and me."

There's so much tenderness and love in his eyes at this moment that I wish I could freeze time to never forget that look, never forget that someone once looked at me in such a way. Like I was the answer to every question he ever had or could have, like I was the key to everything he ever wished for.

The timer for the edamame pods goes off, and Gabe kisses the top of my head before letting me go. "I think the kale is good now. Why don't you move on to cutting the yellow cherry tomatoes in half and adding them into the bowl while I let these cool down in cold water."

I move onto my next task, and Gabe soon joins me to dice up the avocados and slice the toasted almonds. When I'm done with the tomatoes, I add in the blueberries to the quickly filling up salad bowl and crumble some goat cheese in. While Gabe pops the beans out of the pods, he then moves onto making the dressing with olive oil, lemon juice, honey, minced chives, Dijon mustard, and salt. He whisks all the ingredients together before drizzling it over the salad and tossing everything until it's well combined.

"Would you look at that." Gabe beams down at the two bowls now filled with my new favorite dish. "We just made our very first salad together like a real couple."

I snort and turn in his arms, wrapping my own around his neck. "That's because we *are* a real couple, silly boy."

He grins again. "That's right. You're my girlfriend. My fucking sexy-ass, perfect girlfriend." His arms circle my waist as he lifts me off the ground and spins us around.

Chapter Thirty-Five

GABRIEL

Set me free.

I watch from the outdoor couch as Ronnie gently caresses a small brown bird's back. I'm convinced that bird is the same one that comes by every single day to see her. She keeps telling me no, that there are millions that look the same, but I swear, every time she steps out here, that little feathery creature pops out of nowhere and instantly goes to her. Hell, it even lets her pet it, while if I get close, it flies away instantly. That's her bird, and she knows it.

When she's had her fill of spending time with her little friend, she turns to me with a warm smile and finally comes back to my side, plopping down on the couch next to me. I take her wrists in my hands, softly gliding my thumbs over the bandages a little higher. I hate that we did this to her, that we put her in a position that made her feel like she needed to hurt herself.

"Stop, Gabe. I'm fine. You guys are overreacting with this." She takes my hands in hers, stopping me from touching her arms.

"Still, we should have realized you weren't ready for anything like that. We've been careful not to step over your limits, but today we pushed you too far, and that's not okay. How can you truly trust us with your body when we can't even read you properly or in time to stop this from happening? The last thing I want is to put you in a situation that will make you struggle mentally, Vixen, and I hate that we did that today."

"Baby, stop," she says again, climbing over me to straddle my lap. "You and Noah didn't do anything wrong. He asked for my permission before putting me in that position, and if I hadn't wanted you to join or him to hold me in such a way, I would have said something."

"I know, but—"

"No buts." She grabs my face between her palms. "I wanted it, Gabriel. And there are a lot more things that I want to try with you both, but you need to understand that despite how much we try to avoid it, there will be moments that set me back slightly. This is all new to me as well, maybe not the sex part, but the trusting someone else entirely with my body. Just like Dr. Hallaway said, you can't expect it all to be sunshine and roses." She smiles tenderly, her thumb brushing back and forth over my cheekbone.

"I may be tough on the outside, but there are parts of me inside that are still fragile and healing, parts that still hold fear. And sadly, the only way we'll get through them is by facing them." She shrugs, and fuck, do I love how brave she is through every step we take. "You need to stop worrying so much about me. I'm a big girl."

I chuckle and fist her hair, bringing her lips to mine. "We'll never stop worrying about you, Vixen. That's just something you'll have to get used to."

"Hm, I guess I could *try* to get used to it." She rolls her eyes, but I don't miss the way her eyes light up.

"Think of it this way, you know how Hayes is with Cece?" Her eyes instantly widen as I bring my hands down to her waist and give it a little squeeze. "You'll be the lucky lady to get two of those just for you."

Throwing her head back, she lets out the most beautiful laugh I've ever heard. "Oh God! That did not sound as lovely as you thought it di—" Ronnie's face suddenly falls as she stops abruptly and looks past me.

Fear instantly rises within me, and I quickly look back through the glass windows that gives a view inside the penthouse. I'm expecting to see Victor, or something to indicate that he was just there, but all I find is Noah standing in the middle of the living room, looking down at whatever it is he's holding. Ronnie quickly climbs off my legs and hurries inside as I follow behind her.

"Babe?" She takes tentative steps toward him as he looks up from the bottle of Scotch in his grasp.

"I... I saw a liquor store on my way out of my appointment," he admits and slowly lifts it up, holding it out for her. "Can you get rid of it? Don't tell me where you put it."

Vixen takes it from his hand with a nod and holds it to her chest while searching his eyes that are red-rimmed. She doesn't say anything and instead gives him time to express himself.

"It was harder than I thought it would be... I was going to open it."

She tosses the glass bottle to the couch and quickly steps closer to him, taking his face between her hands like she did to me earlier. "But you didn't, Noah; that's what really matters. You may have been tempted, but you stopped yourself when it mattered most. Those are good steps, babe. Don't see this as a failure."

"How can I not? We barely fucking talked about anything, Veronica, and I couldn't even handle that without wanting to drink..." he admits, his voice cracking slightly with emotions.

"But you're trying, Noh, and you did the right thing by coming back here and giving it to me," she tries to reason with him, but I can see it in his eyes; he's struggling more than he's letting on.

Fuck, does it pain me to see my best friend like this, but if anyone can help him, it's that beautiful girl right there.

"And what about next time? What if you aren't here when I get home?"

"Then I'll fucking make sure I am. Hell, if I have to, I'll come with you and sit in the car to make sure you don't have to go through this alone. If you need me, Noah, I'll be there. Just say the word, and I'll do it."

He swallows and nods, then rests his forehead against hers as his arms wrap around her waist, pulling her in. "Fuck, you're too good for me."

"She's too good for both of us," I add, chuckling.

"Is she okay?" Noah asks, looking up toward the stairs.

Ronnie disappeared about two hours ago, claiming she was going to take a shower, yet she still hasn't returned, and I was honestly starting to get worried as well. Despite her repeatedly saying she's okay with what happened this morning in the elevator, it's still hard for us to take her word, and we've been trying to give her a bit of space. Hence why neither of us has gone up to check on her despite thinking about it for the last hour and a half.

"I wouldn't know any more than you do." I shrug from where we're seated on the couch watching TV. "She keeps saying she is, but we're not in her head, so it's hard to tell."

"So she didn't say anything to you while I was gone?"

I shake my head. "Nothing aside from telling me we need to stop worrying about her."

Noah snorts. "Like hell if she thinks we will."

"Precisely what I said." I chuckle.

Just then, the sound of delicate footsteps coming down the stairs catches our attention. *Because yes, we muted the sound on the TV one hour ago to make sure we could hear her if something was wrong. Holy shit, we really are obsessed with her well-being.* We both turn in our spots to see her walking over to the kitchen island with a bag in hand.

She sets it down slowly, then lets out a breath and looks our way. "Could you boys come here, please."

We frown at each other before standing and walking over to her. Noah looks from the bag to her, then back to the bag. "What's going on?"

"I've been doing a lot of thinking since this morning," she starts. *God damn it, I knew she wasn't really okay.* "Mostly about something I said to you," she looks at me, "about how I'll never truly be able to deal with my fears if I don't face them." *Where is she going with this?*

"But also concerning a comment both of you made today, about how I may not be at a stage where I trust you enough to do things that scare me." Ronnie looks down at the ground and shakes her head. "But that couldn't be further from the truth. I do trust you both, more than I've ever trusted anyone else in my life, in ways that I didn't even know I was still capable of trusting." She turns her gaze to the bag next. "That's why I brought this down with me."

"What's in it?" I ask, trying to look inside, but I'm not close enough to see what it contains.

"Do you remember when I went on that little shopping spree with Em and bought a whole bunch of things with your card but pretended I didn't?" She smirks when Noah and I laugh.

"Oh, trust me, we remember very well." Noah smiles at her and folds his arms over his chest.

"Good. As you recall, I went to a few… specific boutiques, and I'm sure you were both dying to know what exactly I had bought."

"Still very curious." I chuckle.

"Well, you won't have to wait much longer." She finally turns toward the bag, placing her back to us, and reaches in with both hands.

I can hear packages being tossed around, and with the size of the bag, there's clearly a lot of things in there. Finally, she grabs hold of something and stops moving. I see the way her shoulders stiffen slightly, the way her back moves as she takes in a deep breath. But the thing I notice the most is how her hands tremble as she finally removes them from inside the bag. My eyes widen instantly when I see what she's holding, and a quick glance at Noah tells me he's just as shocked.

Ronnie lays them out on the countertop and faces us once more. "Three years ago, I promised myself that I would *never* allow another man to tie me up or put me in a position where I had complete loss of control. That I would *never EVER* allow myself to trust a man to a degree where I would give him permission to do such things to me."

She picks up the first item to her left and lifts it. "I am not ready for this one. I'm not saying it's a hard no, but it won't be any time soon." Despite the hint of a tremble in her voice, she speaks with confidence.

Vixen sets down the blindfold and instead picks up the next items in each hand, a pair of leather handcuffs and what looks like satin bondage restraints. She slowly takes a few steps forward until she's standing right in front of us.

She holds out the handcuffs to Noah, then the satin ties to me. "This is me trusting you with more than just my heart. This is me showing you that I do trust you with my mind, my body, and my soul," she whispers.

We both take the items from her hands, looking them over without a clue what to say. "You want us to... tie you up?" Noah asks, feeling as uncertain as I do about this.

"Yes." Vixen nods.

Sliding my fingers over the soft material, I feel a frown forming and find myself shaking my head. "No... I won't do this."

"Gabe..." She steps toward me, but I shake my head again and bypass her, putting the restraints back on the counter.

"No. Just this morning you tore your arms open because he was holding you with his hands! And now you want us to restrain you with these? No, fuck that shit. You're not ready for this, Vixen, and it's completely okay if you never are. But don't force yourself just to what? Prove a point? Please us? No. I'm not doing it."

"We'd need a safe word, something you could tell us if it gets too real for you," Noah suddenly says, and my jaw nearly hits the floor.

"You can't seriously be entertaining this idea! Noh! You saw her this morning, you know as much as I do that she's nowhere close to ready for this bullshit mentally."

"But I am ready, Gabe!" She quickly grabs my hands and forces me to face her. "I am ready, I'm just scared, that's all, and I'll never stop being scared if I don't do this." Tears well in her eyes as she searches my gaze. "I don't want to be scared anymore, Gabe. I don't want my heart to race and feel like I'm fucking suffocating every time one of you squeezes my wrist too tight or holds my legs in a certain way for too long. I fucking hate it. I just want to be free of this fear consuming me, and I trust you both to finally set me free."

"How is tying you up going to set you free when it's the exact thing that caused you that fear?" I don't fucking get it, and like hell if I'll be the reason she ends up with more trauma. I've already done enough of that.

"Because I'm taking back control, Gabriel. I'm *choosing* to take back something Victor forced on me and *willingly* handing it over to you. These are *my* thoughts, *my* desires, *my* actions. No one is forcing them on me. I am choosing to do this with you both because I *know* you will keep me safe and will do it right. Because I know you won't truly hurt me, and in that, I'm reclaiming what was taken from me."

I want to keep refusing, not entirely comfortable with this yet, but now that I understand why she wants this so much, it's hard to deny her. *And am I really capable of ever saying no to her?* "Are you sure about this?"

"Yes." She nods firmly.

I sigh, knowing I won't convince her otherwise. "Fine... but Noah's right. We need a word, something to tell us to stop if it gets too much."

"Hm," she thinks for a moment, then smiles. "Blueberry salad?"

"Jesus, she really is obsessed with that salad." Noah laughs and shakes his head.

"What? It's good! Besides, saying that during sex would quickly throw me off, so I'm thinking it will do the same for you both."

"It would certainly have me pausing." I chuckle.

"Okay, so we're doing this?" She looks from Noah then to me as we both nod. "Good." She takes a few deep breaths, shakes out her arms, then pulls herself up on the kitchen island.

"You want to do this here?" I frown.

"Yes, there's more lighting here; I think that will help with my mind not... you know, going to dark places if I can see what you're doing."

Noah comes closer and picks up one satin tie; he kisses her cheek before beginning to tie one end around her ankle. She watches with wide eyes while focusing on her breath with every loop and tug he makes.

"Is this okay?" he asks her and waits for her nod before continuing. "Can you scoot back a bit on the counter? I'm going to tie it to this handle right here," he points to the very one right beneath the island, "and leave it in a bowtie. Like that one quick tug will set you free, just like I did around your ankle."

"Okay," she murmurs in a small voice and moves back, leaving her foot resting above the counter.

I get to work on her second ankle, mimicking the same knot Noah made, then tie that end to the other side of the counter, leaving her with both legs bent and spread toward either side. We wait a few seconds as she wiggles her toes, then moves her feet around slightly, noticing how we left a bit of looseness to the ties.

"Where do you want these?" Noah picks up the handcuffs next.

"In the front, please. I... I need to see them."

He nods and slowly wraps one around her wrist, once again leaving a bit of wiggle room, which I'm sure if she tried, she could squeeze her hand through it, then does the same to the other.

I stand back and watch as her entire body begins to shake, no longer just her hands. It's like she's standing outside naked in the middle of a blizzard, unable to control the shiver coursing through her, and it fucking guts me to see her responding this way just at the sight of seeing her hands tied up. I quickly step closer and wrap my arms around her, kissing her temple repeatedly.

"I'm okay. I'm okay. I'm okay," she repeats while sniffling, but all it takes is letting her go to see just how not okay she truly is. She curls up on herself the moment Noah releases her wrists and hides herself with her arms, crying quietly.

I fucking hate this. I hate seeing this version of Ronnie. I want to fucking kill that asshole for creating this broken and terrified version of my beautiful and brave girl.

"Shh, everything's okay. You're safe, Veronica." Noah glides his fingers through her hair, trying to soothe her. He then takes her hands in his and gently brings them back down. "Look at me." He waits for her tear-filled gaze to reach his, then smiles tenderly. "I want you to take a few deep breaths, and then you're going to repeat after me, okay?"

"Okay..." She takes several deep breaths, letting them out slowly past her lips.

"Good girl." He pecks her lips, then brings his eyes back to hers. "Now say it with me. You're here, you're now."

Her face scrunches up with more tears when she realizes what he's doing, and her entire body begins to relax. "I'm here, I'm now."

"You're with Noah and Gabe," I say next, taking her other hand when Noah releases it.

"I'm with Noah and Gabe." She smiles tearfully at me.

"They don't want to hurt you." Noah cups her cheek.

"They don't want to hurt me."

"They won't hurt you," I promise her.

"They won't hurt me." A tear slips down her cheek as I reach up to wipe it away.

"You're here, you're now." Noah leans in and kisses her again.

"I'm here, I'm now," she whispers against his lips.

"You still with us, pretty girl?"

Vixen smiles, letting out a small laugh and nods. "I'm always with you."

"That's our girl." I kiss her next.

We give her a few more minutes to collect herself and see the change in her demeanor once she's ready. "There are several different items in the bag, all of which you are free to use on me. These were the hard parts,"—she lifts her cuffed hands then nods to the bag—"those are all fairly easy to me."

Now that we're right beside the bag, I peek in and my eyebrows skyrocket. "Damn, you really went all out." I laugh and pull out three different sized and shaped dildos, two vibrators, a set of nipple clamps, two anal plugs and anal beads, a magic wand, a ball gag, a flogger, and several other things that I'm not sure what they do or what they're used for.

Noah chuckles, looking over everything, but then grabs the ball gag. "This one is off the table. We want to hear you if you need us to stop. But if you ever want to revisit this at another time when you're more comfortable, then we can." He tosses it back into the bag.

Okay," she says.

"Hm, what to start off with?" I pass my hand over every item, smirking when I land on the wand. Our girl is so sensitive, she'll lose her mind over this. I turn it on, making sure it has power, and smile when it buzzes to life.

Noah cradles her cheek and seals their lips together, distracting her from what I'm doing and getting her into the moment. I start off by gliding a single finger up her bare leg that quickly erupts with goosebumps, then take the same trail with the wand while it's on the lowest setting.

She giggles at the contact but moans when Noah squeezes one of her breasts. I do the same to the other leg, first with my finger, then the wand, but this time trailing it higher to the junction of her legs, right over her covered pussy for barely a second.

"Holy shit!" she yelps, jumping slightly when it makes contact with her sensitive nub.

"So sensitive." I chuckle and turn the wand off before setting it down on the counter beside her.

I grab one side of her panties and quickly tear the fabric apart, exposing her already glistening greedy cunt to us. Thanks to our girl coming down in nothing but a long white shirt and her underwear, this is making it super easy for us to gain access to her treasured places.

I grab her hips next and pull her slightly toward the edge of the counter. "Place her on her back. Staring at this beautiful pussy all spread out for me is making me hungry."

Noah smirks and helps Ronnie lean back against the counter, delicately laying her head down as her legs now fold against her body and slightly in the air. He lifts the shirt on her body, exposing her tiny, pebbled nipples to the cool air, and quickly captures one between his lips. Her back arches as she moans once more, and it only gets louder when I drag my tongue from her puckered hole, over her entrance, and to her clit.

Vixen fists my hair with her cuffed hands as I feast on her pussy and Noah continues to devour her breasts. I look up just in time to see one of his hands slither past her belly and over to the array of toys beside her. He grabs the nipple clamps that are chained together and brings them closer to her, letting the cold chain drag along her ribcage.

"These are going to pinch. Are you sure you're okay with these?" he asks as she nods. "Okay. Distract her," he says next, looking my way.

I smirk and dive in, sucking on her clit as I bring two fingers up and push them inside her tight entrance. I pump them back and forth, getting her closer to the edge, but slow down when I feel she's seconds away from detonating.

Noah quickly gets to work on clipping both clamps on, and Ronnie hisses and groans with each one. "Oh God!" she cries out loudly when he pulls on the chain that connects them. "Fuck, fuck, fuck!"

I quickly distract her by adding a third finger and curving them upwards as I press against that soft pressure point that always sets her off. Then I repeatedly flick my tongue against her clit until her legs are trembling and she's pulling against the restraints at her feet. Her hand in my hair yanks painfully while she screams her release, but nothing stops me from devouring my beautiful girl until the counter beneath her is soaking with her juices.

"Holy fuck..." Vixen pants, finally letting go of my hair while staring up at the overhead lights.

"I think you've had enough." Noah suddenly shoves me out of the way and wastes no time to bring his mouth down to her slightly swollen flesh. She whimpers instantly, body jerking, but they quickly turn back into moans as she relaxes and gives in to the feeling.

I walk over to Ronnie's side and claim her tasty lips. "Are you still okay?"

"Yes." She grins. "More than okay."

"Such a good fucking girl." I peck her lips and reach for the wand once more right as Noah grabs one of the anal plugs.

I switch the vibrating wand on as he works the plug into her ass while eating her out, then slightly pulls and pushes it back in repeatedly while I bring the toy down to her chest. I glide it over her breast that is covered in goosebumps, circling her clamped nipple and making the clips vibrate in the process.

"Holy fucking shit! This is like torture in the very best way," Ronnie says breathlessly as she pushes up her chest, pressing the vibrator harder against her nipples.

Once Noah has had his fill, he pulls back and smirks at me while grabbing one of the dildos. He rolls it over the countertop that's still very wet with her juices while kissing her inner thigh, then brings it to her entrance and slowly pushes it in. I watch that huge purple thing slide in and out of her, all veiny with Noah's length and my girth. It's definitely not the size of an average cock, and with the screams and moans our girl is letting out, I'd say she's enjoying the stretch quite well.

I tug on the chains attached to her breasts slightly while trailing the wand over her ribcage, then down to her bellybutton and lower. I graze it lightly over her clit, and she lets out the most sensual sound I've ever heard. My cock instantly jerks in my pants, and with the way Noah growls in response, he's clearly just as affected as I am.

"Fuck, do I love hearing my Kitten purr like that." He bites the inside of her thigh, fucking her faster with the dildo.

"Oh, she's going to do more than just purr." I turn the vibrations onto the highest setting and rub it over her clit vigorously.

"OH FUCK! HOLY SHIT!! YES! YES! YES! OH GOD! I'M COMING! I'M COMING! I'M COM—"

"THAT IS ENOUGH!"

Noah and I instantly turn around, nearly jumping out of our skin from the unexpected booming voice. Vixen, on the other hand, screams at the top of her lungs out of fear while also unable to stop her orgasm from consuming her.

Julian quickly strides over, picking up a blanket from the couch on his way, and in one swift move throws it perfectly over Ronnie, shielding her body from his view. "There are cameras there, there, there, and there! All with a perfect view of what is going on here!" He points at every corner of the main floor. "Will you *please,* for the love of Christ conduct this madness in the bedroom?!"

We all stare at him with wide eyes, not expecting our evening to turn out this way. *Fuck needing the safe word, Julian does the trick all on his own.* Noah finally snaps out of it first and clears his throat. "Sorry, we got a bit carried away." He pulls on each tie around Ronnie's ankles, quickly setting her free, then gets to work on her wrists beneath the blanket.

Julian glares at each one of us. "So it would seem. Where are your phones?"

"Um, I think we left ours over there." I nod toward the side table next to the couch.

"Mine's upstairs," Ronnie says quietly, securing the blanket around her properly.

"From now on, you will keep your devices on you at all times. We have all been trying to reach you for the past half hour. I should not have to be getting involved every time you three decide to act like horny adolescents." He fixes his cufflinks, grumbling something to himself before straightening. "Now that I have your attention. Please refrain from traumatizing my employees. I do not want to have to remind you every single day that you are under constant watch."

"I'm pretty sure traumatizing isn't the word they would use," Ronnie snorts, which earns her another glare.

"I mean it, Miss Masters. Control yourselves." And just as quickly, he spins around and storms out of the penthouse.

"Well, that's one way to kill the mood." I chuckle, shaking my head.

"Definitely." Vixen laughs, then passes her hands through her hair. "Fuck, I don't think I'll ever be able to see these toys without thinking of Julian now."

Noah and I both make displeased faces. Not at all what we want our girl to think about when we're playing with her. "How about we change that?" I smile and quickly scoop her off the counter and into my arms. "I'm pretty sure we could get you back in the mood relatively quickly."

Kissing her neck as she giggles, I turn us toward the stairs and run up to the second floor with her in my arms while Noah gathers the toys from the counter and follows behind us.

Chapter Thirty-Six

NOAH

The big guy and his fear of rats... cats?

~ One Week Later / September ~

I wake up to my favorite warm body pressed to my front. Her soft purrs have become the thing I look forward to the most when I wake up. I open my eyes slowly and am instantly mesmerized by the view before me. Veronica lies on her side, facing away from me, her hand holding onto mine that circles her waist.

Our girl always looks like a goddess, but in these moments when she's at peace, she's everything that is beauty. She's that feeling of bliss you get when you hold the thing you love the most in the world. When you're a kid and you find your favorite plushy after weeks of losing it. She's day and night, the sunrise and sunset, she's the cool summer breeze and the first snowfall. She's the star at the top of the Christmas tree lighting up the night and the presents lying under the tree on Christmas morning.

That's just it. She's everything.

As I watch her body rise and fall slowly with every breath she takes, it hits me how much our lives have changed since June. Gabe and I went from bachelors who only ever indulged in one-night stands, never waking up to the same woman twice. Never having them stay for breakfast or taking them out to dinner. Never talking or making plans about the future, never keeping them around long enough to know their favorite color or what shampoo they use.

And now, now we have Veronica. A woman we can't imagine a day going by without. A woman who constantly haunts our minds in the very best way. A woman who's fighting for us, who's doing everything she possibly can to make us better. A woman who was afraid to love and now loves us unconditionally.

How could we ever go back when we now hold a piece of paradise?

I delicately remove my other arm from beneath Veronica's head and lift onto my elbow. I then use my hand to smooth her hair away from her shoulder and lean in to deliver a gentle kiss to her warm golden skin. She lets out a happy sigh, her body arching into mine, ass pressing against my morning wood.

"Good morning, beautiful," I whisper against the shell of her ear as I continue kissing her exposed skin.

"Mmm, this is my favorite way to wake up." She reaches back with her hand, nails scratching at my scalp.

I grab her hip tightly and grind my erection against her. She moans, head leaning back into me. My fingers leave her hip and slide down between her legs, where I caress her soaking wet pussy a few times.

I twirl the tip of my finger around her clit until she's jerking into my hand, craving more. Bringing my hand back, I grab the underside of her thigh and lift her leg over mine, then fist my pulsing cock and plunge it deep inside her tight channel.

I groan into her hair as she moans loudly. Pulling out, I slide back in leisurely, taking my time to savor this euphoric feeling between us. I love our morning sex; it's slow and soft, passionate yet consuming all together.

Thrusting my hips slowly, I reach up and take hold of her jaw, angling it toward me until I can capture her lips with mine. Then we make love with our mouths as I make love to her with my dick.

Our morning sex never lasts long, as if the feeling is too intense to hold back. Within minutes of my soft strokes, her walls are closing in on me, trembling against my length as she begins to writhe against me. Then she's crying out into my mouth as I swallow every beautiful sound.

Her hand fists what she can of my short hair, hips bucking erratically, pussy leaking onto our thighs. And a few seconds later, I'm coming apart with her, moaning and groaning as my balls tighten, holding her in place as I shoot my cum deep inside her throbbing core.

We're both panting and gasping for air as we come down from our high. I kiss her shoulder, neck, ear, back of the head, then return to her shoulder. "I love you, Veronica."

She takes my hand, interlocking our fingers. "I'll never get tired of hearing that." She smiles tenderly, then looks over her shoulder at me. "I love you, too, Noah."

Her eyes shine with so much adoration, my heart squeezes painfully in my chest. I'll never tire of this feeling. But then something flicks through her mind, and her eyes lose some of their joy.

I turn her to me, brushing her hair behind her ear. "What is it, Kitten?"

She looks down at my chest, where her nails trace patterns over my pecs. "I just wish Gabe was here with us..." she whispers with heartache.

I kiss her forehead. "Soon, love. Let's just give it another week before we try spending the night together. Things are looking promising, and I don't think it's only Blubber. I really think the therapy is helping, too."

We had our second session all together with Dr. Hallaway yesterday, and by some miracle, she seems to be getting through to Gabe, to all of us. I understand why Veronica likes her so much, even if my first session alone with her was rough. I had never had a therapist before, but from what I've heard, her methods are very different than most.

Gabe hasn't had a full nightmare in a week, but that might be more Blubber's doing. He told us that every time one starts up, Blubber bites him until he jolts out of sleep. His arms are now covered in bite marks and scratches, but at least it's working.

The day after our first therapy session, we went out to a local shelter and found this little bugger. A little gray and white male Sphynx with pale blue eyes. Ronnie and Gabe were instantly smitten with him, and if they could have, they would have brought him home the same day. But the adoption process took a full week and a house visit before we could finally bring our little guy home, the day after our incident with Julian.

Veronica looks up at me with a sweet smile. "Me too. I can't wait for us to finally be all together." She bites her lip. "Do you think we'll need to get a bigger bed? Or do you want to continue using separate rooms? Maybe we could take down the wall dividing the two but keep two beds?"

I chuckle at the excited yet inquisitive tone to her voice. "Or we could buy a house, or even have one built to our liking?"

She pushes off me, needing to sit up for this conversation. "You're serious?" Her eyes are wide as she watches my smile bloom.

I sit up next to her, cupping her cheek and kissing her swollen red lips. "Of course, I am. I love the penthouse, but I think a home for the three of us would be a better move. I'd like for us to have our own place, with no previous bed partners. A place we can make ours."

"I'd really like that. I hate thinking about how many women have been in this bed before me." She blushes slightly as she admits to her feelings.

I cringe, feeling embarrassed and bad for her. "Sorry about that. We can get a new mattress if you want."

She waves me off as she stands from the bed, heading to the attached bathroom while I follow her. "Don't be ridiculous, it's fine. We'll just get another one when we move."

We step into the shower and she turns it on. "You realize this is a big step for us, right?"

An extremely big step if we think about how we've technically only been dating for nearly three months. But everything between us three has been moving so quickly, and I know what Gabe and I feel for Veronica is real. So, why wait?

Holy shit, now I get why Silas was so quick to get settled down with Cecilia.

She begins to lather her hair with shampoo, eyes closed, and face angled toward the ceiling. "I do, but I think we're at that stage. It's either buying a house or having a baby, and I am not ready for that one just yet." *Good to know she wants this to keep moving forward as well.*

She stops moving, opening her eyes and looking intensely at me. "Unless you think you'll get tired of me at some point and move on."

I furrow my brows, taking a quick step toward her and bringing her close by the hips. "Absolutely not. Never. You've made us yours, Veronica, and that's forever. Just like we've made you ours. Forever."

She gazes deep into my eyes, comprehension and devotion blazing through hers. "Forever."

Forty-five minutes later, we're finally heading down for breakfast, where Gabe waits for us. Veronica goes up to Gabe, throwing herself in his arms as he catches her with a laugh. Her legs circle his waist, arms going around his neck as she smacks her lips against his, then pulls away just as quickly.

"Good morning to you, Vixen." He laughs at her enthusiasm.

"Good morning, Pretty Boy. We're buying a house!" She beams at him.

His eyes widen with excitement. "We are?" He looks from Veronica to me as I nod. He laughs again, grabbing her by the nape and crushing his mouth to hers. "Fuck yeah, we are!"

Blubber pops out from behind Gabe's legs and sits by his feet, meowing for attention. Gabe puts Veronica down, and she instantly drops to the floor to cuddle the hairless cat. "Good morning to you, too, Blubs."

She peppers his head with kisses, and I swear he looks at us smugly every time she does that, as if he's saying, *"Ha-ha, see? She loves me more."*

She lifts him in her arms, cuddling him to her chest. "Did you have a good night's sleep? I bet you did. You're such a good boy keeping Daddy company. And did you hear the good news? We're going to have a new home! Maybe even a big backyard where we'll be able to let you play in the yard. I'm sure you'll like that a lot."

She stretches out her arms, holding him between her hands. "God, aren't you just the most adorable thing I've ever seen? Look at this cute little outfit!" she gushes, looking over the knitted sweater he's wearing that looks like a tuxedo. "My handsome little boy."

Ever since the nice lady at the shelter told us all we needed to know about Sphynx cats and how they get cold easily and need to be kept warm, Gabe and Veronica have made it their mission to buy every single little outfit they can find that will keep his hairless body warm. He even has a heating pad under a blanket in his little kitty house. I swear, that thing is way too spoiled already.

"Green smoothie?" Gabe asks Veronica as she sets Blubber back on the ground.

"Please." She grins and watches him get to work on their daily drink as well as breakfast.

Suddenly her phone chimes twice on the counter, and we all freeze. It's pretty much become our usual reaction every time her phone goes off. We're constantly waiting for the next shoe to drop.

Victor hasn't made a single appearance since the night in the penthouse, and we're all getting agitated. We have no idea what he's planning next, and I refuse to believe he simply gave up. Whatever he's plotting now is much bigger, I can feel it.

She tentatively picks it up and unlocks the screen. Within seconds, her shoulders drop, and she lets out a sigh, an indication that it's not from him. "Just the girls asking if they should bring anything over later," she informs us as another notification comes in, her brows furrowing as she reads the message.

"What is it?" I step forward, fearing the worst.

"It's from Julian, he says he's on his way..." She drops her phone on the counter and looks up with a worried expression. "Do you think he found something?"

"We'll have to wait until he gets here to find out." I play with her hair, hoping to soothe her as best as I can.

Just then, the elevator dings its arrival, and Julian strides into the penthouse, coming over to us with a laptop in his grasp like he owns the place. "Good morning, everyone."

"Wow, that was quick." Gabe blinks.

I frown when I realize this is the second time he's entered the penthouse without even needing us to authorize him up. "How did you get in?"

"My brother is not the only smart hacker in the family. I know my way around a simple keycard scanner," he says, clearly annoyed with us already. *I wonder what bit this guy in the ass. Whatever it is, it's constantly biting.* "And I am fairly certain I announced my arrival before entering. I am not quite sure where this confusion is coming from." He turns to Gabe with a frown.

"He just meant we thought you were on your way from your home, or office, or whatever. Not that you were on your way *up*," Veronica clarifies for us.

"Ah." He nods. "I can see where there may have been a miscommunication. Apologies." He sits down at the kitchen island, without asking, I may add, and opens his laptop. *Why the hell does he always talk like that? As if he's so superior to us all. It grates my nerves.*

He types at his keyboard for a few seconds, then slides the laptop over to the next stool. "Veronica, I'd like you to go over these images, please." She quickly comes around the island and sits down in front of the computer, scrolling down through more pictures of people I don't recognize.

"Agent Callahan has informed me that he and an associate have gone door-to-door at every unit in the building. Most graciously let them into their home, and those that did not were not present. I have gathered the names of all those people and looked up their whereabouts," Julian tells us while Veronica goes through the list.

"Five are currently out of the state, and two must have simply been away during the time of visit. My guess is he is hiding out in one of those seven units. But unfortunately, we cannot just break into their place of residence. So it is once again a waiting game until we get more leads or a warrant letting Agent Callahan in."

I sigh as Gabe passes his fingers through his hair, both of us clearly irritated with the whole situation. It feels like we're just sitting ducks waiting for something to happen. Veronica finishes looking over the images and pushes the laptop back to Julian. "I'm sorry, I really don't recognize anyone."

He frowns. "And you have not been approached by anyone in the building? Someone asking unusual questions? Maybe even attempting to get friendly?" She shakes her head.

He closes his eyes, fumes practically bursting out of his ears as his nostrils flare. This situation is obviously pissing him off as much as it is us. When he opens his eyes, Veronica looks down with self-reproach.

"Forgive me, my frustration is not aimed toward you, Veronica. I am simply exasperated and displeased with myself." He swipes his hand over his hair, the first sign that he isn't in complete control. "I have never had trouble finding someone who was well hidden. I can find someone who has been off the grid for the past decade. And if I cannot do it, then Jessie will. But neither of us can seem to locate this man, despite him being right under our noses."

He stands from the stool, buttoning up his suit jacket and adjusting his cufflinks.

"I regret that I cannot offer you better news, or any news at all. But I promise you, we will not stop until we find him."

Blubber suddenly comes up to him, passing between his legs and sitting at his feet with a meow as Julian looks down with disgust. "That thing is monstrous."

"Hey! I don't come into your home and call your things ugly!" Veronica glares at him.

He looks up at her, his lip twitching with a bit of amusement. "You are right, my sincerest apologies." He gathers his laptop and nods our way. "I will be seeing myself out, thank you for having me." He turns and heads for the elevator.

"We didn't really have a choice in the matter," I grumble under my breath.

Veronica jumps from her stool, rushing after him, my steps not far behind hers. "Wait, Julian!" He turns just as she catches up to him, elevator doors already open. "There was something I wanted to talk to you about."

He looks at his watch, then back at her. "I am listening."

"Aubrey would like to move back into our condo. She was wondering if that would be possible, although she would be alone." Veronica chews on her lower lip, visibly not liking that fact.

"If she would like to move back into her home, I cannot physically stop her, but I would like to put in one condition. It is the only way a certain someone will not rip my head off for letting her live alone." Amusement shines in his eyes once more.

Veronica smiles, then nods sharply. "I understand. What would the condition be?"

"Around-the-clock personal security. Meaning in home living until this situation is rectified. Wherever she goes, he goes." Now he smirks wickedly.

"Oh..." Veronica's eyes widen. "And you think this certain someone will be okay with that?"

"Oh, I know he will not be. But that simply makes it more fun." He turns, stepping into the elevator. "Talk to her and let me know when she has come to a decision and when she plans on moving back. She will be introduced to her security personnel beforehand." The door shuts, ending the conversation there.

"Why does that guy always sound like such an asshole?" Gabe asks from behind us as we turn to him.

"Because he is an asshole," I clarify.

"Stop it, he's helping us when he didn't have to. He might be rough around the edges, but I think deep down he's a good guy."

Veronica passes me, only stopping for a quick kiss, then heads for Gabe and does the same before grabbing the nasty smoothie from his hand. "Thank you, baby."

"Anything for you, milady. Breakfast should be ready in five," he tells us, turning back to the kitchen.

Veronica takes a sip of her drink and sighs happily, then points it out toward me. "Want some?" She smirks.

I make a face, repulsed by the idea of drinking that concoction. "No, thank you."

She shrugs. "Your loss." She takes another sip then her eyes fall on the elevator doors. "Is it okay if we skip our run this morning?"

True to her word, my Kitten has been running with me every single morning, as well as working out with us. She's not exactly up to my speed, but I admire her determination. And thanks to her, I haven't touched anything strong in two weeks despite being tempted once, which means I was granted my car privileges back yesterday. It really sucked not having a car of my own, and everywhere we went, she would drive me.

So much for having a car no one was allowed to drive. But of course, our girl is the exception to every rule. I'd give her the fucking world if I could.

I take a step closer, placing my hand at the back of her head as I kiss her temple. "Yeah, Kitten."

"But we're still working out, though, right?" She blushes slightly as she bites her lip. I can't help but chuckle.

I know exactly why she likes to work out with us. Claiming she's actually working out would be a lie. Mostly, she pretends to while watching us do our sets. The whole thing gets her pretty worked up until she decides she's had enough with just watching.

That's when she starts stretching, or whatever she wants to call it, in very suggestive positions. Right in our faces. It usually only takes a minute or two before Gabe snaps and jumps her, right there in the middle of the gym while I watch. It's come to my attention that our girl really loves it when I watch her get fucked by my best friend. And I am all for it.

"Of course, we are." I smirk and grab her hand, pulling her to the kitchen island for breakfast.

I focus on my breathing as I turn the corner and spot my building just down the block. I decided on a shorter jog today, since Veronica wasn't joining me and I left the penthouse later than usual.

Normally we start our day early with a jog, then get back home and have breakfast, and an hour or so later we work out. But today we clearly started backwards with breakfast and Julian showing up. So now I'm full and exhausted, which is making jogging relatively harder than normal. I definitely won't be putting much effort into my workout later.

As I come to an intersection right before our building, I stop and jog on the spot, looking both ways for any oncoming cars. With my headphones at full blast, I can't hear anything around me but my music, so my eyes are truly the only thing to help me know if there's a car coming. Thankfully, I don't see any moving vehicles coming my way, only a few cars parked along the side or idling.

I start jogging across the road and make it halfway when movement to my left catches my attention. I look just in time to see a red car that was just idling to the side now speeding straight toward me with no intention of stopping.

My heart pounds in my chest and blood pumps in my ears as I realize just how close it truly is. I force all my strength into my legs and jump out of the way as quickly as I can. The side of the car knocks into my foot and sends me tumbling to the pavement as the car speeds off.

I hiss as I lie against the ground, an ache quickly spreading through my back and ankle, but not in a painful way that tells me anything is truly wrong. "Noah!" someone shouts my name as I sit up. "Are you okay?"

Ricky kneels beside me, looking me over before grabbing me by the arm and helping me to my feet. Liam, one of the newer guards who jogs behind me every day, comes running back from the direction the car went with his phone to his ear. He puts it away once he reaches us with a look that tells me everything I need to know.

This wasn't an accident or coincidence. It was Victor.

I fucking knew this asshole hadn't given up. Fuck, Veronica isn't going to like this...

"Fucking bastard sped up too fast, I couldn't catch the plate in time," Liam says, panting slightly. "God damn it. I spotted that car yesterday but didn't bother with it. Should have trusted my gut," he growls angrily at himself.

"Give Jessie our location, I'm sure some camera nearby caught something. Although I doubt he's dumb enough to use his own plates or show his face, so probably won't lead to much," Ricky tells him as he releases me.

"Already did. But you're right, there's no way that car is his, and we'll probably never see it again after today. That would be a major rookie move, and clearly, he's far from stupid." Liam shakes his head. "You good?"

I nod. "Yeah, just hit my foot, but I'm fine."

"Good. Let's get you to safety while our bosses go over what just happened and hopefully get a lead." Ricky scans up and down the street before telling me to start moving. We've gathered the attention of a few bystanders, but no one that looks suspicious.

I take the first step on my foot and immediately know I'll need to ice it. *Fuck, how am I going to hide this from Veronica without her freaking out?* Both Liam and Ricky frown when they notice me limping, but I try to shake it off and walk normally.

"I'm fine. Nothing that won't fix itself with a bit of ice and rest," I try to reassure them. "But if you could keep this to yourselves and not mention it to Veronica, that would be really appreciated." They give each other a look, not certain that hiding this is the best course of action.

"Look, I just don't want her worrying even more. He came after me, not her. She's already stressed out like crazy waiting for him to show up again, I don't want to cause her more anxiety and fear every time I leave the house."

"Fine, we won't say anything. But from now on, Liam will be jogging closer to you, and no more taking the same route, certainly not if Veronica is with you. Change it up daily. I don't want this fucker trying some shit like that again."

"Deal." I nod as we make it back to the building.

I head up to the penthouse and barely make it three steps in when my Kitten catches me trying to sneak in. She quickly runs over and holds onto me, worry shining in her eyes. "Babe? What happened? Why are you limping?"

"It's nothing." I cup her cheek. "Just tripped over a damn rock and hurt my ankle slightly. Nothing major."

"Are you sure? You don't want to get it checked out?"

"Yes, I'm sure. I'll just ice it a bit before our workout, then keep it up the rest of the day." I kiss her temple, walking slowly over to the kitchen as she follows closely behind.

"Absolutely not. No working out in this condition. I don't want you making it worse."

I chuckle at the serious motherly tone she's using. "Kitten, it's my foot, not my entire body. I can still work out without putting much pressure on it."

She rolls her eyes and grumbles something beneath her breath. "Fine, but if I see you forcing it in any way, there will be consequences." She points her finger at me. "Now sit. I'll get the ice pack."

Two hours later, we're getting close to finishing our workout in our home gym.

And as predicted, Veronica is getting hotter and more bothered by the minute. Her slender fingers run down her neck to the tiny slope of her breast, caressing her skin back and forth.

Her eyes are trained on Gabe as he gets down to the ground, doing his regular goalie stretches. Her breath grows by the second, her pupils dilating as she licks her lips sensually. She then pushes off the wall she was leaning against and walks to the middle of the room, pretending to stretch out. She starts by bending in half into a downward dog, then onto her knees as she pushes back her ass, swiveling her hips from side to side.

"I've been thinking of taking up yoga," she starts. "It's really good for the mind and body and helps with flexibility." She lowers the top portion of her body, cheek and chest against the mat, ass high up in the air. "What do you boys think?" She smirks.

Once again, like I had seen the future, Gabe stands quickly and strides over to her with purpose. He drops to his knees behind her, grabs her hips, and brings his mouth down to her covered pussy, biting her through the material of her workout shorts.

Her yelp quickly turns into a moan as she wiggles against his face. He fists her waistband and pulls her shorts down to mid-thigh, giving him just enough room to lick at her mound. Then he devours her like a hungry beast as she squirms but doesn't move from her position.

I move around and settle down on a bench beside them, giving myself the perfect side view. Gabe laps up at her a few more times, edging her on, but never bringing her to climax. He then straightens behind her as she whines and pleads for him to continue, which only rewards her with a sharp slap to the ass as he chuckles.

He pulls down his shorts just enough to expose his hard, thick erection and drives into her without warning. She cries out, nails biting into the floor mats. Her head turns my way, eyes hooded as she watches me with her bottom lip stuck between her teeth.

Gabe doesn't give her time to adjust before he starts plowing into her at full speed. Powerful thrust after powerful thrust. Her screams echo through the room as she tries to hold on for dear life. He brings a hand down to her back along her spine, forcing her to stay down.

I push my gym shorts past my hips and fist my cock when it springs free. Precum already leaks out of the tip, and I swipe it with my thumb, using it as lubrication. My eyes never leave Veronica, never leave the way her eyes roll to the back of her head, the way her lips form a perfect 'O' every time he rams his fat cock into her tight pussy.

I watch him slide in and out of her, the way his abs clench with every pump, the concentrated frown set on his face as sweat drips from his hair. Watching Gabe isn't what's turning my dick to stone, it's the act itself. Watching people fuck, the way they react—it's hypnotizing.

"Fuck, Vixen. You feel so fucking good like this. Your pussy is fucking suffocating me," he grunts out, removing his hands from her back and taking hold of her hips, slamming into her even harder with extreme fierceness.

I squeeze my fist tighter, my strokes becoming rough and frantic. My chest rises and falls with each heavy pant as my balls tighten and tingle. Veronica's screams get louder by the second, the slap of their skin vibrating through the walls.

"FUCK! Oh God! Don't stop! YES!" she cries and moans, whimpering from the assault he's delivering but loving every moment of it. Our girl has changed so much since this all began. We never could have taken her like this before, but now, she craves it.

Her eyes refocus on me, and I watch the hunger take over as she zones in on my hand pumping my cock with brutal force. "I want you to come on me," she says breathlessly.

I smirk. "Yeah?"

She nods eagerly and bites her lip. Her eyes close momentarily as she cries out when Gabe delivers another intense slap to her ass cheek. I get up and kneel beside her, ignoring the ache in my ankle at how it's placed, and brush her hair to the side.

"Where do you want me, love? Want me to come all over your back?" I caress her cheek. "On this pretty little face? Or deep down your throat?"

Her eyes fill with lust as she looks at me. I already know what she really wants—our girl loves taking us in her mouth. I look over at Gabe for his permission to lift her onto her hands and knees.

He nods. "But hurry up because I can't hold on much longer."

I chuckle. "Don't worry, I'm right there with you."

I move in front of Veronica and help her up onto her hands, then fist her hair as she opens her mouth wide on another cry and shove my dick into her mouth. Hitting the back of her throat, I slide back out. "Relax, Kitten." Then I push in once more, deep into her throat with a groan.

Barely two seconds later, she screams around my shaft, body jerking as she falls over the edge and climaxes. Her throat constricts against me, sending me tumbling along with her. I roar as Gabe pounds into her one last time, crying out along with me as we fill her from both ends.

When we pull out, Veronica gasps for air and drops to the floor like a ragdoll. Gabe laughs as he watches her body continue to twitch sightly, her eyes closed as she hums and pants loudly. "I love seeing her like this, completely spent."

I smile and lean over, pushing her sticky hair out of her face. "You okay, Kitten?"

"Mhmm," she hums. "I can't move." She lets out a breathy laugh.

"That's okay, baby. We'll carry you," Gabe says as he replaces his shorts properly, then hers, and crouches down to pick her up into his arms.

"Let's get her upstairs. I think we all need a shower." I pull my own back up and walk out of the gym and down the hall but stop when I hit the kitchen and notice we're no longer alone.

Aubrey sits at the kitchen island, eyes wide and red as a tomato. She won't meet my eyes as she speaks, only looking straight ahead. "I texted and called before coming over... I should have waited in my car..." I'm guessing Marcos or Ricky brought her up the moment they spotted her since that's what they've been instructed to do.

Gabe explodes with laughter, Veronica giggles against his chest, and I shake my head with a chuckle. "Yeah, may have been a better idea." I point toward the stairs. "We're gonna shower and be right back."

"Mhm," she says tightly. "I'm just going to... bake something... anything... busy myself just in case you guys... go at it again." She stands and goes around the island. "I'll put music on... loud music."

"Won't be necessary, baby Ford. I think Vixen is done for now." Gabe smiles and heads for the stairs as I follow behind.

Thirty minutes later, we're all heading back down the stairs to our kitchen that now smells like chocolate cupcakes. Aubrey holds a mixing bowl in her hands as she dips her finger in to taste the icing she's just made. Her clothes hold dust marks, most likely from the flour she used in her baked goods, as well as a smear on her cheek.

She sets the bowl to the side, wipes her hands on a cloth, and looks down at her outfit with a smile. "Don't worry, I brought spare clothes. I know, I'm a mess. I was a little distracted while baking. I'll clean up the kitchen too."

"It's fine." I wave her off. "Gabe and I will do it."

Ellis and I have been very, *very* careful not to leave any mess behind. Ever since our second disastrous dinner, where I attempted to make grilled cheese and ended up burning the whole thing. To which Veronica still forced us all to have a bite before shivering with disgust as she pulled away from her sandwich and realized I had forgotten to take the wrapper off the cheese slice.

Veronica giggles, clearly understanding why Gabe and I are so eager to clean up, then sits down at the island with Aubrey as they start chitchatting about the rest of the gang arriving later for dinner. We never usually host here, but with our new addition to the family, we thought it would be nice to have everyone over and introduce him.

As if hearing my thoughts, Blubber comes trotting into the kitchen, stopping at Veronica's side, and lifts onto his back paws. She leans over and collects him, kissing his head and petting his furless back over his sweater.

"Oh my God, you guys got a cat?" Aubrey looks at our little guy sweetly.

"Yeah, his name is Blubber. He's ten weeks old." Veronica smiles with love.

"Can I hold him?" Veronica nods and passes him over to Brey. "Aren't you adorable?" Aubrey beams, then looks up at us. "Wow, this is a big step, you guys having a pet together. Don't babies come next?" She laughs with a blush forming on her cheeks.

"Actually… we were talking about buying a house as well…" Veronica says with a bit of hesitation in her voice and eyes as she looks over Aubrey's reaction.

It hits me now why she's bringing the subject up delicately. She and Aubrey are technically roommates. If Veronica moves in with us, it means Aubrey would be living alone.

"Oh…" Aubrey frowns but then quickly replaces it with a small smile. She sets Blubber down on the ground and straightens, taking Veronica's hand in hers. "I'm happy for you, really, I am." Even though her smile is small, her words are genuine.

"I understand this is a lot of change for you. I'd offer you to come with us, but I know how you feel about all that." They both laugh softly. "Are you going to be okay… living on your own?"

"Yeah, of course. I mean, if I can move back into the condo, I'll already be alone. So, it will only give me an idea of what that will be like. But I'm fine, I promise. I want you to be happy, and I can tell that's here, with them."

Veronica lets out a breath. "Okay, thank you. I was a bit worried about telling you. But I did talk to Julian this morning, and he said you could move back with one condition…"

Aubrey's eyes widen. "Which is?"

Veronica chews on her lip for a second. "He wants you to have someone with you at all times… like a personal bodyguard… around the clock."

Her face turns red as she takes in Kitten's words. "He would have to live with me…? I've never lived with a man aside from my brother before… I… I don't know if I can do that… you know how I am." She removes her hands from Veronica's and bites her thumbnail.

"I know, but you would meet him beforehand, and he would be very professional. He can take up my room. It's only until all this is over." Veronica then smiles with a hint of mischief. "Or you could always take Shane up on his offer…"

Well, this is the first I'm hearing about it. What offer? My back is now to them as I place things into the dishwasher, listening in to their conversation. Gabe looks over at me from where he wipes down the counter, a clear question in his eyes, wondering what the offer might be. I shrug, telling him I have no idea.

"I can't do that…" Aubrey whispers in a panic. "It would be too… no, I can't live with him." *Well, shit. Coach offered her a place to stay… Why doesn't he just ask her out already?*

"You're right, you two would probably be jumping each other's bones by the end of the week." I look over my shoulder in time to see Veronica nod as she sucks in her lips, refraining from laughing.

"Ronnie!" Aubrey's neck and ears turn red, even her nose is taking on the shade. "We would not… That… It wouldn't happen… He's—"

"If you say he's not into you one more time, I might smack you," Veronica cuts her off.

"I second that." Gabe laughs. "Seriously, baby Ford. Coach probably jerks off to you daily."

Brey buries her head in her hands. "Oh God, please stop. I don't want to think about that. He's a gentleman, he wouldn't do that."

"All men jerk off, Brey. It's second nature." I shrug. "Gabe is right, though; that man can't take his eyes off you when you're in the room, he's definitely doing it."

The timer on her phone goes off, letting her know the cupcakes are ready. "Okay, no more talking about that. Tell Julian I say yes."

A few hours later, everyone arrives, minus the kids since they are with their grandparents for the night, from what we were told. They all settle into the living room while Gabe finishes up preparing dinner.

"It's so strange to come back here." Cecilia smiles as she looks around. "To think this is where our story began." She turns to her husband with so much devotion in her gaze.

Silas lowers and kisses her passionately. "You and me," he whispers to her.

"You and me," she breathes back.

Gabe comes over, a wide grin on his lips as he wipes his hands on a dishcloth. "We have some news," he announces to the room.

"Now she's pregnant!" Emma exclaims.

"No. Once again, I am not pregnant." Veronica sighs with a head shake.

"Maybe in two weeks." Gabe winks at her glare. "We're buying a house!"

"You are?! Where?" Morgan asks excitedly.

"We haven't decided yet, but we think it's the next step for us," I inform her.

"You should move near us. We'll all be neighbors!" Cecilia says with enthusiasm, liking the idea.

"AH!" Silas jumps onto the couch beside her, pointing at the floor. "What the hell is that?!"

Veronica laughs while picking our boy up. "Everyone, this is Blubber, our newest addition."

"That thing is hideous. That's not a cat, it's a fucking rat!" Silas says loudly.

Cecilia smacks him. "Don't be rude, he's a cutie, and look at his tuxedo!"

"You named the cat Blubber..." Clay frowns.

"Yeah, I'm trying to wrap my head around that one, too." Greyson chuckles and scratches his head. "The thing doesn't have an ounce of fat on him."

"Stop judging him. He's perfect." She stands with Blubber in her hands, bringing him over to Silas. "Here, just hold him. You'll see, he's a sweetheart."

Silas shrieks and jumps over the couch. "Get that thing away from me!"

We all explode with laughter. For such a big, tough guy, he sure is scared of a little kitten.

Chapter Thirty-Seven

VERONICA

Goodbye bubble, hello world.

~ One Week Later ~

I wake up to two different pairs of hands roaming my body, two different lips kissing my quickly heating skin. I hum with pleasure but keep my eyes closed, loving the sensation and how my whole body erupts with desire with every soft press of their lips and caress of their fingers.

This is our last free weekend before training camp and preseason start up. The boys are excited to get back to work, but they also know it means spending less time together. I guess that's why they've been sticking to me like glue for the past week.

Let's just say we haven't really left the bedroom—well, more the penthouse—since we tend to get it on whenever the mood strikes. Which resulted in receiving numerous texts from a *very* annoyed Julian telling us to '*KEEP IT IN THE BEDROOM!*' Oopsie.

"Wake up, Kitten," Noah murmurs near my ear.

"Uh-uh. Just keep doing what you're doing." I smile, eyes remaining closed.

"But we have a surprise for you, Vixen." Gabe kisses up my spine to the back of my neck.

"I already know what the surprise is." I lift my ass, rubbing it against his erection. "Just give it to me already."

He laughs. "It's a better surprise."

I peek one eye open, turning my head slightly to find Noah kneeling at my side and Gabe over my back. Satisfied with having them both in bed with me, despite us still not spending the night all together, I shut my eye once more.

"What could be better than having sex with my two favorite men?"

"We're your *only* two men," Noah grumbles.

I smile. "Yes, you are, and the best ones I could ever ask for." I reach out blindly with one hand, touching Noah first and then Gabe. "So, what's this surprise that's apparently better than sex?"

Gabe nibbles my shoulder. "How does two orgasms with our mouths while having breakfast in bed sound?"

"Hmm, pretty good. But still not better than sex."

Noah chuckles, his fingers sliding through my hair as he massages my scalp. "That's because you didn't hear the best part."

I open my eyes, watching the grin spread on his face. "Okay, I'll bite. What's the best part?"

"Shopping spree on Fifth Avenue," Noah says with a knowing smirk. *Damn him for knowing how much I love shopping!*

"Then a nice day at the beach. They say it's supposed to be warm and sunny. Probably our last chance to go this year before the cold comes in." Gabe beams when I turn my head to see him. *Ugh! I do miss our time at the beach. Damn him for knowing that too!*

"And finishing the night off with a romantic dinner at a fancy restaurant." Noah comes in to kiss my lips. *Ooh, a public outing?* We've been out all together before, but never something that will make it obvious we're dating.

I scoot out from under Gabe as he sits back on his calves, bringing myself to a sitting position against the headboard. "What's the occasion?" I raise a brow.

"No occasion, Kitten. We've just realized that we never took you out on a proper date yet."

"We just want to show you how much you mean to us. We want to give you a special day," Gabe finishes, tucking my hair behind my ear.

I bite my lip, looking from one to the other, before an ear-to-ear grin spreads across my face and I throw myself at them. One arm around each. "AH! You guys are amazing! God, I love you both so much!"

"Now hurry up and eat your breakfast while we have ours." Gabe grabs my ankles and drags me down to my elbows, while Noah comes over with a tray that was set aside. Fruits, croissants, French toast, waffles, pancakes. *Jesus, they really went all out.*

Gabe doesn't waste time on delivering his part of the breakfast. He quickly spreads my naked legs and settles in between them, feasting away at me as Noah tries to feed me. *Let me tell you this, eating while having an orgasm is really not easy.* A few minutes later, once Gabe achieves his goal, he switches places with Noah and proceeds with the feeding.

A quick shower later, we're dressed and heading out the door. It's only eight in the morning by now, and I'm a little curious why they felt the need to rush us out. After forty-five minutes of driving, it becomes clear. Also, the fact that we are nowhere near Fifth Avenue made it obvious they had something else in mind, since we live right next to it.

"What are we doing at Maze's shop?" I smile as I jump out of the car, excited to see my girl.

"Well, we know you get your hair done at the beginning of every month usually, and you haven't done it yet. So, we took the liberty in booking you an appointment." Noah puts his hand along my back, guiding me toward the door as he kisses the side of my head.

"We also chose the color. Well, I chose the color." Gabe grins as he throws his arm over my shoulders and pulls the door open.

We pass through the threshold with difficulty, since neither one wanted to let me go. It was pretty comical to watch us come in sideways, but I love it.

Bear greets us from behind the counter the moment we step in. "Well, shit. You brought both your men today!"

I laugh. "Can't go anywhere without them." I smile and peck both their cheeks.

"Damn, I wish I could have two women to love me like that," he jokes.

"Who knows, maybe one day you will." I wink as I pull my men along toward Maze. "Hey, babe." I hug her once we're in her section of the shop.

"Look at you, all glowing and shit. It's almost nauseating." She laughs while holding me at arm's length and looking me over.

"What can I say, I'm happy." I grin.

"Of course, you are. If I had two fine ass men taking care of my needs like yours do, I'd be as bright as the fucking sun." Maze turns her gaze to Noah and Gabe. I know they aren't her type, but that doesn't mean she doesn't admire the view.

"So, what color are we doing today?" I ask with a bounce in my step as I walk over to the chair.

"Ah, can't say. Blondie told me it was a surprise." She thumbs toward Gabe, then swivels the chair around and away from any mirrors. "Let's get to work, my lovelies."

Three hours later, we're back in the car and grabbing a quick bite to eat before finally heading to the shops. I'm not sure how Gabe and Noah plan to do everything in one day, but they swear we'll have time to go shopping and go to the beach. I don't think they know what it's like to shop with a woman.

I watch my hair run over my shoulders through the windows reflection, a happy smile playing along my lips. I was really surprised when Maze finally spun the chair around and let me see the end result. It wasn't at all what I was expecting, but I love it. Dark green from the roots that falls into a bright yellow at the ends, giving a beautiful ombre hairstyle.

"You sure you like it?" Gabe asks for the millionth time with a nervous tone.

I take hold of his hand above the restaurant table where we wait for our early lunch. "I love it, I promise. It's perfect. Thank you." I take Noah's hand as well. "Both of you."

The waitress comes over with our food, peering down at our hands with surprise before setting down the plates as we pull apart. She then stands to the side, awkwardly shifting her weight from one foot to the other, wringing her hands.

"I don't mean to be a bother... but I was wondering if I could maybe... get an autograph and a picture?" Her eyes keep bouncing back to mine, like she's afraid I may get mad that she's interrupting our date. She swallows and continues. "My dad's a really huge fan and he'd kill me if I didn't ask."

Normally, I probably would get mad. Most times when women approach them it's for different reasons. But this girl sounds genuine and maybe even too young to try anything with them.

Noah and Gabe look at me for permission and I shrug. Gabe looks back at the waitress with his megawatt grin. "Is it okay if we have lunch with our girlfriend first? Then we'll do the pictures and sign whatever you want. We're kind of trying to give her a special day."

Her eyes go wide as she blushes. "Yes, of course, take your time." She looks at me with an apologetic smile. "I'm sorry for interrupting your day."

I wave her off. "It's fine. It's the kind of thing that happens when you're dating two famous guys I guess." I laugh.

We eat the rest of our lunch in peace and by the end, as promised the boys give the waitress what she asked. I suspect she felt a bit guilty because she asked me to be in one of the pictures with them as well.

When we exit the restaurant, deciding to walk down to Fifth Ave since we aren't far, I laugh to myself. "How long do you think it will take her to post that picture of us and tell the world we're together?"

"I give it by the end of the day, and we've gone viral. The media is going to have a field day with that." Noah chuckles.

"Good. I want the world to know your ours." Gabe kisses the side of my head.

Gabe's arm rests along my shoulders, while Noah's is around the back of my waist, and I hold both by the back. Thanks to my height and reaching theirs in my heels, it makes this position a lot easier.

"And I want the world to know you belong to me. If I have to wear two engagement rings on my fingers to make it clear, I will." I nod my head with determination.

"Hmm, that's not a bad idea." Gabe winks.

"Or we could just get them tattooed on." Noah shrugs.

I stop in my tracks, stunned by his words. Removing myself from their hold, I turn to face them. "You two, skin virgins, would get a tattoo for me?"

"Well, it wouldn't be huge, just a ring on our finger. Make it pretty obvious we're taken for good." Noah smirks, while Gabe doesn't look so sure.

"You okay with this, Pretty Boy?" I giggle because I swear, he's sweating just at the thought of doing it.

"I..." He laughs nervously and rubs the back of his neck.

"Is it the permanent commitment part that freaks you out? Or the ink?" I ask slowly, worry surfacing at the thought that he might not think what's happening between us will last.

"No! It's the needle part, not the commitment. I promise I want to commit to you in every way possible. I just... I've seen my parents use needles my whole childhood. I know it's not the same, but it's a fear I kind of developed." He looks down at his feet with shame.

I take a step into him, cupping his face with my hands. "Hey, you have nothing to be embarrassed about. A lot of people are afraid of needles, most without actual reason. Yours are very valid and I can understand why you might be a bit hesitant to do this."

I smile tenderly at him. "If it's too much we don't have to, but if you think it's something you can get past, then we'll take our time. Maybe sitting through a session will help you overcome your fear. We don't have to do it right now either."

"Yeah, okay. I'll think about it." He gives me a sad smile.

"I love you, Gabriel. I'd never force you to do something you aren't comfortable with." I press my lips to his softly.

"I love you, too, Vixen." He kisses me back.

I pull away and turn to Noah, feeling the need to kiss him too. So I do, telling him I love him as well, then I take both their hands and continue our way to the shops. "This is going to be so fun!"

"You're going to make us hold everything, right?" Gabe asks while laughing.

I roll my eyes. "Of course, I will. Why else do you think you two are here?"

"Maybe for our money that will be paying everything?" Noah chuckles.

"That's reason number two." I beam at him.

"Reason number two? Really?" He cocks a brow. "How were you planning on paying for everything?"

"I think you're forgetting that I still have one of your cards." I peck his lips when he laughs.

Three hours later and a lot of shopping bags in our grasp, we make our way back to the car. I now have ten new pairs of heels, a few new dresses, shirts, skirts, and pants. I even got an evening gown for tonight since the boys said it was an extremely fancy restaurant.

When I tried it on, their faces said everything—it was perfect. I had never seen them speechless, certainly not Gabe. His jaw just hung open the whole time, then he swallowed and let it drop again.

Noah looks at the time on his watch and groans as he and Gabe set all the bags in the trunk. I giggle with amusement as I watch him. "I told you we wouldn't have time to do everything."

"What time is it?" Gabe asks, shutting the trunk.

"Three," Noah tells him.

"Fuck... maybe we could still go for an hour or two? Our reservation is only at eight." He scratches his head.

I place my hands on both of their chests, running my palms up until they slide over the side of their necks and my fingers caress at their napes. "Or we can say *'fuck the beach'* and go home and have a little fun before we go out to dinner?"

"I like the sound of that, but we promised you the beach," Gabe says.

"We can just go tomorrow if it's nice." I peck his lips. "I don't need the beach, baby. The only thing I want is you two. And I'd much rather go home and make you both mine than go spend an hour in the sand crowded by people."

Noah grabs my hip on one side and pulls me in, capturing my lips. "Make us yours."

And I do just that. For the next three hours, I make them mine in every way possible. Just as they make me theirs.

We're now getting ready for our dinner reservation, and my stomach is in knots. I'm not sure why; we've been out in public all day, but this feels different. It feels like we're finally stepping out of our bubble and saying hello to the world for the first time. Like our relationship is really about to begin.

I'm already expecting there to be stories about us tomorrow morning. Speculations, pictures, and opinions. But I'm ready for it all; I know it might not be accepted by many, and I'm okay with that. All I care about is that I am theirs and they are mine.

My hair has grown again and now reaches almost halfway down my back. It amazes me the difference in two months; I'm not sure what's making it grow so fast, but I'm not complaining. Neither are the boys. They really like being able to pull it and watch it fall down my back when they fuck me from behind.

I finish up my smokey-eye makeup and apply a coat of deep red lipstick over my lips. I've already curled my hair and passed my fingers through it numerous times to give it more of a wave effect. Once I'm satisfied with my look in the mirror, I step out of the bathroom and over to my dress that waits for me on the bed.

I quickly slip my feet into a new pair of open-toe stilettos and secure the ankle straps in place. Then I pick up the dress and pull it over my hips, passing my arms through the small straps, then walk over to the stand-up mirror to look it over.

At first, I thought the dress might be too much for a fancy dinner, but Noah and Gabe assured me it was perfect and that they wouldn't accept any other dress than this one. The dress itself is a form-fitted silver gown, covered in rhinestones from head to toe, and almost gives off a nude effect.

The length drops down to the floor, with a slit up my left thigh. The sides are cut out, exposing my waist and back, with a deep V-neck. Only a thin strap at my back ties the whole thing together, preventing the two over my shoulders from slipping constantly.

I reach back with my hands just as Noah enters the room looking dashing in his suit. "Let me," he says as he walks over and secures the back of my dress. He kisses my neck and looks me up and down through the mirror. "You look divine, Kitten."

"Thank you. You look mighty handsome as well." I smile, turning to face him. He's dressed in charcoal gray dress pants, black dress shirt, and a black suit jacket.

He reaches behind his back, retrieving a small rectangular box from I'm not sure where. "I have a little something for you." He lifts the lid to the box, and a beautiful diamond necklace winks back at me.

I gasp, my hands coming over my mouth. "Noah...this is beautiful." I look up at him with a smile. "Is this where you ran off to while we were shopping?"

While I was in one of the shops trying on clothes, I came out of the dressing room to find Noah gone. Gabe told me he had gotten a call and went outside to take it, but I now know that was a lie.

"I couldn't exactly tell you about your gift." He smirks. "Turn around, I want to put it on you." I do as he asks and watch him through the mirror as he secures the clasp behind my neck.

I feel my eyes grow misty as I'm suddenly overwhelmed with emotions. These two beautiful souls have been nothing but exceptionally great to me from the very beginning. They're attentive and loving, loyal to a fault, and I have no idea where I'd be without them. I never want to live a single moment without them ever again.

"I love you, Noah Adler." My whispered words come out broken as I hold back the tears that threaten to spill.

He looks up once he hears me, his eyes filled with worry as he quickly turns me to face him. "Hey, what's wrong, love?" he asks, cupping my cheeks.

I place my hands over his wrists, smiling and shaking my head. "Nothing's wrong, I promise. I'm just so happy right now, and I haven't been this happy in a long time. It feels like a lot and may even seem silly, but everything you guys have done for me since the beginning means the world to me, and I want to thank you for that. I love you both so much it fucking hurts when I think about possibly losing you."

"Then don't. Don't think about it, because you'll never lose us, Kitten. We aren't going anywhere. We love you too much to ever leave you. A world without you would mean nothing to us." He kisses the two tears that managed to slip out on either cheek, then my lips. "I love you more than life itself, Veronica. Never forget that. This is forever."

"Forever," I whisper back. I turn back to the mirror and curse myself for ruining my makeup. "Fuck, now I need to redo it. I really need to start investing in waterproof makeup."

Noah chuckles. "I'll go wait downstairs with Ellis. Take all the time you need." He kisses my head then walks out of the room while I make my way back to the bathroom.

Ten minutes later and my makeup once again properly in place, I head down the stairs, finding both my men waiting for me at the bottom. With every step down I take, their eyes grow hungrier and hungrier.

"Fuck, baby. You look incredible." Gabe steps up, passing an arm around my waist and pulling me in as I laugh, my hands falling to his chest. "I can't wait for the world to see you."

"And I can't wait to come back home and get you out of this suit." I glide my fingers over the lapels of his navy-blue suit jacket.

Beneath it, he's wearing a white dress shirt and the same color dress pants as his jacket, with fancy brown shoes. His hair is pushed back with the top portion mostly falling to one side. It gives him a sexy, naughty boy look.

"I was just thinking the same thing." He grins then comes in to bite my earlobe. "But about this dress. I believe I may have the missing pieces to complete your outfit." He pulls away and brings forward the hand he had hidden behind his back. Another gift, this one a small square, but not small enough to be a ring.

"For you, my queen."

I open it, revealing a stunning diamond bracelet and diamond earrings that seem to match the necklace Noah gave me earlier. "God, you guys!" I look up toward the ceiling, blinking rapidly and fanning my face. "Damn it, I'm going to cry again. What is happening to me?!"

"Maybe you're pregnant. I did say we might be announcing it soon." Gabe laughs.

I quickly look down and point a finger at him. "Do not joke about that. I am not pregnant." I gaze back down at the box in his hand. "They're amazing. You two spent way too much on me today."

Gabe takes the bracelet out and gives the box to Noah. "It will never be too much if it's for you." He passes it around my wrist when I hold it out and straps it in place.

I glide my forest-green nail over each diamond as Noah hands me the earrings. Once I've secured them in place, I look at these two marvelous men who stand before me, ready to offer me the world, ready to move mountains, and capture the moon and stars for me. And without a doubt, I know I'd gladly do the same for them.

I never thought I'd let myself feel this way again, that I'd never let myself go again. That I'd never let another man consume me entirely. And yet, it's all I crave from these two, and I'll let them do it over and over again.

I'd willingly let myself fall into an abyss if it meant finding them at the end of the seemingly endless journey through the dark. Because they are my home, the only place I ever want to be.

My forever.

And I'd do anything for them.

Chapter Thirty-Eight

VERONICA

Where we belong.

We arrive at the restaurant in Gabe's Porsche, and a valet comes over immediately. I startle when the door is pulled open for me while Gabe and Noah step out from the front. I'm so used to New York City's street parking that I was expecting us to have to do the same even if it is a fancy restaurant.

There's a carpet along the floor leading up to the doors, where a man dressed in a suit waits patiently to open the door for us. I thank the young gentleman holding the car door and step onto the carpeted sidewalk with Noah and Gabe at my side, while the valet runs around the hood of the car and leaves with the Porsche.

I quickly notice the few paparazzi waiting on the sidelines with their cameras in hand. From what Noah told me, this is a hotspot for celebrities, so it would make sense for them to hang around the place. Both men give me their arm, and I slide my hands above the crook of their elbows, smiling at each one as we step toward the doors.

Within a few seconds, a few cameras go off, but nothing exaggerated. One of them comes up closer and asks politely for us to stop and take a picture. I'm a little surprised by how nice he was that I found myself stopping and nodding at him.

I'm so used to how we see paparazzi and reporters in movies that I expected them to be aggressive. I guess at the end of the day, they're just humans trying to make a living for themselves.

"One last outing before preseason?" he asks with a smile.

"Something like that. We wanted to treat our girl to a nice night before the season starts," Noah says with a nod.

The guy's brows skyrocket as he registers Noah's words. "And may I ask who this young lady with you tonight is?" *Damn, if all reporters could be this nice, celebrities might not be so against them.*

"This is Veronica Masters," Gabe starts, turning his head to me with a wide grin. "Our girlfriend."

And just like that, the news was out, and cameras started flashing galore with questions being shouted at us from every angle. Noah quickly turns us back toward the door and ignores the rest of their questions, walking us in.

After two hours of fine dining, as they call it, we're finally walking out of the restaurant. And I'm guessing news traveled fast because there are even more reporters waiting outside, and they instantly begin to take our pictures the second we hit the carpeted walkway. Thank God the valet shows up quickly with our car, and we get to jump in and drive off within the next few minutes.

The restaurant was beyond chic, clearly made for the rich and famous. I almost felt out of place with my tattoos, piercings, and crazy-colored hair. But with all the thirsty male eyes that turned my way as we were led to our table, that feeling quickly evaporated.

There's something satisfying about gaining all male attention in a room, although the women accompanying them didn't seem too pleased. Neither did Noah and Gabe. I could feel their jealousy radiating off them as Noah walked me down to our table, with his hand at the small of my back. Which was then followed by Gabe taking out my chair and kissing my cheek as I sat down.

We sat at a circular table with both my men reaching across the table to kiss my hand and show any form of affection possible while in public. We had a great time, despite feeling a lot of eyes on us, but once again, it was expected. It's not every day you go to a restaurant and spot three people having a romantic dinner together.

"Well, that was something," I say, giggling from the back seat.

"Yeah, we'll definitely be all over the tabloids by morning." Gabe laughs.

Noah looks back, between the seats. "Did you have a good time at least?"

I reach in front and put my hand on his shoulder. "I did; it was amazing, and everything was delicious. Thank you for taking me there." I smile, but a thought lingers in my mind.

Noah smirks as he assesses my features. "But?" *God, these two really know me too well.*

I sigh. "I'm starving! All the portions were so small! I swear it was like they ran out of food and divided everything into eighths. Can we please stop at McDonald's or something and get some food that will stuff my little belly? Please, please, pleeeease?"

"She's right, for the price we paid, I would have expected to be full by the end of the night." Noah turns to Gabe. "What do you say, health nut? Want to give yourself an extra cheat day for your month?"

Gabe groans, throwing his head back against the seat but keeping his eyes on the road. "That's like the unhealthiest thing in the world. I feel like I'm being punished for breaking a rule when you know we've been careful."

"I know, baby. But I don't think I can wait for us to get home and make something. I need to eat now, like right now. Please?" I grab onto both his shoulders. "If you say yes, we'll spend all day in bed tomorrow, and I'll let you do anything you want to me. I'll let you live out your dirtiest, darkest fantasies." I waggle my brow.

He laughs. "That does sound pretty tempting."

"Come on, say yes. Anything for me?" I pout my lip and flutter my eyelashes.

He turns his head quickly and looks at me, and instantly, I know I've won. A heavy sigh leaves his lips, his left hand coming up to rest above mine that's still on his shoulder. "Anything for you, Vixen."

Half an hour later, my belly is full, and I am well and truly satisfied. We're finally home from our long and exciting day, and I'm more than ready to get into bed. But there's still one more thing I want to do before that.

I walk over to Blubber, who sleeps soundly in his little heated kitty home, and kiss his head. He stretches his paw out and purrs with content. When I stand up and turn around, I find both men watching me closely.

I rotate to the side, giving them a profile view of myself, and slowly bend in half. Keeping my legs straight, I reach down to my ankles and unstrap my heels. When I'm done, I come back up the same way I went down and kick off my heels. Flicking my hair over my shoulder, I face them once more and leisurely make my way to them, swaying my hips from side to side. I glide my fingernails across Gabe's chest, then over to Noah's, who stands at his side.

Rounding his body, I grab one lapel and then the other once I'm standing behind him. Slowly slipping his jacket down his arms, I throw it over to the back of the couch once it's off. I go over to Gabe, taking the exact same steps and placing it beside Noah's. I turn to them and take their hands in mine, walking backwards toward the stairs.

"No rules tonight. I promise I won't punish you for this tomorrow." I release their hands only long enough to face the stairs, then head up with my men behind me.

Once in the room, they stop as I take an extra step toward the bed. I face them once more, reaching back to unclip the strap at the back of my dress, then let the thin shoulder straps slip down my arms. The dress pools at my feet, leaving my body in only a tiny excuse for panties. Their eyes hood and fill with lust as I slowly walk up to them, placing a hand on each of their chests.

"I want to try something new tonight."

"Yeah?" Noah asks quietly.

"Mhmm," I hum and bite my lip. "Remember that thing you mentioned the first time in the cave that I was confused about?" I turn my gaze to Gabe with a smirk.

His eyes widen the moment it clicks. "Oh fuck…"

"Yes, oh fuck." I trail my pointer finger down their chests until I hit their waistbands, hooking my finger in. "I want you both to fuck me… I want you both to fuck my pussy tonight… at the same time."

"It's going to be a lot, Kitten. Are you sure you want this?" Noah asks with worried eyes.

"I do. I want to try at least." I nod.

"If it hurts too much, you tell us, and we'll stop, okay?" He cradles the right side of my face with his palm.

"I promise."

Gabe brings his hand to my left cheek. "We'll be gentle with you. We'll go slow."

I look at both my men with so much love and devotion. "I trust you both."

I remove my finger from their waistbands and take a step back before turning around. I shimmy out of my panties, bending to give them a view of my ass until they hit the floor. I straighten and crawl onto the bed, sitting facing them with my knees bent and wide open as I place my weight on one hand behind me.

"Now undress while I touch myself." I smirk and bring my other hand up, licking the tip of two fingers and gliding them down my body, over my breasts, down my smooth stomach, and finally where I want them most. "The first one to undress gets my mouth around their cock." I bite my lip on a moan as my fingers run through my slick folds and back up to circle my clit delicately.

"And the other?" Gabe asks, his hands halting at the buttons on his dress shirt.

"The other gets to eat my pussy until I come." I wet my lips.

I watch as they continue undressing, rubbing at my clit, then sliding one finger into my channel as I moan. Pumping slowly, I insert a second one, feeling my juices leak from my core. I drop my head back, letting my body enjoy the feeling as my hips leisurely grind against my fingers.

When I bring my gaze back to the handsome men before me, I find that they've only removed their shirts. Shoes, socks, and pants are still in place. They look at one another, slowly taking one shoe off, then the other. Stopping. Then toeing out of their socks at a snail's pace.

I laugh when I realize what's going on. "Are you two seriously fighting over who gets to eat me out?"

Noah smirks with a shrug. "What can we say? We like your pussy."

"More than a blowjob?" I quirk a brow.

"Definitely more than a blowjob." Gabe nods in agreement.

I shake my head and giggle. "How about you both get to eat my pussy? I could go for two orgasms." I shrug like it's an everyday thing. *It is.*

Suddenly, the rest of their clothes are flying off, and they're both jumping at me, fighting for who gets to do it first. Gabe manages to bump Noah out of the way and doesn't waste time sealing his lips to my mound. He smacks my hand out of the way as my laugh quickly turns into a moan.

Noah chuckles and comes over to my side, sitting next to me. He cups the back of my head tenderly and brings me in for a kiss. "I don't need your mouth unless it's against mine." He deepens the kiss, angling my head back and slowly pushing me down until I'm lying on the bed.

His hand leaves my head and trails down to my breast, circling my erect nipple, then pinching it with a small tug. "Noah..." I cry into his mouth as he pulls harder, twisting and turning.

His lips leave mine and come down to my other breast, sucking it into his mouth and nibbling on the skin around my peak, leaving love bites in his wake. My mind quickly grows dizzy when Gabe laps up at my pussy, then slides two fingers in. He quickly replaces them with three and pumps in and out while flicking my clit with the tip of his tongue.

"Oh God, Gabriel..." My hips begin to buck along with him.

One hand comes down to fist his hair as my other goes to Noah's head. This ever-real feeling blooms in my body, my core tingling and burning with each wet kiss, each suck, each bite, and lick. Within minutes I'm squirming, wiggling in every which way, crying out as the sensation consumes me and I tip over the edge.

But they don't give my orgasm time to dwell, within seconds both men rip themselves off me and switch places. Gabe capturing my breasts into his mouth and hands, while Noah flicks at my overly sensitive flesh.

He laps up my wetness, poking his tongue into my contracting pussy, then back up to my clit, where he sucks it into his mouth as I continue to throb and squirm against him. One of his arms loops around my leg and settles over the bottom of my stomach, where he presses down to keep me in place as he pushes four fingers into me.

"Oh shit!" I cry out, arching my back off the bed and forcing my breast even more into Gabe's mouth, who happily accepts it. It takes all of three pumps and a bite to my clit for me to detonate once more on a scream. "FUCK!!!" I feel myself spilling over, the sheets becoming wet beneath me, and my thighs feeling slicker by the second.

When I finally come to, I'm gasping desperately for air, my arms thrown above my head and completely limp. Gabe pulls away from my bruised breasts with a huge grin on his face as he looks down between my legs. Noah lifts his head, beard and chin dripping with my wetness, and a cocky smirk playing on his lips.

"Now that's what I call coming on someone's face." Gabe chuckles. "That was fucking hot, baby. Even I got little splashes from how hard you squirted. Fuck, I want to make that happen again."

I shake my head. "No, I need you inside of me. Now." I reach out, placing my hand at his nape, and pulling him down to me as I take his lips. "Please."

"Anything you want, Kitten." Noah climbs up the mattress beside me, lying on his back as Gabe lifts me off the bed and flips me over Noah, putting us chest to chest.

One hand comes into my hair, while the other holds my hip. I grind down on him, fusing my lips to his, tongues dancing as we moan together. Suddenly, hands push against the back of my thighs, placing my knees higher up against Noah's sides.

Gabe lifts my ass a little higher, and then I feel Noah's cock at my entrance as he pushes me back down onto it. I moan as Noah groans with displeasure. "Hey! Don't get mad at me for helping out; you were taking too long, and I want in."

I giggle, pulling my mouth away from a frowning Noah. "What's wrong, Casanova? Don't enjoy another man's hand on your dick?"

"I never enjoy having a rough male hand grabbing my cock unless it's my own."

I move up and down his length a few times. "There, is that better?" I say breathlessly as my clit rubs against his pubic bone.

"So much fucking better." He bites my bottom lip, pulling it out slightly, then flicks my septum piercing with the tip of his tongue.

Gabe settles in behind me with a bottle of lube in hand, while Noah's legs rest between our spread ones. "Noh, hold on to her while I try to ease in. Baby, I'm going to need you to stay still and focus on breathing, okay? It's going to hurt, but I promise it will feel good after."

"Okay." I nod while Noah wraps one arm around my back, securing me into place as I rest on my forearms on either side of his head.

Gabe squirts some lube in his hand and rubs it over his length, then drops it down beside him and places a hand at the base of my back. Seconds later, I feel something trying to squeeze in beside Noah's cock.

With a little stretching and deep breathing, it slips in. "That wasn't that bad," I say with a sigh.

Gabe chuckles. "That was only my finger, baby."

"Oh God..."

"We don't literally want to hurt you, Vixen. So, we're stretching you out as much as possible first." He leans in and kisses my back, then slips his finger back out, pushing two in instead.

"Ahh..." I suck in air and let out a shaky breath.

"Shh... it's okay, Kitten. You're okay." Noah's free hand caresses my hair as he kisses my cheek. He pumps his hips barely a fraction, but enough for me to feel it, just as Gabe pulls his fingers back and slides them back in.

"Oh, fuck!" I drop my head against Noah's shoulder, feeling his rapid heartbeat against me.

"She's as ready as I'll get her," Gabe tells Noah while removing his fingers. I hear the cap of the lube being popped open, more squirting, some leaking along my folds, then closing again. He replaces his hand on my back, shifting on the bed until I can sense him closer. "Ready, baby?"

When I don't answer, Noah cups my cheek. "We don't have to do this if you changed your mind, it's okay."

"No... I'm okay." I take a deep breath, then let it out slowly. "I'm ready."

"Such a good girl. God, she's perfect." Gabe kisses my back then nudges at my entrance, and I can immediately tell that isn't his finger. With a bit of pressure, he slips in, just the head, and holy fuck, it feels like I'm about to rip in half.

"OH FUCK! Oh, fuck. Oh, fuck!" I squeeze my eyes shut and bury my head into Noah's neck, holding my breath and praying for the pain to fade.

I hear Gabe make a choking sound behind me like he's in pain. "Baby, I need you to relax," he growls out. "Holy shit, I swear she's cutting circulation to my dick." His hand fists at my back as he growls again.

Noah's hand rubs along the top of my spine, up and down as he tries to soothe me. "Breathe, Kitten. You need to breathe, or else the pain won't go away. Concentrate on my voice, okay?" His whispered words flow through my ear.

I nod, taking deep breaths as tears well behind my eyelids. "That's it, my love. You're doing so well. We're so proud of you. So, so proud."

Finally, I feel my body relax a bit, and Gabe breathes out in relief. "I'm going to push a little more in now."

"Okay..." My voice comes out wobbly.

I'm starting to doubt myself, doubt that I can do this. I researched it, I know it's possible, and some women do it. But fuck, I was not prepared for that kind of pain. *Is this what labor feels like?*

He squirts more lube on us and pushes in an inch more. "OW!!" I clamp down on Noah's shoulder, teeth digging into his flesh as I cry out. My body goes tense once more as I begin to shake violently.

Noah hisses and curses but doesn't push me away. Instead, his hold on me tightens to the point where I feel like I'm suffocating. Even Gabe now holds my hips, trying to stop me from shaking so much.

"Breathe, baby. You need to breathe. It'll get better once you do, I promise," Gabe says, trying to calm me down, but it's too much. Their voices are distant in my mind now, and all I can feel is this blinding pain coursing through my body.

"Kitten." Noah tries to gain my attention, but I can't focus on anything but the pain. "Kitten, listen to me," he says a bit louder while gliding his fingers through my hair, but again, not getting a response from me. "Veronica!" He fists my hair and yanks on it, hard enough for my teeth to unlatch from his skin as I whimper, his stern voice finally filtering through.

He releases my back and hair and grabs my face between his hands as tears track down my face on their own. "It hurts so much..." I sob, unable to stop myself from trembling.

"I know, love. But we're past the worst, and you did beautifully. You're so strong, Kitten. Just breathe with me." He wipes away my tears. "In... out... in... out..." I instantly feel myself relax, slowly the pain fading away, turning into a dull but bearable sting. "How do you feel now?"

"Better..." I sniff. I hate that I'm crying, but it's like my body is reacting on its own.

"You're beyond incredible, Veronica." He kisses my lips tenderly. "You're doing such a good job."

"I don't know if I can..." I admit in a broken voice, feeling like I've failed them.

"That's okay, Kitten. We can stop if you want. We told you we would if it were too much. You've already done a lot, and we completely understand if this is too much. We would never want to force you into something you didn't want." He kisses me again. "We love you, Veronica. We only want to make you happy."

"But I want to make you happy too..."

"You already do, baby. You make us happy every single day, just by being here, with us." Gabe leans in to kiss my back once more. "By being ours."

"Do you want to stop, Kitten?"

"I..." I chew on my lip, their words hitting me deep inside my heart and soul. Somehow, they've managed to soothe me enough that I hardly feel the pain anymore, all I feel is them. And this is what I want—for us to be connected this way, entirely. "No... I want to keep going."

Noah searches my eyes for a moment, looking for a sign of hesitation or doubt. But when he doesn't find any, he looks past my shoulder and nods to Gabe.

"I'm going to push in all the way this time, I'll go slow, but I won't stop, okay?" Gabe says, his hand now running up and down my spine.

I feel their hips moving slightly, most likely to keep themselves erect since we have been just lying here for a while, and my crying probably didn't help. Although the feeling is a lot and intense, the tiny movements send shockwaves through my body, and I begin to crave more of it.

"Okay, I'm ready." I take another deep breath as he pushes deeper in, focusing on my breathing the whole time.

My eyes trained solely on Noah, mouth gaping. "Holy shit! Oh, fuck! Oh my God!" I drop my head back down against Noah with a groan and a whimper.

"That's it, baby. I'm almost there, just a little more." Gabe grunts; I can hear both of them breathing hard. I can't imagine what this feels like for them.

Ten seconds later, I feel Gabe's thighs pressing against me as he fully seats himself. "Holy fuck, Vixen. You have no idea how incredible this feels."

Noah groans, the veins in his neck popping as his nostrils flare. "I'm not afraid to admit that I won't last long." He chuckles but groans again when I giggle along with him. "God, Kitten. My dick feels like it's seconds away from exploding."

"How are you feeling, baby?" Gabe shifts slightly and I moan.

"Good, full. I feel like you're everywhere. But I need you to move, please," I say breathlessly.

"Fucking finally." Noah closes his eyes. I kiss his jaw, his neck, then his shoulder where my teeth marks are clearly visible.

Gabe's hands come back to my hips, while Noah cradles me like he did earlier. One hand at my nape, the other arm wrapped around my back. And then they pull back at the same time, and I swear, I see stars. Right before they push back in, and I jump off the cliff. Crying out as I come, my body shakes violently, hips jerking uncontrollably. All it took was one pump, and I was gone. My body shattering for them, giving myself away in the most blissful way.

Apparently, that was the cue they were waiting for, because the second my slick pussy contracts against them, they begin to thrust harder, faster. They stay in sync, hips plowing into me simultaneously, and all I can do is scream and cry as another orgasm crashes into me, and another. The wave never fully extinguishes before the other rolls in.

My mind shuts off, my vision blurs, and my ears ring. All I can hear is my breath, the heavy pounding of my erratic heart. All I can feel is them, their hands, their shafts sliding in and out of me, stretching me beyond repair. To the point where every thrust feels like I'm being ripped in half in a marvelous way.

My toes curl, my back arches, my eyes roll back into my skull as I scream for the last time. My fourth climax since they've entered me, swallowing me whole until all that's left is a gasping, boneless vessel lying between them.

Wild, vicious roars erupt around me, the walls rattling with how loud their voices are propelled as they fill me to the brink. Their warm seed planting so deep within me I can almost taste it on my tongue.

Gabe's hands slip from my hips as he collapses above me, squishing me into a sandwich. Noah grunts with a huff, then somehow, with what little strength he has left, rolls Gabe off from above us until he's lying on his back at our side.

We stay lying down, no one talking for a few minutes until a bubble suddenly pops in my brain, and I begin to laugh. Noah then starts to chuckle beneath me, his chest rumbling against my ear, and within seconds, Gabe is laughing along with us. I think we've all lost a bit of our minds by now.

"Why are we laughing?" Gabe asks breathlessly as he continues, unable to stop the contagious effect.

"I don't know. But there's so much cum leaking out of me right now, it's ridiculous." My giggles slowly fade until all that's left is a dreamy smile on my lips.

"We'll get you cleaned in a minute, Kitten." Noah kisses my crown. "Thank you for giving us this. Thank you for trusting us."

"I'd do anything for you, both of you." I kiss Noah's chest and reach a hand over to caress Gabe's jaw as he watches me with adoration shining in his eyes.

A short while later, we've done our in-shower routine, where I wash them as they take care of my hair, then finish off with my body. I usually wait at least forty-eight to seventy-two hours before my first wash after getting it done, but after sex with these two, it's impossible not to wash your hair.

We've also changed the sheets of the bed and now have it all ready and set for nighttime. Noah and I climb in, and I watch as hesitation dances in Gabe's eyes, where he stands by the side of the bed, ready to wish me goodnight.

"Don't go, baby, please..." I reach for his hand, trying to pull him in. "You haven't had a nightmare in two weeks. Blubber has stopped every single one of them since. Please, just stay. We can just try it out, if anything happens, Noah will be there as well as Blubber. But I know it won't. I trust you, Gabriel."

He doesn't seem convinced, his mind working up reasons to say no.

"Ellis, she's right. I think it's time we tested it out. We won't know if the therapy and Blubber are actually helping until we try," Noah says calmly.

Slowly, Gabe nods, and my heart nearly explodes. Tears rise to my eyes as I stand on my knees and throw my arms around him. "Thank you."

"Let me just go get our little guy from downstairs, and I'll be back." He steps out of my hold and leaves the room, returning with our little furless ball in hand.

He climbs onto the bed, completely naked, just like Noah and me. Settling in on my other side, I turn to face him as Noah comes to spoon my back. He places Blubber between us and strokes his back with a nervous, shaky hand.

I cup his cheek, bringing his lips down to mine. "I love you, Gabriel. Remember that. Whatever happens, I'll always love you."

"I love you, too, Vixen. More than you'll ever know." He takes my hand and kisses my wrist, then places his palm on the back of mine and intertwines our fingers, letting our locked hands rest between us.

I turn my head to the side as Noah leans over to kiss me as well. "I love you, Noah."

"I love you, too, Veronica."

And we fall asleep like that, for the first time since the beginning of our relationship, all together in one bed, in each other's arms.

Where we belong.

Chapter Thirty-Nine

VERONICA

He definitely knew.

~ One Week Later ~

Well, that explains why I've been so emotional... and no, I am NOT pregnant.

Aunt Flow's in town!

Stupid, dumb, period!

And of course, it has to happen when I'm home alone. The boys are away for an exhibition game in Boston and won't be back until tomorrow. When I woke up this morning with horrible abdominal cramps and sweat sticking to my forehead, I knew what was happening.

I quickly got out of bed, ran to the bathroom to get my medication, and got into the bath. It helped for a few hours, but now it's acting up again, and I really wish I wasn't alone. I wish my boys were here to take care of me and help me feel better.

I don't want to bother the girls since I know they have their own lives, and asking them to come over for stupid period cramps would be silly. I'm a grown woman; I can deal with it on my own. Just like I did before they all came into my life.

I throw the blanket off my body and step out of Noah's bed, the one we've been sharing with Gabe every night for the last week. I've never been happier. Waking up to both my men cuddling me and kissing me has to be the best feeling in the world.

There was one night when Blubber's hissing noises woke me up. When I looked over, I found him by Gabe's head. His back was hunched in the air while he watched Gabe's face contort in pain as he shifted from side to side, clearly the beginning of a nightmare commencing.

I expected our little Blubber boy to attack him, but instead, he got even closer, sniffed around him, and then started licking away at his cheek and mouth. Within seconds, Gabe's whole demeanor changed, face and body relaxing until he sighed and went back to a peaceful sleep. Blubber then purred and rolled up in a ball against Gabe's neck, and that was the end of it.

Tears sprang to my eyes as I watched them, watched how much change had happened in just a short amount of time. I knew it, deep within my soul, that the worst was over, and my brave and handsome Pretty Boy was finally healing.

Walking out of the room, I head down to the kitchen to make myself some herbal tea as well as grab the heating pads, then settle in on the couch. A few seconds later, Blubber jumps up and nestles against my stomach, most likely wanting the heat from the pad over my lower abdomen.

"Hey, little Blubs. You gonna keep me company while your daddies are out?" I stroke his back. "You're such a good boy. I'm so proud of you," I whisper as my eyes begin to droop, and I fall asleep.

A few hours later, my phone rings on the side table, jolting me awake. I reach above my head and grab it, noticing Gabe's face filling my screen with an incoming video call. A quick glance at the time tells me they are minutes away from hitting the ice for their game.

Staying in my lying-down position on the couch, I swipe to answer the call and smile when my handsome boy comes into view. "Hi, baby."

"There's my pretty girl." He beams for a second before it drops, and a frown appears along his forehead. "Baby... what's wrong?"

My eyes well with tears at how quickly he picked up on my mood. "I'm okay. I promise, nothing to worry about..." My voice wobbles as I try to hold it together for them. I don't want them to be distracted before a game, even if it's a friendly one.

"Oh no... is it that time of the month?" he asks in a soft voice filled with concern.

Noah suddenly pops into the frame as well, looking displeased. "Why didn't you tell me this morning when I called you?"

"Because I didn't want you two to worry about me while you're away. I'm okay, I took my pills, and I have the heating pads on." I try to smile, but it's tight and weak.

"Kitten, you look pale as fuck, and you're clearly sweating. You aren't doing okay. You should have said something."

"And what would you have done? I'm here, and you guys are in Boston." I laugh with little humor, then instantly regret it when my stomach cramps up and pain shoots through my abdomen. "Ahh..." I scrunch my face and curl into a ball.

"Fuuuck..." Gabe looks on the verge of saying, '*fuck it,*' and marching out of that arena to get to me, while Noah looks down furiously at his phone.

"I'll be okay, I'm due for another dose, and it will be over by tomorrow morning."

I try to reassure them some more, but they aren't even listening to me anymore. Gabe still holds the phone but looks over at what Noah is doing. "Guys, it's fine, I swe—"

"Aubrey will be over in fifteen minutes," Noah finally speaks as they both look up with relief.

"Babe, you don't need to do that," I tell him, even though my heart warms at the action.

"I do. There is no way we're going to leave our girlfriend in pain all alone. So, it's either Aubrey or Marcos and Ricky. You pick," he says sternly, not taking no for an answer.

"Okay, yeah. I'd prefer Aubrey."

"That's what I thought." They both look up at the same time, someone calling their attention.

"Baby, we have to go. But we'll call you when we get to our room tonight." Gabe smiles with warmth.

"Okay, have a great game. Pretty Boy, block all those shots. Casanova, kick some ass." I giggle softly.

"It's a friendly game." Noah chuckles.

"And will that stop you from sending someone sailing into the boards?" I quirk a brow.

He laughs. "Absolutely not."

"That's what I thought. I love you both, have fun, and I can't wait to talk to you tonight." I blow them a kiss.

"We love you, too, baby," Gabe says as Noah nods.

"Take it easy until we get home, Kitten." He smiles and they hang up.

Ten minutes later, Aubrey steps out of the elevator followed by a big, burly dark-skinned man. "Hi, babe. I came as soon as Noah texted." She comes to my side, kneeling on the ground. "Why didn't you call me this morning? I would have come right away."

"You have your own life, Brey. And I know you were supposed to work tonight. You didn't need to drop everything for me."

She takes my hand. "Of course, I would. You're my best friend, Ronnie. My sister. You'll always come before work. They can survive without me for one night." She turns to look at the man she came in with. Standing, she waves a hand out to him. "Ronnie, this is Lionel. My personal bodyguard." She blushes slightly.

The man smiles at her in a fatherly way, then steps toward me as I sit up on the couch. He reaches out a hand and I shake it without hesitation. "Hello, Veronica.

Thank you for allowing me into your home."

"As long as you keep her safe, that's all that matters to me." I smile, then take the time to look him over.

He's very tall and bald-headed; I'd say early to mid-forties but clearly still in amazing shape. Although he seems threatening with his massive frame, he has that fatherly warmth in his eyes that makes you instantly trust him. I have a feeling Julian picked Lionel specifically for Aubrey, knowing how uncomfortable she is around men.

"That's the plan." He releases my hand and straightens to his full height, which must be at least six-foot-six. "Now, what can I help you with?"

"Oh, no. Please, just make yourself comfortable or explore. Anything you'd like."

"I know my job is to guard, but I do enjoy being helpful as well." He waits patiently for me to give him a task.

"He really does. He helps me out with my baking and even cleans the condo." Aubrey laughs as her blush spreads wider on her cheeks.

"Okay, well, I was just about to get my medication upstairs and make another tea," I tell him.

"On it, just let me know where everything is, and you two can settle down."

After informing him of everything, he goes up to Noah's room as Aubrey comes to sit beside me. "I did something," she says quickly in a hushed voice.

I giggle, taking the heating pad off my stomach and placing it on the table beside the couch. "What did you do?"

She brings her hand up to her lips and chews on her thumbnail. "I made some muffins two days ago."

I frown, confused. "Okay…"

"And I put them in a Tupperware and left them at Shane's office door," she mumbles around her thumb as she flushes a deep red, her ears taking on the same shade.

"Awww, why didn't you just give them to him personally?"

She lets go of her nail and turns to me with wide eyes. "I was going to, I even knocked on the door, and he shouted, *just a sec!*' through it. But then I freaked out and just left the container on the floor and ran away."

"For a small girl, she runs pretty fast." Lionel's deep laugh flows through the room as he comes down the stairs and wanders into the kitchen for the tea.

I turn in my seat, looking over the back of the couch. "You were there?"

"Of course, I was. I never leave her side. And for your information, no, she did *not* tell me she was about to bolt." He points a finger toward me.

I throw my head back as I erupt with laughter, then groan when a new wave of cramps comes through. Aubrey quickly stands and grabs the heating pad. "Let me go plug this one in."

"Thank you, there's a second one in the last drawer." I point toward it in the kitchen. Lionel takes it out and exchanges the heating pads with Aubrey. She scurries back and helps me place it over my belly. "Better?"

"Yes, thank you." I lean back against the couch as Lionel sets the tea beside me and a coffee for Aubrey. We both thank him as he takes a seat on the second couch beside us. "So, Lionel, did you make it out of view on time, or were you caught in the act?"

He chuckles. "I barely made it. I heard the door open just as I rounded the corner." He shakes his head. "It was honestly the last thing I expected her to do, so it caught me by surprise. I couldn't stop laughing once we were hidden, and she had to put her hand on my mouth to silence me." He laughs harder as he remembers the moment.

"You were going to get us caught. I didn't have a choice!" Aubrey glares at him.

"Brey, I can assure you that even if he didn't see you, Shane knows they were from you." I pat her leg, then take a sip of my tea.

"We don't know that." Her eyes go wide.

"We do," Lionel answers for me.

I watch with a happy smile as they continue to bicker about whether or not Shane knows who the baked goods are from. I'm happy to see Aubrey getting along so well with him; it reassures me that she'll be safe at the condo alone.

Now if only this asshole could show his face and get this all over with.

GABRIEL

~ Two Weeks Later / October ~

Next week is our first home opener of the season, and I am beyond thrilled to get back in the game. I know we've been having exhibition games, but that's not the same. I want to get back on the ice, hear all the fans shouting with every victory. That exhilarating sensation that flows through your blood as the puck comes flying your way, and you catch it just in time before it passes the red line and into the goal.

God, hockey is where I belong. It feels like home.

But that's not the only place that feels like home. No, the only other place is in the arms of a five-foot-ten, slim, blue-colored hair beauty. *Fuck, how did I ever get so lucky to have this amazing creature in my life?*

I lean against the doorframe to the bathroom, watching her finish straightening her hair in the mirror. She had it changed yesterday to a vivid dark blue with pure white ends. It's sexy as fuck and gives her this naughty glint in her eyes.

When I asked her why she was straightening her hair, since it's naturally straight to begin with, she gave me the *'are you dumb?'* look and didn't say anything. So, I quickly shut up and instead have been standing here for the past hour, taking in every step of her beauty routine.

"Don't you have something better to do? Like maybe get ready?" She looks over from the corner of her eye. She's being sassy, but I don't miss the little smirk playing along her lips.

I look down at my dark blue jeans and gray sweatshirt that cling to my muscles with the sleeves pulled up to my elbows. I even have my black sneakers on my feet. I don't know how much more ready I can get.

"I am ready." I narrow my eyes at her. "I've been ready for the past hour, compared to you," I finish with a smirk that earns me a glare.

"Yes, well, having you standing there is distracting me."

"Oh, is it?" I step into the bathroom, coming behind her and wrapping my arms around her waist as I rest my chin on her shoulder. "How so?"

"Because you keep looking at me like you want to eat me, and it's making my panties wet. Again." She smiles at me through the mirror.

Twenty minutes ago, she left the bathroom without saying a word and headed for the closet, where she quickly took off her thong and exchanged it for another. When I chuckled, she told me to shut up and went back to getting ready. I like knowing I affect her this easily.

"But I like getting you all wet." I nibble at her neck. "I could take care of you right here, right now, if you'd like," I whisper into her ear.

"Don't you dare, we're already five minutes behind schedule. Now go away. I'm nearly finished." She turns her face to the side and pecks my lips before shooing me away.

"All right, all right. I'm going." I lift my hands in surrender and walk backwards out of the ensuite, taking one last lingering look at her.

She's wearing a tight black leather skirt that reaches her mid-thigh with a white long-sleeved shirt that's glued to her body and tucked into the waistband of the skirt. Instead of her usual thigh-high stockings or socks, she has a pair of black heeled boots that reach just above her knees. Her makeup is pretty simple, with cat-eyed black eyeliner, a bit of gold eyeshadow, and nude lipstick. She looks sexy as sin.

I finally leave her alone and head down to make sure Noah's ready as well. We're about to head over to Burkley's for their gender-reveal party. And unlike Cecilia's, where Silas couldn't keep his mouth shut, no one knows the sex of the babies, not even the parents.

I find him standing in the living room, fingers tracing over one of the picture frames Ronnie hung in the living room for him. All the pictures he apparently had of his sister and father. Of the family he no longer gets to see, but that follows him everywhere he goes.

He's been doing this a lot over the past week, where he's present, but we can tell his mind is elsewhere. Dr. Hallaway said it was all a normal step of grieving. That we should simply let him be but remind him that we love him and are here for him if he needs to talk.

"Hey," I say softly, stepping up beside him.

His hand drops from the frame, but his eyes remain focused on the picture. It's one of him as a young boy, holding his baby sister in his arms. She must have been only a few weeks, old given the tiny onesie and newborn hat on her head.

"Hey."

He's dressed similarly to me. But instead of blue and gray, he has light-gray jeans on, with a white sweatshirt, sleeves pulled up, and white sneakers on his feet.

I place my hand on his shoulder, giving it a light squeeze. "You know we're here for you, brother. Anything you need, just say the word."

He finally turns to look at me, a small smile lingering on his lips. "Thanks, man."

I look back to the photograph, smiling at the tiny baby sleeping soundly in his grasp. "I can't wait for us to live that."

"Live what?"

"A baby. Holding that tiny little fragile life in your arms, knowing it will forever own your heart. Watch it grow and become its own person. Figuring out if it takes more after Mom or Dad." I chuckle. "If we have a girl, I hope she looks exactly like her mother." My heart constricts. "She'll be the most beautiful girl on this earth."

"Just like her mom," he finishes for me.

"Yeah…" My cheeks hurt from how wide my grin is until it drops. "Fuck!" I turn to face him with wide eyes. "You do realize how hard it will be to keep men away from our little girl, right? I mean, look at Vixen. They are drawn to her everywhere she goes…"

He nods with a frown. "We'll probably have to hire one of Julian's men to follow her everywhere. No way in hell am I letting any fucking prepubescent jock get near her."

"That's a good plan. We should probably mention it to him in advance. You know, so we can go through his guys and choose the best-fitted one."

"You mean the one who looks like he could crush you with his bare hands," Noah says.

I snap my fingers at him. "Exactly."

A giggle sounds behind us, making us turn toward it. Ronnie stands a few feet away, arms crossed over her chest with a raised brow and an amused look on her face. "You do realize that you two *are* jocks and that this child you are talking about doesn't exist, right? And before talking about hiring someone to follow her around, maybe mention it to the mother first."

I walk up to her, taking hold of her hips. "We just want to protect our little girl as best as we can."

"A little girl that isn't even in the making yet. And what if it's a boy?" She smirks.

"Simple, we'll teach him how to play hockey and how to get girls." Noah comes up and kisses her cheek.

"And what if he likes boys?" She narrows her eyes, still holding that side smile.

Noah and I exchange a wide-eyed look, unsure how to respond to that until I finally shrug. "Then you'll teach him how to get boys. I mean, look at the two you picked up; you know what you're doing." I wink and kiss her other cheek. We have no issues when it comes to that and will support our child no matter who they choose to love.

"Oh, you two are unbelievable." She laughs and pushes me away, picking up her purse from the side table. She kisses Blubber on the head who's sleeping on the couch, then walks toward the elevator. "You guys coming? And don't forget the gifts."

We arrive at Clay and Morgan's house a little over half an hour later, and apparently, we aren't the only ones late. Aubrey's just stepping out of her car as we park behind her.

"Oh, thank God! I thought I was the only one not on time." She rushes out as we walk over with our gifts in hand, hugging her quickly.

"Nope, this one was taking forever." I nod toward Ronnie as I lower to kiss Aubrey's cheek. "How are you doing, baby Ford?" I look around with a frown. "Where's your man?"

She turns pink. "He's not my man. You all need to stop calling him that," she whisper shouts.

I suck in my lips, holding back my laugh as Noah chuckles and Ronnie hides her face against my shoulder. "Umm... I was talking about your guard."

Her eyes go wide, the pink along her cheeks turning a bright red as clear embarrassment shines in her eyes. "Oh... um, he's down the street somewhere. He said I didn't have to worry and that they were around here watching from a distance."

"That's good." Noah nods.

"Yeah, although he thought someone was following us yesterday. He reported it back to Julian with as many details as he could give. He thinks it was Victor. I just don't understand why he would be following me." Aubrey frowns as Noah's eyes find mine quickly.

He told me about what happened a few weeks ago during his morning jog, but we both agreed it was best to keep that information from Vixen, not wanting to cause her more worry.

Ronnie goes stiff beside me. "What?! He went after you? Why didn't Julian tell us?"

"Because we are still going over all the details and street surveillance." Julian pops up out of nowhere behind us with his two brothers. "We did not want to worry you without having actual proof that it was him."

"And did you? Find any proof?" Noah asks, turning to face him as we all do.

"From what unclear footage we can get, yes, it does appear to be him. But I would like to think he was not intending any harm to Miss Ford. With the length of space he was leaving between the two vehicles, I believe he was only sending a message," Julian informs us, like he's talking about the weather and not a man clearly threatening us in some way.

"What message?" I ask.

"Not to get too comfortable. That he is not going anywhere."

"And the car he was using? Do you have anything on that? Maybe that could be a lead," Ronnie questions next as she chews her lip.

"We've already looked into it. It was a rented car under fake registrations." Jessie smiles sympathetically.

"So, another dead end." She sighs, coming into my chest for comfort.

She's always acting so bravely, but I know deep down this is still affecting her. I see her looking over her shoulder every now and then when we're out in public. I see the way her eyes search the place when we pass through the lobby at home.

How she jumps slightly every time the desk clerk asks if she needs him to call a town car because she was too focused on looking around that she didn't even notice him standing there. I wish I could end this all for her right here and now, help her the same way she's helped me.

"Look, I know it feels like we aren't helping," Jessie starts as he takes a step closer and puts his hand along her back; her muscles tense under the contact, but she doesn't say anything. "But I assure you, we're trying. We haven't stopped searching. I have people looking into any possible lead around the clock, no matter how small or unlikely it is. We even had three more out of the seven missing units searched. We're narrowing it down. We'll get him. I promise."

She nods against me but doesn't look at him. Finally, he retreats and goes back to standing between his two brothers. It's as I watch them that a thought occurs to me. "Wait, why are you guys here?"

Julian sighs with annoyance. "Apparently being a friendly neighbor extends to baby shower invitations."

"It's not a baby shower, it's a gender-reveal party. And I, for one, am excited and happy to be invited. You could do with having more friends, you know." Jessie nudges Julian in the side with his elbow.

Julian glares at him with daggers in his eyes. "I do have friends," he says through gritted teeth.

"No, you have Shane and us. We don't count." Jessie grins at his brother just as a purring engine pulls up to the curb. Shane steps out of his black Audi R8 and rounds the hood with a gift bag in hand. *Fuck, that's a beautiful car.*

Aubrey gasps then spins on her heels. "Oh God, I need to go... Yup. We... we should head in." She takes a step forward but stops when she's asked to.

"Aubrey, wait." Shane skips over, catching up to her. He stops a foot away from her, then looks at us all with a nervous, awkward smile.

Coach is a pretty confident guy, who seems so sure of himself and stands tall and proud all the time. But when he's around Aubrey, this nervous, boyish side of him comes out. It's comical to see the change happen.

She turns to face him, a spatter of red blotches all over her neck and cheeks. Jesus, these two are hilarious. We should start filming them and a few years down the road show them how embarrassing and awkward they used to be around each other.

"I just wanted to... um... thank you." He slides his fingers through his hair, pushing it back off his forehead, then gives her a charming grin, dimples popping out.

She sighs, clearly swooning, then her eyes turn wide, and she straightens. "Oh... I don't know what..." Ronnie snorts against my chest, giggling under her breath. Aubrey looks quickly over, then back at Shane with a defeated look in her eyes. "You're welcome," she finally says, admitting to whatever she did.

Then they just stand there, smiling at each other like two lunatics, while we all watch with amusement and second-hand embarrassment. *God, tell me that's not what Noah and I look like when we look at Ronnie...*

"There you guys are!" The front door flies open and out comes an exhausted-looking Morgan with her hand on her round belly. She's only twenty-one weeks along, but it's clearly showing there's more than one in there.

Aubrey and Shane quickly take a step back from each other, as if they were doing something inappropriate just as the rest of our gang comes to join us outside in front of the house. *I guess the party's happening out here then.*

"What's taking you all so long to get inside?" She stops in front of us as Clay comes up to her side and places his arm around her hip, the rest joining in as well.

"We were just talking before going in," I tell them with a smile.

"Okay, well, while we're all out here... Mind telling us why we have big goons following us around everywhere we go?" Emma quirks a brow with a knowing smirk.

Well, shit. I guess we weren't as sneaky as we thought.

Chapter Forty

NOAH

Sneaky kids and cupcakes.

"You all know?" I frown at Emma's question, looking from one woman to the others.

"Clay told me what was going on, he didn't feel safe letting me wander around without me knowing what was happening." Morgan smiles tenderly.

"And Silas can't keep a secret; you all know that." Cecilia giggles.

"Why am I not surprised these men could not keep anything to themselves," Julian mutters under his breath as I chuckle.

"That's not true! I simply tell you everything because you're my wife and best friend." Silas narrows his eyes at her.

"Yeah, well, Greyson didn't tell me shit. But the big gorilla of a man made himself known when Tommy cornered me at the store last week." Emma crosses her arms over her chest and pops her hip.

"He what?" Grey glares down at her. I guess this is the first time he's hearing about it. "Why didn't you tell me this?!"

She waves him off. "It's fine. For some reason he thought that we still had some unfinished business and that I was playing games with him. I told him to fuck right off. I was even about to punch him when he grabbed my arm. But then this muscle man came out of nowhere and picked him up by the back of his shirt. Told him if he ever touched me or came near me again, he'd rip him in half." She smirks wickedly.

"I don't even know how to process all of that," Greyson mumbles with a frown.

"What exactly did he tell you?" Julian asks with a displeased expression. I'm guessing that was against direct instructions.

"Not much, he was about to walk away and act like he was just at the right place at the right time. But it wasn't the first time I saw him, so I asked him to cut the crap, and that's when he said that I had nothing to worry about, that he was hired to protect me at all costs from any harm that came my way." She shrugs, to which Julian nods.

"I do wish you had told us what was going on, sweetie. You shouldn't have had to go through all this alone." Morgan reaches out and places her hand on Veronica's arm.

"I know, but it wasn't your problem to deal with. And I was afraid that you would distance yourselves if you knew everything..." She looks down, vulnerability taking place in her gaze.

"Never! How many times do we have to remind you all? We're family, and family sticks together." Cecilia steps up, wrapping her arms around Ronnie.

"So, back to my question. Can someone fill me in, please?" Emma waits patiently, looking at all of us.

Finally, Veronica gives them a quick résumé of what's been going on with Victor, and the more she talks about it, the more weight I can see lifting off her shoulders. This is how she'll heal from her past, by talking about it openly.

Once all is said and done, it's time to head in and join the rest of the celebration. Everyone is already here, parents and the rest of our team with their spouses mingling about. Their large entertainment room is covered in blue and pink baby-themed decorations, with little games and activities to guess what the babies' genders are.

Veronica, Gabe, and I stand by a table set out with three different types of brooches lying all over it. The first is a full blue pin written with, *Double Boy'*. The second is all pink and says, *'Double Girl'*. And the third is cut diagonally, pink on one side, blue on the other, with *'Boy + Girl'* written in the center.

"What do you guys think she's having?" Gabe asks, smiling down at the table. "I'm going with all girls." He picks up a pink brooch and fastens it to his shirt.

I reach for an all-blue one. "I'm thinking two boys. I can totally see her being a mama to a couple of boys." I secure it in place while Veronica continues to look over each one, her fingertip tapping against her bottom lip.

"I think you're both right." She picks up the boy/girl one and hands it to me. "I bet she'll have both. It only makes sense she'd have it all."

She smiles at me as I pass the pin through her white shirt, making sure not to poke her. When I'm done, she leans in and kisses me. I love these little tender moments between us.

We go around the room, greeting everyone along the way until we reach a beverage table filled with anything you could ask for. Despite it being a gender-reveal party, Morgan still offers alcohol to everyone, and I could kiss her for that right now.

I haven't touched anything but the occasional beer since we started therapy, but today I'm craving it more than usual. I can't explain why today, out of all days, I'm feeling off, but it's weighing down on me.

Maybe it came with the realization that when I start creating my own family, mine won't be there to see it grow. That they'll never get to meet this beautiful, incredible woman I get to call mine and spend the rest of my life cherishing. I'm not sure, but those thoughts must not help my mood.

I walk over to the beer cooler and take three out, handing one to Gabe and another to Veronica. When I hold the last in my hands, I instantly feel guilty taking it, but I need something to take the edge off. I look up to find Veronica watching me. "Is it okay?" I'm not sure why I feel the need to ask her permission, but I do it anyway.

"Of course, babe." She comes up, wrapping her arms around my neck. "I know it might feel like I'm punishing you sometimes by not letting you drink more, but I only want to help you." She pecks my lips. "I know today isn't a great day, so tell me what I can do to make you feel better."

I place my free hand on her hip, brushing my lips against hers. "Just being here with me, like this, is enough."

"Okay. But if ever you want to sneak off into a room later, I promise to make you feel so much better." She giggles against my smiling lips.

"I'll keep that in mind."

She pulls away smiling. "The offer stands all day." She winks and heads off to join the girls in their conversation.

Two hours later, it's finally time for the big reveal. Everyone is seated or standing around the room while Morgan and Clay stand in the center, surrounded by their guests.

"We wanted to take the time to thank you all for being here today, to celebrate with us something we've all waited patiently—" Morgan giggles when the girls clear their throats the moment she says the word. "Or not so patiently for."

Clay rubs up and down her back, his other hand resting on her belly as her eyes tear up with emotions. "We decided the best way to do our reveal today was to have you all participate in it," he says with a smile as his mother, Johanne, and Aubrey come into the circle, carrying large platters filled with cupcakes with blue and pink swirled icing.

"You'll all be given a cupcake—please wait until we tell you before biting into them!" He glares at some of our teammates who were just about to devour theirs. "Amongst all of them, two contain colored icing inside the treat. Either pink or blue, determining the gender of each baby. When you find it, please let us know."

Aubrey comes over with her tray, letting us pick out the ones we want. They're all identical on the outside, but it's fun to get to choose the one that's calling to you, in hopes that it will be the right one.

Gabe, Veronica, and I are all seated at one end of a couch, with little Gracie in my lap. She walked up to me thirty minutes ago and stretched out her arms in the air, clearly letting me know she wanted to sit on me. I didn't hesitate to pick up the little princess, placing her back against my chest, and she hasn't tried to leave since.

Every few minutes she turns her body to the side and pats my cheek with a warm and tender smile. It's the cutest thing I've ever seen, and I swear Veronica melts in her seat a little more with each time it happens.

Gabe groans beside Veronica as he looks down at the sugary treat in his hand. "Do I have to eat it?"

She smacks him in the arm with a glare. "Yes, you do. It's one cupcake, Pretty Boy. You aren't going to die." She rolls her eyes at him as I chuckle, then she refocuses her attention on the couple in front of us, waiting for everyone to have their baked goods in hand.

"Okay, is everyone ready?" We all nod, a chorus of *'yes'* tumbling around the room. "All right then, dig in!" Morgan clasps her hands together over her chest as she waits for someone to say something. Clay's eyes bounce around the room, looking at everyone's reaction.

"OH MY GOD! I got a blue!" Cecilia shouts from the opposite side of the room, bouncing in her seat.

Morgan and Clay hug each other, happy to find out one of the babies' gender. I look to my left, finding Veronica and Gabe already taking a bite of their cupcake and looking disappointed when it comes up empty.

I quickly peel back the paper cup from mine while trying to keep it away from the toddler in my lap, then bite into the moist cake. Instantly, I feel my teeth sink into something gooey in the center of the small cup, and I pull it away. A big pink blotch of icing right in the center catches my eye.

"Pink," I say out loud without even realizing it as I continue to stare at the soft color.

Morgan gasps as tears roll down her cheeks; her hands are now covering her mouth as she tries to control her emotions. Her eyes bore into mine when I look up at her, something flickering through them, but I can't tell what it is.

"Oh! I'm so happy!" Johanne reaches the happy couple and hugs them both. "I can't believe I get one of each." She sighs happily. "Now I know you've talked about boy names, but you haven't mentioned any girl ones. Did you have any in mind?"

Morgan beams widely at her. "Yes, actually we had one."

She then turns her gaze to me, and without her even needing to say it, I know the words that are about to leave her mouth. "We agreed that if we had a daughter, we'd like to name her Trinity... for you. If that's okay?"

I drop my head into the little girl's hair that sits before me, emotions quickly taking over as I try to swallow them down. I take deep breaths as my eyes fill with tears, and I squeeze them shut, not wanting to cry in front of all my friends and teammates once more.

I feel Veronica's hand gliding up and down my back soothingly as she sniffles a few times, just as many emotions coursing through her as well.

Suddenly hands press on my knees and when I lift my head, I find Morgan kneeling at my feet. "I know we didn't get to personally know her, but I wish we had. And I wanted to do something in memory of her, for you. To show you just how much you mean to us, Noah." She cups my cheek, stroking my cheekbone tenderly. "Your family is our family. When you miss them, we miss them too."

"Thank you," I croak out, then tilt my head up, pressing the thumb and finger of my free hand into my eye sockets as the tears slip out. I use the hand that still holds my half-eaten cupcake to tighten my hold around Gracie's body as Morgan stands and returns to her husband.

"Little Tulip, no!" Emma shrieks, hands fisting her own hair, while Greyson drops his head back and groans loudly.

"Oh, no..." Veronica giggles at my side when I finally look down at the sweet little girl. I find her face buried in my cupcake, icing all over her nose and cheeks; hell, she even has some on her eyelashes.

I quickly try to pull it away, but her grabby hands latch onto it, refusing to let go. "No, princess. You're gonna get all dirty. Damn it, I'm sorry I wasn't thinking." I look up to her parents.

Greyson finally laughs with a shrug. "It's fine. We expected this to happen."

"Clearly, she knows what's good for her." Cecilia giggles.

Veronica snorts. "And she's not the only one apparently," she says, nodding her head toward Dante, who just finished a small cupcake that was made especially for him and is now licking away at his father's cupcake, who isn't paying attention.

"Oh God! Dante!" Cecilia quickly grabs him.

Silas bursts with laughter. "Damn, you sneaky kid."

Laughter erupts around the room as we decide to just let the kids be. Eventually when it dies down, Cecilia leans into her husband, bumping him with her shoulder. "See, honey. This is how you properly do a gender-reveal party. Take notes!"

He frowns at her. "Hey! It's easy to not spill the beans if you don't even know the sex yourself! No one knew, so how did you expect someone to find out before time?"

"I knew," Aubrey says from her seat near Gabe.

"You did?" Emma asks her.

"Yeah, I was in charge of the cupcakes. They gave me an envelope that revealed the gender of each baby." She nods, slightly flushing now that the focus is on her.

"Wow... your parents were right, you really can keep a secret. Damn, I wonder what else you know and haven't told anyone." Emma narrows her eyes as if she could magically see inside Aubrey's mind.

"Here's a trick for the future, Cece. Next time you get pregnant, don't tell him the gender. Like that, you're sure he won't spill it to anyone until you're ready," Greyson tells Cecilia with a chuckle.

"Or better yet, don't find out the sex at all and wait until the birth." Em shrugs.

Greyson turns to her. "That's a good idea. We should do that, Bunny."

"Absolutely not! It's a good idea for them, but not for me. I want to know what's hiding in there so I can plan in advance." She shakes her head.

"Would you want to wait until the birth to know?" I ask Veronica when everyone goes back to their own conversations and congratulates the couple on their new discovery.

She puckers her lips as she considers the idea before a heart-stopping grin transforms her features. "No, I don't think I could wait the whole nine months. I'd want to know what we're having. I think I'd be too excited."

She then looks over at Gabe, who's now holding Dante's spare hockey stick and playing the goalie as he pretends to stop the puck from sliding between his legs. "And I know someone who's going to go crazy with shopping once we know what we're having."

I chuckle, passing Gracie over to her mother to get her cleaned up. "You have no idea. Our house will be filled with kids' toys and clothes. We might even go bankrupt."

"Well, we can't have that, can we? Who's going to fund my hair dyes every month?" She giggles. "I'm kidding, I'm kidding." She takes my hand and laces our fingers. "But I have been thinking about what we talked about not too long ago."

I frown in confusion. "What's that?"

"About starting my own organizing business. Once we buy a house, I'd like to look more into it seriously." She smiles.

"Then we'd better get moving on finding our forever home." I lean in, capturing her lips with mine.

Chapter Forty-One

GABRIEL

In love with a nutjob.

~ One Week Later ~

I finish adjusting all my equipment then rest back against my bench, waiting for the call to hit the ice. Music plays on a Bluetooth speaker to get us into the zone, but there's really no need; we're all ready. We have so much to prove this year. Prove that we are the best of the best, and that we will bring that cup home once more.

With one minute left, Silas gets up in the center of the room and begins delivering his speech as captain. "All right, boys, this is it! Let's go out there and make our fans proud!"

"*Yeah!*" everyone in the room yells.

"Let's remind them exactly why we took that cup home last season!"

"*FUCK YEAH!*"

"And exactly why we're gonna take it home again this year!"

"*WOO-HOO!*" we all shout as we jump up and head down the players' tunnel to the rink.

Fog billows through the tunnel and onto the ice, screams and shouts vibrate down the hall as fans cheer us on, excited to get the game started. Blue, yellow, and white lights flick around the arena, the music dying down as the announcer comes on and begins naming every player and jersey number as they hit the ice.

Noah stands before me, jumping up and down on his skates as he waits for his name to be called. "Ready to stop all the pucks from making it in?" He smirks.

"Ready to stop those fuckers from coming at me?" I smile back at him.

"You know how much I love sending them flying back where they came from." His grin widens, a wicked glint shining in his eyes.

"*Number Seventy-Nine! Noooaaah Adleeerrr!*"

Silas slaps him on the ass as he races off onto the ice.

"Come on, guard dog. Make sure we win that game! Show them who's boss tonight!" Silas yells over the cheers and slaps my ass just as the speaker announces my name.

"Number Eighty-Six! Gabrieeelll Elliiiissss!"

My heart pumps as I step onto the ice, stick held high in the air as an explosion of screams comes along with my name. I look up at all the filled seats, people standing and throwing their hands up. A beaming smile stays glued to my face as I skate around the ice and into my spot, waiting for the rest of my teammates to join us.

My eyes drop to where the girls are bouncing on the spot, clapping along with everyone, and despite the dim lighting and flickering lights, blue hair catches my gaze just as she blows me a kiss.

God, I love this girl.

Once the whole team is here and the announcer has finished his speech, we speed off to do our quick warm-up before the national anthem and the start of the game. I make my way to the goal, throwing my bottle above the net and placing my mask on properly. I skate to the side, leaving the net free to practice shooting pucks, and sink to my knees. I stretch out my groin and rock back and forth, keeping one leg straight, then the next.

"She's looking at you like she wishes she was beneath you right now." Noah drops beside me, chuckling. He places himself in a similar position as me but keeps both his legs bent and drops lower to the ice.

I laugh and look over to our woman. "Yeah, it's not just me anymore. I'm pretty sure if I squint, I can see some drool on the corner of her mouth."

"Don't tell her that, she'll smack you." He stands, shaking his head with a smile.

"Maybe I like it when she smacks me." I wink at him.

"Fuck off." He laughs and heads over to Ronnie.

From there I do the splits and bring my chest toward the ice, feeling the satisfying burn in my hamstrings and groin. Then I jump back onto my skates and do a few butterfly pushes and slides before joining the girls just as Noah, Clay, and Silas vacate the spot.

Greyson bends to pick up a puck just as I reach them, purposely bumping him with my hip and sending him toppling over. When he picks himself up, he turns to face me with a glare. "Was that necessary?"

"Sorry, just a habit. Whenever Ronnie's bent over like that, I just can't help myself and need to ram into her. I guess I got a little confused." I give him a shit-eating grin.

The girls giggle at my comment, except for Ronnie, who folds her arms over her chest with a raised brow. "You got confused? And how often does that happen?"

Oh fuck...

My smile instantly drops. Greyson snickers beside me as he passes a puck over to his daughter through the hole, his every-game tradition when she's present. My eyes are wide and filled with horror.

"No. Nooo! Never. Baby, that's not what I meant at all. Promise. No one but you," I rush out, hoping to save my ass from my stupid comment.

She then laughs and the tension lifts off my shoulders, letting me breathe again. "I'm kidding, baby. I know you wouldn't."

My smile returns as I watch her. She's wearing a jersey just like mine, blue with white and gold bands at the bottom and on the sleeves, with a huge white *'G'* in the center and a golden griffin crawling out from it. We had hers custom-made, since they don't have any jerseys with both our numbers on it.

On the right sleeve, she has Noah's number, *79*. And on the left one, she has mine, *86*. But the best part is at the back, where it says *'Mrs. Ellis-Adler,'* and both our numbers are below it, side by side. I think that makes it pretty damn clear she belongs to us.

"You look beautiful, Vixen," I tell her, checking her over. She has her blue and white hair curled, gold eye makeup on, and below her jersey she's wearing white skintight jeans. Her entire look fits with our team, and I love it.

"Thank you, baby." She bites her lip and blushes slightly. "I love you. Now go and get in the zone."

"I love you, too." I smile while skating away, feeling different for the first time on the ice. Feeling like I finally have a reason for everything. And that reason is right there, sitting with the rest of my self-made family.

VERONICA

"Fuck, he's so hot," I mutter to myself.

Cecilia snickers beside me. "Which one?"

"Both of them. I mean, look at that." I point with my hand toward Noah shooting pucks at the net with all the strength in his body. "All I'm picturing right now is him slapping my ass like that as he takes me from behind." I wet my lips as I change my focus onto Gabe next.

I'm not exactly sure what the technical term for what he's doing is, but he's skating in place with this angry, savage look on his face, the cage of his mask making him look even more menacing. "And that! What even is that?! He looks like a caged beast preparing to break free. Tell me that doesn't look dark and dangerous, yet you'd gladly let it attack you."

I fan myself with one hand, shifting in my seat and feeling the heat pool between my thighs. "I am definitely letting those two go feral on my body tonight."

Emma bursts with laughter beside Cece. "As if that's different from any other given day."

"Oh, shut up. You know exactly what I'm talking about." I chuckle, shaking my head, then look down at Gracie, who stares at me. "Oh, shoot! I'm sorry, I haven't been paying attention to my words." I place my fingertips over my lips.

Cecilia shrugs me off. "It's fine, they can't hear much through the noise-canceling headphones anyway."

Relief fills me and I let out a sigh, I really don't want to be the reason these kids start cussing like a sailor.

"How do they know who you're talking to when you call them?" Aubrey suddenly asks from my opposite side.

I turn to face her with a confused expression. "What do you mean?"

"Well, when you call them *'baby,'* how do they know if it's for Noah or Gabe?" she clarifies.

"Oh! It's simple; I only call one of them baby."

"Wait, you call Gabe *'baby'*, But for Noah, it's just *'Noah'*?" Emma frowns. "That doesn't seem fair. Poor guy."

"No! I call Gabe *'baby'*, and Noah *'babe'*. Just like they have their own nicknames for me. Gabe calls me *'Vixen'*, and Noah calls me *'Kitten'*. Also, only Gabe ever calls me *'baby'* or *'babe'*, but never Noah. He calls me *'love'*." I shrug.

Aubrey stares at me with wide, unblinking eyes. "That's a lot of information to remember."

I laugh. "You kind of get used to it after hearing it every day."

"Okay, but here's the real question we all want to know. Can you tell the difference between them?" Morgan leans over from beside Emma, waggling her brow.

"Oh, she definitely can." Emma giggles.

"Really? That much of a difference?" Cecilia questions next.

"Yeah, but in a good way. Noah is longer and curvy, but Gabe is thick as hell. Like, *really* thick. Sometimes I think he may have ripped something up there." I laugh, even though I'm only half joking.

"Oh God!" Aubrey covers her ears. "Please, can we not talk about male genitalia right now? I really do not need a visual of their... things."

We all giggle, watching poor Aubrey getting extremely uncomfortable. I really wonder what her first time is going to be like if she can't even say the word penis.

"I totally get what you mean, though. The first time I saw Gabe's junk, I was convinced I'd need to get stitches at the ER afterwards," Emma jokes with a giggle.

"Oh, that's true! Sometimes I forget you've been with them. It's a little weird, right?"

Despite me being uncomfortable when we bump into their former bed partners, I don't feel that way with Emma. Yes, it's strange and awkward to think that we've both slept with the same men. But it doesn't make me jealous or hate her in any way.

"I mean, maybe a little, but she's slept with my soon-to-be husband, so I guess it's just a natural thing in this group." She points at Cecilia, who gives her a displeased look for bringing it up.

"Um, no. That will not be a natural thing to happen in this group. No one is coming near my husband. I will cut you. I swear." Morgan throws her finger in all our faces, then quickly pulls it back and blinks. "Wow, I'm sorry. I have no idea where that came from. These pregnancy hormones are turning me into a crazy woman."

"Been there!" Cecilia laughs, squeezing Dante in her arms.

"Doing that," Emma grumbles, since she's clearly going through it as well. She's now sporting this cute little baby bump at seventeen weeks.

"I can't believe you're getting married to my brother in just two months." Aubrey smiles and leans in, reaching across to Emma as she does the same to take her hand.

We've all been helping out wherever we can with wedding details, since Em's already crazy busy as it is. And planning a wedding with only five months to go on is really not easy. Luckily, we know Emma pretty well, so making decisions for her isn't a super hard task. And whatever we aren't certain about, we make sure to ask before taking any liberties.

Brides don't usually appreciate it when others get involved with the planning, but Emma practically throws tasks our way. We actually have dress fittings next week, which Em and Morg are really worried about. Since they seem to be growing at rapid speed and are afraid that they won't fit in their dresses when the time comes.

"I know! I can't wait to call you, my sister." She looks back to the ice with a dreamy sigh, eyes following Greyson. "Who knew this is where we'd end up? Getting married where we fell in love, just one short year later."

"I told you it would. Just like I told him on Christmas morning up on the hills," Aubrey tells her softly.

Emma's gaze turns back to hers with a gratified smile. "You did."

We refocus on the ice from there just as the anthem starts, and then it's game time. By the end of first period, we're ahead by two points, while Buffalo still sits at zero.

I'm still not a pro at this sport and don't know the names of every pass or block, but I've gotten a little better at following the puck and understanding what position does what. *I only started watching hockey a year ago, give a girl a break.*

By third period, we're now at four-to-one, and that's only because Buffalo got lucky. When their centerman and two wingers came at Gabe, it was like watching a battle to the death. I couldn't even tell who had the puck, because Gabe was blocking every shot coming at him on repeat.

Until he was sprawled out on the ground right before the net, continuing to dodge every attempt with Noah and the other Griffins defenseman trying to regain control of the puck. But with one last well-placed shot from the Buffalo's right-winger by the side of the goal, it went flying over Gabe's shoulder. Hitting the bar with a loud ping before falling behind him, scoring them their first goal of the night.

Gabe gets back to his skates, shaking out his head a bit. I can see the frustration radiating through his caged mask. I know he takes every opponent goal to heart as if he's personally responsible for letting them score.

It's even worse when they lose a game; he beats himself up over it. Noah says it's just a natural goalie thing to feel more pressure than the rest of them.

Gabe lifts his mask above his head, picks up his water bottle over the net, and squirts a huge amount into his mouth. Then some all over his sweaty face, before putting it back down and replacing his mask properly.

He gets back into position just as the puck drops, and Silas sends it off to Clay. He takes it down the ice toward Buffalo's net but smacks it back to Silas just as he's pushed into the boards by their defenseman.

Buffalo's centerman manages to reclaim the puck and skates off with it like a bolt of lightning, while the whole team chases after him. Noah blocks the centerman by smashing into him, the puck springing free right as their right-winger nabs it.

He raises his stick, firing a shot at Gabe, but Gabe deflects it to the left with his blocker. The left-winger picks it up, striking another shot to the net, but Gabe sees it coming too and catches it with his catcher right before it passes the line.

The whistle blows and the play stops, starting up again quickly, this time our men keeping the puck and making it over to the other end of the ice within seconds. When I look over at our empty end, except for Gabe, who stays by his little house for the night, I find him moving around on his skates. He goes from one side to the other and shakes his booty out on the spot.

"What the heck is he doing?" I narrow my eyes, trying to make sense of what he's up to.

Cecilia looks over and starts laughing. "He's dancing."

"Jesus, he really is a goofball." I shake my head and giggle.

I keep my eyes on him for a few more seconds as he makes a quick spin, jumps on his skates, and shakes out his hips some more. My laugh gets deeper as I watch the big, massive man really getting into it while his team tries to get one final goal in. If I thought my boys were huge before, they're simply enormous with all their gear on. Certainly, Gabe with his huge pads.

The shouts in the arena grow louder as the timer on the clock runs down. I turn back to the play in time to see the final goal happen. Greyson passes to Silas, who then sends it back to Noah when he notices he's trapped.

Noah sails it off to an open Clay and Clay doesn't waste a second to shoot it through the goalie's five-hole just as he goes to close it. But it makes it in, the buzzer sounds one second before the time runs out, and cheers erupt all over the arena.

Clay raises his stick and points it toward Morgan, sending her a kiss with his gloved hand just as he's tackled by all his teammates. Gabe leaves his post, skating over to them and wanting to join the celebration.

Midway down the ice, he jumps down onto his stomach and glides over to the group, crashing into them. Everyone laughs around us as they see him in action. *God, I can't believe I'm in love with this nutjob.*

Noah

Gabe and I hurry out of our equipment and get in the shower quickly. Scrubbing away the sweat as best as we can before getting back into the dressing room and pulling on our suits, excited to see our girl after a great win.

My phone rings with a notification just as I pull it out of the cubby, smiling as I see Kitten's name pop up. It's a text from her telling us she's just down the hall with the girls and kids.

They usually wait for us elsewhere, not wanting to deal with the reporters that are waiting just outside the dressing room. We've already had a few inside the locker room before undressing, but there's always a handful more waiting for us with more questions.

As predicted, the moment we step out of the room, cameras and recorders turn to us. Questions are being shot out, one after the other, hoping to gain our attention. I stop in front of one I recognize that has been interviewing us for years now.

"Noah, what a great way to start the season with a five-to-one win, on home ice above that. How are you feeling about this season?"

"We're definitely excited to be back on the ice after such a win last season and hoping to make it just as far this year."

"I have no doubt you guys will. Now, I have to ask." He smirks when he sees the smile spread on my lips, because I knew this question would come up. Ever since our date night, we've been all over the tabloids with speculations about whether or not the rumors surrounding Veronica, Gabriel, and I are true.

"There have been rumors flying around about you and Gabriel Ellis being off the market and taken by the same woman. Will you give us and all your lady fans out there that are dying to know the truth and answer? Are the rumors true? And how serious is this relationship between the three of you?" He aims his recorder back at me, his cameraman to the side, capturing every moment.

It's at that moment that I spot our girl just above his shoulder, with the widest grin plastered on her beautiful face. I keep my eyes trained on her as I give them what they want.

"Yes, it's all true. We've fallen madly in love with the same woman, and we're just lucky that she happens to love us just as much." I wink at her as she mouths, *'I love you'*, clearly hearing what I've just said.

The reporter catches my action and looks behind him, directly at Veronica. Before he can even ask, I wave her over. She hesitates for a second but then comes, sliding her hand right into my extended one.

"This must be the woman we've all been hearing about." He smiles at Veronica.

"Yes, she is." I lean in and press my lips to hers for the world to see. She sighs against me, melting as she rests her hand over my chest.

Gabe finishes with his reporter and comes up quickly, taking Veronica away from me as he scoops her up into his arms. "There's my baby!"

Her legs go around his waist, arms circling his neck as he holds her up with one hand on her ass and the other at the back of her head, devouring her mouth like a starved man. Veronica laughs as he finally sets her back down beside me and wraps his arms around her neck from the back, head leaning to the side of hers.

"Well, I do have to admit you both look smitten." The reporter chuckles.

"Oh, we are." Gabe beams at him.

"And for my final question, how serious is this relationship between you three?"

Veronica takes my hand again and places her other above Gabe's crossed forearms. "We're actually looking at houses right now," she tells him.

"Wow, that's as serious as it can get! Well, thank you for answering my questions, and I wish you all the best of luck. I'm sure you're eager to get out of here and celebrate your win of the night."

"That we are," Gabe answers as I thank the reporter. Then we both take our girl's hands and join the rest of our friends waiting down the hall.

"Did you boys want to go out and celebrate with the team?" Veronica asks us as we make our way to the car.

"Nah, I'm ready to get home and celebrate with you, Kitten." I wink at her.

She laughs. "My favorite type of celebration."

"It's all I've been thinking about all night." Gabe sighs happily.

"Really? Not defending our goal?" I smirk at him.

"Okay, it was fifty percent the goal and fifty percent burying myself deep in our girl." He laughs as Veronica and I join in.

"You two are ridiculous." She swats us both with her hands as we reach the car.

"But you love how ridiculous we are." Gabe holds on to the back passenger car door, stopping her from closing it.

"That I do." She smiles. "Now hurry up so we can get home, and you can defile me properly." She yanks hard on the door as he loosens his grip and slams it shut.

Gabe and I sprint into action. "That's one way to get us moving." I laugh as we jump in and Gabe starts the engine, driving us home.

Chapter Forty-Two

NOAH

This doesn't feel like forever...

~ One Week Later ~

Something's wrong.

I'm not sure what, but I feel... off.

I've felt it since I woke up this morning, a knot in my gut that won't go away. Like when you forget something super important, and all day, your mind will sense that you're forgetting something. But this time, it doesn't feel like something forgotten.

It feels like dread.

It's the same feeling I had when I walked into the care facility—the day we found out Trinity wasn't doing well. It's that feeling of knowing something's about to happen but not being able to put your finger down on *what* exactly.

When I was on my morning jog with Veronica this morning, she could sense something was off, and when she asked, I told her I felt strange. She said I probably just slept wrong or was hungry and that it would pass. But I didn't sleep wrong, and I wasn't hungry, and it still hasn't passed.

The problem is, I'm not the only one who feels it.

Gabe, who's usually happy-go-lucky throughout the day, woke up with a sour face. He told me he kept having a strange dream but couldn't remember what it was. All he remembers is a loud crashing sound and running. And since then, he's had a strange look on his face, like he's anxious about something.

We're currently on our way to the training facility in my Aston Martin for our late morning practice, and I find myself worrying the farther away we get from home. Just leaving was rough; I didn't want to go, and neither did Gabe. I think he held on to Veronica for a good ten minutes before I forced him into the elevator.

Gabe is looking out the window, chewing on his lip with his phone in hand. He

427

keeps sending texts to our girl and breathes out when she replies a few seconds later. My fingers drum against the steering wheel, desperately wanting to grab onto the wheel and turn us around.

"Should we tell her to go to one of the houses? Maybe she could go spend the day with Aubrey and her guard," Gabe asks, looking at me with uncertainty in his eyes.

"I don't know..." I work my jaw, unsure what to do about this feeling. *What if we're just overreacting? Maybe we're just growing impatient with the whole Victor thing.* "I'm sure everything is fine. Let's just get through our practice, and then we'll go straight home."

Or maybe we're just anxious because in two days, we're leaving for an eight-day away stretch, and it will be the first time we leave Veronica alone for so long.

"Yeah, okay..." He nods, but he doesn't seem convinced.

"She has security. Marcos and Ricky are right outside the building. Nothing's going to happen to her," I tell him, trying to ease his worry and mine at the same time.

"I know."

A few minutes later, we arrive at the training facility and make our way into the building. But we get stopped right at the entrance when we notice the whole team waiting around, with Coach and our General Manager talking to someone who works here. There are big yellow caution tapes blocking our access to where we need to go.

"What's going on?" I ask as Gabe and I reach Silas, who stands in the front near Coach.

"One of the main pipes burst overnight, flooding the rink and gym," Silas says, listening in on the conversation happening beside him.

"I don't think we'll be doing any practice or training today," Clay mutters as we wait for the verdict.

Finally, the worker leaves, heading down the hall behind the yellow tape as Coach turns to us. "All right, boys, listen up. Practice is canceled for today since we were unaware of this situation and don't have a spare place to train with such short notice." He gives us all a tight smile.

"Luckily, we won't be needing the facility until we get back from the road, so let's hope all is back to normal by then. We'll notify you all if there are any changes. You all head home and enjoy your time off with your families, I'll see you all at the airport in two days."

We all turn and head back out to the parking lot, not in the least upset about getting an extra day of rest. "Hey, you guys want to come over for dinner later?

Morgan's finally past her nausea stage and started cooking again; she's been going at it for the past two days. Claimed she missed it," Clay offers as he heads over to his SUV.

"Sounds good to me," Silas tells him as he jumps into his Range Rover.

"We'll be there," Grey says, opening his truck door.

I look at Gabe, who shrugs. "Yeah, sure. We'll see you guys later," I tell him as we get back into my car.

My foot's heavy on the gas as we drive home, that feeling inside of me growing by the second. I don't know what it is, but I know we need to get home. Even Gabe is getting antsier with every mile we pass, his knee bouncing up and down as he drums his fingers on his thigh.

"I don't like this... I feel like I'm gonna be sick."

I look over to him. "Do you want me to pull over?"

He shakes his head. "No. Just get us home."

I give him a curt nod and step on the gas once more, going over the speed limit and praying we don't get stopped. Apparently, luck is on our side because we make it to the underground garage in no time, without being pulled over by the cops. Except the second I shut the engine, the whole garage goes into blackout mode.

"What the hell?" Gabe steps out of the car, looking around as I do the same.

It takes a few seconds for the backup generator to kick in, and small lights along the walls light up, giving us a dim view of our surroundings. Gabe and I quickly head over to the elevator, but it isn't responding.

"Shit, the power's out. Try the other," I tell him as he jogs over to it and presses the call button, but nothing happens.

"Noh..." Gabe starts.

"I know. Let's take the stairs."

We hurry to the stairwell, skipping steps as we make our way up to the twentieth floor. "I have a bad feeling, Noh. This... I remember this from my dream."

"Let's just hurry up, we're almost there," I say, feeling the muscles in my legs burn the higher we climb.

We've just reached the seventeenth floor when the worst happens. A loud explosion sounds above us, violently shaking the walls and ground, making us trip on the stairs.

"FUCK!"

VERONICA

I finish placing the dishes in the dishwasher and start it up, then look over at my phone and notice a message from Gabe. A smile spreads on my face as I pick it up and read his text.

Husband #1

Practice canceled. On our way home. Love you, baby.

It's dated ten minutes ago, so I don't bother replying since they'll be here soon, and I'd rather tell him I love him in person.

I'm just about to put my phone down when the power goes out. It was pretty gloomy outside this morning, so I kept the blinds shut and turned on the lights around the penthouse, not wanting to see the depressing weather outside. But now that all the lights have gone out, it's dark.

I quickly turn on my phone's flashlight and walk over to the breaker in the laundry room, trying to see if maybe something jumped. But everything's still on, which means it's either a power outage or the whole building that went off.

My phone shrills in my hand, and I jump out of my skin, heart pounding in my chest. "Jesus," I mutter as I look at who's calling. *'Ricky'* flashes on my screen, and I hurry to answer it. They probably noticed something and want to check on me.

"Hey, Ricky."

"Miss Masters, are you all right?" His deep, rough voice filters through the phone as I switch him to speaker, making my way back into the kitchen.

"Yes, but I think the power went out. Nothing's working up here." I try the switch on the wall as I say it, making sure I'm not going crazy.

"Yes, we're aware. We just entered the lobby. We'll try to find out what's caused the outage. Marcos will come up to stay with you until it's back on."

"Oh, there's no need. I'm fine, and everything is locked up here. No need to come up." Then I chew on my bottom lip as a thought pops into my mind. "Are the cameras in the penthouse still working?"

"Yes, they work through cellular data, just like your phone, so they weren't affected by the power going out. We've already informed our boss of the situation at hand, and he assured us that someone is monitoring the live feed as we speak," he reassures me, and some of the tension in my muscles relaxes. "Now are you certain you don't want one of us up there right now?"

"No, it's fine. Just let me know what you find out," I say, remembering that Noah and Gabe should be back soon.

"All right, but the minute we find out what's going on, we'll be up to make a sweep. Just to be sure."

"Okay." We hang up and I put my phone down with a sigh, keeping the flashlight aiming upwards as I look over at the curtains covering the floor-to-ceiling windows.

"Stupid automatic curtains that only work with a remote. How the hell am I supposed to open them now? Didn't think about that, company, did you?"

I shake off the icky feeling creeping up my spine and turn toward the living room, ready to try and pry them open somehow. But stop dead in my tracks with a gasp when I spot someone already standing there, someone I prayed I'd never see again.

"Hello, Veronica."

"Victor." My hands instantly begin to tremble, but I clench them into fists, not letting him see the effect he has on me. Not showing any weakness.

"Not a very smart move telling them not to come." He tsks me. "Although it does play in my favor. So, thank you for that." He smirks.

"What do you want, Victor?" I keep my eyes trained on him, looking for any sign of a weapon before making an exit strategy. *Just like he taught me to do.*

He chuckles and reaches behind him, pulling out a knife with a sharp-looking blade. "Is this what you're looking for? Don't forget who taught you, little one. I know all your tricks."

"I asked you a question," I bark out, done playing his stupid game. "What do you want?"

"That's a good question." He brings the tip of the blade to his finger, pressing it in as he twirls it around.

He then pulls his finger away, looks at it, and brings it to his lips, likely licking the blood from where the blade punctured his skin. It's his way of showing me just how threatening the weapon he holds is.

"You almost cost me my life, you know that? Did you think I wouldn't find out it was you? That I didn't know it was you who snitched us out to the feds?" He takes a step closer, and I go to take one back, but his booming voice stops me. "Don't even think about it!"

My body instantly freezes up, just like it used to whenever he'd raise his voice at me as I waited for my punishment to arrive. I swallow past the bile in my throat while thinking of a way to get to my phone that rests on the counter not far behind me and then hiding somewhere.

But where?

"You know, it's a nice disguise you have going on; too bad it wasn't enough to fool me." He takes another step. "You used to be such a good girl for me, but I should have known better. I think it's time I make you pay for everything you've put me through."

"Me?! Everything *I* put *you* through?! You tortured me for years! You beat me and raped me repeatedly! Then you passed me around to your friends and had them do the same!" I yell at him, tears springing to my eyes as I shake violently.

"You deserved everything you got! If you had followed the rules, I wouldn't have had to punish you!" He takes an aggressive step forward, making me flinch.

His words ring in my head, sounding too familiar. *Aren't I doing the exact same thing with Gabe and Noah? Punishing them when they don't follow my rules. Is that where my obsession with organizing and wanting everything to be perfect comes from? Has he really been living in my head this whole time?*

A loud booming noise sounds from somewhere below us, shaking the floors as I lose my footing slightly and grab onto the island to stabilize myself. "What was that?" Worry laces my voice.

He smiles diabolically. "A distraction."

My instincts kick in. I spin quickly on my heels and lunge for my phone, but he tackles me to the ground before I have time to catch it. I scream as he lifts me off the floor and puts his hand over my mouth, stopping my yells from echoing through the room.

I try to fight against his hold, but he's too strong. He pins my front to the kitchen island, keeping his body pressed up against my back and his hand over my lips. He lifts the hand that still holds the knife and brings it to my throat as tears track down my face.

"Shh, it's okay, little one. All you need to do is be a good girl for me one last time, and this will all be over quickly."

He licks up the side of my face, capturing my tears, and I shiver in disgust. Just then, the sound of the door unlocking in the foyer that leads to the main elevator and stairs echoes in the quiet penthouse.

"Hmm, seems your little boy toys are home earlier than planned. That's okay, we'll just have to make some quick adjustments to my plan," he whispers into my ear. "I wonder how they'll react when I tie them up and force them to watch as I fuck you and then kill you." He chuckles wickedly against my ear, his grimy breath stinging my nostrils.

"VERONICA!!" The door smacks against the wall, and seconds later, Noah and Gabe come into view.

They stop the moment they see us, taking cautious steps toward the island. My hands grip the edge of the counter, and I breathe hard through my nose, blinking away the tears in my eyes. With every inhale and exhale, I feel the blade press into my skin.

"I wonder how I should do it. Maybe a quick slice to the throat? Ending your miserable life within seconds." He presses the blade deeper against my neck. I hiss at the sting as it cuts through the skin slightly.

"Or maybe I should torture you, cut off body part after body part. Skin you alive. Cauterize everything so you can't bleed out, and I can continue to make your life hell, the same way you made mine." He smiles at them as he paints a gruesome visual.

"Don't you fucking touch her!" Gabe steps to the side, going near one end of the island, while Noah stays near the other. *They're trying to corner him in.*

Victor laughs loudly. "And what are you going to do about it if I do, boy?"

"I'll fucking kill you," Gabe answers without hesitation.

No, baby! Don't play the bluffing game with him!

I try to shake my head, telling him to stop, but end up cutting myself deeper with the sudden movement. I cry out beneath his hand, sobbing at the pain. Noah quickly takes a step closer and stops when Victor turns his gaze on him. But Gabe takes advantage of his distraction and gets closer from the opposite side.

"Oh yeah? You think you can kill me? I'd like to see you try, blondie." He throws his head back and laughs, clearly not believing Gabe would be capable of such a thing.

Clearly, he's been following us around long enough to know my Pretty Boy isn't a fighter; that's why he doesn't feel threatened by his words.

Gabe and Noah jump on the moment, coming in from each end. Victor catches on quickly, and everything happens in the blink of an eye. One second, Victor has his arms around me, the next, I'm being thrown to the side, crashing into Gabe's body as we both tumble down against the bottom kitchen cabinets.

When I manage to climb off Gabe, I scramble to my feet and find Noah and Victor wrestling each other. I look around quickly for a weapon, something to hit him with, but I'm too late. Victor manages to get his hand free, still holding on to his knife, and plunges it deep inside Noah's gut.

"*NOOO!!!*" I scream frantically.

Noah's eyes widen on impact, his mouth parting as his hold on Victor loosens. Victor pulls his hand back with an evil twinkle in his eyes and a chuckle, the blade sliding out covered in blood.

A gutting sound leaves Noah's parted lips as his hands come down to clutch his stomach, red blood seeping through his fingers. He takes a wobbly step back, then another, until his back hits the wall behind him and he drops to the ground, still holding on to his wound.

I don't think twice as I run over to him, not caring about Victor, not caring that he still has the knife and could turn it on me as I pass by. The only thing I care about in this instant, the only thing that matters, is to get to Noah.

I fall to my knees beside him with a loud sob and quickly press my shaky hands to his stomach as he groans, applying as much pressure as I can to stop the bleeding.

Just then, a loud thumping sound echoes behind us, seconds before a thud vibrates the wooden floor beneath me as a heavy body collides with the ground. The head smacks against my foot, and when I look back, I find Victor face down against the wooden planks, dark red blood spilling out from the back of his head and pooling around him and onto my feet.

My gaze travels up to Gabe standing behind him with his glass blender in hand. A red blotch along the side from where he must have hit Victor in the head with it. "I told you I'd fucking kill you," he mutters. His eyes widen as his words register in his own head. "Holy shit... I... I killed him." He releases his hold on the blender, letting it drop to the ground.

Noah suddenly coughs, bringing my attention back to him. "You're okay, babe. You're going to be okay. Just hold on," I tell him with a weak smile as tears continue to spill from my eyes.

He removes his hands from beneath mine, leaving a gap between my palms and his stomach. "No! No, don't do that." I push down harder against his wound, but the blood keeps spilling. My hands are now covered in blood, and I don't know if this is normal. *He was stabbed just once, is it normal to bleed this much?*

"I... I can't stop it! It won't stop! Gabe! Call 9-1-1, please! I can't stop it!" I'm panicking, growing more and more frantic by the second.

Blood pumps through my ears and my heart feels like it's about to burst through my chest with how hard it's beating. *This is not the time to have a panic attack, Veronica! Pull yourself together!*

I shake my head, trying to focus as Noah's bloody hand reaches my cheek. My eyes fall to his, those beautiful deep brown eyes that seem to have lost their light. He wipes at my tear-stained cheek and offers me a wobbly smile.

"I love you, Veronica," he croaks out, the color slowly draining from his face as his skin turns an ashy white tone.

"No... no, don't say it like that. Don't say it like you'll never get to say it again. You're going to get through this, help is coming. I promise, Noah..." I sob louder, gasping for air. "You can't leave me... you can't. You promised me forever. This isn't forever, Noah... It's just the beginning, we still have so much to see, so much to live..."

His head starts tipping to the side, body sliding sideways down the wall until he hits the ground. I quickly lay him on his back and climb over him, putting all my weight into my hands against his stomach. His eyes are still open, but I can tell he's quickly losing focus, about to go unconscious from all the blood loss.

"Why is no one here?! Why is no one coming?!" I look around the empty room, then up at Gabe, who hasn't moved an inch. Frozen in shock as he continues to stare down at Victor.

"Gabriel!! Why aren't they here yet?!" Ricky said they were watching the feed, so they must have seen what happened. *Why aren't they coming?*

Just then, the lights flicker back to life throughout the penthouse. Fifteen seconds later, the elevator dings, and in rushes Marcos and Ricky, along with Agent Callahan and two paramedics.

"Why did it take you so long?!?" I shout as Marcos comes down beside me, pressing his hands over mine. Ricky wraps his arms around my midsection, lifting me off the ground and away from Noah.

"NO! Don't take me away from him! Please don't take me away!" I scream and cry, kicking my feet and trying to break free from his grasp.

"It's okay! It's okay. I'm not taking you away, but they need room to help him," Ricky tells me as he tries to calm me down.

"Why did it take you so long..." I weep, losing my strength and feeling my body turn numb. I know it most likely all happened pretty fast, but at this moment, it feels like it's been hours.

"The explosion caused a fire and spread to the stairwell. We couldn't make it past the 18th floor. Luckily, it wasn't too big, and they're shutting it down as we speak, but we can't stay here any longer. We need to go."

He brings me over to the couch, taking a throw blanket and wrapping it around my body as he looks over my cuts quickly to make sure they aren't deep. He then lifts me back into his arms and carries me toward the elevator.

Marcos stands as the paramedics take over, controlling the situation as best as possible and getting Noah on the stretcher. He goes over to Agent Callahan, who kneels beside Victor's dead body, confirming he is in fact dead.

He then steps up to Gabe slowly, who still isn't moving. Marcos whispers something to him, and instantly, Gabriel snaps back to life, blinking a few times then turning to look at me.

The paramedics run back to the elevators with the stretcher and Noah's now unconscious body strapped to it. "I want to go with him! Please, I can't leave him!" I cry, pushing against Ricky to get down, but he tightens his hold, stopping any attempt I throw at him.

"No, they need room to work. I understand this is scary, but we'll follow them to the hospital, okay? He's in good hands. If you want him to live, then let them do what they need to do."

I don't want to agree with him, but I know he's right. "Okay..." I say in a small voice, praying this won't be the last time I see my lover.

He has to live. Noah has to live. Because I'm not ready to say goodbye to my Casanova.

Ricky waits a few seconds, then calls the elevator back up as Marcos and Gabe reach us. Agent Callahan says something about coming to the hospital later when they've taken care of everything at the penthouse. But I'm not sure; I'm having a hard time focusing on anything but Noah.

We go to step into the elevator, but a thought occurs to me. "Wait! Blubber! We have to take Blubber," I rush out. "I... I haven't seen him since... I don't know where he is. We can't leave him here."

"We'll go find him," Gabe tells me, cupping my cheek quickly then heading back into the penthouse with Marcos.

It doesn't even take them two minutes, and they return with a confused little bald cat wearing a striped red and white sweater over his body. He's currently sitting in his carrier with his heating pad and a blanket.

"He was hiding in our room under the covers," Gabe says, lifting the carrier to let me see Blubber up close.

I reach out with a hand to pet him through the caging, but when I spot my blood-tainted skin, another wail leaves my lips, and I quickly cover my mouth, not caring that I'm getting it all over me. It was like my brain momentarily forgot what had just happened, but now seeing the evidence, everything is crashing back into me at once. Every image, every smell, every noise, every feeling. And it's suffocating me.

From there, everything is foggy. I don't remember the elevator ride down or getting into a car. I don't remember driving to the hospital or entering it. I don't remember getting placed on an examination bed while a nurse looks over the cuts on my neck and makes sure there aren't any others.

She keeps asking if I'm bleeding somewhere else and where all the blood came from, but I don't answer her. All I do is sit on the edge of the bed, looking down at my hands that are still covered in my lover's blood, then down to my bare feet that are soaked in the devil's. The man responsible for all of this.

I didn't even remember that I was barefoot. I didn't remember that all I'm wearing is one of Noah's shirts that barely covers my ass. I guess that explains why Ricky put the throw blanket around me at the penthouse and carried me around everywhere we went, like I couldn't walk on my own.

But the truth is, I don't think I could walk if I tried. Everything feels numb, and I feel weak. Like if I tried to stand, I would collapse.

I hear the nurse tell someone that it's normal I'm not responsive or talking, that I'm still in shock. Maybe she's right, maybe I am in shock, but I also don't want to talk. Because every time I try, every time I go to speak, all that comes out are screams as reality crashes back into me.

Talking makes it real. And if I stay quiet long enough, my mind goes to this vacant place where I can't feel the pain ripping at me from the inside. Where I don't remember the look on my Casanova's face as he told me he loved me like it would be the last time.

She cleans my cut and places a bandage over it, then takes my hands and begins to wipe at them with some sort of disinfectant and a cloth before doing the same to my feet. I look down at my palms, at my nails, seeing all the missed spots, the pink tint still engraved in my skin.

"I'll go try and find her some slippers and clothes to wear. You can bring her back to the waiting room for now," the nurse says calmly as she stands and pulls the curtain open to leave. Leaving me alone on this bed, and suddenly that's all I feel—alone. Because that monster took something away from me, half of something I don't know how to live without. *Half.*

"Gabriel... Where's... where's Gabriel?" I whisper, needing to feel seen, needing to feel like I'm not alone in this chaos. Needing to know that my other half is still here, with me.

"I need Gabriel!" I shout, growing frantic by the second as I begin to look around the tiny enclosure, hands shaking and desperate to grasp onto some semblance of hope.

"I'm right here, baby!" He steps out from behind Ricky and wraps his arms around my back as I clutch onto his shirt like he's my lifeline, and right now, he is. "I'm right here," he whispers into my hair.

"Please don't leave me, too... please," I cry into his shirt, body racking with desperation.

"I'm not going anywhere, I promise. And neither is Noah. He's going to pull through this, I know he will." He kisses my head repeatedly, trying to soothe my pain.

I only wish I could believe his words...

Chapter Forty-Three

GABRIEL

Unbreakable blenders.

I can't explain how I feel at this moment. It's like I've just woken up and taken everything in. My red-rimmed eyes sting with unshed tears as I hold my beautiful girl's shaking body while she cries for our missing piece.

I don't feel worthy of her at this moment. I don't deserve to be the one holding her, the one she seeks out through her pain. Because I froze. When she needed me most, when my best friend was bleeding out on our kitchen floor and she needed my help, I froze.

I fucking froze.

All I could do was stare at the body lying at my feet, the one I hit hard enough to kill. I didn't mean to kill him. My intention was only to knock him out. But as I reached for the blender and lifted it in the air, every emotion I had ever felt from the moment I was born to now resurfaced.

Every hit my parents gave me, every broken bone, every night I cried myself to sleep in agony from the torture they inflicted on me. It all came rushing back, and when I let my hand come down with the heavy object, it was with all the strength I'd wish I had back then. I didn't see him, I saw them, and that was it.

It took Marcos telling me to snap out of it, that my girl needed me and that she couldn't go through this alone, to pull me out of my fogged state. And from that moment, my eyes haven't left her. They've been glued to her like she's the only thing holding me together. *My center.* She needs me right now, just as much as I need her.

I lift her into my arms as she cradles against my chest like a wounded animal and take her back to the waiting room, with Marcos and Ricky not far behind holding Blubber's carrier. I know I shouldn't make promises like the one I just did, telling her Noah would pull through, but I can't think of the worst right now. I need to stay strong for all of us.

Because if I don't, I'll break down, and there won't be anyone there to support my girl. The thought of losing my best friend, losing my brother... it guts me and makes it impossible to breathe. So no, I can't think of that. Because we aren't losing him. I won't accept it...

I can't.

When we get back to the waiting area, I find it filled with familiar faces. Friends, family, teammates—they're all here. Silas stands, coming over to me immediately.

"We came as soon as we heard." He looks down at Ronnie in my arms and strokes the back of her head with his hand.

"How?... Where?... Who?" I'm confused, unable to think clearly.

I'm glad they're here, but I don't know how they found out. I haven't even thought about calling anyone. I don't even know where my phone is right now.

"Jessie. He went to Burkley's and told him what happened when he got word of what was going on," he confirms for me.

I nod and bring Ronnie over to a chair between the girls, who all stand with tears running down their faces. When I set her down, needing a moment to collect myself, they gather around her, holding her in their arms.

I turn my back to them, taking deep breaths as all my teammates come by and hug me, showing me their support as best as they can. Clay, Greyson, and Silas stay by my side as the first tears begin to spill. I look up at the ceiling, trying to keep my composure.

Silas presses his hand to my back, rubbing up and down with his palm. "He's going to be all right. Noah's a tough motherfucker. Nothing will knock him down."

"I hope you're right, because I promised Ronnie that he would... and I don't know what I'll do if he doesn't..." I choke on the words, not wanting to think about him not pulling through.

"I'm going to kill that piece of shit when I see him," Greyson grumbles out with rage.

"He's dead," I say, looking back down and making eye contact with each one.

"He is?" Clay asks curiously.

I nod. "Killed him with my blender..."

"Damn..." Grey's eyes widen.

"It didn't even break."

Clay frowns. "What?"

"The blender. It didn't break." I have no idea why I'm saying it, why this particular detail is sticking with me. I guess trauma just works in weird ways.

"Well, shit... that's one strong-ass blender. We should probably all get one of those," Silas says in a low voice, but apparently not low enough.

"Silas!" Cecilia rebukes him. "This isn't the time or place."

"You're right, I'm sorry." He looks down with shame.

"It really is a good blender," I say after a moment of silence, and we all kind of lose it, me included.

We're all suddenly chuckling quietly; I can even hear some of the girls trying to control themselves. But not Ronnie. Ronnie just stays quiet in her seat, eyes staring down at her hands. I know this isn't the time to laugh, but there are so many emotions coursing through my body right now that I have no control over it.

Morgan comes up to me, taking me in her arms as the tears start flowing again. "I'm going to take Blubber back to our place and get some spare clothes and shoes for Ronnie." She pulls back and holds me by the arms. "Do you need me to get anything else?"

I shake my head. "No. Thank you."

She smiles with glassy eyes, sniffling as she turns and heads over to Ricky. She takes the carrier from him and walks out of the emergency's waiting room, just as the Storm brothers walk in. Marcos and Ricky reach them a few feet away, whispering to their bosses as Shane joins them as well.

They finally come over, and I see the moment Ronnie finally snaps out of her silent state. The second she spots them, she throws the blanket off her shoulders and stands, marching up to them and smacking Julian in the face. A loud cracking sound resonates through the room as her hand makes contact with his cheek.

"YOU SWORE! YOU PROMISED YOU'D PROTECT US!" she shouts in his face, then smacks her fists against his chest. "You said nothing would happen to us! You said you wouldn't let him hurt us! But you lied!" She hits him harder, but he doesn't attempt to stop her. He takes every hit that comes his way, letting her release the frustration she's been holding on to. "You lied, and now he's going to die!" she cries harder.

I move in to pull her away, but Clay beats me to it. He wraps his arms around Ronnie and lifts her off the ground as she fights against his hold, screaming and crying. He gets down to the floor against the wall and cages her in by holding down her arms and placing a leg over hers to stop her from trying to kick him. She grows more and more hysterical by the second, thrashing her head from side to side and screaming at the top of her lungs.

The nurse that saw her earlier returns with a pair of cheap hospital slippers and a hospital gown. "I'm sorry, this is all I could find." She looks over to Ronnie, who's still losing it in Clay's arms while Cecilia kneels at her feet trying to calm her down.

"Oh, dear." She presses her hands to her lips. "We can give her something to calm down, but we'll have to admit her for the time being."

"Do it," I say without hesitation.

I know I should go over there, take her in my arms, and hold her until she settles. But I can't. Watching her like that is killing me and I feel like it's my fault. Maybe if I had snapped out of it sooner and helped her, Noah wouldn't have lost so much blood.

Maybe if I had stayed home this morning like I wanted to, I could have stopped this from happening. But I didn't listen. I didn't listen to my gut, just like I didn't listen when she told me she couldn't stop the bleeding.

She hurries over to the nurses' station with Julian following behind her. I'm not sure what he tells her, but she nods and rushes off. Coming back a minute later with another nurse and a syringe in hand. They gather around Ronnie and Clay, holding her as still as possible, and stab her in the arm with it.

"It will act quickly. In the meantime, we'll set you up in a room for her to rest," the nurse tells me as she comes back to my side, then looks on at everyone gathered here for us, for Noah. "They can all come up too. The room is pretty spacious."

I nod and walk up to Clay and an already calming down Ronnie, her eyelids slowly drooping as her head falls back against Clay. I crouch down and take her from his arms while her body grows heavy and she falls unconscious, then follow the nurse as she leads us to her room.

Two hours later, we're all up in Veronica's room as she sleeps soundly on the hospital bed, still knocked out by whatever they gave her. It's been three hours in all, and we still have no news about Noah. We know he was taken into surgery the moment he arrived, but this feels like it's taking too long, and I hate it.

Everyone is lying around, waiting. There's a couch at the far end with Greyson, Clay, and Silas on it. Emma, Morgan, and Cecilia sitting in their laps. The nurses also brought in a few chairs that have been claimed by a few of our teammates.

The rest are all scattered around the room, sitting on the floor with their backs against the walls. A few of them went home an hour ago, asking for updates when we get them. I'm not mad that they left; I get it, they have their own lives as well. Just the fact that they showed up was enough.

Aubrey is sitting on the bed behind Ronnie as she passes her fingers through her hair, keeping her calm even in her sleep. While I sit on the opposite side, Ronnie's hand lies over my thigh, holding on to me.

Shane walks back into the room with two coffee cups in hand, the three brothers following not far behind him. He walks over to Aubrey's side and hands her one of them. "I added some hazelnut creamer. I figured since you bake sweets, you probably like your coffee the same way," he whispers as his cheeks take on a tiny light-pink shade.

"Oh, thank you." She takes the coffee from him, and instead of a tiny shade of pink, hers goes bright red.

"Of course, he only gets coffee for the pretty girls." Jessie chuckles, earning him a glare from Shane.

Jessie brushes him off and looks at the table that was set up and is now covered with food Morgan brought over for everyone. "Oh God, I'm starving, and that smells amazing. May I?" He turns to me, pointing at the food.

"Yeah, help yourself. It's there for everyone."

Julian walks over to me, rubbing his jaw as he looks down at my girl, probably still feeling the sting she imposed hours ago. "I understand that I may not be very high on your list of likability at the moment, but I assure you, we truly did try our best to keep you all safe. We could not have seen this coming, although we should have. And for that, I am truly sorry."

"I don't blame you, Julian. And neither does she. She was simply emotional and needed to put the blame on someone. I'm sorry it was you," I tell him genuinely because I know my girl, and I know deep down, she knows it wasn't his fault. Just like it wasn't mine.

He nods. "I called in a favor and had the best surgeon ready to work on Noah the moment he came in. He will pull through. If Dr. Willensteed cannot save him, then no one can." He places his hand on my shoulder, giving a light squeeze. "But he will."

He lets go of me and straightens, adjusting his cufflinks and clearing his throat. This guy clearly isn't used to showing any form of affection or support. "I have some information for you and Miss Masters regarding Mr. Cordova, but it can wait until later in the week." And with that, he heads back to his brothers.

Ronnie stirs beside me, her fingers flexing against my thigh until she blinks her swollen eyes at me. I brush the little hairs out of her face and lean in to kiss her forehead. "Hi, baby."

"Anything?" she asks in a small, broken voice.

I try to smile, but it's hard. "No, not yet. But it will be any minute now."

Her eyes well up as she nods, face scrunching up as she tries to hold back her tears.

"Morgan brought you some clothes and shoes if you want to put them on." I cup her cheek, brushing my thumb back and forth.

"Okay..." She sits up on the bed, then tries to stand on shaky legs.

I wrap my hand around her waist, supporting her. "Come on, I'll help you."

I bring her over to the bathroom with the bag Morgan had left here for her. I get her into a pair of leggings and put socks on her feet with a pair of slip-on shoes. When I grab for her bloodstained shirt, she rips the hem out of my hands.

"No, please... it makes me feel close to him... please don't take it away from me..." She begins to cry, and I instantly feel bad for making her tear up once more.

"Okay, baby. I won't take it. You can keep it." I wrap my arms around her shoulders, cradling the back of her head. "It's okay, Vixen. He's going to be okay. I know it doesn't seem like it, but this is good news. If something had gone wrong... we would have heard by now." *It's what I keep telling myself.*

"I know... it's just hard... it's hard to wait around without worrying."

"I know, baby. I know."

"I didn't say it back..." she whispers against me.

"Say what back?"

"That I loved him... The last thing he said to me was that he loved me, and I didn't say it back... What if he dies thinking that I don't..." She whimpers into my chest, soaking my shirt with her tears.

I release her and hold both sides of her head, kissing her crown, her forehead, her cheeks, and then her lips. "He's not going to die. And Noah knows more than anything just how much you love him. Don't ever doubt that."

She lets out a shaky breath, then nods, letting me know she's ready to go back out there. I take her hand and open the bathroom door. When we exit the small enclosure, everyone in the room is standing, and a man in scrubs stands near the door.

I can immediately tell this is Dr. Willensteed, the man we've been waiting on. Ronnie's hand tightens around mine, a small tremor in it as we wait for him to speak, to tell us something.

His face is stoic, void of any emotions, and I can't tell if this is good or bad. My own hands begin to shake and become clammy. But then my breath catches when a smile spreads over his lips and he nods.

"The surgery was a success. Mr. Adler is now in recovery."

"Oh God!" Ronnie exclaims, throwing herself into my arms as she loses control over her emotions once more. Everyone is reacting pretty much the same, with cries and words of relief. And finally, fucking finally, I feel like I can breathe again.

"Now," Dr. Willensteed raises his hands to gain our attention. "Recovery will not be easy, and we will need to keep him under observation for at least a week, if not more. His small bowel was hit as well as one of the blood vessels, but thanks to your quick actions, we were able to save his life."

None of that felt quick, but I understand what he means. In our heads it seemed like hours before help arrived. But when Agent Callahan came by earlier, after reviewing the security footage, he said it took exactly two minutes and thirty-eight seconds for the paramedics to arrive from the moment Noah was stabbed. Since they were already on the scene and only waiting for either the power to come back on or the fire in the stairwell to be contained.

Apparently, whoever was watching the live feed immediately called it in when they noticed Victor in the penthouse. They planned a worst-case scenario and sent the paramedics as well. And thank fucking God they did, because from the sound of it, Noah wouldn't still be with us if we had waited a minute longer.

"I'll leave you all to digest the good news together. And I'll be back shortly to explain everything in detail to you both, as well as what his recovery will look like." He nods toward Julian and Shane, who go to follow him out.

"Wait!" Ronnie stops him and he turns. "Can we... can we see him?"

Dr. Willensteed smiles warmly at her. "Shortly, yes. His room is being prepared as we speak. A nurse will come get you when you may see him."

"Thank you," she says quietly as he leaves with the two men. Shane, most likely wanting to know what this means for Noah's career.

Ronnie throws herself at me once more, one arm around my neck, her other hand cupping my cheek as she captures my lips with hers. Every raw emotion in her body flows from hers to mine. She pulls back, pressing her forehead to mine, nose touching, eyes closed as we breathe each other in.

"He's okay," she whispers with relief.

"He's okay."

Chapter Forty-Four

NOAH

To family.

~ Ten Days Later ~

Ten days.
That's how long I stayed in the hospital.
Ten.
Freaking.
Days.
God, am I glad to be heading home.

"Now remember, six more weeks before you can do anything. No heavy lifting, no baths, no sex! And I mean it, Noah, we don't want you back here in a few weeks because you ripped yourself open." Nurse Wendy narrows her eyes at me with the point of her wrinkly finger. She's my favorite out of all of them.

I laugh, holding Veronica closer to my side with my arm draped around her shoulder. "I can promise the first two, the last might be hard to follow." I wink.

"Noah…" She gives me a stern look.

"Don't worry, Wendy. I won't let him get near the goods." Veronica giggles when I frown at her.

"And don't forget to take your painkillers. I know you athletes think you're all high-and-mighty, but you need them. So stop being a big baby and take your damn pills when you're in pain."

"I'm not a big baby." This time it's my turn to furrow my brows at her.

Wendy rolls her eyes. "Not a big baby, my ass," she murmurs. "The guy was in so much pain, couldn't even get out of bed. Yet he refused to take his pills." She shakes her head.

"I'll make sure he takes them. Simple, if he doesn't take them, then no sex."

Veronica shrugs with a smile, and Wendy's mouth drops as she flaps her arms at her side. Veronica bursts with laughter. "I'm kidding! No sex, take your meds. That's my motto for the next six weeks."

"You kids drive me insane," Wendy mutters as she heads for the door, with us following suit.

She sighs once we stand outside my latest housing and reaches a frail hand up to pat my cheek in a grandmotherly way. "We're going to miss seeing your pretty face around here, but I'm glad you finally get to go home."

I crouch down slightly and wrap my arms around her. "I'll miss you, too, Wendy girl."

She pushes against my chest. "Now go on, before I get emotional and ruin my makeup."

She waves a hand at her face, because yes, she's the oldest nurse here and still wears makeup. She might be close to her seventies, but that woman is as sharp as they come. "I know you have some friends at home who are excited to see you back on your feet."

"That he does." Veronica beams at me seconds before she goes in for a hug of her own. "Bye, Wendy. Thank you for taking such good care of my man."

"It was all my pleasure."

We wave goodbye to everyone on our way out of the hospital and over to my car. And of course, Veronica is driving and I'm in the passenger seat. I lower myself, getting seated into the bench with a groan. Even though I can now walk around and move pretty fine with ease, certain movements still cause a pull inside my gut that's pretty damn uncomfortable.

"Are you okay?" Veronica searches my face with worry.

"Yeah." I drop my head against the headrest and close my eyes, letting out a breath. "Just the car is pretty low."

"Shit, I should have thought about that and taken a bigger car." She frowns at herself.

I reach out and cradle the back of her head. "It's okay, Kitten. I'm just happy to be with you and finally get home and back to our normal life."

Despite my annoyance with having to stay in the hospital for so long, I was lucky to have Veronica by my side the whole time. The only time she left was to get us spare clothes and see Blubber for a few hours. The rest she did here; shower, eat, sleep, although the nurses weren't too thrilled about her sleeping in the bed with me. But she needed comfort, and I needed her.

I haven't seen Gabe since my first two days here, except for when he videocalls during his free time. He's been gone with the team for their series of away games and came home early this morning. He wanted to drop by, but since we knew I was being discharged today, we told him not to bother and rest instead.

We made the news again. Word spread really fast about what happened, and everyone wanted to know if I was okay, what this meant for my career, and if I would ever play again. They've been harassing Gabe at every game to get as much information as they can out of him. But he's kept his mouth shut about it all, only telling them that I'm out of the woods and recovering. Even Coach and our GM haven't said much about it to the press. Only that they were waiting to see how things went before making any major decisions.

That's another thing that's been rough on my spirit. No hockey. I miss my morning runs with Veronica, I miss working out with my brother, I fucking miss playing hockey with my friends. And knowing that I'll most definitely be out for the whole season sucks.

Despite our management team not saying anything to the reporters just yet, Coach and our team doctor don't think I'll be ready to hit the ice until the playoffs, if I've completely recovered by then and my physical therapy goes well. And that's a *big* if.

The only upside to this whole shit show is that I get Veronica. I'll have her at my side every step of the way. Day and night. And after a scare like that—where I thought that I would never get to see her beautiful face again, never get to hear her voice, to hold her and kiss her—the only thing that matters to me at this moment is *her*.

We drive through the city and past the penthouse. My brows furrow as I notice we aren't taking the right route home. "Where are we going?"

Veronica swallows as her eyes gloss over. "I can't go back there, Noah... I tried, but I can still see it all... it's still too fresh in my mind..."

A tear spills out, and I quickly catch it before taking her hand in mine. "Hey, it's okay, Kitten. We don't have to go back to the penthouse. If anything, I'm kind of glad."

"You are?" She peeks at me quickly before refocusing on the road.

"Yeah. I mean, I'm fine. But stairs are still a little rough on me." I chuckle, a bit embarrassed that I have a hard time going up and down stairs at my age. Although getting stabbed is a pretty good excuse for it.

"Then you'll be happy about where we're going, because there are no stairs." She smiles and heads down roads I know too well.

I laugh. "Who got roped into hosting us for the time being?"

She looks over with a twinkle in her eyes. She's been doing that a lot, just stares at me like she can't believe I'm really here. I know this hasn't been easy on her, and she's still shaken up by the whole thing. I wish I could take all her pain away, make her see that I'm not going anywhere. That I never will. Not just yet.

"No one," she finally says as we pull up at Burkley's place. "Morgan and Clay offered us their pool house for as long as we need."

"The one they turned into an apartment for Cecilia back in the day?"

"Yeah, that's what I was told. I know it's not big, certainly not for three people and a cat. But we're already used to being all together, so I thought we could stay here until we find a house." She smiles at the thought of buying our first home. We have been looking during my time in the hospital and have found a few potential ones.

"Plus, there's no stairs." She giggles as she climbs out of the car.

She rushes around to my side while I'm opening the door and helps me climb out. That's the worst part, getting up. Sitting down sucks, or walking up and down stairs, as I've mentioned, but standing up from a seating position? Holy fuck, does that shit pull on my abdomen.

"Are you okay? Do you need a minute?" Veronica asks me once I'm standing by the car with my hand on the roof.

"Nah, I'm good." I wrap my arms around her neck and kiss her. "The only thing I need is you."

She smiles against my lips. "Well, that's going to have to wait another six weeks. Doctor's orders."

I groan, pressing my forehead against hers. "Don't remind me."

She dips out of my hold and stretches a hand out. "Come on, everyone is waiting inside to see you. But we don't have to stay long. If you get tired or in too much pain, we'll head out back to our place."

"Okay." I take her hand and walk up to the front door that has *three. Fucking. Steps.*

I can't wait for this shit to clear up. From what Dr. Willensteed said, it should be better in a couple of days. At least I'm eating normally again. Well, not as normally as I used to, but it doesn't hurt my stomach when I eat normal portions now.

"Just take them slowly, there's no rush," Veronica says, to which I say fuck it, and get it over with as quickly as possible.

When I hit the landing with a satisfied sigh, she looks at me with a disapproving frown. "I'm starting to see what Wendy was talking about."

I laugh and push the door open, excited to see my friends again.

"Oh my God! He's here!" Emma shouts as she throws herself into my arms, crying.

"Careful!" Veronica rushes out with worry.

"It's fine," I huff out.

"Right, right. I'm sorry." Emma lets go and wipes her tears, taking a step back beside Morgan, Aubrey, and Cecilia, who are all in tears as well.

"We just missed you so much," Morgan says with a sob. *Jesus, these two are really emotional with these pregnancy hormones.*

"Ladies, you all saw me two days ago," I remind them with a smirk. They all came by to see me at the hospital, and I was really grateful for that. It was a nice change in scenery compared to the usual staff.

"Yeah, but that's not the same. You were in the hospital, now you're home for good," Cecilia says, coming in slowly for a hug as she sniffles.

Once she lets go, Aubrey steps up next. "Hi, beautiful," I say with a grin as she flushes her usual blush.

"Hi," she says softly as she lays her head against my chest.

When the girls finally back off, the boys come in next, starting with Silas. "Hey man, it's good to see you standing." He hugs me a bit tighter than necessary, but when I groan, he quickly lets go. "Shit, I'm sorry."

"It's fine." I wave him off and go to Greyson next.

"We've missed you on the ice, man. It's not the same without you."

"Yeah, well, it's going to be a while before I can get back on it." I give him a tight smile, hating the feeling in my stomach at the thought of not playing.

"Just take all the time you need and come back to us when you're even better than before," Clay says, hugging me delicately compared to the other two.

"That's the plan. And thanks for letting us crash out back."

"No need to thank me. You guys are welcome here as long as you'd like." He steps to the side, making way for the last one of my friends, the most important one that I've been dying to see most.

Gabe stands back, looking uncertain and emotional. So, I take the few steps toward him and wrap my arms around him as he drops his head against my shoulder. "I've missed you, brother."

"Fuck, man," he croaks out. "I thought... I thought we were gonna lose you."

"Never." I rub my hand up and down his back. "I'm not going anywhere."

He pulls back, wiping the evidence of his tears away. "You better fucking not, because I'm not ready for another funeral. That shit's depressing as fuck." Everyone chuckles at his comment, and the mood is instantly lightened.

We all wander over to the living room, and I take one of the armchairs, using the armrests to lower myself slowly into it. Everyone watches me carefully, and I hate the pitiful look in their eyes, but I get it. They're worried about me, and I love them for that.

Morgan comes up to me, rubbing her belly. I swear she's getting bigger by the day. "Can I get you anything? Water? Juice? Soda? Beer?"

"No soda or beer," Veronica answers before I can, and I narrow my eyes at her. "What? You can't."

I chuckle and turn back to Morgan. "I'm good."

"Okay, are you hungry? I can make you something."

"Not at the moment, thank you." I smile as she nods and goes to settle at her husband's side while I look around the room, searching for the two toddlers. "Where are the kids?"

"Sam kept them at our place. We were afraid they might try to jump on you or something like that, and we didn't want to cause you any more pain," Cecilia says as she sits down on the couch beside Silas.

"It would have been okay. I miss the little buggers." I shrug with a smile.

"They miss their Uncle Noah too." Em smiles back. "We'll do something next week with them. Give you some time to adjust being back home." I nod in response.

"Hey, Morg. How come you guys didn't decorate for Halloween this year? I was told it was the thing to see every year. And it just hit me that Halloween is in a few days, and I don't see any decorations," Veronica asks, as she stands beside my armchair, her hand on my shoulder.

She's right; Morgan is the queen of holidays. She always goes all out and decorates her house from top to bottom on the first of October. Same with Christmas. Then we usually have a huge Halloween party with the whole team and whoever else has been invited.

And for Christmas, we always have a team Christmas dinner before everyone heads off to spend the holiday with their families. Although I'm guessing with Greyson and Emma's wedding being the twenty-third, we won't be doing that either this year.

"Oh, honestly, my mind was so busy focusing on the babies that I didn't even see the time go by. When my brain finally caught on at the beginning of the month, I was still pretty nauseated, and Clay didn't think it was a good idea to put myself through that kind of stress," she answers her with a sad shrug.

"So, there won't be any celebration at all?" Gabe asks while frowning.

"Well, we're still going to have the usual party. I was planning on asking you boys to decorate the place tomorrow. Just a bit, nothing extreme. Noah, you're off the hook." She giggles when the rest of the guys whine.

"Fuck, yeah. Never been happier to be injured," I joke with a laugh.

Veronica smiles as she leans in, sliding her fingers along my jaw and pressing her soft lips against mine. "I love you." She's been saying it a lot since I woke up from surgery, at least ten times a day. And I am not complaining.

"I love you, too, Veronica." She pulls away with a beaming grin, then heads over to Gabe, who sits in the other armchair next to mine.

She climbs onto his lap and wraps her arms around his neck. "Hi, baby. I've missed you." Since she's been with me all night and morning, this is the first time she's seen him in person since he left.

Gabe fists her hair and devours her mouth. "Fuck, you have no idea how much I've missed you. I can't wait to show you just how much later." He bites her bottom lip, giving it a tug as they pull away.

"Umm..." She chews on her lip.

"What?" He frowns, confused.

"Six-week sex restriction." I snicker when his eyes bug out of his head and his jaw drops.

"No..." He gapes, then looks back at Veronica with a nervous look. "Oh, no... please tell me I'm not included in that restriction. Please say I'm not, Vixen. Don't make me suffer like that! I'll do anything!" he pleads with her as everyone around us laughs.

"We'll see." She smiles and pats his chest.

"So, since everyone is here. We have an announcement to make," Emma says, sitting beside Greyson with her hand on his thigh. "We had a doctor's appointment early this morning and found out what we're having."

We all wait in anticipation for them to tell us what's about to be added to our rapidly growing family.

Greyson beams down at his fiancée with such pride. "We're having two boys."

A chorus of cheers erupts around the room as Aubrey gets up and hugs them both. "Congrats, you two. I can't wait to meet my nephews."

"Have you picked out names already?" Morgan asks with an excited grin but then drops it and points a finger at them. "No Theo, though, that name's taken already."

"You guys decided on Theo for your boy?" I ask Morgan, unaware that they had finally made a decision between the three names they had.

"Yes, just yesterday. It's weird, but I was napping and had a dream that I was chasing my kids in the backyard, and I called him Theo. I think it was a sign." She takes her husband's hand as they grin at each other, then turns back to Emma. "So? Names?"

"We're naming them Maddox and Parker," Greyson tells us.

"For Maddison Parker Ellery," Emma finishes as tears rise in her eyes.

"Aww…" Cecilia gets up and quickly hugs her friend. "Have you told Bryan?"

Em nods, wiping at her tears. "We called him right after finding out. He was happy and couldn't stop crying and thanking us. It was a lot of emotions in one morning." She lets out a sad laugh.

"How is he doing?" I ask them.

"As best as a parent can do after losing a child." Em sighs. "He started going to therapy to help cope with it all, and he's taking the rest of the year off from work to deal with everything and get back on his feet."

"We try to help him out wherever we can and see him regularly, but it's not easy with hockey, and it's a lot of emotions for Emma every time. I don't want her stressing too much with the babies," Greyson adds with a defeated look.

"That makes perfect sense, and I'm sure Bryan understands," Gabe tries to reassure them.

"Yeah, he does. He's always telling me to stop worrying, but it's in my nature to worry about others. I can't help it, and it's even worse since I became pregnant." Emma chuckles.

The doorbell rings and we all look at each other with a curious gaze. "Are we expecting more people?" I laugh when no one gets up right away.

"Not that I'm aware of." Clay finally stands and heads over to the front door as we wait for him to come back with whoever is there.

Suddenly a tiny little guy I've actually missed enormously jumps onto my legs and rubs his head against my hand when I start to pet him. "Hey, little Blubs. Missed you, boy." He purrs louder, a little meow at hearing his name, then finally lies down and rolls into a ball on my lap.

"Hm, I see that thing is still in your possession." Julian's voice pulls my gaze up to where he stands behind the couch with Shane and Clay.

"Yes, and he's not going anywhere until he's lived out all his cat days," Gabe tells him. "What are you doing here, Julian?"

"If you would all remember correctly, I informed you of having some things to discuss regarding Victor. I thought it would be best to wait until Mr. Adler was well enough to be present for this conversation."

"How did you know we were here?" I ask him next.

"I know you may not believe me when I say this, given the recent situation, but I do know everything." He walks around the couch and takes a seat facing us, beside Silas and Cecilia, while unbuttoning his suit jacket.

Clay returns to his seat on the second couch with his wife at his side, and Shane comes over and grabs my shoulder, squeezing lightly. "It's good to see you back on your feet and healing, Adler. I know it's got to be tough not playing this season, but we just want to make sure you're good before trying anything."

"Thanks, Coach. It definitely sucks, but I get it." I nod and swallow past the thickness in my throat.

He nods and straightens, looking around the room at everyone. "Yeah, I was just with Julian when he said he was coming over here and thought I'd tag along to see how you were all doing." He scratches at the back of his head, eyes falling on Aubrey.

Yeah, nice excuse to see your girl, Coach.

Veronica scoffs from her spot in Gabe's arms. *Clearly, I'm not the only one who doesn't buy his excuse.*

"Well, not that we just spent the last eight days with you, Coach. But we're doing pretty great. We actually found out we're having boys this morning," Greyson says with pride, placing his hand on Emma's baby bump.

"That's awesome! Congrats again. You planning on making a hockey team or what?" Shane jokes.

"Something like that," Greyson agrees with a laugh.

"Absolutely fucking not! I wasn't joking about getting your balls chopped, Wolf!" Emma barks out, making us all laugh.

"Julian." Veronica's voice pulls our attention back to the matter at hand. "I wanted to apologize for my behavior the other day, I didn't mean to come at you like that. I wasn't in my right mind, and I lashed out. And for that, I am sorry."

"No need for apologies. I understand the situation was a tender one and could make even the strongest of us react in such ways." They both nod in agreement.

"So, what is it you wanted to talk about? The man is dead and finally out of our lives; what could we possibly need to know?" I ask with a frown, not really up for hearing more about the man who could have ruined everything for us.

"I thought you might want some answers on where he was and how he was gaining access to your home." Julian waits.

"How?" Gabe finally bites.

"Does the name Antoine Fisher ring a bell?"

"The lobby desk clerk?" Gabe and I both look at Veronica with surprise. When she catches our gaze, she frowns. "You seriously don't know who that is? He's the young-looking one. He even called you when your mother was in the lobby." She looks at Gabe.

He raises his brows. "I didn't know that was his name."

"What did I tell you both about making an effort?" she scolds us.

"Right... sorry?" Gabe gives her a big apologetic smile that only gains him an eye roll.

"Then you do know him?" Julian asks, intrigued.

"Well, yes. I've seen him often, and he was always really nice to me. He would offer to get me a driver every time I was leaving the building without—" Her eyes widen. "Oh my God... He... he wouldn't have gotten me a driver... right?"

"That was the plan. He confessed to everything when Ricky and Marcos were trying to find the source of the power outage. They noticed he seemed nervous and kept looking at the time, as if he was waiting for something," Julian confirms.

"But I don't understand. Why him? What does he have to do with this?" Veronica searches for answers, looking at him in complete disbelief.

"He was simply a target, just as you all. Mr. Fisher happens to have a three-year-old daughter by the name of Priscillia. Victor discovered this information and threatened Priscillia's life if Mr. Fisher did not cooperate."

"Oh God..." Cecilia gasps.

"He went after a child? Are you freaking kidding me?!" Emma shouts. "I wish I could bring that fucker back to life, just to kill him again!"

"I'm right there with you, Bunny," Greyson agrees.

"And I'm guessing they weren't empty threats?" I question Julian.

"They were not. He had photographs of Fisher's daughter at their home, her daycare. Everywhere that little girl went, he was right there. Fisher gave Victor access to your penthouse the first time. But once we changed the keycodes, he handed him a key for the main entrance," Julian informs us.

"He also informed Victor about one of the tenants having a condo in the building that was rarely being used, since the owner is away half the year for business. Which is where Victor was hiding out on the nineteenth floor."

"So, what? His plan was to stay hidden there until I accepted a car ride, and instead of it being an actual driver, it would have been him?" Veronica frowns, trying to put all the pieces together.

Julian nods. "Originally, yes. But he became impatient and decided on a different course of action. He had Fisher close the main breaker to the entire building and instructed him only to turn it back on five minutes later, not a second sooner," he says before continuing.

"When the power went out, Victor snuck into the penthouse through the main entrance at that exact moment. He knew the camera would need a second to regain focus once it switched from day vision to night vision, making him a smidge too blurry for our sensors to alert us of movement. The asshole was a lot smarter than we anticipated."

"And the explosion?" Gabe asks next.

"Fisher was unaware of that part. But my guess is that Victor knew it would be impossible to keep the power off for so long without someone checking on the breaker. The explosion was planted in the condo Victor was using as housing. And had you two not already been on your way up, it would have made it impossible for anyone to make it up to the penthouse before the five minutes were up." Julian explains it like it's all so simple.

But it's not. We had this guy pegged out as just a petty criminal biker, but in the end, he was a fucking mastermind.

"He said it was a distraction…" Veronica mumbles to herself, looking down at her hands. "He knew all our schedules. He knew how the cameras worked. He knew about the guards. He knew everything." She finally looks up. "God, we were such idiots to think we could ever get him. This whole time, he was right under our nose, literally! And we never once caught sight of him."

"He definitely was significantly more intelligent than any of us could have imagined. Do not blame yourself for this, Veronica. None of us could have seen it coming, myself included," Julian tries to reason with her.

"And what was he planning on doing once he was in the penthouse?" I wonder because we still don't know what his big plan was.

"I do not believe he intended to harm Veronica, at least not in the building. From what Fisher told us, he needed the five minutes to get her out of the penthouse. My guess is he would have waited the five minutes to then take the elevator back down once it was up and running. Thinking my men would have been waiting at the stairs. The moment they would have slipped in, he would have already been riding it down with Veronica."

Julian looks down and shakes his head, elbows resting on his spread knees. "And that is exactly what would have happened. If Marcos and Ricky had not picked up on Fisher's strange behavior, one would have been waiting at the top of the steps to get through the fire. And the other would have been on the closest floor, waiting by the main elevator in case the power came back, to get to her as soon as possible."

He lifts his head with a dejected look I've never seen on him. I think it's the most human expression he's ever shown us. "He would have slipped out that front door with Veronica, and we would have just missed him. Even if the cameras had seen him, by the time my men would have run back down, he would have already been gone." His eyes fall to Veronica. "And now knowing just how well orchestrated his plan was, we likely would have never seen you again."

She nods, a tear slipping down her cheek. "Not until he would have wanted you to find me."

Fuck, I hate seeing her like this. "Come here, Kitten." I put Blubber down on the ground and open my arms for her.

She shakes her head. "No, I don't want to hurt you…"

"Please, just fucking come here. I need to hold you right now. So, it's either you come here on your own, or I'll pick you up and carry you myself."

She gets off Gabe quickly and tentatively climbs onto my lap, making sure not to press against my stomach. I palm her cheeks, forcing her to look at me. "I'm right here, Kitten, and so are you. We're all safe now. It's over." I press my lips to hers. "It's all over."

"But there's still one thing I don't understand. How was he getting in and out of the building unnoticed?" Gabe asks Julian.

"Fisher uses one of the residence parking spots in the underground garage, although he should not be. Victor would wait at the end of his shift to leave the building in the back seat of his car and would not return until his next. He would show up at Fisher's house before he would leave for work to get back into the building unnoticed," Julian clarifies the last puzzle piece to this whole shit show.

"Well, it's over now, and that's all that matters." Greyson stands. "I need a beer after all that."

"Indeed, it is. You may all go back to living your lives as you wish." Julian lifts from the couch, straightening his suit jacket. "We will leave you to your celebrations. Thank you for having me, and for trusting me despite the outcome."

"It may not have gone as planned, but it could have been worse if we didn't have your help," I tell him, shaking his hand when he comes over and offers it to each of us.

Shane stands as well, saying goodbye with one last lingering look at Aubrey, then leaves as well.

"What do we do now?" Veronica asks now that the room is silent.

"We celebrate like he said. We celebrate life, and friendship, and family." I kiss her cheek. "We celebrate love and all the beautiful things it brings into our lives."

Morgan and Clay head over to the kitchen, where Greyson is pulling out a few beers as well as non-alcoholic ones. They come back carrying the lot, handing one out to everyone. Except for Morgan and Emma, who get the non-alcoholic versions, and me, who gets a damn water bottle.

"Sorry, man. Your woman said no beer or anything bubbly." Greyson chuckles as he hands it over.

Everyone rises from their seats, standing in a circle in the center of the room. Veronica gently slips off my legs and takes my arm as I try to stand from the armchair. *Fuck, I'm going to need my pain meds again.*

"I'll get you them right after," Veronica whispers with a tender smile, reading my mind.

I nod and stand beside Aubrey, Veronica at my opposite side with Gabe at hers. Silas and Cecilia hold each other beside Gabe, followed by Clay and Morgan doing the same, as well as Greyson and Emma between them and Aubrey.

I bring my arm around Veronica's waist, just as Gabe places his around her shoulder. Both of us holding on to our girl. We all lift our bottles toward the middle, pressing them together and looking at each and every one of us.

It's a beautiful thing to see, this life we've all built together. This group that started off as strangers, then friends, and now family. People we would do anything for. People we would die for. Kill for. None of us are perfect, but we complete each other. We're a team.

"To family." I lift my water bottle a little higher.

They all join in, hitting their beer bottles to my plastic one. "To family."

I take a sip of my drink then look at the beautiful goddess in my hold, just as Gabe does the same. And without needing to communicate, we're in sync, just like we've always been. We both lean in simultaneously and kiss her cheek on either side.

"To loving you," I whisper into her ear.

"To making babies," Gabe whispers in her other. She giggles and pushes us away as we laugh.

Gabe looks at me over her head, since this is one of the rare times she's not wearing heels and matching our height. "She didn't say no," he whisper-shouts.

I smirk at him, then grin down at Veronica rolling her eyes at me. "She didn't say no."

Chapter Forty-Five

EPILOGUE
Hell unleashed...

VERONICA

~ Four Weeks Later / End of November ~

We finally found our home.

It's not near our friends, like we originally planned, but it's perfect. We're closer to the boys' training facility, just on the outskirts of Scarsdale, New York. It's a beautiful three-story, five-bedroom, seven-bathroom mansion. *Yes, I said mansion.* With a large in-ground pool, a four-car garage, and a huge, and I mean huge, backyard. The place is gated and gives us complete privacy. Our master bedroom takes up the entire top floor with its own balcony overlooking the backyard.

The second floor has four bedrooms that we aren't sure what to do with yet, but the boys are excited at the idea of filling it with kids. I have to agree; there is more than enough room here to have a whole herd of them.

The main level contains two living rooms, an entertainment room, kitchen, and two dining rooms. Along with a wine cellar, gym, two offices, and library that we most likely won't be using again. A laundry room, mudroom, way too many closets and storage rooms, and a fully finished basement that we are thinking of turning into a game room for when the gang is over. We also have a pool house at the back that has an apartment above it. *I should ask Aubrey if she wants to move in up there, she'd love it here.*

There's so much space that I have no idea what we'll do with it all, but I'm sure we'll figure it out. We came to visit it last week while Gabe was away, but I fell in love with it the moment we stepped in.

I video called Gabriel and showed him everything and told him this was it. This was our forever home. The boys made an offer right away, and now we are back to sign everything and make it officially ours, and Gabe finally gets to see the place in person.

I wander around our future bedroom, looking over the huge space and what we could fill it with. The realtor just left after handing us the keys and showing us how to change the codes for the front door and garage. We plan on moving in slowly, since we don't have any furniture or anything yet except for clothes. But we'll hopefully be in our home within the next two weeks.

Gabe, Noah, and I haven't been back to the penthouse since the whole incident. None of us really feel comfortable going back there. But we're lucky enough to have great friends who went to collect all our things for us, and Silas has officially put it up for sale.

You'd think having a murder in a place would bring down its value, but apparently that isn't the case for New York. He's been receiving crazy offers from the second it was listed.

I stroll out onto the balcony, setting my hands on the cold railing as I look down at the beautiful snow-covered lawn. We had our first snowfall just yesterday, and it makes the place look even more picturesque. Being here feels like a vacation home that you get to live in for the rest of your life, and that's exactly the feeling I was looking for when we were visiting places.

Noah comes out a few minutes later, joining me with his arms circling my waist from behind around my winter coat. He's been doing really well and says the pain is all gone; he even stopped needing his painkillers, so I guess he means it. But I can tell he's excited to get back to his life. He misses working out and moving around.

Sometimes I find him lifting canned goods as if they are weights, and it makes me laugh. Although I stop him every time, I can understand this is hard for him. But I think what he misses most is sex. He's always cornering me and trying to get it on, hoping I'll fold and give in. *But I don't.*

I haven't punished Gabe with the sex restriction, but we still try to be respectful toward Noah. We only have sex occasionally, either in the shower when we're alone or when Noah is sleeping. He knows what we're doing and keeps telling us it's okay, that we don't have to hide. But I can tell he appreciates us being discreet.

"God, I miss you so much." He kisses down my neck.

"Two more weeks, babe. And then I promise to ride you from the moment the sun comes up all the way until it goes back down." I smile, tilting my head to the side and kissing his lips.

"Damn, that's going to be some intense sex." Gabe joins us as well, laughing. "She'll probably break your dick, and then you'll have a new sex restriction."

"Don't jinx him!" I point at Gabe. "I miss his cock just as much. I don't think I can wait any longer than two more weeks."

"We could just end the waiting now, christen our new home. Start up here and work our way down through every room," Noah says, hands roaming up and down my body. *God, this is torture.*

I push him off while giggling. "No. Two more weeks."

He huffs out with a pout. "Fine."

I can't help but smile at his reaction, then turn back to the scene before me as I sigh.

"What are you thinking about?" Gabe steps up, passing his fingers through my hair. It's now black at the top and hot pink the rest of the way down to my waist.

"Just how much our lives have changed in just five months. I went from hating you two to not being able to live without you," I finish with a laugh.

"I don't think you ever really hated us." Noah smirks.

"You're right, I don't think I did. And now here we are, buying our first home together. Planning a future together." I bite my lip and look away from them, feeling the emotions rise.

"What's bothering you? I can see there's something going on in your mind," Gabe asks softly.

"I just... I guess with the whole wedding planning for Emma, reality has been hitting harder than I thought." I turn to them, wanting to make things clear.

"I don't want you to think that I don't love our life and what we have. I do, and I never want to change any part of it. I know at the end of the day, all that matters is that we have each other. I just hate that we'll never be able to live that moment together, you know?"

Noah and Gabe exchange a look that I can't decipher. They nod at each other before Noah takes out his phone and starts tapping away at it. Gabe takes my hand and brings me back inside.

"Where are we going?"

"We have somewhere to be." He grins at me. "You'll see."

And one hour later, I understand exactly what we're about to do. I stand outside the car in front of Maze's shop and look back at the boys, to find them both smiling at me. "Are we really doing this? Gabe?"

They nod. "I think it's time we did it. I can go through this for you."

I wrap an arm around each of their necks and kiss their cheeks. "I love you both so much. Thank you."

We head inside and Maze takes me aside right away, while the boys go off with Bear. The plan is for Noah and Gabe to get a black band with an intricate design inside of it that will give it a hollow look. While mine will simply be the detailed design, making it look like I'm the missing piece to their rings.

"Hey, do you think you have time to give me another small tattoo? It's nothing extreme, maybe five-ten minutes tops," I ask Maze in a low voice, making sure the boys can't hear me.

"For you, girl, I always have time. What were you thinking?"

Thirty minutes later, I walk back to the front with my two new tattoos to check on the guys. They're both waiting around, chatting with Bear and another customer about hockey. When Noah sees me, he comes over asking to see my ring tattoo. As we planned, they match perfectly, and my heart beats harder as I look down at them.

"It's not the only thing I got."

He frowns, looking me up and down. "What do you mean?"

I turn my arm that is covered in ink and show him the new addition right in the center of my wrist. His eyes widen as he stares down at it, his Adam's apple bobbing as he swallows. "Kitten…"

"It's the Trinity knot," I tell him softly, but it's not the only thing with it. On either side of the knot are the numbers seventy-nine and eighty-six, for my boys. "Three hundred and sixty-eight reasons to be happy forever."

"Fuck…" He wraps his arms around me, squeezing me tightly in his hold. "I love you, Veronica. Hell, that's not even a strong enough word to describe what I feel for you."

"I know exactly what you mean," I whisper into his ear.

We pull apart and I go over to Gabe, wanting to see his tattoo. But when I reach him, I notice his ring finger is empty, and something in my heart breaks. My eyes well with tears on their own.

He stands right away, taking me in his arms. "Vixen…"

"I'm okay. I understand that this was too much for you; it's okay," I rush out, wiping my tears away.

He pulls back, holding onto my arms with a smile. "That's not why I didn't do it."

"I… I don't understand?"

His hands drop from my arms, and he reaches into his back pocket, taking out a small square jewelry box and drops to one knee. "I had a different kind of ring in mind."

He beams up at me, popping it open to reveal a deep sapphire-blue engagement ring with what looks like tiny diamond vines wrapping around each side of the ring.

My hands fly to my lips on a gasp. I look around at everyone who watches us. Bear and Maze hold each other with a smile on their faces, while the client now has his phone out filming us. And then to Noah, who watches me carefully.

"I... I thought we agreed we wouldn't do this?" Tears track down my face. "That we... we wouldn't get married if I couldn't marry you both..."

Noah takes a step closer, cupping my face and wiping my tears away. "Marriage was never my dream, Veronica, but it's always been his. Ellis and I talked this over for a while, and we both agreed that you deserve a wedding, just as much as he does. I don't need you to wear my last name, to have a ceremony, and be recognized by the law. All I need is this," he holds up his ring finger, "and you."

He kisses my lips tenderly as I sob against his, overcome with emotions. "Are you sure?"

He pulls back, looking me in the eyes. His deep browns swimming with so much love, it's breathtaking. "I'm positive."

I nod as he steps away and refocus on Gabe, who patiently waits kneeling on the ground in front of me. He holds out his hand for me to take, and I slip mine in his without an ounce of hesitation.

"Vixen, before you, my life was great. I won't lie about that." He chuckles when I frown. "It was easy and simple. I knew what I wanted out of it, but I wasn't in any rush to get it. I thought I already had everything any man could want. The career, the money, the friends, and the ladies."

"Gabriel, this isn't how these speeches usually go," I interrupt him with a raised brow.

"Well, if you'd stop interrupting me, I could get to the good part." He laughs.

"Okay, okay. Go on."

"I thought I had everything. But then one November afternoon, a little over a year ago, you walked into my life, and I thought I had died and gone to heaven. You were the most beautiful creature I had ever seen, a goddess. One of those celestial beings we crave to witness all our lives. And there you were, standing right in front of me. And as crazy as it sounds, I knew it, in that moment, I knew I needed you."

I go to open my mouth, but he lifts his finger that holds the ring, shushing me. "And before you say it, no, it wasn't just about sleeping with you. That was a major factor, I'll admit to that, but it was always more. I always wanted more of you. Wanted to uncover every little quirk you have, understand why you go left instead of right. Why you smile, why you frown. I wanted to know it all, every single inch of you—I wanted it." I sniffle, letting out a shaky breath as he goes on.

"But you never gave me the time of day, no matter how hard I tried, no matter what I said or did, you always looked the other way. And at some point, I thought of stopping, of giving up. But then I realized it would be impossible to walk away from you, impossible to pretend you didn't already own every aspect of my heart. And what kind of idiot would I be to give up on such a beauty like you?" He smiles wider, thumb caressing the top of my hand that he holds as tears pour from my eyes.

"And then finally, fucking finally, you looked my way and gave me a chance. You took my hand, and never let it go. You made me face my fears, you accepted me as I was, and have only made me a better man. One I hope will always be worthy of you."

"You'll always be, Gabriel. You always were," I whisper through the thickness in my throat where my free hand lies.

He grins. "Now it's my turn to take your hand and never let it go." I nod enthusiastically. "Veronica Masters, will you do me the honor of becoming my wife?"

"Yes! Yes, Gabriel, yes. A thousand times yes! Every day for the rest of our lives, yes!"

He slips the ring onto my newly tatted finger, making sure not to push it all the way down, and I throw myself into his arms as the few people around us clap and cheer. I capture his lips, promising to love him forever, then let go and do the same to Noah. Despite this engagement being between me and Gabriel, it wouldn't be the same without my Casanova.

After a few minutes of receiving congratulations from Maze, Bear, and his client, who's already forwarded us the video, we head outside and back into Gabe's car. "What do you want to do now, baby? We could get the gang together and tell them the good news," Gabe offers, looking back from the driver's seat.

I shake my head. "Not just yet." I bite my lip, looking down at my rings. "I wish I could tell my parents..." I lift my gaze to both men who watch me intensively. "It's crazy, right? That after they threw me out and pretended that I didn't exist, I still miss them? That I wish I could share this news with them... even knowing they would never approve."

"Have you ever thought of going back?" Noah asks softly.

"I've wanted to... many times. But I was always afraid they'd just shut their door in my face... They probably wouldn't even recognize me." I shrug, the sadness creeping slowly into my heart. Knowing my father will never be there to walk me down the aisle, or that my mother will never tell me how beautiful I look on my wedding day.

"Why don't we go see them? It's only like a five-hour flight to Arizona. We could leave tomorrow morning, be there before noon, and take a flight back at night. I don't have practice or a game tomorrow," Gabe tells me with a warm smile.

"You'd really do that for me?"

He twists in his seat, cupping my cheek. "I'd do anything for you, Vixen. Anything."

When his hand drops and a new tear rolls down, Noah does the same, cupping my other side and swiping away my tear. "You've made us yours forever, Kitten. Facing your parents comes with that territory. We'll forever do anything for you, Veronica."

I swallow, my eyes soaking up and spilling over once more. "Anything," I whisper, looking at Gabe, then turn my gaze to Noah. "Forever."

By ten-thirty the next morning, we're standing outside my childhood home, and nerves eat at me from the inside. I could have texted or called in advance, since I still have their number and am sure they haven't changed it. But I was too afraid to face their rejection through a phone.

I needed to see them face-to-face. To tell them how much it hurt me when they banished me. How much I've been through since the last time they saw me. That I know I'm not the daughter they wanted, but I'm proud of who I am today.

"Whenever you're ready, Kitten." Noah rubs down the back of my coat.

"Or we can turn back around if that's what you want. Whatever you choose, we're here for you." Gabe squeezes my hand in his.

I take a deep breath and slowly let it out, working through my anxiety. "I'm ready." I nod, capturing both their hands in mine and taking a step forward toward the front door.

But before I can make it any closer, it flies open, and my mother stands in the doorway. "Oh, my lord! Stephan! She's home! Our baby's home!" She comes running down the steps in slippers and a robe and throws her arms around me, sobbing against my winter coat.

I'm frozen in shock as I stand there with my arms glued to my sides. Out of all the reactions I imagined coming from them, this one wasn't one of them, and I have no idea how to deal with it.

She finally unwraps her arms from around me and grabs my face, looking me over. "Oh, look at you. My beautiful baby girl. You've grown so much," she cries, touching every inch of me, from my hair to my piercings to my hands that are still being held by Noah and Gabe.

She gasps when she sees my ring. "Oh, sweet baby Jesus! She's engaged, Stephan! Hurry up and come out here!"

My father suddenly emerges as well, wearing slippers and pulling on his winter jacket. He's wearing a simple T-shirt and jeans underneath, and I'm extremely confused by the look. My father's a pastor; I've never seen him dressed like this.

He comes in as well and takes me in his arms, similar to what my mother just did. "Oh, sweetheart, we've missed you immensely." He then takes a step back and holds my mother as they both look at me with such joy radiating from their features.

Noah and Gabe squeeze my hands simultaneously, jolting me back to the moment. I clear my throat and force a smile onto my face. "Hi, Mom. Hi, Dad."

"Oh, where are our manners? Please, come in. Come in before someone catches a cold." My father waves us in as he turns with my mother and heads back into the house.

I'm so baffled by what is going on that I don't move from my spot, not until Noah releases my hand and places it on my back, guiding me forward. We shrug out of our coats and boots then head into the living room, where my mother tells us to sit down while she prepares coffee for us all.

I look around the room, noticing all the changes. There used to be religious artifacts all over the mantel and walls, but now every space is filled with random decorations and pictures of me. There's even a Griffins' jersey hanging up on the wall, and all I can do is stare at it, blinking.

What in the hell is going on?

"So, which one of you proposed to my daughter?" my dad asks from his spot in his favorite recliner. It's still the same one he had before I left, only now it's much more worn out and covered in patches.

"That would be me, sir." Gabe grins at my father and reaches forward, shaking my dad's hand. "Gabriel Ellis. It's a pleasure to meet you."

"I know who you are." Dad smiles back at him. "Stephan Masters." He lets go of Gabe's hand and offers his to Noah next. "And you must be Noah."

Noah nods. "That's right. Pleasure to meet you."

"Likewise."

"Wait," I lift my hands. "Just... wait a minute." I shake my head and close my eyes, needing this to make sense for a minute. "You know who they are?"

My mother comes back carrying a tray with five coffee mugs. "Of course, we do. We've been watching all their games." She hands out a coffee to each and introduces herself as Lucia to my boys.

"You and Dad? Hockey fans? And of the New York Griffins, instead of Arizona's own team?" I blink, entirely perplexed.

"It was our only way of feeling close to you," my mother says with a saddened smile.

"You've..." My eyes well up. Noah places his hand on my thigh while Gabe takes my hand in his, both encouraging me to go on. "You've known where I was all along?"

"When you left Arizona, we had no idea where you'd disappeared to. We feared the worst, that maybe... maybe Victor had done something to you..." My mother begins to tear up, grabbing a tissue from the coffee table and wiping her eyes and nose.

"But then we just happened to be at a friend's house while one of your games was playing a year ago, and we saw you in the front row with the wives," my father continues for her.

"I knew it was you the moment the camera aimed your way. You may have changed your look a lot, but I'd never forget my daughter's face," Mom says through her tears.

"Your mother nearly lost it when she recognized you. She wanted to jump on a plane right away and find you."

"Why didn't you?" I frown, not understanding what would keep them away.

"We wanted to, but we feared you wouldn't want to see us after how things ended between us. We never intended to throw you out of our lives for good, sweetheart. We just wanted to teach you a lesson, but now we realize it wasn't the right approach. We knew Victor was bad news, and we had hoped that making you dependent on him would make him reveal his true colors," Dad admits with a guilty look.

"Well, he sure did. Only he waited until I was completely trapped to do it." I close my eyes as the horrid memories resurface. But when I feel hands caressing my thigh and back of the hand, it makes them vanish.

"When we realized who he really was, it was too late. We tried to get you back, to come and get you. But he threatened us and said he would kill you if we ever tried to reach out to you." My mother sobs louder.

"You've wanted me to come home since the beginning?"

"It's all we've prayed for. It's the only prayer we've allowed ourselves to give," my father says with so much regret in his voice.

"I... I don't understand..." My father practically prays for a living. Teaching the good from bad and guiding people in the right direction. Praying is part of his job.

"When we couldn't get you back, I stepped down from my role as pastor. I couldn't live with myself knowing what I had done. How can I help people stay away from evil when I forced my daughter right into its arms?"

My eyes widen. "You're no longer a pastor?"

He shakes his head. "No."

"But Dad, you loved the church and the community."

He reaches over the table, taking my free hand in his. "I do, but I love you more."

This time it's my turn to sob. I take both my hands back and cover my face as I cry into them. All these years. All this time wasted on living in fear that they would never love me again when the truth is they never stopped.

"I'm so sorry it took me so long to come back."

"No, we're the ones who are sorry. We're just glad you're here now. And I hope you'll give us another chance to be the parents we always should have been to you." My mother smiles as she wipes her face.

"That's all I want," I whisper, then let out a breath. "So, you're not mad about this situation?" I point to Noah and Gabe.

My dad laughs. "We were surprised, but we always knew you were more adventurous than most. And from what we can see, they do seem to treat you well. That's all that matters to us."

"We're also sorry to hear about what you went through." My mother addresses Noah, then looks at Gabe and me. "What you all went through. But we are happy that that evil man is finally where he belongs."

"Yeah, we all are," Gabe says, taking my hand once more and kissing the back of it.

"So, when's the wedding?" My mother beams as her entire body lights up, excited to talk about wedding plans.

We arrive back in New York at almost midnight, and my life finally feels whole again.

My parents promised to come down once we were settled in our new home and seemed really excited to get to know Noah and Gabe more, as well as all my friends. It feels good having them back in my life, like that was the puzzle piece missing all these years.

As we drive through the city on our way over to the apartment behind Morgan and Clay's home that we're still using, I tap on Gabe's shoulder. "I know you're probably exhausted, but do you mind if we stop at my old condo? Aubrey should be on her way home right now, and I really want to tell her the news in person before everyone else."

"Yeah, no problem." He looks back quickly at me and smiles before refocusing on the road as he takes us to my old home.

We park a few cars down from the building as I look at the time. "She should be walking down that street any second." I point ahead of us, knowing her routine by heart.

And on cue, Aubrey turns the corner, heading for the entrance of the building. But she's not alone. "Is that...?"

"Coach?" Noah leans in, squinting to make sure we're all seeing the same thing.

No one moves in the car, and the lights are off, so we aren't drawing any attention. Shane walks her to the door, seems to wish her goodnight, then turns and begins to walk away as she goes to unlock the entrance door.

"Did you know he walked her home at night?" Gabe asks in a hushed voice, like we might be heard if he talks any louder.

I shake my head. "No, she's never mentioned it before."

Suddenly, Shane stops walking. He says something, and Aubrey turns quickly to face him. He says something again, then marches up to her with quick steps, grabs her face, and kisses her.

"Oh my God!" I shout, then quickly cover my mouth, unable to tear my eyes away from them.

"Well," Noah starts. "Seems hell's about to be unleashed."

Afterword

And we've reached the end once again!

Thank you to everyone who has helped and continued to support me on this incredible journey as I prepared to gift you all the third book in my series. Every one of my books holds a special place in my heart and a personal connection to myself, and I am so grateful I get to share them with you.

If you enjoyed reading Veronica, Gabriel, and Noah's story and couldn't get enough of them, be on the look out for the fourth book in the Sticks and Stilettos series, where you'll get to see this amazing found family continue to grow.

Always Been Yours will be coming in July 2026.

Featuring the couple you've all been waiting for! Our famous head coach, Shane Jefferson, and our blushing beauty, Aubrey Ford!

And if you haven't checked out the previous books yet, go ahead and give it a try, I promise it will be worth it. Although some are an emotional rollercoaster, so prepare the tissues!

Eternally Yours, book one in the Sticks and Stilettos series features the couple that started it all, Cecilia and Silas Hayes!

Unexpectedly Yours, book two in the Sticks and Stilettos series features our wild couple, Emma and Greyson Ford!

Acknowledgements

There are so many of you I'd like to mention here, but I fear if I did, it would never end and we'd end up with an even thicker book! So I'll just try to cut it short and start off by saying a very deep thank you to all my readers who have been around from the very start.

To those who follow my every post, comment on anything I have to share, who laugh and cry with me even though I'm a complete stranger who simply wrote a book you liked. I know I say this often, but I don't think you realize how much just a simple like or share really means to me. Some of these obstacles we face as authors are truly hard to overcome, there's always that "fuck it. It's too hard." voice echoing in my mind every time I encounter a new one. But seeing your names pop up on my screen, reading your sweet comments even when they're as little as a heart emoji, those are what push me through every time, what keep me going. So this may be my book, my journey, my dream, but it wouldn't be the same and may never have come true if it wasn't for all of you. I don't think I have to give any names as you all know who you are. But once again, thank you from the bottom of my heart.

To my Slay Sister, Victoria Pauley, author of the Silver City University series. To my Wordy Mama, Emerson Reign, author of the Season Sisters saga. To my Brilliant Brina, S.J. Reid, author of the Tainted Throne series. To my queen B.A.B Dannielle. And to my BFTR Kylie. You girls are my rock and I have no idea where I'd be without any of you. I'll never stop shouting out your names the same way you've all done for me over the past year. I love you all so so much.

To my Lemonyy girl. You my darling girl, are like a breath of fresh air I didn't know I desperately needed. Our friendship started so unexpectedly, but I wouldn't trade it for the world, I certainly wouldn't want to go without all those juicy reels we send each other daily haha. Talking to you has brightened every single one of my days and I consider myself the luckiest to have found someone as extraordinary as you from across the world. I feel like I found a sister I can hold on to forever, and I intend to do just that. I love you, my juicy lemon and may we keep sending each other HR thirst traps until the end of time! xx Also, Liam can go suck a dick.

To my IRL Minnie. I still remember the first time I fell on your IG profile, and immediately knew I wanted you in my corner. I don't know what it was, but something drew me in and I knew I had to do everything possible to get you to read my books. And then you actually showed interest and I started freaking out. I wanted you to love them so badly, but I was so terrified to disappoint you. It was like suddenly nothing else mattered, and all I needed was Minnie's approval because that would be like winning the lottery. And then you did, you loved them and raved about them and showed me so much support, and through that, I found an unforgettable friend. One that I can vent with, talk about anything and everything, one that I know will always be there when I need a shoulder to lean on. You are the true kind of reader every author dreams of having in their corner, and I am beyond grateful I get to have you by my side through it all. I love you and thank you for everything xx

A HUGE thank you to Ali of @juniper.charm, my amazingly talented and wonderful cover designer. You truly are one of a kind and I have no words to describe how much I love working with you. The way you captured Ronnie's hair so perfectly never ceases to amaze me! I swear, I could look at that beautiful cover all day long and never get tired. Hell, I already do it, all of them! They are everything and even more than I expected and I can't wait for all the future covers we'll do together.

A deep thank you to Ashley, my PR girl, who has helped me through every step of the ARC process and taken SUCH a huge workload off my shoulders! Time was already not on my side with this book, but you helped me make it all happen and I'll forever be grateful to you! Thank you so much for everything and I love you!

And of course, one last thank you to my family, my friends, and anyone else who has been along for the ride and has supported me through every step.

About the Author

Chloe Rouxel is a Canadian writer who lives for romance and good books. A hopeless romantic at heart, you can always find her writing down notes about the perfect love story. Whether that involves a golden-retriever hero, or a morally gray alpha, she'll think of a way to make you fall in love with him.

When she's not spending her days trying to tame her three young wildlings, she's lost to the voices in her head with her laptop in hand. Daydreaming about her many many book boyfriends.

She loves to sit around the house with her friends, laughing about her wild and vivid imagination. Brainstorming about scandals and plot twists together over a glass of wine. (Can't forget the wine!)

You can find out more about Chloe and her upcoming books, or even just to chat and be along for the ride on her social media pages. She loves to here from her fans, so don't hesitate to reach out!

Instagram: @chloerouxel.author

TikTok: @chloe.rouxel.auth

Facebook: /ChloeRouxelAuthor

Website: chloerouxel.my.canva.site

Email: chloe.rouxel.author@hotmail.com

ALSO BY CHLOE ROUXEL

Series